RUSSELL KIRKPATRICK

The RIGHT HAND of GOD

FIRE OF HEAVEN
BOOK THREE

orbit

www.orbitbooks.net

ORBIT

First published in Australia in 2005 by Voyager,
HarperCollins*Publishers* Pty Limited
First published in Great Britain in 2007 by Orbit
Reprinted 2007, 2009

A CIP catalogue record for this book
is available from the British Library.

ISBN 978-1-84149-465-4

Typeset in Goudy by Palimpsest Book Production Limited,
Grangemouth, Stirlingshire
Printed and bound in Great Britain by
CPI Mackays, Chatham, ME5 8TD

Papers used by Orbit are natural, renewable and recyclable products sourced from well-managed forests and certified in accordance with the rules of the Forest Stewardship Council.

FSC
Mixed Sources
Product group from well-managed forests and other controlled sources
www.fsc.org Cert no. SGS-COC-004081
© 1996 Forest Stewardship Council

Orbit
An imprint of
Little, Brown Book Group
100 Victoria Embankment
London EC4Y 0DY

An Hachette UK Company
www.hachette.co.uk

www.orbitbooks.net

To Iain, with love

ACKNOWLEDGMENTS

I received help and encouragement from a great many people while writing these books. Foremost among them were the members of my family, Dorinda, Iain and Alex. I'd particularly like to thank Iain, my elder son, for his enthusiasm and astuteness. He became plot critic and draft reader for the conclusion of the series. This book is dedicated to him.

I would like to formally acknowledge the assistance of my readers. I salute the patience and good humour of Margaret, Martin, Gillian, Tony, Malcolm, Phil, Dereck, Jaynie, Daniel, Simon, Deborah, Tim, Tracey, Richard, Robin, John, Hannah, Anna, Alan, Glenda, Ella and Trudi. These people made helpful suggestions and, more importantly, kept my morale high when writing threatened to become nothing more than a task.

I owe a huge debt to my editors. The work benefited immensely from the vision of Stephanie Smith and Lorain Day, the skill of Annabel Blay and the assistance of Davina MacLeod, pronoun pruner, metaphor muncher and editor extraordinaire. Grateful thanks also to the proofreaders.

Steve Stone was responsible for the stunning covers. I was fortunate to have a cover artist of such high quality.

Finally, thanks to all at HarperCollins Voyager Australia and New Zealand for their professionalism.

CONTENTS

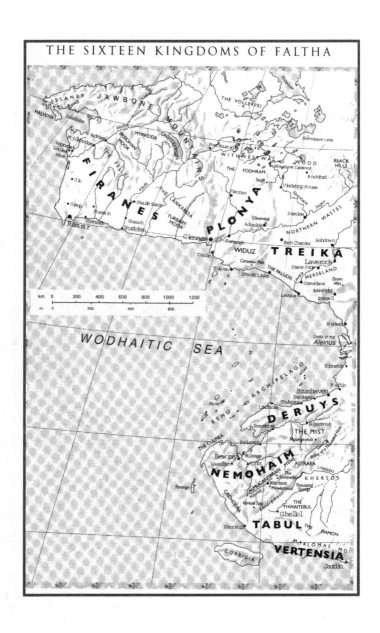

THE SIXTEEN KINGDOMS OF FALTHA

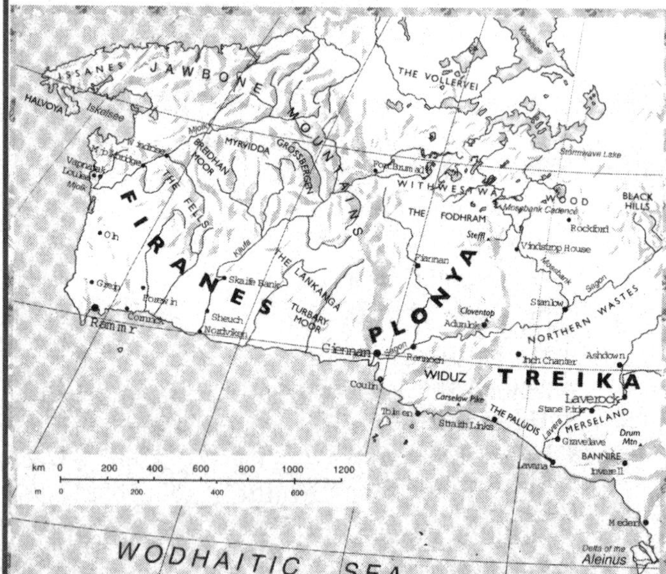

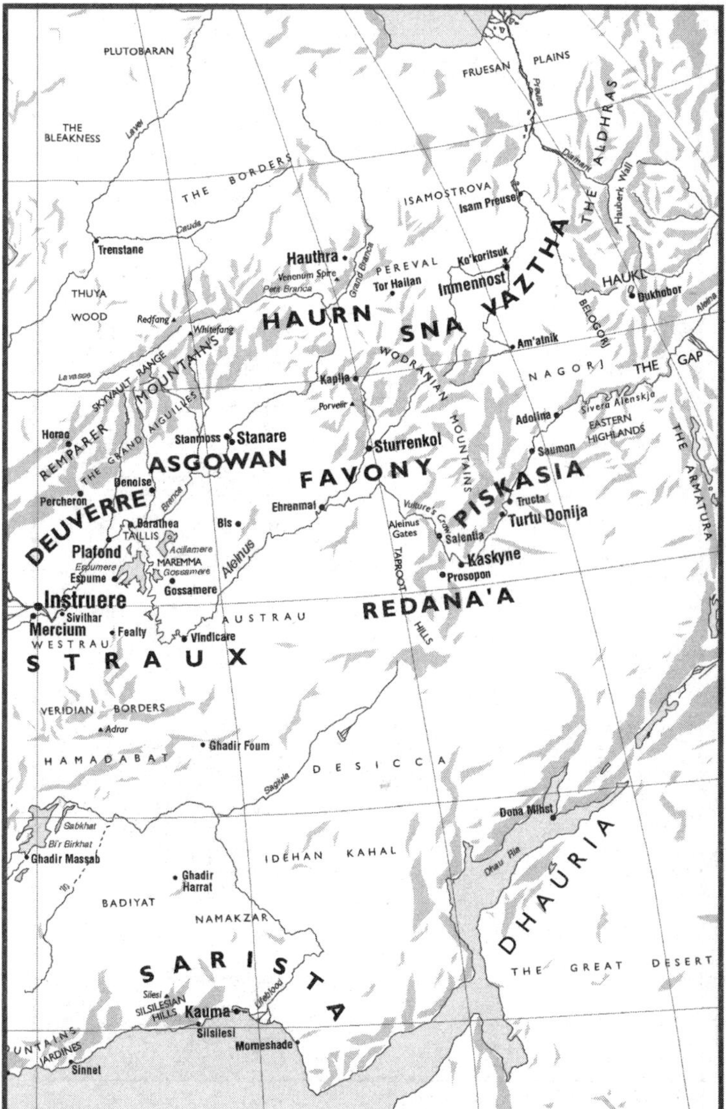
PLUTOBARAN
THE BLEAKNESS
Lavei
THE BORDERS
Cauda
Trenstane
THUYA WOOD
Redfang
Whitefang
Lavasse
SKYVAULT RANGE
MOUNTAINS
HAURN
Hauthra
Venenum Spire
Petit Branca
Grand Branca
PEREVAL
Tor Hailan
FRUESAN PLAINS
Preuss
Diamant
THE ALDHRAS
ISAMOSTROVA
Isam Preuse
Hauberk Wall
Ko'koritsuk
Immennost
SNA VAZTHA
HAUKL
Dukhobor
BELOGORI
Aleina
Am'atnik
WODRANIAN MOUNTAINS
NAGORJ
THE GAP
Kaplja
Porveiir
THE GRAND AIGUILLES
REMPARER
Horaq
Stanmoss
Stanare
ASGOWAN
Sturrenkol
FAVONY
Adolina
Sivera Alenskja
EASTERN HIGHLANDS
Sauman
PISKASIA
THE ARMATURA
Denoise
Percheron
DEUVERRE
Branca
Ehrenmal
Tructa
Turtu Donija
Barathea
Bis
TAILLIS
Aleinus Gates
Vulture's Craw
Salentia
Plafond
Acillamere
Aleinus
Kaskyne
Espumere
Espume
MAREMMA
Gossamere
TAPROOT HILLS
Prosopon
Gossamere
Instruere
REDANA'A
Sivithar
AUSTRAU
Mercium
Fealty
Vindicare
WESTRAU
STRAUX
VERIDIAN BORDERS
Adrar
Ghadir Foum
HAMADABAT
DESICCA
Sagiule
Dona Mihst
Sabkhat
Bi'r Birkhat
Ghadir Massab
IDEHAN KAHAL
Dhau Rio
DHAURIA
Ghadir Harrat
BADIYAT
NAMAKZAR
SARISTA
THE GREAT DESERT
Silesi
SILSILESIAN HILLS
Kauma
Lifeblood
Silsilesi
Momeshade
JARDINES
Sinnet

WESTRAU, STRAUX

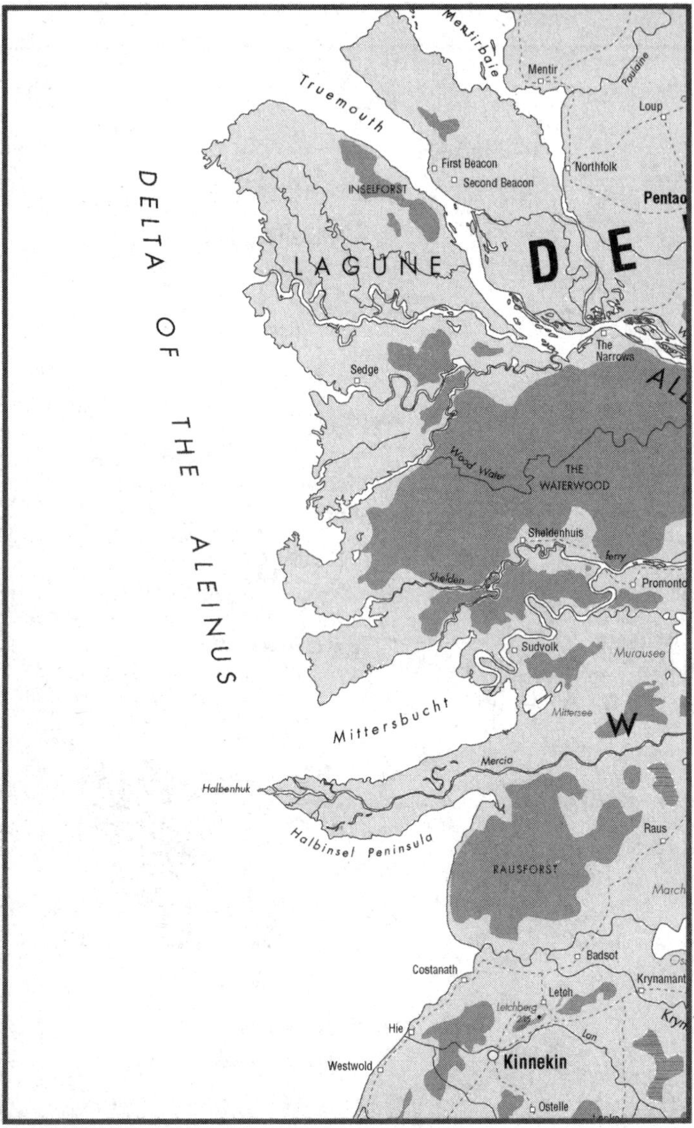

Westhalba
Alrance
Laco Serie
Lommes
THE
MARAIS
UVERRE
Somatan
Chere
Sallas
ferry
Ponty
SURTENDE
Lac Neuve
Lac Pontaumere
Remenoir
Lac Remenal
Lac Remenette
Sallastria
Lac Ankar
Ankar
BOISDEAU FOREST
Bois d'Eau
Caussenere
CHEMIN REMENOR
Lac Bonne
CHEMIN SEGUE
Yosse
Lac Etang
Isle Paran
Mormorion
Pania
Fools' Borrage
Instruere
Blokhuis
Mercium Ship Canal (abandoned)
Chieme
Gabi
Chihillac
Pontau
Mormor's Reach
Dachanne
Sudvolk
MERCIUM ROAD
Strasvolk
Kingtide Reach
Meribor
Sivithar
MERCIA
Sumtal
Endra
Merbrucke
Mollin
Mercia
CENTRE PLAINS ROAD
Collines Hill
Eddale
Merluch
Alkover
Wyvarne
Collines Reach
Flache
Tomacher
Pensel
Umerung
Szano
Mercium
AUSTRAU ROAD
Nyscha
Alino-bogon
Dex
ESTRAU
Gelf
Eneit
CENTRE PLAINS ROAD
Oneiro
GREAT SOUTH ROAD
Hansa
TYRINAFORST
Wencel
TYRINA ROAD
Abinada
Tyr
Asim
MARCHFELD
Tyrina
TYRINA
Rosenweg
STRAUX
Oberfelden
OBERFELD
AMADAN ROAD
Flockwold
Amadan
Bellholz
Lynanth

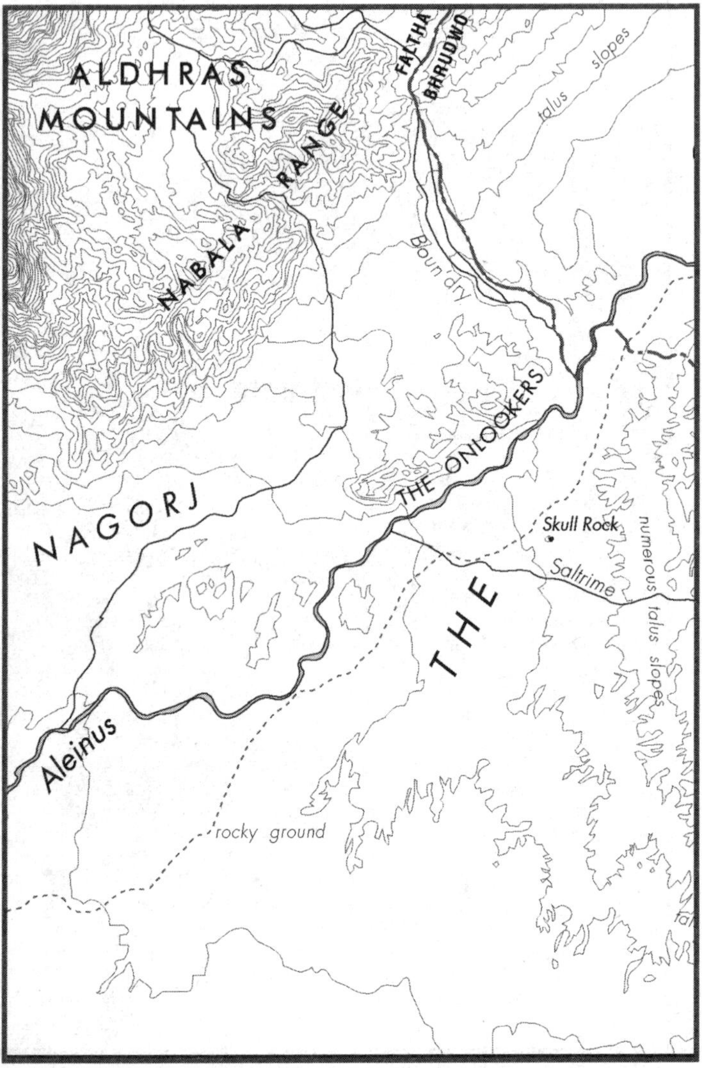
ALDHRAS
MOUNTAINS
NABALA
RANGE
FALTHA
BHRUDWO
talus slopes
Boundry
THE ONLOOKERS
NAGORJ
Skull Rock
numerous talus slopes
Saltrime
THE
Aleinus
rocky ground

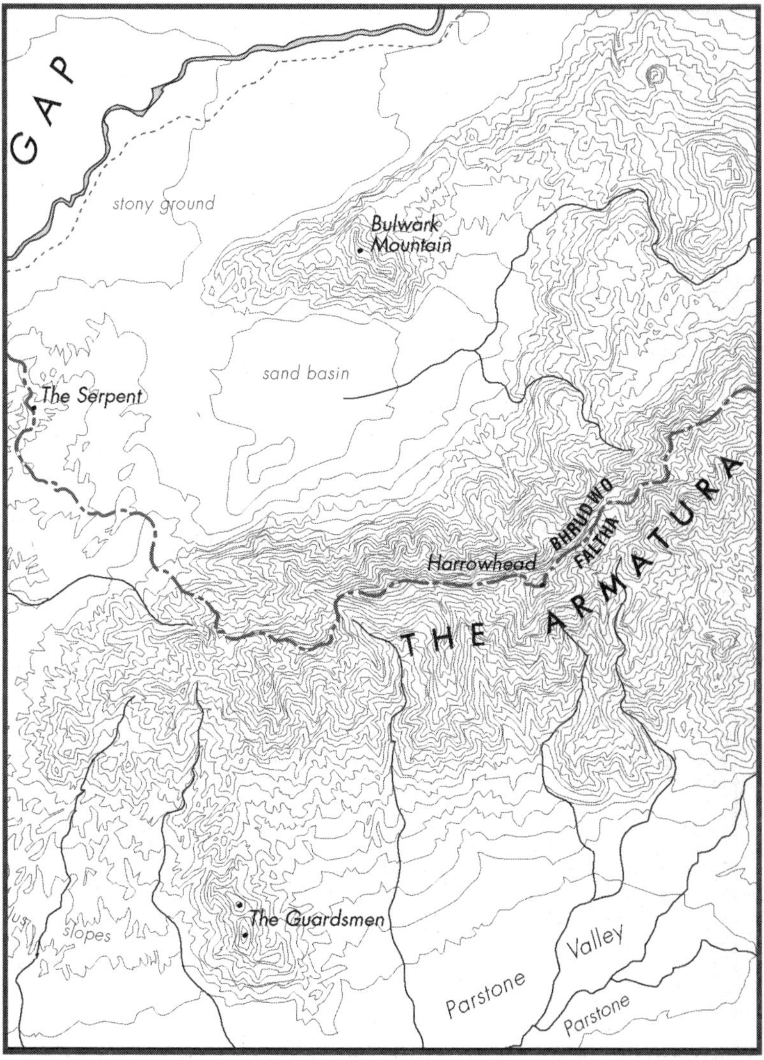
GAP
stony ground
Bulwark Mountain
sand basin
The Serpent
Harrowhead
BHRUD WO
FALTHA
THE ARMATURA
The Guardsmen
slopes
Valley
Parstone
Parstone

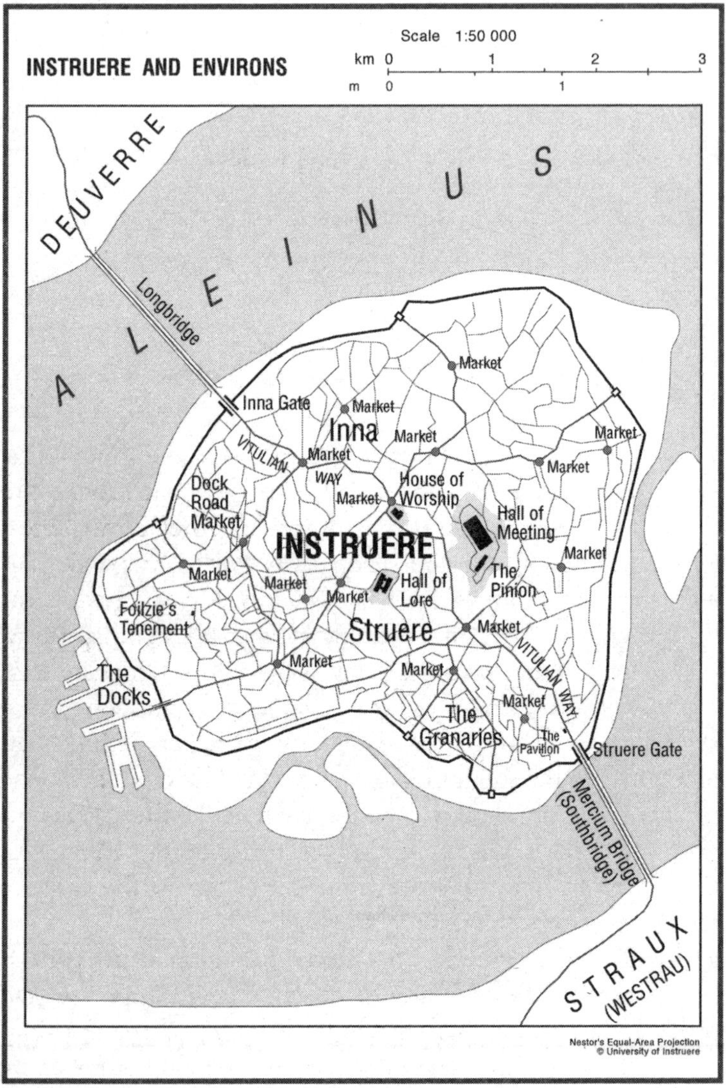
INSTRUERE AND ENVIRONS
Scale 1:50 000
km 0 1 2 3
m 0 1
DEUVERRE
ALEINUS
Longbridge
Inna Gate
Market
Inna
VITULIAN WAY
Dock Road Market
House of Worship
Hall of Meeting
INSTRUERE
The Pinion
Hall of Lore
Foilzie's Tenement
Struere
The Docks
The Granaries
The Pavilion
Struere Gate
Mercium Bridge (Southbridge)
STRAUX (WESTRAU)
Nestor's Equal-Area Projection
© University of Instruere

PROLOGUE

TWO PROUD MEN FACED each other over a low stone table. Both men nursed deep anger and bitterness. Each hated the other. They found themselves drawn together nevertheless by expediency and desire. Each man sought to govern his emotions, successfully so he thought, and each watched scornfully the other man's pitiful attempts to retain his equanimity.

'Escaigne remains well hidden, despite the treachery that saw us betrayed,' the Presiding Elder said. For a moment he considered confessing just how many of his people had been taken by the Instruian Guard, but decided to keep secret the paucity of his remaining force. Better to make the agreement first; better to avoid ceding the leadership of any alliance to the deranged man opposite him, especially on the basis of the number of followers.

The Hermit smiled. The man's thoughts were written plainly on his face. Watcher of the Sixth Rank, he had proclaimed himself. Watcher indeed! He could see nothing!

'Unlike you, I have lost no followers,' he told the Presiding

Elder. 'But some of them will die, I have seen it; holy martyrs who will be enthroned above us at the right hand of the Most High. Their example will serve to inspire the remainder of the Ecclesia. They will be seeds sown into the fertile ground of belief, and as the fire falls on Faltha I will reap a harvest of true believers.'

The older man snorted. 'I wouldn't be so sure about that if I were you. I predict that many of your Ecclesia will come flooding into Escaigne once they realise the emptiness of your promises. We offer them a chance of revenge against the corrupt Council, of setting real fires, not running after some numinous spiritual flame that achieves nothing. Your most sensible option is to join with us. Commit your people to Escaigne, the next rulers of Instruere, and I will see to it you are given an exalted place among our ranks.'

'I forbear to remind you of the many Escaignians who found real meaning in the Ecclesia,' the Hermit answered testily. 'Perhaps a few of them may return to your dubious care, but even they will come back to me when they discover you offer them nothing but the darkness of a windowless room.'

'Not for much longer!' The Presiding Elder stood and leaned forward over the table, his arms spread wide, hands on the cold stone. 'With or without your help we will reclaim the leadership of Instruere.'

'Reclaim? You've never led Instruere!'

'The Watchers were always involved in leadership,' the Presiding Elder growled.

'As were the true believers of the Most High!'

'Then why can we not work together?' The leader of Escaigne tried reason for the last time. This fool was probably not worth the effort, and everyone knew how badly his ill-equipped, untrained rabble would fare against the

Instruian Guard. Still, the Presiding Elder's plan required expendable soldiers, people to blunt the swords of the guardsmen, and he was unwilling to preside over the deaths of any Escaignians. These religious fools would serve him well.

'Of course we can,' the Hermit replied with forced sweetness, nearing the end of his patience. Why should the Anointed Man of God be subject to the wishes of an unbeliever such as this one? The day would soon come when all such would be placed under his heel!

Pulling himself together, he continued. 'The question is, who leads? Since both of us are men unaccustomed to following the wishes of another, it seems that we will not easily arrive at an answer. So, in the interests of our common goal, why do we not share command?'

'How would that work?'

'Simple. We do nothing without the agreement of both. Should this agreement not be sought, the alliance will be considered broken from that moment. And be warned! I have many ways of seeing, ways a Watcher cannot comprehend.'

'Save your mysticism for the gullible,' the Presiding Elder snapped. 'You are more persuasive when you trouble yourself to think. Very well, we will join our forces together – for a time. But at the first sign of treachery I will have no hesitation in abandoning you and your followers to their fate.'

'And I yours,' the blue-robed Hermit agreed, stretching out his right hand. The sallow-faced Elder took it in his own, and for a moment the two men were linked as one, each squeezing as though to break the bones in his ally's fingers.

CHAPTER 1

THE GATES OF INSTRUERE

THE CAMEL TRAIN SNAKING its way up the Pass of Adrar looked like all the other summer trains from Ghadir Massab – heavily laden, slow moving, and shimmering in the scorching heat. The train halted again and again like some hesitant reptile as the drivers stopped to water themselves, their beasts and their slaves, in that order. But, the bandit leader reflected as he watched it draw closer to his ambush, unlike all the other trains that travelled through Hamadabat on their way to the Central Plains of Faltha and to Bhrudwo, this one appeared here. Why not on one of the longer but less dangerous passes to the east?

The bandits could hardly believe their good fortune. What fool would take a fully-laden train over the highest pass in the Veridian Borders? Straux, the kingdom to the north of these mountains, had recently declared war on the slave traders and their cargoes of human misery. It hardly seemed credible the slavers would risk their lives on this northern road, even if it meant they would avoid having to pay off the marauders who lined the more easterly route out of Hamadabat. Nevertheless here they were; and the band of robbers awaiting them, cutthroats and murderers sloughed off from more successful groups, knew that their luck had finally turned. Until now the bandits had managed to construct a meagre existence from preying on the few lone travellers foolish enough to venture across the Borders without an armed escort, but it had not been enough. They were hungry, tired and starved of the various entertainments a captive could supply.

The Veridian Borders were the worn-out nubs of old mountains, beaten into submission by the hot southern sun and the clash of winds from the desert and the more fertile, rain-swept Maremma Basin to the north. The winds had carved the yellowing, grassless hills into a myriad of odd shapes. Adrar himself, the Golden Lion, presided over the head of the pass, while many other figures, most conjured up from local myths and legends, adorned the winding pass from mouth to crest. The best place for an ambush was directly below the Claws of Adrar, where the road narrowed between two steep talus rock slopes, just before it darted to the right, crested the mountains and began its journey down into Straux. Here the bandits waited.

Let the merchants think they'd made it all the way through the mountains, that was the game, then take them at the very last minute. Take them and have some fun with them, in the usual bandit style; then let one lucky merchant escape with his life, thereby ensuring their ruthlessness became a byword, all the better to attract more desperate men. This robber band had more to prove than any of the others, and each member had secret plans for any merchant or slave who remained alive after the initial exchange. The excitement rose as the camel train inched closer. One of the lieutenants drew his sword to clean it, and his arm was slapped down by the bandit leader in case the sun glinted on the exposed blade. *Not that it matters*, he thought. These merchants were either so foolish or so overconfident they had posted no scouts. They probably wouldn't notice if he knifed one of his men in the back and sent him plummeting to the road. Briefly occupied with this thought, it was all the bandit leader could do to stop himself laughing out loud.

As the camel train passed a predetermined point the robbers divided into two groups, one to block the head of the pass in front of the train, the other to block the road behind them. Once the road was secure, they could take as long as they wanted over what would happen next.

At a signal, the still afternoon air was rent by the ululations of two dozen bandits scampering down the slope towards the hapless merchants. The bandit leader noted something minor had already gone wrong. When the group led by his second-in-command reached the road below the camel train, the merchants and their slaves had contrived to place themselves further down the road. Rather than trapping their prey up against the frightened camels, the robbers themselves were trapped. The bandit leader shrugged his shoulders. Killing rather than planning was his lieutenant's strong suit. It wouldn't matter to him which direction he faced when he killed.

The dozen or so robbers who ran shouting on to the path in front of the train found not the panic and terror their surprise attack was supposed to create, but an eerie silence, and one man standing to meet them. He wore a long, flowing black robe in the Bhrudwan fashion, though the cowl was thrown back to reveal a close-cropped head, a young but weather-beaten face punctuated with deep-set eyes. He stood the way an experienced fighter stands, balanced on the balls of his feet, ready to counter any thrust from his enemy. *A Bhrudwan*, the bandit leader mused. *And a warrior. I might lose one or two of my men – it's time they were culled anyway. I have nothing to fear. I have faced men said to have fought alongside the Lords of Fear themselves.*

Perhaps the bandits might have had a chance of survival had they abandoned their original plan and focused all their attention on the lone warrior. But they did not, deeming him the sacrificial bait in some desperate gambit. Angered his trap had been sprung, at least to some degree, the bandit leader cried out a command, throwing his hindmost group at the merchants and their slaves, and ignored the lone man for the moment.

As the merchants threw back their cloaks and drew their weapons, the bandits' second-in-command received his first of many shocks. These were not the sleek Falthans he was familiar with, men who had grown rich trading in the misery of others; instead they wore the look of hardened fighters. That one there, the dark-skinned one wielding a huge stone club as if it weighed nothing at all, he would not scream for mercy as soon as a knife was set to his skin, promising to reveal hidden treasures in exchange for his life. Neither would the man beside him, a long-haired Falthan wearing a tunic marking him as a Deruvian. That woman there, she would scream, but the fierceness that distorted her face made him realise this one would kill or be killed before she let anyone get their hands on her. And the truly fat man wearing a red robe, he had the light of madness in his eyes, as though some dark hunger lurked within. He had seen that light in the eyes of one or two of his former companions, a death wish that had eventually been granted. Some of the arrogance the second-in-command habitually cloaked himself with began to drain away, to be replaced by an unfamiliar fear. *Caution*, he told himself.

Then it dawned on him that the supposed 'slaves' were not shackled together. They, in their turn, drew weapons and now stood opposed to his men. To his left stood a young girl, trying not to be scared; beside her another fat man strove to keep the fear off his face; a thin man with a staff; a cripple who held his sword awkwardly but with confidence; and still others the bandit did not have time to identify.

Even as he tried to think this turn of events through, the merchants and their slaves set upon him. Instantly two of his men were down, slow-witted enough not to have realised that something was wrong, paying the price for overconfidence. No coward, the second-in-command moved towards the man with the stone club and his long-haired Deruvian companion, rightly identifying them as his greatest threat. Immediately he regretted his decision. The sheer speed of their strikes and thrusts was unlike anything he'd ever experienced. The stone club howled horribly as it swung through the air, just missing his unprotected arm. He could not parry the club, and had to duck and weave, backing away more and more quickly just to stay alive. The Deruvian took a wicked swing, and next to him one of the bandits – he couldn't see which one, but it sounded like Hamus – shrieked in agony. He found himself ducking again and again, without respite, trying to keep the savage man off him, cursing the bandit leader, cursing their bad luck, certain now they would all die here. Back, back again; then he heard a wheezing behind him, felt a sudden thump in his back and something burned hot in his lungs. He looked down through blurring eyes to see the tip of a sword protruding from his chest, and he cried out in fear as the day he had told himself would never arrive finally came upon him.

A hundred paces further up the pass the bandit leader awoke to his peril and, far too late, decided to cut down the lone Bhrudwan and make his escape. With a shrill cry he sent his second band of men at the warrior.

The narrow path allowed only three bandits to come at the Bhrudwan at one time. The bandit leader watched transfixed as the sword moved from one place to the next with blurring speed, often in a quite different direction to which the Bhrudwan sent his body. The man's strength was clear. His first real blow took off a sword arm and ended embedded in the unfortunate man's hip. He delivered it with only a casual flick of his arm, his body already moving to meet the stroke of his next assailant. The bandit leader noted this in a dry place at the back of his mind. Not one of the Bhrudwan's strokes could be said to have finished: all flowed into a graceful dance where sword tip counterpointed feet and head, all seemingly going their own way, but meeting together to deliver a death blow. It was music, it was poetry, it was slaughter.

Six men down, and only now did the bandit leader realise he had met something he never would have believed could exist. Surely the dreaded Lords of Fear themselves could not fight like this – this spirit-being! He abandoned the half-dozen remaining men to their fate, and began to scramble up the slope.

Within moments there were only two robbers left standing on the path, one of whom already emitted a dreadful wailing, a keening for the death that even now reached out to claim him. The other seemed to be a good fighter, one who might have given any of the others pause, but the Bhrudwan warrior's cruel blade had inflicted the killing blow and was withdrawn before the man moved to duck.

The Bhrudwan took a moment to check his victims for any sign of life; then, satisfied, he hefted his sword and in a powerful overhand motion threw it up the slope. The bright blade took the bandit leader in the back, and the last sound of the conflict was that of the body rolling back down to the path accompanied by a number of small rocks.

'Most High, Most High,' Wiusago breathed as he made his way back down the path to meet the others. For a moment he stopped on the path, hands on his knees, as the urge to vomit almost overcame him. He had seen death before, but not like this.

'What happened?' Phemanderac asked him and Te Tuahangata, both of whom had sprinted up the path in what turned out to be an unnecessary effort to help Achtal deal with the bandits. 'Did you see?'

'Yes, we saw,' the Deruvian prince replied, unable to keep his voice entirely level. 'And I, for one, wish I had not.'

Achtal came down the path to join the others, wiping his sword clean as he walked, showing no sign of arrogance or pride that Kurr could see. Apart from the sweat beaded on Achtal's broad face and the dust clinging to his robe, nothing indicated he had killed some twelve bandits unaided. Te Tuahangata, who still breathed heavily from his own exertions, shook his head in simple disbelief, and Prince Wiusago, his friend, his enemy, returned the gesture.

'I was raised as a swordsman,' the blond man said, still struggling to control his voice. 'I've sparred with the best in

Deruys. Were I to tell them what I've just witnessed, they would counsel me to stop frequenting taverns.'

'I was born a warrior,' Te Tuahangata countered angrily, 'and we do not fight as others do. Neither strength nor skill alone makes a warrior. We Mist-warriors are taught to live like fighting men. Larger than life, intimidating in everything we do. That is part of being a true warrior.' He sounded as though he was trying to convince himself.

The Deruvian laughed at his companion's words, not unkindly. 'Yes, my friend, you are right. I have seen you fight. Gestures, war cries, swinging your club in huge, extravagant arcs, the howling noise it makes, those things are enough to break the spirits of all but the bravest of foes. Yet the Bhrudwan teaches us a different way. He does nothing for show. Everything has an economy about it, which speaks of care and devotion, of calm and heart's peace, of having nothing to prove, unlike you and I. He makes no hasty moves and so comes to no hasty conclusions. He never overcommits himself and so can flow from one move to the next without effort. You, dear Tua, are hot-blooded in all you do. He is cold. While I prefer your way to his, there is much we must learn from him before we can truly call ourselves warriors.'

His companion merely grunted, clearly unwilling to accept either the compliment or the judgment implied in the words. But from what Kurr saw, the Child of the Mist had plenty to think about.

A much different and darker set of thoughts occupied the old farmer's mind. He, too, had run some way up the path to give whatever help he could to the Bhrudwan, in itself surprising given that a few short months ago this man had tried to kill him and his friends. And this, really, was the nub of his problem. He had just seen this implacable warrior do something otherwordly, something which must have required the dedication of a lifetime to perform. Yet he and his little band of village peasants had faced four of these monsters, of whom this man was the least, and defeated them. Watching the Bhrudwan kill a dozen bandits brought home to him how unlikely their own victory had been, and he mentioned his concern to the Haufuth as they readied the camel train to move on.

The village headman stood silent a moment, stroking his chin, before answering. 'Well, you benefited from some luck, I can see that. From what you've said, had all the Bhrudwans walked across that swingbridge with their captives, you would never have executed your ambush, no matter how clever it was.'

Phemanderac spoke up from behind them: he had just finished applying a damp cloth to the swelling on Belladonna's temple. The injury, incurred in the Deep Desert, seemed for some time to have given her a deathly hurt, but had recently healed somewhat. The swelling was still evident, however, and the magician's daughter still had trouble keeping down solid food.

'According to Mablas of Dhauria, who made a study of these things, the Lords of Fear are not only great warriors, but are also masters of the Realm of Fire, and can use illusion, the Wordweave and dark magic to achieve their ends. When Leith first told me of your Company, and how you had overcome four Lords of Fear, I assumed he was being modest about his own abilities, and you were the greatest of your people, life-trained and hand-picked to oppose the Destroyer's servants. But then I saw it was not so, and it became evident you had not overcome the Lords of Fear by strength or by magic. How, then, could you doubt the favour of the Most High rests on you? How else could you have defeated them?'

The Haufuth scowled, and Kurr muttered under his breath. The lean philosopher had been talking like this for days, ever since their deliverance from the slave markets, in spite of the anger it engendered among his fellow travellers. There had been a time, Kurr admitted, that he had almost been persuaded. Almost he had believed they were the chosen of the Most High, his instruments of salvation destined to bring deliverance to Faltha. To his credit, the Haufuth had never gone along with the words of this outlandish man, words echoed by the equally suspect Hermit, and even by Hal, their own fey prophet. Yes, there were things he couldn't explain, rightly or wrongly, he acknowledged that. He'd seen the castle of Kantara with his own eyes, had witnessed the power of the Jugom Ark. His friend the Haufuth bore the physical scars on his hand in testament to that power. But knowing these things and not being able to explain them fell a long way short of the unquestioning belief others professed.

'Answer me this, then, O Prophet of the Most High,' Kurr grated. 'If his favour rests on us, where is the Jugom Ark? Where is Leith? Strange way to show favour is that, burying Arrow and Wielder alike under a pile of rubble.' He knew his words hurt Phemanderac, he meant them to hurt, because the philosopher seemed not to care for their feelings, so often did he bring up the subject. Phemanderac turned away without a word and busied himself with one of the packs. Perhaps he did care, but not enough. Leith was not from *his* village.

The old farmer returned to the problem. How had the four Bhrudwan warriors been defeated? How had the Company bested even one, this Acolyte, as Mahnum named him?

The question would not leave him, and every time Achtal the Bhrudwan aided them and then deferred to Hal the cripple, unease grew in his mind like a blight taking hold in his apple orchard back on Stibbourne Farm. He remembered giving up hope of anything but a slave's life in that terrible city by the Lake of Gold, until miraculously their purchaser turned out to be the Bhrudwan, complete with camel train. They had been totally in his power then, yet he acted as their servant. What sort of hold did Hal have on the man, and how secure was it? It was as though the Company held the sun in a jar and made it do their bidding. At any time it might break out of its prison and incinerate them all with its power.

Perhaps that was the plan all along.

The travellers took a moment to tend their animals, then set off again to climb the few remaining steps to the top of the pass. Already the huge desert flies buzzed lazily around the pools of drying blood. Achtal did not spare the bodies even a glance: it was as though the people who until a few moments ago inhabited them no longer existed for him. Kurr and the former Captain of the Instruian Guard, who shared with Achtal the vanguard of the camel train, exchanged uneasy glances.

Further down the train the Arkhos of Nemohaim wiped sweaty palms on his red robe. The last few weeks had proven extremely taxing for him, but he was alive, a victory of sorts. Even his dark inner voice was quiet now, sated for the moment by the bandit stepping back on to his sword.

The Arkhos received as deep a shock as anyone to be redeemed from the slave market of Ghadir Massab by the Bhrudwan. He'd fully expected to be killed. Indeed, his captain had made to defend him, but the traitorous Bhrudwan did nothing but lead them to a camel train he had persuaded one of his countrymen to give him. The Arkhos was not clear over that – the Bhrudwan must indeed be high in their complicated hierarchy to have commandeered such wealth – but it proved the perfect disguise. The Bhrudwan even produced their cloaks, packs and swords, having gained them from the slavers as part of the purchase price he paid.

The hatred the Arkhos of Nemohaim bore towards these northerners had not lessened, he knew that, everyone knew that, there was no point pretending otherwise; but while that cursed Bhrudwan served them he could do little but agree to a temporary alliance. Strangely, the crippled boy had suggested it, arguing it would be sensible to recognise the informal partnership originally forced on them because of the attack by the Sanusi of the Deep Desert. In the uncertainty of their rescue it had been agreed to by the northerners, no doubt for the same reason as he gave his swift assent. Sharing the road with his enemies was better than the alternative, which was to lose contact with them – or worse still, to be hunted by them.

The arrangement, therefore, met with the Arkhos's approval. Without their support it was less certain that he would be able to return to Instruere. And he desperately wished to return. He had plans for that city, and for its new leader. The loss of the Jugom Ark did not change that.

The camel train crested the pass; and suddenly the green basin of Maremma lay spread below them like an irregularly patched cloth. A spur of the Veridian Hills stretched a brown finger into the smoky distance, and along this spur, high above the plains, wound their path. Through the town of Fealty it would go, the birthplace of Conal Greatheart and still the seat of his knightly order, then down to Sivithar on the great river, and thence to Instruere; two weeks or more at walking pace. There the travellers would go, having failed in their quest. They were bereft of the Jugom Ark, had lost one of the Arkhimm, and faced an uncertain future.

The Arkhos smiled. He was certain about one thing. The future would involve blood and fire.

The abiding impression created by the Wodhaitic Sea was one of peace. Each morning Leith invariably found his favourite position, lying on his stomach in the prow of the outrigger, letting the silent, turquoise depths slide by mere inches from his face, taking in deep breaths of the astringent salt air. He would spend the day talking with Maendraga, or perhaps with Geinor and his son Graig, while they fished for their evening meal. Then in the evenings, after the warm rains, the glorious red-green sunsets and the swift darkness, Leith talked with the navigator, the only Aslaman willing to make conversation with him.

In spite of all that had happened to Leith, he did not truly appreciate how exotic his life had become until these nights on the ocean. On his travels he had seen so many places unlike the green, rolling hills and chalk cliffs of Loulea, his home: barren, snow-covered moors, cold rearing peaks, deep green woods, wide white deserts. An amazing variety of people had crossed his path, from the ragged villains of Windrise to the laughing Fodhram, the simple but proud Fenni, the sophisticated yet confusing urbane Instruians. Yet the most unsettling land Leith had yet travelled was no land at all, but the sea, the wide, pathless Wodhaitic Sea.

Two weeks on the ocean had given Leith his first respite, his first chance to really think, since that Midwinter's night many months ago. He found himself relaxing, unclenching like a hand held as a fist for too long – or, perhaps, like the hand learning to hold the Jugom Ark more and more gently. So, for the first time on his journey, he was in a position to appreciate the unfamiliarity surrounding him.

Relentless heat served as a constant reminder that he journeyed far beyond the lands he knew. Coming from a Firanese winter to the warmth of late spring in Instruere felt odd enough, but with so much to occupy them all in the great city of Faltha he hardly noticed the warmth, or perhaps became accustomed to it. The Valley of a Thousand Fires assaulted them with unbearable ferocity, but their journey through the valley lasted only a few days, and they gained some respite at night. But here on the Wodhaitic he found no escape, day or night. The night heat was the worst, leaving him gasping for breath, sweating like a horse after a day's hard riding.

Along with the heat and the vastness of the pitching, heaving ocean came the astonishing skill of their navigator. The archipelago to which they had travelled had been made up of a few dozen tiny islands, none more than half a day's walk around, scattered like crumbs on a tabletop; yet the Aslamen guided their craft straight to them, travelling a hundred leagues or more northwards across the west wind in just over a week. Leith felt sure, in spite of the confidence the Aslamen displayed, they would miss their target and go sailing on forever, until the ice swallowed them or they came to the end of the world; but had since learned in conversations with the navigator that a combination of secrets, wielded by one with experience and skill, made the islands difficult to miss.

The islands themselves were tiny outposts hidden like secrets in the midst of the sea. Leith had expected small mountains rising out of the water, miniatures of the lands he knew; but the island upon which they made their landing was raised no more than a man's height above the waves. As they had sailed through a narrow gap in the coral reef and into a wide lagoon so startlingly blue it seemed to have been mistakenly coloured by a child, Maendraga leaned over to Leith and whispered in his ear: 'No talking now. This is Motu-tapu, the sacred island of the Aslamen. No word may be spoken until we leave, save the passing on of the Name.' Leith nodded his head in earnest reply, though he had been told this before, and had little idea of what the magician meant. All he knew was that Maendraga desperately wanted to bury his dead wife's name, and he had usurped the quest to do so. The Guardian of the Arrow had claimed that travelling on the dugout canoe would be the speediest and safest way back to Instruere, but Leith suspected that Maendraga would have insisted on this particular journey even if it proved the slowest path of all.

Once on the island, little more than a strip of land that cleverly escaped the notice of the sea, the four outsiders were instructed to wait under the palm trees until it was time. There they waited in silence through the long morning and longer afternoon, watching the white clouds gather and lifting their faces to the warm rains; until the evening when, the air washed clean and fires burning along the beach, they were summoned to the Burying.

Perhaps a hundred people, maybe more, assembled before the largest of the bonfires on the shores of Motu-tapu on the night of the Burying. Leith and his companions were the only people not Aslamen, and they felt a keen discomfit. The islanders did not need words to communicate their disdain, even hatred, of the White-skins. The air seethed with a barely restrained violence, as though the four intruders were committing innumerable acts of sacrilege simply by standing under the trees. For a while Leith thought it might be provoked by the presence of the Jugom Ark; but, curiously, none of the islanders indicated any interest in the flaming Arrow he carried, or showed any fear of it. Leith kept his tongue, in spite of his curiosity and growing nervousness, and did not ask Maendraga what was so important about his wife's name that they needed to brave this suppressed malice to return it to the island. And now, it seemed, the secret was about to be revealed.

A man wearing a long robe and carrying a blazing brand came forward and with the fiery stick pointed to a woman. With great dignity of bearing she walked to the fire, pulling something out from under her robe as she did so. In the half-light Leith could not be certain what it was, but he fancied it was a doll. The woman held it up for a moment, then cast it into the flames.

As she stood watching it burn, a small child came up to her. The woman bent down and whispered something in the little girl's ear. A shy smile spread over the child's face, then she and the woman shared an embrace. A moment later the little girl danced off into the shadows, obviously happy.

What's all that about? Plainly Leith would get no answers here, as talking was forbidden. He would have to wait until they left the island and he could question Maendraga. Whatever had just happened, its significance escaped him.

<A Name has been buried and reborn,> said the voice in his mind.

Leith started, and let slip an involuntary gasp that, fortunately, no one heard above the crackling and sighing of the fire.

He would never get used to the voice in his head. He certainly never wanted to.

<Here on this shore the Names of the dead are returned to the Pei-ra. They are committed to the fire, thereby freeing the Name to be given to the next generation.>

So the Name is cast into the fire by the symbolic act of casting some object in? Something personal that belonged to the dead person?

<Yes. The doll was owned by a little girl called Laya, who died of a sickness in her bones. She was loved very much, and all the islanders miss her. But now her Name has been reborn, and whenever they see the new Laya, they will remember and be glad. And the new Laya will try her best to be good like the old Laya was.>

Do you believe all that stuff? Leith asked, though he was profoundly moved by the simplicity of the ceremony.

<Believe it? If you mean to ask whether their interpretation of events is totally accurate, then the answer is no. But no more inaccurate than yours. And somewhat more meaningful.>

Then why is this silence necessary? Why is no one allowed to talk?

<Names are sacred to the Pei-ra, nowhere more so than on this island. The only words to be spoken here are the reborn Names, and then only at the moment of rebirth. Thus they are sealed to the next generation. The Names are never an islander's personal property. They are held communally, and loaned to the person using it. But at death they must be returned to the heart of Pei-ra, names gathered to the secret Name of the Aslamen, and from there redistributed. I like the system. It teaches respect for the achievements of the dead, and fidelity to the living.>

So Maendraga's wife Nena? Is that why Maendraga came here – so that her Name can be reborn?

<So his memories of her can find rest. So he can pass on the Name in the belief that someone, somewhere, is striving to be faithful like his Nena.>

And if she doesn't? What if she shames the Name by her deeds?

<Watch and see. Look at her face. Then decide if Nena's memory and Name will be honoured.>

Hold on. You called these people Pei-ra! Weren't they the ones driven out of Astraea by the Tabuli and the Nemohaimians? Didn't we see the battle mounds in the hills north of Kantara? How can these people be Pei-ra if they are Aslamen? Why did you call it their secret Name?

But the voice had apparently finished talking with him, and gone back to wherever it came from. Leith couldn't help feeling he was being conditioned by the voice, just like the sheep back home in Loulea Vale, herded in directions they themselves would not have chosen by a taciturn shepherd and his dogs. He remembered the morning he had helped Kurr with the sheep for the Midwinter Feast, and felt a growing sympathy with the sheep when they tried to escape the voice of the shepherd.

As Leith watched, the man with the blazing torch walked towards where the outsiders stood, arm outstretched and pointing. A hundred pairs of eyes gazed at Maendraga as he stepped forward. In the ochre light of the fire the magician looked old, tired, as though he carried a burden too heavy for his back.

He shuffled over to the fire, and flicked aside his robe. From a fold he brought out a carving, about a forearm's length tall: it gleamed in the firelight, visible in the flickering light even from where Leith waited. A carving of a woman, a young woman, with sadness etched on her face, surpassing in some indescribable fashion any art Leith had ever seen. To one who himself had the soul of a carver, who once carved a replica of his own father from birch bark, the sight brought tears to Leith's eyes. Only too poignantly did he appreciate what that carving must mean to Maendraga the magician. How many nights must he have sat by his fire, alone with his memories, trying to recapture something that faded from his mind, eluded his heart?

Tears streamed down the old man's face as he raised the carving to the heavens, as if in declaration of his undying love. Then, in a moment that cramped the heart with aching, he cast it on the fire; and wept silently.

A young girl with black hair to her waist detached herself from the others and stepped forward. Leith wiped the tears away from his eyes so he could better see her face. She could be no more than eight years old. With a start, Leith realised she must have lived those eight years without a name, and this night must be very important for her also.

Her small face was set in determined lines: below her black fringe her large brown eyes contained no doubt, her wide mouth set in a slight smile. Her hands shook slightly, yet she strode quickly, confidently up to Maendraga, and smiled encouragingly at the stranger who held her Name in his heart.

For an awkward, fearful moment Leith thought Maendraga was not going to respond, that he might even reject the girl, or do something that would see them all killed. But he did not. Instead, he placed his hands on her shoulders and looked searchingly into her eyes for what seemed like an age. Then, as if satisfied at what he saw, he bent his mouth to her ear and whispered a name.

'Nena.' Even though it had been whispered, Leith imagined he heard it spoken aloud. Lost in beauty, he had no idea the voice he heard was his own.

The girl's smile was immediate and genuine, reflected in the lustre of her eyes. Leith watched her carefully: undoubtedly the islanders would know Maendraga's wife Nena had been an outcast, and had lived among strangers, far from the sacred shores. This little girl may not have known what Name she would receive, but she would have known the story. She showed no shame as she accepted the Name, only pleasure and a determination to be worthy. She too had seen the carving and the tears it brought. Perhaps she even understood what it meant to the old man.

The Burying ceremony continued for some time after this, but Leith, lost in thought, noticed little until he was suddenly shoved roughly from behind, then propelled towards the fire. For a confused moment he thought he was being made part of the ceremony, but the fire burned untended now, and the people had withdrawn into the darkness. Geinor and Graig were somewhere behind him, and Maendraga was nowhere to be seen. If anything, the faces of the Aslamen surrounding him, jostling him forward, were more hostile than they had yet been. Unease turned to panic. Leith realised this was certainly no part of the Burying. *What is going on?* Now, when it would have been truly useful, the voice remained silent.

Strong arms steered him past the Burying fire, guided him to the water's edge and thrust him into a small boat; joined there by three Aslamen. Leith resisted the urge to shout. Maendraga had impressed upon him the danger of speaking, the offence it would cause, and Leith did not wish to bring the wrath of these people down on himself. The men cast off, paddled silently but with angry strokes across the moonlit lagoon, then hove to on the seaward side of the reef.

'What—' Leith began, then stopped as a stone-blade knife drew a line lightly across his throat. He stiffened in shock. A harsh voice rasped in his ear: 'No sound. More sound, I cut out your voice.'

The Jugom Ark flared in his hand, reminding him of its power. For a moment he considered using it against his captors – stabbing them, slashing them, driving them away with the weapon of the Most High. He even raised his hand fractionally.

No, he told himself, *no. It's not that kind of weapon. If I ask the Most High for help every time I get into trouble, I'll end up a servant with no control over anything.* So he sat there, bleeding from the neck, trying not to move, not to give offence, but knowing he had offended, and he continued to offend.

Another canoe pulled alongside and Maendraga clambered in beside him. 'Listen carefully to me, Leith,' said the magician in an urgent whisper. 'The Aslamen want to know why you spoke a name on the sacred island. They want to know why you stole someone's Name.'

For a moment Leith was at a loss, and again he considered using the Arrow, or asking the magician to cast some spell that might save them. Then he remembered the moment Maendraga had spoken the name, remembered watching, remembered how it had affected him, remembered the Name being spoken aloud – and suddenly his transgression became clear. No use arguing it had been unintentional, done out of ignorance. He had spoken where it was sacrilege to speak. He nodded, summoned up enough saliva to enable him to speak, and waited until the knife eased away from his throat.

'I was caught by the moment,' he said simply. 'I saw the girl receive her Name, and I spoke it aloud without realising.' He turned to face Maendraga. 'How can I be sorry for that? Should I apologise for being moved?' It was a reckless reply, he knew, but it brought a grunt of understanding from at least one of the men surrounding him.

'You are First Man,' said the voice of the man holding the knife. 'You say you were first, but you were last. You came to our island and broke our rules. When we break your rules you kill us all. What should we do to you?'

In that moment, as the Aslamen waited for his answer, Leith's mind turned over the puzzling thing the voice had said during the Burying ceremony. 'He called you Pei-ra. He said it was your secret Name. I saw your battle mounds in the hills of Astraea, and took sable armour for myself. I—'

The Aslamen backed away from him, thrusting themselves towards the stern of the canoe and nearly swamping it, forgetting their seamanship in their haste. The eyes that stared at him in shock were rimmed with fear and loathing.

'The burial mounds . . . they remain?'

The question was hesitant, and layered with a number of undercurrents. Anger that one of the despised First Men had something they wanted, fear of the answer he might give, shame at the reminder of their debased state and the loss of their homeland, all were mixed into the few words spoken.

It did not seem possible that Leith might read such great significance into those words, but he did. He told himself it must be the Arrow, that possessing the Jugom Ark gave him magical insight into the words of others. After all, he reasoned, how else had he bested the King of Nemohaim but a few days earlier?

'The Pei-ra lie untended and unregarded in the land of

Astraea,' Leith said, almost dreamily. 'The land is uninhabited, while the Tabuli and the Nemohaimians go about their business elsewhere, having forgotten their quarrel with you.' And, hoping his insight ran true, he added: 'There will be no one to interfere when you return to bury the many, many Names in the great fires you will set there, and the Pei-ra will have their Name restored once more.'

Is this your story? he hissed a thought, but there came no answer.

Maendraga looked at the youth with something approaching awe. The Aslamen – the Pei-ra – began to mutter among themselves, and there was no more talk of what ought to be done with Leith.

I'm still doing it, Leith realised. *Still gathering*. Someone from the Pei-ra would come to Instruere, to be part of the salvation of the First Men . . . He wasn't understanding fully, he did not have the whole picture; something greater, perhaps, than he yet appreciated was still to unfold. Nevertheless, as he watched the men talking with each other, still reluctant to meet his eye, he was content.

That night the Pei-ra held a meeting on the sacred island and, for the first time in a generation, voices were raised above a whisper in that place, and something other than Names were spoken. Leith, Maendraga and the two Nemohaimians were excluded, but needed no interpreter to tell them what topic dominated the energetic discussions they could see and hear from the other side of the lagoon. Children talked with the women and the men as the fires burned on into the early morning. Then, as dawn smudged the sky with a pale light, a great cry rang out across the water and the Pei-ra sprang for their canoes.

'They're leaving for Astraea?' Leith said, surprised at the lack of preparation. 'Just like that?'

'No, they won't go for a long time yet,' replied Geinor of Nemohaim. His voice, unused during the long evening and night, sounded reedier than ever. 'They will wait until the turning of the winds later in the year, when the summer is over and the rains come. They could not easily sail to the coast of Cachoeira with the wind from the west, as it will be for months yet.'

'Well, where are they going, then?'

The old counsellor paused over his reply. 'I know not, but guess that the Aslamen will travel to their own islands to bring their people the news. You did not think these few were all of the Aslamen, did you? They occupy a hundred or more islands spread across the southern Wodhaitic Sea. It will take them many weeks to prepare.'

Geinor continued, hands clasped firmly together in front of his tunic like a young boy accounting for displeasing his parents. 'Were this to have occurred without our knowledge while I was responsible for Nemohaim's intelligence network, the king would have dismissed and exiled me instantly. It is – was – my business to know everything about the lands and the people who surround us. I have to admit to having given the Aslamen little or no thought. That they are in truth the Pei-ra come to live in these islands is something neither I, nor anyone else in Nemohaim, would ever have guessed.'

The man was obviously having trouble not behaving like a functionary of the Nemohaim court. It was as though he looked for someone to whom to apologise for his oversight.

Leith turned to the magician. 'Did you know?'

Maendraga nodded slowly. 'I ought to have. My great-grandfather was the last Guardian to encounter the Pei-ra, and he told us terrible tales of the wars that ravaged Astraea. One or two of the Pei-ra escaped into the Almucantaran Mountains, and he cared for them until they died or were well enough to leave.

'Leith, I don't think you realise what you've done. Now that you've told them Astraea is uninhabited, the Aslamen will try to return to their ancient home. I have no doubt they will succeed, and I also have no doubt they will be seen. What will happen when some fool from Tabul or Nemohaim – no offence, Geinor – decides that if the Pei-ra want Astraea enough to return from the dead, then he wants it too?'

'It'll be a bloodbath,' Graig said sadly. 'Like it was last time, like Vassilian on the Plains of Amare, like it always is.' He glanced at the Jugom Ark which, though subdued, still commanded his attention as it had since the day he intercepted Leith and Maendraga on the road south of Bewray. 'Unless something can be done about it.'

But Leith no longer listened. He did not see how all this could possibly be part of the task that lay ahead of him. Uniting the Sixteen Kingdoms of Faltha would be difficult enough without concerning himself about the Pei-ra – or the Children of the Mist, or the Widuz, or the Fenni, or the Fodhram, or any of the *losian* who lived on the margins of Faltha, regrettable as their plight was. The Bhrudwan army was coming, and he and his friends, scattered as they were across southern Faltha, represented Faltha's best hope – maybe Faltha's only hope – of turning them aside.

Though the ocean had many moods, and showed them all to the seafarers, Leith and Maendraga never felt unsafe. The Pei-ratin navigator exuded an air of confidence in, even command of, the sea. It was as though the Wodhaitic forbore to trouble them, respecting the seamanship of the men from Pei-ra and the artistry of their navigator. Certainly, the dark-skinned Pei-ratin revered the sea, almost to the point of worship; and surely no deity would willingly take the lives of such a devoted subject. Or perhaps the vast open ocean feared to offend the even vaster power held within the Jugom Ark. Whatever the reason, the Wodhaitic Sea declined to trouble the fragile canoe, preserving its inscrutable serenity, venting its puissance on some far-distant shore.

Little talk disturbed the silence on the boat. While the pilot at least had a rudimentary grasp of the common tongue, and Leith had much that was needful to discuss with Maendraga, the overwhelming majesty of the sea kept them quiet, leaving the youth from Loulea to deal with the poignancy of his memories. His birthday had passed him by somewhere on the long journey. He had lost track of the days somewhere south of Instruere, probably in Hinepukohurangi, the land of Mist, or perhaps in the Valley of a Thousand Fires. Though now seventeen, of an age where boys in his home country of Firanes became men, left their parents' house and 'took to the land', he was by no means ready to bear the burdens the peril of Faltha thrust upon him. By intuition – Leith was still reluctant to put a name to his inner voice – he had found and taken hold of the Jugom Ark, when no one else dared to touch its flaming shaft. Right then, in Joram Basin high above Kantara, the quest was still on track, and its fulfilment lay burning in Leith's hands.

Then the Sentinels jerked into life. Leith's heart quailed at the memory. The Arkhos of Nemohaim pursued the Five of the Hand, climbing up to the sacred Joram Basin, and something in the magic of the place, left there by Bewray himself, set the mountains shaking when the feet of traitors desecrated the holy site. Though he had since spent much time reflecting on those fraught hours, Leith could still make no sense of the confusion that struck them all, scattered them all, and claimed lives. The shriek of the Instruian archivist as he fell into the chasm bound itself into his dreams. And, when the mountains finally stopped their shaking, he had lost his companions. The Arkhimm was no more. All that remained was the Jugom Ark.

After searching fruitlessly for the rest of the Arkhimm, Leith abandoned that high and holy place and, with Maendraga, the Guardian of the Arrow, made his way sorrowfully to Bewray, capital of Nemohaim. There, with the aid of the Arrow, he performed a miraculous healing, and gained the friendship and assistance of Geinor the counsellor and his son Graig, making an enemy of the king in the process. The healing was still a difficult knot in his memory, deliberately left unexamined for fear of what he might find. Had it been the power of the Arrow? Or was he, Leith, like his brother, able to tap into (*enhance*, Hal called it) healing and other magical powers? Or was this all the work of the Most High, and were Leith and his brother – were they all – merely pawns? Of any possibility, that was the one Leith feared: that nothing he did, no risk he took, really mattered; that some divine protection ensured success by removing freedom of choice; that, like Hal, he was incapable of making a mistake, or at least admitting it. He wanted to be more than one of the stars fixed in the sky, forever set to follow a predetermined course around the locus of the plans of the Most High.

And now he was here, out in the wide Wodhaitic Sea, sailing towards Instruere and whatever was to come. Here with Maendraga the magician, the Guardian of the Arrow, with Geinor and Graig of Nemohaim, and with a Pei-ratin pilot and a crew who could not decide what to make of him. Here with the Jugom Ark, a mind full of doubts, a few haggard memories and the tattered remnants of a quest.

The last few miles of the journey up the Aleinus River were made against the wind and the tide, so Leith and Maendraga joined the others in paddling with those strange, teardrop-shaped oars the Aslamen used. Ahead of them Instruere rose from a low bank of fog, or perhaps a morning haze; certainly the air felt heavy, making it difficult to see any real distance even though the sun beat down on them and the day was otherwise clear. Few boats plied the River, fewer than Leith remembered from his morning walks on the walls when last he'd been part of this place. Far fewer than anticipated by those Aslamen who had made this trip before, raising a number of puzzled comments from the stern of the dugout. Still enough river traffic, however, to force the navigator to continue his conversation with Leith in a series of snatches separated by careful perusal of the waters ahead.

'You say we are hostile to strangers,' said the curly-headed Aslaman pilot, picking up a conversation he and Leith had shared since sunrise. 'If we are hostile, why did we allow you to set foot on Motu-tapu? And when you broke our laws, why did we let you leave?'

Leith nodded, conceding the point. 'But we've met other *lo*— other people who are not First Men, and they were very friendly.'

'Hmph,' the pilot snorted. 'They must have been people who still have their land. If they knew the history of the Pei-ra they would not think so kindly of First Men.'

Again Leith was forced to concede. 'But neither Maendraga nor myself have maltreated such people. We are not your enemies! On my travels I attacked nobody, but was captured twice by people who are not First Men. The Fenni would have put us to death but for the intervention of one of their number, and the Widuz tried to sacrifice us to their god. How can you say that we're the ones to blame?'

'Whose land were you on when these things happened? Your own?'

For the third time Leith acknowledged the point. Even as he talked he remembered the words of Farr at the inn in Windrise, his assertion that the *losian* were not real people, ill-chosen words that probably led to the attack on the Company in the Valley of Respite.

'That's true, but—'

But the Pei-ratin navigator turned away, and Leith noticed they drew level with the city docks. The air here tasted acrid, filled with smoke and sulphur. The pilot called out politely to a dock worker, asking for permission to put ashore.

'You can't land that thing here, you savages!' Leith could hear the words, but the speaker remained hazy, though only twenty paces from them. 'What kind of craziness is this? With all that's happening, do you think we have time now for the likes of you? Go and see if you can land on the Straux shore, then take your chances . . .' The rest of the man's angry words faded away in the thick air.

The navigator directed his crew to paddle towards the centre of the River, then turned and faced Leith, his eyes sad and resigned. 'You say we're hostile. Perhaps we are when it comes to letting people set foot on our sacred island, especially to those whose kind drove us from our land. Yet I have never heard Instruere called a holy place. People from all over the world are encouraged to come to this island. Why, then, are we met with hostility when we try to set foot on it?'

Leith nodded again, as he had throughout the argument, but his mind was no longer on the issue of the *losian*. Smoke rose from a number of places inside Instruere's walls, and now he could hear an intermittent booming sound drifting across the water. Fires occurred often in Instruere, whether deliberate or accidental, but he did not remember it being like this. Perhaps Instruere was always like this in the autumn. But even as he considered these thoughts doubtfully, a new plume of thick black smoke curled over the walls and bent towards them, driven by the downriver breeze.

They drew close to the Straux shore, and there before them stretched Southbridge. Oddly, none of the soldiers set to guard the bridge looked in their direction as they beached the outrigger. Their attention was engaged with, of all things, a group of people in outlandish dress accompanied by a long line of unusual-looking animals with long necks, bulbous, horse-like faces and peculiar lumps on their backs which Leith at first mistook for baggage. Traders come to peddle their exotic goods in the Great City, no doubt. The booming sounds continued to echo across the River as Leith and Maendraga bade a cordial farewell to the Pei-ratin navigator. None of the others in the canoe acknowledged their departure, reminding Leith yet again that the agreement to take the two outsiders to Instruere had not been universal. Leith turned to the scene before him.

'Just let us across this bridge, boy, and that'll be the end of it!' snapped the leader of the traders. Leith's head jerked up, all else suddenly forgotten. 'We'll take the risk, if risk there is, if this isn't just a story to keep us out of the city.' Leith plunged forward along the riverbank towards the bridge, ignoring Maendraga's surprised cry.

'I've told you, none can cross today,' a bored voice replied. 'We are not prepared to expose visitors to our fair city to any risk until we've ascertained the nature of the problem—'

'Leaving us out here is a risk! What if it rains again like it did last night?' the trader yelled back.

By now Leith was sure, even though he could not yet see the speaker clearly. He filled his lungs with air, ready to shout – and at that moment an enormous boom shook the ground and knocked him off his feet. On hands and knees he turned towards Instruere. A great sheet of flame erupted from behind the walls. A second boom rang out, then a third, and slowly, ponderously, the Struere Gate collapsed into a pile of rubble.

CHAPTER 2

TANGHIN AND DEORC

DEORC, LORD OF INSTRUERE, settled into his austere, high-backed chair. He'd destroyed the red velvet monstrosity used by his predecessor. A palpable sign of weakness, one of many the overrated fool had allowed to cloud his judgment. The Arkhos of Nemohaim had not come through his last visit to Andratan at all well, his ambition and arrogance all too obvious even to Deorc, let alone to the subtle devices of the Master of All. The Undying Man told Deorc the Arkhos would need replacing. He'd had the fat man thrown out, just like he'd disposed of the red chair. A momentary twitch of unease spoiled his benign mood. Not quite like the red chair. While he'd set flame to the chair the Arkhos had used, the man himself continued to evade him. *But not forever*, the Destroyer's lieutenant told himself. The harrowing of Instruere was at hand, and eventually the hiding place of the Arkhos of Nemohaim would be revealed, along with many other things.

He leaned back, content with his day's work, and admired his favourite trophy. On the wall, hanging from chains, placed for him alone to see, was Stella, the northern girl. He knew his master would not exactly approve of the decoration, since he had said she was to be kept for his arrival, but if pressed Deorc would explain that the arrangement was part of the breaking process. It had certainly been effective. The struggling, arguing and weeping had passed into a sort of numb acceptance, and soon she would begin to believe she deserved this kind of treatment. Then it would be only a matter of time until the self-hatred surfaced; and at that point she would agree to whatever her master demanded of her. Perhaps she might even be returned to her former friends – if they still lived – to be eyes and ears for the Undying Man. He had seen such things before, had been party to them.

Time for reflection later, the Lord of Instruere told himself. The Ecclesia was due to meet soon, and they would expect Tanghin there to offer his words of wisdom. He wouldn't disappoint them, he thought as he rose and pulled on his cloak.

'I'm off to preach to your friends,' he taunted the girl. 'Do you have a message for them?' She turned her face towards him, but no reply came from her, and soon her dull eyes turned inward again. He laughed shortly, eased on his calf-high boots and strode from the room.

As soon as the heavy wooden door closed and the noise of the bolt sliding home died down, the dullness faded from Stella's eyes. She could touch the floor if she stretched her toes, though it sent agonising waves of pain up her pinioned arms. 'I must exercise my arms and legs,' she said aloud, as much to keep the memory of her own voice alive as to remind herself not to surrender to hopelessness.

Unable to keep track of time and deprived of contact with anyone apart from a small, frightened woman who cleaned the room – and of course, the beast that was Tanghin – Stella spent hours and hours exploring her own mind. She'd been thinking a lot about her family. A weak father, a shallow, superficial mother and her brother the wastrel drunkard. She began to realise she hated weakness in all its forms: the wanderings of old age, the helplessness of babies or of cripples like Hal, ineffectual people like her father – or like Leith before the journey changed him – and especially the weakness she found in herself. She hated her inability to resist the strength of others, her unreasoning fear of Druin and of being trapped in a life of helplessness, of being tormented by someone strong and merciless, unable to escape. She had fled from all of that, and here she was. Here she was, led by her fears.

She remembered a time when she was very young. Her older brother would sit on his father's knee and listen to the stories he told. Once she crept out of her room and sat unregarded at the door to listen to a goblin story, where the hero had been trapped in a lightless cave, surrounded by evil creatures intent on catching and eating him. Paralysed by terror as the words washed over her, Stella missed the part where the hero had been rescued by his companions, and was caught up instead in a never-ending tunnel of clawed hands groping at her, wide open mouths leering, teeth clashing, hot breath covering her . . .

She bit her lip until she drew blood. Thinking like this did her no good. Ignoring the needle-like pain in her arms and legs, and the greyness that closed around her like a tunnel without end, Stella began her exercises.

The Ecclesia has grown like a mighty tree, the Hermit reflected. Well watered, its roots extended to touch the wealthy and influential as well as the poor and powerless. Branches had been set up in Deuverre and Straux as day workers returning home to villages north and south of the Great City exported the Fire. The Mercium meeting now rivalled the Basement as the largest branch of all, an especially pleasing development for the Hermit, who remembered with bitterness having been driven from that iniquitous town many years ago. In the few short months since he set foot in Instruere many hundreds of people, he didn't know how many exactly, declared themselves for the Ecclesia, contributing much to the welfare of the people of the Fire. Last week the contributions tallied over four and a half thousand pending; he had the exact figure written down in a notebook.

More importantly, he told himself as he walked out on to the raised platform in the Basement, the Fire continued to fall. There they all were, waiting on his word or gesture. There! He pointed dramatically, and half-a-dozen fell to the floor cackling loudly. And there! A few more went down. Others lined the sides of the platform, their prophecies at the ready. Some of them were crackpots, going from one meeting to another trying to peddle their own vision, but he had trustworthy men tending the branches of his great tree, and they would not give place to the fakers or the deranged. He thought of Tanghin and his heart swelled with pride. Soon he would leave Instruere and the movement he had started to take charge of the Mercium branch, but only after installing Tanghin in the Basement. The man Tanghin had deep insight into the ways and plans of the Most High, and was a true disciple of the Ecclesia.

Across the City, in a disused storehouse close by the Hall of Lore, Tanghin strode through the crowd, touching foreheads as he went. Inevitably the result was the same; down the people fell, to lie prone on the stone floor for hours at a time, enjoying some mystical cathartic experience. He could have used his true power to push them over, but they did it themselves! It continued to amaze him just how suggestible these people were, and he was beginning to realise how his master might have come to his power. Had he merely tapped an innate weakness in everyone? 'The Fire is falling tonight!' he cried, enjoying himself immensely. 'Open yourselves to the flame! The Most High wants to burn within you!' There existed a kind of unspoken agreement between the crowd and himself: he agreed to perform, and they agreed to fall for him. Oh yes, and they were falling! Laughter welled up in his chest, and for a moment he checked it, but nothing he did tonight would offend or bring suspicion on him, so he let the laugh ring out. 'The joy is here tonight. Can you feel it?' he cried. As though joy was a commodity to be plucked out of the air. Simpletons!

Time to get to work. He fashioned a strong Wordweave, then began to declaim. 'The Most High is doing a new thing,' he intoned. *I am about to give you new orders*. 'He says: "I am about to raise another group to do My will. Escaigne are My chosen instrument, and they shall bring Fire to this City, setting neighbours against each other."' *Escaigne is about to attack the Council of Faltha, and I want you to support them.* 'They are the winnowers of the Most High, separating the chaff from the wheat and setting it alight. Hear the words of the Most High and obey them!' *Hear my words and obey them!* 'The proud City of Instruere will be brought low, and you are His instrument!'

He lowered his voice, and the chorus of shouted agreement dropped away to a whisper. 'Even now the Master of All draws near to your walls.' *The Undying Man is coming with his great army*. 'Prepare to open the gates and let Him in, no matter what your earthly leaders might say.' *When the time comes, you will betray Faltha in the name of your religion.* 'Many of you will be required to suffer in His name.' *He will torment you and kill you, and you will regard it as an honour.* 'But, in the end, you will be victorious!' *In the end, he will be victorious!*

Now the prophecies began. He continued to be amazed at how accurate some of them were, although he suspected many people susceptible to the Ecclesia were also susceptible to the Wordweave, and their very thoughts were shaped by his will. The idea that he was bending thousands of lives like reeds before a rod of iron drove him into a frenzy of excitement, and it was all he could do to restrain himself and listen to what was being spoken. Something about the Arrow of the Most High drawing near. Well, wasn't that what he'd just said? He began to tremble and recognised the itch. He'd need to visit The Pinion tonight. Or perhaps Stella could provide him with some more entertainment. He might not be allowed to touch her – a command he would not break, would not think of breaking – but there were many other things he could do.

He drifted through the rest of the meeting in a red haze, palmed off the many supplicants to his assistants, and headed back towards his rooms in an annexe of the Hall of Lore, rubbing his hands in anticipation.

'Who is that?' whispered Petara. 'Is it one of the Council?'

The Presiding Elder put a finger to his lips, indicating silence, a gesture wasted in the darkness. This one was indeed a puzzle. They had been observing him for a few days, a man who was a part of the Ecclesia, who actually ran one of the meetings, but who lived in the Hall of Lore, in rooms reserved for important visitors to the Council of Faltha. He obviously didn't want people to make the connection, because he was seen to use this path only when no one else was about.

The leader of Escaigne's army whispered a command for absolute stillness. Now, of all times, they could not risk discovery and the loss of all they had worked for, not when they waited on the very cusp of their assault on Instruere. Though it might be interesting to capture this man and find out what he knew, the Presiding Elder resisted the temptation. A lifetime of operating on the fringes of society, first in Sivithar and latterly in Instruere, taught him to make no hasty decisions.

Without warning the figure turned from the path and walked briskly towards them. The Presiding Elder panicked and, fearing they were about to be discovered and denounced, made to signal his archers to strike the man down; but, to his horror, found he could not move as much as an arm or even a hand in response to his urgent thought. He could not cry out. His voice seemed locked in his throat.

'I know you're there,' the man said casually, peering through the foliage towards where the Escaignians hid. 'I know who you are and what you intend to do. In fact, I'm helping you with your plans. Some of your best ideas are mine! But I don't want you to know who I am, not yet, not until it's too late. So – let's see – I'll take one of you,' – he beckoned, and Petara rose woodenly to his feet – 'and let the rest of you go. But first, it seems you have all become very forgetful. Ah well, just don't forget to launch your attack on the Granaries at dawn tomorrow morning.' He came close to the helpless Escaignians, close enough for them to see his face, then his eyes flashed red and they fell to the ground, unconscious.

Deorc beckoned to the remaining Escaignian. 'Come with me to The Pinion. I have a number of things I want to show you.' He would turn this man without placing a hand on him. Perhaps he would show the result to Stella before he returned the unfortunate man to the Escaignians.

After a brief but heavy shower overnight, the next morning dawned clear and bright, as though someone had spent the night scrubbing all the dark deeds from the city. The Presiding Elder rubbed his temple. He had picked up an annoying headache, dampening his spirits somewhat. Still, the culmination of a decade of planning had arrived and, as the first rays of sunlight broached the walls of the wicked City and illuminated the high tower of the House of Worship, he signalled the commencement of their long-awaited campaign. He could surely be forgiven the surge of excitement flashing through him.

Within a few moments a lamp was lit and one of the Granary buildings, located near the Struere Gate, caught fire. This was purely a diversionary tactic, as those who planned this attack did not want ordinary Instruians to starve; but the fire would ensure the authorities, and many of the Instruian guardsmen, would be occupied in putting it out. Being able to predict the movements of the Guard was crucial to the Escaignian plans.

Smoke began to rise from half-a-dozen places around Instruere, all close to the walls, designed to draw the Guard away from the centre of the City. The attack of Escaigne on Instruere had four main targets, the Four Halls of Instruere: the Hall of Lore, the House of Worship, the Hall of Meeting and The Pinion. Capturing these four buildings would give them command over Instruere. It would offer control over the decisions made and the people who made them; over the guards who enforced them; and over the minds and hearts of the Instruians who looked on these four buildings every day as representing the tangible link to the founding of Instruere by the First Men. Whoever held these places held Instruere in his hand.

The plan was to harry the Guard rather than to engage them in battle. The Presiding Elder was smarter than to think his men and women could hold out long against a concerted attack by the well-trained, well-equipped guardsmen. The Escaignians were to emerge from their hiding places, ambush the guards as they ran from one fire to another, then melt back into the tangle of narrow streets and alleyways, of rooftop paths between tenements and disused buildings they knew far better than did the Guard.

By the midst of a morning full of shocks, their plan had been abandoned. Far fewer guards than anticipated arrived to deal with the fires, and because of this things began to go wrong for the Escaignians. The Council, having tumbled to their strategy, held a large reserve of guards in The Pinion, which meant the attack on both it and the Hall of Meeting nearby had to be delayed. Further, the fires which ought to have been extinguished by the Guard now raged out of control. The Presiding Elder fumed, having never considered the notion that the Council might rather see Instruere burn than empty The Pinion of guardsmen. Finally, the appearance of only a few guards emboldened many of the Escaignian fighters, who saw a real chance of success when confronted with small knots of confused guardsmen. Some of his generals encouraged sustained attacks, believing this would help draw reinforcements from The Pinion, but had forgotten how well-trained the Guard was. The situation collapsed rapidly from there.

'Turn aside! Turn aside!' screamed the Presiding Elder to a group of Escaignians armed with all manner of cast-off weapons. Inflamed beyond reason, they ignored the cries of their leader and continued to chase half-a-dozen guards down a lane, pursuing revenge. Around a corner they went, there to be confronted by another dozen of the Guard. The Escaignians had been lured into a trap. Fifty yards behind, the Presiding Elder saw what was about to happen, but could do nothing. He turned helplessly and ran from what already sounded like a slaughter.

His plan was ruined, and his men were dying.

The Granaries burned beyond saving. Many ordinary Instruians joined with the firefighting efforts of the grain workers and the Guard, but made little impression on the fires. High up in the largest of the grain silos, the heat and pressure finally reached the point where something had to give. With a loud boom the silo exploded, showering those below with flaming wood, white-hot fragments of metal and burning grain that settled on their exposed skin and found its way inside their clothing. Within moments the whole area began to come apart in a series of explosions, dooming many of the people who rushed to put out the fires, and the Escaignians who hoped to pick off the guards, or at least delay their return to The Pinion.

'Back, get back!' Mahnum cried, dragging Indrett away from a large, jagged piece of glowing metal, from the shrieking of a man whose legs jutted out from beneath it, and from the terrible smell of burning flesh. 'We can do nothing! We must leave!'

'Always we can do nothing,' Farr growled. 'Run from this, run from that, never staying, never standing to fight!' But like the others he ran, barely outpacing another explosion, joining with the crowds trying to escape the sudden destruction reaching out to them.

'If Stella is held in the Granaries, or anywhere around them, then she is dead,' concluded Perdu.

'As will we be, if we don't run faster!' Mahnum urged them on. He longed to scoop Indrett up but knew she wouldn't allow it. Just four of them left. They couldn't afford to lose anyone else.

They had lost Stella the morning after their confrontation with her over her proposed marriage. She was not in her room, and could not be found. Mahnum and Indrett immediately suspected she'd run off to be with Tanghin. The man denied it, and he'd been very convincing. He expressed shock and sorrow, added a mild rebuke of those who would have counselled such a headstrong girl as his Stella to lay aside her feelings, and incidentally disappoint his hopes. He offered to help them search for her, but as yet his duties with the Ecclesia prevented him from joining them as they scoured every part of Instruere for news. To Mahnum his words simply did not ring true. How much did he truly love her, if he was not willing to put the Ecclesia aside for a short while for her sake? Stella had been wrong in her judgment of him, and Indrett had been right, he decided. The man was a social dilettante, one who played with the affections of others, who liked the sound of his own voice and the effects of his own power. She was well rid of him. But where was she?

Over the last few weeks they felt they'd searched the whole of Instruere, inside and out, every alley, every crooked street, marketplace and business house. Yet they knew this could not be so, as in all their inquiries they had not once come across any sign of Escaigne. And if Escaigne could hide itself effectively in Instruere, so could whoever hid Stella. They knew from their time at the markets that every year a number of people went missing in the Great City, never to be heard from again. The general opinion was that these were made up of some who vanished to escape bad debts or a wrathful lover, others who had been murdered for any number of reasons, from robbery to revenge, and a few who, so the whispers went, ended up as slaves to the rich and powerful. Still, none of the searchers seriously considered any of these possibilities had befallen Stella.

Just behind them and to their left a tall wooden building burst into flame. Mahnum cried a warning. The fire kept pace as they fled, running parallel with the southern wall, herding them towards the Struere Gate. Panic spread throughout the district as people tried to avoid the accelerating destruction. Perdu stumbled and fell, and was immediately trampled on by people desperate to escape the ruin of the Granaries. Without warning a bright orange flash lit the street, then a pulse of sound followed, so loud it blew them off their feet. Debris rained down from above. Just as the first of the crowd regained their feet a second, louder blast felled them again; then before they could do anything other than curl up, hands over their ears, a third explosion seemed to lift the very skin from the earth.

Indrett hauled herself to her feet, using a doorframe for support. The explosions had blown her across the street, where she fetched up against a tenement. Her left side hurt, her lip bled where she had bitten it involuntarily, and her ears rang so she could hear nothing else. Even so, her first thought was for Mahnum, and for a few awful moments she could not find him. Eventually she located him lying with his legs in an open sewer, his torso half covered by the body of a man who had been pierced through by a piece of smouldering roofing timber. Mahnum groaned, coughed a little, then raised himself to his knees and retched.

First Farr, then Perdu, came to find them. The two men staggered out of the smoke and ruin of the street. Black smoke filled the air, billowing out from the shattered windows of warehouses and tenements set on fire by shrapnel. People struggled to their feet, looking for friends in the choking gloom, or tried to make their way somewhere, anywhere but here. A few prone figures made no movement. Indrett glanced to her left. Close by, at the end of the street which she now recognised as the south end of the Vitulian Way, lay the wreckage of the Struere Gate.

A cold thought stabbed through her mind. *Is this the beginning of the Bhrudwan assault?*

As she watched, half-expecting the armies of the Destroyer to come howling through the gate, a lone figure stepped into the gap, framed by chaos. The figure raised an arm. Something flared brightly in his hand, piercing the gloom. Indrett staggered forward a few feet, careless of the danger from further explosions. As the smoke cleared, thinned by a fresh wind blowing through the open gate and by the light that pulsed like a heartbeat from the flame above the figure's head, she knew; and the tears began to flow. Indrett was joined by her husband, and together they called his name.

'Kurr! Haufuth! Over here!' The old farmer heard the shouts, but too much noise, too much movement all at once made it difficult for the voice to register. Around him men and women struggled to calm frightened animals and children, or dodge the occasional red-hot missile that fell from the enveloping darkness descending on them. Kurr hung on grimly to the reins of the lead camel, while at the same time trying to see through the smoke to ascertain whether all the travellers were unhurt, and wondering what had just happened to the Great City. Could this be the Bhrudwan army?

Then a figure materialised out of the smoke. Astonishingly, beyond all joy or hope, like a figure from a dream, the boy Leith stood before them. Mahnum's boy, grinning from ear to ear, with the Jugom Ark flaring brightly in his hand. He was almost unrecognisable in outlandishly foreign clothing, and there seemed to be a broad cut across his cheek and blood smeared across his face, which healed and disappeared even as he watched. The boy didn't seem to realise it had happened, and continued to grin widely at the old man.

'Took your time, didn't you, boy?' Kurr growled, trying to keep an answering smile from growing on his own face. 'Where did you get to? Never mind for now: I see you still have that pretty arrow thing. Well, I suppose we'd better have a think about what to do with it. Did that magician come with you?'

'I did,' said a stocky figure stepping up on to the road beside Leith. But what else he might have said was lost as Belladonna threw herself into his arms, crying inarticulate words of delight.

Now the remainder of the travellers gathered around, fractious animals forgotten in the joy of the unexpected reunion. Leith found his hand shaken and his back slapped, and though his friends were reluctant to embrace him, perhaps for fear of the bright arrow he carried, the boy from Loulea found himself weeping for sheer happiness. He was even able to look Hal in the eye and tell him sincerely that he was pleased to see him again. Most startling of all was seeing the Arkhos of Nemohaim standing at the back of the group, obviously eyeing the Jugom Ark with a mixture of covetousness and nervousness. He wanted to ask his friends what had happened, how this man came to be standing with them, but there were more immediate things he needed to do.

'So what happens now?' the Haufuth inquired of them all. As one, the travellers turned to Leith – who was already walking across the bridge towards Instruere.

'My parents are in there,' he called back over his shoulder. 'They are why we started on this adventure in the first place. I'm not doing anything else until I find them.'

He picked his way across the bridge, stepping over debris from the City and ignoring the soldiers who tried to accost him but who drew back when they saw what he carried. Kurr and the others looked on as Leith walked right through a sheet of flame without seeming to notice. As they tried to keep up with him, they were forced to hug the railing on the far side of the bridge to avoid a place where the timber roadway had caught fire. They were still some distance behind when he stood, framed in the wreckage of the Struere Gate, and raised the Jugom Ark aloft.

He saw them as the smoke parted momentarily, then heard them call his name. He felt no surprise that of all the places they might have been, his companions were here to see him enter the City in triumph. Then he saw his parents, and all pretence of power, all confusion over what was happening to him, all his fears about what the future might bring were forgotten in an instant as he ran to his mother and father and their deep, enfolding embrace. The Jugom Ark flickered quietly, unregarded in his hand, as the man and the woman were reunited with their son.

Deorc strode purposefully into his room, slammed the door shut behind him and took a key from his desk. Stella knew that key, and she took a deep breath to keep control of the fear that rose up within her.

'Time to inspect the progress of the battle, my queen,' the hateful man said as he undid her chains. She whimpered a little as feeling returned to her arms. Though Deorc did not seem particularly aware of her, preoccupied as he was with the conflict he had fomented, Stella did not attack him or try to escape. She remembered what he had done when she first tried, and kept still.

'Up to the tower, my queen!' he cried, almost gaily. She was to be married to the Destroyer, he told her – not quite truthfully, she thought, as she understood the Destroyer's words from the blue fire – so she would be Deorc's queen. But he had all the power, and he delighted in taking every opportunity to drive despair into her heart.

Pushing her ahead of him, Deorc and Stella made their way to the highest room in the tower above the House of Worship. They met a few people in the corridors, but so thoroughly had Deorc cowed those who worked there that none remarked on the bedraggled girl accompanying the dapper Head of the Council. Indeed, none gave any sign that there was anything amiss. Stella thought she recognised one man she saw as a member of the Council of Faltha. She couldn't remember his name, but dragged at the memory until she retrieved it, taking any chance to keep her mind working, focusing on anything but her predicament. The Arkhos of Firanes, that's who he was. *Firanes! That's where I'm from!*

He dragged her to a window, one of four quartering the circular room at the top of the tower. 'Gaze on the fruit of my master's plan!' he boasted. 'Look there!' He pointed out over the City, towards the south-west, where a vast plume of smoke hung. 'Escaigne, the sworn enemy of wicked, debauched Instruere, does his work! They have set fire to the Granaries, believing it would draw the Guard away from the heart of the City, leaving the Council vulnerable. It was a good plan! The only problem is that it was *my* plan! Ah, listen, my sweet. Can you not hear?' Against her wishes she heard faint cries and the sound of explosions. 'That is the sound of Escaignians and the Instruian Guard killing each other. I play them both like stringed instruments, one counterpointing the other, sending just enough reinforcements from The Pinion to keep the battle even and ensure the greatest number of deaths on both sides. See how I weaken the City, thus fulfilling my master's commands!'

Stella turned her head away, her mind's eye filling with imagined scenes of battle in which people died, people she knew from the market and the Ecclesia. Because of this man, the one she would have wed. His hand snaked out, grasping her jaw in a harsh grip, turning her head back to the window.

'Don't make me angry, my queen,' Deorc said from between clenched teeth. 'I have practised some new tricks which I long to show you. Is that what you want?' She shook her head, stomach icy with fear.

'Good. Since you desire so much to watch the destruction of Instruere, I will allow you to remain up here all afternoon. Keep a close watch, my queen. I shall ask you questions about it later. You wouldn't want to give me any wrong answers.' His level voice was more of a threat than any shout might have been.

'Now wait here until I bring back your jewellery.' He laughed his dry laugh and turned on his heel, as though grinding something in to the floor.

As soon as the door closed, Stella moved into a series of exercises. She needed the defiance, the self-assertion, whatever the risk, though she kept a careful ear for his footfall on the stone stairs. When he returned she acquiesced, as she always did since those terrifying first few days, not resisting as he chained her to a single bolt high on the wall, facing the south and east windows.

'I'll make sure you have plenty to look at,' Deorc promised her. 'And tonight, if you're good, I'll leave you here to watch the death of the Ecclesia.'

Stella tried to keep her renewed fear from showing on her face, but she must not have entirely succeeded, for the brute drew close and leered at her, his foul breath hot on her cheek. 'Oh, I neglected to inform you. I've invited the Ecclesia to join my party. We can't have a battle without allowing the fanatics to take part, now can we?'

The girl said nothing, but clearly Deorc enjoyed hurting her. 'Your friends will be invited too, don't worry. If you're lucky, you might just see the heroic dreams of your northerner friends end at the tip of a blade right below this tower. And if all goes well, I might let you be the one to tell our master of His great victory – and mine, of course.' He sneered at her, then left the room. Stella heard the key turn in the door. When she was sure he had truly gone, she hung her head and wept bitterly.

'What is happening here?'

Leith's question spoke for them all. They had no time to tell each other their stories. Still the explosions continued somewhere behind them in the Granaries district, not as violent as those that brought destruction to the Struere Gate, but threatening nonetheless. All around them buildings burned, with one or two of those ahead starting to smoke, and there was a very real possibility they might not escape this place if they remained much longer. Already they stood alone on the street, apart from a few unclaimed bodies.

'Somebody fired the Granaries,' Mahnum told them. 'Started at dawn. We were out on the streets looking for Stella – it's a tale we will tell when we can—'

'Stella is missing?' The Haufuth moved to the front of the group. He turned his head this way and that as though he might see her somewhere on the street.

'As I said, it is a tale we will relate when we can. For now, let's go back to our lodgings, if we are able, if they're not on fire as well.'

'Who started the fire?' This from the Captain of the Guard as they began to walk hurriedly along the Vitulian Way, the Struere Gate behind them.

'And who are you to ask?' Mahnum retorted.

'*Now* who wants to ask questions?' the Haufuth said gently. 'The man's question is a fair one. He serves this City loyally, no matter how evil his master might be, and might be able to do something to save it. So who did start the fire?'

'The general belief among those helping put out the Granary fires is that it must be Escaigne. They've committed similar acts before, apparently, but nothing on this scale.' The grim captain nodded, as if the information confirmed his own guess.

Indrett added: 'A few of the locals I spoke to tell of seeing strangely-clad men and women, and even some children, grappling with the guards. This likely convinced them the Escaignians are involved.'

Farr spoke up. 'I have a question. What is *he* doing here?' The mountain man indicated the Arkhos of Nemohaim, who walked among them without apology. 'More to the point, why is he still alive? I have the will and the skill to change that, if no one else has the stomach for it.' He put a hand on his sword hilt.

'There is much to explain,' Hal put in. 'He gave us aid on the journey north, and we agreed to respect each other for the time being. We have a bargain to honour, and until the man proves unfaithful he may remain with us.'

'Are you collecting enemies like stray dogs?' Farr asked the cripple with a sneer in his voice. 'Such dogs turn on their masters when hungry. I, for one, do not want to make a meal for them!'

'We would have made a meal for a band of robbers, were it not for Achtal,' Kurr responded sharply. 'We would not have escaped from the Deep Desert if he had not rescued us. Don't be too quick to condemn others. Perhaps your brother might still be with us if those who knew him best had been more tolerant.'

'You have no right!' Farr cried, his anger blazing hot. 'You know nothing!'

'Enough!' The Haufuth stood between them. 'I thought you two had resolved your differences. Can't this wait until we're somewhere safe?'

The two antagonists glared at each other and lapsed into silence. For some time the group walked briskly northwards, along the road. Clear sky opened up above them.

'So how do we stop the burning?' Leith asked eventually, glancing back behind him. 'Surely that is the most important question?'

'That, and then to decide what we do about the thing

you carry in your hand,' Phemanderac stated firmly. 'We could spend our time battling the flames, or the Escaignians who started them, but surely we have forgotten our purpose? The Arkhimm has succeeded! We have reclaimed the Jugom Ark and brought it to the heart of Faltha! Now all we need to do—'

'—Is what?' the Haufuth finished for him. 'So we have an arrow that burns people's hands, all except his.' Involuntarily he lifted his own hand and placed it under his armpit, as though sheltering it from pain. 'It was never clear to me how this talisman would suddenly make everyone do as we tell them to.'

Geinor spoke, throat working, his thin voice barely under control. 'How can you doubt? Are you not a true Falthan? This is the Jugom Ark, the Arrow given to unite all true Falthans against the Destroyer, as spoken by the Most High Himself and relayed to us by Bewray of Nemohaim. I can testify personally to its efficacy. My hand was burned, and was instantly healed!'

'And you are?' the Haufuth asked, holding his own hand against his chest. Tempers threatened to flare in the heat of this extraordinary morning.

'He is here at our place of lodging,' Indrett said brightly, keen to avert open argument. 'This is where we are staying. We have left the fire behind for the moment. Let us go inside and talk things over there.'

Tanghin strode up and down the platform in the Basement. The fervency of his delivery drew the crowd close to him so that even more of those waiting outside could squeeze in to listen. Though it was late afternoon, and the nightly meetings did not begin until after sunset, a large crowd gathered.

Tanghin knew they would, after the great fires in the southern districts. To make sure, he spread word that something extraordinary would be happening. The curfew would be strictly enforced tonight, he whispered, so the meeting would begin early. Expecting the blue-robed Hermit, their usual speaker, the crowd was confused by the appearance of the handsome man from the Lore Market branch. Tanghin counted on this, and threw all his skill into the Wordweave he spun. This was a critical moment.

'We have been guilty of placing spiritual interpretations on the prophetic words we have been given,' he cried. 'We have mistakenly thought the fire would fall only in our hearts. Our founder, the Hermit from the north, gave us that interpretation. He had the message straight from the mouth of the Most High, but he failed us in its interpretation. Beware! Do not get caught up in deception! The Most High has come to visit us with fire, but not just a fire within. He has set the city of sin alight! He seeks to purge the Great Harlot of wickedness, of all her evil! He will not work with an unclean vessel. He will have us cleansed!'

The preacher ran a careful eye over the crowd. Despite the force of his words, and the underpinning of the Wordweave, a few people made their way from the Basement, faces set in puzzlement or anger. *Troublemakers and wiseacres*, he thought. *Better off without them.*

'Last night I gave my flock from Lore Market a word from the Most High Himself. I prophesied He would raise up a new movement to execute His will. See how I am proved correct! See how the City burns for its sins, as I foretold! The anointing has passed from the Hermit, the one who prepared the way, to me, the appointed one. I am here to immerse Instruere in fire, to supervise the spread of the flames across Faltha, until all the worldly governments are brought down and the greatest Power in the world is installed in their place.

'This new movement is made up of the men and women of Escaigne, whom the Most High caused to be set apart from their worldly fellows, dedicated unto purity. They have been raised up to tear down the ungodly Council of Faltha. Even now, right now as we speak together, they are fighting and dying on our behalf. Outnumbered and ill-equipped, Escaigne continues to challenge the Instruian Guard. They are fighting and dying for us! While we talk, they act!'

He paused for effect, and noticed the usual formulaic chorus of assent was absent. Good. *They're listening. They're hooked.* On cue, a voice came from the crowd. 'So what do we do?'

Ah. The months of conditioning pay off. I could ask them to put their neighbours to death, or sacrifice their own children, and many of them would do it.

Quietly now, he continued. 'So what do we do, my sisters; my brothers? We fight. It is time for what has been placed inside us to come out. It is time to live – and to die – for the Most High. And where do we fight? It has been prophesied we are the spearhead of the next move of the Most High, and so we are. We are pointed squarely at the heart of Instruere. The Most High hurls us at the Council of Faltha! Go now, seek out your friends and acquaintances from other branches, and tell them to assemble in front of the Hall of Lore at sunset tonight. Bring your swords, bring your sticks and your clubs, bring your torches and your fire. Bring your wives and your husbands, your parents and your children. Bring the fire that has been set in your hearts, your courage and your purses to receive the largesse of the Most High Himself. For we will burn the buildings of the ungodly to the ground, we will take their treasures for our own, and we will lift high the standard of our master!'

Cries of assent rang around the Basement. Really, he needn't have bothered with the Wordweave.

'Go now! Today is the day of decision, when you find out whether your faith is of the heart or of the mind only. If your faith is indeed of the heart, then meet me in front of the Hall of Lore at the setting of the sun. I will be there, revealed as the appointed one, and I will see that justice is delivered!'

With a mighty roar the crowd surged toward the door, which burst open. Within ten minutes the Basement emptied out, leaving Tanghin alone, laughing, laughing.

The hot autumn sun beat mercilessly on Stella as she hung from the wall of the high tower room. She could feel her skin burning in the glare, but could not move to protect herself. Sweat blinded her, the salt stinging her eyes, and the joints in her tortured arms screamed their pain. For a time she rehearsed the bones of a plan in her mind. A desperate plan, a plan of revenge, not of escape, but even revenge would most likely be denied her. Yet she now hated Deorc – Tanghin – with a passion far exceeding her former regard for him; a hatred born of pain and humiliation. Her plan relied on what the Destroyer might do to her if ever he came to claim her. She practised and practised what she would do, what she would say, which thoughts she would display and which she would hide. She polished the plan like a precious stone, honed it like a sharp knife to slip between Deorc's ribs. Eventually her mind wandered, her thirst for revenge dissolving in the face of a bleak tiredness, her precious disciplines abandoned.

Some time later her skin cooled, and a light breeze caressed her arms, waking her from fractured dreams. The breeze seemed the most beautiful thing ever to happen to her. She hung there for some time before opening her eyes. The sun had set, and the stars were out.

Stella blinked, and blinked again. The stars were below her, and they were moving. What had Tanghin done to her? What new illusion was this? No, they were not stars, but torches. Hundreds of people carrying torches filed down the streets that converged on the open space in front of the Hall of Lore. Coming to the slaughter.

The reconstituted Company spent the afternoon in deep conversation. Tales of remarkable adventure were told frankly and without embellishment, and listened to with few questions and little comment. All present realised the urgency of the moment. They heard about the journey of the Arkhimm, of the disaster of Joram Basin, of the separation of Ark and Arkhimm, and of the adventures encountered on the way back to Instruere. Leith told them of Nemohaim and the Pei-ra, and his companions marvelled anew at the flame in his hand.

The Company now numbered over twenty. Kurr sat with the Haufuth, Mahnum and Indrett at one end of the table, with Leith and Hal to their left, along with Farr and Perdu, an empty seat in their midst to remind them that Stella was not with them. At the other end of the table the Arkhos of Nemohaim and his Captain of the Guard sat side by side, with Achtal the Bhrudwan flanking them to one side and Te Tuahangata on the other. And to their left Prince Wiusago had been joined by Belladonna and Maendraga her father, by the Escaignian woman who sat the slave girl on her lap, and by Phemanderac, who was currently speaking. Geinor and Graig his son sat on the floor behind them.

There came a knock at the door. Indrett opened it to find a woman she knew vaguely from the markets, and more recently from the Ecclesia meetings at the Basement. She held a burning brand in her hand, and a fever burned in her eyes. Indrett searched her mind for a name.

'Pelasia! What can I do for you – and what do you have in your hand?'

'Can't stay, dear,' she breathed excitedly. 'I know you used to go to the Basement branch, so I thought I'd pass on the word: the Most High has commanded us to attack the Council of Faltha! If you can still hear the Most High in your heart, He will confirm the truth of it.'

'Pellie!' came a cry from somewhere out on the darkening street. 'Come on! We'll miss the excitement!'

'Think about it,' the madwoman added. 'The world is changing, and we're the ones changing it!'

'Come on, Mother!' the voice called, and a hand reached out and pulled her away before she could say another word.

'Did you hear that?' Indrett asked the room. 'Something awful is about to happen.'

'Something awful has been happening all day,' a wheezy voice said from the far end of the table. 'My city is under attack from within, and I know who's responsible for it. I've listened to your stories with patience, forbearing to correct the more grievous of the exaggerations and untruths they contained. Are you willing to repay the courtesy and listen to me, and consider the advice I bring to you?' The Arkhos of Nemohaim adopted an air of studied reason that belied not only all the Company knew about him, but also the glow of excitement in his eyes.

Graig stood, clearing his throat. 'Begging your pardon,' he said diffidently, then waited, looking to Leith.

'You can speak, Graig,' the youth said gently. 'I am no king, and this is no king's court. We're all the same here.'

'But you have princes and chieftains here among you,' his father said incredulously, standing beside his son.

'And the former leader of Instruere,' Leith replied, 'who might have something important to say.'

'Yes, but – but we of Nemohaim know this man, and his behaviour and appetites shame us all. He was able to coerce the king to appoint him as ambassador to the Council of Faltha, and now we learn he has betrayed us to Bhrudwo. He is ever scheming, ever on the watch for any advantage he can find. We dare not trust him!'

'I wondered where I remembered you and your brat from,' the Arkhos replied amiably. 'The king's old counsellor, ever timid, and his famous offspring, so skilled with the blade he once stabbed himself in the foot without even unsheathing his sword. Did they put you out on the Southern Patrol where you could do no harm?'

Graig tried to restrain his anger. 'I was the first of Nemohaim to behold the Jugom Ark in its glory, and to look on the face of he who carries it. I could do this because I was not in Instruere plotting against my king!'

'Ah, but as a result of your . . . goodness, you have no insight into what is happening in Instruere today. I do. Many things Deorc said now begin to make sense, and I see his plans. Now, youngster, for once in your futile life you might actually have some power. You can prevent these people listening to what I have to say. Tell them all the stories you know about me, and make up some new ones to go alongside them. Nothing will surprise them. They know me well by now. Nonetheless, their goals and mine are the same for the moment. You want the man destroying Instruere defeated?

So do I. You want a chance to show the Council your Arrow? I'd like to see their faces when they behold it. Who else can give this to you? Or will you sit here waiting, discarding one plan after another, while people like the foolish woman who just knocked on your door die bleeding in the streets?'

'Let us hear the man,' Kurr said, and beside him the Haufuth nodded his head. 'Then we can decide what to do.'

The view from the top of the tower rapidly became truly appalling. Stella watched like an impotent god as The Pinion disgorged guards like ants abandoning an anthill. It was as clear to her as if Tanghin had left a script: a crowd had gathered on the lawn in front of the Hall of Lore, and the Guard were going to put them to the sword. There they were now, circling quietly around the massed group; hundreds of them, lining the shadows. She didn't know who the people were, but she could make out the smaller shapes of children in the flickering torchlight. Her captor often described the enjoyment he derived from the death of children. Stella did not want to see him derive any enjoyment this night. She cried out through a dry, swollen throat, but the desperate noises she made were swallowed by the evening breeze, and she knew she could not make herself heard.

A figure stepped forward from the shadows, a hated figure. Raising his arms, he stood in front of the crowd. *Strike him down! Don't let him live!* Even if she was to remain chained here as a result, unknown and unregarded until she died of hunger or thirst, it would be a small price to pay for his death, especially if she could witness it.

By some perverse trick of the wind, his voice drifted up to her, faint but clear. 'Citizens of Instruere! Members of the Ecclesia! You are here tonight to confront the Council of

Faltha, to demand their evil be cleansed from this City of God. As your leader, I will deliver your demand to the leader of the Council!' He turned and knocked on the door of the House of Lore, which opened and swallowed him. The crowd moved uneasily.

The Ecclesia! He is Tanghin – and he is Deorc – and he betrays the Ecclesia to the Instruian Guard! Oh, Most High!

The door opened, and the figure re-emerged. But it was Deorc, not Tanghin, who stood before the stunned Ecclesia. Dressed in a sable cloak and with a cowl over his head, he lifted his arms high.

'Hear me, scum of Instruere!' he screamed. 'I am Deorc, leader of the Council of Faltha, keeper of Andratan and servant of the Destroyer, the mortal enemy of all Falthans. I am Tanghin, the usurper of the Ecclesia. I am here to declare your doom. The fire will fall on Instruere tonight, *and you will be the first to burn*!' With that, he lowered his arms and the Instruian Guard streamed out from the shadows, swords raised.

Stella wept burning tears, her body shaking as grief and pain racked her, even before the slaughter began.

CHAPTER 3

THE MAN FROM SNA VAZTHA

THE MAN FROM SNA VAZTHA rode his white horse at a measured pace towards the City and the dark cloud that hovered over it. The setting sun illuminated the dense pall of smoke, rays of light spreading through the upper cloud like a vision of paradise, though the flicker of orange and red at the base of the cloud might have heralded the portals of the underworld. The situation in Instruere had obviously deteriorated since the messenger left over two months previously. The man nodded: it was to be expected. Indeed, it was to be welcomed. If things were now in the open, it would make his task much easier.

The guards at the Longbridge Gate were in a panic, as were their Southbridge counterparts, and had been since midmorning when word of the happenings in Instruere began to filter out. An increasing stream of refugees from the City had, at first, been held at the northern end of the bridge, but as their numbers increased it became pointless to hold them back, despite the absence of instructions. So the gates opened and people allowed to leave, whether or not they carried a yellow identification card.

Night now lurked just below the horizon, their relief had not appeared and they had grown anxious, having been forced to watch the rising columns of smoke and gouts of flame rising from within their city's walls. Frightened people hurried across the bridge, adding further tales of fire and destruction to those the nervous soldiers had already been told. The Granaries were destroyed, they heard, and the Docks razed. Fighting in the streets. A rain of fire and death. Escaigne had arisen at last to challenge the Council of Faltha. No one could escape south of the City, some claimed, because the Southbridge was burned to the waterline. Every boat in the City had either borne their owners far away or were making fortunes for those greedy enough to ferry others to shore for profit. No orders were forthcoming from the Council of Faltha, and the City lay open to its enemies.

And now someone approached from the north, a lone rider on a dusky mare. Hardly the threat to take advantage of a vulnerable City, but such a one might carry news of that vulnerability to its enemies. The rider reined in at the guardhouse, dismounted briskly and waited by his horse.

'No one's getting into the City today, card or no card,' he was told. The guard spoke in a nervous voice, tinged with worry. His house lay on the southern edge of town, perhaps half a mile from the Granaries.

The stranger pulled back the hood of his cloak. The face revealed was old, startlingly so given how he carried himself. Heavy brows and deep-set blue eyes were capped by a close-cropped shock of white hair. His mouth appeared little more than a slit in his face and his nose an eagle's beak. His stare was that of one used to mastery.

'I have no card,' the man said in an astonishingly deep voice.

'Card or no, you cannot cross. The City burns. Can you not see it?'

'I have been summoned by the Council of Faltha. I must cross.'

'Friend, no one may cross. None have gone into the City since the ninth hour. Perhaps in a few days . . .'

'I am the Sria Vazthan replacement on the Council of Faltha,' he said, holding up a piece of paper. 'I must cross today. If there is strife in the City, I should be there to assist.'

'You are not yet of Instruere, my lord,' the guard said respectfully but firmly, 'so I am not required to obey your commands. Once you have stepped foot in the City, thus confirming your commission, then I will be authorised to obey you and convey you to the City.' The guard crossed his arms on his chest, clearly pleased with himself. His fellows exchanged smiles behind him.

The Sna Vazthan pursed his lips, then without warning his hand flashed to his waist and a shining blade lay across the guard's throat. The movement was impossibly fast.

No one moved.

The stranger raised a questioning eyebrow. His captive signalled frantically with one hand and the other guards made way.

'You shall come with me to the City to verify my commission. I shall then return to this guardhouse and you shall issue me with a card. I would not wish to do anything illegal.' The words were all the more menacing for their gentleness.

'Actually, it seems that this may not be necessary after all—'

'No, it *is* necessary, I assure you. I want no one to claim I am here illegally.'

'They won't let you in at the gate.'

The stranger smiled then, the gap-toothed grin of an old man. 'That is another reason you are coming with me.'

So, much to the consternation and embarrassment of the guard, he was forced to lead the man and his horse first to the Inna Gate, through the guards' entrance and into the city proper, where by setting foot on Instruian soil he activated his commission, and back out across the bridge to the gatehouse. The procedure took half an hour, by which time dusk had descended.

'You have not yet checked my letter of appointment. It is signed by Her Majesty Ylisane, Queen of Sna Vaztha. See, here is her seal.' He handed the letter to the guards, who looked over it for what they guessed might be an appropriate time, then gave it respectfully back to him, along with a yellow card. He turned then, mounted his patient horse and trotted away across the bridge towards the gate.

'Will they let him in a second time?' one of the younger men asked.

'If they have any sense,' answered his captain, rubbing his throat.

The Company arrived at the Hall of Lore at a dead run, spurred on by the awful sounds growing clearer as they approached the open, grassy space. Leith held the Jugom Ark high, and his anger and shock at what he saw caused the Arrow to flame like the sun. The Arkhos of Nemohaim had been right. In the brightness they beheld a scene of terror.

The guardsmen present that night were specially chosen for the task. Deorc knew many of the Guard would object to killing their own people, no matter how the command was phrased, so he had asked his newly-appointed captains to choose those whose lack of personal scruples would permit them to take part. The names of the others were recorded. Deorc had plans for them, plans involving placing them at the forefront of the next battle.

The guards rushed the stunned Ecclesia, ensuring panic. The first brutal wave felled perhaps a third of those gathered there, some of whom had not seen the transformed figure of Deorc emerge from the Hall of Lore and so died without understanding how they were betrayed. The screaming drowned out the shouts of those few who kept their heads, who tried to organise people into groups, the better to be protected by the few men and women who knew how to fight.

The glare of the Jugom Ark revealed three knots of people bravely, hopelessly resisting the guards. In the brightness of the moment, a tableau that branded itself on Leith's memory, he heard a woman cry: 'Please, not my child—' but the plea was ended mercilessly. A raw sound came from behind him, and he realised it came from Farr, from deep in his throat. It was the sound of purest anger. Then he realised the sound came from his own throat as well.

'They are skilled at killing the innocent,' said Wiusago. 'Let us see how skilled they are at facing real warriors! Come, my friends!' And with a cry, the Company pitched themselves into the battle.

Leith transferred the Arrow into his left hand and drew his sword with his right. Again for a moment he wondered about using the Jugom Ark as a weapon of war, but again he forbore, afraid of what might happen. Along with Wiusago, Te Tuahangata and Graig, the last of whom attached himself to Leith like a liegeman, he rushed towards a ring of guardsmen so busy harrying a knot of poorly weaponed people they did not see their doom approaching. With a cry Leith launched himself at them, aggression making up for lack of skill. Graig fought at his side, deflecting any well-aimed blows away from Leith. Swiftly they interposed themselves between the guardsmen and the Ecclesia, then turned and faced the ranks of the Instruian Guard.

The rest of the battle seemed to Leith a terrible dream. Some of the guards plainly recognised the Arrow for what it was, and abandoned the field in fear. Others fought half-heartedly. Few there were who could call upon more than their training; none had the recent battle experience of the Company. From time to time Leith held up the Jugom Ark. In its light he could see that though the guards were being turned from their purpose, the inroads the Company made were too slow. Too soon their captain would call for reinforcements, if he had not already. Leith could see no way for the Company to stand against the full Instruian Guard, and the remnants of the Ecclesia proved more of a hindrance than a help. At any moment one of the Company might fall, whatever charm that had protected them up to now having run out. He reached out in thought to the Arrow in his left hand, and again considered how it might be used as a weapon.

Then his eyes opened wide in disbelief as one of the slain Ecclesia lying in front of him rose to his feet and, with a shout, pulled a broadsword from thin air. To his left, a dead woman rose from the ground and joined him, her ghastly wounds gaping, her face bloodless. To his right, a third; then many more, even children, each the ghostly simulacrum of someone who lay dead on the grass. Joining them, flanking this army of the dead to left and right, stood Maendraga and Belladonna. The magician laughed, and then Leith understood. Illusion. The looks of concentration fled the faces of the guardsmen, replaced by superstitious fear.

'You have taken our lives without just cause!' boomed a voice, somehow amplified beyond normal human volume. 'So now we return to take yours!' To a man, the Guard turned and ran from the phantom army, many casting their weapons aside in their fright.

'It's an illusion, you cowardly fools! Return and fight!' The shout, equally loud, came from the sheltered entrance to the Hall of Lore, some distance across the open ground. A man stood there, a man dressed in black with his arms spread wide in frustration, or in a gesture that summoned a mighty power.

Maendraga's laughter changed to a grunt of effort, then he was on his knees, supported by his daughter. The phantom army flickered and disappeared. 'There is a magician here – very powerful—' He groaned, then fainted away. Leith's gaze fastened on the figure in the doorway, whose arms were now raised. Could this be the man the Arkhos of Nemohaim had told them about? The Keeper of Andratan?

Others in the Company asked themselves the same question. 'Achtal!' the Haufuth cried. 'That man, he is the magician pitted against us!' The Bhrudwan warrior already realised this, Leith saw, for even before the speaker finished Achtal turned from the opponent he faced, leaped lightly over the large mound of dead and dying guardsmen surrounding him, and began sprinting across the lawn towards the door.

Deorc could not believe what he witnessed. From the safety of the entrance to the Hall he directed the slaughter; in fact, early on he had snatched a spear from the hands of a reluctant Guard and thrust it through a small figure trying to flee. Within moments the attack seemed certain of success. He savoured the pleasure of watching the fool who, last night, offered a self-satisfied prophecy about an arrow approaching

Instruere, struck down by a double sword blow. *So much for your God.*

Then things changed for the worse. First, a great light turned night into day, then a new force charged into the battle. For a time he thought this might be some fighting brigade from Escaigne come to join the Ecclesia: if so, all the better. Deal with all the rats in one trap. Soon, however, he was firmly disabused of this happy thought. The fighters were too fierce, too well trained, to be from that source. Some unknown enemy? Some rival for his place at the Council?

At that moment two things happened: the Arkhos of Nemohaim appeared in the midst of a group of fighters, and someone somewhere on the battlefield began to weave a powerful illusion. The explanation for the night's disaster suddenly became clear. *The Arkhos has found powerful new allies. Someone in Bhrudwo plots to overthrow me as the Undying Man's right hand.*

He watched as the shades of the dead chased his guardsmen from the field of battle, and cried out at their stupidity. He knew he wasted valuable time, but frustration overwhelmed him. Getting control of himself, he probed the illusion which, for all its power, was diffuse, hastily constructed and lightly held; probed, and attacked it with a raw magic drawn from deep within himself. He could feel it draining him, knew he would pay the price, but he had no choice. Even as the wraiths disappeared, he looked on the ruin of his plans – *the temporary ruin*, he told himself firmly – and one thought burned itself into his brain.

Someone will pay for this. Someone will pay.

As he stood, indulging his anger, he caught a glimpse of a figure rushing towards him, sword held in a manner he knew only too well. Tip forward, angled just so. Without conscious thought he leaped back through the open door and bolted it firmly shut. Then, just to be sure, and in spite of the extra strength it drew from him, he placed a sealing spell on the door.

Swords were held like that in only one place: at the cruel training grounds of the *Maghdi Dasht*. Impossible as it might seem, he had been about to confront one of the Lords of Fear. How many others were out there, serving his enemy? And he was so weak, so recently drained!

This confirms my belief, he told himself. *Someone high in the service of my master seeks to destroy me. But is it with or without His blessing? No matter. I will be just as dead either way if I make a mistake.* He turned and made his way swiftly to the tower, resolving to think on this further when he was out of danger.

Out on the field the Company herded the shocked, terrified remnant of the Ecclesia away from the Hall of Lore and back towards the roads leading to the southern areas of the City. Wiusago had fallen victim to a dreadful wound in his chest; he bled freely, and was ghostly pale. Te Tuahangata hovered over him, raising his head to call for help. Leith wondered, distraught, where Hal might be. The wound, though, looked beyond healing. Then he remembered the Arrow still alight in his left hand. He transferred it back to his right, stepped over a broken body and bent down to examine the stricken Deruvian.

'I told him not to be fancy,' Te Tuahangata growled. 'But no, he has seen the Bhrudwan fight, and suddenly the way he was trained is not good enough. He is lucky not to have been killed outright, but I think he is dying. Can anything be done?'

Leith desperately tried to remember how he did it before,

how Geinor's hand had been healed. He had used ointment, he remembered. Had it really been necessary? No time for ointment. Time to find out if the Arrow could work its magic without it.

Not magic, came a thought. *Enhancement. Speeding up the natural healing of the wound. Many wounds heal without ointment.*

He placed the Jugom Ark on the dying man's chest, and the Arrow flamed in response. When he lifted it away, the wound had closed, leaving nothing but a fresh scar.

Exultation flooded through Leith, along with a strange bitterness: again he had been used, a conduit for the power of another. But he could not afford to let his pride cause the deaths of others, so he turned from the open-mouthed Child of the Mist and went in search of other injured people.

The Company surrounded Leith as he went about his task, swords outward in case the Guard returned; but the streets remained eerily quiet, the shadows empty of foes. The only sound was that of sobbing and crying as the newly-healed wept over their dead.

Maendraga supported the strange young man from the north, the chosen vessel of the Most High. Though many were healed of their wounds, Ecclesia and guardsmen alike – some argued against the restoration of the guardsmen, but Hal would have insisted on it, and Leith agreed with him – the Jugom Ark could do nothing for the dead.

'I raised them up as an illusion,' Maendraga said sadly. 'If only they could be raised up in truth.'

Finally the last child was healed. The Company looked at each other, at the sweat and grime that covered them, then turned as one and left that terrible place.

* * *

'I've gathered you here this morning to discuss the events of yesterday,' Deorc said to his fellow Council members, his voice deep and resonant in the inner chamber behind the Iron Door. *I'm here to placate your fears, to reassure you that everything proceeds as planned.* But a stray thought leaked into his Wordweave. *Is everything really under control? Am I safe even here?*

'We've had a minor disturbance down by the Granaries, an accident and subsequent fire that unfortunately saw a number of workers killed. Our friends from Escaigne, miscreants and rascals all, decided to take advantage of what was for a while a confused situation. My captains faced a difficult choice. They knew whether they chose to fight the Escaignians, thus following our Council decree of two months past, or helped the worthy residents and businessmen fight the fires that threatened the buildings of Old Struere and the Docks, they would be criticised for having chosen wrong. So, alas, they decided to divide their forces, which left them prey to the Escaignians, and a number of our brave guardsmen met their deaths yesterday. I propose that we do not leave their deaths unavenged; and to remind us of their bravery, we will all stand for a moment's silence.'

The rising Councillors scraped their chairs back and stood silently while Deorc took their measure. The Arkhos of Nemohaim deserved credit, he acknowledged. He had wooed the most intelligent and gifted men of the Council to the Bhrudwan cause. Some of them still did not appreciate what that meant, how completely they had been bought, and the price they would pay when their master came calling. Nevertheless, there were two or three here who, if circumstances had been different, might have served Bhrudwo long and loyally. Firanes, there, proved himself an expert with figures, having bled the City's reserves dry without anyone realising it, including the powerful House of Commerce. Favony, who stood beside him, spent money as fast as his colleague saved it; but as a consequence of his gambling developed an extensive and useful network of informants throughout the City. It turned out one or two from Escaigne liked to gamble and had amassed large debts, which provided Deorc, through the Arkhos of Favony, a way to whisper his plots to the inner council of Escaigne.

The Council was not yet restored to completeness after the purging of the loyalist group. Replacements for Sna Vaztha and Redana'a were yet to arrive, having the furthest to travel. The rest were firmly in his pocket, including the new Arkhos of Deruys, which had been a surprise: all the information he had suggested the Raving King would not send anyone corruptible. Yet this man suggested new strategies to the traitorous Council's advantage. Deorc had taken him to the cells below The Pinion, seeking to test him, but the fellow had not been squeamish. Another one in the eye for the supposed purity of Faltha!

Talented or not, useful or not, this Council would be swept aside when the Master of All took Instruere for his own, as he would before the year was out. They would surrender the City to him, then find themselves bearing the punishment on behalf of the people for being Falthan. Deorc already had the perfect place picked out, and would ensure the executions were public and prolonged.

They had barely resumed their seats when the first question came, from the mouth of Haurn the Craven. This was odd: he seldom spoke in front of his betters. He was barely tolerated here and he knew it. 'Forgive me,' he said quietly, 'but why did we not send the main force of the Guard against

Escaigne? We have guards enough to put down Escaigne and to put out the fires. Why did we miss the chance to destroy them while they were out of their holes?'

The question gave Deorc pause. The identity of the one asking it, the content of the question, and that anyone would question him after the Wordweave he'd applied, all these things worried him. He was still weak, he realised. The magic he'd been forced to use last night, including the forbidding spell, had depleted his abilities more than he guessed. In his weakness he had broken one of his master's commands, though not badly. He'd found the wretch Stella with a smile on her face when he'd gone to retrieve her, and so nearly lost control. His level of attachment to the girl frightened him. Despite having ordered her taken down to The Pinion, her face still haunted him.

He dragged himself back to the moment. Damn his wandering thoughts! His powers were low, as evidenced by how easily the councillors shrugged off the Wordweave and asked their foolish questions. He could not afford to lose concentration.

'If we had committed our whole force to the extermination of the rats from Escaigne,' he replied stiffly, 'we would have been severely exposed here in the centre of the City. What would you have done, O master strategist, if they had sent a force here to deal with the Council? No, you didn't think of that. We needed to keep guards in reserve. The attacks by Escaigne may have been a feint designed to draw us out – as, in fact, was proven by the shameful assault on the Hall of Lore last evening, which I dealt with. That's why I sit here and you are fortunate to sit there.'

As the Keeper of Andratan leaned back, satisfied with his answer, the door to the Council chamber opened and

Furoman, his personal secretary, stepped through. Deorc's annoyance flared. 'You are forbidden to enter the chamber while the Council is in session. What emergency do you announce?'

The man's face paled, but he continued into the chamber. 'My lord, the Arkhos of Sna Vaztha has arrived to take up his place at the Council. He has presented his credentials to the protocol officers, and the papers are in order. He awaits your pleasure.'

'Could you not have put him off until this session was at an end?' Deorc asked, again caught off guard. *Sna Vaztha? How could the man have arrived so speedily? He should have been a month or more yet on his journey*. The report on the queen's nominee had not yet arrived, even though his Sna Vazthan spies had been admonished to hurry. Was the man a loyalist? Could he be bought?

'Is that the usual procedure for the Council?' asked a deep voice. A tall man in a white robe had padded silently into the room, unnoticed by Deorc in his preoccupation. 'No matter. Please show me to my seat, and acquaint me with the business of the day.'

He waited, arms folded, until Furoman found a chair and seated him between Deruys and Haurn. *Good*, thought Deorc, recovering. *Where I can keep an eye on him. Let's see what the Wordweave will reveal.*

The Arkhos of Tabul, today's designated recorder, spoke quickly, reading through his notes. When he finished Deorc stood, giving the newcomer a brief welcome, who responded by nodding respectfully to the rest of the Council. *A man of few words*, Deorc decided. *Perfect*.

But this illusion lasted only as long as it took the thought to form. The Arkhos of Sna Vaztha leaned forward, fixed them with his deep-set eyes, and began asking questions. 'What of the attack last night? I have walked the streets this morning, and heard it said that it was not an attack at all, but merely a gathering of religious fanatics called the Ecclesia. Why were they put down so severely?'

Deorc scowled. He'd tried to keep that information quiet, but it was bound to have spread sooner or later. 'It was indeed the Ecclesia, but they were dupes of Escaigne, nothing more. Do you know of Escaigne?' Acknowledging the man's nod, he continued. 'Somehow they were persuaded it was in their interests to rid the City of the Council of Faltha. They were armed with a variety of weapons, and inflicted heavy casualties on the guardsmen I sent in to disperse them.'

'I took a walk on this battlefield this morning,' the infuriating old man continued, running a hand through his grizzled white hair. 'There were over seven hundred corpses there, the guards outnumbering the Ecclesia by more than two to one. How is it this group of untrained, poorly armed citizens were able to inflict such losses on your well-trained Guard? I assume they are well trained, for you receive a large sum annually from my kingdom to support them.' His lined face showed nothing but steel.

'Really, Sna Vaztha, don't you think you might wait until you learn how this Council works before you have your say? the Arkhos of Straux said plaintively. Always a bit of a dandy, Straux was the person Deorc would least have liked to try putting the newcomer in his place.

'The Arkhos deserves a reply to his sensible question,' the leader of the Council bit off. 'I have not yet spoken to the captain in charge last night.' Nor would he, for the incompetent fool lay near the bottom of a large mound of dead, precisely where he belonged. 'But it is my reasonable guess the Guard operated under restraint, trying not to inflict fatalities among what are, after all, our own citizens, however misguided.'

'I visited the local apothecaries,' the hatchet-faced man said in his gravelly voice. 'There was not one single wounded person in their care, either of the Guard or of the Ecclesia. If the guardsmen tried not to kill, why are there no wounded?'

Deorc fashioned a strong Wordweave. 'Perhaps, my friend, the unfortunate Ecclesians took their wounded with them.' *The time for questions is over. You will be satisfied with what you have learned.* 'Now, we have many other matters—'

Astonishingly, the old man waved a hand in front of his face as though dismissing a persistent insect, then spoke again, interrupting Deorc. 'There are no matters more important than the welfare of our people. What is happening here in Instruere is symptomatic of what we hear throughout Faltha. My queen has sent me here to get to the heart of what ails us all, and I will do so. I respect no authority, no individual placing himself in my way, whatever his title, wherever the land of his birth. I have my orders, and as a representative of Sna Vaztha, I will follow them without compromise.'

Deorc was shaken to the core. The man was unaffected by his Wordweave. Even in his weakened state, there was not a man here, none in all of Faltha, who could resist him. Or was there? He remembered the magic he'd encountered the previous evening. Was this man the magician, sent here to undermine his position? Did the Undying Man have an undeclared enemy, one who might be a rival for Deorc, an inheritor of Andratan's power?

The handsome Bhrudwan cast off all civility, his face distorted into a frightening grimace as though something fought to explode from his skin. 'Tell me, old man, who are you?'

The man from Sna Vaztha raised his eyebrows, then told the Council of Faltha his name. The name meant nothing to Deorc, but cries of anguish came from around the table, faces turned red and his normally restrained Councillors, who had remained calm even in the face of the northerners' accusations a few months earlier, began shouting at the Sna Vazthan and each other. In the midst of the uproar, the white-robed man with the frightening name stood, bade them a solemn if unheard farewell, and left the chamber before a hand could be laid on him.

His feet took him south, away from the corrupt heart of Faltha, back to the devastated Granaries. How could men in leadership ignore the needs of those they purported to serve? None of them had troubled to investigate the damage for themselves. All they had done was to send soldiers to fight with their own people.

Here, in the old city of Struere, a smoky haze still covered the sky, making it difficult to breathe. He recalled the last occasion he spent time in this district, over four decades earlier. He remembered the tall tenements, built close together here, some well over a thousand years old, having been occupied continuously since well before the Bhrudwan invasion. He had stayed in a five-floored tenement on this street, if he remembered rightly – yes, there it was – or, at least, there was a pile of smoking timber where it had once stood. It, and the buildings to either side, had fallen victim to the fires that still burned in places throughout the old city. A line of people ferried buckets from the river, perhaps half a mile away, trying to damp down the smouldering ruin. He watched them for a moment, people who knew little more than the fact that their homes and possessions had been destroyed; then he walked quietly over to them and joined the line.

The choking smoke made talking difficult, but after a while the scope of the devastation became clear to him. It was not quite of the scale of the burning of Inverlaw Eich – he'd been through the ruins of that city less than a month after the fire razed it to the ground – but it seemed to have struck hardest at the most vulnerable citizens, people with menial jobs and nowhere else to live. Apparently a group of outsiders was coordinating a resettlement effort through the local markets. The old man smiled. Leadership would always arise in the absence of good government. He worked for a while longer, then moved on.

All over the old city the picture was the same. Struere always suffered most in times of devastation, the old man reflected. Instruere began life as two separate settlements, Inna and Struere, founded by Raupa and Furist on the northern and southern shores respectively of the large island located near the place where the River of rivers ceased being tidal. These settlements fought with each other for centuries, until they grew together, sharing in the prosperity generated by their advantageous location and casual disregard for the rules of fair trading. However, in the fifteen-hundred years since the island had been walled around and known as Instruere, the northern city of Inna had become the residence of choice for the wealthy and respectable, while Struere was used as a dumping ground for the less respectable of the city. *It was this that contributed in large measure to the destruction*, the Sna Vazthan observed as he walked the unpaved lanes. Houses built flimsily, too close together, with no water supply save the open sewers. Warehouses set cheek by jowl, so fire in one spread easily to the next. Narrow roads, making escape difficult for the residents. So much different to the clean, wide streets of Inmennost of the Snows.

The man spent a further hour with another group of neighbours trying to douse a burning building. The bravest among them would take it in turns to rush up the stairwell and tip his or her meagre bucket over the flames. Here again the people were too weary to say much, but they, too, told him of a small band of northerners who were trying to organise everyone's efforts, so the people in most desperate need might receive help first. He shared a flask of wine with the firefighters, accepted their grateful thanks, bade them farewell and moved on.

It was near sunset when he came upon a gathering near the ruin of the Struere Gate. Perhaps five hundred people stood patiently in a series of lines moving slowly forward. The man from Sna Vaztha joined one of the lines, and without betraying his ignorance learned he was waiting in line for some bread. Apparently a group of people – not from Struere, but where they were from was unclear; some said Deuverre, some said further north – had organised food and shelter for those who had suffered loss in the fires. These were the same people, said one woman, who had rescued the Ecclesia last night. It was true, a young man agreed. He had been there, having been promised a part in the cleansing of the hated Council from the City. But the whole thing turned out to be a trap, he said angrily. The Instruian Guard had been waiting for them. On and on the boy talked, painting in their minds a graphic picture of the confrontation. The youth told them how his sister had been struck down by a guard, though she had begged for mercy. He himself received a wound to the leg, he said, though when he was pressed, he showed them a scar that looked weeks old. He had been healed, he claimed, along with many others. No, he wasn't imagining it, he wasn't making the story up. He repeated these claims in spite of the scepticism of those around him.

The Sna Vazthan found himself puzzled by the boy's story. Though it seemed to verify much of what he had heard, and hinted that serious questions needed to be asked of the Council at their next meeting, it contained elements that were clearly fantastic. A great light? A swordsman who raised a mound of dead guards around him? Ghosts of the dead causing the guards to flee? A man who healed with a touch of fire?

The crowd's attention turned to the man in the white robe. Who was he, they wanted to know, and where did he come from? The Sna Vazthan admitted he was a stranger to the City, but told them he had spent the afternoon labouring to put out fires. Dubious glances followed his words, until he was able to satisfy them of the truth of what he said, supplying them with names and descriptions of enough local identities to finally be believed. By the charcoal stains on his expensive robe, by the cuts and bruises on his hands, and by the way he listened to their tales of woe, he convinced them he was a friend.

The sun set, and still the line crept forward. Children cried from hunger and from fear, adults bore their grief stoically, dirty bodies rubbed together uncaring as the tide of citizens, ignored by the rulers of the City, sought a morsel of bread and whatever else could be spared. Ahead of them someone had installed a torch which shed much-needed light over the food distribution area.

Finally the Sna Vazthan arrived at the head of the line. In front of him half-a-dozen trestle tables contained what this committee had managed to gather: bread, clean water, some fruit, dried meats, a treat or two for the children. He glanced up: the light he assumed was coming from a torch actually came from something a young man held aloft. He looked more closely . . .

An arrow. On fire. Not burning the boy who held it. The obvious explanation took some time to work its way into his mind, steeped though he was in the history of Faltha. *This cannot be, it cannot be. Not here, not in the humblest part of the City; not now, when the borderlands are at peace . . . unless . . .*

A great chill passed through the man's spare frame. A hundred unconnected incidents came together in a rush, the signs and portents aligned themselves into a clear message, and suddenly the man realised he was in the presence of the Jugom Ark.

'Would you like some bread?'

'What? Pardon me, what did you say?' His normally unflappable mien shattered into a thousand pieces. This is why he had been called out of retirement, this explained the appointment to the Council of Faltha. *This* is what he had trained his whole life for. The years with the Haukl, the decades as a Trader, the service in the court at Inmennost; all pointing to this moment. To take service with those who wielded the Jugom Ark.

'I asked you if you would like some bread,' the woman repeated gently. She was forty, perhaps, still a beauty, a cheerful face framed by long dark hair. He read patience in her face, and long-suffering, but also joy. Right now she waited for him with the pity of one who had served many who suffered from the shock of seeing their homes, and perhaps their friends and family, consumed by the flames.

'No, no, I need neither food nor shelter,' he said to her. 'What I need is to speak to the people in charge here. If you are one, I apologise for my rudeness. And I also need to speak to the one holding the Jugom Ark. I would dearly love to hear his story.'

At the mention of the Arrow the woman's face paled, and she turned and signalled to a man standing some distance away. 'Mahnum,' she called, 'this man wants to know about the Jugom Ark.'

'Tell him to come back later tonight. We'll be talking about the whole thing then.'

'I think he's from the Council,' she said carefully.

At that, the man called Mahnum put down the parcel he had been holding and came over to where the white-robed Sna Vazthan stood. He looked up into the old man's eyes, his own widened in shock, and for ten long seconds neither man moved a muscle. Indrett moved forward, about to speak – there were many people to be fed, and the hour grew late – when Mahnum spoke.

'It is you,' he said in a flat voice. His face had gone grey.

The old man nodded, his countenance in turn drained of all colour.

With a snarl of rage, Mahnum leapt over the food-laden table and tackled the old man, driving him to the ground. There he began to beat the man where he lay, fists pumping, arms flailing, shouting incoherently all the while. Shocked members of the Company came to the old man's aid, dragging their maddened friend from on top of him. The stranger had not raised a hand in his defence. One eye was already swollen shut, and as he stood, aided by Hal, it was clear his right arm had been damaged in the unprovoked onslaught.

'Mahnum! Mahnum! What are you doing? What has this man done that you would attack him so?' Indrett held on to her husband; along with Kurr, she was barely able to restrain him from renewing his assault on the old man.

Mahnum shook an arm free and pointed at the stranger. 'That man – that man,' he said, breathing heavily, 'that man is my father.'

'Is it true?' Indrett said, unsure which man to ask. 'How can it be true?'

The old man nodded. 'It is true. I am Modahl. Mahnum is my son.'

'But you are dead! You were executed for your part in the war between Sna Vaztha and Haurn!'

The Sna Vazthan spoke through swollen lips, his voice heavy with irony. 'This is manifestly not the case, though some here might wish it.'

'They tied him to a chair, weighted him down and put him out on the thin spring ice of the Preuse River to wait for the afternoon sun,' Mahnum said bitterly. 'Apparently even that was not enough to finish the old demon off.'

'That story effectively ended the life of Modahl the Trader of Firanes.' The old man accepted the offer of a chair. Others of the Company made their way over to the scene of the altercation, leaving Geinor and Graig, the Escaignian woman, Perdu and the former captain of the Instruian Guard to serve the lines of people. 'It allowed me to begin a new life, which by a fateful irony has brought me here to face my old life, and the fully justified wrath of my son.'

'Excuse me,' said Kurr roughly, 'but are you saying that you are Modahl of Firanes?'

The old man nodded wearily.

'I remember Modahl clearly,' the old farmer said. 'I remember bidding him farewell, one Watcher to another, as he set out for Haurn to take their part in a hopeless defence of their little country against the might of Sna Vaztha. I remember his anger at what had already been done to that land. I remember hearing about the day the mighty Modahl, the finest Trader ever to have lived, was taken captive on the very summit of Tor Hailan in a battle so fierce the midwinter snow would not settle, such was the heat of combat. I wept to hear it. I heard he was borne in chains to Inmennost and executed on the day of the spring equinox, his death the finale of the events celebrating the Sna Vazthan victory. I feel sure I would recognise such a man if he still lived. Come, stranger, and step into the light.'

But the light came to the stranger. Leith walked quietly over to where the two old men stood, and the Jugorn Ark bathed them both in its flickering light, giving their visages the look of legendary heroes.

'It *is* you!' the old farmer cried. 'By the Most High, it is!'

'Yes it is, friend Kurr. Do you want to attack me too?'

Kurr's reply was lost as the two men embraced, slapping each other on the back. Eventually they separated, and the Company could see tears sparkling on their cheeks.

The Sna Vazthan turned to Mahnum. 'You and I need to talk, my son.' Mahnum spat and turned away. 'You wear a great sword,' the old man continued, undeterred. 'I have seen that hilt before. It belonged to my old friend Jethart of Treika. You attacked me with your fists when you could have cut me down with his blade. Does that not say anything to you? It says to me that you know we have unfinished business.'

Mahnum spun around on his heels and stabbed a finger at the white-robed old man. 'My father is dead. It makes no sense to kill him again. He has sullied my soul enough! Who you are, old man, no longer interests me. Go away and wander the earth! Go and delve into still more secrets, go and interfere in the politics of yet more countries! But don't ever talk to me again. There is only one person to whom you need to talk, and she's been dead for twenty years. She now lives in a country that even you can't return from. Go and talk to her!'

'Son, I—'

'*Don't call me son!*' cried Mahnum, and lunged at his father once again. This time Kurr was ready, and he and the Haufuth kept the two men apart. The younger man squared his shoulders, turned and stalked away.

The older man sighed deeply, his face lined with regret. 'I fear there is too much between us for me ever to find his heart again. We have much talking to do. I owe him an explanation.' He looked up, and the light of the Jugom Ark was reflected in his eye. 'Might I be permitted a question?' Taking silence for assent, he asked: 'Who is the boy who holds the Arrow of Yoke?' The glittering gaze rested on Leith, who took a step towards the old man.

'I am Leith Mahnumsen, and I seem to be the only person who can hold on to this thing without getting burned.'

'Then you are my grandson,' Modahl of Sna Vaztha said simply, 'and you are the Right Hand of the Most High.'

The Company invited the Sna Vazthan to dine with them. On hearing Kurr issue the invitation to his old friend, Mahnum announced angrily that he would take his place serving food to the homeless of Struere. Indrett accompanied him, though obviously torn between trying to comfort her husband and finding out more about this legendary stranger who happened also to be her long-dead father-in-law. The serving lines had thinned somewhat, although a large number of people milled about in front of the gaping hole that had been the Struere Gate, so Mahnum and Indrett were sufficient to take care of their needs. *Good*, the Haufuth thought, *he needs a chance to talk to someone*.

The weather drew in and a light drizzle began to fall, taking the edge off the late summer heat. The waxing moon made little impression on the heavy overcast, being only a few days past new. Willing Instruians had that afternoon erected a pavilion of sorts, open to the south, at the juncture of the Vitulian Way and a narrow side street, not far from where the lines still lingered and within sight of the Struere Gate. Under the canvas shelter the Company took their meal, gathered around one large board formed by putting four tables together. Basic fare, of the kind handed out to the locals, supplemented with two dozen honey cakes baked that morning by Hal, hindered more than helped by Prince Wiusago. A veneer of good cheer ruled at the table, derived in part from the work they shared and from their happiness at being together again. During the meal Maendraga was asked to repeat the story of his and Leith's adventures, and the slightly embellished description of the drunken soldier at the King of Nemohaim's unruly court set them all to laughing. But underneath the laughter and jollity lurked a sombre mood. Farr spoke of his frustration at what he saw as the lack of activity in Instruere while the others had been away, emphasising their failure to find Stella. While he spoke, the thoughts of many drifted to the Firanese Trader and his reaction to the appearance of his long-lost father.

Modahl stood. 'I wish to thank you all for your welcome,' he said, without a hint of irony. Indeed, he sounded genuinely glad, as though he considered he deserved the anger his son had offered him as a greeting.

He reached into a small pack and drew out a bottle of clear liquid. 'In Sna Vaztha we celebrate the reunion of friends long separated by sharing a special drink. Actually, we celebrate anything with this drink. To be truthful, we drink it even when there is nothing to celebrate. I would be grateful if you would share it with me. Pass it around, and let each one here mix a small amount into their drink. A small amount, mind: it is very strong.'

As he began to talk other conversations dropped away, and gradually the night drew quiet. 'I have heard only a few of the tales of this Company tonight, and yet already I am amazed at what you have done. Nowhere in Faltha were there people like you when I was younger, particularly in places like Loulea. Or, perhaps, people like you were everywhere but not yet called out by the needs of the time. It seems much has changed! I am eager to hear more of your stories, and I have many, many questions for you all. But before I begin to ask for your tales to be told, I believe I need to tell you mine.'

'We know your tale, Great One,' Geinor said, deep respect in his voice. 'The greatness we see in your village, as manifested by the Five of the Hand, and in your son and grandsons, is explained by who you are. We of Nemohaim have heard the stories of your journeys, of how you, alone of any of the First Men, travelled through Jangela and the swamps that kill, south to new lands where vast cities are built entirely in the branches of trees, and where in one kingdom the entire capital city is made of solid gold; and how you brought home to Faltha precious metals, rich spices and news of exotic peoples as proof of your journey. We have heard of your exploits in the Borderlands of Rhinn and Bannire; of how you forged a treaty in the Lankangas, uniting warring cities;

and of how, at the last, you were made captive while a general in the army of Haum, defending the smallest of Faltha's Sixteen Kingdoms against greedy Sna Vaztha. You have lived many lifetimes, it seems to us, or had adventures enough for many at the least. Your name is known and revered throughout the Sixteen Kingdoms.'

Modahl laughed, a full, rich sound that seemed to come from deep within his soul. 'The passage of time makes legend of many a person,' he said, 'but twenty-five years ago I was barely tolerated in the Court of Firanes, and hated in many other cities by those I had bested in trade or diplomacy, including Bewray, I must say.' He nodded to Geinor. 'I made powerful enemies in this very City, defying the Council of Faltha a number of times after they ordered me to stop interfering with their rule. My journeys in the Southlands were held up to general ridicule, and at home my wife and child wanted nothing more than for me to retire from my adventurous life and return to them for good.

'Ah, that I had! And yet – no, that is a tale best left for the time when he who needs to hear it is ready to listen. Instead, I will tell you of my supposed death, and what happened to me after.

'As my friend Kurrnath said, I went to Haurn because I had for some time been troubled by rumours that Sna Vaztha once again planned to extend their borders by swallowing up their small neighbour, in spite of the treaty I helped them devise. I arrived there at winter's heart to find the Sna Vazthans had taken the capital city of Hauthra and held the king hostage. A small band of brave men aided me in his rescue; but we could not save his family from the stake. The king was driven mad by the bitter news, and climbed to the top of Verenum Spire, from whence he cast himself to his death.

'Within a month the Sna Vazthans pinned the remnants of the Kingdom of Haurn inside the ruined city of Tor Hailan. Their general agreed to spare the women and children if I would surrender only myself, which I did; but after he made me captive he scoured the city, leaving not one soul alive. Over five thousand were killed, the corpses fed to the wolves. He then carried me off to the Sna Vazthan capital, a trophy of his famous victory against a peaceful nation one-tenth the size of his, and with no standing army.

'What I did not learn until much later was that this general was an ambitious man, and his conquest of Haurn was conducted without the authority of his king, as part of a campaign to win the throne for himself. His king was greatly angered at the news, and was made more so when I supplied an account of the darker deeds done in Haurn, which his general omitted to mention.

'The king faced a dilemma. How was he to rid himself of a famous and well-loved general without risking public wrath and a possible revolt, but at the same time make use of his prized captive, Modahl the Trader? His answer was ingenious. The general found himself enthroned on a chair in a mock ceremony, placed on the thin ice of the Preuse River, and left there to await the afternoon thaw, as my son Mahnum rightly told it. The crowds were told the man on the chair was me. None could approach close enough to tell the difference without risking death themselves. The bells of the great Tower of Inmennost rang when finally the ice cracked and the Robber of Firanes, as I was known to them, disappeared into the icy waters. I cheered along with the crowd, for the man on the chair was responsible for atrocities that should not be perpetrated even on the hateful battlefields of war. I cheered from the king's balcony, for I had not been released, but rather taken into the old king's service. And there for ten years I was forced to stay.

'In truth I found my time there a great delight, even though my heart was heavy with the knowledge that my king, my friends and my family would all have heard the news that I was dead. I longed to return to them, but as that was not allowed, I threw myself into the governance of the king's affairs. I became the shadow behind his throne, his closest and most secret adviser, and within a few years I was making policy for the most powerful, proud and independent of all the Kingdoms of Faltha.

'Ten years after my capture and enslavement (for that is what it was, however kind), the old king died. In his will he granted me my freedom, and here I reveal my sinful heart, for I was afraid to return home, afraid of what my loved ones would think of me. I took enough food for a week and, with the new queen's blessing, went up into the Aldhras Mountains, the highest in Faltha, there to await the judgment of the gods – or, most likely, death.

'I will not tell you of the great storms that came, of the days I spent in a snow cave by the banks of the frozen Diamant River, nor of my scaling of the precipitous Hauberk Wall. What I will say is, I was rescued from starvation by a mysterious race of people who called themselves Haukl, and taken to their city of Dukhobor on the shores of the ever-frozen lake.'

'The Haukl!' Kurr cried. 'My friend, I do not doubt you, but everyone knows the Haukl are a myth, the bastard offspring of men and the giant she-bears who live on the Roof of the World. Are you saying the Haukl are real?'

'I am, and I would add that stranger things than the Haukl are to be found within the kingdoms of Faltha. Indeed, one such wonder burns in the hand of my grandson no more than a few feet from where I sit. Speak not to me of myths!

'The Haukl are a gentle race, far advanced in the arts of survival. I could not believe the cruel conditions in which they make their home, could not understand how anyone managed to stay alive in the white waste; yet they took me in and taught me their secrets, how to sense the rhythms of the land and align myself to them. For ten years I studied with them, the strangest, most ineffable people I have ever met, including all the races I encountered south of Jangela.

'I learned that once they were the people of eastern Faltha and western Bhrudwo, and their stewardship extended unchallenged from the Wodranian Mountains in the west to the land of Birinjh in the east. They told me how the First Men drove them from their homes, killing many and forcing the rest into the mountains, there to be starved or frozen to death, so they supposed. Yet the First Men had not reckoned on the hardiness and will to live of the Haukl.'

Te Tuahangata stood, and his body trembled with rage. 'Again and again we hear this story! The accursed First Men are found unworthy of their own lands, and so come north to steal ours! Is there no end to their evil?'

Prince Wiusago stood and laid a hand on his friend's arm, but Te Tuahangata angrily shook him off.

'You have every right to be angry,' the man from Sna Vaztha said to him. 'I learned far more than I cared to hear about the sins of the First Men from my gentle hosts. One day, they say, they will come down the slopes of their beloved mountains and share the plainlands with the First Men; but not until the First Men have grown, as they put it.'

Te Tuahangata sat down, but growled: 'One day we will come down from the Mist and murder every one of the

First Men. Then will we win back our lands and our lives with honour.'

'That is not how the Haukl see it. They are listening to the mountains, they would say; and when they finally hear the mountains speak, they will descend and live with us. I fear for them should they ever leave their secret home. I fear what we would do to them.

'I came down from the high places reborn,' said Modahl. 'I entered the service of the new Queen of Sna Vaztha, consumed with the notion of preparing the way for the Haukl; but I found the courtiers and functionaries self-opinionated, braying their shallow thoughts to those around them as though no one noticed how empty those thoughts were. Though Sna Vaztha has vast tracts of unoccupied land, we could spare none for the land's original occupants. For three more years I served, until I could stand it no longer. I resigned and once again set out for the Aldhras Mountains, but this time the way was closed. I could not scale the Hauberk Wall, and no Haukl came to my aid, though my cries echoed among the cruel peaks. I lived for a year in the wild valley of the Diamant, witless like an animal, eating whatever came to hand, relying on my Haukl-learned senses to survive until I learned something of humility; then returned to Inmennost and begged the queen to let me serve.

'I served as her Chief Minister for another year, until she learned her representative at the Council of Faltha, the Arkhos of Sna Vaztha, had died suddenly in a terrible incident, an act of sabotage by the Escaignian rebels. Apparently the Arkhoi of Sarista, Redana'a and Deruys died also, according to the official communication we received some time after the event. This made my queen very angry because, unknown to the Council, the Arkhos of Sarista had sent a letter to loyal Falthan monarchs warning of treachery in Faltha, and named names. We misbelieved the Arkhos of Sarista – as everyone knows, Sarista has long been our chief opponent in matters of state – but in his letter he named the very Arkhoi who died as the members of a loyalist group working to expose the treachery of the Council. Further confirmation came when a similar letter arrived from our own Arkhos, though by that time it was posthumous.

'In the light of this the queen felt my talents and experience would be invaluable in Instruere, and so appointed me as Arkhos to the Council of Faltha. I left Inmennost no more than four weeks ago, travelling with an Imperative from the queen authorising me to change my mount for a fresh one at every stage of my journey. I doubt the journey has ever been made more quickly. And so, here I am. Treachery I expected, and treachery I found. The Council of Faltha reeks like an open sewer, and its leader is a dark magician not above trying his powers on new members of the Council. But old friends and family members I did not expect to find. I see that part of my mission here is to atone for the selfishness that drove me to search for enlightenment rather than return to my family.

'So now my story is finished. On behalf of my queen I ask you, bearers of the Jugom Ark and the Hope of Faltha: how may Sna Vaztha serve you?' And with that he raised his glass in a salute, and downed it in one long draught. The Company followed suit, acknowledging the old man's speech, though a few of their number choked on the sharp taste of the liquor Modahl shared with them. He laughed deeply, and poured himself another drink.

*   *   *

Leith sat quietly and listened to this strange man who said he was his grandfather. His grandfather! The word meant nothing yet; he felt a strange numbness in the place where joy should be blooming. What bothered him was the hurt his father obviously felt. Seeing his own father so angry about the neglect he had suffered made Leith feel better about him: there was no logic as to why this should be so, it hadn't changed what had happened to Leith – and Hal, he remembered grudgingly; and to his mother. Mahnum in his turn had left them alone for two long years, becoming no more to Leith than a wooden carving and the blurred memory of a face.

And something else ticked away inside his mind, connected in some way to the stories of the Haukl he'd just heard, to the Pei-ra and even the Children of the Mist. Something that took root on the quiet days spent sailing the Wodhaitic Sea, something . . . but no matter. Slow and methodical, his mind was; the thought would form when it was ready.

More important by far, at least as Leith saw it, were the questions facing them; issues so important yet so intertwined with politics, danger and death that even now the Company danced around them as though they were snakes rearing to strike. In a City as divided as this one, how were they to use the Jugom Ark to achieve unity and raise an army to oppose Bhrudwo? How had finding the Flaming Arrow advanced their cause? And was Modahl right when he acclaimed Leith as the Right Hand of God?

CHAPTER 4

THE FLAMING ARROW

THE COMPANY ROSE FROM their evening meal, their thoughts already turning towards sleep after a wearying day. Yet each of them knew many hours of debate lay ahead. The Jugom Ark had been brought to Instruere, and there was no one to tell them what to do with it.

Leith held the Flaming Arrow in his upturned left hand. So attuned to him was the talisman, it now no longer mattered how tightly or loosely he held it. No one else could come within an arm's length of the Jugom Ark without wincing in discomfort. Leith had hoped his return to Instruere might signal an end to his stewardship, so he could turn it over to someone braver and wiser than he; but it seemed appointed for his hand and none other.

If only, if only someone would step forward and claim the Arrow for themselves, he might then be rid of the voice in his head. *If only*. Failing that, he resolved not to speak to the voice, not to ask any questions of it. Certainly the voice had remained silent since the sacred island of the Aslamen, weeks ago now. Perhaps his growing familiarity with the Jugom Ark meant the voice was no longer necessary. He could only hope.

Or, more worryingly, maybe the voice was his own, the voice of a troubled boy trying to be heard. Perhaps he was crazed. Had he confessed his inner voice to his friends in Loulea, they would have considered him mad. He remembered a man with a young family from a farm near Garrison Hill who took to living in a tree, the better to hear the teachings of the Most High, most of which seemed to revolve around the care of cattle. His sons had been forced to run the farm. It was as though their father had left them and been replaced by another man, so complete was the change.

Feeling the stirrings of a strange pity, Leith left the tent without a word and went in search of his own father. The food lines had finally disappeared, either satisfied at last or maybe driven off by the light but persistent drizzle. Neither of his parents was in view. He cast about for them somewhat anxiously, wondering where they might have sheltered. Then he noticed the crowd.

They were gathered near the broken arch of the Struere Gate, huddled under the City Wall, which provided a measure of protection from the southerly showers sweeping over the City. Leith raised the Arrow without thinking, simply seeking to shed some light so he might find his mother and father. As he did so a collective gasp rose from the crowd. Leith gasped in turn as he realised the magnitude of the gathering. *There must be thousands!* Twenty and thirty deep against the wall they stood, spilling out on to the street, quietly waiting for something; their numbers still being reinforced by others walking down the Vitulian Way or even coming through the Gate itself. Leith wandered over to them, wondering what they waited for.

'Look!' came a man's voice from the throng. 'There it is! It's the Arrow!'

'It is, it truly is!' a woman echoed. 'Hold it up again; let us see it!'

Other voices joined in. 'Please, sir; come and bless us! Shine your light on us! You fed us, you healed us, you rescued us from the swords of the wicked! Grant our prayers, we beg you!' Within a moment the noise became deafening, and the crowd surged forward. Leith was momentarily overwhelmed by panic.

All of these people are standing in the dark, in the rain, to see me.

Then his parents appeared at his side, flanking him, right and left; and Mahnum cried out in a loud voice: 'Hold! Please, good people, hold back! The Arrow is dangerous. It will burn anyone who approaches too closely!' Indrett put an arm around Leith's shoulder and whispered in his ear: 'Be brave, my son. Remember these are people, not just a crowd.'

'What do you mean? What is happening?' But his voice was drowned by the crowd thronging towards him still. They parted left and right, taking Mahnum's warning seriously. Others of the Company drew up behind him, having heard the commotion, and it took only a moment for them to realise what was happening. Something they should have anticipated. Hundreds had been rescued from the Instruian Guard the previous night, hundreds more fed and clothed today: all of them had seen the Jugom Ark, and of all the cities in Faltha, this was the one whose inhabitants best remembered the legend of the Arrow of Yoke.

Here on this island, two thousand years ago, Furist and Raupa quarrelled and divided Faltha in two. They had argued over who should have charge of the Flaming Arrow, the symbol of the Most High's judgment on Kannwar, the

Destroyer. Bewray emerged victorious from that conflict, and from the island he had travelled southwards, the Jugom Ark entrusted to his safekeeping. Here the Bhrudwan wrath descended a thousand years later, a thousand years ago. The Destroyer hated Instruere, the unofficial capital and most powerful city of Faltha, to him a potent symbol of the regard the Most High held for the First Men. And to this great City the Jugom Ark would return, so the legends said; heralding a time of trouble, yet bringing unity to Faltha and giving true Falthans strength and light against their dark Enemy. So it was said.

And on this day, all over the city, it had been said again and again. People drifted together, talking in groups on the streets or meeting together as neighbours, friends or extended families. Those who had been there told of the miraculous intervention of the Flaming Arrow on behalf of the Ecclesia. In the afternoon the Arrow had been sighted again, this time in the company of a group supplying food, shelter and clothing for those affected by the fires. The largesse had apparently been wrested from reluctant businessmen, not from the City Fathers. Word of the new sighting spread swiftly through these clusters of Instruians. In every knot of people discussing the strange events someone could be found who knew the prophecies of the Arrow and was only too willing to share that knowledge. The excitement and speculation grew with each retelling.

No one called them, but they came. The Jugom Ark was the talk of the town, the whisper in the darkest alleyways, the topic of discussion among the well-to-do, the subject of the moment in the markets and a distraction to all who wanted to conduct business. In the midst of their troubles, many Instruians believed their salvation was revealed. Some remembered how the northerners braved The Pinion a few months previously, and that deed was added to the list of reasons why it seemed a good idea to brave the rain and the dangerous streets to catch a glimpse of the flaming Arrow. In their thousands they came. And now they waited for the Bearer of the Arrow to speak.

'You'll have to say something to them, boy,' Kurr hissed in his ear. 'They're not here to look at your pretty face.'

'But – but I . . .' He could say no more. *The truth of it*, Leith realised, *is this is more than I can bear*. He would not ask the voice for help, and he could not think of words of his own to say.

'Leith! This is the moment! This is why we risked everything to find Kantara!' Phemanderac's voice whispered urgently, but Leith felt rooted to the spot.

Hasty whispers from somewhere behind him produced a wooden box, which willing hands placed in front of the crowd. In an instant Phemanderac stood on it, arms outstretched, pleading for silence. 'Citizens of Instruere!' he cried. 'In a moment you will hear from the Bearer of the Jugom Ark. But first, listen now as I tell you the tale of the Flaming Arrow.'

Even though his friend the philosopher had earned him a brief reprieve, Leith found it hard to breathe. What would he say to them? What hope could he offer these people? What counsel could he give? A thousand thoughts swirled in his head, like starlings seeking a field on which to alight.

Phemanderac raised his voice until it could be heard throughout the open space in front of the Struere Gate. *Perhaps it's Hal enhancing again, or maybe the magician and his daughter*, Leith thought. Whichever it was, the illusion made it possible to address the crowd.

'More than two years ago I left my home, the legendary land of Dhauria,' the tall philosopher told them. 'I have dedicated my life to studying the ancient prophecies of Hauthius, who foretold the return of the Arrow of Yoke, which would bind the peoples of Faltha together. I travelled the wide world in search of the Hand that would wield the Arrow, with few clues to help me in my search. "The one you seek will be found in a Lowly Vale, in the Cape of Fire," the old books told me. So I travelled towards Firanes, and on the way there was captured by a fierce tribe known as the Widuz, imprisoned in a dark dungeon and readied as a sacrifice to their gods.

'But I was rescued by a brave and valiant warrior, a member of a company of northerners travelling to Instruere to warn Faltha of a great danger. One of their number had learned that the Destroyer plans an invasion of Faltha. Even now the Black One amasses his evil armies, and aims them at Instruere, the heart of Faltha. Before year's end, perhaps, the Undying Man and his army will be camped outside your gates.'

He pointed to Mahnum. 'Here is the man who spent two dangerous years in Bhrudwo uncovering the Destroyer's plans. He braved the dungeons of Andratan and wrested the knowledge of our fast-approaching doom from the hand of the Destroyer himself. Without his courage we would be ignorant of the black tide drawing near our borders. And my rescuer, the one who saved me from the Widuz execution pit, is this man's son. It is he who holds the Jugom Ark. His name is Leith, son of Mahnum, and he is the Bearer of the Arrow.

'The northerners came to Instruere to warn the Council of Faltha. But the Council of Faltha, your rulers, would not listen, for among them were traitors, men who sold their souls to Bhrudwo in exchange for promises of wealth or power to be delivered when the Destroyer takes the City for his own. They have gained control of Instruere, and even now plot to render her defenceless when the brown hordes are thrown against us. They are prepared to expend your lives, and those of your children, to curry favour with their new master.

'Leith and his father were thrown into The Pinion by the Council of Faltha, but they escaped, eluding the Instruian Guard and setting others free in the process. Perhaps there is someone here tonight who was rescued by their bravery?' Three or four voices called affirmation from near the rear of the crowd; heads turned to look. 'For a time Escaigne hid them from the vengeance of the Council of Faltha, and sought to enlist their aid in the overthrow of the City. However, it is not their desire to replace one regime with another, but to unite all Falthans in opposition to our great enemy. The northerners rejected Escaigne's offer, instead setting out in search of the Jugom Ark.

'Citizens of Instruere! It is obvious the quest for the Jugom Ark was successful. Leith Mahnumsen is the first man to hold the Arrow of Yoke in two thousand years, the first since Bewray hid it against this very hour. So I need not regale you with our many adventures, or the suffering and loss we endured, in order to find and redeem the one hope of Faltha. It is here, it is truly here, and we are saved!' A great cheer arose from the crowd.

Phemanderac, arms raised, waited for quiet. 'Yet not completely saved.' He paused. 'If our leaders were loyal servants of Faltha, we would gladly turn over the Arrow to them and trust them to find ways to use it to deliver us from the evil about to fall upon us. But they are part of that evil. We must take up the Arrow of Yoke ourselves and try to raise an army to defeat the menace of the Destroyer.

'Listen to me! We are like insects drawn to the light of the Jugom Ark. Yet I do not believe it has any magic of itself that will heal all the divisions between us. We have much to do before we can present a unified front against the cruel enemy that comes our way. Look around you! Struere is set against Inna, Escaigne opposes Instruere, and northerners and southerners still treat each other with suspicion. It is time to put aside the things that divide us – money, old quarrels, misguided loyalty to the place of our birth – and unite under the banner of the Jugom Ark. Thus we will drive out the traitors in our midst, and raise an army to defend Instruere and all of Faltha from the hatred and greed of Bhrudwo.

'So be ready! Prepare! Await the call of the Flaming Arrow, and together we will go into battle!'

Phemanderac stepped down from the impromptu platform amid the cheering and excitement of the crowd.

'A stirring speech,' the Haufuth told him. 'Maybe this is how it will begin. We will find our army amongst those who have been oppressed by the rich and powerful.' Others of the Company gathered around the philosopher, congratulating him on his oratory. Clearly assuming that the evening's entertainment was over, the crowd began to disperse, perhaps turning their thoughts to the journey home through the light rain that continued to fall. The flames from the Jugom Ark reflected from every puddle, every rain-slick surface, until it seemed that the whole neighbourhood had caught alight.

Everyone had forgotten Leith. He stood there, a little apart from his friends, surrounded by thousands of faces flickering in the supernatural light of the Arrow, yet no one looked at him. Those who remained gazed at the bright light they saw as their salvation. The figure bearing the Jugom Ark might as well have been a torch-holding stanchion.

It's not right, Leith realised. *That's not how it's meant to be. Phemanderac's got it wrong.* Simplistic black-and-white rhetoric, the philosopher's words papered over the huge cracks in Faltha's façade. *Faltha's not like he said. He told no lies, but what he said wasn't the truth.* He continued to worry away at it. *We're not entirely good*, he admitted. *And if we're not entirely good, then the Bhrudwans aren't entirely bad.*

The thought opened something in his mind. Words and thoughts flickered in his head; slow at first, then faster and faster. '*You five are the fingers of a gatherin' hand*,' he heard Kroptur say, in the house under Watch Hill. '*A hand has five fingers*,' the voice of Phemanderac explained, as they hid together, planning their journey south to find the Jugom Ark. Another voice hissed: '*You are First Man. You say you were first, but you were last.*' He recalled the feel of the knife held to his throat, the sweet fragrance of the sacred island in his nostrils, sharpened by the moment. The memories quickened: Te Tuahangata's anger, the cruelty of the Widuz and the cowardice of the people of Inch Chanter, the glorious, all-encompassing laughter of the Fodhram; and through it all like a discord came the voice of Farr of Mjolkbridge, angrily declaiming in the inn at Windrise; 'Losian! Losian *to a man, the abandoned of the Most High, discarded misfits who rejected the Way of Fire! Arrogant, ill-tempered half-breeds! Save your dealings for descendants of the First Men, and keep yourself pure!*' Images swirled through each other, finally resolving to a warm night in a forest, Leith sitting with two old ones by a fire, and hearing the old man say: '*We wanted to ask you a boon*' and hearing the old woman say: '*When you come into your own, remember the Children of the Mist. Remember all those peoples who live in Faltha, yet are not of the First Men*'.

Pressure began to build in his chest. The voice was about to speak to him; Leith could feel it. And in a flash of insight he knew what the voice was going to say. The words had been forming in his mind for months, making him uneasy, making what seemed a simple battle between good and evil into something much more complicated, much less certain, where the heroes grew black wings and inflicted sickness and suffering on others, or kept dark secrets from each other, little different to the villains. He would speak now, before the voice had a chance to echo through his head, robbing him once again of his own will, of his self.

He stood. Thoughts coalesced in his mind, a multitude of memories coming together to form a single idea, and he shook with the enormity of it. The Arrow responded by exploding into life, burning with a fierce, white-hot flame. The crowd moved back, stunned. None of the Company could brave the heat and flame to get near the youth from Loulea, who stepped on to the box and stood before them enveloped from head to foot in a pillar of fire.

'Leith! What is happening?' Kurr cried, his face a surprised mask, his eyebrows singed. 'What are you – what is it doing?'

Flames roared in Leith's ears. He heard the old farmer, but could not make out what he said. The flames distanced him from the others, as though he was some mad prophet in the grip of a supernatural ecstasy. *These are my words. My words!* he told himself. *Nobody else's!*

'I am Leith Mahnumsen from the village of Loulea in Firanes,' he said. His voice carried over the crowd, which quieted to hear his words. *Truth, tell the truth as I see it. My words.* 'I am the bearer of the Jugom Ark. It does not belong to me. I carry it on behalf of the Arkhimm. It's just that I seem to be the only one who can pick the thing up,' he said, indicating the Arrow in his hand, which continued to blaze like a captive star. 'But I do have a question for us all to think about, and it is this: how do we unite Faltha?'

He paused, taking a moment to look about him. To his right and left stood the Company, which had grown from the original five members to a large group of people from most parts of Faltha – *and beyond*, thought Leith, glancing at Phemanderac, who watched expectantly. They were all there: his family, enlarged so dramatically by Modahl's reappearance; friends old and new; a few acquaintances, even an untrustworthy adversary with whom they had a temporary alliance; all gathered to debate how to make use of the Jugom Ark. Before him, spread out until it filled the open space between him and the Struere Gate, waited the crowd. Some had made their way into the adjacent tenements, and now leaned out of windows and sat on balconies and even roofs, the better to see and hear what the people with the Jugom Ark had to say. *They will expect more inspirational speechmaking*, Leith realised. *They will expect me to instill courage in them, courage to face their enemy.* They *will expect us to lead them.* They want someone to follow.

And, with a suddenness that shocked him, Leith realised what he was about to say might ruin the whole quest. Might cost them the war. Might damn them all to defeat. He took a deep breath.

My words. Mine!

'The Undying Man of Bhrudwo is bringing a vast, well-trained army to take Faltha and make it his own,' Leith told them, his words echoing in his own ears, the squeaky voice of a nervous youth. 'Half of the kings of Faltha have gone over to him. Yet we will need the strength of a united Faltha if we wish to defeat the Dark Lord of Bhrudwo.' *Good, so far. They're listening.* 'You recognise the Jugom Ark, the ancient heirloom of the Most High, and are willing to put your trust in it. It is his promise that he will not forget us in our time of trial. But many of our leaders will not recognise the Arrow. They will refuse to acknowledge the leadership of a group of peasants from lowly Firanes. Or they will try to take the Arrow from us, and bend it to suit their plans.

'So what do we do to win over the kingdoms ruled by traitorous kings? How do we get the message out to the furthest corners of Faltha, and gather an army swiftly enough that we can meet the Destroyer before he brings his force through the Gap? How can we make our army powerful enough that it can defeat the might of Bhrudwo? These are the questions we must answer. My friends will tell me this should be talked about in secret, that there may be spies of the enemy right here in the crowd. But I say nothing should be hidden! I tell you we have choices, and tonight we can decide how this whole war is going to proceed.'

His father came as close to him as he dared; Leith could see the heat drawing sweat from his face. 'Leith! Leith! What are you saying? What are you doing? Should we not talk about this first?'

Leith spoke no word to him, untouchable in his fiery cocoon, and continued. 'We could ignore the kingdoms of the traitorous kings, and halve the potential size of our army thereby,' he told them. 'Or we could somehow subvert each kingdom, perhaps by identifying people still loyal to Faltha, and encourage them to begin a rebellion; but this will take far too long, and will result in Falthan deaths long before we face the might of the Bhrudwan army.'

Leith sighed. Now for it, the vast risk, the great idea that had been building in his mind for months, though he had not been aware of it until a few moments ago. He began to shout, aware how he must appear to the crowd: smothered in fire, flames coming from his mouth as he spoke, like an apparition of the Most High.

'There is another way, a way to bring together an army so vast it will outnumber the Bhrudwans, so fierce it will cause them to fear. This way arises from the meaning of the Jugom Ark itself. The Flaming Arrow was given to Falthans as a symbol of unity. It is a brightly burning idea which, if we have the courage to accept it, will bring together all true Falthans for the very first time. It is an idea so large its effects will be felt far beyond the end of the battle with Bhrudwo, no matter who is the victor. It is an idea so frightening in what it asks of us I would not suggest it unless we were in the last extremity – but that is where we are.

'*Who are the true Falthans?* Are true Falthans the same as First Men? No, they cannot be, for we know many of the leaders of the First Men have betrayed Faltha. They are not true Falthans. So what makes a true Falthan? I declare to you by the Flame that burns brightly in my hand – may I be consumed to ash if it is not so! True Falthans are those who remain loyal to the land and the people of Faltha, no matter where they live.'

'Where do they live?' a man called out.

'How can we tell the true Falthan from the traitor?' asked another.

'True Falthans don't short-weight their goods, that's for

sure!' yelled some wag who clearly knew the previous speaker. A section of the crowd laughed, but were shushed by those around them.

'Let the boy speak!' they cried. 'Listen to the Arrow-bearer!'

The disturbance barely registered on Leith's consciousness, so far into his message had he gone. As soon as the crowd quieted, he continued.

'Where do we find these true Falthans? Not only within the walled city of our own small prejudices. True Falthans also live beyond the borders of our Sixteen Kingdoms. They live in secret valleys where we drove them. They remain in hiding on small islands on the fringes of Faltha. They dwell in the deep forests as yet unexplored by the so-called First Men. They occupy hot southern deserts and icy northern wastes. They were once free to roam throughout Faltha, but now are penned in their small lands, the lands we First Men have not yet claimed for ourselves. That is where we find our army. They are under threat just as we are. Their ancestors died just as ours did a thousand years ago when Bhrudwo last defeated Faltha. They will fight for their people and for their land: but unless we make room for them, they will not fight alongside us.

'Where are the hidden armies that will come to our aid? Who are these true Falthans who live on the margins of what we call civilisation? They are the *losian*. *They* are the real First Men – and First Women – of Faltha.'

His pronouncement was met with stunned silence.

'Anathema!' an old man cried into the void. 'Anathema! The *losian* refused the Fire of Life! How can we fight alongside such as they?'

'We ain't joinin' with *losian*!' came another voice from the back of the crowd. 'Animals, that's what they are!'

'He's right, young sir,' a woman shouted. 'You dursn't say such things. Were your family murdered by savages from the desert like mine were?'

The crowd began shouting – at the man holding up the burning arrow, at each other, at anyone who would listen. As Leith watched, people began to leave the street, unwilling to accept what they had been told. First one, then another, then dozens and dozens of listeners drifted away into the shadows, until perhaps two-thirds of the crowd remained.

'Very good, you young fool!' Farr cried bitterly. 'Rather than doubling our army, your ill-advised plan has halved it!'

Leith turned on him. 'Be patient!' Around him the flames roared, forcing the Vinkullen man back a step. 'Withhold your judgment until the whole plan is revealed to you. I am tired of your constant opposition to things you don't understand!'

Farr drew back even further, shocked to hear the youngster speak like this. In an instant Leith softened. 'I'm sorry, Farr. You've done much to help us. But the die is now cast, and nothing anyone does can unsay what has been said. Please be patient with me a little while longer.'

The youth from Loulea raised his voice: again, it carried easily to the remnant of the crowd, again the flame rose until he was cloaked in fire. 'I have placed my life as forfeit once already tonight, and now I do so again. In the crowd, and within our very Company, there are people we call *losian*, people not descended from the First Men exiled from the Vale of Youth. Let us see whether the Arrow of Yoke, the most sacred object known to Falthans, accepts or rejects the *losian* amongst us.'

Well, you've challenged me to say and do strange things, he said to the voice. *Now it's my turn. Do I do this or not? I'm going to wait until you speak to me.*

<I don't need to speak. You're in tune now with the Arrow. Its desires have become your desires. Do what you plan to do.>

'Behold!' Leith cried, feeling like a hawker at the local market, but knowing what he was about to do was necessary. 'The Jugom Ark tries the *losian* by fire!'

A dozen gouts of flame burst from the Flaming Arrow, arced over the heads of the crowd and landed in a dozen widely separated places. Louder and louder roared the fire. One of the fiery arcs descended on Te Tuahangata, standing only a few yards away. Immediately he disappeared in a blaze of light. For an awful moment Leith thought the man had been destroyed, and he cried aloud, along with many of the crowd, expecting to see nothing but ashes. But no! In a scene eerily reminiscent of his own dream, the arcs of fire held firm, each one immersing a dark silhouette in flame. The Flaming Arrow burned brighter and brighter, until none could look upon its radiance. Then, in a final burst of light so bright it seared the very darkness, the filaments of fire disappeared.

'Look around you,' Leith spoke into the preternatural stillness. 'The *losian* have been judged. They have been touched by the Fire of the Most High, and they still live. Have any been found wanting?'

The people standing around the fire-drenched figures had already pulled well away from them, and retreated further when they saw that each figure glowed, as though the fire still rested on them, though already the glow began to fade.

'We have been answered,' Leith declared, trying to keep

the relief out of his voice. 'Now, does anyone here wish to put their prejudice against the *losian* to the same test? There is plenty of fire left!' He held the Arrow aloft, and it burned with an angry red glow.

No one took up the challenge.

'Return now to your homes,' the figure bearing the Flaming Arrow told them. 'Think on what you have heard, and decide if you can still stay loyal to this new vision of Faltha. Then come back here tomorrow at dawn, and bring everyone you know with a like mind. We will then decide what to do.'

The Company drifted back to the pavilion, stunned by the turn of events. Leith noticed rain now fell steadily, and his friends were wet through: he, however, was completely dry. The Arrow flickered quietly, the vast energy it had displayed replaced by a gentle glow.

Leith waited until everyone else found a seat, then took his place between his parents. Twenty faces and more stared back at him, with only a few betraying anything but anger. Hal, he noticed, wore a smile of immense satisfaction.

I've been played for a fool again, Leith realised angrily. The Arrow, the voice, his brother. All in league against him. Just when he thought his great idea would take him forever away from the clutches of the voice, he discovered – had been told – the Arrow itself exercised control over him. And he had thought he controlled it! That it matched his moods! That it was his tool! Now he knew who the tool really was.

Putting the rising anger to the back of his mind, Leith waited for the inevitable questions.

'How could you have done this thing?' Kurr began, his face drawn and pale. 'Surely you could have spoken with us before announcing your plans to the world? Don't you think we deserved some say in the matter? Or have we merely been bystanders in all of this, bit players in the drama of Leith Mahnumsen and his Burning Arrow? Have we, boy?'

'It wasn't like that—'

'I want to know where you got this scheme from,' Farr interrupted, clearly unable to wait a moment longer. 'Whose idea was it to involve the *losian*? Even if such a thing was conceivable, even if they should agree to fight with us, what's to stop them turning traitor and selling us out to the Bhrudwans halfway through the battle? They can't be depended on, mark my words. I won't march alongside them! I swear this on the grave of my dead brother: if but one *losian* fights alongside our army, I will leave this Company forever!' Then he sprang to his feet, knocking his chair to the ground, and marched from the tent.

The silence following his hasty exit impressed upon everyone present just how serious the situation had become. At that moment the whole quest rested on the edge of a knife. Leith bit back the replies fighting with each other for control of his tongue. Someone else had to carry the argument forward . . .

'Earlier tonight I told you all a story about the Haukl,' rumbled a deep voice. Leith had to turn and look to attach a name to it. *Grandfather*. 'It appears you did not listen. I watched the Jugom Ark mark out the *losian* as true Falthans. It appears you did not see. If we spend time now debating our course of action, who among you will understand?'

'Is that all you have to say, old man?' Mahnum snarled. 'You, who came late to Haurn, who came late to this quest, and who came to your family not at all? You presume to teach us?'

Modahl stood quietly and with dignity, but with a troubled

expression on his proud face. 'You are right, my son. I have no right to speak here. I will wait outside the tent until you have reached a decision. Perhaps without me here you will be able to concentrate on the matter at hand.'

As the night closed around the white-cloaked figure, Mahnum put his head in his hands. 'Everything is falling apart, just when we should be victorious,' he muttered.

'Anyone else want to leave?' Te Tuahangata asked them. 'You, my prince?' he inquired of Wiusago mockingly. 'Could you stand to share a battlefield with the likes of me? Or you, wise one?' This to Phemanderac. 'Do you find our grasp of the world a little too primitive for your taste? Anyone else?' No one moved.

The Child of the Mist snorted. 'And *you*,' he said, turning to Leith. 'I am angriest of all with you. Who gave you leave to speak for us? When did we agree to fight in your Falthan army? Did you think we *losian*, as you call us, would be so fawningly grateful to have your god's approval that we would gladly march like fodder in the van of your mighty force, to shed our blood so your precious First Men might hold on to *our* land? You who have been honoured by my ancestors beyond your wit to recognise, did you even listen to what they said? We are not of the Fire like you; we follow a different path. We are of the Earth. We are tied to the land. We cannot leave it to fight in your war. The *losian* say "No" to your generous offer!'

Leith made to speak, but Geinor spoke before him. 'Be not too hasty to throw away the offer extended to you,' he said unctuously, no doubt enraging the warrior all the more. 'It is no trivial thing to be invited to fight with the armies of Faltha.'

'No,' Leith said, and silence fell. 'No! They will not fight alongside the army, they will *be* the army, along with all the rest of us. We will make no distinction. How else can we avoid destroying each other before we ever face the Destroyer himself?' He turned to the smouldering Mist-man. 'Whether we fight together or not, the time has come for First Men and *losian* to talk. Tua, we have set Fire to your Earth and consumed it, leaving you little more than nothing. If you are truly to be a part of Faltha, then we must make room for you. We must aid you in reclaiming your lands for your own.'

'Fine words well spoken,' Tua conceded, though he did not look satisfied. 'But we have sat together with our foes on the sacred mound and exchanged well-meaning words, while behind our backs the First Men continue to steal the Earth away from us. Is that not so, Wiusago?' The blond-haired man gave a slow nod of agreement.

'Leith,' Perdu said gently, kindly, as a father correcting a much-loved but wayward son. 'I admire your heart. You are young, and for the first time you see the injustice in the world. With youthful enthusiasm you think to change all this; you seek to enforce your own benevolent rules, and in your hand, you think, is the power to enforce them. But the land is not yours to give. What would happen if you took the land from the people who now live on it? Who have lived on it for generations? You will have created a new list of injustices.

'Leith, I live with a race who once ruled over most of Firanes. The Fenni were masters from Iskelsee to the Jawbone Mountains. Now they are confined to the moors. Were you to offer them their ancient lands back, they would refuse, for they have grown to despise the soft coastlands. They have become hard, like the land in which they dwell. They wish for no other.'

As Leith sat amongst them, looking from one to the other, his mother took up the thread. 'And what of the Widuz?' she said. 'Mahnum told me what they did to those they captured. I saw what they did to Parlevaag, and I will never forget her face as the blade pierced her. Should people like that be given more lands to corrupt? Would they be satisfied even if they were given the whole of Plonya, the whole of Treika? Would their cursed hole in the ground stop crying out for sacrifices? Leith, dear Leith, you ask too much.'

'Then this has all been in vain,' Leith said, voice heavy. 'Five set out from Loulea, the five fingers of a gathering hand. Farr and Wira from Mjolkbridge we gathered, and from the Fenni came Perdu and Parlevaag. The Hermit joined us on our travels, as did the Warden of the Fodhram for a time. Amongst us sit men and women from Escaigne, from Nemohaim, from Deruys, from Sna Vaztha and from Hinepukohurangi. Even some from outside Faltha have joined us. Phemanderac of Dhauria, and Maendraga and Belladonna, do not serve any of the Sixteen Kings. We have Achtal from Bhrudwo itself. This is the true nature of the Arkhimm! We are appointed as gatherers! Could we have gathered any more widely? Please, answer this: what were we doing wrong, that so many who are not of the First Men have been gathered to our cause? Or could it be we have done what was planned from the beginning? That this conflict with Bhrudwo, serious as it is, has been allowed to happen to force us to look in each other's eyes? Isn't the spirit of the Jugom Ark the friendship we see around this table? Are we to be the forerunners, the very first to enter into a partnership that will not only drive Bhrudwo from our lands, but also see that those lands are divided with greater fairness amongst all true Falthans?

'I have held on to this Arrow when none other could,' he

said, and his voice was edged with bitterness. 'Time and again I wanted this burden to pass to someone else. Someone older, wiser, stronger than I. It is a responsibility I do not want. I would rather go back to Loulea and sit on the front step of my house, carving wood and talking to my friends, and let someone else worry about the defence of Faltha. But no other hand has stretched out to take the Arrow, save one.' Here he nodded to the Arkhos of Nemohaim, who wore a scowl like the entrance to a deep cave. 'And he could not bear it.

'I have held on to the Arrow when no one else could,' he repeated stubbornly. 'Surely that counts for something! I have become attuned to it. I know what it wants; I sense its spirit. Let me tell you what it is like. It burns with a passionate fire, ready to consume anything or anyone who seeks to divide and destroy; ready to defend anyone who seeks to build up and to unify. It is pleased with the plan I have outlined. It wants us to oppose Bhrudwo with one heart. If you do not believe me, all you have to do is to take up the Arrow yourself and listen to what it says to you. Perhaps it will tell you a different story! Perhaps a story like the one it told the Arkhos of Nemohaim!'

He stood, anger finally consuming him like fire, and raised the Arrow above his head. 'If anyone here wishes to take the burden from me, then all that is required is to take up the Jugom Ark. If you can do this, then I beg you, please take it!' And, with a cry, he struck the table with the Arrow, then stepped away, leaving the point stuck fast in the wood.

Long into the night the Company talked, ideas and arguments flying around the table, where in the centre the Flaming Arrow burned low. Leith said not a word. Eventually they either left or fell asleep where they sat. The talk died down until the only sounds in the pavilion were the gentle snores of the Haufuth and the whispering crackle of the Jugom Ark. Long after everyone else had closed their eyes, the Arkhos of Nemohaim remained sitting upright in his seat, eyes fixed on the glowing Arrow.

CHAPTER 5

THE CLASH OF FIRES

THE HERMIT OF BANDITS' CAVE sat hunched over a low table, his head resting in his hands. Opposite him the leaders of the various branches of the Ecclesia sat, talking earnestly; sometimes one after the other, sometimes all at once. He gave no sign he listened to what they said.

The news of Tanghin's betrayal was a devastating blow. For twenty years the dark, isolated recesses of Bandits' Cave had been his home, a place of purification, of preparation for the time that was to come. In countless dreams and visions he had foreseen it. The coming of the Right Hand of God, the one who held the fire of the Most High in his hand, the Anointed One who raised a mighty army to deliver Faltha from the mouth of her enemies, the one to usher in a new golden age. Perhaps even to rule it. For a time the Hermit had believed the youngster from out west was the one, but since his arrival in Instruere it was clear this was not so. In his humility, which he now realised had held him back from his true destiny for years, he ascribed the object of the vision in his heart to someone other than himself. Yet where was the boy now? Where were the northerners, for all their self-importance? They had turned their back on the Ecclesia, which proved their timidity, their lack of vision. And where was he, the Hermit so beloved by the Most High? Here in Instruere, at the forefront of the next move of God.

The setback perpetrated by the duplicitous Tanghin, undoubtedly motivated by jealousy, seeking to destroy what he could not rule, was a test, a trial of the Hermit's faith. All this talk from his leaders about joining with Escaigne, or with the rumoured group of outsiders supposedly doing good works in the south of the City, he took to be a sign of their weakness. Tanghin would be overcome by strength, not by weakness. They were unfit to carry the vision, Tanghin was unfit, they were all unfit. It was time to take the burden back on his own shoulders. There would be no more alliances.

The Hermit slammed his fists down on the table, silencing his followers. *For that is what they are. Followers, not leaders. They will serve me; they will* all *serve me. The Fire would not be snuffed out by the fear and timidity of cowardly men.* So, gathering them together, he told them what they were to do.

The blue fire burned dully as Deorc chanted his foul words. They hurt Stella's ears as they rumbled across the room. Moving his hands backwards and forwards over the bowl, he drew the flame upwards until the cold light steadied and the familiar voice began to speak. The girl from Loulea writhed in agony at the mere sound of that voice. She desperately wished she could clap her hands over her ears; but forced herself to listen for anything she might be able to use to her advantage. While she listened she felt the dreadful pull of the flames. Deorc had carefully explained to her that the blue fire drew strength from all those nearby. Each time it was used, he said with pride, it would take maybe a month, maybe a year or even more from the life of those it drew from, depending on the length of time it burned. Strong men could be reduced to husks by the blue fire, he told her. The hateful man seemed to think spending his life in this way was a badge of honour, and kept him high in his master's favour. Stella could feel the fire pulling at her, draining her dry.

'I will hear your report,' the loathsome voice commanded. Deorc abased himself like a whipped dog.

'Great Lord, I find I must report a setback in your plans,' he said, licking his bloodless lips. 'The deposed Arkhos of Nemohaim has raised a force in opposition to me, and thwarted my attempt to destroy the Ecclesia.'

'How is this possible?' the voice thundered. Stella thought it would rip her heart out, such was the anger behind the words.

'My lord, he has a mighty magician to aid him. By the power of this mage the shades of the dead were raised against the Guard. It took me all my strength to break the spell. Moreover, at least one *Maghdi Dasht* is in his service.'

'Impossible!' This time, Stella was sure her heart stopped beating for a moment. 'You know the number of the *Maghdi Dasht*; thirteen thirteens, one hundred and sixty-nine, never more, never less. The whereabouts of all my greatest of servants is known. Unless the rumour of four renegade *Maghdi Dasht* is true, and they survived their reported deaths. Could this be so?'

'My lord, I trusted the words of those you sent to investigate the stories of *Maghdi Dasht* in western Faltha,' Deorc answered carefully. 'The messengers I dispatched to the kingdoms of Firanes and Plonya discovered the bodies of men who were undoubtedly *Maghdi Dasht*, according to the descriptions they gave me. Some calamity had befallen them: their broken bodies were found at the bottom of a gorge, below a bridge that looked to have given way under them. There was, however, evidence of a great battle, with more than a hundred dead in a clearing a short walk from where the renegades were found. Would you care to interrogate these messengers? At least two of them are within the City.'

'You will bring them before me at this hour tomorrow. But first I will search your mind. I wish to learn more of this magician who has you so thoroughly cowed. Draw nigh the fire!'

Gritting his teeth, the head of the Council of Faltha moved closer to the flame, which instantly enveloped him in a fierce blaze. Stella shrieked along with her captor as the Destroyer sifted his servant, searching for any clue as to what had temporarily slowed his inexorable victory. After a minute or so the flame withdrew. Deorc collapsed to his knees, gasping and retching his pain. The voice spoke again, ignoring Deorc's distress, as though the suffering of his servant was of no account.

'I have seen something in your mind that gives me pause. Do not be alarmed!' the voice cried as Deorc backed away from the blue flame, though there was precious little reassurance in the cold tones. 'You, my faithful servant, have not tried to deceive me, which has saved your life thus far. Know that the first falsehood you tell me will be written on your tomb. I am concerned by something you saw, a great light . . . reminding me of something I beheld a long time ago. I shall take time to think on this further.

'In the meantime, you will strike early and strike hard. Put this rebellion down in the same ruthless fashion you dealt with the insurrection in Jasweyah. When I ride into Instruere I expect to see the crow-picked head of this dull-witted Arkhos adorning the city walls, along with those of his followers. Put forth all your strength; the time for secrecy is past. Find this magician and his renegade *Maghdi Dasht*. Find them and defeat them!

'Now, on your face, my faithful servant. Open your soul to me! I am about to infuse you with the strength you need. You will not fail me!'

As Stella watched in horror the flame reared up, then drove Deorc to the floor. Gobbets of red pulsed through the blue tendrils of fire, washing over the twitching figure like old blood, entering in to his mouth, his ears and eyes. And, in the eerie light, the woman from Firanes quailed as the malice of the Destroyer beat at her like the winds of a mighty storm. Finally, blessedly, she lost consciousness, overwhelmed by the power behind the flame.

As the darkness paled towards dawn Leith sat alone at the table in the pavilion, his eyes closed, feeling the flicker of the Jugom Ark on his eyelids, a cornered animal hiding from the torchlight of the hunter. At some stage during the night the others woke and made the short journey back to their lodgings, but Leith remained. He told himself it was a matter of comfort. Now that twenty-two members of the Company were crammed into the five rooms that comprised their lodgings, it seemed he had nowhere to think, nowhere to be alone. So much to think about. Stella lost and they could not look for her, prevented as they were from doing anything until they had decided what to do with the Jugom Ark. *That cursed Arrow!* he reflected bitterly, and the talisman flared in response. *I have lost Stella, whom I loved; and I have this Arrow with its hateful voice, which I do not love. Yet I tried to do what is right, speaking what the Jugom Ark wants spoken, and no one will follow its lead. I can do no more. Why won't they listen to me? Why can they not see there is a price to be paid for unity? How can they expect to gain aid from the* losian, *and afterwards have everything the way it was before? I wish the Firanese king had never ordered my father to Bhrudwo! Then at least I might have had one more year to myself before I died. One more year to climb trees and swim in the lake!*

He thumped his fist on the table, opened his eyes, and the light before him lurched for a second. There, seated around the table, was the Company. For a moment he thought it was an illusion, but then realised they must have returned to the pavilion while he dreamed. *But no, I did not fall asleep. I'm sure I didn't!* A moment's reflection confirmed he had indeed slept: his father was now absent, replaced by his grandfather Modahl, who had left the tent earlier. From the looks on their faces, Leith knew he had spoken his thoughts aloud, and he hung his head, shamed that he should have been overheard.

The Haufuth stood. 'Dawn comes,' he said. 'We have heard your anguish, Leith, and if we could do anything to spare you this task, we would. While you remained here alone, we took counsel with each other. There are many among us who are stronger and wiser than you, and yet none of us knows what to do with the Jugom Ark, let alone take hold of it and constrain its wild magic to our service. No one has stretched forth a hand to take the Jugom Ark; there it remains, embedded in the table. Take it, Leith. The Five of the Hand may have left Loulea together, but there is only one hand able to lead us to victory.'

Three seats to his right, Phemanderac began to pick a gentle tune on his harp. Three notes repeated, then played again in a different key. *Told you so*, it seemed to say; *told you so*.

Kurr stood up and moved to the Haufuth's side. 'It doesn't all make sense, boy, but what pieces of the puzzle we have uncovered all seem to have your face on them. It was your father who uncovered the Bhrudwan plan, and your grandfather who against all chance has returned to aid us. Your family is wrapped up in this mystery. When you stretch out your hand and take up the Arrow, you take it up on behalf of your family, of the Arkhimm, of the Company. Perhaps on behalf of all Falthans.'

'All Falthans?' Leith retorted. 'Or just the ones like us?'

'When it comes to that,' Prince Wiusago answered quietly, 'you know the answer. We of the Company have been gathered by the Five of the Hand. We represent all Faltha. Therefore whatever we do must be done with all Faltha in mind. Yet as the son of a king I must add that this idea of yours is fraught with danger. We may end up with an army that fights with itself before it ever faces the real enemy. A true soldier would counsel that it is better to have a small army of one mind than a large army with many minds. Nevertheless, I do not see how we have any choice. Let the Arrow have its way, if indeed we have read its will aright. After the war is over, those of us who remain can sit together and decide what to do.' Unnoticed, the harpist picked up the pace of his tune, becoming a little more insistent.

Modahl eased back his chair and faced his grandson. 'My bones are old and my wits are not what they were,' he said in his deep voice. 'Yet this does not seem a difficult riddle to me. Whether I was to find the Jugom Ark in the hands of a small child or an old woman on her deathbed, I would serve that hand without question, and with whatever ability remains to me.

'This should be of encouragement to the Company. Many

others will be of similar mind to myself, including people in positions of influence. They will not hesitate to send the men at their command to join with us, once the discovery of the Jugom Ark is verified to them. I but need to send the word to my queen and ten thousand Sna Vazthan soldiers will be dispatched to aid us; or a still larger army could be sent to the Gap to hold it for a time against any army Bhrudwo could muster. This I shall do, no matter what the Company decides, for Sna Vaztha will not tolerate any army passing their southern borders. The passage of the Gap will cost the Bhrudwans many lives, particularly if they are foolish enough to attempt it in winter.

'Leith, I barely know you, and yet already I suspect the Flaming Arrow has chosen its keeper well. Do not be discouraged! You have wise heads and strong arms at your service.'

'You must lead us, Leith,' the Haufuth declared, picking up the thread; and it seemed to Leith a great relief lay behind his words. 'Last night you gave us an ultimatum: in effect, to accept your terms or to forfeit the use of the Jugom Ark. That is the act of a leader. We have decided. We will follow.'

The Haufuth sat down, his broad face clearer than it had been since this journey had begun.

'The sun is rising,' Modahl reminded Leith. 'Soon people will gather, waiting to hear what the Arrow bids them do. We wait on your word. In the meantime I have a responsibility I must discharge. Do I have leave to absent myself for a little while?' No one raised any objection, so he left the tent swiftly.

The harpist brought his playing down to the very edge of hearing.

Leith gestured to the people facing him. 'I see four empty seats,' he said, thinking furiously, choosing his words carefully.

'The number of the Company is not complete. Where is my father? Why will he not even sit at the same table as my new-found grandfather?' Turning to Kurr, he said: 'You talk about our family as if it's something special. Maybe we are, I don't know; no one told me anything about my grandfather. But it is a divided family. How can a divided family be involved with the Arrow of Yoke?'

He pointed to another empty chair. 'Where is Hal? My own brother keeps secrets none of you know about. I could take an hour and tell you things about him that might change your opinion of my family. Even you, Mother, don't know all Hal has done since we left Loulea. He's not what he seems. Hasn't anyone else noticed his silence? Why does he no longer say anything? Doesn't anyone else remember his harsh words in the Hermit's cave? His counsel against bribing the functionaries of the Council of Faltha? Or his ready advice at the Haufuth's house, before the quest even began? Shaping us, always trying to influence what we do. But now he says nothing. He's not said anything since the Jugom Ark was found. Doesn't anyone else think that's strange?'

'Leith, Hal is a special boy. We all know that.' Indrett spread her hands. 'Perhaps he's keeping silent to give you a chance to come into your own. When he comes back from making the breakfast, you might ask him.'

Leith grunted in frustration: that would be just like Hal, once again claiming the moral high ground. 'I see another gap in the Company's ranks,' he continued. 'Where is Farr? Has he abandoned us?'

'We've seen nothing of him since he left us last night,' Perdu replied. 'That one is little loss.'

'I disagree,' Kurr said, surprising everyone, perhaps even himself. 'He showed more spirit than most. Who is to say how any of us might have turned out in his circumstances? I did not have to watch my mother, my father and then my brother die while I was still a young man. My hope is that he finds somewhere to reflect on what remains to be done.'

'Yet Farr is lost for now,' Leith concluded. 'As is one other. Less than two days ago I walked through the gates of Instruere to learn Stella had gone missing. I still haven't got the straight of it.' He turned towards his mother. 'You say she fell in love with a man from the Ecclesia, but was not given permission to wed him? How could this be? I was only away for one season!'

'Leith, Leith; Stella is a woman. At least, this journey has made her one before her time. Perhaps we should have granted her permission to follow her heart, trusting that her heart might prevent her making a disastrous marriage – as any such union would be, for she wants something from a marriage that no marriage can provide. We will continue to search for her.' Indrett nodded to emphasise her words.

'I want all the members of the Company together,' said Leith. 'I don't like the thought of any empty seats.'

'I don't like to harp, but it grows lighter outside every moment,' Phemanderac reminded them, the smile on his face lessening the gravity of the moment. 'What, then, is to be done? Do you, Leith, accept the burden of the Jugom Ark?' He played a last chord, which echoed through the pavilion, then faded into silence.

The moment hung in the air above the table like a storm about to break. In the cave under the island in the Joram Basin Leith had taken the Jugom Ark without knowing all that it meant, clasping his hand around the burning shaft in obedience to a voice that seemed to be a friend. Now it was different. He knew that the Arrow would not burn him, at least on the outside, but he could feel himself being inwardly seared by the potency of the flame. The same flame had visited him the night of the Firefall in Foilzie's basement, the same voice that had spoken through him to Stella on the icy lake in Withwestwa Wood. It spoke of love, but sought to constrain. It offered freedom for Faltha but bondage for him. He desired the voice, yet wanted nothing to do with it. This time, if he stretched forth his hand, he would not be parted from the Arrow and its voice until all was won – or lost. And even should the war be won, what would he lose in the process?

I don't know why I hesitate. There really isn't any choice. There never has been.

He opened his fist . . . and the Jugom Ark burst into life, jerked itself free of the table, crackled through the air and flew to his open hand like it had been loosed from a bow.

'I accept leadership of the Company,' Leith announced, 'until a better hand than mine can be found.' The Arrow of Yoke flared, as though expressing contentment with the situation.

'You've made me leader, but that doesn't mean I will no longer ask for advice. So,' he said, signalling for them to draw closer, 'here is an idea that seems good to me, and I would like your thoughts on it.' He spoke rapidly for a few minutes, and as he spoke first one, then another of the Company began to nod.

When the Arkhos of Sna Vaztha arrived at the Iron Door, the Council secretary informed him the meeting had already begun, and he couldn't possibly be admitted until after the morning session, and then only if Deorc allowed it. A quick glance back along the corridor told Modahl the first of the day's supplicants had yet to arrive. He drew his sword and asked the secretary a second time, knowing what would be waiting for him as the great door slowly rose on its chains. Nevertheless, his queen commanded it, so he must obey. He had little hope of returning to this side of the door alive.

'That is why we cannot let the present situation continue,' the handsome magician was saying as Modahl drew near the half-open door to the Inner Chamber. 'A man such as he loose in the City, even if his powers are less than legend makes them, will be a focus for all the discontent currently troubling us. The news that he is related to these northern peasants is yet another reason to act swiftly.'

Modahl made to push open the door; and at once the speaker was aware of him. He could feel the leader of the Council as though the man stood right beside him.

'Come in,' said the voice, and the Arkhos of Sna Vaztha was forced to obey. Around the Council table the treasonous Arkhoi sat, open-mouthed that he would dare to return. Directly opposite the door sat Deorc, owner of the voice.

'Sit down,' it commanded, full of power, and again he did not resist. *Save your strength for when it counts*, he told himself.

What sat opposite him was no longer human. Something had happened to it since last he had been in this fearful place. A fierce and harrowing presence stared out of those eyes, and for the first time Modahl looked into the face of a man possessed.

'You've saved me a great deal of trouble,' said the voice, the mouth jerking the face in a number of directions, as though in parody of normal human speech. 'I was about to order a search for you. I have some questions for you, Arkhos.'

It hurt horribly, but Modahl resisted in the Haukl fashion, not directly confronting the power beating at him, but stepping aside in his spirit, allowing the malice of the voice to slide past. He could do nothing to attack it, that was not the Haukl way; but he fashioned a place of resistance.

'I have a message for you from my queen,' he began.

'Be quiet!' snapped the voice in front of him, and the words whipped at him like ropes cut from a sinking vessel. The compulsion was nigh irresistible, yet he had prepared.

'I – I have a right to speak,' he continued, swallowing hard, and the eyes in the terrible face opposite him narrowed in surprise. 'My queen suspects treachery in the Council of Faltha, and it is confirmed by the use of dark magic in the halls of the First Men. She bids me say that Sna Vaztha withdraws from this false Council, and considers it disbanded. She seeks like-minded monarchs with whom to appoint a new Council of Faltha. Her association with this group is now at an end, and her representative will now leave.'

'Oh, he will, will he?' Deorc shouted, but though the voice poured at the Arkhos like blood and fire, it could not hold him captive. Enraged, Deorc stood and gripped the table, which began to smoulder under his hands. 'You will not long escape the power of the Great Master, base-born fool! Peasant! I choose to let you go, for my master has entrusted me with power to put your pitiful band to the torch, and I would not waste it before time! Beware!' And now it seemed to Modahl in his distress that actual flames spurted from the man's mouth in bloody gouts. 'We come for you! Rally your useless defences, for the Undying One will enjoy your struggles. Now go! See if your old legs bear you to your road ahead of the Instruian Guard, who are being loosed upon your friends this very hour!'

With that, the power exerted by the magician slammed into Modahl like a blow from a giant hand, and he flew through the open door, to land on his back in the Outer Chamber, the wind knocked out of him. He struggled to his feet, then ran from that place in fear, in a desperate attempt to outrun the doom that would soon descend upon the Company.

The rising sun silhouetted the Bearer of the Arrow as he stood on a small wooden platform facing the vast gathering. He raised his arm so that sun and Arrow joined and made one large conflagration, casting long shadows behind the thousands who stood silently before the Struere Gate. They had gathered here for many reasons. Fear and uncertainty, despair and loss motivated some, anger and hatred others. There were those who came to see the magic, as though the whole business were of no more importance than the entertainment generated by a passing band of players. Most, however, sensed the changing of the times. The Jugom Ark revealed. Modahl the legendary Trader back from the dead. The City in an uproar. It was the end of an Age, some said, or even the end of all things. Some said the Destroyer himself was but a few days' march from the walls, bringing with him an army to wipe every trace of Instruere from the earth.

The silhouette spoke to them in the simple voice of a young man, amplified by some strange magic so that all who stood there could hear it clearly and understand it, even if the common tongue was not their own. As the figure spoke, the Arrow in his hand pulsed gently, flaring occasionally as if emphasising what the voice said.

'The Council of Faltha is made up entirely of traitors to Faltha, according to Modahl the Trader, who was appointed to the Council as the Arkhos of Sna Vaztha,' said the voice earnestly. 'It is corrupt to the core, and is led by a Bhrudwan magician. Therefore, as the Bearer of the Jugom Ark, I disband the Council of Faltha and declare them anathema. Should anyone capture a member of the former Council, I would ask that you refrain from killing them, although their lives are forfeit, but instead bring them to me.

'There shall be a new Council, chosen from all the peoples of Faltha. Each country or kingdom will elect a Councillor, and they will meet together when they may. Until such time, I appoint the Company of the Arrow as the interim Council.' The figure pointed to the left and to the right, where those who had helped put out the fires and served them food and drink stood silently. A few members of the crowd cheered.

'Lest you think we have replaced one tyranny with another, I declare that all meetings of the interim Council will be held in the open. Anyone who wishes to hear what is discussed may do so. We have no secrets from you, no interest apart from the salvation of Faltha.

'We are aware the interim Council is incomplete. We place our faith in the Jugom Ark to draw representatives from the lands who have none.'

The voice continued on in its boyish, almost shy manner, explaining how a great army would be raised. This army would confront the Destroyer by marching eastwards to secure the Gap against him. They dared not wait until the brown hordes laid siege to the City, as happened a thousand years before. The army would be made up of trained soldiers in the main, the voice told them, but there would be room for any who wished to defend Faltha.

'We are fighting to defend far more than just the Sixteen Kingdoms,' the voice said. 'Therefore we will invite warriors from many other lands to join with us.' On the voice went, explaining how the *losian* might help in the perilous task ahead.

'What d'you think?' one man said to his neighbour. 'Ever heard of a war where they ask you if you want to fight?'

'Not as though I'd be unwilling,' came the reply. 'It doesn't bear telling what those Bhrudwans might do if they break open our gates. But I've got the ashes of my house to sort through. Take weeks, that will.'

'So will raising an army,' an older man put in. 'Sounds like he's wanting people to come from all over. It'll be months before they march east, see if I'm right.'

'I don't like the thought of that Destroyer coming here again.' The speaker, a middle-aged woman, gave voice to their fears. 'I've three sons, two of them married. How many will I have once this is all over, whether they join the army or no?'

'Where will they get the armament, that's what I'd like to know,' the first man asked those nearby. 'Takes ages to make swords, good ones at any rate. I used to work for a blacksmith, and swords took months. One poorly-aimed blow and snap! All that work wasted.'

At that moment heads jerked around: something appeared to be happening near the platform. A man in a white robe had just arrived, after a hard run, it looked like. Two of his colleagues held him upright as he spoke urgently to the Bearer of the Arrow. The figure stepped down from the platform and out of sight of much of the crowd. Talk spread through the assembled throng, much of it agitated. What was happening?

The former blacksmith felt a hard bump in the back, and turned angrily, ready to quarrel with whoever had been careless with their elbow. His curse died in his throat. At the back of the crowd a solid line stretched along the length of the City wall. The Instruian Guard. Directly behind him a knot of guardsmen pushed forward, bludgeoning a path through the gathering with the butts of their swords and spears.

'Stand aside!' they cried. 'Make way, or you'll finish up on the end of a spear!' One or two scuffles broke out, and a scream came from somewhere away to the left, but in the main the crowd parted.

Leith looked on with concern as his grandfather struggled to speak. 'The – Council – is coming!' Modahl forced out between gasps. 'They plan to – wipe us out!' Mahnum and Indrett could barely keep him on his feet.

A commotion in front of them made Mahnum lift his head. People moved to the left and right, opening a path back to the Struere Gate – through which poured hundreds of guardsmen. Leading them towards the Company was the Council of Faltha, and at its head strode Tanghin of the Ecclesia.

Groans of recognition went up from the crowd. Some of the survivors from the Ecclesia were among them, and they remembered Tanghin and his betrayal. With half an eye on the approaching Guard, Mahnum heard Modahl explain that this Tanghin was in fact Deorc, the leader of the Council of Faltha. For a moment he believed his father mistaken; but as the Council drew near, the realisation settled into his spirit like a hot stone. Tanghin and Deorc were one man, the man at the heart of the evil in Instruere. Someone shouldered Mahnum aside. The Arkhos of Nemohaim stared at the man with hatred on his face, his wheezing breath expelled in a series of hisses.

'This is the man that would have wed Stella,' Mahnum said quietly. 'We have all been so blind!'

The man with the handsome face and the dire eyes raised a hand. The Guard halted. He stood there, a few scant yards from the Company, scorn on his face.

'The speechmaking here this morning was weak,' he said, almost conversationally, addressing the Arkhos of Nemohaim, whom he seemed to regard as the leader. 'Insipid. Double-minded. It is clear you and your rabble know nothing of power and the manipulation of minds, nor will you ever. I was right to replace you. Why did your new friends not recommend Tanghin of the Ecclesia to make speeches for you? He would have gladly spoken on your behalf!' His words spat from his mouth as though they were weapons.

'Beware the Wordweave!' Phemanderac cried from beside Mahnum. 'Keep your thoughts unmixed! Hold in your mind the image of this man as a liar and destroyer of lives!'

Deorc cast a venomous glance at the tall philosopher, who stared back at him unblinkingly.

'I listened to your attempt to inspire these men and women to rebel against their rightful rulers,' said the man with the mask-like face, his voice carrying to all corners of the open space, just as Leith's had done. 'I have been sent by the authority of the Council of Faltha to put down this rebellion and to take its leaders into custody. If the leaders surrender voluntarily, the rest of the people standing in this square may go free.'

A relieved cheer went up from the crowd. Most were already under the magician's spell.

Mahnum took a step forward. So this was the Keeper of Andratan? He had memories of that dark place. Perhaps taking the life of this cruel man might enable him to sleep more soundly at night. He put a hand to the hilt of his sword, the Sword of Jethart.

Deorc saw the gesture and laughed. He raised a hand and instantly the hilt burned with a feral heat. Mahnum jerked his hand away before his skin could burn.

'Illusion!' Phemanderac hissed.

'I do not think so,' Modahl dissented. 'Look at his eyes; see how they glow. And his uncovered wrists! They pulse with a beat not of this man's heart. He carries the power of another. Ah, the price he must be paying!'

'Well, he can pay it and more,' Mahnum said, forgetting for the moment his unwillingness to speak to his father. 'But it appears we are the ones who will be doing the paying here today. We are trapped.'

'What have you decided?' the unclean thing in front of them asked in his dreadful voice.

'We have no decision to make,' Mahnum replied. 'There is no Falthan law requiring us to submit to Bhrudwo.'

Their enemy laughed. The monster's throat glowed red, as though a great furnace burned within him.

'So my master predicted! Very well: many hundreds of honest Instruian citizens will pay the price for your pride. You have only a few moments of life remaining – just as long as it takes to prepare the blue fire. My master would watch his triumph!'

The leader of the Council turned to call for something from the arms of one of his captains. In that moment the spell loosened. Te Tuahangata sprang forward with a fearsome cry, swinging his war club at the figure. Scant inches from the man's unprotected head it struck an invisible barrier. The warrior cried in pain, clutching his right arm to his side.

Deorc – Tanghin – whoever it was – turned to face them again, apparently not having noticed the attack upon his person. He set a bowl of some oily substance on the ground in front of him, then raised his eyes to those of the Company.

'You account yourselves great,' he said, mocking them. 'You have scholars among you who can read mighty books and almost understand them. Children who can fell members of the Guard with a single cowardly blow from a water-filled jug. Magicians who can contrive a spell that holds together for a full minute. But there are others of your number who are of some interest. Before you die, the Master of All would know you.' He waved his hands over the bowl, and a sickly blue flame rose slowly from the liquid. As it grew, he continued. 'Your cup of despair is not yet drunk down to the dregs. Tell me: is the number of your little band complete? Or have you missed someone?' Without waiting for an answer, he signalled a guardsman, who turned and strode back past the waiting ranks of soldiers towards the Struere Gate.

'Have you guessed yet?' Deorc asked them. 'Soon you will see!'

He raised his arms above his head, and the blue fire leapt into the sky with a roar. 'Behold the Undying One, the Lord of All!'

Something began to take shape in the flames, three red stains in the blue; an open mouth set below two eyes. A voice spoke, shaking the square.

'See my faithful servant! Bow before him!' And a vast weight like a mighty hand drove them all to their knees. In the stillness, laughter rippled across the bent backs of the crowd, causing many to stop their ears. All felt the terror of the voice.

'Arise, my worshippers!' the voice commanded, and at once the weight lifted, and they could stand again. And to their horror, a slender figure, bound with chains and dressed in rags, stood between them and the horrible flames that even now reached out towards them, searching, searching.

'Oh, no,' said the Haufuth. 'He has Stella.'

The next few seconds seemed to last forever. Hal was there beside Leith, where a moment ago he had not been among the Company at all. Placing an arm on his brother's shoulder, he whispered: 'Wait! Do nothing yet!'

His words had quite the opposite effect. With a cry of rage Leith leaped on to the platform, and the Jugom Ark exploded into unbearable brightness. 'Stella!' he cried, and the thin figure turned her face towards him. For a brief moment their eyes met; his filled with rage and fear, hers with despair and hopelessness – and something else, something deeply held. Defiance.

Then she was lost to his sight as the blue flame surged in response to the Jugom Ark. The voice within the flame bellowed in words Leith could not understand, a cry of loathing and hatred. Blue fire met the white light of the Flaming Arrow. Everything dissolved into noise and vibration, as though the earth wrestled with the sky. For a moment the world went dark, then flickered and cleared. It was morning again. The blue fire was gone. A broken bowl lay on the ground at his feet.

As Leith shook his head to clear it, a voice cut through the clean light like a swathe of darkness. 'For this you will pay,' it said in a voice thick with anger. Under the arch of the Struere Gate the figure of Deorc stood, shaking his fist at the Company. 'You will pay! You will burn, burn forever, pleading for release but never finding it. Just as your companion Stella now pleads. Think on that!' Then, with a snarl, the figure turned aside and vanished from his sight.

Desperately Leith looked about him, searching for any sign of Stella, but could see none. Every person in the crowd lay on the ground, whether dead or merely insensible he could not tell, nor did he care. The Instruian Guard fared no better, having been toppled where they stood by the clash of the two great powers. Even the members of the Company lay still as death all around him. It seemed as though he was the only person left alive.

Someone groaned beside him. Phemanderac struggled to his feet, holding his head. One by one the Company stirred. 'I saw her,' the philosopher whispered, horror in his voice as he relived some terrible sight. 'I saw the flame reach out and take her! O Most High! It pulled her into its mouth! I hope she is still alive, but I fear – I fear . . .' He came to himself, and realised Leith stood beside him, mouth open abjectly. 'Oh, Leith; I'm sure she's all right . . .' His voice tapered off. 'I'm sorry. She cannot be all right. I am a fool.'

Ignoring his friend, Leith ran into the crowd, calling her name. Not a single guard stirred, but a number of the crowd had made it to their feet, some leaning on each other for support. Most were still unconscious. No sign of her.

Looking back at the Company, now all on their feet, Leith saw his brother make his way towards them, as though only just arriving. His mother embraced him. 'Hal! Where have you been?'

'Preparing our morning meal,' he said. 'What has happened here?'

'Much,' Mahnum replied. 'But before we can talk of it,

there are some things that must be said and done. Leith?' He turned to his younger son.

Leith nodded. The madness had passed. Pushing sorrow and anger aside, he stood once again on the platform. More than half those gathered had now regained their feet, but still not a guardsman moved.

'Today the enemy has revealed himself,' Leith told them. 'He set his dark magic against the Jugom Ark, and he failed. His lieutenant has been forced to flee, and his army lies stricken on the ground at your feet. The first battle in the War of Faltha has been fought here in Instruere, and you are the victors!'

The onlookers cheered, but it was a less than convincing sound. Forces far beyond their comprehension had clashed, and they were alive only by some lucky chance. Hundreds of frightened people scurried away from the scene, heartily regretting their earlier curiosity: at close quarters, magic had not proved to be the kind of spectacle they wished for. Nevertheless, they told themselves, they were alive.

Leith continued on, choosing not to refer to those who were leaving. 'Now the Destroyer knows that the Jugom Ark has been found. He has seen it raised up against him. His preparation for war will be much the swifter for that knowledge. He will not be surprised to find us prepared.

'So let us prepare! Let us debate no longer! Those of you with courage and strength of arm, take the swords from the guardsmen near you, and be ready to guard them when they wake. The new Council of Faltha will meet, and before the day has ended we will send out emissaries to every land in Faltha. Let the Jugom Ark unify us, as the prophecies have said!'

Within a few minutes the Instruian Guard found itself

captured by the very people it had been charged with striking down. A few fools tried to fight their way free, but they died under a rain of sword blows. However inexpertly the steel blades were wielded, the sheer weight of numbers ensured none survived who did not surrender. The others were marched to the space they themselves had cleared with the butts of their spears, then made to sit down with their hands on their heads. Hundreds of enthusiastic citizens stood over them, watching for any move towards escape.

Leith stepped down from the hated platform for what he hoped was the last time. He found a shadowy area away from the light, sank to his knees and began to weep.

Stella tried to scream, but there was no breath in her lungs. She tried to struggle, but could not move. She was inside the flame, absorbing and being absorbed by it, reduced to nothing more than an ember flickering in a cold grate, barely alive. She was beyond help, beyond redemption, in a place where mere pain would have been a welcome relief. She moved neither forward nor back, neither up nor down, could not tell how long she'd been inside the flame nor when the agony would end, if ever. She begged the flame to snuff her out, but it paid her no attention, its cold blue heart bent on some other matter.

Then, horribly, the blue flame began to scream in rage at an old memory rekindled. Stella knew she was about to be consumed, and gave herself up. Paradoxically, this saved her. She drifted upwards like a nearly-spent spark. Had she retained her will to live, the flame would have burned it and her with it. Below her the red mouth roared, enlarging as though intending to swallow the world, but even in her extremity Stella could tell the bite was too large for it.

There came an enormous detonation, a coming together of light and dark, of oil and water, a conflagration so large it threatened to destroy everything. Up, up the blast came, but it was weak by the time it reached her, and merely drove consciousness from her like a dove from a lake of fire. Stella sighed blissfully as the darkness claimed her.

She awoke in the dark. Her senses returned to her in a flood, sharpened somehow by the flame. Beneath her, rough flagstones radiated an intense cold, and the air was damp to the taste. She could hear the sound of someone breathing raggedly.

Disoriented, Stella at first thought she had been returned to The Pinion. A dreadful day and night she had spent there, chained to the inner door of an empty cell, exposed to smells, sights and sounds she told herself could not possibly be real. Certainly this must be a dungeon of some sort – but, she realised in surprise, she was not fettered. Somewhere in the darkness the breathing steadied and deepened. A witless dread crept over her.

'Are – are you there? Is anyone there?' Her voice came out no louder than a whisper, but it was enough. A flame burst into life, small but steady. Behind the flame a figure came into view. Then, as the flame grew and blue light flooded the room, Stella saw him.

He was tall, broad of shoulder and clad in grey raiment so dark it stole the light from around him. His eyes burned faintly red. A silver crown rested upon his brow. And his face – his face was old and haggard, scarred and lined, a wasteland where no rain had fallen for centuries, a face from beyond the grave. Then, as she watched, his face began to heal. Scars faded, lines smoothed away, until the man wore the visage of a king.

The Destroyer.

He looked on her and knew her. This was the northern girl, the one Deorc was keeping for him, the one with the echo of the bright flame set within her. The bright, bright flame . . . the memory of his recent defeat tightened his shoulders and sent a spasm across his noble face. But was it truly a defeat? He had exchanged a few useless soldiers, and perhaps a skilled but replaceable servant, for the knowledge he had been seeking these past years. Who and where was the Right Hand? The question had been nagging at him ever since he squeezed out the dying words of the Dhaurian spy twenty years ago. And now that question was answered, and more, much more. The flaw in his plans was finally laid bare, and early enough that it could be mended. His mistake was that he had neglected to ask the obvious question: *what would the Right Hand be holding?* Now he knew the answer. The cursed Arrow.

The Undying Man had made it a policy not to dwell on that day, two thousand years ago, when he had confronted the Most High in the Square of the Fountain; but now he forced himself to relive the moment the Flaming Arrow flashed past his eyes and sliced through his wrist, when he felt the agony and the shock, and looked up to see the silhouette of his nemesis standing over him. However, nothing the Most High might have done to him could rob him of the exultation that coursed through his body in that moment. The draught he had drunk fizzed through his veins as though boiling his blood. He remembered it clearly, he felt it still; a life beyond anything mortals knew, burning, burning,

burning. The water of the Fountain of Eternal Life. Worth the price of a hand. But the Jugom Ark represented the anger of the Most High and the threat he still posed to the Undying Man's grand designs. More than that, it symbolised his favouritism for the puerile First Men. And, as he had just discovered, it was more than a mere symbol. It contained a potency of its own. The Jugom Ark, and the Right Hand that bore it, would have to be faced at some time; but not now, not yet.

Now to the matter of this northern girl, cowering on her knees in obvious dread of him. Two thousand years was a long time to live, but there were many new things to learn. He had not known the blue fire could be used to transport people from one place to another. He had not even considered the possibility. Of course, it might have been the backwash of the power generated by the clash of magic, and might not be repeatable. It would require further investigation. He had plenty of time.

Of more importance was the connection between this girl and the Right Hand. She had received the Fire from the Most High, of that there was no doubt; and this was a worrying development, for he had been certain the Most High would never again gift the *Fuirfad* to descendants of the First Men. She was an enigma. He could sense no talent, none of the soul-stretching the use of the *Fuirfad* engendered. How well he remembered it! She was either woefully weak or masked her power with a skill surpassing his own highly developed spiritual senses. There were ways to find out, of course, some of which would do relatively little damage to her. He might need her at least partially intact – though bound to him, of course – if the ideas seeding themselves in his mind were to bear fruit. That she was unaware of the power set within her, he did not consider for a moment.

'So, Stella,' he said in a surprisingly gentle voice, lifting her name from the surface of her shallow mind. 'You have come to me. There are things I would know about you – and your friends.'

As the questions began Stella bravely tried to resist, but the voice that until now she had only heard from out of the blue fire was dreadfully, infinitely more powerful in person, and her efforts were futile. Though the words were mild, they washed her away like a stick before a storm, and in a horror of self-loathing her mouth opened and she told him everything he asked, everything, everything.

CHAPTER 6

REPOSITIONING

'WE HAVE NO TIME to waste! We must act this very day!' Perdu said.

It was just before noon on the day of the Battle of Struere Gate – as it was already being called – and the Company seemed inclined to take his words, and the similar urgings of others, to heart. The consensus of opinion was that with the victory their position had actually worsened slightly. Deorc and his blue fire had been driven away, that was true, but no one could say what the limit of his power might be, or how quickly he could recover. And while the main force of the Instruian Guard was gifted to them by the clash of fires, there might be hundreds more not currently on duty, or still hidden in The Pinion, waiting to be unleashed on them all. Less important, but more immediate, was the problem of the crowd. Few wanted to leave, most preferring the perceived safety of numbers and closeness to the Jugom Ark, but they had little food. They could not be sent home, for who would then guard the captive soldiers? Something had to be done, and quickly.

Not much time remained. Hours, not days. While Leith's

employment of the Jugom Ark in opposition to the Destroyer's blue fire may have rescued them from the present danger, it had alerted the Ancient Enemy to its discovery after two thousand years. The element of surprise the Company counted on was lost. There was nothing else he could have done, Leith explained desperately to the Company when they asked him what had happened. He had felt compelled to try to free Stella, he told them. Was he supposed just to look on as she stood there in chains, at the mercy of the Destroyer? Some were sympathetic with his actions, but Phemanderac cautioned him on the danger of surrendering to his emotions, a view seconded by Kurr. 'You're going to have to retain a level head, boy,' the old farmer said gruffly. 'As much as I love the girl, it would have been better to have kept the Arrow hidden. As it is, you did not save her, and our position is much more perilous than it was.'

Leith's feelings for Stella still ran deep; seeing her for those few moments made him realise she meant more to him than arrows or armies. He had listened to his fair share of fairy tales as a child, where the protagonists fell in love and risked all for each other. The tales made a virtue of such behaviour, but Leith knew any suggestion he was considering setting aside the future of Faltha in order to search for Stella would not be well received. So he said nothing to those who offered criticism of his actions. There were more important things to decide than the rights or wrongs of what he had done, at least that's the way they would see it; especially when nothing could be done to mend it. He kept quiet because, fairy tales aside, he knew his friends were right.

Geinor and the Escaignian woman stood respectfully at the entrance to the pavilion as the Company talked together.

Eventually, taking advantage of a quiet moment, the woman came over to the table. 'There are people waiting to speak to us,' she informed them. 'They say they have been chosen by the Jugom Ark. Some of them are very angry.'

'What?' Leith asked, confused. 'What people? Why are they angry? How were they chosen?'

Kurr placed a steadying hand on his shoulder. 'Why don't we go and find out?'

'There are so many others we need to talk to,' Leith replied flatly. 'Te Tuahangata for one; Hal for another. Can't these people wait? Most likely they just want another look at the Arrow.'

'We refuse help at our peril.' The old farmer tightened his grip on the boy's shoulder.

'Very well,' Leith conceded, then smiled ruefully. 'I'm not used to this! I naturally feel as though I should do what I'm told; but I'm supposed to be the leader, so I try to resist the feeling. But then I become harsh. I'm not sure I'll ever get used to this.'

'They await us outside the pavilion,' Geinor reported. 'There are many people there; some, I think, were identified by the Arrow of Fire yesterday when you challenged the crowd about the *losian*. Remember?'

The members of the Company made their way out into the late-morning sunshine. Several groups waited for them, sitting and talking quietly in what had been, until yesterday, a busy city street. As the Company approached them all chatter ceased.

Leith scanned the faces, and noticed one man sitting aside from the others. 'You!' he cried, and ran forward to him happily. It was the Pei-ratin pilot, who nodded darkly at the greeting. Leith stepped back, puzzled.

'I do not want to become involved in this,' the navigator told him, his black eyebrows bristling in anger. 'I returned to the city yesterday to buy supplies for our return voyage, and came upon a crowd inside the gate. Your fiery arrow picked me out. What am I supposed to do? My people prepare to return to Astraea, and they cannot leave without their navigator. What help can I be? Why should I do anything for the First Men?'

Still feeling his way, Leith called some of the others over. Maendraga, Phemanderac, Kurr, Geinor, Graig, Indrett and the Haufuth came in answer. Others of the Company moved amongst the remaining groups. After Maendraga briefly explained to everyone who the dark-skinned man was, and how he knew him, Leith sat down opposite the Pei-ratin pilot.

'Would your people consider a longer route to Astraea?' Phemanderac asked the navigator. 'If Nemohaim and Tabul signed an agreement with the Council of Faltha to cede to the Pei-ra all of ancestral Astraea, would your kin set aside their plans for a season and come to our aid?'

'No – and yes. Most would not, but some might. They owe you a debt, after all, for revealing that the ancient places lie unoccupied.' He sighed. 'It seems that even though we sought refuge in places untouched by the First Men, we are continually drawn into their affairs. Many of our people will resist this, no matter how many pieces of paper are signed.

'I am a navigator, however, and my people look to me to see the currents that otherwise might drive us on to the reefs. Many of us may be swept up into your wars by the currents to come. For myself, I want nothing more than to journey home to Astraea, to finally bury my grandsire's name and live out my life. But I listened when you and the magician

Maendraga spoke in the days and nights you guested on my canoe. You are right: whatever land *losian* dwell in becomes an object of desire for the First Men. I fear that our hold on Astraea will be short, and again end in blood.'

He sighed, then sat on his haunches and looked up into the philosopher's face. 'Bring me a map,' he said.

'A map? Of what?' Leith had never taken much notice of maps; the lines and names confused him. Phemanderac seemed equally puzzled at the request.

'Of southern Faltha,' Graig said from behind Leith's shoulder. 'Surely Instruere must have a supply of maps.'

'They will undoubtedly be in the hands of the rulers,' Phemanderac commented. 'Gone are the days when any of us could visit the Hall of Lore to search the City archives. More is the pity; for there are precious books in the library I wish to read more closely.'

'Some parchment, then?' the curly-haired man asked. 'I will try to sketch out something.'

Phemanderac was able to supply parchment, pen and ink, and seemed now to understand what the Aslaman intended. With a few bold strokes the navigator sketched out the coast south and west from the mouth of the Aleinus down to Nemohaim, then east past Tabul, Vertensia and Sarista, where his knowledge ended. Rivers he drew, and mountains; under his hand the paper came alive, and for the first time Leith could see the lie of the land represented by the map. There on the paper was Deruys, clearly marked; inland must be the Mist, and that heavy line, like a wound on the parchment, had to be the Valley of a Thousand Fires. If he looked closely he could almost see the Company climbing out of the valley and crossing the northern borders of Astraea, which occupied a large space in the centre of the map.

From his pocket the navigator drew a paddle-shaped object, slightly smaller than a hand's-breadth, with teeth at one end. 'This is a kai-nan, a stick we use for eating,' he explained to the small group gathered around him. He placed the object on the map, and positioned it over where he had drawn Astraea; the wider, toothed end he set to the north-east, overlapping the Valley of a Thousand Fires, the narrow handle to the south-west, just touching the sea. Then he took the pen, dipped it in the ink and drew a line around the kai-nan, enclosing it. When he took his eating-stick away, the outline remained.

'This is the land we desire,' he said in a voice of utter conviction. Almost, Leith imagined, he heard the Wordweave in it. 'From the fires in the north to Cachoeira on the coast, from the Almucantaran Mountains in the east to the Escarpment in the west; this we claim as ours for all time. None from Tabul will cross the Lifeblood without our permission. None from Nemohaim will enter the Vale of Neume unless we permit it. This land shall be the price for our participation in the war against your enemies. For this price you will receive a thousand of the Pei-ra, who will fight for you unto death. Do you agree?'

Leith turned aside for a time, and gathered the rest of the Company around him. When he returned to where the Pei-ratin navigator waited patiently, he said: 'This offer is what I had hoped for, and to me it sounds good, whether you fight with us or no. For my part, and in ignorance of claims to the land, I see no argument; but there may be others, from Tabul or Nemohaim perhaps, or from your own people, who might dispute the boundary as you have drawn it. Let this document be held by the interim Council of Faltha for one year. Copies should be sent to the kingdoms of Nemohaim and Tabul, as well as to the Sanusi and to the islands of the Aslamen. If in twelve months from today all objections can be satisfied, the boundary will be confirmed. You shall then have a seat on the Council of Faltha, if that is your wish.'

'Then let us seal the agreement with a meal,' said the navigator. 'The Aslamen will come within the City walls and eat with the First Men. Of course,' he added wryly, 'it is only a beginning. I have no doubt many of my kin will object; but that does not make this agreement worthless. We are not a kingdom whose people must obey the word of one, wise or otherwise. Each one will do what seems right to them. So do not be surprised if not all of my people wish to eat with you. Some, however, will come.'

Leith smiled, and waved farewell as the navigator walked proudly through the remains of the Struere Gate.

That afternoon the Company spoke to others who had been fire-touched by the Arrow, marked out as *losian* and as True Falthans. The Jugom Ark was less discriminating than the Company might have wished. One man turned out to be a rogue who once served the Knights of Fealty, but more recently had abandoned that high calling to become part of a roving band of thieves that plagued camel trains out of Ghadir Massab. This last item brought a scowl from Kurr, who remembered the Pass of Adrar. The tousle-haired rogue seemed reluctant to answer questions directed at uncovering why he had left the Knights of Fealty, but did tell them he was born a Wodrani, a reclusive people living in the folded hills north of Favony, far to the east of Instruere. Of the Company only Modahl knew of the Wodrani, and even he had not travelled to their hidden land.

'There are other'n like me,' the man slurred, his soft accent difficult to follow. 'We all leave'n the birth-home and find'n livin' in the Falthan lands. I took up'n with the Fealty ones. If'n you'm want'n soldiery, can't go past'n the Fealty ones.' It turned out the ill-favoured man, who went by the name of Lessep, thought he could win the aid of the Knights of Fealty to the Company's cause. 'Talk'n a lot of the Arrow, they did,' he said. 'Had'n a carvin' of it in the Meetin' hall. Picture of it on the ceilin'. Lots of pictures.' Kurr remained dubious, but knew enough not to mistrust the Arrow.

Lessep was not the only Wodrani touched by the Fire. A woman, so old her face appeared made from leather left too long in the sun, came from an ancient lineage, she told the Company. Or, at least, her sons told them, for she did not speak the common tongue. 'We will return to the Old Land,' they said. 'There are many people who look to fight in wars for money.'

'Mercenaries!' the Captain of the Guard spat in professional disgust. 'We can't rely on such as they! All I see today are the untrained and the weak, people who will be a liability on the field of battle. This is not a task for ordinary men. We need warriors, mighty men, each of whom would be worth fifty, a hundred of these!' He spread his arms wide to indicate the rabble gathered in front of the pavilion, and the crowd still waiting between the pavilion and the Gate.

'So you think this task is beyond anyone but heroes?' Indrett asked him pointedly. 'You think the Most High made a mistake entrusting the Arrow to people like us?'

'You can carry the Arrow, but don't bother carrying a sword,' he replied in the crisp voice of a professional soldier. 'Your task is complete. It is time for others to take on the burden. Strength, not stealth, will be our protection.'

Indrett frowned, but said nothing.

The other *losian* gathered by the Arrow came from various little-known parts of Faltha. None seemed very promising, certainly not the kind of people of whom the former Captain of the Instruian Guard might approve. There was a young family from a village somewhere south of Redana'a, from the harsh semi-arid steppes on the margins of *Khersos*, the Deep Desert. They were descended from the Sanusi of Ghadir Massab – a tale made less unlikely by their likeness to the slavers Kurr had encountered only a few weeks ago – but they had not ventured south into the desert for generations. Two or three men hailed from the deep-sided valleys of the Remparer Mountains which divided Deuverre and Asgowan from Treika to the north and west, and belonged to related clans that traced their ancestry back thousands of years. A family from Instruere itself, bemused as to why they might have been selected, protested that they were pure First Men. Eventually, however, it turned out there might have been a connection with a northern tribe that lived somewhere near Whitefang Pass, the notorious northern passage of the Remparer Mountains.

Late in the afternoon Kurr called them all together in the name of the Arrow-bearer, whose weariness had finally caught up with him. 'The young man deserves a rest,' the old farmer explained. 'This afternoon I will speak in his place.' Not everyone was happy at the news: it seemed the Arrow inspired more loyalty than those entrusted with its care. Kurr had little patience with them, and began to speak before they could mount any serious objection.

'Now is the time of sending,' he told them. 'If we are to gather any kind of army, we must send you back to your homelands in haste. Our best guess is that the army will depart Instruere in three months' time, and set forth for the

Gap, a further three months' journey. The earliest we can hope to engage the Destroyer, therefore, is in late spring. This means we must march through winter. Some of you, therefore, will be sent ahead to prepare for our passage, as our army will require food and perhaps shelter as we journey to the east. We will call upon people from the lands of Favony, Redana'a, Piskasia and Sna Vaztha to aid us in this task, as well as those of you gathered here who come from the eastern lands.

'Others of you we send home to raise a fighting force. From our Company Te Tuahangata of Hinepukohurangi, Prince Wiusago of Deruys, Geinor of Nemohaim, Modahl of Sna Vaztha and Perdu of the Fenni will journey home to their respective lands, there to entreat their sovereigns for aid. In the event that this takes longer than three months, we request that they make their way to the Gap with all possible speed, ready to reinforce us.

'Those of us who remain have our own appointed tasks to complete. We are loath to leave Instruere in the hands of traitors: there is no point in defeating the armies of Bhrudwo only to find the City stoutly held against us on our return, or razed to the ground. We give ourselves three months to wrest control of Instruere from the remnants of the Instruian Guard. On the last day of September we will leave the City, whether it is under our control or not.'

The named members of the Company came forward, bowed once to Kurr and then left. *Just like that*, Kurr thought, *without ceremony*. Their loss was hard to bear. All had shown themselves faithful and true, good friends and advisers. Perdu was a particularly heavy loss to the Company: though Kurr had spoken little to him, he admired the Fenni man's directness and humility. He had been a balance between himself and

Farr, the two mercurial antagonists, and would be missed even in the absence of the latter.

Perdu would travel north from Instruere, accompanied for the first part of his journey by Modahl, the two Wodranian families and by three men from the Remparer Mountains. A few days north of the City the others would depart for the north and the east, leaving the adopted Fenni to journey on his own to the west. Even with Wisent, who, surprisingly, had thrived in the stables they found for him, the journey would take him many weeks. Modahl's journey to Faltha's far east would take longer still.

Another party would leave Instruere by the ruined Struere Gate, thence to the Docks and the canoe of the Aslamen. Wiusago and Te Tuahangata, the latter having overcome his initial reluctance to the Mist's involvement, would be set ashore at Brunhaven, and Geinor and his son, who perhaps had the most difficult task of all, were to continue on to Bewray. The Aslamen would then return to their islands. Various others, mostly of the *losian*, were also to leave from the Struere Gate. They would make their way to their southern and eastern homes, and see what assistance they could raise in support of events far away.

For three glorious days the number of the Company had been full, Kurr realised; always excepting Stella. Now they were being sent all over Faltha, and would be together again – if at all – only when they came face to face with their enemy.

Deorc strode impatiently down the noisy corridor leading to the Iron Door. The hands of a dozen or more supplicants reached out towards him as he passed; angrily, he slapped them away with a fraction of the power still burning redly within him. The great door was slowly raised in anticipation of his return, too slowly for his mood. With an imperious gesture he sent the Iron Door crashing up into its housing. He stormed into the Outer Chamber amidst falling gears and broken machinery, the ruined craftsmanship of an earlier, greater age.

There the Council of Faltha waited for him, the Arkhoi of Haurn and Deruys at their head, themselves newly returned from the site of his failure, ready to question him on the day's disaster. Deorc would have none of it. With a snarl he spread his arms wide, and the Councillors were struck dumb. It took only a crook of his finger to drag a gurgling Furoman into the Chamber, the secretary struggling as though he had a rope around his neck.

'Set the blue fire,' he commanded his servant. Furoman tried to obey, even though his face was turning blue, invisible fingers at his throat. He managed to lay the bowl on a table, but collapsed halfway through pouring the oil.

'You,' Deorc hissed, pointing at the Arkhos of Favony. 'Set the fire.'

Favony had never done it before, though he had watched with some distaste as the new Head of the Council had in his view behaved like a common conjuror, summoning a voice from the flames in an unnecessary display of intimidation. Setting the fire was servants' work, but he knew better than to argue with the man. The Arkhos of Favony was about to learn that the conjuror wielded real power.

With shaking hands he picked up the oil pitcher, which now lay on its side on the floor, slowly leaking sticky fluid on to the marble. As soon as he began to pour, a strange, terrible power sucked at him. To the frantic man it felt as though his strength, his soul, was being poured into the bowl along with the oil. He could not scream, he could not move, he could not halt the dreadful pouring. He could do nothing but die.

To the others it seemed as though the Arkhos of Favony slowly dissolved in front of their eyes, first his flesh, then his bones. The Council cried out as one man, protesting to Deorc: 'What are you doing?'

'I need blood for the fire,' the Bhrudwan replied acidly. 'Would anyone else like to volunteer?'

'But we are your allies!' shrieked Vertensia. 'We're on your side!'

'You are of no account,' Deorc responded. 'You are straw, and I come to set fire among you. Now be silent, or you will burn before your time.' He turned towards the fire, set his face to it, and put the foolish conspirators to the back of his mind as the eager blue flame leaned towards him.

The Destroyer stood tall, looming like an avalanche over the girl who only now began to stir. He had wrung her out, drained her of all she knew, which was not much – on the surface. A simple northern peasant girl, nothing more, not worthy of his attention. Dungeon fodder. But he had dug down deeper, remembering the time he first sensed her through the blue fire, remembering the touch of the Most High on her. No one could resist him when he dealt with them in person. And there, like a light hidden inside a shuttered room, he found it; a so-small kernel, an opening to the Realm of Fire, a jewel in a setting of dross. A life so ordinary, filled with petty fears; a small, mean spirit, with no capacity for greatness. A slave, not a master. What had attracted Deorc to her?

The Undying Man could answer his own question with little difficulty. Somehow – she attributed it to a dream – she had been given the Fire of Life. This hint of power, wrapped up in an attractive, vulnerable package, would have drawn a man like Deorc. She did not know what she had, knew nothing of the power she could draw on, and was no threat to his plans, though he would keep her alive until he solved her mystery. But for what purpose had she been given the Fire?

This girl had to be a decoy, he concluded. The Most High had obviously not entrusted his defence of Faltha to such as her. Though she saw herself at the centre of the Most High's plans, this was plain self-deception. She must have received the Fire incidentally, as part of a larger group. If the rest of them were like her, he had nothing to be concerned about. He knew how unlikely that was. Others of her party must be more powerful than she, for with his own eyes he had seen the Jugom Ark, had felt the power of the Arrow wielded expertly by a shining youth, such as he himself had once been, two thousand years ago in the Vale. A shining youth who was undoubtedly the Right Hand.

And now, thanks to the knowledge embedded in the mind of the girl grovelling before him, the mystery began to unfold. Less than two years ago he had interrogated a man in Andratan, a Falthan spy from far Firanes sent to uncover Bhrudwan secrets. He squeezed that one dry, he remembered; but like all the Falthans he put to the question, this man knew nothing of the Right Hand. According to Deorc, who was Keeper at the time, he was put to death some time later. Only it transpired he had not been put to death at all. This Falthan spy had somehow returned to Firanes pursued by four *Maghdi Dasht*, sent, the Destroyer presumed, by Deorc in an attempt to put right his blunder. The *Maghdi Dasht* finally caught up with the spy, and that should have been the end of it – but, staggeringly, they had not killed him and whoever else might have learned of the plan to invade Faltha. Instead they made him captive and dragged him back towards Bhrudwo. Blunderers! Or was there something more sinister behind this? A subordinate positioning himself to take Deorc's place by winning the Undying Man's favour? Or – it hardly seemed possible, he knew the mind of Deorc inside and out – was his most faithful servant finally aiming higher?

Surely it could not be. And yet . . . he cast his mind back to his arrival at Malayu several months ago. He spoke through the blue flame with Deorc that night, and his lieutenant denied sending the four warriors westwards. People had been sent to find out what became of them, Deorc told him. He remembered sensing a resonance through the flame . . .

Now, thanks to the memories of this girl still twitching on the floor, he knew what had happened to the four *Maghdi Dasht*, if not who sent them west. They had been defeated and slain, save one. Their captives rescued, not by great warriors, but by peasants from their home village. This northern girl was one of them! The one *Maghdi Dasht* remaining alive was taken into the service of the northern peasants. Tamed and set to work. Moreover – and this troubled him most of all – this spy named Mahnum, the man he had interrogated, had held in his own fortress, turned out to be *the father of the Right Hand*. Of this the girl's memories were unequivocal: she had seen the youth with the Arrow for only a moment, but recognised him beyond any doubt. The Undying Man sifted her mind to find out more about this Arrow-wielder, and uncovered her affection for him, hidden in a secret place, as though she herself turned from it. The youth had a name, and it echoed through her deepest thoughts. Leith Mahnumsen.

This information raised many questions, the most immediate of which was the role of Deorc. The Keeper had either been deceived as to the supposed death of this Firanese Trader in his own dungeons, or had lied to his master. Certainly he was evasive about the activities and the fate of four *Maghdi Dasht*. He must have lied. Certainly there was now enough evidence to destroy the man. And, disturbingly, he found something else in the girl's mind, a package of fresh memories from two days ago when Deorc held her prisoner in a high tower. Her memories clearly indicated he had done things to her, touched her, tortured her, in violation of the express command of his master. The images were there, half-formed, as though seared into her mind against her will. Worse, according to her memory, he boasted to her that the Undying Man would never find out what he, Deorc, had done.

At that moment, as he considered the unthinkable treachery of his servant, the Destroyer was startled to see the remaining oil in the Bowl of Fire begin to smoke. Deorc was trying to contact him. In an instant his anger burst all restraint, and the bowl roared into flame. Barely conscious, Stella was thrown across the room, ending in a crumpled heap against the far wall; and as she came to herself, her mind aching with the agony the black-robed man had inflicted on her, she was able to watch what happened.

In the Outer Chamber of the Hall of Meeting, the blue fire erupted into a howling inferno. The Arkhoi of Vertensia and Firanes disappeared screaming into the flames, as did the table. The remaining Council members scattered, some running, others thrown by the force of the blast. Deorc alone withstood the furnace that began to eat into the marble floor, holding his ground, awaiting his master's response to his failure.

What emerged from the conflagration was not a voice. Instead, the red mouth spewed blue flame like a vast rotten hand. It reached out and took him around the throat, then jerked him forward into the heart of the fire. Before he had time to protest, Deorc found himself ripped away from Instruere, transported through a tunnel of shrieking agony and deposited at the feet of the Undying Man.

'I command your soul,' said the voice, with a sharpness that cut at him like the daggers in the hands of the torturers of Andratan. He could not breathe, let alone reply. He could not take in what had just happened to him. 'You kept secrets from me. You schemed against me. You disobeyed my word by taking the girl for your own.' The evidence was laid out in front of Deorc, who scrabbled and retched on the cold concrete floor.

'I entrusted my power to you, power enough to deal with the opposition in Instruere, but you wasted it. Now learn how I deal with those who are untrue!'

Stella hauled herself to her knees, unable to believe she was watching the one thing she had wished for so fervently. She remembered hanging from chains in the tower of the House of Worship, going over and over an imaginary story in her mind, one in which the hated Deorc abused her and boasted of it. She remembered trying desperately to force the story deep into her memory, so that when the Destroyer questioned her, as she knew he eventually would, he might come across the memory and believe his lieutenant false.

And so, beyond every hope, it had proved. The day of her revenge had come.

Farr Storrsen walked with an angry stiffness, a rage that drove him forward. Had anyone asked him in those first furious days where he was going, he would not have been able to supply them with an answer, even if he had been inclined to speak.

He felt he had a right to his rage. He had been involved in a quest the like of which he had never heard, had for the first time in his life been right at the heart of things, had witnessed the finding and the raising of the Jugom Ark. Right there, at the Bearer's side! And suddenly, so suddenly, everything went wrong. His counsel had not been listened to, and the Company elected to make allies of the *losian*. When he walked out, no one had come running after him, begging him to return. Well, then. He would return home, would stop only to gather the ashes of his dead brother, and scatter them on the grassy tops of the Vinkullen Hills. Wild, open and free, where no one told you what to do and no one forced you to befriend half-men. Where the cold winds would shrivel your soul.

Day and night he walked, powered by his anger and deep bitterness. With the long strides of a mountain man he covered many miles between sunrise and sunset, and as many again at night. He had food in his pack, so did not need to forage or purchase meals from the inns he passed. Water was plentiful on the northern roads of Deuverre; shallow, swift rivers crossed the road regularly on their journey down from the Remparer Mountains over the horizon to the north-west. He stopped for nothing but brief snatches of sleep, spoke to no one, and did not turn aside from his road. Within a week he was high up on the Rhinns of Torridon, near the borders of Treika, having left Deuverre, civilisation and the Jugom Ark far behind him.

The moon, almost full, hung low over the Westway in a cool night sky clear of cloud. Farr crested a grass-clothed saddle, and glanced up at the shadowy ruins of castles on the brows of high hills to the right and to the left. Quite possibly the builders of these ancient holds had been enemies, ranged against each other, separated only by this valley he now walked through, a no-man's land of hatred that prevented people working and playing together. As he drew level with the broken walls, he imagined children's laughter coming from within in times of peace, then the screams and cries as siege was laid and walls torn down. He wondered how Instruere might look in a few years' time, whether people would wander past the ruins of the great City and wonder who used to live there. It would serve them right. How could friendship with the *losian* please the Most High? He shrugged his shoulders and carried on, but could not get the ominous image of the ruined walls out of his mind, the sound of laughter suddenly silenced. *The brown armies will not reach Vinkullen*, he told himself, but his mood did not improve.

The moon rose into the silver sky like the eye of an accuser, and he lowered his head to be rid of it. Thus it was he did not see the hundreds of lights spread out ahead of him, coming up the slope towards him, bobbing slowly as though on the back of ponderous beasts. The sound of singing finally jerked his head up, and in a moment he would never forget, Farr Storrsen beheld the Army of the North marching to Instruere, moon-washed and night-cloaked, arrayed for battle.

There were aurochs in the van, dozens of them, none so mighty as Wisent, but great beasts nonetheless, shaggy hair gleaming in the silver light. Other warriors were mounted on tall warhorses. The vast bulk of the army travelled on foot, rank after rank spread out on the silver grass at either side of the paved road, each man carrying a torch in his hand, a sword at his hip, a staff on his back, a quiver on his shoulder. At the head of this impossible army walked a small, squat figure, one which, as it drew close to the astonished Farr, gave him a shout. Laughter followed the shout, and three other small figures emerged from the front ranks of the army and ran towards him.

Farr thought his heart would burst with joy as the four men surrounded him, crying his name aloud, slapping him on the back, miming the carrying of fur bales or the shooting of rapids, and laughing, always laughing. Tears flowed from his eyes at their greeting; unashamedly he wept, and a shadow left him on the Westway that night, never to return, as he laughed with the Fodhram.

The thing on the stone floor could not possibly still be alive, but it was. Stella begged for the punishment to stop, for that which once had been a man, however evil, to be granted release; but the grunting and twitching continued unabated. Thus Stella learned there are limits even to revenge.

'I trust this is instructive,' said the voice. 'You would do well to remember this for the rest of your life. This is what happens to those who think they can keep things from me. This traitor will not die. He will be collected and taken to the fortress he once ruled, where he will be imprisoned in the deepest dungeon, among the instruments he knows so well. Some of those who served him in the past will be delighted to meet him again in such circumstances. Do not be mistaken: worse than this will happen to you should you ever think to deceive me.'

Oh, but I have, she said silently, in that secret place of defiance. *I have*.

The evening of the day of the Battle of Struere Gate began with a dull sunset, red rays peeping from under a blanket of cloud, momentarily bathing the grey city walls in a sombre light before fading quickly into darkness. The sun's last rays lingered a moment longer on the Tower of Worship, the tallest of the City's buildings. Built by the First Men in remembrance of Dona Mihst, as were all the Four Halls of Instruere, the slender tower rose plain and unadorned from the squat Hall of Worship. High up in the tower, in a room with windows facing to the four points of the compass, nine men watched the sun slip behind the Veridian Borders far to the south-west.

The Arkhos of Deruys turned to his fellow Councillors. 'So ends a day of dread,' he said to them. 'If you follow my advice, so also ends the Council of Faltha.'

Haurn the Craven added hesitantly: 'Deorc is gone, the Arkhos of Nemohaim is gone, half the Instruian Guard is gone, and we are left to face the wrath of the City. I don't want to be executed just to appease the anger of the masses!' He made no attempt to hide the fear in his voice.

'Haurn the Craven indeed!' cried the Arkhos of Treika from beside the eastern window, from which the spreading darkness reached into the room. 'We may yet hold the City! Or if not, at least the parts that matter!'

'We have hundreds of loyal guardsmen ready to do our

bidding,' added the Arkhos of Straux. 'We do not need recent arrivals from insignificant kingdoms' – he cast a glance towards the Arkhos of Deruys – 'to tell us how to order our affairs. If no one else has the courage to stand by the Grand Alliance we have made, then we three remaining of the original signatories to that alliance will be happy to arrange its defence.' He indicated Treika and Tabul, who made their way in silence and stood either side of him.

'Ah, the positioning,' murmured the Arkhos of Deuverre to his friend the Arkhos of Plonya, in a voice unwisely, or perhaps purposely, loud. 'And in the unfortunate absence of Deorc, the Arkhos of Straux would be happy to lead us in that defence.'

'If not I, then another of those who first sought the favour of the Lord of Bhrudwo, and under no circumstances one who is but recently bought!' A fatal anger, fuelled by fear and masked by a veneer of politeness, threatened for a moment to overtake them all. Deuverre flushed and lowered his head, muttering an insincere apology and defusing the moment. Though by agreement there were no swords here in this room, no weapons of any kind, it was foolishness to make enemies. A word from one of the others and he might not make it out of the Hall of Worship alive.

Deruys seemed to have no such concerns. 'So your counsel is to stay and make a fight of it. I do not agree. It is time to put aside alliances foolishly made and accommodate the present realities. There is no merit in entrusting ourselves to one who is blinded by loyalty to a cause that is lost. In fact,' he continued as the Arkhos of Straux took a step forward towards him, 'such a person, rather than being promoted, may need to be removed from the office he currently holds.'

'So, that's how it stands, is it?' Straux growled. His hand flashed under his tunic and emerged holding a thin-bladed knife. 'Then, in the name of the Undying One, you should die!' Joined by the Arkhoi of Tabul and Treika, he advanced confidently on the weaponless Deruys.

Only to discover he was not weaponless, and neither were the two other Arkhoi who moved quickly to support him. Short swords and knives were drawn from secret places and held at the ready. 'Betrayed!' the Arkhos of Straux snarled. 'You have planned this in secret!'

'As you have,' Deruys laughed. 'The problem for you is you have fewer supporters for your plan.' He moved to the door, rapped on it with the hilt of his throwing blade and was answered by a servant, head deferentially lowered. 'The chains?' Deruys asked him.

'They are being fetched, my lord,' came the answer. 'Forgive our tardiness, lord; we had some difficulty on the stairs with servants of the Arkhoi over there.' He pointed to the three crestfallen figures in front of the south window. 'Two of your servants are dead, I am sorry to report, as are all of theirs.'

The chains arrived some minutes later. The Arkhoi of Straux, Treika and Tabul were disarmed briskly and, in spite of repeated protests, were chained to hooks set in the walls as though there expressly for the purpose.

The Arkhos of Deruys moved over to where Straux hung, feet not quite touching the floor. Already the strain was beginning to show on the captive's face. 'From here you can see much of Instruere,' Deruys said to him conversationally. 'Perhaps the view might help you consider how you might better have looked after these people's interests.' Then he added, in a voice so low that only Straux could hear: 'Did you never wonder at my easy adoption of your traitorous cause? My king would never have sent anyone who might have been corrupted by the likes of you.'

'But – I saw you in The Pinion. I watched what you did! Do the others know of this perfidy?'

'Of course the others do not know, and would not believe you if you told them. As for The Pinion, I paid the price my king decided I had to pay. I have nightmares about it every night. Do you?' And with that he turned his back on the man in chains.

Before closing and locking the door to the Room of Four Windows in the Tower of Worship, he put his head back through the opening. 'I will have no nightmares over your fate,' he said quietly.

In the same hour the servants of the remaining Councillors were fighting and dying on the stairs to the Tower, members of the Instruian Guard now under the control of the Company were being addressed by their former captain. Disarmed, dishonoured, surrounded by merchants and labourers, peasants and city-dwellers, men, women and children armed with makeshift weapons – and now also equipped with their own – they listened with downcast hearts as they were told what lay behind their ignominy.

The Captain of the Guard was a persuasive man. The Arkhos of Nemohaim owed much of his former power in this city to the love these soldiers held for their tall, raven-haired captain. Firm but fair, this quiet, practical man always placed himself at the forefront of any task he asked his guardsmen to perform. He had joined the Guard as an under-age recruit, escaping from the sewer-gangs of the old city of Struere. Working his way through the ranks, the handsome soldier gained himself a following. A series of wise commanders recognised his usefulness by setting him the most difficult tasks, which he had completed unquestioningly. So it was that the Arkhos of Nemohaim found him, promoting him over a number of those commanders to be the youngest Captain of the Guard ever known. Loyal to a fault, the captain came to realise what his master really was, but could not oppose him without undoing his soldier's code, and thereby his own meaning, his personal centre of balance.

This he explained to his men. He told them about his journey south with the Arkhos. He emphasised his respect for the youth from the north, the Bearer of the Arrow; described how he'd seen the boy stretch out his arm and summon the River Aleinus to refill its banks, destroying his pursuers. He told them of the coming of the Jugom Ark, the Arrow which they had seen for themselves, and shared his version of events as they had unfolded in the Joram Basin, a story none of them had heard.

Then he told them of the Destroyer, and of the bitter betrayal planned by the Council of Faltha. The murmuring and muttering among the men increased in volume as he described how the Council had promised to open the gates of Instruere to the Destroyer's hordes. Not only did they understand that they, as soldiers, would have been the first victims of this betrayal, but they also despised this lack of loyalty. Soldiers such as they recognised the value of oath-keeping.

Now their captain's words were accompanied by angry shouts, which only grew louder when they were told the people they attacked in front of the Hall of Lore three nights ago were not Escaigne, as they had been told, but instead were merely untrained citizens. Among the Instruian Guard, commissioned to protect the Great City, the news that they were tricked into killing their own citizens came as a shock to many.

The Captain of the Guard seized on the moment. 'The

Council of Faltha is corrupt. Their actions render void the oaths we swore to them,' he said bluntly. 'But our oath to uphold order in the City still holds. I propose that we pledge allegiance to the Jugom Ark, and to the man who bears it. Choose swiftly! Look, the sun sets!' He pointed to the north-east, where the upper part of the tower glowed a dull red above the roofs of the city. 'By the time the last ray of sun leaves the Tower of Worship, I expect you so to swear. You will do this by coming forward and standing in this open space in front of me. There you will be reissued with your weapons and await your command. Those who choose not to swear will be held prisoner until such time as the threat to the City has ended. There are but a few moments left. Choose!'

In less than a minute only a few dozen guardsmen remained seated in front of the Struere Gate. A number of these men tried to come forward but were prevented by their fellows, who suspected them of being too deeply entwined with the old Council. Others were not willing to forsake their hope of reward, and placed their faith in being rescued by the bulk of the Instruian Guard, who must even now be preparing to attack this renegade Company. The very tip of the Tower of Worship flickered, then the sun withdrew its finger and shadow came to claim it.

The Haufuth turned and shook the hand of the Captain of the Guard. 'Thank you,' he said with feeling. 'Your words may have saved hundreds of lives.'

'Thousands will be spent before this is done,' the man responded gruffly. 'Yet that is as it should be. We will not stand for the betrayal and slaughter of our people.' He turned on his heel and directed a level gaze at the huge figure of the Arkhos of Nemohaim, then deliberately spat on the ground and walked away to speak to his soldiers.

'Eloquent,' Kurr said approvingly, 'especially the last part. He raises an excellent question with his gesture. What shall we do with the Arkhos of Nemohaim?'

The question remained unanswered as Kurr and the Haufuth stepped into the pavilion to report to Leith, who had just awoken from a much-needed sleep. Three fraught days had taken their toll; in truth Leith had experienced about enough decision-making to last him a while. He felt anew the wonder, the continued awkwardness of the situation, as the man who had been his village headman – who still was, technically – and the farmer from whom he had drawn back in fear a few short months ago brought him a respectful report of what had taken place outside.

'Ensure they are fed,' he said to them, and they nodded. 'We should have some stores remaining. Encourage those of the crowd who remain to bring enough for one soldier when they return tomorrow.'

Sage words, he thought, but they were not his. Hal spent a few moments talking to him earlier this afternoon: he had anticipated the defection of the Guard to the Company.

'Bring the Arkhos of Nemohaim to me,' Leith added, as a thought occurred to him. Hal was not the only one who could come up with clever ideas.

'Is that wise?' the Haufuth said, eyebrows raised. 'At least he will require a guard.'

'No guard. I have a defence he will not challenge, not while he has a deep scar on his right hand to remind him.'

'But—'

'No guard.' His voice was edged with a finality that even the old farmer chose not to argue with.

Some time later the Arkhos of Nemohaim entered the

pavilion and sat on a wide, low bench which groaned under him. 'You've decided to be rid of me, haven't you,' he said flatly, before Leith could offer a word. The youth from Loulea could not miss the deep, dark hunger in the man's eyes, as though Leith's confirmation would be the best news in the world.

'I have not,' Leith answered him. 'You will decide that.'

'How so?' The eyes deepened, if that was possible.

Leith laid the Jugom Ark on the table between them. Quiescent since the battle with the blue fire, the Arrow nevertheless began to char the wooden surface of the table.

'Take it,' Leith said. 'Pick it up. If you can. Then take leadership of the Company and do what you will with us.' He sat back and watched the man's eyes carefully.

For an instant they hollowed out, as though two passages had opened into a cavern at the dark centre of the world. Then they changed again, became hooded, and the Arkhos laughed.

'Grown a lot, haven't you,' he acknowledged. 'You know I can't touch it. You know that I want to.' The wheezing voice was heavy with bitterness.

'Then swear allegiance to me. Swear on the Arrow. Do service to this City, to this land, that might make up in part for the things you have done.'

'And the alternative?'

'If you will not make a contribution to the care and protection of Faltha, you will be tried and judged for your crimes,' Leith said. 'No one knows of the offer I am making you now. Will you swear?'

The Arkhos of Nemohaim held his gaze, saying nothing, but a shrewd look slowly settled on his face. Leith waited, disconcerted, feeling that somehow the knowing silence was draining his authority.

The obese man smiled. 'Certain things become clear to me. Your older brother has exercised mercy against all advice, to good effect. He befriended the *Maghdi Dasht* warrior, turning his heart. Others would have used him, then had him put to death out of fear. I would have. Your older brother now has a powerful weapon at his disposal. And you now wish to emulate him?'

'Why are we talking about my brother?' Leith snapped angrily. 'And why do you keep saying that he's older?'

'Is he not? Forgive me if I am mistaken.' The smile became wider.

'What does that have to do with it? Will you serve me, or not?'

'Is that really the question?' The Arkhos appeared to be struggling to contain his mirth. 'Should you not be asking why you wish to copy your crippled older brother?'

'I wish no such thing! My feelings are my own concern!' But even though he was not touching it, the Arrow flared briefly, betraying him.

'Is that so? Then why are you here, unless it is to prove you are his equal in intellect, in compassion, in wisdom, in power? Why am I here, unless it is to make me your servant in the same way the Bhrudwan is his?'

He's taunting me, he's taunting me, Leith knew, but he could not formulate any way of rebutting the Arkhos. There he sat, with the power of the world at hand, completely powerless in the presence of this man.

Because he spoke the truth.

'Now things are clear between us,' the Arkhos of Nemohaim continued. 'I know you better than you know yourself. In spite of what I have said, you will continue to deny it to my face. Ah well, let me consider your offer. You will never make a tame pet of me. I will not perform like a trained dassie so you can convince your friends and family of your worth. Perhaps there is nothing I can do for you.'

'I won't beg you, but I won't kill you either,' Leith said, his voice strained with the effort of keeping it level, free from betraying emotion. 'I need advice, and you might be able to help. Go and think about it. If by this time tomorrow you cannot swear to my service, I will have you sent for trial.'

Slowly, insolently, the Arkhos of Nemohaim stood, pushing himself up from the table, his eyes never leaving those of the Arrow-bearer. 'Having access to power does not make you powerful,' he whispered, then left the pavilion.

Leith watched him go, feeling very young, wanting desperately to ask the voice of the Arrow what to do, but afraid.

Graig burst in to the tent to find him slumped over the table, head in his hands. 'My lord, my lord Leith!' he cried, startling the young man out of wherever his mind had taken him. 'Come quickly! There are people here to see you!'

'Bring them here,' Leith said wearily. 'Bring them to the pavilion.' Graig left the tent before Leith realised he had not asked who the people were.

He found out soon enough. In came six cloaked and hooded figures, with two of the Instruian Guards as escorts. 'Graig! Graig!' he shouted, suddenly aware that these guardsmen had weapons, when all were supposed to be weaponless.

'No need,' said one of the figures, throwing back his hood to reveal steely grey hair and deep brown eyes. 'We are not here to harm you. Even if we were, I am not certain we could, if all I hear around this City is true.'

'I remember you!' Leith said, astonished. 'You sat beside me at the evening banquet, at the palace of the King of Deruys. Why are you here and not with the king?'

The man nodded soberly. 'I am here at his request,' he said. 'The king sent me to Instruere to replace the previous Arkhos of Deruys, who was put to death by Deorc. I deceived the Bhrudwan into thinking I had betrayed my king.' He smiled then, and the sight of it chilled Leith's blood, for it held a menace for his king's foes. 'With me are five other Arkhoi who believe the betrayal has gone far enough. We are here to turn over the rule of the City to your Company and, with it, the remainder of the Instruian Guard. It must be said that not all of the Arkhoi here are entirely innocent, but with your agreement we seek to exchange the keys to the Four Halls for your pardon. Only by paying this small price will you achieve control of the City without bloodshed.'

'And with it, the chance to leave for the Bhrudwan borders even earlier than we had planned!' Graig cried. 'That's why I let them in. It seemed too good a chance to miss!'

Without thinking, Leith formed a question in his mind, and was about to ask the voice, but caught himself just in time. *Who cares what the voice thinks*, he admonished himself. *This will be certain evidence I am worthy to hold the Arrow.* He knew the thought was wrong, but he was still angry over what the Arkhos of Nemohaim had said.

'Very well then,' he said. 'You will swear allegiance to the Jugom Ark. No doubt you've heard stories of what it can do to those who try to deceive it.' *Actually*, Leith thought, *it has done nothing but help and heal.* He said nothing of this as the six Arkhoi knelt and swore.

Just then the Company began to file into the pavilion, readying themselves for their evening meal. Leith tried to explain who these people were, what he had done, what it might mean to them, but even to his ears it sounded as though he had acted thoughtlessly, without asking the others.

As he finished his explanation, in walked the Arkhos of Nemohaim. The six Arkhoi froze as one man.

'Leith, oh Leith,' his mother said, in the moments before the shouting began. 'What have you done?'

CHAPTER 7

BATTLE OF THE FOUR HALLS

THE STRUGGLE WAS BRIEF. No one suffered serious injury, but it was a close thing. As soon as the Arkhos of Nemohaim entered the pavilion he was recognised by four of the Arkhoi – Haurn, Plonya, Deuverre and his own replacement, the new Arkhos of Nemohaim – and the other two were not far behind in drawing their conclusions, then their swords. They were joined by the two guardsmen who had accompanied them, and for a moment it seemed the Arkhos of Nemohaim would be slain. Someone made a lunge. No one was sure who it was and, as it missed, there was no point pursuing the matter, but at that moment Achtal the Bhrudwan strode into the tent armed only with a staff, deflecting blows aimed at the Arkhos, who appeared to be making no effort to defend himself. A few moments of blurred motion and half-a-dozen Arkhoi were left holding bruised arms and hands, and their swords lay on the floor. Bitter curses hung in the air.

'What is happening?' Leith cried into the sudden stillness. Every head in the tent turned in his direction.

Surprisingly, it was the Arkhos of Nemohaim who answered him, an avid gleam in his eye. 'Someone has not thought things through,' he said, directing his disconcerting gaze at Leith. 'Someone who would privately entertain members of the Council of Faltha and not plan against the chance of them discovering their former leader walked free and unrestrained.'

'Ungently put, but accurate,' Kurr said. 'Leith, if you had informed us that the Council of Faltha had come calling, we would at least have ensured the Arkhos of Nemohaim was kept apart from them.'

'What is that man doing here?' the Arkhos of Plonya asked through lips thin with anger. 'He should be made to answer to the Council of Faltha for his deeds!'

'You are hardly in any position to make demands,' Mahnum replied quietly. 'You are here to surrender, if Leith's explanation is correct.'

'Not quite,' said the Arkhos of Deruys pleasantly. 'There is a delicate balance to be obtained here. A number of my fellow councillors are guilty of reprehensible crimes, treason not the least, which might cost them their freedom or even their lives, depending on the mercy of the new rulers of the city. I myself am not entirely innocent, according to the law; although I acted on the orders of my king, and remained loyal to Faltha at all times. We turn the City over to you, but do not surrender ourselves. Is the distinction clear? Some here might want to make a swift journey home to their king on their fastest horse, while others might want to avoid such a journey. I do not know. But none want to find themselves in The Pinion.'

'What prevents us from making you captives and dispensing justice as we see fit?' Maendraga wanted to know.

'I would have thought honour might prevent such a betrayal. Or if not honour, common sense would suggest that receiving the keys to the Four Halls and being granted the allegiance of the Instruian Guard, both of which require our cooperation, might be worth consideration.'

Maendraga nodded. 'Please excuse my shortsightedness. Leith is not the only thoughtless one here today. We have been many weeks on the road, and have taken little rest since we came to this city.'

Leith wanted to protest, to say something that might wrest some control back for himself, but circumstances had run away from him. He risked a glance at Hal, and discovered that his older brother was gazing at him with something akin to compassion on his face. He'd seen that look many times before. He remembered it, for example, when he'd been wrongly accused of breaking the shutters on Malos's kitchen window, Hal had sat opposite him while their father gave him a telling off. There was a clear message on Hal's face that day. *I know what you're going through*, it said, *and it is undeserved.* Not pity, exactly; more a knowing, understanding, sympathetic look. Nothing Leith could think of at the moment could have made him angrier. Something of this must have been reflected on his face, because Hal turned away suddenly, a hurt look clouding his features.

Geinor and the Escaignian woman had been busy organising the evening meal, and began serving the others as the discussion continued. Hal ventured a rare opinion: as Leith expected, he supported the idea of accepting the Council's offer and letting them go where they might. 'After all, had we been offered this choice four months ago, we would have accepted it without question,' he said. Mahnum and Perdu were disinclined to agree, worrying about the possibility of further treachery. But, as Kurr reminded them, their victory over the remnants of the Instruian Guard was by no means assured, and even if it was to be achieved, would be bought at a great cost. 'Doing the Destroyer's work,' was how the old farmer summed up the consequences of rejecting the Council's offer.

The Escaignian woman spoke up. 'What of the other Council members? There are sixteen of you: what happened to the others?' The slim, round-faced woman had said very little since their return to the Great City. According to Indrett, she suffered the frustration of separation between herself and her family still in Escaigne. Though they were undoubtedly close by, she could not make contact, as the normal entry points were boarded over.

But with these words she occasioned groans from a number of the Company. 'How could we have been so foolish?' the Haufuth said. 'What were we thinking? Six cannot speak for sixteen!'

'There are no longer sixteen,' said the Arkhos of Nemohaim, the former leader of the Council. 'There were not sixteen even before I left. There will be fewer now. Associating with such as Deorc the Bhrudwan has a way of whittling down the numbers until only the fittest, most ruthless – or luckiest – survive. How is my old friend Deorc, anyway? Is he asking after me? Does he approve of your negotiations?' His piggy eyes pierced his former fellow councillors.

'The fat man is right,' said the Arkhos of Plonya, directing a baleful stare at him. 'Much has happened since his poor judgment led us, and the City, away from the path of wisdom. Let me tally it for you!' He held up the fingers of both hands, and began counting them off. 'Twenty men have served on the Council of Faltha since Nemohaim recruited those he called his "Patriots" two years ago. Sarista was assassinated, first fruits of betrayal, he and his family and all his servants, at this man's direct order. Then followed Asgowan, who sided with Deorc and was denounced by Nemohaim because of it. We all watched Deorc torture and kill him, and though he deserved it, his death was unpleasant to behold. The four remaining loyalists were executed, burned at the stake, and their deaths can also be charged to Nemohaim's account. Deruys, Redana'a, Sna Vaztha and Piskasia. They died well, unlike Asgowan, but were accorded no dignity: Nemohaim ordered their ashes scattered into the sewers. Then, of course, the Arkhos of Nemohaim himself was driven out of the City after the Escaignian fiasco; driven out, I repeat, no matter how much he might claim he left of his own accord.

'Three Patriots – Firanes, Favony and Vertensia – perished when the blue fire raged out of control just a few hours ago, when Deorc was forced to report his failure to his master. Ten councillors eliminated, ten to go.' He closed his fingers into two fists, then opened them again. 'I do not know what Deorc said or did to offend his Bhrudwan masters. I'm not sure any of us understood what happened with the blue fire. I know I was uncomfortable with it. Some kind of dark wizardry. In my opinion those who tamper with such powers deserve their fate. And that is what happened, for Deorc also perished in the fire.'

The hiss of indrawn breath from the Arkhos of Nemohaim was audible throughout the tent. *The breath of ambition rekindled*, Leith realised.

'Some things might have been better left unsaid,' Kurr said regretfully. 'It seems that no one is immune from unwise thoughts today.'

'Detail a guard on the man until we decide what to do with him,' said the Haufuth to the Captain of the Instruian

Guard, who nodded and moved closer to his former master. 'With this news, there's no telling what he might do.'

Plonya acknowledged his error with a shrug of his shoulders, then went on. 'Let me continue with my count as I started it. I include Deorc, who was never appointed but did serve, after a fashion. This is what has happened to the other nine: only three of the original traitors remain as councillors, and they chose not to support our initiative. Treika, Straux and Tabul are now being taken to The Pinion. Of the rest of us, three were replacements for those executed earlier, and three came over to the "Patriots" only under duress. We six are all that remain. When we evaluated our position, and our sources told us of the exploits of your Company, in particular the revelation of the Jugom Ark, it seemed to us there was little point in continuing to govern.'

'You forget the twenty-first councillor, the replacement Arkhos of Sna Vaztha,' Indrett pointed out. Beside her, Mahnum's face hardened.

'So we have,' the Arkhos of Deruys said, faintly amused. 'How could we have forgotten? Such a grand entrance, and his credentials were impeccable. I think his appearance did something to Deorc, drove him to swift actions he would otherwise have taken more time over. Certainly he had been planning to confront your Company at some appointed time, but hurried down here with his Instruian Guard almost as soon as the Arkhos of Sna Vaztha left for the last time. Where is Modahl, by the way? He showed great courage in a tight place. I would like to shake the hand of a living legend.'

'He is gone, along with others of our number.' Kurr was reluctant to say more.

The Arkhos of Plonya took a step forward. 'And the Jugom

Ark is in the hands of the legend's own grandson! I take it that the arrow in the young man's hand is indeed the Arrow of Yoke, returned after all this time? There are signs and proofs of such?'

'There have been,' answered the Haufuth soberly. 'If you choose to remain with us, you may see more. Leave us now, while we discuss whether we will accept your offer.'

After they had been escorted out, Phemanderac hustled over to the Haufuth. 'Surely we will accept?'

'Without a doubt,' Kurr replied, and his village headman agreed with a nod. 'Their spokesman was right. This is the least expensive way of doing what we need to do.'

'There are some implications, however,' Hal said. The others turned to him, unused to him offering his opinion. 'Well, we will have to take the Arkhos of Nemohaim and the six councillors east with us when we march. If we do not, we leave people behind in Instruere who, even if they don't want to assume leadership of the City themselves, might be proposed by others with ambition.'

'Good thinking.' The old farmer nodded his appreciation. 'Of course, there are other ways we could render them ineffective.'

'And you would use them?' This was more like the Hal they remembered from their journey to Instruere.

'No,' Kurr admitted. 'None of us have the stomach for executions, but we must not let on that this is so. There are many people in this City who would hastily move into any perceived gaps in the leadership. We must take the keys and lay claim to the Four Halls before anyone else realises what is happening.'

'Would it help to let the City know that we have the blessing of the Council of Faltha?' Belladonna asked.

'That's a good question,' said the Haufuth reflectively. 'It might reassure some people, but turn others against us.'

'Nevertheless, it is a question we can consider after we've actually taken control.' Phemanderac's eyes blazed with urgency. 'We must move quickly. Are we agreed?'

'What does the Arrow-bearer say?' Graig asked, a little stiffness in his voice. 'We would still be begging for help if it was not for him.'

Leith smiled gratefully at the young Nemohaimian. 'I don't think they care any more,' he said to him, unable to keep the hurt from choking his voice. 'I'm just a candle-holder, shedding light so everyone else can get on with their tasks.' The other members of the Company showed that they heard him, as he intended them to.

'Come, Leith, much has changed even in the short time I have known you.' Leith looked for signs of sympathy in Phemanderac's deep blue eyes, and was relieved not to find any. He was not sure he could stand any more sympathy. 'You are an important part of the Company. When have you ever not been listened to?'

'We don't have time for this,' Kurr growled. 'If Leith has something to say, we'll listen. Otherwise, we need to make a decision.'

'It seems to me the decision is made,' Mahnum said quickly, perhaps to cover his son's embarrassment. 'Does anyone think we should refuse?' No one spoke; a few shook their heads emphatically. 'Then let us call the councillors back and set things in motion.'

'So swiftly?' Belladonna asked.

'A vast army descends upon us,' he replied. 'No matter how swiftly we move, we may already be too late.'

* * *

The Company spent a restless night back at their lodgings. Events, already outpacing their capacity to take them in, moved even more quickly from that point onwards. What had taken months to prepare unfolded the next day in a matter of hours.

They ought to establish a presence in the Four Halls, it was decided. They were the key to authority in Instruere, everybody knew that. Even with the Jugom Ark, it would not be enough to remain in Old Struere, from where it would be difficult, if not impossible, to win support from the rest of the City. Initially they were all going to go to the halls, but Hal cautioned them to leave some of their number behind. He remained, along with Achtal, the Haufuth, Mahnum and Indrett, and the Captain of the Guard, who kept a watch on the Arkhos of Nemohaim. The Arkhos of Plonya surrendered the keys to the Four Halls into Kurr's safekeeping. The six Arkhoi then donned their cloaks and put up their hoods, somewhat incongruously in the autumn heat, and led the rest of the Company through the busy City. Overhead clouds began to build up, though it was only mid-morning, promising rain or even thunder later.

For the first thirty minutes or so the signs of the recent destruction were obvious everywhere. A few buildings still smouldered, mostly at the ends of narrow lanes some distance from the nearest source of water, left to burn themselves out. Behind the block of residential tenements to their left, to the west as they walked north along the Vitulian Way, lay a large area of warehouses and the skeletal remains of the Granaries. Black smoke rose from half-a-dozen places in that direction. Closer to their path fully one in four of the houses were damaged in some way, either by fire or by falling fragments from the warehouse district. On these houses carpenters laboured, assisted by swarms of locals, including many whose jobs in the warehouse district were at least temporarily suspended. Weary voices called to each other across the streets, exchanging materials, offering or asking for assistance, calling workers in for food or drink. A number of them waved to the Company, recognising the Arrow if not the person who held it, and within minutes a small group of children gathered, cheering and dancing around them. They at least acknowledged something special was happening, if their elders would not yet – either because of the taxing events of the previous few days or because of their reserved, private natures down in the poorer southern part of Instruere.

Their path took them beyond the environs they had frequented since their return to the City, the change marked by a gradual improvement in the standard of accommodation, wider, cleaner sewers, and better-dressed people on the streets. They began to encounter many who had not seen the Arrow, and the news of their passage spread ahead of them. Citizens came to their doors and spilled out on to the road, pointing, talking, shouting. A few of the older children from Old Struere still tagged along, telling the people all about the Company of the Arrow.

The ground began to rise as they approached the Hall of Meeting, the largest and most important of the Four Halls, a large building squatting over a wide area of parks and gardens. They knew this building well, having many times made the hour-long walk from Foilzie's tenement to the Appellants' Hall during the frustrating weeks they were seeking an audience with the Council of Faltha. The attendant crowd waited outside while the Company walked silently through the colossal Outer Chamber. Deruys showed them where earlier that day the blue fire had consumed a marble table and eaten into the floor. No remains of Deorc or the three councillors had been found, Deruys said. Leith remembered that evil face gloating over Stella in chains. Stella! Had Phemanderac seen truly? Had she been burned by the flames like the others? Had it hurt? Was she really gone forever?

Leith glanced upwards, his vision blurred by tears he had not yet taken time to shed. Something inside him ached unbearably, and seemed to be taking control of him, thickening his throat, burning his chest, robbing the strength from his arms and legs. He knew this was grief, and that soon he would have to give way to it – he could almost hear Hal giving him well-intentioned advice to that effect – but not yet.

High up in the vaulted ceiling, centuries-old shadows flickered in response to the Jugom Ark, and began to withdraw as though being driven away by the light. Intuitively, Leith realised this great Hall had been designed with an artefact like the Jugom Ark in mind, even though it had been built hundreds of years after Bewray's time, if he understood Phemanderac rightly. Could it be? How could the builders have known? Leith sighed. It made no more or no less sense than many other things that had happened to him.

One of the keys they had been given opened the small door to the Inner Chamber. 'Not in there,' said Kurr and Leith in the same moment; then laughed at themselves, the man ruffling the boy's sandy hair, and then leading the Company back out into the Outer Chamber.

The Arkhos of Plonya tried to deter them. 'It is cold here most of the winter, and sound plays odd tricks. Not at all suitable for a small group to meet.'

'We're used to the cold,' Leith said in reply, 'and we don't plan to be here for long anyway. Just time enough for the City to settle down and for us to raise our army. Then we'll be off east, and those we leave in charge can meet wherever they want.'

'What about one of the other halls? Why can't we use the Hall of Lore?' Belladonna asked. Phemanderac turned to her and nodded his head eagerly in agreement.

'No, it has to be here,' Kurr said with finality. 'This is the hall the Instruians associate with authority, so here we must stay.'

The far door sprang open and a young man burst in, wearing the livery of the Hall of Meeting. 'Please, you had better come,' he said to them, unsure exactly who it was he ought to be addressing, but eventually settling on the Arkhos of Deruys. 'A large group of people has gathered outside. They are calling for the Council of Faltha, and they sound very angry.'

The Company was able to observe the new arrivals from the marbled mezzanine floor of the entry annexe. Six or seven deep, the crowd formed a line that curved away out of sight to the left and right. 'Surrounding the hall,' Kurr muttered.

'What do they want?' Leith asked.

'Let's listen.' Deruys threw the shutters open, an action that did not go unnoticed by those below. A tall, blond-haired man in a blue robe turned and pointed, then cried: 'Look on them! There are the craven councillors! The ones who brought darkness to this City of Light!'

'Burn them! Burn them!' cried the crowd, on cue.

Deruys snapped the shutters closed. 'Who are those people?' he asked, puzzled. 'What do they want?'

'The man in blue is our old friend the Hermit,' said Kurr sourly. 'The man who formed the Ecclesia.'

'Ah – the dupe of Deorc.' Plonya smiled. 'Whatever one

thinks of the Bhrudwan, he certainly proved effective in subverting the designs of others.'

Leith spoke his thoughts aloud. 'If that line goes all the way around the hall, it must be thousands strong. Surely there are not that many remaining in the Hermit's thrall after the atrocity in front of the Hall of Lore?'

'You are right,' the old farmer said, edging open one of the shutters and peering out. With mounting anger in his voice, he turned to the others. 'Down there, standing beside the Hermit, is the Presiding Elder of Escaigne. They appear to have joined forces. This is something we should have foreseen!'

'We're trapped here, you know,' Leith said nervously. 'If they don't want us to leave, we won't be able to. What fools we are!'

'I don't see how you could have foreseen this,' growled Maendraga. 'You seem to think you ought to divine all the secrets of the western world. From what you've told me, these are two proud men of ambition, unwilling to share glory with another. It is a mark of their desperation that they feel the need to form an alliance.'

'A fragile alliance at best, easily undone if we can find the knot.' Kurr leaned forward, easing the shutters open a little further. 'I knew this Presiding Elder when he was a double-dealing youth. I'm sure I could find his weakness.'

'What if they manage to break in?' Leith asked. It seemed cruel that just as they achieved what they had worked so hard to attain, something should come along to threaten it. How many more obstacles would be raised in their path?

Phemanderac scratched his head. 'Let us talk with them, and perhaps we can determine what their grievance is and defuse it.'

Belladonna agreed. 'We mean no one harm. Surely when we explain our plans and show them the Jugom Ark, they will be won over to our cause.'

Her father laughed derisively. 'I know you had a sheltered upbringing, my daughter,' he said gently, 'but our experiences of the last three months should have taught you that nothing is that simple. Those two down there want power, not peace. Both will believe they can more effectively serve Instruere than we might. Both will believe the heirloom of Bewray is rightly theirs, and their hand alone should raise it.'

'Maendraga is right, I believe,' Kurr said. 'I wish the Haufuth was here. He spent more time with the Hermit than anyone else, and would know more of his motivation. Hal warned us of him back when we first met him, remember?'

Leith remembered. Hal had embarrassed the man by deriding him publicly, and later that same night inflicted a near-fatal injury on him. He remembered the black wings, the insect-shape hovering over the Hermit's cot, the words they exchanged . . . *Perhaps Hal's actions made the Hermit into what he is now*, Leith speculated. *Maybe if Hal had left well enough alone, the Hermit might have been an important part of the Company*. The Hermit had the gift, the second sight. He proved it in Leith's case, a cold puddle on the Southern Run, the knowledge of Wira's secret, a hidden passage in the fortress of Adunlok. And predicted that Leith would be a leader of men, far-fetched as it sounded at the time.

The hermit had taken him aside and predicted 'a high and lofty destiny' for him. For him alone, not for any of his fellow travellers. Others had echoed those words, the latest being his own legendary grandfather, openly calling him the Right Hand. Bearer of the Jugom Ark, the one hand that could hold it without being consumed. Touched by the Fire, hearer of voices. Son of a Trader, grandson of the greatest of them all. Healer and worker of miracles. At the centre of everything. He saw himself seated on a high throne set on a pedestal in the Outer Chamber, the Flaming Arrow in his hand, a thousand people assembled, minstrels playing, food on tables, the Company seated below him, emissaries from foreign lands bowing their obeisances to him. With wisdom he dispensed justice tempered by mercy, and every eye rested on him, filled with love.

<You make a pretty sight,> said a familiar voice in his mind. <Look at those clothes you're wearing! Did you see raiment like that at the Court of Deruys?> Irritatingly, there was a hint of laughter in the voice.

Where have you been? Leith was not amused: it felt like being spied on.

<Waiting for you to reach this point,> came the laconic reply. <I am impressed, actually: the young lad I called out a thousand years ago believed himself king of the world, and nothing I said or did changed him. That's how he died, believing himself invulnerable, climbing the waterfall alone, leaving the others behind him; choosing the wrong side to climb and trapping himself on an unreachable ledge. Too proud to cry out for help. His bones lie there still. Just a stable-boy, but in a few short months he became overconfident. Not like you, Leith. Mature as you have become, you still lack confidence.>

You're not going to give me a telling off, are you?

<No; just offer some advice. Look for the balance. Don't get carried away by grandeur or the praise of others, but don't pretend you remain a simple northern shepherd boy. Keep a level head. Learn to laugh, that's the key!>

Leith snorted. *A homily from the voice of the Arrow? The greatest power in the world offers sensible advice?*

Now anger infused the voice. <Do you think there is anything more powerful than good sense? With your vantage point of millennia of wielding power, you have a different view?>

No, Leith snapped back. *But common sense is just that: common. It doesn't lift you from the fringes of civilisation and put you in place to resist the Destroyer. If I had used common sense, I would still be playing by the pool in Loulea.*

With this reply the anger dissolved, and Leith imagined he could hear a smile in the voice. <You are right! You took many risks, each one justified according to what you knew at the time. But my advice remains. Keep a level head. Try not to make decisions based on the emotion of the moment.> There was a finality to the voice that Leith remembered. It had said all it was going to say.

Come back! I wanted to ask you a question about Stella! Is she all right?

Silence was his only reply.

Unsettled and angry, Leith turned to the others. It seemed no time at all had passed. Kurr was telling them what Mahnum and Indrett had told him: that the Hermit had imposed his will on the Ecclesia, believing himself the Anointed One, the chosen vessel of the Most High. Carried away by his own vision, the result had been the shaping of followers who thought little for themselves, relying instead on the pronouncements from their blue-robed leader. This development led the Company to abandon the Ecclesia, and eventually to the deaths of many of the Hermit's followers at the hands of Tanghin/Deorc and the Instruian Guard.

The Arkhos of Plonya threw the shutters open and called out: 'What is it you want with the Council of Faltha?'

'Kill them! Burn them! Destroy them!' came the raucous cries from below. A more cultured voice added: 'Submit them to our judgment, thus bringing the City under the authority of the Chosen of the Most High!' This was followed by another, older, voice which cried: 'Turn the City over to the Watchers. It is time for Escaigne to rule!'

'The leaders are irrelevant,' Kurr said quietly. 'There's something dangerous down there. I've seen it before, in the Sivithar riots when I was young. The people down there are angry because many of their friends were hurt or killed in the last few days. They will not walk away quietly, mark my words! All it will take is for someone to do something foolish—'

'Like that?' Leith pointed down.

'O Most High, what is he doing? He is a dead man.' Kurr's voice went flat.

The Arkhos of Deruys had vanished from among them, having obviously taken it into his head to speak to the crowd. Now he strode out from the entrance to the Hall of Meeting, towards the crowd that wanted his blood, and as they noticed him a feral howl rose from their throats. He held up his hand to treat with them, but what he had to say was lost as he was overrun. For a moment he disappeared under a few dozen figures – men and women both – and then Leith saw him again, lifted off his feet, his arms pinned behind his back. His mouth opened to cry out, and someone thrust something into it.

From left and from right others came running. With a dim part of his awareness Leith realised they could, in all probability, escape out of some back door, if there was one. *There must be a servants' door of some kind.* But even though he could guess at what was about to unfold, he could not move his feet.

'They've got a pole – someone's bringing wood,' Kurr said. 'They're going to – they're going to burn him!' He leaned out of the window. 'You down there! Listen to me!' he cried urgently, at the top of his lungs. 'We need to talk!'

'You need to burn!' came the reply from a hundred throats.

'Can't you do something with that Arrow of yours?' The Arkhos of Plonya faced Leith, hands on hips. 'They're going to kill him!'

'I – it doesn't work like that, seemingly,' Leith mumbled. 'I'd be as likely to kill the crowd as save the Arkhos.'

Maendraga leaned over, saving Leith further embarrassment. 'You'd be a fool to go out there. The Arkhos is beyond saving. I could hazard an illusion, but such things work at this distance only if I show people something they'd expect.'

'They're hammering the stake into the ground . . . they've bound poor Deruys to the stake . . . now they pile wood around it. He struggles, he can't escape what they are going to do.' Kurr kept up his running commentary on what was happening below. 'They are waiting for something. No one can find any fire! Perhaps there is hope! But no, no, here's a woman with a burning torch . . . the Hermit stands by and watches with his arms folded, and Feerik eggs them on, shrieking at the top of his voice . . . how I hate that man! They've set the flame to the wood . . . it's caught fire. Aahh, no! They've turned away from the Arkhos and are facing us . . .'

'Come and warm yourself by the fire!' It was the voice of the Presiding Elder, serrated like a knife, crazed beyond belief by what had just been done. 'Come and burn! Come and burn! Or we will come up and get you!'

Kurr swung the shutters closed, but Leith could see a flickering light dancing insanely on the wooden slats. 'He's burning, he's burning, aahh, he's burning,' groaned the old farmer, peering through the slats. 'Some of the mob are coming this way.'

His words were punctuated by heavy thumps on the door below. Now Leith could hear the clamour of the mob, a wild, abandoned sound, swirling, intoxicating, burning. No words were distinguishable in their howling, but their message was clear. The fire had fallen on them, but not the fire of the Most High. A fire of madness.

'We need to get out of here,' said the Arkhos of Plonya, a quaver in his normally calm voice. 'They'll break down the door soon. It wasn't designed to stand up to a prolonged assault.'

As if to confirm the Arkhos's words, a servant came scurrying up the stairs, red-faced and out of breath. 'We've been looking for you everywhere! There's a mob—'

'We know!' Plonya snapped. 'How do we get out of here?'

'My lord, I don't know! Galen tried to get out the back way, but they saw him and – and – my lord, they tore him apart. We're all terrified.'

'How many are you?' Kurr asked.

'Fifty-two staff on normal days, my lord,' came the quick reply. 'Though with some of the councillors absent, the exact number—'

'Yes, yes,' the old farmer responded distractedly. 'And the others?'

'My lord?'

'The appellants!' Kurr's impatience was obvious to all.

'Oh, yes, a hall full of them,' the servant said dismissively. 'But—'

'So how many in total?'

'Perhaps a hundred and fifty altogether, my lord. But the appellants will be no use—'

'When the mob break in, they will not distinguish between

councillors and servants and officials and appellants. They'll kill them all. Those appellants, who you seem to think don't count, are our responsibility. Now, do we have any weapons in this cursed place?'

The servant led them back to the Outer Chamber, where the staff had assembled. Before them was a pile of old swords. 'Ceremonial, my lords,' said the frightened man. 'Taken from the walls and storeroom upstairs. Enough for perhaps half of us.'

Banging came from behind the massive Iron Door.

'Have they broken in already?' Leith gasped.

'No, the appellants bang on the door in their fear,' the servant said.

'Then, by the Most High, let them in!' Kurr was clearly beyond reasoning with this obsequious man.

'But, lord, the rules say—'

'Damn your rules to the pit! Open the door or I'll throw you to the mob!'

'But the machinery—'

'OPEN THE DOOR!'

Without another word the servant grabbed two of his fellows and hauled at the chains. Slowly, in small jerks, the Iron Door rose; but as it did so, gears, springs and other small items showered down on them. As soon as it was a foot from the floor, people began scrambling under it. Leith was relieved to see frightened rather than crazed faces. Perhaps two feet from the ground the door ground to a halt, wedged open by broken lifting machinery. A few moments later all the appellants had gathered in a nervous group beside the staff.

'Close the door!' Plonya cried.

'It's jammed open! I tried to tell you it was broken, but you wouldn't listen!'

'We must close the door,' Plonya said to the others, calling them over to the chain, where the three servants struggled in vain. 'Come on, lend a hand. Our lives are at stake!'

Ten pairs of hands heaved on the chain. For a minute or so the only result was the sound of gears grinding together. Then another sound intruded on them. A door splintered, then crashed to the ground; and then a renewed howl came from the far end of the Hall of Appellants.

'They're coming!' The cry came from a dozen of those in the Outer Chamber.

'Quick! Take a weapon!' Phemanderac instructed the staff, needlessly.

With a shrieking of gears the Iron Door began to lower, but slowly, too slowly. More hands hauled on the chain. Sweaty palms slid from the smooth steel links, replaced by others. Pounding footsteps echoed down the hall. An inch, and another, and another, but there was more than a foot to go when the first of the mob arrived. A body slithered under the door, then another; both were cut down by sword-wielding servants before they could rise. This occasioned a pause from behind the door, followed by some shouting; then twenty or more came through. The Iron Door let out an enormous groan, as though in the throes of death. Kurr gave a cry of triumph as suddenly the great door dropped, slamming to the floor, pinning a dozen or more underneath its huge weight, killing the lucky immediately.

In the relative silence that followed, disturbed only by the dying moans of those trapped by the Iron Door, the few members of the mob who had succeeded in getting through looked around them, their courage fading fast. They were faced by sixty or more determined-looking people holding swords. A few of them spun around, but their way out was blocked by the huge door and the bodies of their fellows.

The old farmer let out a fearsome shout, darted forward and grabbed one of the mob by his tunic. 'Feerik!' he snarled. 'I would have thought you would operate in the shadows! So you finally had to lead by example, did you!'

It was the Presiding Elder, hiding in the midst of the small group. He glanced hopelessly around, his bird-like face white and small as the old farmer took up a sword and unsheathed it. 'See what has crawled under our door! A snake! But a snake with no venom, and soon to have no head!'

'Kurr! Don't do it!' Leith cried. 'Don't kill him! He might be able to negotiate a way out for us. If you start killing, there's no telling where it will stop.'

'I was not intending to kill him, though it is the fate he has earned,' rasped the farmer, obviously having difficulty keeping himself under control. 'I merely intend to separate him from his precious Escaigne.'

Further banging came from behind the Iron Door as, undeterred, the mob continued to call for the Council of Faltha to be given up to them. 'Talk to them,' Kurr growled in his old adversary's ear. 'Tell them to go home!'

The Presiding Elder replied by spitting in the old farmer's face.

Leith waited for the explosion, but it didn't come. Instead, Kurr calmly took a handkerchief from his pocket and wiped his face clean, then guided the Presiding Elder to a stone bench. 'Sit down, old friend,' he said in an eerie calm on the far side of anger. 'We have things to do. Later we will talk, you and I.' He signalled a couple of servants to watch over the slump-shouldered figure.

'In the meantime,' he said, 'we must escape this place. We

might be able to outwait the mob, but we have things to do, and we must do them swiftly.

'We seek suggestions,' he said more loudly, 'as to how we might leave this building undetected by those waiting outside.'

'Who are you?' asked one of the servants, not unreasonably, Leith thought.

'We are your new leaders,' Kurr replied brusquely. 'Leith, hold up the Jugom Ark. Surely you recognise this? We are the guardians of the Arrow, which arrived in our midst at just the right time. The Council of Faltha are turning control of the city of Instruere over to us for the time being. And now, before we do anything else, we will make the transfer of power official. Plonya? Leith!' And with that he called them all over to him and, under the light of the Jugom Ark, with the sound of the mob outside the door and with the Presiding Elder a reluctant witness, the remnants of the Council of Faltha surrendered their authority to the Company.

Minutes later an elderly servant approached Kurr and knelt before him. 'If it please you, my lord, I have a thought to offer. There is a door on the south side of the hall which leads—'

'Don't they have the building surrounded?' Plonya said irritably. 'Why is this man wasting our time?'

'I asked for ideas, and I will hear this man!' Kurr snapped. 'Learn to live without power!' The Arkhos of Plonya stepped back a pace, surprise on his face, then nodded shortly.

'The door is very close to The Pinion, lord,' the old man continued. 'No more than fifty paces. It may be that a swift runner could cross that space before those outside reacted to the attempt.'

'Then what?' Kurr asked him, not unkindly. 'How does that help us?'

'My lord, I am the one entrusted with notifying The Pinion of the changing of the guard, which I have done for fifty years, and my father did so for just as long before me. I have the key to a small side door which is used to gain access to the belltower.'

'The belltower?'

'Yes, lord. The bell rings out twice to signify the change. Surely you have heard it? Unless you live too far away to hear, of course. But there is also a peal known only to a few, which is used to summon the Guard in times of danger. That peal could be rung, and the Guard would rally to your command.'

'To his? Or to the Council of Faltha? Is there any authority here they would recognise?' The Arkhos of Plonya stood, his legs wide apart, arms folded, a broad smile on his face. 'Our ceremony was perhaps a little premature. The old Council is still needed.'

Kurr ignored the man. 'So you tell us we might be able to send one or two through this door and summon the Guard to disperse the crowd?'

'Yes, my lord,' the old man nodded, pleased.

'Who will go? Our brave friend, the Arkhos of Plonya, will obviously be one of those to try, as he points out. Maendraga, an illusion would serve us well here. They don't expect to see people come out of this door: can you make sure they see what they expect? We would also benefit from someone who can use a sword, but we seem to have left them back at the pavilion or sent them home to their kings.'

'Not all of them,' said Graig boldly. 'I will go, and keep the magician and the Arkhos safe.'

Kurr nodded. 'Very well, then. The three of you will bring help.'

All the way to the hidden door the Arkhos of Plonya whined and pleaded to be spared this honour, but no one would listen to him. The elderly servant produced a key, then bowed and withdrew, leaving the three of them to oil, then unbolt the door. Graig eased the door open a fraction: outside, a small knot of ordinary-looking people stood talking to each other, no doubt discussing what might be happening inside the hall.

'Go with the guidance of the Most High,' Kurr breathed, patting the young Nemohaimian on the shoulder. He swung the door wide open, and pulled it shut after them.

The Pinion bells rang out over the great City, three peals for an alarm. The Captain of the Guard jerked his head up at the sound, one he thought never to hear. The Arkhos of Nemohaim sat on a narrow chair, his huge bulk hanging off the seat on both sides, his arms tied behind him to the chair's tall back. His face was raised, jaw thrust forward, and set with a stern look: he had been trying to persuade his former liegeman to let him go. But with the sound of the bells his arguments were forgotten. The Captain of the Guard brusquely checked the Arkhos's bonds, then hurried from the small room, leaving Nemohaim in the care of two guards. A moment later he emerged from Nemohaim's prison, a nondescript tenement a local family had loaned to the Company for the purpose, a few hundred strides from the pavilion. He ran swiftly to the Struere Gate and his guardsmen.

'Attention! Form up ranks!' he barked. Soldiers scattered right and left, rushing to lay hands on swords and shields, regretting their heavy armour was stored in The Pinion; but, within minutes, the Captain of the Guard had over a thousand fighting men ready to do his will.

The flurry of activity had not gone unobserved by those of the Company who remained near the pavilion. Mahnum woke the Haufuth, who had indulged in an all-too-rare early afternoon nap. Together they left the pavilion and went in search of the Captain of the Guard, but could find neither him nor the Arkhos of Nemohaim in the small back room being used as a cell. 'The captain must've taken Nemohaim with him,' the Haufuth commented, still rubbing sleep from his eyes; being woken before his time always left him with a headache, but he supposed he could see the sense in Mahnum alerting him to this, whatever it was. 'Sensible,' the Trader muttered. 'Just wish he'd told us. I'm not sure I trust that man with the Arkhos.'

They met up with Indrett and the Escaignian woman back at the pavilion. The two women were dispensing the last of the food and drink donated by various benefactors on the day the Granaries burned: some had already been thrown out, as it had spoiled. There seemed a never-ending supply of people in need – though, as Mahnum wryly pointed out, a large proportion of them would have lined up even if there had been no fire. Old Struere had not done well recently under the Council's hand.

'Did you hear the bells?' the Haufuth wanted to know.

'We thought they were telling midday,' said Indrett.

'Perhaps. But the Captain of the Guard has lined up the Instruian Guard. It may be something more serious. I've never heard the bells toll at noon like that, have you?' The big man turned to Mahnum, who shook his head.

The three Firanese and one Instruian made their way to the Struere Gate, which still lay unattended and in ruins.

Ranks of the Instruian Guard filled the large open space in front of the gate. The captain shouted orders to his guardsmen, preparing them to march.

'What was the bell?' Mahnum asked, a little more harshly than he intended.

'The alarm,' the captain replied tersely.

'What does it mean?'

'A general emergency. It means the Council of Faltha is threatened in some way. When the bell peals three times, make your way to The Pinion and await orders.' He sounded as though he quoted from some service manual.

'But – there is no Council of Faltha. What if it's some ruse?'

'By whom?' the Haufuth asked Mahnum. 'Deorc is gone, the Council has surrendered and the Arkhos of Nemohaim is here under the control of the Captain of the Guard.'

The captain turned on his heels to face the big man. 'No, not here – the Arkhos remains in his cell, guarded by two of my most trusted men.'

The Trader shook his head slowly, his mouth open. 'No, no. The Arkhos, he is not there.'

'He has escaped, then.' The Captain of the Guard spoke in a flat voice.

Mahnum and Indrett both sighed deeply. 'It seems so. Instruere is in trouble.'

'Nonetheless, the law requires the Instruian Guard to gather at The Pinion when the alarm bell rings. If we delay, it is as though we have disobeyed the law. We must restore the confidence of the Guard, not undermine it further. Do I have your permission to obey the summons?'

'Yes, but we will come with you,' Mahnum said, speaking for them all.

* * *

The delay was no more than fifteen minutes, but it proved costly. By the time the Captain of the Guard marched his men up the Vitulian Way to The Pinion, the Arkhos of Nemohaim had ordered everything as he desired, short of having more soldiers. He could not have wished for a better circumstance than the alarm bell, following so soon after discovering his mortal enemy had been destroyed. He knew what the alarm meant, was quick to grasp the opportunity it afforded. While the Captain of the Guard had a strong, disciplined mind and was not open to his word tricks, the two guardsmen were another matter. After the captain left, it had been the work of moments to gain control of one man's mind and get him to cut the throat of the other, then dump the body in a sewer. Five minutes later the Arkhos was free and laughing at the foolishness of adversaries who never considered the long view. *Patience*, he told himself, *is the only virtue worth cultivating.*

The Arkhos of Nemohaim could move very quickly when he chose. He'd proved it to the peasant fools when he climbed the scree slope and managed the rope across the waterfall. They'd not expected that! They wouldn't expect him to *run* to The Pinion either, but he did. He had been an athlete in his younger days and, though now dissolute, could draw on hidden reserves when required, as long as he was prepared to pay the price later.

'Ho, the Guard!' he cried in his loudest voice when he strode up to The Pinion, hardly out of breath. Five hundred elite guardsmen thundered: 'Ho, the Arkhos!' in reply. Five hundred throats crying his praise, when he thought never to hear it again. It brought a tear to his eye.

'The Council has been betrayed!' he cried. 'Deorc the infiltrator is dead, and a few fearful Council members have surrendered the keys to the Four Halls to a handful of northern peasants. This must not be allowed!'

'But what of the Jugom Ark?' came a voice from the rear of the serried ranks.

'Coat an arrow with pitch, set fire to it and you have an instant heirloom,' the Arkhos snapped. It didn't matter so much what he said, he'd learned many years ago, but rather how he said it. Soldiers looked for confidence in their leaders.

'How could you hold such an arrow without getting burned?' the same voice asked.

'That is your last anonymous question!' There was so little time; he could not afford to waste it in pointless debate, but this did give him a chance to re-establish his rulership. 'If we knew how it was done, we could expose it as a fraud. If it was widely known, we would have a hundred Jugom Arks discovered every year. Now! The alarm has sounded, and we have a City to defend. Are you with me?' The response was deafening.

Leith called to Kurr and the others in a voice filled with urgency. They had been inspecting the pile of swords, sorting out the best of them for use. *Me, a swordmaster*, Leith laughed at himself. His own sword sat snugly on his hip as though it belonged, reminding him of their adventures and the men he had killed; the nameless Windrisian and the Bhrudwan Lord of Fear. Then a different kind of noise from outside attracted his attention. He went to the window and his eye was immediately drawn to the obese, eminently recognisable figure standing in front of The Pinion, barking orders to ranks of guardsmen. Leith gasped with shock.

'Where are the others?' he asked urgently. 'Why is the Arkhos on his own?'

Kurr ground his teeth in frustration and pointed to the right, where another force could be seen marching up the Vitulian Way. 'Because he has escaped, somehow. Look! The Captain of the Guard comes, leading those of the Guard who surrendered to us. What has happened? Why has the Arkhos of Plonya not taken control of the guardsmen? There may have been some double-dealing here.'

'I don't see how,' Leith replied. 'Graig wouldn't allow it.'

The old farmer laughed shortly. 'Neither he would, boy; neither he would. Worships the ground you walk on, that one.'

'I don't want to be worshipped by anyone,' Leith growled. He only had a moment to wonder: did Graig hear Leith's voice in his head?

With the arrival of the Captain of the Guard the situation became irretrievably confused. Leith and the others were pinned in the Hall of Meeting, surrounded by Escaigne and the Ecclesia, the former of whom were still in the throes of finding out they were leaderless. These two groups, numbering perhaps three thousand in total, were in turn surrounded by the Instruian Guard, less than half their number and together for the first time since the Battle of the Hall of Lore. Yet not together, as the Arkhos of Nemohaim began to issue instructions to the five hundred soldiers under his control, commanding them to engage with their fellows. Fighting began to erupt on a front about fifty paces wide, guard against reluctant guard.

The Captain of the Guard, however, sent orders to his men to disengage, forming them instead into a narrow wedge and throwing them against those of Escaigne and Ecclesia between his force and the Hall of Meeting. A few moments' furious thought had led to only one conclusion: his task must be to take possession of the hall. The guardsmen who issued from The Pinion had obviously not caused the alarm to be sounded. Instead, they had responded to the alarm, and had been suborned by the opportunistic Arkhos of Nemohaim. Therefore the alarm must have been sounded in response to the threat posed by those surrounding the Hall of Meeting, where the former Council had gone with the northerners. For the sake of order, for the sake of the City, for the sake of Faltha, the boy with the Arrow must be protected.

The captain, an experienced campaigner, set a rearguard, a convex semicircle of swordsmen and pikemen arrayed against whatever the Arkhos decided to throw at them. It would not hold for long, he knew; perhaps only minutes. Forward he threw his remaining men with a roar, and set as a wedge they smashed into the nearest of their foes, who happened to be Escaigne – and who now knew they had lost their leader inside the hall.

For the Escaignians the next few minutes were filled with confusion and fear. Three of the remaining elders came up with different battle plans. Two of them ended up screaming at each other in the middle of the battlefield, while all around them their friends, sons of the men they had grown up with, were dying on the ends of swords. In a matter of seconds ten, twenty, fifty or more fell like autumn leaves in a storm. Where was the Presiding Elder? Why was this so different to the years of careful planning? How could it all collapse so quickly?

The Ecclesia fared even worse. For all his vision, the Hermit realised he had relied heavily on the Presiding Elder to organise and execute the battle tactics, and the man had disappeared on an ill-advised foray into the hall. Crushed by the Iron Door, some said; captured by the northerners, said others. The plan of attack had been to take the Four Halls before anyone realised what was happening, but they had not bargained on the northerners getting there ahead of them. The Presiding Elder had tried to draw them out: the burning of the Arkhos raised a twinge of guilt in the Hermit's breast, but he consoled himself with the thought that sometimes the sacrifice of one man was necessary to save the lives of many others. So it would have been, if the northerners had only given themselves up.

But they did not, and he was left in charge of a confused and divided force suddenly trapped between the hall and the Instruian Guard. On came the Guard, forcing a passage directly towards him. He stood surrounded by a troop of the Ecclesia's supposedly best fighters, who began to melt away in front of him. The roar of battle resolved itself into shouts, curses and screams, death cries uttered by people he had met, spoken with, eaten with, laughed with. Who now died before him. The guards were stern of face, laying about themselves with swift, economical strokes of their blades. One of them looked straight at him, surely the face of evil, less than ten paces away and closing; and suddenly the blue-robed Hermit remembered he was unarmed and unable to defend himself. From somewhere to his left he heard a hissing noise, and at the same instant felt a sharp pain in his left arm. He was knocked to the ground. An arrow stuck out from the fleshy part of his forearm. The pain increased tenfold and he let out a howl. The shocking intrusion of sharp reality on his world of vision and prophecy was more than he could bear. He hitched up his robe and ran, ignoring the shouts of the followers he left to die on the field of battle.

The thing that turned Leith, watching all this helplessly from above, was the smell. Since he was very young he had played at soldiers with his friends, usually on the receiving end, but always with his dreams of glory. Cutting a swathe through the foemen, defeating the enemy champion, people shouting his name. But he had never imagined the dreadful odour of battle. Bodies should not smell like that, but they did. Broken, bleeding, leaking; moaning, screaming, dying, all the while giving off a reek that turned his stomach.

There is no glory in this.

He turned from the window without a word and strode down the long, winding passage to the small side door, opening it over the protestations of Kurr and the others who could do nothing to stop him. It was as though he did not hear them, did not see them, did not acknowledge their existence. Out into the sunlight he walked, out into the field of battle, out into the stench, out into the shouting and the screaming and the sobbing; and the Jugom Ark flamed until all eyes were filled with the brightness of it. Those there on the field that day, those that lived, told of a ghostly figure filled with light marching across the battlefield, as though the Gatherer had come to collect the souls of the dead for their journey to the afterlife. Past fleeing members of the Ecclesia he strode. They turned and beheld the Fire of God on the field of battle, and some remembered the first time they had seen it.

There were arrows on the battleground now, loosed by archers set by the Arkhos of Nemohaim against the superior forces of his former captain. Fighting men in light armour, such as those summoned in haste, could do little to defend themselves against such tactics, and the soldiers of the Captain of the Guard began to die. A hail of arrows overshot their mark and landed amongst the Ecclesia, felling at least three unlucky men. Eyes turned to this threat from the sky. Fighters from all sides watched an arrow, shot with fatal aim, sail straight at the shining figure holding the Jugom Ark, and saw it consumed by the fire without touching him, the fletch reduced to ash blown away by the breeze, the red-hot point falling harmlessly to the ground. One man scooped it up with his cloak, a holy relic to his awestruck eyes.

Through the battlefield Leith came, shining like an angel of vengeance, stepping over the slain, with no regard for the swords and spears flashing around him, until he found a slight rise; then stood there, feet wide apart, braced as though leaning into an invisible storm, and cried 'Halt!' in a loud voice, one that penetrated into the heart of battle. Throwing his arms wide, he cried again: 'HALT!'

All around him the battlefield fell silent.

Save one voice only. The Arkhos of Nemohaim knew this was his last chance, and so urged his men onwards. They were so close to breaking through the screen thrown against them! But his soldiers, superstitious Instruian fools to a man, no longer listened to him. There on a low hill in the middle of the battle stood the hated, hated boy with his Arrow. *His* Arrow! The Jugom Ark, the heirloom of Nemohaim, rightfully the property of the descendants of Bewray. Rightfully his!

With a cry of anguish and frustration, the Arkhos of Nemohaim fled the battle.

CHAPTER 8

LORD OF INSTRUERE

NEWS OF THE COUNCIL of Faltha being deposed swept through Instruere faster than the Granary fires. Even as the battle was being fought a crowd gathered, and there were hundreds of witnesses willing to swear they beheld the Jugom Ark appear from nowhere to bring the battle to a sudden, miraculous end. The story of the hail of arrows sent to strike down the Arrow-bearer, but instead being consumed by fire, spread quickly amongst the crowd. Rumours added to stories, visions grafted to dreams; the Ecclesia emphasised the supernatural, Escaigne spoke of the heroic; all the citizens soon heard of the Jugom Ark, the Heirloom of the Ages, and came to see its glory.

Thus the whole City attended the Acclamation of the new Lords of Instruere, two weeks after the Battle of the Four Halls. The wide open space in front of the Hall of Meeting, which a fortnight before was the scene of slaughter, now held a hundred thousand cheering citizens decked out in bright colours, full of noise and exuberance, eager to acknowledge their new leaders. It mattered not at all to the crowd that these new leaders were self-appointed and not delegates from the far-flung Sixteen Kingdoms; they cheered just the same. More, in fact, and louder. The old Council had been hated for at least a generation. With high taxes that crippled trade and business expansion (according to the traders and businessmen, at least), with the gradual decay of basic services such as roads and the maintenance of the sewers, with the curfews and the beatings, with the evil reputation of The Pinion growing worse each year, and with the active persecution of the Watchers to the point where they were driven underground to become Escaigne, opposition to the Council of Faltha had fermented for at least a decade. Given the ruthless methods the Council employed to suppress any opposition, such sentiment, though widespread, was muted, spoken behind closed doors and to trusted friends only. For many long-time residents of Instruere, the great City had gradually become a grey and dangerous place.

For all of these reasons the Acclamation took place in a festive atmosphere, like that of a gala or feast-day. People abandoned their sickbeds to catch a glimpse of the northern lords and ladies who had come to save Instruere from the Council. The elderly were carried on pallets, children held tight to their parents' hands, babies on their mother's backs, the injured in the Battle of the Four Halls accorded a special place at the forefront of the enormous crowd. Impromptu markets sprang up at the four corners of the square, though all but the flower sellers and purveyors of authentic relics – arrowheads and the like – did a desultory trade, as they found it difficult to interest people in anything other than the Flaming Arrow. Hawkers moved hopefully through the crowd, supplying food and drink to those who had neglected to bring enough. And inside the hall itself stood a hastily-erected stage where city officials and business leaders sat nervously, along with a thousand invited guests, waiting for the ceremony to begin.

Leith, too, waited nervously, looking down on the staggering crowd from the annexe above the Hall of Meeting. Too much could still go wrong, even at this late stage. The last fortnight had been a blurred succession of events with little time to relax, and not everything had gone well. He remembered the evening, six days ago now, when the King of Straux himself held an acrimonious meeting with the Company. The king was angry at being forced to come from his seat in Mercium to attend on them like a supplicant seeking their favour; which, Leith supposed, is exactly what he was. He protested his undying loyalty to Faltha, and asked his advisers, against the Company's advice, to attempt to authenticate the Jugom Ark. That resulted in a number of burned hands which Leith healed – *the Jugom Ark healed*, he reminded himself – somewhat reluctantly. The King of Straux hurriedly declared himself satisfied, pledged his cooperation if not his allegiance to the Company, promised ten thousand men for the army Leith was raising, and submitted a list of names for their consideration, one of which was to be chosen for the new Council of Faltha. *Why were kings so pig-headed?* Leith wondered.

'I don't trust the man,' the Haufuth had said.

'And well you might not,' Mahnum agreed. 'He was prominent on the Destroyer's list of traitorous kings. I told you so before he came to visit. Nothing he said convinced me otherwise.'

'But he has repented,' said Hal quietly. 'How long can we refuse forgiveness to those who ask for it?'

His brother's comment had outraged Leith. The King of Straux was a vain and proud man, with all the airs and graces of an aristocrat, and made them all feel like peasants. Leith ignored the small voice that reminded him the description was accurate. The king had not apologised, had not admitted his betrayal of Faltha, and had not shown a shred of humility. How could Hal then call the man repentant?

This was so typical of Hal, and it angered Leith. He exercised a naive type of goodness; one which professed to see the best in everyone, and was prepared to believe that anyone could change their ways after having their errors explained to them. He'd behaved that way with the Arkhos of Nemohaim and now with the King of Straux, men obviously steeped in evil. He'd done the same with Achtal, in the days before the Bhrudwan had proved himself. Who next? Was he willing to make an alliance even with the Destroyer?

Or perhaps he wasn't naive. Perhaps he was so self-righteous he needed to parade his goodness in front of everyone, at every available opportunity, whatever the cost. A kind of cynical behaviour not concerned with anything other than the recognition of its own goodness. Not caring about the effect too much trust might have on anyone else when people took advantage of it. Encouraging people to think positive thoughts even when the armies prowled around outside the gates. Admitting no guilt even when he was shown that his actions had led to those armies—

'It's time, boy,' said a gruff voice, and a gnarled hand clamped on to his shoulder, spinning him around and out of his train of thought. 'They're waiting.'

Leith drew a deep breath and adjusted his robes. He'd wanted to wear his old clothes, the ones given to them by Kroptur for the journey along the Westway, but they were too warm for the late autumn sun this far south. Anyway, his mother insisted on him wearing this finery.

He walked reluctantly across the stone floor of the annexe, through the door and down the stairs to the Outer Chamber. His long purple robe flared out behind, and his shiny black boots clacked unnervingly on the stairs, drawing the thousand or more pairs of eyes directly to him. Or, in truth, not to him; rather, to the Arrow that flickered in his right hand. He brushed his grey waistcoat and fingered his neck, where a ridiculously large ruff scratched against his skin. He imagined missing a step, falling forwards and landing in a heap at the bottom of the stairs.

The Company and their retainers, most of them servants of the former Council of Faltha, followed him across the marble floor of the huge hall. It made sense to use the servants, Hal had argued. While not all may be innocent, they knew much more than anyone else about the running of the City, of the protocols, of the taxation system, of how to deal with the merchants, the lords and the kings whom the new Council would have to deal with. Innocence or guilt could be determined later, when they all had more time, and the guilty could be offered a second chance.

Hal and his second chances!

Leith stumbled, tripping on the hem of his robe, and for an awful second thought he was going to fall. He recovered his balance without anyone noticing. *Well, they probably all noticed,* Leith admitted to himself, but no one said anything. *As if they would! I've got this great big Arrow of Fire to curse them with!*

Clack, clack, clack. No one else in the party wore big heavy boots. They all followed him silently. Oh yes, this had been carefully planned to focus everyone's attention on him. *And it is working,* he noted as he carefully climbed the steps to the wooden dais, nodding as instructed to the luminaries seated to his right and his left. He halted at the correct place, and saw that someone had painted the outline of a pair of boots in the place he was supposed to stand, so he deliberately stood just to the left of the outline. This meant those following had to squeeze past to get to their seats, but he was angry now and didn't care. Finally everyone found their seats. He deliberately waited a few seconds longer than he'd been told – a sidewards glance showed Kurr looking at him with daggers in his eyes – then finally sat in the one remaining seat.

The ceremony began, but Leith was too angry to take any of it in. *I'm a child*, he thought to himself. *Wear this, wear that, stand here, sit there, do this, do that, carry this arrow, save Faltha. They treat me like a child.* Lead us, lead us, they said, then, when he made the decision on his own to get the Arkhos of Nemohaim to swear to him, and again when he met with the remnant of the Council of Faltha, everyone had criticised him. They went back to making decisions without even asking him. *This will be just the same.* Lead us, lead us, the crowd was saying. He could see it in their eyes. *Look at them out there, staring at the Jugom Ark! But as soon as I tell them what to do, they'll find reasons to ignore me and do exactly as they please. So what's the point?*

'Leith! Leith!' His mother's voice woke him from the depths of his thoughts, and as his attention returned to the moment he noticed the loud murmur of conversation in the hall. He turned in his seat to find that everyone had been forced to move back, away from him, leaving a wide space around where he sat. He glanced down and saw the Arrow blazing like the sun in his hand. The floor below was scorched, and threatened to burst into flame at any moment.

Warily, the Arkhos of Plonya came as close as he dared,

then turned to face the nervous gathering. 'As I was saying, the power of the Jugom Ark cannot be denied. Behold it burning in answer to our need! The former Council of Faltha acknowledges the claim of Leith Mahnumsen and his Company of followers to the leadership of Instruere, and to all of Faltha, in these troubled times. I have spoken to you of treachery, and explained the way in which the Council of Faltha itself was suborned to the will of the Destroyer. I have told you the tale of how the Jugom Ark arrived in our midst. I have faithfully reported how close we of Faltha stand to the brink of ruin. Your own eyes confirm how dire is the predicament we face, for the Jugom Ark would not have returned after two thousand years unless our need was truly great.

'So let us stand now, all united in the presence of each other and of the Jugom Ark itself, as Leith Mahnumsen assumes the Mantle of leadership.' He turned to the northern youth, whose normally pleasant demeanour had for some reason been transformed into something menacing, and said: 'Leith Mahnumsen, will you lead us?'

If the crowd thought the Jugom Ark bright before, it was nothing to the way in which it erupted into flame at these words. With a roar the fire billowed outwards and upwards, and the representatives of the City fell over each other to get off the stage. Leith rose to his feet: fire was in his hand, and all behind him was shadow. He strode forward as though stamping Faltha's enemies under his feet, seemingly unaware he was mantled in flame.

'I will lead you,' he said, each word a flame that roared and shook the hall, so that dust and small fragments of plaster fell from the ceiling.

'And now I place the Mantle on your shoulders,' said the

Arkhos of Plonya bravely. 'Er – ah . . .' He stepped forward, the blood-red garment under his arm, but could obviously get no closer than three paces without being consumed.

'Put it down,' Leith said, and somewhere at the back of the hall a suit of armour collapsed in a crash of dust and rusted metal.

'But I have to – but the ceremony demands . . . yes, lord,' said the Arkhos, placing the Mantle on the wooden floor and stepping hurriedly back to the extreme edge of the platform.

Leith stood erect, and somehow – no one could say how, whether because of some enchantment or because the Arrow in his hand was simply too bright for mortal eye to penetrate – the Mantle lay draped across his shoulders.

'I will lead you,' he repeated, and a chair fell from the dais with a clatter. A few people, their nerves stretched beyond endurance, ran from the hall.

'I will lead you,' he said for a third time. 'Not because I want to, but because I must. I have no choice in the matter! Our task may be hopeless, and many of you here today will die before it is over. I expect to die. One of my best friends is already dead! Dead!' The hall shook again, and a large chunk of plaster crashed down from above, narrowly missing a section of the crowd.

Visibly taking hold of himself, the fire-cloaked Arrow-bearer continued. 'Like me, in these terrible days to come you will not be able to do what you want. I will take your sons and your daughters from you and feed them to the cruel god of war. I will increase your taxes to pay for our defences. I will try to be fair, I will favour no one, and my own family will be at the forefront of the battle. But I will have little patience with those who oppose me. Disagree with me if you must. Tell me to my face that you don't approve of what I am doing. But don't work against me, I beg of you. My task is to save you, not to destroy you. I do not want to be a destroyer.'

Leith stepped back from the front of the stage, and as he did so the Arrow in his hand dimmed, the flame drawing back until it did little more than flicker in his hand. The next part of the ceremony, as it had been explained to him at least, was for the rest of the Company to come forward and receive the keys of office, confirming them as the interim Council until such time as a proper Council could be chosen. But no one moved. A thousand people sat motionless, stunned into silence by the raw power of command in the voice they had just heard.

Finally an old man in the front row of seats rose to his feet, bowed in the direction of the platform – *he's bowing to me*, Leith realised with a shock – then turned and made his way down the aisle and out of the hall. Another followed suit, then a woman stood and curtsied to him. Within a few moments the whole hall rose to its feet and did obeisance to him, then filed out quietly, without any of the usual chatter.

When the Outer Chamber finally emptied of all save the Company and their servants, the Haufuth climbed on to the dais and strode over to Leith.

'What on earth was that all about, son? That certainly wasn't what we agreed upon. All that threatening talk! We want to encourage them to follow us, not frighten them into it! How was your performance different to that of Deorc's? And we were not confirmed as a Council. We'll have to arrange another ceremony!'

By this time Kurr stood beside the village headman. 'I hardly think that matters, old friend. Do you really think, after what they've just seen, that anyone will take any notice at all of the Council? By the Fire, boy, the Most High Himself could hardly have been more impressive. I would have done anything you commanded me in that moment.'

'That – that wasn't me. That wasn't me!' Leith said awkwardly, not looking his companions in the eye. 'I know that wasn't what I was supposed to say. I don't know what happened!'

'Don't give us any nonsense about the Arrow taking over your mind,' the Haufuth growled. 'It's an arrow that keeps burning, nothing more.' But he looked askance at Leith's right hand as he said it, then glanced at his own, undoing the intent of his words.

'Whoever it was, whatever happened, I don't think any harm was done.' Phemanderac smiled down at him. 'No one should expect you to be able to control it. It took years of training for the First Men to learn how to control the Fire of Life set within them, and this is the same, it seems to me. But you do need to learn about the Fire, Leith. You need to learn about the *Fuirfad*, the Way of Fire. I can teach you. It's why I'm here, I'm sure of it.'

'No harm done? No harm?' Mahnum looked angry. 'How much harder is it going to be to get cooperation from the people of Instruere now we've threatened them with the Arrow?'

'Easier, I would have thought,' Kurr shot back. 'Anyway, I'm not sure Leith threatened anyone. All I recall him saying was that we all have to make sacrifices in the days to come. Is there anyone here who does not agree with that? No, I didn't think so. It's just that he said it very forcefully.' The old farmer glanced down at Leith's right hand. Leith held up the Arrow in response to the old man's unspoken request.

'What kind of weapon is that thing?' he wondered aloud. 'What can it do? What about it do we not yet know?'

He looked Leith in the eye. 'The most important thing you can do in the next few weeks, boy, is to sit and listen to Phemanderac here. You might just have the weapon to save Faltha right there in your hands.'

The Company walked through the Corridor of Appellants as a group. Kurr pushed open the tall wooden door and they emerged into the sunlight – to an enormous cheer beginning at the front of the vast crowd, then swelling even further as people some distance back realised the new Council of Faltha had arrived. Phemanderac waved cheerily, occasioning a renewed roar, and the other members of the Company – the Council, they reminded themselves – followed suit. The crowd made way for them as they walked slowly across the churned-up lawn, quieting down only when they stopped for a moment by an impromptu monument to those who had fallen in the battles of the last three weeks. Looking behind him as they renewed their slow march back to their lodgings, Leith saw the people closing up behind them, eager to get a glimpse, a touch, a word. *The whole thing is crazy*, he thought. *A month ago none of them would have given us a second glance.*

Day after day of weariness had stretched Leith far beyond anything he had known before. Even the days in the Vale of Neume, the struggles in the Joram Basin when the Sentinels came to life, had not been like this. There he had needed to deal with only one thing at a time, and in most cases his path had been clear. Here there were so many people to see, advisers to listen to and things to read, with a multitude of choices to be made for each. But finally the bulk of their quest was over; they had turned the focus of Instruere, and much of Faltha, towards the Bhrudwan threat. Leith longed for an afternoon's rest, and decided that one last afternoon at their lodgings, where he could spend some time thinking – sleeping, more likely – was something he desperately needed.

At that moment a guardsman burst through the crowd and threw himself down at their feet, gasping for air as though he'd just run to save his life.

'There's an – an army, a great army outside the gates – coming across Longbridge! Strange men from far away, horses and terrible beasts! We must summon the guards!' The man knelt on the grass, trying to recover.

'Ring the alarm!' cried the Captain of the Guard. Instantly two men sprang forward, and set off at a dead run towards The Pinion, a few hundred yards away. The crowd scattered, but not quickly enough to prevent one or two being knocked off their feet.

An army outside the gate. The thought seemed to hover somewhere outside Leith's mind, as though unable to find a way in. The only thought that went through his head was: *after all this, we are too late*.

The captain dispatched a company of guardsmen to check the Struere Gate, and they ran off down the Vitulian Way, knowing they might discover their own deaths there. Others were sent to prepare horses, though it may already be too late to organise a sortie or to cast down Longbridge. Nevertheless, the captain set as many plans running as he could think of. With a frown he glanced across at The Pinion: the alarm ought to have been sounded by now.

The journey east from Instruere, the journey south to Kantara. Leith recounted the deaths in his mind: Wira,

Parlevaag, Illyon, Stella. All to no purpose. *There's an army outside the gate, and we're trapped here.*

Now the crowd, alerted that something was wrong, scattered in every direction. Leith had no idea what they knew, and spared no thought for their fate, so paralysed had he become by the news. Someone – Phemanderac – grabbed his arm and pulled him along the street to the north, towards the Inna Gate. He couldn't hear what the tall philosopher said to him: everyone was shouting, and there was a roaring in his ears. He had enough strength left to curse the voice that had led them to this place, then sat on the cobbled street and rested his weary head in his hands.

'Leith!' It was his mother's voice, but it was muffled, as though she was wrapped in blankets. 'It's all right. Everything's all right!'

His eyes snapped open. Immediately to his right stood the Inna Gate, firmly closed and bolted. The members of the Company were ranged around him, some of them with concerned looks on their faces.

Embarrassed, he sat up. 'What happened?'

'Come with me, Leith,' said Phemanderac in a tender voice. 'There's something you should see.'

The youth struggled to his feet, trying to make his rubbery legs work, and followed his tall friend with difficulty as he strode to the nearest stair and climbed to the top of the wall. Leith shook his head to clear the fuzziness, and looked out over the Great River Aleinus to the plains of Deuverre.

There, indeed, spread out on the far side of the river, stood a large army. But what attracted his attention lay directly below him: four small figures, jumping up and down and calling his name, two of them with their arms around the shoulders of a seemingly drunk Farr Storrsen. Beside Leith, Phemanderac laughed out loud in sheer delight, pointing out the young man's shocked face to the others of the Company now joining them on the wall.

'Wha – what?' Leith got out.

'The *losian* Army of the North!' announced the Dhaurian Philosopher in ringing tones. Leith looked more closely, and saw the aurochs, the furs, the multitude of colours that spoke of Fodhram, Fenni and Widuz, and knew he beheld a miracle. Phemanderac drew close, and said in a much quieter aside: 'Though that's not what they call themselves. Arrived just in time to join our march eastwards. And what's most magical of all, they were led here by our *losian*-hater!' He laughed again, a carefree sound.

And as the Company rushed through the reluctantly-opened gate and embraced their old friends from the Woods of Withwestwa, then joined with them in dancing and singing – to the surprise and bemusement of the Instruians who watched from the walls – it seemed as though the tide had indeed turned in their favour, and the defeat of the Destroyer would be only a matter of time.

The celebrations had barely begun when a worried Captain of the Guard called Leith over to him. 'I don't wish to alarm the others,' he said quietly, 'but perhaps you would come with me. Something unpleasant has happened in The Pinion.'

After some thought, Leith gathered Kurr and the Haufuth (the latter reluctant, having spied a haunch of roast beef being passed around) and followed his captain back into the City. It was a brisk half-hour walk to The Pinion, but a horse was found for Leith as he still felt somewhat weak.

As they approached the low, long building, Leith saw

groups of guardsmen standing silently, nervously eyeing him and his Arrow, as though waiting to find out how their new rulers would react to what they would see.

'It appears someone has taken advantage of your investiture ceremony to attack The Pinion,' said the Captain of the Guard. 'See here how the sewer has been diverted. Whoever did this got the drain to flow into The Pinion – see here – and down into the dungeon below.' He paused beside the trapdoor. 'You might want to put these on,' he said, indicating a guard standing nearby who held a number of rags. The captain took one and wound it around his mouth and nose; the three northerners copied him and, when they were ready, the guard opened the trapdoor.

The stench was beyond belief. A dreadful cloud of ammonia rose out of the pit, burning Leith in the back of the throat and bringing tears to his eyes. A glance down into the awful depths revealed where the sewer water had ended up, and Leith clamped his eyes closed so he didn't have to see what was down there.

'I recall we imprisoned the traitorous Arkhoi in the dungeons,' drawled the Arkhos of Plonya, coming into the room. 'I imagine their last few moments were extremely unpleasant.' The Plonyan seemed to be trying not to smile.

'How many prisoners were in The Pinion?' Leith asked, appalled.

'We're not sure,' came the captain's reply. 'I did ask, and sent someone off to the Hall of Meeting to check the records. The cells can hold up to two hundred people, it is said.'

'Murder,' Leith breathed. 'Cruel murder! As much as the three Arkhoi might have deserved death, many others down there did not.' Pointedly, he turned to the Arkhos of Plonya, who traded stares with him.

'My lord, this act has the finger of Nemohaim all over it,' the Captain of the Guard said in his ear. 'He will want revenge on the Arkhoi who were content to see him driven from Instruere. All of them,' he emphasised, turning to look at the Plonyan, who now wore a worried look on his face. 'He'll have some sort of plan,' the captain continued, speaking with deliberation. 'But before he enacts it, he will want to take care of all the perceived insults and injuries he has received. I would not sleep very well if I was on the Council of Faltha when Deorc supplanted him.'

'I want the Arkhos of Nemohaim found,' said Leith, a deep and grinding anger working away inside him. 'I want him found before we depart for the Gap. I don't want to leave any enemies in the City when we leave. I want him found before anyone else dies. By the fire I hold in my hand, I want him found!'

'Yes, my lord,' the captain said.

'But before I do anything, there is someone I need to talk to. I've put this off for far too long.' Kurr and the Haufuth looked at each other with puzzled expressions on their faces, but they could do little else than follow their young leader as he set out once more for the Inna Gate.

At least Stella wasn't down there, Leith told himself as he strode northwards along the Vitulian Way, completely ignoring the horse offered to him. *At least I had the good sense to check on The Pinion last week. Wherever she is, whatever happened to her, she didn't die in that dreadful dungeon.*

Stella blinked and looked around her. She had just emerged from the mouth of a deep, stone-lined cavern out into watery sunshine. Perhaps there would be something lying around that might help her, someone nearby she might be able to call on . . . but she could see nothing of use. In front of her stretched a wide, snow-streaked plain, devoid of grass or other vegetation, a dark smudge in the centre. In the distance low hills bulwarked the steel-grey sky. Behind her, prodding her forward, came the searing presence of the Undying Man. *He's bringing me up here to make my death more painful,* she thought. *Death in the dark I was prepared for, but not out here in the light!*

She was pushed forward by nothing but his irresistible will, still blinking against the harshness of the sun. Something was different about the light. It hurt her head. Was there a problem with her head, she wondered. With the rough treatment she'd received, this seemed likely.

Slowly the dark smudge on the plain came into focus, and her heart sank. An army. She knew what it was for and where it was headed.

The Destroyer led her to a rocky platform, from where he could look down on his army and their last, their very last drill before they marched forth. There were many thousands assembled on the plain before them, before just the two of them, so it seemed.

'Raise my arm,' he commanded her, and she obeyed without thinking, shuddering at the touch. As his arm was raised his army gave a great shout, then began to manoeuvre. Left and right they marched, splitting apart and re-forming with a frightening precision, their war cries echoing across the plain.

All that day the army paraded for their master. Stella held up the arm of the black-robed man until she could bear it no longer, and slumped to the cold stone, hands on her aching head. Yet she was not allowed to rest. His power compelled her to her feet, and she did not have the strength to resist as he forced her to raise his arm again. In an agony of exhaustion, she found strength to do his bidding. She dared not think where it came from, what it was doing to her. Deorc had told her in detail how the Destroyer gained the strength to do his magic.

As the sun set and the deep cold of this far northern clime began to bite, the Destroyer finally allowed her to lower his hand. He laughed at her extremity as she grovelled on the ground, then yanked her to her feet with his one hand. 'Behold my handmaiden!' he cried, and Stella felt the gaze of the great Army of Bhrudwo turn to her. 'Behold my future bride!'

Fifty thousand throats cried 'Hail!' and the woman from Loulea swooned into unconsciousness.

Farr was indeed drunk, the first time in his life, so he claimed. A fortnight of celebration with the Fodhram had been enough to overcome his reserve, and now he was sharing the forest-dwellers' deep mugs of ale. Gaily he greeted his friends from the Company, a broad smile never far from his face, all anger seemingly forgotten.

Time and again he told the Company how he found the *losian* army on the road north of Deuverre, his tongue tripping over lyrical descriptions of the singing and the moonlight on the open fields of the Borderlands. He talked of his friends the Fodhram, and of new friends he had found among the Fenni and the Widuz. He made his own part in their arrival sound comical, as though they had rescued him from being lost, and the four Fodhram laughed with him every time he told it.

'I have a few questions for you,' Perdu began, but Farr wasn't listening. 'How is it that enemies match together as friends?' Perdu persisted, to no effect. 'How can Widuz and

Fodhram sleep back to back?' His cousin just laughed at him and offered him his mug. 'Aaah!' Perdu exclaimed after a few minutes of this. 'I need to speak to my clan chief. Is he here?'

'He is beyond the river with the other leaders, waiting for an invitation into the city,' said a woman's voice from just behind him, the sweet voice speaking a language he had not heard for months. 'Will you speak to me instead?'

'Haldemar!' the adopted Fenni cried, spinning around to catch his wife in an embrace. 'You're here! And the boys . . .'

'Safe at home on the vidda, where they should be. Where you should be. Come and speak with me, my husband, and tell me why you should not be beaten for staying away from me.' Her words were sharp, but there was a playfulness about them. Then she could speak no longer, as Perdu pulled her face down on to his breast.

Leith brushed past Perdu and Haldemar, his mind on one person only. He strode up to his crippled brother, who was talking quietly with his parents and with Achtal the Bhrudwan, and grabbed him by the shoulder. As Hal spun awkwardly around, a stray thought flashed through Leith's mind: *how long since I last touched him?*

'Leith! We were just talking—'

'That's all you ever do!' Leith snapped, pulling Hal aside, away from his shocked parents. Achtal watched them walk away, a frown on his face, then turned and muttered something to Mahnum. The Trader nodded agreement, and went looking for Kurr and the Haufuth.

'Leith, what's the matter—' Hal began, but again his younger brother didn't let him speak, pulling him down to sit on an upturned barrel close to the shore of the River.

'What's the matter?' he threw back at his brother. 'Perhaps

two hundred people dead, killed in the foulest possible way by the Arkhos of Nemohaim, that's what's the matter!' *Don't look at his face, don't get pulled into his arguments.* 'This is the man you made a bargain with, Hal. You knew he was a traitor, a killer, and that he would betray us too as soon as he could. Why didn't you put him to death in the desert when he was in your power, like he deserved?'

'Leith, it doesn't matter what he did, he deserved—'

'And don't use words like honour or forgiveness or sacrifice!' Leith growled. 'Always you have a justification for your noble acts. Two hundred people, Hal!'

A troubled look creased the cripple's face, as though reflecting unfamiliar doubts. Leith drank it in like the elixir of life.

'I – I did not think he would do such a thing. But even so, it was right to give him the chance.' Despite his words Hal looked uncertain, Leith was sure of it.

'It was not right. He deserved no chances. It could never be right to give him the chance to murder more innocent people. You haven't even asked me how the people died. Don't you care?'

'I thought you were talking about the Battle of the Four Halls,' his brother replied. 'Is there – was there another time?'

'Just now,' said Leith wearily. 'Somehow he flooded The Pinion and finished off his former fellow traitors, and no one knows how many others as well. Hal, they died choking on the city's excrement. They died horribly because you provided the Arkhos of Nemohaim a way to return to Instruere. Because you wanted to prove to everyone just how holy you are, how full of goodness, how pure and untainted by evil.' The words flew like fiery darts across the pace or so between them, and as they were spoken everything else around them faded away, such was their vehemence. 'Your hands are tainted. You might as well have drowned them yourself. Two hundred people paid the price for your pride.'

Leith could not believe his eyes. Silent tears began to run slowly down Hal's face. A small place deep within him exulted at the sight.

A voice intruded upon their private world of pain. 'Leith! Leith! What are you doing?' His mother's voice.

'Make it short, boy,' came another voice, a voice that had once intimidated him but now had no power over him. 'You have leaders to meet, an army to inspect. You don't have time for this.'

Without turning his head, Leith waved his right hand behind him in the direction of the voices, signalling for them to stay out of it, and did not see the blue-tinged flame surge from the Arrow, driving his parents and fellow villagers back.

'Don't do this, Leith,' his father's voice warned him.

'If you wish to remain, then do so,' Leith said. 'What I have to say should be said in front of witnesses.' He turned towards them, and only then noticed the Haufuth patting down scorch marks on his robe.

'I accuse Hal of siding with the Destroyer,' said Leith deliberately, and again the words took on a life of their own, cocooning them from the real world, enclosing them in a weaving of words. 'Not only did he make an alliance with the Arkhos of Nemohaim, he counselled friendship with the traitorous King of Straux. And he made a pawn out of Achtal, the Bhrudwan warrior. To what purpose, Hal? To what purpose?'

'Leith!' his father cried angrily. 'What are you saying?'

'Whatever it is, it needs to be said,' the old farmer growled, surprising the others. 'I want to hear the answer to his question. I have often wondered about Hal Mahnumsen on this journey.'

'He's just a boy!' Indrett exclaimed. 'He wouldn't hurt anyone!'

'You can't see it,' retorted Kurr. 'You're too close to him, too familiar with him. But I see it. He knows too much to be just a boy.' There was an ache in his voice like old pain.

'What do you mean?'

Leith took up the thread. 'Tell them about your enhancing, Hal. Tell them about how you influenced us at Kantara, pulling our strings like the puppet show at the Vapnatak fair. You can do magic, Hal. It was you who overpowered Maendraga and Belladonna, the guardians of the Arrow. Do you deny it?'

Indrett let out a derisive snort at her son's words, but Mahnum put a hand on her arm.

'No. No, I don't deny it. I know how to use the Way of Fire to change the way things happen.' Hal's voice was quiet, strained, bereft of its usual knowing timbre. Behind him, his mother gasped. Kurr grunted agreement.

'It's true,' the old farmer said. 'I thought you were just fey, a kind of throwback to the days when the First Men were closer to the land, closer to the old gods. But you can actually do magic. Where did you learn to do it?'

Hal swallowed before he replied, and as he spoke he had a hunted look in his eyes. 'I spent a lot of time by myself, owing to – well, I observed what happens in the forest and the field, and somehow found I could bend – enhance – speed up many things that happen. Leith, I hear the voice of the Most High. You want me to say that I do not. How can I make what *is* into what is *not*? Why does it matter so much?'

'Because we want to find out what you are,' said Phemanderac, dread in his voice at what he was hearing. 'Because you might be an agent of Bhrudwo without knowing it. Hal, you were found as an infant. No one ever claimed you. In every village there are children born out of wedlock, and some girls feel so ashamed they abandon their babies. Perhaps that's where you came from. But what if there is a more sinister explanation?'

During the philosopher's speech Kurr had been trying to interrupt, and finally he burst through. 'No! You've gone far enough! You don't have a right to know the private stories of people who had to make terrible decisions because men like you told them what they'd done was wrong! Leave this alone, I'm warning you – or you might find out something you might regret knowing!'

Indrett stared at the old farmer, her face suddenly white.

Unsure of what Kurr meant and confused at this change of heart, Leith was reluctant to lose the thread of his argument, so pressed on, filling the rapidly darkening silence with his questions. 'There were other times when Hal could have intervened to help people, but didn't. Isn't that right, brother? You left the Haufuth's hand to heal itself. You could have enhanced the healing process, but you didn't. What sort of lesson did you hope he'd learn?'

'Sometimes pain can—'

'I don't want to hear it!' Leith shot back. 'A homily on the benefits of pain? What gives you the right?'

Behind Leith the Haufuth took half a step forward, visibly rubbing his hand.

Leith took a deep breath. 'Tell them what happened at the Hermit's cave, Hal. Tell them now.' His voice was flat, hard, irresistible.

'Leith, please don't get me to talk about that. It will do so much harm.'

'And you are the judge of what will do harm?' Leith yelled. 'You, who have done so much harm? Speak, or you will be cast out of the City!'

The others listened, appalled, as Hal told them of that night. He told them how he crept into the Hermit's room late in the evening, how he recognised the effects of black fly poisoning in their host and enhanced the venom for a swift effect. Leith interjected with a lurid description of Hal changing shape, taking on the form of the fly, hovering over the helpless Hermit with huge black wings. In the background Indrett sobbed, but Leith ignored her.

'You told me you wanted to give the Haufuth a purpose, and so persuaded him to stay behind to nurse the Hermit back to health. But what gives you the right to injure one man to help another?'

'Leith,' came the reply, and to the younger brother's ears the voice sounded broken, defeated. 'Leith, I can't explain how I knew what to do. I hear the words of the Most High, and act on them. It seemed right to me that the Hermit should be given time to reflect on his misuse of the gifts given him, and the chance to help the Haufuth regain his confidence was very important. Are you saying I did wrong?'

'Yes! Yes, I *am* saying that! Your voice is so *right* that it is wrong!' Leith was beside himself, and didn't stop to consider what he was saying. It was too late, anyway: the dam had burst, and all that was in him came pouring out. 'The Hermit came to Instruere and led thousands of people astray with his cursed Ecclesia. Who knows what he would have been like had you not interfered with him? Perhaps he would not have been so holy, so fanatical, so much like you. Perhaps he might never have come south at all if you'd left him alone. Perhaps the children I saw die outside the Hall of Lore might never have died. Perhaps Stella might never have met Tanghin! Perhaps she might still be with us now if it wasn't for your evil goodness!'

'No, Leith, listen to me—'

'*No, I won't listen!*' Leith howled. 'I'm tired of listening to you. I've had a life of listening to you! You've always acted as though you're better than me. But you're not!'

'Leith—'

'Be quiet! I'm sick of hearing your voice. I hear it all the time. For a while I thought it was the Arrow itself talking to me, but now I realise that whenever I think of doing something for myself, whenever I go to make any sort of decision, I hear *your* voice in my head. No more! I will not listen to you any longer! I will not be your negative, your shadow, a useless echo of my older brother. I want to be more than the weakness that sets your strength into sharp relief! I want to be myself!'

Slowly Leith became aware of the silence around him. Dimly, as though in the far distance, he could hear the noise of the *losian* army as they prepared for a night outside the walls, but the silence smothered everything close by as effectively as a blanket of snow. No one dared trespass on the words just spoken. Hal said nothing to defend himself, and just looked at Leith with eyes filled with hurt.

'Hal, you are the reason we are in this state,' Leith said quietly. 'I don't want to hear you telling us you thought you were doing the right thing. I don't want you to tell us about the voice of the Most High, or whatever it is you imagine you hear. I just want to hear you say you were wrong. Just tell me, tell me to my face that you're not perfect. Please.'

Hal remained silent, his face like stone, and Leith walked away, leaving his parents and his friends to make sense of what had been said. As he left his brother sitting there on an upturned barrel, his heart burned with shame and guilt at what he'd said, and it was all he could do not to turn back and beg his brother's forgiveness.

That evening the leaders of the *losian* army came across Longbridge and were taken to the Hall of Lore, where they were formally welcomed into Instruere in the name of the Jugom Ark. Leith took little notice of the formalities. His mind was full of his conversation with Hal, and the old farmer's words – which he had ignored at the time – raised questions for which he could not find answers. He had succeeded in humbling his proud, self-righteous brother, which should have made him happy, but he felt dreadful, as though he'd put an injured lamb out of its misery.

The Fodhram leader, who formally named himself Axehaft of Fernthicket, introduced the Company to the *losian* leaders. Leith hardly spared a glance for the clan chief of the Fenni – not the man whom they had met on their journey across the vidda, but the chief of all the clans – and his High Priest. He did allow his gaze to rest, for a moment, on the leaders of the Widuz, but their faces were not those he remembered mocking Parlevaag's death and their names meant nothing to him, less than nothing. All he could concentrate on was how he had pushed his brother into a deep hole of suspicion and mistrust. The leaders discussed the circuitous nature of the politics involved in the formation of the *losian* army with the Company, but he followed little of it. Kurr and the Haufuth asked many questions, and Leith sat there with Hal's face in the forefront of his mind, obscuring his vision; his broken voice blotting out all other sound. Then, finally, an old man came forward from the shadows and spoke, and his voice sounded like that of the Most High himself. Leith came to himself long enough to recognise Jethart of Inch Chanter, the man everyone hailed as responsible for welding the *losian* army together. The man turned his face towards Leith, and there was something in his gaze that the new Lord of Instruere could not look upon. He stood, excused himself, and left the Hall of Lore at a run, fleeing from the eyes that held a question in them he could not face.

CHAPTER 9

THE FALTHAN ARMY

PHEMANDERAC FOUND LEITH THE next morning, sitting alone on a low stone bench, shivering in the early winter chill, watching the river roll past. Raindrops from a large oak tree dripped down the back of his neck, seemingly unnoticed. He grunted when the philosopher called to him, and had to rub some feeling back into his cold, stiff legs before he could stand to greet his friend.

'Leith, it is time I spoke to you of the *Fuirfad*,' Phemanderac said tenderly. 'You must learn about the Way of Fire.'

'I'm not interested in anything to do with fire,' came the truculent reply. Beside him the Jugom Ark guttered on the stone bench.

'You must listen to me, Leith. Soon we leave this place to do battle with the Destroyer himself. It will be too late to wish you'd learned everything you could about the power in your hand when you're running from him, trying to avoid the crushing power of his might and his magic. Will your stubbornness be of any use when he reaches out to take the Jugom Ark from your dying fingers?'

The melodramatic words earned him a harsh laugh. 'Why

don't you use the Wordweave on me while you're at it?' Leith said stonily. 'Or was that all from Hal, and none from you?'

'I did talk to your brother,' Phemanderac replied, and the stress he laid on the last word could not be missed. 'Like the rest of the Company I was surprised by your revelations last evening. Hal admitted he added some of his power to my own when we confronted the guardians, but my knowledge of the *Fuirfad* was still instrumental in countering the wiles of Maendraga and his daughter. The rest of the Arkhimm contributed to our success at Kantara. Hal is a wild magician, nothing more. Leith, not everything that happens, whether good or bad, happens because of your brother.'

Leith snorted. 'It feels like it, Phemanderac. Do you know the Arrow speaks to me in my brother's voice?'

'I heard you say that last night, and wondered at your words. Leith, have you considered you might *think* you hear Hal's voice because you associate him with wisdom and good sense? I'm sure it's not really Hal's voice you hear, otherwise why did the Most High take us through peril and loss to fetch the Arrow from Kantara? We might all have done just as well to listen to Hal, and with a lot less bother.'

Leith sat silently on the bench. Phemanderac could see him digesting this.

'Phemanderac,' he said, after some time, and the philosopher's heart melted at the anguish in the boy's voice. 'It comes down to this. I feel like I'm losing control. All my friends are doing what they want, but there are dozens of people I have to ask before I can do anything. If I give in to the Arrow things will only get worse. I'm afraid I'll lose myself, be swallowed up. I don't want that to happen. I don't want to be controlled like a puppet.' The Jugom Ark flickered uneasily, as though trying not to draw attention to itself.

'Then you will have to learn how to control it!' said Phemanderac triumphantly.

'I don't want any of this.'

'Then lay it aside,' the philosopher said. 'But you won't do that, I know you won't. Leith, we're trying to be patient with you, but every hour spent here in Instruere is an hour's less time we have to bring our army successfully to the Gap. Please, Leith, you don't have to feel like saving Faltha. Just go through the motions for a while. Your feelings will catch up eventually.'

Leith grunted a non-committal reply, then stood, stretched and began to walk towards the Inna Gate.

Worried, Phemanderac tried to engage the sullen youth in further conversation as they made their way through the City, but could get no response. *Just like Maufus*, he thought to himself, remembering his carefree childhood friend and the change that elevation to the Dhaurian Congress had wrought in him. *Too young for it, they asked too much of him.*

As the Hall of Meeting drew closer, Leith found himself surrounded by well-wishers, all oblivious of his moody silence. A great deal of activity focused around the building: tents had sprung up overnight on the lawn, and people burdened with baskets and barrows wove their way between them, pouring into the square from other parts of the City, and moving in and out of the hall.

'What's going on?'

'Supplies,' Phemanderac answered shortly. 'The army will need food and supplies. They will be ferried up the river to a place far inland where the Aleinus is no longer navigable.'

'Who decided this?'

'You did. At least, your officials did, in consultation with the Company. You would have been asked, but no one could find you.'

'I thought I was the head of the Council!'

'You can't have it both ways,' the philosopher said, and laughed to take the edge off his remarks. 'If you don't want the responsibility, just lay the Arrow aside, and we'll see if there's someone else who can pick it up. Otherwise . . .'

Leith was saved from having to reply by the appearance of Kurr and the Haufuth, followed by Perdu and a glum-looking Farr. The village headman and the old farmer greeted Leith as though nothing was out of the ordinary, but each took an arm and led him, gently but firmly, towards a tent with a large yellow-orange flag flapping in the morning's land breeze.

'What is that?' Leith asked, pointing at the device, which looked like . . .

'A fiery arrow,' Kurr said. 'Or as near as the City's best seamstresses could come to. It's to be our device, the symbol of a reunited Faltha.'

'Another decision I took?' Leith said, arching an eyebrow in Phemanderac's direction. The tall man shrugged his shoulders in an exaggerated show of ignorance, and Leith struggled to suppress a smile.

'The people of Instruere are on a war footing,' said the Haufuth as he drew aside the tent flap for Leith to enter. Inside were a number of low tables, each laden with maps, charts and sheaves of paper, and people – some of whom he recognised, and others he did not – bent over them, discussing and arguing various matters. As he entered the tent his father waved to him. His mother looked up, her face turned to his with recognition in her eyes and something else, then she turned away and continued a conversation with someone he'd never seen before.

The Haufuth continued talking, leaving Leith no opportunity to find out why his mother had behaved so strangely. 'We have a great deal to decide before we can leave Instruere on the long march east,' he said, thrusting a roughly sketched map into Leith's left hand. 'Look at this. Instruere is here, by the sea, near enough. This line is the Aleinus River. Over here' – he pointed to the rightmost edge of the parchment – 'is the Gap. See how the Aleinus River issues from it? We can follow the river all the way to Bhrudwo.'

'How long will it take us?'

'No one is really sure,' said the Captain of the Guard from over Leith's left shoulder. 'Our best guess is a hundred days, but so much depends on the weather. A northern winter . . . well, you would know about that better than I.'

Mahnum leaned towards them. 'The ground frozen so hard it drives the ice up into hillocks and makes paving patterns out of the plains. A wind from the east that drains your strength, no matter how well you protect yourself. Ice falling from the skies like shards of broken glass. A pitiless place, the Nagorj.'

'Nagorj?' Leith repeated, though as he, spoke he saw the word on his map.

'The Sna Vazthan name for the Gap. The land immediately to the west of the Gap is not really part of any Falthan kingdom, so harsh is the climate, and no one lives there. But nearest is Sna Vaztha, to the north, and Piskasia, to the south-east.'

'Sounds like the vidda to the north of Breidhan Moor,' said Perdu uneasily. 'And we plan to take an army there in winter?'

'It is worse than the vidda, and we go there because we must,' said Mahnum resolutely. 'The Destroyer showed me his plans, remember, and they depend on a winter invasion. He has trained his army to travel in winter, and they will have the advantage over us.'

'So why do we not wait until they come down the river closer to Instruere?' Leith asked. 'It will be spring by then, we can fight on our own ground, and we won't have to march as far.'

'Because of what will happen to the farms and villages, the towns and the cities between here and there, if we do nothing,' replied his father, with old pain rimming his voice. 'The Bhrudwan army will tear any Falthan opposition apart on their way to Instruere. Look at the map! Piskasia, Redana'a, Favony, Straux; all will fall. And even if we were victorious, the Bhrudwans would be impossible to root out from Faltha's heart. We cannot allow a single Bhrudwan on this side of the Gap.'

'It's a risk we are taking, a grave risk,' said Jethart of Inch Chanter, his voice carrying across the tent from where he sat. 'The essence of successful warfare is to choose the ground that best suits your forces, and most disadvantages your enemy. We don't yet know the numbers or experience of our own army, let alone that of our foe. One blizzard could wipe out the lot of us.' He sighed. 'Perhaps no ground will suit us, perhaps no ground will disadvantage the Bhrudwans. Nevertheless . . . nevertheless, we must fight.'

'Yes, Jethart, we must,' Mahnum said, and something passed between Leith's father and the old man. I *remember hearing them talk about this old fellow, last night in the Hall of Lore. They said Jethart travelled into Widuz and persuaded the warriors of Adunlok to join the* losian *army. My father carries his sword, taken as payment for saving captives of the Widuz originally of Inch Chanter. There was talk about how he was the greatest swordsman in the west, in his day*. That day was clearly long past.

The insistent murmuring all about him drew Leith away from his thoughts, and in a few moments he became immersed in the planning around him. At one table people debated the best way to get supplies for the army up through Vulture's Craw, the notorious gorge where the Aleinus became non-navigable. At the next table, hunched over the best map of the Nagorj that could be found, a group of older men listened as one of their number held forth about tactics. Leith listened for a while, but could understand very little of what was being said. Nearby another knot of officials sat opposite some obviously senior members of the *losian* army, and from what Leith could make out, the discussion centred on the chain of command. At every table Leith was politely acknowledged, and asked to contribute his opinion, although he couldn't help but notice their furtive glances at the Arrow burning in his right hand, and the uneasy, even fearful glances he attracted.

Leith gleaned a great deal of information during the morning he spent in the tent. Spies had been sent out at dawn to scout the possible routes the army might take, to determine possible obstacles, food sources and level of support. Other riders on fast horses were already heading east towards the Gap, with instructions to find the Bhrudwan army and report on its strength. 'Knowledge, my lord, knowledge is everything,' people kept saying to him.

Emissaries had been sent, men whose job was perhaps equally risky, to make contact with the rulers of each Falthan kingdom. In some cases the message to be delivered was blunt: their treachery was known, and would be forgiven only if the king put his entire army at the new Council's disposal.

In other cases the appeal was friendlier, if no less urgent, informing the king of happenings in Instruere and beyond, explaining the threat to the east and witnessing to the return of the Jugom Ark. These ambassadors of the Arrow were to beg the kings' help, and would accept armsmen, supplies or gold. Much was hoped for from these emissaries, but little could be counted on. As yet.

City officials purchased food, weapons and medical supplies from all over Instruere. According to the clerks, the City's coffers were being emptied at an alarming rate, though apparently a great deal of gold had been recovered from the private rooms of certain of the former Councillors of Faltha – some of the coin of obvious Bhrudwan origin – and was already proving very useful. Hal was out in the City, so Leith was told, organising the collection of supplies: a difficult job, apparently, with the firing of the Granaries only a fortnight earlier having depleted food stocks in Instruere. Traders scoured the countryside, buying up supplies from nearby towns and cities as well as directly from farmers.

The mighty Falthan army would march within three days, Leith was informed. This was the target he himself had apparently set for the citizens of Instruere, one which was repeated to him enthusiastically by those hard at work on his behalf, and the source of which he never tracked down. An army from Deuverre would join them on the plains north of Instruere, as would their king. They would then be ferried across the Aleinus to Sivithar, avoiding the vast swamplands of the Maremma, from where they would march across Westrau, the western province of Straux, until they reached Vindicare. There they would take ship on the Aleinus, sailing upriver directly towards the Aleinus Gates and Vulture's Craw. To keep to schedule they must arrive at the Aleinus

Gates within fifty days of leaving Instruere. Shipbuilders were already making the large rafts which would take them upriver from Vindicare to the Aleinus Gates.

'What about Straux?' Leith asked, interrupting a senior official as he explained this to him and other members of the Company.

'Pardon, my lord?'

'What happens when the army has left Instruere behind? Won't the King of Straux take Instruere for himself? I hear he has long desired it, believing it a natural part of his kingdom.'

'My lord, he met with you only a few days ago, and agreed—'

'He was named a traitor to Faltha, and I do not trust him,' Leith snapped. He looked at the map on the table, and slammed a finger down on it. 'We will leave from the southern gate, cross Southbridge and march to Mercium. We will demand a proof of his loyalty. He will supply us with his best soldiers, and he will accompany us eastwards on our journey, or he will be put to death as a traitor.'

'But, my lord, the agreement—'

'The agreement demands he support the Council of Faltha on matters of war. He will not be left behind to threaten the vulnerable citizens of this City,' Leith declared. Behind him a few onlookers cheered, then put their heads back down to the discussions they had been part of.

'Such a decision will cost us valuable time, boy,' said Kurr quietly. 'Are you so determined to undo everything your brother counselled?'

Leith turned to face the old farmer, and for a moment the Arrow in his hand flared brightly, flames surging dangerously close to the old man, who stood there, his arms folded, an unreadable expression on his face. Then the youth visibly took hold of himself, and the flame receded to a yellow flicker.

'Hal is not the only Mahnumsen with ideas,' Leith said flatly. 'I think this is the right thing to do, but I can't predict how these people are going to react. A year ago I was just some peasant child, and you were a sheep farmer. Can you honestly tell me that you know what the King of Straux will do?'

Kurr pursed his lips, obviously biting back a retort, and nodded his head reluctantly. 'You may be right, boy, you may be right,' he said. 'We've taken a thousand risks up to this point. Why not take a few more?'

The next three days passed in a blur of meetings. It rained on and off outside, a cooling drizzle that signalled the end of warm weather to the locals, though to Leith the temperature still seemed agreeable. It sufficed to remind them all there was little or no time to spare if they were to beat the worst of the weather. Leith began to assume command. He was the only one who shared in the knowledge generated at each of the tables, and gradually earned the grudging respect of his commanders. He left the tent only to sleep in a luxurious chamber attached to the Hall of Lore, a room that made him uncomfortable with its richness, its velvet curtains, its tapestries and exotic rugs, and the servants who stood outside his door. Most discomfiting, however, was the loneliness. He missed the sounds of his brother stirring, of the discussions they had, of him shuffling across the room in the morning. He didn't know where Hal slept, hadn't seen him for days.

And now three days had passed, and he sat astride a tall white horse, weighed down by ceremonial armour, a sword held awkwardly in his left hand, the Arrow in his right.

Another duty to perform. It was a fog-bound morning, and the Falthan army – really three thousand of the Instruian Guard accompanied by ten thousand ill-trained civilians and the *losian* Army of the North – was ready to march. Ahead of him the mostly-rebuilt Struere Gate stood closed, awaiting his order to open. Behind him the Company sat uncomfortably on their mounts, none more so than Indrett. Though Leith himself, and Mahnum his father, begged her to stay behind, she was coming east with them. Beyond all expectation she had proven to be tactically astute, regularly defeating the generals of the Falthan army on the wargaming table through an unfathomable combination of conservative and outrageously risky tactics. A legacy of years at the Firanese Court, she explained. The defeated generals, far from being resentful, requested Leith to allow her to come with them. 'She may save many lives with her tactics,' they told him, and he relented, secretly pleased.

In the end none of the Company was left behind. Even the slave girl they had rescued from the markets of Ghadir Massab came with them, unwilling to be separated from Indrett, to whom she attached herself as though a long-lost daughter. The government of Instruere was to be managed by a committee of businessmen, all of whom had been made aware of the price of treachery. Most frustrating to Leith was the necessity of leaving behind a thousand of the Instruian Guard, but there had been no sighting of the Arkhos of Nemohaim since the Battle of the Four Halls. No one wanted to return, whether in victory or in defeat, to find the City held against them.

So now all was made ready for their departure. Or, at least, as ready as three days could make. Leith stood up in his stirrups, raised the Arrow high above his head, and cried: 'Forward!' at the top of his voice. Crowds gathered in the square in front of the Gate, on the balconies of the tenements and all along the City wall, cheered and shouted as the Struere Gate opened and their army filed slowly out of the City and across the partially repaired Southbridge, soon to be lost in the swirling fog. All too soon. The army vanished, and the citizens made their way home or to their places of work, steeling themselves for the long wait ahead.

The Company and the leaders of Instruere had thought hard and planned carefully for the campaign ahead, making the best of the experience they had and the little time at their disposal. But they had forgotten one man. That man now stood alone in the shadows of the Struere Gate, his blond locks hidden by a hood. Tall enough to see over the heads of the crowd in front of him, he directed a stare of pure hatred at the youth on the horse. This was not how the Most High had ordained it; the words he heard from the Most High himself had been sabotaged by the glory-seeking Company. But now they were gone, and he could make those words come true before they returned. With a sweep of his blue robe the man turned on his heel and strode away into the depths of the city. With luck the army would not return.

Stella awakened to a sickening motion. Everything around her glowed a bright white. Disorientated, for a moment she thought she lay in a cave of ice, though she felt warm, not cold. As she came to herself she realised her dazzling surroundings were made up of pillows, sheets, lace, hangings and curtains; not the snow and ice she had taken them for. Everything was in motion, a regular rolling from side to side as she was borne forward in a conveyance of some kind. In the few moments before the awful memories flooded back,

Stella imagined she was in a palace somewhere, a resting place on the Company's journey to Instruere, the sort of grand place she dreamed of seeing on her travels, not all those backwoods hovels the others seemed to delight in.

But then the cruel memories returned, and the Stella who now huddled in the small white chamber, arms wrapped protectively around her knees, was not the Stella who might have complained at the rustic accommodation of the Great North Woods. Her dreams had been pulled apart by a man infinitely more cruel than the boy Druin – now a distant and almost pleasant memory, a boy who did little worse than trapping moths and pulling off their wings. She was a remnant, something discarded after the essence had been distilled from a person, something that found itself centred around an immense inner ache, a sea-deep sense of loss, and an uncontrollable fear of what was to come.

The curtain jerked aside and a round-faced, shaven-headed man smiled emptily at her. 'Is the Shining One ready?' His voice, soft and oddly high, was respectful.

'What shining one? What do you want? What is happening to me?' Each question was higher pitched, more frantic. Before the man could answer her, she pulled back from him and began to weep.

'No, no! No crying! Crying is not allowed!' He thrust a pudgy arm into the white chamber and pinched Stella on her shoulder. Instead of a mild discomfort, his touch sent a surge of agony through every joint in her body. It took fully five minutes for her to recover her breath and to relax enough that her muscles stopped twitching. Her shallow breathing seemed to rip through the serenity of the chamber.

The shaven-headed man waited patiently, seemingly unaware of her distress. 'Please!' she whispered hoarsely, as soon as she was able. 'Is the Destroyer nearby?' She tried to peer past his bulk, but found she could barely move. 'Could you help me escape?'

Abruptly his hands jerked wide, his face seemed to change its shape and his eyes rolled until only the whites showed.

'The Undying Man is indeed nearby,' said a voice from the man's mouth. A deep voice, the Destroyer's voice. A dark pit of despair opened up underneath Stella. She shrieked and shrieked, and all the while the Destroyer's voice laughed and laughed.

Stella tried everything. She refused to eat, but her shaven-headed keeper tickled her throat to make her swallow. She held on to the edge of her travelling cot, but with no seeming effort he dragged her wherever he wanted her to go. She fought her captor, punching, scratching, biting; he only had to touch her to turn her into a quivering wreck. On some occasions she fouled herself, trying any method to subvert whatever plan the Destroyer had for her, but with unflappable patience the round-faced servant would bathe her, clean her, change her as though she was a baby. Always she was returned to the white chamber, a litter carried by four bearers drawn from a pool of eunuchs, servants of the Undying Man, of which her keeper was one. She learned to fear the chamber, to fear the high voice of her keeper, to hate her own helplessness. But most of all she feared the unpredictable moments when her keeper's large frame would stiffen, his eyes would roll up and his voice deepen. It was worse, she decided, than encountering the Destroyer in person.

The Bhrudwan army was on the march. Stella had no idea where they were, how far it was to the borders of Faltha or how long it would take them to get there. She did know that the army she had witnessed marching, drilling and preparing was invincible. Even she could see that. And on the long march westwards she learned the extent to which this army shared its Dark Master's ruthlessness.

A week or so on the road west – she quickly lost track of time, and truthfully it didn't seem to matter – the army halted early in the afternoon, not marching a full day as was their wont. Stella was permitted to observe proceedings from her litter, no doubt as a further caution to her. Had she been forbidden to watch, she would most certainly still have heard enough to understand what was taking place.

During their westward progression Stella had noticed the army was divided by colour. Each soldier, whether cavalry, infantry or support, wore a coloured bib. Clearly this division was not rank-related, as generals and the lowest saddler might share the same colour. She guessed the colour referred to the land of origin. For the last three days her litter ended up beside a part of the army bibbed in blood-red, and the soldiers seemed to share an easy familiarity. They certainly did not seem to be the evil, ravenous horde she might have expected, and the red-bibs were the friendliest to each other of all those she had yet seen.

The early halt was called when the general of the red-bibs, the Duke of Roudhos, a land far to the south, received a report from a mounted outrider. This scout was one of those whose task it was to keep the army well contained and marching in the right direction, to harry any stragglers (or apprehend any deserters, but Stella supposed there would be few of those) and to requisition supplies from the surrounding countryside. As they were passing through a folded land, with little sign of pasture, she guessed this last task would occupy most of their time.

And so it proved. The scout's report told of a village, half a day's ride to the south, which refused to supply the army. Their leaders spoke of a recent plague and the failure of their crops, but there was a suspicion this was merely dissembling, and the villagers were holding out for more money.

At that moment a black-clad horseman rode up. Stella had learned these black riders were the Destroyer's personal servants and, though they had no standing in the army, wielded more real power than even a general. He overheard the latter part of the scout's report, and his eyes glazed over for a moment. Stella could guess exactly what was taking place, and she turned away, fighting another wave of the fear that seemed to define her existence.

'We will round up their women and have sport with them, and then there will be a burning,' announced the black rider.

'My lord?' The Duke of Roudhos stared open-mouthed at the messenger of the Overlord.

'Fortunate are the ones who have been chosen as the spear-head of our glorious invasion,' continued the servant, as though he had not been interrupted. 'The Red Duke and his men will be the first to enjoy the fruits of our master's plans.'

'A test of loyalty!' the Duke growled, his proud, stern face growing pale. 'Your master knows my abhorrence of "sport", and seeks unquestioning obedience to trap me. Well, it had finally come to this. I always knew it would.'

He stood tall and pushed his chin forward. 'I am ready to invade this barbarian land, and shed the blood of its fighting men in the service of my Overlord,' he replied bravely. 'But I will not ravish the women, nor will any man under my command. I will not fight against people living in my lord's domain. And we will certainly not allow women to be burned.'

'My master anticipated your response,' said the messenger

smugly, as though he himself had devised the plan rather than merely commanded to enforce it. 'He bids you know that any refusal will require the forfeiture of your own life. If you do not do what he commands, you will burn at the stake as an example to the massed armies of Bhrudwo that no one is above obedience to the Master of Andratan.'

'A clever plan,' the Red Duke said bitterly. 'My house has ever been a hindrance to the machinations of Andratan. He will gain land and power at no cost to himself, and with the support of my neighbours. Yet how can I set a torch to women? It is better to refuse some things and die.'

The red-bibbed man drew himself up even further. 'I refuse his command, as he expected I would,' said the Duke of Roudhos proudly. 'I would rather be slain by flame than use it to buy a craven life.'

The messenger struck him a blow across the mouth with his glove, and the massed army groaned as one. Though most had not heard the words, they understood their import.

'Let it be so,' declared the messenger. 'Any of your House who harbour similar rebellious intent should step out at once to share their master's fate. Otherwise, you will ride south in the morning and teach these villagers some manners. Are there any who will burn beside their foolish duke?'

At once twenty men stepped out into the dry, sandy space in front of the army. The face of the Red Duke broke into a wide smile: he had obviously not expected anyone to share his death. Then two, three more joined them; and, most surprisingly, one from the vast House of Birinjh, green-bibbed and strange of features.

'You are not on trial here!' the messenger shouted at the grizzled Birinjh warrior.

'Indeed I am not,' came the proud reply, in a barely

recognisable rendering of the common tongue. 'It is you and the master you represent who are on trial – yes, you, he, and all of us. The deed you ask the House of Roudhos to do is abhorrent to the true soldier, and I will not stand by and let it pass unremarked.'

'Then join in their punishment, old fool!' cried the sable-clad messenger, a look of chagrin on his face.

'I choose death with honour!' the old man cried as they bound him to a hastily-fashioned stake. The red-bibbed followers of the Duke of Roudhos let out a ragged cheer at this defiance, then they too were staked, branches and twigs brought and the fire set. Stella wondered at their bravery, but could not honour it by watching what transpired, instead seeking the refuge of her chamber. An hour later, as the last screams died away, she doubted her wisdom: surely what had actually happened could not have been as bad as the scenes her imagination conjured for her. Yet she knew that whatever the Destroyer had in store for her, death by burning would undoubtedly be preferable. It was a terrifying thought.

There was no way the King of Straux could have known the army of Faltha would descend upon him, Leith thought. But when they drew near the gates of Mercium, late on their second day out from Instruere, he was waiting for them, his crown atop his long flaxen hair, flanked by a ceremonial guard. *I have a spy in my midst.*

The king put on a brave face, but he was visibly shaken by the strength arrayed against him. Mercium was a populous city – some said it was the second-largest city in Faltha, behind only Instruere itself – and Straux was the most populous of all the Falthan kingdoms, of that there was no dispute. It would take time to assemble an army to oppose that which now came to a halt outside his city. Nevertheless, the King of Straux brought with him a fair strength of arms, enough to inflict serious losses on Leith's own army.

'My lord, you are well?' the king inquired in his unctuous voice, clearly acknowledging Leith's superior forces, and just as clearly finding it uncomfortable to do so. 'And your adviser? The crippled one? He is well also, I hope?'

The king's gaze darted around the faces at the head of the force facing him, but he could not see the one he sought.

'My brother is well,' Leith responded, 'but I speak for myself today. In the name of the agreement we made, a copy of which I bring you as a reminder of your pledge.' An attendant held the sealed document up, then rode forward and placed it in the king's hand. 'I have come to request your help in a time of war. You will surrender your army to us, that we might have command of it. You may keep a tithe of your force here in Mercium to protect the city from any threat while you are gone.'

'Why, my lord, who are we to fight? I know of no enemy befouling the fair plains of Straux!' Then the king realised the full import of what had been said: 'While I am gone? You cannot mean that I—'

'I do mean it,' said Leith reasonably. 'And before you humiliate yourself further in front of your men, you are invited to come and talk with us in our tent.'

In private the King of Straux blustered and argued, trying to dissuade Leith and the Company from their wishes, but in the end he had no choice. Leith was delighted to find that, though the king had learned of his army's approach only late yesterday evening, he had in the one day available to him assembled a force of four thousand warriors, with the possibility of four thousand more by sunset. It was a simple matter to commandeer this army. The King of Straux would accompany his soldiers east as a surety of his army's fidelity, and his eldest son was to rule in his stead while he was gone.

'Should I ever return,' the King of Straux said bitterly, 'I will require much in the way of goodwill in exchange for this day.'

'If you had chosen your allies more carefully, this day would never have happened,' Leith answered him.

In the midst of the evening meal, which the King of Straux reluctantly shared with the Company, one of his soldiers burst into the tent, despite being restrained by two of Leith's men. 'My king!' he cried, forgoing all the usual formalities in his haste, and grabbing the edge of the table to hold himself up. 'My king! There is an army to the south, marching on Mercium!'

'What trickery is this?' roared the king, standing and upsetting his meal. 'You eat food with me, and at the same time send an army to take my city unawares?'

Leith leaped to his feet. 'We have done no such thing. Let your messenger speak. What banner did this army fly?'

The messenger looked to the king before he spoke. 'Frinwald, this is the new ruler of Instruere. That is the Jugom Ark in his hand. You may speak freely in front of him.'

The man's eyes widened, but his message was important, so he composed himself and replied. 'They flew a banner of green, with a yellow lion wearing a jester's cap. The lion on the green field I recognise, but . . .'

'The jester's cap must be a recent addition, one most befitting the Raving King of Deruys,' finished the King of Straux, scowling.

It was all Leith could do to keep the triumph from his voice. 'This army is not unexpected,' he said confidently, as though everything followed paths of his ordaining. 'Deruys comes to support our cause. All the more reason for Straux to join its southern ally.'

The King of Straux nodded politely, but he could not hide the anger within as he bent his head to his food.

At dawn the next day Leith, along with the Company, the *losian* leaders and the King of Straux, went to meet the Deruvian army. The Raving King greeted them effusively, and beside him stood his son, Prince Wiusago, with a smile spread across his face.

'Five thousand elite soldiers march behind us,' he said to Leith as they rode back to the main army, 'and another five thousand wait at the northern border of Deruys. I will ride back to them, and with my father's blessing, lead them eastwards. They will march when the Children of the Mist come down from the forest.'

Leith did the sums in his head. No one quite knew how many warriors made up the *losian* army: the best guess put it at about twenty thousand. So, in total, including the soldiers waiting at the Deruvian border, his Falthan army had fifty thousand soldiers. He frowned. The lowest estimate of what the Destroyer would bring through the Gap was over twice that.

'Don't worry,' said Wiusago, as though he could read Leith's thoughts. 'The warriors from Deruys and the Mist are combat-hardened. The men of the Mist are worth ten of your guardsmen.'

But far from being reassured, Leith couldn't help thinking the warriors of the Bhrudwan army would be similarly hardened. *More so, if Achtal is any yardstick.*

Over the next few days the army settled into a pattern of

sorts. They made their way almost due east from Mercium, crossing the plentiful plains of Straùx. With the king's grudging permission the army took most of their provisions from the land around them, careful to make payment where possible and making sure they stripped no region bare. 'We want no enemies behind our backs,' the provisions master said. So each day a tenth of the army gathered food for the other nine-tenths, and no food was taken from the wagons that still streamed south and west from Instruere. The army would begin their march an hour after dawn, giving four clear hours on foot until halting for the midday meal. The afternoon saw six more hours of marching, ending just before the sun went down, allowing them barely enough time to make their camp. The fires were lit, the soldiers' kits were inspected and repaired where necessary, blisters and other injuries were ministered to; then the experienced men among them retired early.

But not all did so. Many of the younger men stayed up late by the fire, sharing songs and occasionally liquor purchased or stolen from a local farmer, even though this was expressly forbidden. A number of the soldiers were punished, severely and publicly, before the more unruly men calmed down. 'They're nervous, that's all,' some said; but others counselled the need to conserve all the strength they had. 'Get your sleep now,' they said, 'for there will come a time when you'll need it.'

And then there was the *losian* army. None of them went early to bed: young or old, they danced and sang late into the night, and marched as soon and as quickly as their counterparts. Some of the Falthans grumbled, but their commanding officers would not relent, and so they had to lie in their tents, listening to the laughter and the shouting in the distance.

On the third night east of Mercium, and their fifth since leaving Instruere, Leith paid a visit to the *losian* camp. There, by a massive bonfire, he met with Axehaft of the Fodhram, Tanama of the Widuz and the Fenni clan chief. With them were Perdu, Farr (who jokingly told Leith he had 'gone native') and the unsettling figure of Jethart, who sat in the shadows like a dark cloud on the horizon.

'We read your rising in the stars,' said the clan chief through Perdu, who interpreted for him. 'The Five great Heavenly Houses have arisen to oppose the blue fire coming from the East. The clash of fires is coming, and we have been called out to support the First Men with the gifts the gods have given us, the secret gifts of the vidda known by no man save ourselves.'

'What gifts are these?' Leith asked, and the clan chief answered briefly once the question had been interpreted.

Perdu shrugged his shoulders, puzzled. 'He won't say, and I know nothing of them. I do know the people of the vidda use fire, but do not worship it. They see themselves as people of the Air, from where the snow comes, and in which the mighty eagles soar in search of their prey. There are many secrets the Fenni would not share with me, a child of Fire as they called me. I never knew what they meant,' he said, then glanced at the Arrow in Leith's hand. 'Perhaps I do now.'

Leith thanked the Fenni for making the long journey east. 'You must have left not long after we departed your lands,' he said.

'We left as soon as the priests could meet,' was the answer. 'Your coming confirmed the signs in their mind. We march eastward to see the fire fall.' And nothing clearer than this cryptic answer could Leith obtain.

Axehaft and Tanama sat down together, side by side, seemingly allies, yet Leith could clearly sense the tension between them. 'It was not my idea to join with our enemy,' said the Warden of the Fodhram. 'That gem came from our friend from Inch Chanter, sitting apart from us, as though this had nothing to do with him.' He laughed, a deep chuckle that reminded Leith of pine-scent and the dark depths of forests, or water foaming at the bow of a canoe. 'He turns up one evening, as pleased with himself as a bear having found a honey-tree, as though he was anything but a stranger to our lands, having neglected them for twenty years and more.' Again the laugh, softening the words. 'He had the remnants of the Widuz leadership in tow, suing for peace. Seems they pay him the same kind of respect we do. Anyway, there was nothing we could do but accept. Shamed into it, really.' He saluted the stern-faced Widuz chief sitting next to him. 'We were barely back from avenging our dead at Helig Holth, but Jethart gathered us up over the summer, and we marched together as an army as soon as the leaves turned. Fenni, Fodhram and Widuz. Who could have guessed?' And he laughed at his own credulity.

'What?' Leith managed. 'Jethart just told you to march, and you marched?' He risked a glance into the shadows, but the hunched-over figure gave no indication he was attending to the conversation.

'He explained what the hidden signs meant,' said the Widuz leader. 'He told us of the Earth and of the defeat of the fire. He spoke with the authority of a priest. He drew us out from Adunlok, from Frerlok, from Uflok; from our fortresses and sacred dancing grounds. He promised we will look on the day of our freedom. He told us what we would see in your hand.'

Then, before anyone could shout a warning, the man leaned forward, casually stretched out an arm and, with his gaze firmly fixed on Leith's face, placed his hand on the shaft of the Arrow.

Leith cried out, startled, then his eyes opened wide in shock as the Widuz leader showed no sign of hurt. Behind him the Company gasped in dismay. 'But – but . . .' Leith spluttered, astonished. 'How can you touch it? Is the Jugom Ark yours?'

'No,' came a deep voice from the shadows. 'No, it's not. Haven't you yet guessed, youngster? The Arrow is of the Fire, and can hold sway only over those that are of the Fire. He of the Widuz can touch it, but cannot control it. It is just an arrow to him. How is it you do not know this?'

The old man stood up and stepped forward into the firelight, facing the Company. Though very old, he still retained the shape of a fighting man, and fixed them with a fierce eye. That eye settled on Phemanderac, whom he addressed, speaking right over the top of Leith's head. 'Why did you not tell him, offspring of the House of Sthane? Why else were you called across the desert, if not to instruct the boy?' There was heat and power in the voice, and Leith felt the pull of the Wordweave – now he had a name for the strange power he'd felt time and again since this adventure began – even though it was not directed at him.

'I am ready to teach him, when he agrees to the tuition,' said Phemanderac defensively. 'Though it seems as though you could have done just as well.'

The man from Inch Chanter raised his beetling brows, then laughed shortly. 'He wasn't ready. Still isn't ready. Doesn't want to be ready. Nevertheless, he must learn!' He turned his owl-like gaze on Leith, who tried not to quail at his stare.

'You must learn, and quickly. I thought you would have listened to those provided for your instruction, but you wouldn't have it. This must change.'

'How is it everyone knows what I should do but me?'

'How is it you still don't know what you should be doing?' Jethart responded evenly.

'Do *you* know? I'm asking politely.' Leith's terse, angry voice belied his words.

'I'm not the one appointed to teach you.'

Leith jerked the Arrow out of the grasp of the Widuz leader and forced himself to his feet. 'You don't know, that's why.'

'Maybe you are right,' Jethart responded.

'Then I'll find my own answers,' Leith said stubbornly, and stomped away from the fire.

Phemanderac followed him into the darkness. No matter how fast Leith walked, or where he turned, the philosopher kept up with him. The young man found his angry steps taking him away from the huge camp site, past the sentries who dared not question the youth with the mighty arrow, out into the harvest fields of Westrau, but still could not shake Phemanderac off. Soon he was running, angry anew at the sheer silliness of what he was doing, at his own childishness and at what the *losian* must think of him, but did not stop until his pursuer caught him by the shoulder.

'Sit down, Leith,' said the philosopher's voice, his face hidden in the darkness, the only contact the hand on the youth's shoulder, and the voice in the night. 'Sit down and listen to what I have to say.'

Leith squatted on the ground and listened as Phemanderac spoke. 'I should have told you,' he said. 'I really only suspected at first, and it wasn't until you sent the Fire out to mark the *losian* in the crowd that I realised what it all meant. I must apologise to you.'

'What *what* meant? What are you talking about? Why could the Widuz warrior touch my Arrow?'

'Listen, Leith. Please; this is important. Falthans descended from the First Men are of the Fire. That is how the Most High came to them; that is the nature of the covenant he made with them. But not all people are of the Fire. Other Falthans are descended from people who are of the Earth, like the Widuz and the Children of the Mist; still others are of the Air, like the Fenni, and there are yet more who are of the Water.'

'But they are *losian*!' exclaimed Leith, confused. 'They fled from the Vale, from the Fire, and are lost. How can they have another covenant?'

'Because the *losian* the First Men told us about are no more than a myth,' said Phemanderac firmly. 'There were people of the Vale who rejected the calling of the Most High, but I doubt any of them made it through the desert to Faltha. The people living here in Faltha before the time of the First Men were not refugees from the Vale of Youth. They came to their own understanding of the way the gods dealt with them. When the First Men arrived, they explained the existence of these people in their own terms, and the explanation also served to make the so-called *losian* lesser, which justified the taking of their lands. Don't you see? The Fire is of the First Men, the last-comers to this land. The land was of Earth and Water and Air before the Fire came. The First Men brought death and destruction, a great burning, and the Faltha the *losian* knew was laid waste.'

Leith listened to the earnest voice coming from the darkness. A cool wind picked up from the north, rustling the wheatfields surrounding them and bringing with it the cooking smells of the distant camp: the familiar smell of Instruian fare and, mixed with it, the spicy scent of exotic food.

'So if the only people the Jugom Ark is a weapon against are the descendants of the First Men, why do we see the Arrow as our salvation in the coming war?' he asked slowly, thinking carefully as he spoke. 'Surely the Bhrudwans are not of the Fire?'

'No, they are not,' came the answer. 'From what we've been able to piece together over the years, they are of the Water. But remember, the Destroyer was once Kannwar, strong in the ways of the *Fuirfad*. He can be touched by the Jugom Ark, we know that; he has only one hand because of the Arrow you now hold.'

'If he was of the Fire, how did he manage to subject the Bhrudwans to his will?'

'Ah, this is the great mystery,' said the disembodied voice of his friend. 'Hauthius believed that when the Destroyer drank of the Fountain of Life, in disobedience to the command of the Most High, he entered into a second covenant without breaking the first. Thus, alone of all people the Destroyer is of two covenants, Fire and Water. Together they mix in his veins, keeping him alive past his time – in the same way the spray of the Fountain preserved the dwellers in the Vale, giving them their legendary longevity. This second covenant made him acceptable to the Bhrudwans, and gave him power over them. He is the only one in the whole world who could rule over both Falthans and Bhrudwans. Such is his ambition.'

Leith shifted nervously: the Arrow in his palm seemed to burn with an even greater potency, though the flame did not flare like it often had. 'You say only those not of the Fire can touch the Arrow without hurt,' he said. 'Why can I touch it, then?'

The silence emanating from the darkness went on for some time. 'Leith, I don't know the answer to that. But somehow you and the Arrow are linked: it responds to your thoughts and emotions, it heals where you see hurt, it flames when you are angry. It is an extension of your heart. Anyone who looks on the Arrow sees you, and the strength and beauty and fire within you.' The philosopher's voice sounded suddenly thin, somehow hesitant, as though approaching a thought he did not want to give voice to.

But this fragility did not communicate itself to Leith. 'My heart? Or the Arrow's heart? Phemanderac, I feel like I am an extension of it – as though I am a walking quiver, a place for the Jugom Ark to rest before it is finally used by its rightful owner. Sometimes it speaks to me, and makes me do what it wants! You don't know how many times I've begged it to leave me alone!' Abruptly the youth stood up and stumbled off into the darkness, clearly unable to bear the weight of what was being asked of him. The Arrow flared in his hand like a beacon: bright, clean, pure, beckoning. Desirable.

Phemanderac did not follow. Instead he put his head in his hands, and whispered to himself: 'I see your heart, Leith.' Then, unable to speak the words written on his own heart, he wept.

CHAPTER 10

THE HALL OF CONAL GREATHEART

THE BHRUDWAN ARMY MARCHED westwards, dragging Stella along with them. Somewhere ahead lay the borders of Faltha; and somewhere beyond that huddled the towns and villages of home, places made by ordinary people doing everyday things, unaware of what marched towards them.

Stella shivered in her white cocoon. She knew with a dreadful certainty what marched towards the Falthans. She had seen it in all its pitiless, terrifying violence. She stared at the wastelands outside her cot, seeing nothing but the fire set to Loulea, the cries of those about to die. Nothing she could do was able to erase the horror, so much greater than even her own terror of the man who had her in thrall.

A week ago Stella had woken from evil dreams to find the eunuch leaning over her, shaking her, his eyes rolled back in his head and his flabby body rigid with the control of his master. 'Awake, Gem of Faltha!' rasped the mocking voice, in the way he had taken to calling her. 'Awake, my Morning Star! I have something to show you!' As always, the power of the voice was enough to pull her to her feet and send her stumbling out into the bright morning, still in her hated silken nightclothes.

Before them lay a tattered village, nestled in a dell that obviously protected the few buildings from the winds here on the northern plateau. The houses had seen better days. Old stone walls had been more recently supplemented with animal skins, or with timber, and more recently still with sticks scavenged from the woods nearby. In all, twenty or thirty ramshackle dwellings huddled together as though awaiting a beating.

As Stella watched, the villagers were dragged from their homes and assembled on the rutted track that passed for a main street. The men, women and children were clothed in oft-mended garments; some of the children clinging to their parents went shoeless on the frozen ground. Fear rimmed their eyes and hunched their shoulders, as though even the children knew what was about to happen.

Stella knew. This was the village which refused to supply the Bhrudwan army. Late the previous afternoon the great army had turned to the south, away from the westward road, and followed a seldom-trod path through a low range of ice-striped hills. They were here to punish the village, to make a point to the soldiers in this dark army, to teach them ruthlessness. And, chillingly, to make a point to Stella herself. *Would the Destroyer put this village to the sword just to impress me?* She tried to make her stiff limbs move, though she knew what the penalty would be if she tried to flee. Before she could take more than a step from where she stood, hands clamped down on her shoulder blades, sending shockwaves of pain through her body. *Better this . . . better this than accepting what is to come . . .*

When she came to, the women were being led away. She

could see the last of them walking into a small glade, spear at her back, trying to take a final despairing glance over her shoulder at the loved ones she would never see again. There were two ragged, bloody shapes on the ground in front of the men and the children, and one of the shapes moved still, making noises like a newborn kitten. Someone had resisted.

Soldiers set fire to the houses, and Stella watched. They took the children and cut off their hands and feet, and Stella watched, hollowed out by the sight. She watched as they made an obscene pile of the off-cuts in front of the men. She watched as the soldiers brought pieces of wood – doors, walls, tables – up from the burning village and stretched the men out on them, nailing them to the wood like shoes to a horse's hoof. She listened to the crackling and roaring of the flames, and to the crashing of the timbers as the houses caved in. She listened as the children shrieked and the men shouted out their pain and frustration. She listened as the soldiers cheered and cried with inhuman glee. She could hear other cries in the distance, and tried not to listen to them.

The voice coming from the round-faced man beside her gave her a running account of what was happening, and she was compelled to listen. The voice passed comments on the accuracy of his archers as they stood the pieces of wood up in a row and loosed arrows at human targets. He described in detail the agony the villagers would be experiencing, and how long it might take them to die. With every word he needled her with the inescapable fact of her own powerlessness.

The long hours blurred together into a tableau of blood and suffering, a shattering vision of a Bhrudwan future. Far more directly even than her capture and mistreatment, first by Deorc and then by the Destroyer, this day spent watching the slow death agonies of an innocent village brought home to Stella the fundamental evil of life. Once she had thought the world a fair and pleasant place. Such self-indulgent folly! Now she saw more clearly. The world was a place of power and powerlessness, where the few who had power made the lives of everyone else a hell of cruelty and hate. To think anything else was to deny the truth, or perhaps to not recognise one's own place of power. People in power could do anything they wanted to the powerless.

Anything.

Leith's Falthan army continued on its eastwards march. Two days from Instruere to the time they left Mercium, then five more days to Sivithar, a large city on the south bank of the Aleinus River. There they halted to replenish their supplies, much of which had been barged up the great river from Instruere. More and more Leith learned the wisdom of his generals, who all agreed their success in the coming war depended as much on the provisioning of their soldiers as it did on the tactics debated every evening.

The army was kept well to the south of the city, to prevent desertion, drunkenness and other temptations common to soldiery. Kurr, however, insisted the Company take lodgings at a tavern in the heart of Sivithar. In the hour before sunset he walked them around the city in which he had been born and raised, the city he had fought for in uprisings nearly half a century ago. A bittersweet homecoming indeed for the old farmer. In the many years he had been absent, making a life for himself in the cold north of Firanes, many of the places he remembered were changed beyond recognition.

Some of the damage had been done, he admitted, in the uprising itself, but what surprised him most was how many of the beautiful fountains for which the city had been justly famous had fallen into disrepair. Indeed, on the site once occupied by the best of them, the beautiful Fountain of Diamonds, a squat wooden doss-house now stood, filled with rowdy sailors from the docks. Some of the city's beauty remained, but to Leith and the others even the smell of the place was of something gone slightly to seed.

That night Leith sat on a hard-backed wooden chair, poring over a detailed map of the Aleinus River. He had found a small storeroom at the back of the tavern, empty except for a few dusty mats, and took the opportunity to spend a little time there alone, away from the clamour of the army and all the people trying to get his attention. He stationed a servant at the door with instructions to refuse all callers.

According to the map, the Aleinus seemed to wander over a large area of the Central Plains. He could make out a main channel, broader and straighter than the minor streams, though even this main channel wound back and forth like a worm seeking soft earth. Long curved lakes, channels ending in swamps and streams winding in and out of each other completed a complex picture. His generals had explained to Leith how the army would march west to Vindicare, well away from the river, to avoid coming to grief in this difficult land.

His finger traced its way up the river to Vindicare. There the river seemed to behave itself, keeping to one channel. Disciplined, easier to deal with. He laughed to himself. He knew which type of river his parents wished him to be.

A soft knocking intruded on his thoughts. Without

waiting for permission his mother opened the door and stepped into the room.

'Hello, Leith,' she said brightly. 'We've missed you this last week. How have you been?'

Leith bridled at her words. *How have I been? You meant to ask me* where *I have been.* Keeping his thoughts to himself, he set aside his map, stood up and offered Indrett his chair.

'I've been busy.'

'Anything we could help you with?' His mother smiled still, though the lines around her eyes had tightened. He knew the signs.

'Not unless you can explain this map to me,' he said. 'But thank you for offering.' It was a dismissal. Rude, far too early. He should give her a chance to speak, but he had so looked forward to time alone.

Her eyes tightened further. 'You may not want help, son, but you need it. The Company wants to be reassured you know how to use the Jugom Ark. More importantly, I want reassurance you are going to apologise to Hal for the hurtful things you said to him.'

'You are seriously telling the leader of the army of Faltha how to treat his brother?' Leith was determined not to lose his temper.

'You may hold the Jugom Ark, but you're still my child.' Instantly a look of regret passed over her face.

'Child? Mother, you cannot have it both ways. In one breath you tell me to grow up, in the next you call me a child. How long since you called Hal a child?'

'He's not a child,' Indrett said, her voice rising. 'But he can still be hurt. Promise me you'll seek him out and talk to him at least. Please, Leith.'

'I will,' he said, and his mother breathed a sigh of relief.

'I will,' he repeated, 'when I hear you have gone to him and given him the same message.' He moved to the door. 'Now, I'd be grateful if you could allow me some time to myself. I have much to think about.'

He had left his mother no choice but to leave. *I was right to speak this way to her*, Leith told himself as he closed the door behind her. *If I give in and make peace with Hal, everyone will forget the issues I have raised.*

He sat on his chair, but left the map untouched. *I am not a child. But she is partly right: I must seek Phemanderac and find out more about this Arrow.*

For the hundredth time he thought about asking the Arrow's voice, but didn't know what would be worse: a smug answer designed to draw him further away from his own will, or silence.

Leith sighed. Phemanderac had behaved oddly towards him in the last few days. Why did everything have to be so complicated?

Farr couldn't sleep. The small room above the tavern closed in on him as he lay on a sagging pallet. He'd offered the better pallet to the Haufuth, who snored loudly next to him. For a while he imagined he lay under a canopy of trees, but there was less comfort in the tavern bed than any bed of moss and tree roots he'd found in Withwestwa Wood. Eventually he shrugged aside his blanket and went to explore the tavern, leaving the room to the resonating throat of the big Firanese man.

The hallway creaked, as all hallways do, no matter how carefully Farr trod in his stockinged feet. The tavern below him was quiet. He had no idea how late the hour was, but was surprised to hear a thin sound on the stairs. Someone else was awake. Wounded? He rushed forward. No. Someone was sobbing.

Indrett sat on the top stair, her head bowed, tears falling on to her lap. A pale light filtered under a door to her right, gently illuminating her shaking frame. She seemed completely unaware he stood a few paces from her.

'Indrett? Lady?' he whispered, then spoke her name again more loudly. 'Indrett? Can I be of assistance?'

She raised her swollen face. 'No,' she said. 'Not unless you have some magic word to unlock the stubborn will of the Arrow-bearer.'

Slowly the proud woman unburdened herself to the most unlikely of counsellors. Farr tried to understand how a lad like Leith could argue against a destiny so clearly given him by the Most High himself. The more he listened to the story, the more his incredulity grew. In his experience men faced their tasks square-on, without resorting to sophistry to excuse them from their duty. If only the Most High had chosen Wira, or he himself, for such an honour. He would not have taken a backward step! He would have taken the Jugom Ark and faced the Destroyer in single combat, if need be!

'Indrett, we must talk with the Company about this,' he said to her. 'Leith must be made to see sense, or to relinquish his task to someone more worthy.' Righteous anger filled his voice, making it husky. 'Let us call a meeting and make everyone aware of your concerns. What you have said tonight is far too important to keep to yourself. I will organise it at the earliest opportunity.'

Indrett nodded her agreement. Farr patted her shoulder a couple of times, then made his way back to his room and his pallet.

*　*　*

The Company took their accustomed position at the head of the ranks early the next morning. Leith turned in the saddle and looked back at his fighting force, then lifted his arm, letting the Flaming Arrow blaze out, occasioning a mighty shout from fifty thousand throats and signifying the start of the day's march. Shaking his head, he turned his face to the east. Already his great army had suffered casualties. Two days ago a horse threw a shoe, apparently, tossing its rider into a ditch. The resultant broken wrist invalided the young man back to Instruere. Leith had seen the youth leave: he'd tried to put a sad face on his misfortune, but a week with the army had taught him, like many other volunteers from Instruere, just what an undertaking they were marching towards, and he was unable to keep his relief from showing. His captain reported the mishap to Leith himself, taking the opportunity to see the Jugom Ark at close quarters, and commented on the difficulties he was having maintaining discipline among his young charges. He looked Leith in the eye and spoke deprecatingly, but in a voice devoid of irony, about the callowness of youth. Leith watched the youngster walk slowly away in the direction of Sivithar's docks with more than a little envy.

Of many other mishaps, the worst was perhaps a drunken brawl in which two hard-bitten men from south of Mercium were beaten senseless by a number of as-yet-undiscovered assailants. The blame was being laid squarely at the door of the *losian* army, but Leith seriously doubted this, guessing suspicion of the *losian* was inflamed by their seemingly lax discipline. Maybe he'd have to say something about that.

As was their custom, the generals of his army rode close by early in the morning, passing on any important information about their men. It was merely an act of politeness,

Leith knew. The group of stalwarts who served as leaders of the Instruian, *losian*, Deruvian and Straux forces managed not to be condescending only by the barest margin. The Captain of the Instruian Guard was the youngest of the group, the most willing to hear anything the Company might wish to say, but also the lowest in the informal pecking order. Excepting the *losian* leaders, of course, who were treated with polite indifference. Axehaft made the point privately to the Company that of the War Council only he himself, Kula of the Widuz and the Fenni warrior Nutagval had any real experience in fighting an enemy. The Instruians had fought amongst themselves, not the same in *losian* eyes. From the look of them, the Westrau additions would be more trouble than they were worth. Only the Deruvians seemed to have the bearing and dedication necessary for proper soldiering, according to Axehaft of the Fodhram.

This morning there was little to discuss. The supplies awaited them at the docks, causing Kurr to note that the army itself might have taken the same route, thereby saving valuable time. To Leith's delight the generals did not agree, instead applauding his decision to strike southwards and make certain of his reluctant ally. He tried to restrain his smile at the old farmer's discomfiture, but from the scowls directed at him, he doubted he had succeeded.

They left the Aleinus River at Sivithar and struck out eastwards towards Vindicare, the main city of Austrau, the eastern province of Straux. To the north of their route the wide plains descended into the stinking mires and stagnant lakes of the Maremma, through which the Aleinus picked its way in a never-ending series of snake-like bends, switchbacks and oxbow lakes. To their south, and drawing ever nearer as they marched, were the Veridian Borders, from which, Kurr told Leith, the Company descended on their way north out of the desert slavelands of Ghadir Massab. Indeed, he said on the fourth day east of Sivithar, the army now followed the very road they had used. To the right, in the distance, he pointed out the northward-thrusting spur of ancient rock down which the Hamadabat Road wound, and upon which stood the one-time fortress of Fealty.

Out on the plains of southern Straux the army made good time, as much as fourteen leagues a day. 'It's all a matter of leagues marched per day,' Leith's generals would tell him. 'Ten leagues a day for a hundred days and we will arrive at the Gap ready to fight.' But increasingly he noticed their guarded looks as they told him this, and he wondered how they might keep this pace up in more difficult terrain. He remembered the slowness of their journey over Breidhan Moor. 'Are there any places like that?' he asked them, the reply to which was a shuffling of the feet and the odd equivocal comment: 'The Nagorj can be tricky in places,' or 'You wouldn't want it to snow in the Vulture's Craw.' Leith's anxiety grew as these comments were repeated.

Eventually he made them show him the whole journey on a map. Their progress eastwards from Instruere, a small dot near the coast on the left margin, was marked by a red line with a cross showing every place the army had stopped for the night. Vindicare stood in the path of the red line, still more than seventy leagues to the east, on the banks of the Aleinus River which, as Leith remembered from his own map now lining his cloak, described a huge loop to the north between Sivithar and Vindicare. Their projected route was dotted in charcoal black, and east of Vindicare it seemed to follow the river very closely. 'That's because we're taking to boats between Vindicare and the Gates of Aleinus,' said his generals and strategists. 'We told you all this, remember? That's why we sent anyone with shipcraft ahead on swift horses.' Leith nodded, not bothering to correct their impression he had forgotten their words. From the writing on the margins of the map he could see that shipping the army up the great river would save them many days of walking and cut more than a week off the total journey. 'My masterstroke,' said his chief steward proudly.

The map allowed a total of fifty days for the army to reach the Gates of Aleinus, nearly three-quarters of the way across the parchment, then another fifty days for the last quarter. 'It will be colder then,' he was told. 'We will have to allow for winter storms.' The Aleinus was not navigable above the Gates, and the army would have to negotiate the Vulture's Craw, a narrow and difficult path. The Wodranian Mountains to the north had no paths suitable for armies, and no food supplies to sustain them, while the Taproot Hills to the south were too tall, with high passes unable to bear a winter traverse.

Once the passage of Vulture's Craw had been effected, the remainder of the journey was arduous but by no means impossible, according to his strategists. East of Kaskyne, the Redana's capital, which the map said they would reach after sixty days, they would follow the north bank of the Aleinus through Piskasia to the town of Adolina at the mouth of Sivera Alenskja, the vast and impenetrable upper gorge of the great river. They would reach this small town at the eastern limit of habitable lands after eighty-five days' marching, leaving the army fifteen days to make their way up the Northern Escarpment and on to the Nagorj Plateau. From there they would make their way eastwards to the Gap, a low saddle between the huge bulk of the northern Aldhras Mountains and the cold, dry spikes of the Armatura to the south, where they would dig in and wait for the Bhrudwans to appear.

One hundred days in total, of which eighty-eight remained. As he rode on down the road, doing the sums in his head, farmers paused in their harvest to cheer the passing army and the boy with the burning arrow. Leith did not acknowledge them. He could not stop thinking about the mathematics. Fifty thousand soldiers, one thousand leagues, one hundred days – and one unpredictable enemy, who might already, at this very moment, be pouring through the Gap like a colony of ants bent on picking the Falthan larder clean.

Stella had no maps to tell her where she was. Day after featureless day passed in the company of her keeper, the eunuch who might at any time become the Destroyer's mouthpiece. He would ride beside her litter – which, he told her, travelled at the rear of the Bhrudwan army, in the company of the Undying One's carriage, a position of the highest honour – or, on occasion, would sit with her. At first she simply turned away from him, afraid she would suddenly find herself talking to the Destroyer, and stared out of the window at the grey hills that seemed to follow them westwards. The eunuch would say nothing, but would regard her with his blurred, poached-egg eyes, remaining silent even when she wept with frustration at her captivity.

He used to hurt me when I cried, Stella realised during one interminable afternoon. *He used to pinch me on the shoulder. He doesn't do that any more. Why?* she asked herself. Perhaps she had been conditioned, and no longer stepped over the invisible line of unacceptable behaviour. But no, that couldn't be it, for why did he let her cry? *Perhaps he feels sorry for me. Surely no heart could be so hard as to not feel pity for my plight.*

She turned from peering through the curtain of her prison and stared at the face of her keeper. Close-cropped hair, round, hairless cheeks, a small mouth – except when it was distorted by the Destroyer – and large brown eyes like that of the village dogs she used to play with. *Just like a tamed dog, obedient to his master, denied the pleasure of freedom – just like me. He's just like me.* She tried to read his face. Was there the merest sign of shared suffering, of sympathy, around those eyes?

'Where are you from?' she asked him, her voice hushed, willing him to answer. 'Where is your home?' Steeling herself, Stella leaned towards him, trying to elicit a response.

His mouth twitched, and he drew in a breath as though about to answer her; but, as if he'd been taken by surprise, he mastered himself and his face went blank, expressionless, unblinking, and looking into his eyes was like staring though the windows of an uninhabited house.

Almost, Stella told herself. Almost.

On the sixth afternoon east of Sivithar the Knights of Fealty came down from their rocky castle to confront the Falthan army. One hundred and nine there were, wearing the full ceremonial armour of an earlier age, each mounted on a black horse, each with a flag-bearer and page in attendance, and they were followed down the slope from their castle by the townspeople, dressed in bright clothes and in festive mood.

For a moment worry gripped Leith. He feared the formidable-seeming knights were about to attack his army, but he heard laughter from around and behind him, and looked where the amused generals were pointing. Some of the knights were having obvious difficulty staying in the saddle, while others clearly struggled to bear the weight of their armour, and when they removed their helmets the reason became clear. They were old men. A closer look showed that some of the horses had been blackened to disguise their greying muzzles, and much of their gear, while well kept, was clearly past its best.

But the laughter died as, with immense dignity, the foremost knight rode up to Leith, dismounted and knelt before him. There was something timeless, something noble in his bearing. He remained kneeling, making no sign that he would stand. Discomfited, Leith looked around, searching for guidance.

'You must'no keep'm kneeled, good sir,' said the knight's page, smiling widely. 'Bid'm rise, m'lord. Bid'm rise!'

'Rise, sir knight,' Leith said, in exactly the same voice he had always used by the Loulea lake when he and the other children played at swords. To his amazement, the man arose, and nodded respectfully to him. A dream come true. To his further amazement, he recognised the roguish face of the page with the broken speech.

'Lessep!' Leith cried, surprised. 'You brought me the Knights of Fealty, after all!'

'Was tellin'ee I knowed the knights!' the man crowed. 'Was unbelieved, was I, but knowed them I did!'

'I believe you now,' Leith replied, smiling at the simple man. In the silence that followed his words, he heard one of the generals beside him mutter: 'But what use will they be?'

The knight stepped forward, a small frown on his face. 'I do not judge a man by what I can see of him,' he said in a crisp, clipped voice. 'I would be interested to cross swords with a man who thought he correctly judged my skill by my appearance.' He directed a blazing stare at the Deruvian general who had spoken, then turned to Leith. 'By your leave, Arrow-bearer?'

The sensible thing to do would have been to refuse. Leith knew that. But events funnelled down a track centuries old in its tradition, and it seemed no one could do anything to prevent what was going to happen. Leith nodded, the Deruvian general – Reaf, his name was – dismounted and drew his sword, and before wisdom had a chance to clear its throat, the two men were bowing to each other. Reaf was a portly man in his fifties, who looked bemused that a careless word could lead him to this pass. A sudden thought passed through Leith's mind like a draught of cold air. *Was this to the death?* He was about to call a halt, when the Fealty knight stepped forward and flicked his sword in an impossibly quick motion. Reaf's blade spiralled lazily through the air. By the time it landed point-first in the grass at the side of the road, the knight had sheathed his own sword and extended a hand to the bewildered Deruvian. 'You have a good stance,' the man from Fealty said to his beaten opponent, nodding his approval.

Leith took a deep breath, and the Jugom Ark flamed as though sharing in his relief. Drawn by the brightness, the knight turned to Leith and bowed. 'We are the Knights of Fealty,' he said. 'One hundred and forty-four is our number, though in truth some are not hale enough to make the journey down to greet you. Chalcis is my name. I am a direct descendant of Conal Greatheart, the man whose band drove the Bhrudwans out of Faltha nearly a thousand years ago.' He smiled, removed the glove from his left hand and ruffled the hair of his page. 'My rascally son told me you would be coming, but his is only the latest voice of many to predict your arrival. We have known for many years the Bhrudwans would return to Faltha, and the Jugom Ark would be raised against them. We have a Seer amongst us, one who exhorted us to prepare, and for twenty years we have trained to be ready for what lies ahead.' He smiled again, and nodded to the humiliated Deruvian, who had remounted his horse and was sucking his stinging hand. 'What use can we be? We have prepared a banquet for you, and our town is ready to entertain your soldiers with feasting and music. And tomorrow, with your leave, we will march eastwards with you to make war on our enemies. Will you come to Fealty with us?'

The tall castle presented a formidable outline but, like the knights themselves, seemed a little shabby, a little frayed at the edges when looked at more closely. Again Leith wondered whether these knights would be all they promised. Thus he was not prepared for what he found in the castle's Great Hall.

The Knights of Fealty formed an honour guard, flanking the Company and the generals of the Falthan army as they walked up the ever-narrowing road and under the arched entrance to the castle. Once through the entrance they were led across a substantial courtyard, past a well and towards a rectangular structure with a steeply raked roof, a building the equal of anything to be found in Instruere. Here, at least, the stone looked well maintained. A knight – Sir Pylorus, Chalcis named him – flung open the tall double doors and the Company walked in to a room of wonder.

Leith heard a bitten-off exclamation behind him, in a voice that sounded like Hal's. He hadn't seen his brother to speak to for more than a week. *Not since that night. If it was him, he's losing control. The old Hal would never have . . .* His attention was drawn to the hall spread before him, and he had to work not to cry out himself.

Wambakalven. It was the first word that went through his head. The architect who created this hall had captured the essence of an underground cavern: the shimmering play of light and shade, the golden sand spread across the floor counterpointing the fluted marble columns that rose to the ceiling like a hundred stalagmites. And the ceiling! A hundred swirling scenes chased each other across the vaulted heaven of the hall, each one directing the eye to a vast centrepiece depicting a rainbow hanging over a field of deepest battle.

In the centre of the hall stood a table laden with food, around which the Knights of Fealty began to seat themselves. The single board looked too small to be able to seat them all, but as he drew closer Leith realised this was a trick of scale: anything human-sized, including the largest table he'd ever seen, would be dwarfed by the cavern-like hall surrounding them.

'Please, be seated,' Sir Chalcis beckoned to his visitors, his voice magnified in a way subtly different to the illusions spun by Phemanderac and others. His words seemed to come from all parts of the hall at once.

'Oh, my!' Phemanderac exclaimed, his eyes wide with wonder. 'Perfect acoustics.' He unlimbered his harp from his shoulder. 'May I?' he asked Sir Chalcis.

'Sir Pylorus is the keeper of the hall. It is his permission to grant or to withhold.'

Further inquiry produced a curt nod from the gatekeeper, and at once the philosopher set his fingers to the strings of his instrument.

Leith took his seat as the music began. Others of his Company stood behind their benches or froze halfway to their seats as the sounds washed over them. Now it was the knights' turn to be amazed. His playing began with a descending run of liquid notes, then a second, then a third. A thrumming bass note had been added without Leith noticing its introduction, winding its way around the tune's insistent call. A second tune began – how many hands did Phemanderac have? Leith wondered – an echo of the first. A pause, a drawing of breath: then Phemanderac drew together the disparate notes into a wash of pure sound that winked and pulsed as though it danced through their very minds. The Jugom Ark blazed brightly in Leith's hand; and myriad carven facets in the hall took the harsh light of legend and transmuted it into a glorious brightness, so that light and music conspired together to envelop all present in a sweet, warm embrace.

Some time later Leith found himself still overcome by the majesty of the place, and as a consequence found it difficult to concentrate on the voice of their host. He stole another glance at the swirl of coloured carvings. Here was the sense of power the Hall of Meeting in Instruere had striven to achieve, and had not quite succeeded. Leith could sense that on this ceiling the builders, carvers and mosaicists had attempted to capture something much truer than mere power. Their work paid homage to a glory, a majesty, an awe beyond the more prosaic Instruian artisans. He turned his head, the better to gaze on the rainbow above him. It appeared to spring from rocky hills on both sides of the battlefield, a multicoloured banner of hope flying above a field of despair. The image was so bittersweet as to be poignant. And there, in the foreground . . .

His heart stopped in his breast, his breath caught in his throat.

There in the foreground, standing atop a pinnacle of rock, watching over the battle, stood a figure holding a blazing brand. No, not a brand. An arrow, clearly an arrow, aflame with the fire of God.

'It is a prophecy,' said a voice. Leith tore his gaze away from the incredible scene and back to his eating companions.

'What?'

'It is a prophecy,' Sir Chalcis repeated patiently. 'The whole hall is a prophecy.'

Kurr, seated to Leith's left, glanced up at the mural overhead, his brow puzzled for a moment, then his eyes widened.

'A prophecy of what?' Leith asked weakly.

'Perhaps you had better ask Sir Amasian. It is his life's project, after all.' The knight leaned to his left. 'Sir Amasian? The Arrow-bearer asks about your work. Would you care to speak to him of your vision?'

Opposite Leith, Phemanderac began to play his harp again, eyes closed as if in prayer, fingers barely touching the strings. A few places to his left an old man slowly stood, then shuffled around the table to where Leith sat. The man's shoulders hunched close to his neck, and he wore a robe of deep crimson, his hair a circle of white around a bald pate. He placed a calloused hand on Leith's shoulder and the youth was forced to hold the Jugom Ark away from the old man, lest he catch fire.

'Put it down,' said the old man in a voice as soft as a child's. 'You can put it down. It won't burn anything in this hall.'

Leith nodded, then placed the Arrow on the table in front of his hosts, who all turned from their various conversations to watch and listen. 'You had a vision, Sir Amasian?' Leith asked courteously, barely able to contain the excitement building within him. Perhaps this man could tell him all he needed to know.

'I stood in this hall twenty summers ago,' said the old man in a thin voice, and his eyes closed as he relived his dream. 'Back then the hall was plain and unadorned, though still a work worthy of he whom it honours, and the twelve twelves – the pillars that hold up the roof – did nothing more than record the names of the knights who have passed on since the days of Conal Greatheart himself. At that time I had the task of lighting the torches before the evening meal. I had come from our little chapel, where I opened my soul in agony to the Most High, seeking his guidance; for I was too old to ride with the knights, and was considering resigning from the Order and going to live with my sister in Sivithar. As I stepped forward into Conal's Hall, the burning taper in my hand blazed forth like a thousand suns, too bright to look upon, too holy to endure. I thought for a moment the hall had caught fire, but in an instant I knew it was not so, for the light formed into a vision, a storm-lashed field of battle, of torment, where two mighty armies fought for supremacy. I watched men fall beneath their foes, men unhorsed and crawling on the ground to escape death, and men fighting courageously against insurmountable odds. Their cries came to me as though from a great distance, but even so I could barely contain my fear at the dreadful slaughter taking place before me. I then saw a grey-cloaked figure, a man with one hand, standing on a hill above one of the armies. Opposite him I saw another figure, a boy wearing a white robe, atop a hill rising above the other army. The one-handed man raised his hand, and a vast fist rose up from behind the hills, as though to smash the boy's army. The man opened his fingers, and the fist opened into a hand. But the boy raised his hand, and in it was an arrow, and it burned bright beyond knowing, driving the fist away. Then a rainbow spread across the dark clouds of war, and to my troubled heart it was like a promise. The boy with the arrow cried out in triumph and the arrow flamed brightly, blurring my sight and bringing my vision to an end.'

The old man took a deep breath, opened his eyes and stepped forward so he could look on Leith's stunned face. 'I knew this vision for prophecy. I have the gift: I am on occasion touched with the Sight, and I see true. My lord, I saw the Destroyer and his armies. I saw the army of Faltha. And at its head, with the Jugom Ark as a talisman of victory, I saw . . . you.'

He took a step back, and spoke in a loud voice. 'I beheld the one who will defeat the Destroyer, and he is here in my hall today, seated in the sanctuary I created over many years for his coming. Aah, the honour! The glory! That I should have seen the Right Hand of the Most High! That I should have foretold his coming! Twenty years' labour in this hall is not sufficient to pay the debt I owe the Most High.' And he bowed deeply to Leith, until his bald crown almost reached the floor; and shouts of praise rang out around him.

Lying awake that night in another strange bed – in a splendid room, with servants attending, but a strange bed for all that – Leith found himself unable to shake off the darkness that gripped his heart. Surely news such as that delivered by Sir Amasian ought to have eased his own doubts, since it had done so for everyone else. Yet he felt unable to deal with the dread enveloping him. Was it a fear of death? No – that particular fear he had faced on many occasions throughout his long journeys. Compared to what he felt now, the fear of death was a clean thing, something no one could hold him responsible for. Ah, was that it? Was this the weight of responsibility? The Haufuth had spoken to him of this during their march eastwards from Instruere. But surely even that would feel lighter, somehow. He might make a wrong decision, and people might die. He knew that; knew people would die even if he made every decision correctly. Anyway, who was to judge?

Responsibility, that was partly it. But something more burned away at the pit of his stomach, stealing sleep, stealing peace. It settled deeply into him tonight, after being forced to stand and acknowledge the praise offered him by the Knights of Fealty following the words of their Seer. He felt like an impostor. It wasn't supposed to be him on that hilltop facing the Destroyer. He'd done something wrong, made some wrong choice, and he was disqualified from leading the army. He should stand aside and let someone else lead, or disaster would befall the great Army of Faltha . . . the Destroyer's giant fist would fall on them, crushing them under its might . . . down the fist comes, slowly falling, but still too quickly for his friends to escape death . . . Kurr falls beneath it, still shouting advice to Leith as he dies . . . his father and his mother disappear beneath its shadow, their mouths open in a mute cry of terror . . . Hal his brother waits patiently for the blow to fall, his face full of love and patience . . . Leith cries out but the fist falls, tearing his heart out . . .

The Destroyer speaks to him. 'I couldn't have done it without you,' he says in a mocking voice . . . he leans over and places his hand on Leith's shoulder; the touch is ice-cold . . . 'It was what you said, it was what you said!' and he laughs, a cruel sound that sets rocks to falling . . . and again the victor speaks: 'Now you will be my Right Hand!' The fist opens out, rears up, hovers over Leith for a moment, then picks him up . . . places him on the Destroyer's hill . . . beside the cruel Harrower of Faltha . . . Leith can't breathe, there's a weight on his chest, crushing him like his army had been crushed . . . he can't breathe, can't breathe . . .

O Most High, Leith cried as he came awake with a start, heart hammering, sweat soaking into his bedsheets, *what have I done?*

Clad only in his nightshirt, Leith pushed open the door of his room and took a torch from the brazier set beside the knight assigned to watch his room. The man turned at the sound, then nodded, took up his sword and made to follow him. Though Leith gestured for him to remain behind, the knight padded down the dimly-lit corridor in his wake.

He remembered the way. Within minutes he found himself easing open the door to the Hall of Conal Greatheart, in which a few torches still burned. He'd left the Jugom Ark behind: after thinking about it for a moment, he decided his forgetfulness was deliberate. It could remain on the stone sill of his bedroom window. Perhaps the prophecy on the ceiling of the hall would look different under the illumination of mere torchlight.

There it was, up in the shadowed ceiling. The rainbow, picked out in tessellations that seemed to blend one colour into another, looked in the half-light more like a portent of doom than a herald of victory. The armies fought in the twilight, it seemed, and their deaths went unnoticed. On the twin hills, left and right, stood the two figures opposing each other. Or was it just one figure cunningly reflected, as in a mirror?

He searched the image for the faces of his friends, his parents, his brother, but they were not there. *Just a nightmare, then.* As he turned to leave, his eye was caught by a detail from one of the other images. He followed it outward to the edge of the ceiling, then found another image and followed it back in to the centre. Twelve paths, twelve people led to this great image of victory.

<I did tell you.>

How many of them? How many have you called?

<You're not the first. But you are the only one to have made it this far.>

So I'm supposed to be here?

If the voice could have sighed, it would have. <Why is it people think the most important question is where they are? As though where you live is more important than *how* you live?>

But surely if I'm supposed to be somewhere else, doing something else, I should know about it?

<Leith, there are a hundred ways this task could be achieved. There are a thousand people who could have achieved it. The Seer of Fealty was shown this truth, and on the ceiling of this hall he has tried to represent it by depicting a multitude of paths to the same place. Beware, Leith. This image proved too powerful for his mind. He has not rendered it exactly as it was shown to him. Do not put too much store in it.>

Then why show me at all?

<You overestimate my power in the world of men. I showed Amasian the vision, but it was his to interpret. All I can do is point the way. I cannot compel anyone to follow. However reluctantly, you have followed where no one else would walk, and so now it has come down to you. Already you have made

choices that made your path a harder one to walk, and you will no doubt make it harder still for yourself in the days to come.>

What have I done wrong?

<You find it hard to trust. You have drawn away from the people who could offer you the most help. Perhaps there is no other way for one such as you.> Leith was sure he could hear tenderness in the voice, tenderness mixed in with the weariness of the ages, as though it was the old, old earth itself who spoke to him.

Who are you? Tell me who you are!

<One day you will learn my name.>

Tell me, please tell me! he cried. But the voice had gone silent. He glanced towards the Arrow, as though through some act of will he could bring the voice back – and realised he'd left it back in his room.

When the rest of the Company found him next morning, he was still there in the hall, sitting alone at the great table with a dozing knight standing at his side; and he was laughing softly to himself.

One hundred and twelve knights marched forth from Fealty, accompanied by their pages and heralds, to join the massed Falthan army down on the plain below. As they approached, their heralds blew a great blast on their trumpets, and the army cheered as the morning sun shone on their armour. The cheering grew louder as the knights divided into two lines, drew their bright swords and held them aloft, then brought them together above the path between the two lines. Under this guard of honour came the Company and their generals, led by the Arrow-bearer. Those close enough to see his face noticed a strange smile playing on his lips.

That afternoon the weather turned to the south. A warm wind blew from the desert hidden behind the Veridian Borders, and soon had the army sweating in their cloaks, their horses lathered, the foot-soldiers struggling to keep up. Small clouds appeared above the slopes to their right, but as the afternoon drew on they grew, fed by the reservoir of cool air on the plains, made unstable by the warm air from the desert. Up, up they rose, spreading out like anvils in a celestial smithy, and lightning began flashing from their black bases.

The weather broke the next day. One of the huge storms, wafted north from the Veridian Borders on the desert wind, slowly moved abreast of the marching army. Though the marchers were spread over nearly two leagues, from the Company and the Jugom Ark at the front to the many provision-laden wagons at the rear, the cloud covered them all. Lightning cracked and boomed all around them, then the rain began and within a few minutes came down in torrents, as though trying to crush Leith's army into the muddy road. He could do nothing but call a halt for the day, though there were hours of daylight left. To march on in the storm-darkness risked injury. It seemed to take an age to pass the message down the ranks, though some of the more experienced soldiers had already set up camp, with tents pitched and horses tethered in anticipation of the order.

The storm passed overhead at a snail's pace. At times the rain relented, as though the great cloud was exhausted; but then the hail would return with renewed vigour, battering the tents and the shields of anyone unfortunate enough to be left in the open. The *losian* army bore the hail with stoic silence, having but few tents among them, and unwilling – or uninvited – to share the tents of their First Men allies.

At the height of the storm a horse came galloping down

the road in a tunnel of spray, drawing to a halt in front of the generals' tent. A rider leaped from its back and flung open the tent flap. It was one of the heralds sent out every morning to announce the coming of the Falthan army and to recruit any willing fighters. 'There is a force of arms less than a league east of here, holding the road against us,' he said. 'Many thousands strong. Like us, they wait out the storm, but will march west when the rain stops.'

'Their devices, man!' one of the Straux leaders roared. 'What were their devices?'

'My lord,' he stammered, 'they display a banner of green, slashed left to right with blue and overlaid with a brown tree.' At this, several of the generals sighed their relief, and the man from Straux clapped his hands together.

'You're from Deruys, are you not? Were you not taught to recognise the banner of the northern plain? It is the Army of Deuverre come to join us!'

The good news spread throughout the army, making up, to a degree, for the soaking everyone received. Before nightfall the storm drifted away to worry someone else, rattling and booming in the northern distance. The Deuverrans joined their numbers to what was already the largest army ever assembled in the history of Faltha – at least, according to the old man Jethart whom Leith often saw in the company of his father.

Leith was listening to a detailed recitation of the Falthan army's remaining stores when the summons came. The Falthan army suffered a severe shortage of axles, apparently; a consequence of rutted ground. He believed it important to keep abreast of such things, even though someone else always seemed to have these matters under control. Perhaps if he had been listening to something of greater interest he would have turned the messenger with the summons away. But he recognised his mother's handwriting on the parchment, and knew there were issues more important than axles he needed to deal with. Bidding the clerk a good day, he left with the young woman who delivered the summons and made his way across a muddy half-mile of trampled fields. There, some distance apart from the armies, stood a plain white pavilion topped with his banner.

Ambush. The word sprang into his mind when he opened the tent flap and walked into the pavilion. In the foreground stood a long table, from which servants cleared the remains of a substantial meal. A meal to which he hadn't been invited, and during which he was no doubt discussed. The scrape and clatter of wooden platters served to mask the whispering of his family and friends, his Company, who sat on two rows of benches set up behind the empty board. As Leith approached them their heads drew apart, they fell silent and their eyes settled on him like accusations.

Leith needed no telling what this was about. Mahnum and Indrett sat in the centre of the front bench. His mother had been crying, her red, blotchy face all the evidence he needed. As Farr rose from his bench, Leith began to gather his anger.

Unbidden, an image appeared in his mind. A massive shape, stretching right across his mind's eye. It came from his dream in Foilzie's basement, when the Most High had fallen upon the Company with Fire.

<I told you I'd remind you of this.>

I haven't forgotten, Leith responded. Quiet, even serene, the feelings associated with that dream smothered his anger, leaving him calm. He'd received a vision of sorts in his dream, in which he'd seen a vast cube which stood for the love others had for him. As he beheld this love, somehow rendered in physical form, a voice had spoken: 'Nothing you do will exhaust the love your family and your friends have for you.'

I still remember.

<Your friends and your family will speak out of love, but their words will offend you. They do not understand the struggles you go through in order to hold the Jugom Ark.>

I don't understand my struggles either. Could I talk with you about them?

<Of course, but not now. Others want to talk with you about much the same thing.>

As always, this exchange apparently occupied no time at all. Farr got to his feet, cleared his throat and welcomed Leith to the meeting. 'We're here to talk about your role in the coming war,' he said. 'I've called the Company together because we're concerned about your fitness to lead us.'

'A little blunt, but Farr has the heart of it,' his father said. 'Leith, we can go no further without reassurance you act in our best interest. We have spoken with the *losian* leaders, specifically Jethart, and he has explained to me how those not of the Fire are not harmed by the touch of the Jugom Ark. That is worrying information, Leith.'

Leith made to answer, but Kurr beat him to it. 'So it is, boy. What use is a weapon if it can't be used against our enemies? You're playing with the future of Faltha. How could you be so foolish?'

'People lost their lives on the journey to find that arrow,' said a soft voice from his right. Illyon, the Escaignian woman.

The Haufuth made to speak, but Leith forestalled him. 'You are right,' he said quietly.

This had to be done with care; he walked a fine line. He would not, could not allow himself to be submerged by the voice of the Jugom Ark. Above all, he wanted to avoid Hal's fate. His adopted brother's mystical union with the Most High, whether real or imagined, obliterated whatever personality he might once have had. What Leith said would need to leave him some freedom, while still keeping the confidence of the Company.

'You are right, all of you,' he repeated. 'I don't really know what to do with the Arrow, and I should have found out before now. Phemanderac spoke to me over a week ago, but I haven't seen him since. I note he's not here today. Was he asked?'

Farr frowned. 'What does that matter? Where I come from much is expected of young men. For you to have come this far without fulfilling your duty is just cowardly. How could you value so lightly the sacrifices of those who died to get you this far?'

'Phemanderac did not want to attend today's meeting,' Indrett said. 'Leith, have you said anything to upset him?'

The echo in her voice spoke of Hal. His brother was nowhere to be seen. *No matter what they say, they will not exhaust my love for them.* Repeating this paraphrase of his vision gave Leith the strength to keep his frustration in check.

'Mother, I don't know what's wrong with Phemanderac. I need his wisdom, but whenever I send for him he responds with some excuse. He's busy, or he's sick, or he's got some task he can't get free from.'

'Then you must find someone else. None of us know anything about the Arrow. Find Phemanderac and *make* him talk to you. If he won't talk to you, try Jethart or Maendraga. Or Hal. But please, son, make sure you know everything you can know about the Jugom Ark before we encounter the Bhrudwans.'

The Haufuth shifted his bulk on the bench. 'You know, Leith, if I were you I'd be worried about the Destroyer. We're expecting him to accompany his army westwards. In your hand you hold the only weapon known to be effective against him. Aren't you afraid this whole journey is leading towards a confrontation between you and the Destroyer?'

'Haufuth!' Indrett hissed. 'We agreed not to mention your concerns!'

'We did, but we've asked Leith to face up to his responsibility. We have to face up to ours. We can't leave Leith to work this out on his own.'

Bless you, Haufuth. Leith did not expect to meet the Destroyer face to face: the Undying Man would surely have more important people to deal with. Nevertheless, his village headman's words were the first in the meeting sympathetic to him.

'I have learned *some* things about the Jugom Ark,' Leith said determinedly. 'It is tuned to my emotions, though I'm not sure what to make of that. Any advice would be welcome.' *Put it back on them.* 'I can heal with it. I haven't tried to use it as a weapon. I'm worried I'd do damage I didn't intend.'

'You need to find somewhere alone and practise,' Farr suggested.

'How could he practise?' Maendraga asked quietly. 'Are we going to round up volunteers to be slain by the Arrow?'

'What do you suggest, magician?' Farr leaned towards the guardian as though pressing him for an answer.

'Why not trust the Jugom Ark?' Belladonna stood and walked elegantly over to where Leith stood, Arrow guttering in his hand. 'You talk as though Leith directs the Arrow by his will. From what I've seen, the reality is far more complex. Sometimes the Arrow reflects Leith's feelings, but other times it appears to direct his actions. How else do we explain the way Leith beat back Deorc's unholy blue fire?'

For a moment he debated telling the Company about the voice in his head. *Well, the Arrow speaks to me, but I'm not going crazy, honestly*. A wild thought ran through his mind. He told them of the voice, and as a result his friends and family decided he was insane and demanded he lay the Arrow aside. He complied, feigning sorrow and leaving the task to others more fit than he.

No, he'd made his choice. Twice he'd made it by picking up the Arrow, once at Joram Basin and then again when he accepted leadership of the Company. He couldn't take that way out. He was their leader now: it was time he led them. Ironically, his first act as leader would be to sit and listen to his followers chastise him.

He found the next hour very difficult. He was lectured by Kurr and, more gently but still as gallingly, by the Haufuth – whose abandonment of the Company in Withwestwa Wood seemed to have been forgotten. His father brought up the subject of his brother while his mother nodded in the background. Again everyone ignored Mahnum's difficulties with his own father, Modahl. It all seemed so unfair.

Words formed in his mind. *Just as I've been fair to you by admitting my fault, you need to be fair to me. Until Hal explains why so much of his counsel works against our interests, he needs to be watched. Just as you have called me to account, so you need to call him.*

He gritted his teeth and kept his mouth closed. The vision he'd had in Foilzie's basement enabled him to get through without saying something he would regret. Only two dissenting voices were heard in the pavilion. Maendraga and his daughter continued to suggest there was little to worry about, but Leith knew better. He needed knowledge, and he knew from whom he would seek it.

Waking up a little earlier than usual, Stella slid across her silken sheets and eased open the curtain of her litter. The Army of Bhrudwo had spent the last week slowly winding up a series of steep inclines, ascending to a land even higher than the high plateau of Birinjh, and the previous night they had halted on a broad stair just above the treeline. In the half-light of a pre-dawn sky, the land around her seemed just like that of northern Firanes. The environs of Windrise, perhaps, or the upper Thraell valley. Just thinking of those places set her heart aching, and the tears she seemed constantly to be shedding came to her eyes yet again. Her mind populated the landscape with woodsmen – laughing Fodhram, perhaps – and a village or two, their fires sending lazy spirals of smoke into the pinking sky. She imagined the Company walking up that shadowy defile to her right: the old farmer Kurr in front, Leith and his brother Hal just behind, deep in conversation. Her eyes moved back down the valley, and there she was, it seemed, eyes down on the stony path, walking in front of the Storrsen brothers, Farr and Wira – her heart gave a twist – followed by Perdu and the Haufuth sharing a joke. For a moment the agony of the sight bit at her like a knife in her side, and she screwed her eyes shut tight; but the scene remained spread across her inner vision.

A few feet away to her left, her four guards sat huddled around a small fire, eating the same gruel they fed to her each morning. One of them raised his voice in song, a high-pitched, plaintive chant that sounded entirely in keeping with her despair. After a few minutes the singer rose, put down his bowl beside the fire and began walking towards her litter. No doubt he went to wake her to another day of fear, of hopelessness, of darkness.

Abruptly, Stella couldn't stand it a moment longer. On this bitter morning a slow death in the wilderness seemed infinitely preferable to continued captivity, even if it was in a silken cage. She darted forward, her thin legs pumping, and within moments was gone, swallowed up by the shadows.

CHAPTER 11

VULTURE'S CRAW

WARM SOUTH WINDS CONTINUED for a week or more until, early in the afternoon of the twentieth day since they had left Instruere, the Army of Faltha halted atop a small rise and looked out over central Faltha. Directly below them the Aleinus flowed from right to left in a wide curve, arcing off northwest into the mazy distance of the Maremma where, on the edge of sight, the sunlight reflected from hundreds of nameless lakes. To their right lay the town of Vindicare, the capital of Austrau, Straux's less populous eastern province. Behind the town over three hundred leagues of semi-arid steppeland stretched to the Taproot Hills of Redana'a in the east, and from the Deep Desert in the south to Favony in the north. Across this less promising land the army would have to make their way, but not on foot. Below them, in the broad harbour built in the lee of the great river's curve to the north, dozens of huge barges had been constructed.

'I hope this works,' said Leith to his generals. 'We've emptied the City's coffers to get these rafts built on time.'

'Barges, my lord; barges, not rafts,' said the captain of

the Instruian Guard, wincing. 'Don't let them hear you call them rafts.'

'They might hear more than that if they haven't built as many as they promised,' Kurr growled. 'I can only count fifty. Didn't we order at least a hundred?'

'They had one month, my lords,' said the Chief Clerk of Instruere, the man charged with this task ever since serious thought had been given to moving a large army from Instruere to the Gap. 'One month to find materials, hire workers and build a hundred barges.' He smiled at them obsequiously, then shrugged his shoulders as though making it clear that this turn of events was in no way his responsibility. 'It was always going to be a difficult challenge.' Behind him someone groaned in frustration.

The trek eastward had encountered its first serious check, Leith knew. He sent his generals to make a detailed assessment of the condition of their fighters, while he, the Company and a number of officials made their way down to the Vindicari Docks to find out how many barges were available. Soon they would learn whether they had to abandon their grand idea of poling up the still-sluggish river to Aleinus Gates, and sacrifice at least ten days in a long, slow march across the steppes.

The Falthan army was forced to wait in Vindicare for two excruciating days. The Haufuth tried to tell himself it probably would not matter, that the Bhrudwans might now already be streaming through the Gap, or more likely still be six months short of it. The line of thought only got him wondering how Leith planned to provision an army of sixty thousand men while they waited for the Destroyer to appear, and how foolish the Company would appear if the Bhrudwan army failed to materialise. That could be faced in the future, but for now the task of waiting for the remaining barges to be finished gnawed at his patience.

Leith expressed similar sentiments. The Haufuth used the opportunity to answer his own doubts. 'We arrived a full three days ahead of our schedule,' he said between mouthfuls of breakfast on the second morning. 'Not fair to expect the shipbuilders to have finished their task ahead of time, is it?' He leaned over and patted Leith's hand. 'We did manage to send off a good third of the men yesterday. They'll be well up the river by now.'

'Haufuth?' Leith said quietly. The big man leaned over close to him, drawn by something in the boy's voice. 'What did you do when it all got too much for you? When people wanted more than you could give them?'

The village headman sighed his relief. The Company had talked much together since their meeting with Leith, worrying about how the young man was coping with leadership, concerned he no longer had anyone to talk to. They had all witnessed the falling out between the two brothers, and continued to hide from Leith the depth of hurt Hal suffered that day. A reconciliation seemed unlikely, eliminating one of the people Leith might have gone to if he chose to unburden himself. Then there was Phemanderac. No one had seemed closer to the Arrow-bearer than the curious philosopher of Dhauria, yet something had come between them also, though no one had seen any evidence of ill-feeling, and Leith himself denied it. If anything, the Dhaurian now appeared reluctant to spend time with Leith, even though he had promised to educate the lad in the mysteries of the *Fuirfad*.

The boy needed to talk to someone. All agreed far too much depended on him to allow his potentially destructive silences to continue. Now he had spoken, and the Haufuth knew he must be very careful in the way he answered.

Take it lightly, he told himself. 'I always relied on the village council,' he replied blandly, as though not appreciating the importance of the question. 'If I thought something was too large for me, I could always turn to them.'

'But none of them can carry it,' Leith said in little more than a whisper. 'None of them can hear it.'

'I don't think my size helped me,' the Haufuth continued in his conversational voice. *Don't lecture him!* 'The villagers knew my limitations. Sometimes they saw me as a fool, a big buffoon not to be trusted with anything but food. I had to learn to let others do things I felt perfectly capable of doing myself. I'm not sure how I would cope if I had your burden to carry.'

'You wanted us to leave you behind at Roleystone Bridge.' Leith's voice was tight. 'You wanted us to continue along the Westway without you. In the end, you remained with the Hermit and had a rest from your cares. Who will give me a rest from mine?'

'Leith, back then everything seemed to be lining up against us. The Bridge was torn down, the Bhrudwans taunted us with their captives, and there seemed little chance of our survival, let alone rescuing your mother and father. But now look at us. See how far we have come! We found the Jugom Ark, and with it gathered together a great army. We are well on the way to doing what we once thought impossible. At Roleystone we were a handful, now we are many thousands, and there are many wise and experienced people here who can share the burden.'

'No,' Leith whispered. 'There is no one. No one else. Only me.'

The Haufuth was about to reply when a Vindicari official, just up from the docks, bustled in to the tent. 'You asked me to report when the hundredth barge was launched,' said the man briskly. 'We have worked all night under torchlight, and the last ten barges are ready to be floated. Will you come and inspect them?'

The look on Leith's face as he followed the official out of the tent, his breakfast uneaten, his words unsaid, nearly broke the big man's heart.

Numbers, numbers. Four hundred and seventeen dead, Leith was told, when the seventy-first barge foundered and the following barge drove over the top of it, spilling soldiers into the dark, cold waters. All numbers, not panicking, screaming, drowning men. Just numbers. Over two hundred deserters, most from the Straux army, running from the growing spectre of war, running because the speech-fostered enthusiasm had died. Sixty thousand less four hundred and seventeen, less a further two hundred. Numbers.

Around him soldiers took turns at poling his barge into the slow but inexorable current, making a league every hour, ten leagues a day, two hundred and fifty leagues to Aleinus Gates. More numbers. Less than half the number of days gone, more than half the number of leagues travelled. Good progress, they told him. To Leith they were just numbers. He recalled sitting with other children in front of the Haufuth's house, reciting his numbers. He'd always been good at them. He could feel the shape of them, he could tell when they didn't add up or divide right, when someone derived a careless answer. The numbers in his head had that careless feel. Even though he knew he had not made a mistake, they still felt wrong.

The deaths were regrettable, his advisers said; and in the same breath told him many more would have been lost if they had attempted the long march across the steppeland. Many more, they assured him, their faces lined up in a row in his tent, delivering the news without a tear. Just information. He was doing the best thing.

He couldn't sleep. Every time he closed his eyes, he seemed to slip below the surface of green waters, eyes wide open, watching others sink into the darkness, unable to save himself, unable to save them, unable to breathe . . . Finally, some time in the night, he slipped out of his tent and down to the shore of the cursed river, sat down on the bank and cried out his misery under the uncaring stars.

Ninety-eight barges arrived at Aleinus Gates a full five days ahead of his generals' most optimistic schedule. Only one further barge lost, and that only slowly, gradually falling apart over a number of days. The Falthan army was well rested, ready to take to the path that would lead it through a northern winter to the Gap. Supplies were alarmingly depleted, but agents dispatched from Instruere in the days before the new Council was invested had purchased food and provisions enough to see them through Vulture's Craw to Kaskyne, a two-week trek along narrow paths.

More encouraging was news that another army waited for them at the small town of Aleinus Gates. This army numbered perhaps five thousand, all but a few hundred of which came from Sturrenkol, the capital city of Favony, whose king remained loyal to Faltha. King Cuantha of Favony made the journey south with his army in order to see the Jugom Ark for himself, he claimed; and the Company spent a long evening in discussion with the king and his advisers.

'No one knows Vulture's Craw better than we,' said King Cuantha, a curly-haired, freckle-faced man of perhaps thirty years, indicating his retinue of courtiers. 'If there was another way east, I would recommend you take it; but there is not, since the first snows of winter have already closed the high Wodranian passes. You are walking into difficulty, friends. Vulture's Craw is not kind to winter travellers. Could you not have left earlier in the year?'

'There are passes through the mountains?' asked the Captain of the Instruian Guard. 'We had heard that they were impassable.'

'They *are* impassable. These days the deep highlands are overrun with wild men down from the icy north. They will not hesitate to waylay any travellers on the mountain paths. Many of my people have been slain by these brutes. There have been reliable reports that some of the victims are tortured and eaten. Having said that, I doubt even these *losian* wildlings would attack an army such as yours. You would have been safe had you arrived here even six weeks ago. Now the snows would eat your army more quickly than the cooking fires of the Wodrani.'

'What is so dangerous about Vulture's Craw?' Leith asked. The red-haired monarch turned his not-so-regal face towards the Arrow-bearer, measuring the young northerner who carried in his hand the salvation of Faltha. There could be no doubt, his spies told him: the Arrow was no trick, and thus the threat from the east was no mere rumour. Besides, he reminded himself, one of his eastern villages had been destroyed just over a year previously, and not by the Wodrani. According to the handful of survivors, the attackers had been Bhrudwans; and this story had been confirmed just today by the father of the Arrow-bearer himself.

In the moments before he answered, the King of Favony took stock of the leader of the Falthan army. His informants in Instruere spoke of a mighty magician who ended battles with a word, and who immolated his enemies in fire. Well, the Arrow was undoubtedly capable of great things, but, at first glance at least, its callow Keeper seemed nothing more than a small-minded villager.

Was this the opportunity he had been waiting for?

'Vulture's Craw is a deep gut where the Aleinus roars and foams like an angry bear,' he told them. 'In winter deep snows can smother the paths, while in spring the river floods, sometimes carrying the paths away and all who travel on them. Every spring the floodwaters bring down a few bodies still frozen from the winter snows. When the floods abate, the vultures gather; hence, Vulture's Craw.'

'Why, then, would we take our army through there?' Sjenda of Deruys snapped. The chatelaine of the Raving King's castle, she had proved to be the best at chivvying reluctant suppliers, often procuring essential provisions at a cost far below that which any of Leith's Instruian officials could achieve. She had an open, round face and a demeanour that many mistook for naiveté, an impression corrected the instant she spoke. 'Might as well just tip our supplies in the river and be done with it!'

'Because, fair one, it is neither spring nor deepest winter – yet,' replied the king heatedly, his eyes narrowing. 'Though if you waste time wishing the inevitable would not come to pass, then in spring you might meet the Bhrudwan army right here!'

Leith spoke up at just the right time to avert an argument between people he clearly needed. 'If we must take this path, then let us set foot on it as soon as we can. I don't like the sound of those winter snows, and I am a northman. I don't like to think of southerners caught in a winter storm.'

'I will send expert guides to assist you, my lord,' said Cuantha. 'This is a precious gift, for two days' march east of here a last bridge stretches across the river. There you must choose between the north and the south bank. The road on the north bank is longer, steeper and narrower, but is somewhat sheltered from the north winds, while the south road is perhaps three days shorter, but travellers are vulnerable to storms coming down off the Wodranians. You'll need a local to help you choose.'

Sjenda sniffed loudly, as if doubting that any mere local could know more about the movement of men and provisions than her. Leith leaned forward to get a better look at her, perhaps to quell any argument she might offer, and the Jugom Ark flared in his hand. The officials sitting on either side of him threw themselves from their chairs. Leith's advisers backed away from him, and Sjenda's face wore a frightened pallor.

'Oh,' he said, embarrassed. 'I'm sorry. This thing is attuned to me, or so I'm told. I have yet to learn how to fully control it.'

From that moment the gathering busied itself with mundane matters, heads down and private thoughts unvoiced, but no one approached Leith. And sitting quietly in a corner of his own pavilion, the King of Favony watched the young Bearer of the Arrow and considered how best he could turn this situation to the advantage of his new master – and to himself.

Leith had his mind on other matters. He'd managed to have Maendraga and his daughter assigned to his barge, and had spent three interesting weeks on the wide, slow Aleinus River in the company of the two magicians. They had filled his head with both mysticism and good sense, but he was having a dreadful time separating the two.

The Guardians of the Arrow, Belladonna and her father, had been genial and restful companions. Neither guardian pressed him in the way he felt his other friends had done, trying to force him into some revelation about the Jugom Ark. Instead they had passed their days in simple conversation, only incidentally touching on the subject of most importance to them all. They knew Leith needed to learn, and he knew they knew it, but their unhurried approach opened him without any harsh words needing to be spoken.

'Yes,' Maendraga had said, his rich voice reminding Leith of the time they shared on the Wodhaitic Sea. 'Jethart is right when he says the Arrow only affects those of the Fire.'

'Why is that? Are there talismans for each of the other elements?'

Belladonna laughed, the gap in her front teeth visible in her smile. 'We were told so. The knowledge was passed down from Bewray's time, but no one knows with certainty.'

'Can't see it myself,' Maendraga interrupted his daughter agreeably. 'The Jugom Ark is the product of rebellion and justice. I don't think similar situations prevailed for the people of the Water, Earth and Air.'

For a while the two guardians debated this idea, constantly referring to the writings of Maendraga's ancestors, an increasingly esoteric subject to which Leith could contribute nothing. Eventually the river rocked him gently to sleep.

A few days later Leith had asked the question foremost

on his mind. 'Is the Jugom Ark a weapon?' For a reason he could not yet name, the subject was difficult to broach.

Father and daughter discussed it for a while, but could not make up their minds. Maendraga began by arguing forcefully for the position that the Arrow must have a function as a weapon, but Belladonna opposed him. 'Can a weapon unify?' she wondered aloud, after her father suggested the very shape of the Jugom Ark pointed to its function.

Leith seized on her argument. 'Weapons are made to divide and defeat,' he said. 'How does division suggest unity?'

Maendraga answered immediately. 'Easily, Leith. Especially if the weapon divides Faltha and Bhrudwo. What better reason to unify Faltha? Of course it's a weapon.'

'But if it is a weapon, how does it work?' Belladonna continued to pull at the issue like a loose thread hanging from a garment.

Maendraga turned to Leith and raised his eyebrows questioningly.

'Well, I haven't used it as a weapon,' he said. 'I've healed with it, at the Court of Nemohaim and when Escaigne and the Ecclesia were ambushed by Deorc. I used it to resist the blue fire of the Destroyer. I don't know what other powers it has.' He looked down at the Arrow in his hand.

'The biggest miracle, of course, is the assembling of this army,' Maendraga said thoughtfully.

'Perhaps the Bearer is supposed to heal the hurts of his army, thereby maintaining their unity?' Belladonna uncrossed her long legs as she said this, and began pacing back and forth on the barge.

'Or maybe heal the hurts of the Bhrudwan army, drawing them in to some greater unity with Faltha?' Maendraga put out an arm and touched her, emphasising his point.

'But it took the Destroyer's hand,' Leith said. 'Wasn't that its original purpose? What if I'm supposed to assault the Destroyer with it?'

'I'm not sure how you would go about that,' Belladonna said doubtfully.

Leith pulled out his most convincing argument, the one which had come to him weeks before. 'The carvings in the Hall of Meeting show the Most High loosing the Arrow at the Destroyer using a bow. I wasn't given a bow. Surely, if the Arrow was meant to be used as a weapon, I would have been given a bow? How can I launch this weapon at our foe?'

Maendraga rubbed his chin, deep in thought. 'The Jugom Ark would not suffer an ordinary bow, however constructed. It would set the wood alight.'

'Must I sneak into the Bhrudwan camp, then, and throw it at him? If I throw the Arrow and it does not destroy him, I will have surrendered it to him for nothing.'

'Maybe you need to get even closer and stab him with it.' Belladonna's tone suggested she harboured severe reservations about what she said.

'Through the massed might of Bhrudwo and the Lords of Fear? That's even worse. If they catch me I will have surrendered myself as well as the Arrow.'

The discussion continued on for an hour or so, but seemed to Leith a waste of time. Nothing could be proved anyway. They could conceive of no simple method of testing the Jugom Ark's efficacy as a weapon without rounding up some of their own soldiers and using it against them. He could hear Hal's outraged voice of protest if *that* idea was suggested! *And*, thought Leith, *my voice would be added to his*.

Though their time on the barges was soon over, Leith

hoped to spend more time with the guardians later in the march. They were friendlier, more knowledgeable and less judgmental than his parents would likely be. *Go and speak with Hal*, his mother and father would say. He doubted he could explain to them why he couldn't do that. *Hal speaks in my head*, he'd say to them. *He is taking over my mind. I need to work this out without his interference!* No, telling them about the voice would further harm the already reduced respect in which his family held him.

Leith looked up from his musings: the King of Favony was about to take his leave. *Best to keep my eyes open. Take every opportunity to speak to Belladonna and Maendraga. And Phemanderac, if I can find him.*

'I do not like the look of this weather, no matter what Ruben-rammen says.' Kurr was unhappy, and not afraid to let others know it. 'I know what we'd call this weather in Firanes.'

Farr stood shoulder to shoulder with the old farmer. 'You can smell it, can't you. Up on Vinkullen we'd be bringing in the stock and splitting the firewood. There's snow out there, sure enough.'

Ruben-rammen, their stocky Favonian guide, stared up at them from under bushy black eyebrows. 'So I come to your land, outdoorsman, and tell you how to live on it? You would sit at my feet and ask me when to plant and when to harvest? Not all the world is like your home! Allow someone who lives here to share his wisdom!'

Kurr hissed on an indrawn breath but held his tongue, looking to Leith. Farr, however, had no such self-restraint. 'Snow smells like snow anywhere in the world.' The Vinkullen man gestured around him, to the wide greensward, the narrow bridge across the swirling, deep-channelled Aleinus, and the towering hills on both sides. 'It's calm down here in the valley, but look up on the shoulders of the mountains to the north. See the faint white smear in the sky? That's wind-blown snow picked up from the upper slopes and tossed out into this gorge. Unless snow here behaves in a completely different fashion to the snow of Firanes, there is a gale blowing above us. Who can tell what the wind will bring?'

'Very clever, mountain boy. Always it is windy there, up on the Wodranian heights. Sometimes from the north, mostly from the south, until the tail of winter. Anyone who lives in the lee of the mountains knows this! I say the wind will turn to the south before the day is over, and your army will have a safe passage to the east. One week from now you will be feasting in Kaskyne, remembering to toast Ruben-rammen of Favony.'

'Aren't you coming with us?' Kurr asked, surprised.

'My king requires me at Sturrenkol,' came the short reply. 'I cannot disobey.'

Leith stepped forward. 'We are grateful to your king, and to you, Ruben-rammen. Take these coins as extra payment for advice well given, in the face of adversity.' Here Leith cast a baleful glance at his friends.

'That is undeserved, boy,' muttered Kurr. Beside him, Farr growled his agreement.

'So was the criticism,' replied Leith, angered by the old man's intransigence. 'Why must we always think we know best? Every chance we get, we First Men try to enforce our desires on others. This time we are going to listen to the advice we are given.' In the back of his mind he could hear a dockworker yelling abuse at the Pei-ran navigator on the morning he arrived at Instruere, and remembered the shame he had felt.

'We will take the south road, as Ruben-rammen suggested. The king was kind enough to help us: how would ignoring his advice advance the cause of unity in Faltha? We will use all help offered. Now, please kindly go and tell my captains to prepare their charges. We leave as soon as we are ready.'

Though he hated the stares and mutterings the decision drew, Leith felt strangely satisfied with his choice – as if a decision based on information supplied by people outside the Company redressed some celestial balance in which the First Men were always the beneficiaries. It didn't matter that Favonians were First Men themselves. It was good, Leith judged, that the Company didn't appear to always get their way.

At first the weather stayed clear but cold, as it had done since they marched through the Aleinus Gates, a huge and impressive basalt cliff sundered by the roaring waters of the Aleinus a few hours' journey east of the town. Above this point the great river was not navigable, falling over two thousand feet in the hundred leagues between the Gates and Kaskyne, the chief city of Redana'a. The army woke every morning to a heavy frost, which in many shaded parts of Vulture's Craw did not melt before the early afternoon sun left the valley. Leith stopped to inspect the wooden bridge that led to the northern path, and noted the wooden slats had already become slippery with frost. His army would have experienced some difficulty crossing it, and again he congratulated himself on his decision.

The snow began on the fourth day east of Aleinus Gates, the forty-seventh of their march to the Gap. Light at first, it sifted down in patches from a mostly clear sky, garnishing the hard road with a treacherous granular surface. The air became bitterly cold. 'Issue cloaks to anyone without them,' Sjenda barked, her breath frosting in the frigid morning, her words sending people scurrying for the wagons. 'Prepare extra rations,' she ordered the cooks. 'Include a nip of brandy.' A few of the cooks smiled inwardly. The dragon had a heart after all.

By afternoon snow covered the rutted road. Tramped flat by thousands of feet, it froze into a glass-like icy surface almost impossible to stay upright on. Leith's mighty Falthan army suffered a spate of bruised hands and knees, with a few broken bones. As light faded from the southern hills, Leith looked wistfully across the wide southern banks to where the river cut into the base of the northern slopes. Just discernible on the sun-lit slope was the thin line that marked the north bank path. Leith fancied he could even see a few people travelling on the road – or were they watching the Falthan army picking their way east on the southern path?

The King of Favony called a halt. High above the Aleinus River, he and his most trusted advisers observed the long, snake-like procession make its way haltingly up the valley. 'You have done well,' he said to the stocky man at his side. 'Fools beyond belief, entrusting the leadership of such an army to a child.'

'Yes, my lord,' Ruben-rammen replied. 'He actually rejected the advice of his wildscrafty outdoorsmen.'

'How many do you think they'll lose?' the king asked his liegeman and fellow traitor.

'My lord, the question, really, is how many of them will return?'

The curly-haired monarch laughed. 'Set the fire, Ruben-rammen. Let us see whether this magic works. Our master will be very pleased with our work.'

'Yes, your majesty. So pleased, perhaps, that he will agree to the rest of your plan?'

'The rest of my plan? What do you know, my old friend?'

'Know, my king? Just that if I were you I would be planning a western excursion with the ten thousand soldiers you kept in reserve. I can think of an undefended city that might be a gift well received by our new Friend.'

The king laughed again, loud and long. 'Oh, Ruben, I forget just how clever you are. Would that you were of royal blood: you are worthier by far than the talentless clods that squander the king's purse.'

Ruben-rammen smiled at the delight of his king, pleased he had guessed correctly. Inwardly, however, he tasted anger, and as he unstoppered the small vial of potion he had been given at the dark castle in Bhrudwo, in preparation for the blue fire, he reminded himself of the coup d'état conducted by Cuantha's grandfather. Royal blood indeed! The old man had been half Wodrani!

Stella's first night in the northern snows was agony, and she doubted she would survive a second. Her dash for freedom was instinctive, an unthinking flight from despair. Her first thought was to make for the village the Bhrudwans had sacked days before, hoping to find food and shelter among the houses left standing. She had a vague thought of doing something for any survivors: there had to be some, surely? Someone she could help, something to do to assuage the guilt that racked her every time the sickening images flashed through her head.

For the first few hours she expected discovery at any

moment. When the minutes stretched into hours, and the day came to an end, she began to hope – and to worry. Her cloak was flimsy, barely covering a ridiculous lace nightgown, and a light snow had begun to fall. She was not yet hungry, and there were plenty of streams from which to drink, but where would she find shelter?

At the base of a pine tree, it turned out. With night all but fallen she climbed down into a narrow valley sheltering a woody copse. Shivering uncontrollably, she dug into the soft soil between the roots of a tall tree and pulled a thick layer of needles over herself. The ground was cold, but by huddling into a ball Stella preserved a little of her warmth beneath her blanket of needles.

Throughout the long night she lay there, contemplating her freedom. She had exchanged perfume for pine sap, silk for needles, food for hunger. But for the first time since the night she had so foolishly abandoned the Company in favour of Tanghin, she allowed the faint stirrings of hope to steal around her heart.

By the middle of the following day Leith knew they were in trouble. The snow had slowed overnight, but the temperature fell markedly just before sunrise, bringing more snow; and for the first time the wind began to blow, throwing icy pellets into the faces of the soldiers. Progress slowed to a stumbling walk for the footsoldiers, and by noon – at least, by the time Leith estimated it was noon – they had travelled no more than a league from the place they spent the previous night. The wind howled, spitting snow at them like a million darts, closing down their world to sixty thousand small white circles, at the centre of each a soldier under siege. Heads down, hunched under their cloaks, eyes fixed on the road in front of them, the army moved doggedly forward – but cold, so cold. Captains began to lose contact with their troops. Wagons became mired in the snow. Horses lost their footing, and soldiers cursed their luck in the way soldiers do. The better-equipped *losian* army, more familiar with these conditions, nevertheless called a halt for their midday meal and did not set out again. While the great shaggy aurochs, in particular, appeared to be in their element, unaffected by mere drifts of cold white powder, their captains knew what conditions like these could do to man and beast alike. There was little cheer and much grumbling, even amongst the merry Fodhram. And still the snow kept driving in.

'It's only autumn!' Leith shouted, shrugging his shoulders in exasperation. 'How long can this last?'

Kurr shook his head in reply. Nothing was to be gained by pointing out Leith had chosen to ignore his advice. Farr did not hold back: 'We don't know the answer! We don't live here, remember?'

On and on the blizzard raged. *Finally this arrow is of some practical use*, Leith reflected as he rode on through the snow. He wouldn't freeze to death, he could use it to see a little further than others, he could light fires, and on a couple of occasions used it to melt away snowdrifts that blocked their path. But he couldn't be in every place, and the snow depth could now be measured in feet.

Suddenly the wind died, then burst forth with even greater power; and the snowfall tripled in intensity, hammering at them as though the white world was collapsing inwards. What had been annoying quickly became serious, even fatal. Within minutes the army was in total chaos. While some had the good sense to stay put, huddling together with anyone they found, others struck out along the road – or where they imagined the road to be. Men cried out their confusion, their anger, their fear . . . and eventually their despair, in increasingly weak voices.

As night fell in Vulture's Craw, so did silence.

On her second day of freedom Stella risked venturing on to the road, driven there by hunger. The Bhrudwan army had churned up the surface, but in the bootmarks and beside the cold fire-places she found frozen scraps of food. Carrot greens, bread crusts, chewed jerky ends. An hour of scrabbling and the Falthan girl gathered enough to beat back her hunger. She ate on her feet, pressing on down the never-ending slope, following the broken ground back into the heart of Bhrudwo.

In the middle of the afternoon a cold rain began to fall, gradually turning to sleet, soaking the miserable girl to the skin. She could feel her raw limbs begin to cool, her muscles stiffen, in spite of the effort she exerted just to climb the road. She knew she should be afraid. Unless she turned and ran back to the Destroyer she would die, but she also knew beyond any shadow of doubt she would rather die out here, alone in the snows of a strange land, than ever see that hated litter again. Her death would be clean, a result of her own choice, given at the hands of a nature more merciful in its indifference than the cruel hands of evil men. Were she to return to the Bhrudwans her death would be inevitable, and could come in one of a number of awful ways, like the burning Duke of Roudhos, or the arrow-feathered men of the nameless village, or their handless children. She would walk on until she fell.

Shaking with the cold, she trudged over the shoulder of yet another ridge; and there, lying discarded in the middle of the road, was a soldier's pack, just like those the Bhrudwan soldiers carried. She scuttled towards it like a frantic spider, trying to get her knees to bend. *It is real, it is real*, she told herself, her mind as sluggish as her body as she forced her blue fingers to work at the buckles. Inside, filling most of the pack, she found a great black cloak with a red bib, fringed in red. An officer's cloak. Only officers' cloaks had the red fringe as well as the red bib. One of Roudhos's men, then. Perhaps he'd protested the treatment meted out to his lord. Happy with her reasoning, Stella shook the cloak out, then wrapped herself in its fur-lined length. What else? Stout boots. Too big, but they could be packed with fur from the cloak. Some food, and a flask of some foul-smelling liquor she tipped out on the spot. Wira. Her brother. Both taken by the drink. She would not drink it, no matter how much it might warm her.

Slowly her mind focused. Now she had hope! Already she felt warmer. With the cloak, the boots and the food in this pack, surely she could make it back to the village. Then, some time in the future, spring perhaps, she could try the long paths back to Faltha and the people she loved.

Buoyed by these thoughts, Stella picked up the pack and eased it on to her shoulders, adjusting the straps with warming fingers. She did not for a moment wonder why, when all around was frozen and snow-shrouded, the pack was dry and uncovered.

Leith blundered on and on, unsure of his direction, completely alone in the heart of the blizzard. *Sixty thousand soldiers lost*, he kept saying to himself. *Sixty thousand lost*. He had been transported to some other valley where he was the only one alive, he and his feebly burning arrow. He was unhorsed and without hope, wandering the valley of the damned, reaping the reward for his wilful decision that had cost so many lives, and would cost so many more. Occasionally he would stumble over a solid lump, each time to discover the body of a warrior, frozen to death. The first time he tried to thaw the man out with his arrow, but merely made a steaming, sodden mess which caused him to retch until he threw up. *Most High! Most High! Where are you! How could you let this happen?*

At one point the darkness lifted, signifying morning, Leith supposed, though he could barely raise any interest in the fact he had walked all night. A little while later he nearly fell into the Aleinus River, a smoking sliver of grey foam racing past him from right to left – *east to west*, he remembered, visualising the map – like a runnel of molten metal in a giant's forge. East to west. He had been walking downriver. Was that the right way? Had his army continued upriver to their soft white graves?

Later in the morning, after burning his way through a snowdrift, he met his first living man. He was a soldier of Instruere, blue with cold, and he had his arm under the shoulder of a dead man, trying to drag him along the road to safety. Leith tried to persuade him to put the body down, but he would not: eventually, after an hour of arguing, Leith took the corpse's other arm and together the three of them made their way westwards.

Around a bluff they struggled; and, as though they had crossed an invisible boundary drawn by some cruel weather god, the snow stopped. Ahead of them lay a wide grey smudge on the snowy river flat. As they drew closer, Leith could see movement along the length of the smudge, which eventually resolved itself into a huge gathering of people. His army. Or the remnant, at least.

As heads looked up, and the cry went out at the sight of

his Arrow, Leith collapsed to the ground in tears. Strong hands took hold of him, bearing him aloft like some kind of trophy, carrying him gently to the tents and the fires, but Leith was barely aware of them. He scarcely saw the kindly but worried faces bend over his prone form; his mother and father, his villager friends, others of his Company, and his brother.

The Arrow-bearer was safe, it was announced, and the remnants of the mighty Army of Faltha rejoiced. If a few fools cursed his name privately, none said a word against him in public; for who among them, however blessed with supernatural power, could fight against the heart of a storm such as that? The fact he survived, some argued, was proof enough he remained the Most High's anointed Right Hand. Many soldiers talked about how they had seen the light of the Arrow in the midst of the blizzard, shining like a beacon, directing them westwards out of the storm's grim jaws. No, he was their saviour; he had led them to safety.

As Leith lay in a swoon, the Company listened stolidly to the recitation of their losses. Perhaps ten thousand men unaccounted for – ten thousand! Some of these men would surely have survived, in the opinion of experienced campaigners. March in the winter, they said, and this was the inevitable result. Perhaps, the optimistic among them said, a number had made it through to the far side of the storm and would continue to Kaskyne or some other place of safety, but the members of the Company had all seen enough dead bodies on their struggle through the blizzard to doubt that argument. Then there had been the disaster of the avalanche: just before the last bluff, only yards from safety, a wall of snow had come roaring down the mountain, obliterating many of the wagons and taking hundreds of people to their deaths. Sjenda had been lost, as had many of the men from Deruys who tended the wagons, swept right across the valley and into the river.

Worse, in the opinion of the strategists, the army would lose a week, maybe more. It would clearly take time for the army to recover, they advised the Company. To press on now would risk further deaths from exhaustion. Some of the soldiers would disguise the degree of their hurt, or simply would not realise how badly they were affected until exposed once again to the rigours of the path. Then there was their morale to think about. Perhaps it would be best to take a few days to recover, some said, but the strategists were divided on this.

'Get them back on the road as soon as possible,' said Jethart of Inch Chanter. 'Don't give them time to think about their hurts, or you'll not be able to contain the numbers who want to desert.'

Some of the younger generals accused the old man of having no compassion, but others read him better, realising he wanted the maximum number of soldiers to survive in good enough condition to fight. He argued for his position in a firm voice, and gradually his logic won the day.

Leith awoke to muttering. A voice droned on in the distance, but around him a few voices discussed their situation.

'Any campaign such as this is bound to suffer losses.'

Losses?

'The Sna Vazthan army lost more than ten thousand men on the march home from reducing Haurn.'

Ten thousand men!

'At least the *losian* army survived relatively unscathed. They had those big cow-things—'

Aurochs!

'—to protect them from the worst of the snow. Anyway, they hail from parts like this; used to it, no doubt.'

What have I done?

'We still have the Arrow-bearer. He'll protect us. Did you hear about the prophecy carved on the ceiling of Fealty Castle? We just have to keep him alive – oh, he's awake! Everyone, the Arrow-bearer is awake!'

At the end of a terrible week, Stella finally came to the outskirts of the village she sought. She had been in no danger of losing her way, as the Bhrudwan army had left a trail wide enough for a child to follow, and they had been careless enough to discard many treasures in their haste westwards. She had not wanted for food, and her fur greatcloak kept her warm. Yesterday she found a flint, and spent an enjoyable night by the fire: if it were not for the unfamiliar night-sounds around her little camp, and a dreadful feeling of loneliness, she could almost have convinced herself she was back on the Westway with her friends.

The boards were still there, upon which the men of the village had been nailed, but their dreadful human adornments had been removed, by wild animals, no doubt. A few half-eaten carcasses lay in the snow, some smaller than others, and Stella chose not to examine them too closely. She would have to be careful. If bears or wolves regarded this area as an easy source of food, she might be in danger.

Down a gentle slope she went, eyes wide open, looking for any sign of life. She glanced to her right, where the trees hid what had become of the women . . . she would not go there, even if someone was still alive. Past the first ragged hut, little more than a charred ruin, door swinging slowly in the breeze. The sudden barking of dogs rent the air. Stella started, shrinking into the shadows of the hut, as three thin curs bounded past, the first with something in its jaws, the other two dogs chasing it as though in pursuit of treasure. Their snapping and snarling continued for some time. She waited until they had gone, then continued her progress through the village.

There! Off to the left! A hut that was more or less whole, with smoke issuing from the chimney. Oh, Most High, someone was alive! Breaking into a run, Stella made for the hut. As she reached out for the door latch, it occurred to her she had not been careful enough, she had not thought things through, the people inside the hut might not be pleased to see her.

But she couldn't stop herself; the need for human contact, to sustain her hope, was too great. She grasped the handle, threw open the door, stepped into the hut, saw the blue fire set in the grate . . . saw the four white-robed eunuchs . . . saw the Man in the grey robe stand and turn to her . . . heard his words of welcome, and was engulfed in his wild laughter . . .

She stuffed her fist into her mouth but screamed nonetheless, horror beyond horror, as the Destroyer took her by the arm and led her to a chair by the fire.

'Did you think you had escaped us, pretty one?' he asked her, leaning over her like a vulture, his grip painful on her arm. 'That all you needed to do was run and you would be free?'

Her chest was a fire of pain, despair a flame that threatened to consume her. Surely her heart no longer beat within her chest. She wanted to howl and howl.

'Who watched over you every night to ensure you survived? Who left the pack in your path so that you could make it this far? Who waited patiently in this hut, longing to see the look on your face when you realised what has happened to you?'

Stella could do nothing but moan. His harsh, angular face hovered over hers, blurred by her tears.

'You are mine, now and forever. I declare it, and thus it is so. You are marked, having been drawn through the blue fire. I can track you wherever you go. I know you, Stella. I know your fears, I put them there. We will be married, you and I, a symbol of a world united under my hand. You will rule over Faltha, I prophesy it, so know it for truth. You will be the Falthan queen, dark and terrible, and will reign over a thousand years of torment!'

His words echoed in her head, sealing themselves to her as though a second skin, and she shuddered at their touch.

The Destroyer turned his raging eyes away from her, and she collapsed as though boneless. Dimly she heard the black-robed fiend issue orders to his eunuchs; faintly she felt their loathsome touch as they lifted her up, took her outside and bound her behind the saddle of a horse.

The last thing she heard before she passed out was the Destroyer. 'Hurry, now. My pleasure has cost my army a week's marching. A small price, and one we can easily afford, but we cannot allow the Falthans any real hope.'

'This is a day of mourning, Leith. The soldiers hold memorials for their dead comrades even as we speak. We can't send them back into the snow to dig out dead bodies. We don't have the time.'

'But – shouldn't we bury our dead?'

'We are taking a day to remember them, my friend,' Axehaft said softly. 'If we take the time to bury them, we may end up paying for the time taken by burying many more. All the generals are agreed. One day to mourn, then back on the road. Whichever road we choose.' He glanced around the pavilion, acknowledging the nods of agreement.

'And what road will we take? The north road, the south road, or the road back west?' The King of Straux, clearly unhappy at the deaths of many of his soldiers, placed a small but unmissable emphasis on the latter option.

'We've sent scouts along both western paths, with instructions to go as far as they can without endangering their own lives,' the Chief Clerk of Instruere informed them. 'They should return some time today.' His matter-of-fact voice seemed to render unreal the disaster that had befallen them.

'With their information we can choose which path to take,' Kurr said, masking his shock at what happened in Vulture's Craw, knowing they all had to keep their private misgivings about Leith's leadership to themselves, otherwise the boy would be stripped of what confidence remained.

'We cannot return along the southern road,' said Leith fiercely. 'We cannot! Can you imagine what it would be like? Soldiers stumbling over the bodies of their friends? We must take the northern road, or return to Instruere to await the wrath of Bhrudwo.'

'But Leith, the scouts have been sent—' A wave of the Arrow silenced the Haufuth. Would they gainsay him on every point?

'I will accept no other course! Call the scouts back! We must take the north road! I will be cursed before I ever take that hellish southern road again!' And, having vented his anger, he stormed out of the tent and into the cold but clear air of eastern Favony, leaving behind him a collection of sorrowful faces and worried minds.

The recovering army was spread out across the valley immediately east of the last bridge, the ill-favoured bridge Rubenrammen had advised them against crossing only four days ago. If Leith ever found that man, he would arrange for him the most painful death imaginable. Surely such a blunder in reading the weather could not have been accidental! The sorrowful sights all around him tempered his rage. In groups large and small his army stood, in prayer, in quiet conversation or in contemplative silence; whatever their race considered would best honour their newly-dead companions. For a brief moment he considered joining a ceremony, but thought better of it, reasoning that the appearance of his Arrow would draw attention away from the names and faces being remembered. Carefully he masked the Arrow's bright glow while he threaded his way across the valley, avoiding the many congregations gathered there. Finally Leith found himself at the lip of a small dell, sloping down to a lone tree: the army avoided this spot as though a prohibition rested upon it. A thin mist rested in the basin – probably the reason why no one gathered here, Leith realised, as the cold air drained down to this low spot.

There was a solitary figure in the dell, close to the trunk of the bare-branched tree, not part of any congregation. Leith walked a few paces down into the basin before he realised who it was, then stopped himself going any further.

The figure was his brother Hal. So he had survived the southern road. Leith's anger flared again. *What of your magic now, brother? What of your voice? Did you know about the calamity that hung over our heads, Hal, or did it take you by surprise? I trusted the King of Favony and his expert guide, just like you would have done, and look what happened. Ten thousand! I killed ten thousand men!* He forced his jaws shut so as to stifle the scream that threatened to rip out his throat.

What was his brother doing? Reluctantly he drew a little closer. The cripple had a branch in his left hand, swishing it backwards and forwards as though it was a sword. He seemed to know what he was doing. Undoubtedly Achtal had been training him, but to what end? Feeling like a spy in the stronghold of an enemy, Leith crept around the rim of the dell until he found a rock he could take cover behind. Back and forth the switch went, back and forth; forward and back Hal's crippled legs sent him, as though in a dance with an invisible partner.

Leith wanted so much to talk to Hal, to tell him all about the ache in his heart, to share his sorrow, but there had been too many angry words spoken, too many secrets kept, and so he stayed silent, though his throat thickened with the effort. He felt overwhelmed by a vast sadness. How long had Hal been down in this dell? How was it his brother was so alone? Leith felt a fierce, protective anger sweep through him, not unlike how he felt the times his brother had been teased when they were both young. How dare they treat Hal as an outcast, just because his body was a little different?

Then the irony of what he was thinking hit him, and his shoulders hunched in misery. *O Most High, what have I done?* Leith looked on the mist-wreathed face of his brother from the protection of the rock, and as he watched, he saw that Hal wept bitter tears. Finally he could bear to look on his brother's face no longer, and he left the dell, staggering back to his tent as though drunk. It wasn't until he was lying on his pallet that he realised Hal must have known he was there. The Jugom Ark, unregarded in his hand, would undoubtedly have flamed at various times while he hid behind the rock. But he had said nothing, had not betrayed his awareness of the Arrow or its bearer.

Oh, Hal, what have we done?

The blizzard moved off to the south, and the Army of Faltha was able to take the northern road through Vulture's Craw and on to Kaskyne, albeit much more slowly than they had hoped. Even on the more sheltered northern path the snow was banked up high, and Leith consoled himself with the knowledge that neither road would have been passable at the height of the storm. *But how many fewer would have died on this road?*

Truly, the towering Gates of Aleinus and the extensive gorge of Vulture's Craw set behind them together constituted one of the most wondrous places in the world. In high summer a trip through the Craw ranked as one of the most delightful experiences to be had. Sudden waterfalls, rocky heights, sunless valleys, foaming rapids, small, friendly hamlets. No one made the journey in the winter, so no one spoke of the delicate hoar frosts, the tall, snow-cloaked trees, the mist stirring on the frigid river flats, the sudden smoke of hidden villages.

The Falthan army did not have eyes for the scenery. Slowly at first, then more and more swiftly, they pounded towards Kaskyne, passing through Salentia and fording the wide River Donu just above its confluence with the Aleinus a mere eight days after setting their feet to the northern road. The generals could not keep the army to a measured pace: something took hold of their soldiers, some terrible urgency, and the army drove ahead as if men and wagons sought to make up the lost time by running the rest of the way.

Inevitably the pace told on the Falthan army. They trailed

into Kaskyne on the twenty-fourth day since leaving Aleinus Gates, having spent nineteen days on the northern path, the last seven stumbling and sliding over frozen roads. A day of rest in Kaskyne, a meeting with the Redana'ai regent to express their insincere sorrow at the news the king had recently died, some grudging assistance with provisions (but no soldiers) and a peremptory dismissal from the city. The King of Redana'a, exposed by Mahnum as a traitor to Faltha, would go unmourned by the Falthan army. Despite showing the regent that his kingdom was directly in the path of the Bhrudwan assault, the wizened old man mocked them and bade them depart.

It was not until they left their camp on the outskirts of the city that word came to Leith of an army staged a day's march south-west, near Prosopon, the second city of Redana'a. An army from the west, their informant told them, held at Prosopon by a regent opposed to allowing them through his territory. The regent of Redana'a obviously hoped to prevent the two forces from learning about each other.

'Ten thousand or more,' said the patriot, who wore a kerchief over his face for fear of being identified. 'Some from the lowlands, with a banner showing a yellow lion on a field of green; and some from the highlands, fierce warriors with spears and clubs and no banners. They are penned there by twice as many soldiers, the full force of the Redana'a army, and cannot move without the risk of bloodshed.'

'We will put an end to that!' snapped Leith, a delirious hope rising within his breast. Surely this was none other than the armies of Deruys and the Children of the Mist, come to join with them as promised. 'Alert the army. We'll drive the Redana'a force into the river!'

No one said anything for several seconds. It was as though everyone within earshot had the same thought. How to tell Leith his idea was ill-conceived without offending him? The moment was crucial.

Leith himself laughed, breaking the spell. 'Or perhaps we could go and speak with the regent, and explain to him that we know of his deceit. Would that be a better plan?' The sense of relief as the words were spoken was plainly written across two score faces.

The streets of Kaskyne were quiet as the Arrow-bearer led a force of five thousand men towards the royal palace. Now they knew about the army near Prosopon, they noticed the absence of young men in the Redana'a capital. More, they sensed a frisson of fear about them. Shuttered windows, curtains drawn back just far enough for faces to glimpse the army marching past colourless markets, indicated that Kaskyne was a city under heavy-handed control.

'We haven't got time for this,' worried the Haufuth. 'We're still many days behind.'

Leith frowned. 'But we can't leave our allies penned by a traitor! If only there was a way of unseating this regent, we might consider our time well spent.'

The regent had been alerted somehow, and stood alone in the middle of the paved square in front of his palace, anger contorting his features. 'I bade you leave my city!' he cried. 'Why have you returned?'

'To confront a traitor to Faltha,' Leith barked. 'One who would detain the allies of Instruere without due cause. You hoped we would not find out about our friends, but you did not reckon on the courage of your own subjects. How long ago were you bought? Did you think to receive a reward from your master the Destroyer? Better by far to fear the one nearer you!' He took a step towards the elderly man, who by this time cowered on the ground as the Flaming Arrow blazed with wrath.

'So, intimidation works where diplomacy does not,' Leith snapped at him. 'You shall take me to the camp near Prosopon, or I will let the Arrow test you with its fire. I see you know the power of the flame, and I wonder if the Destroyer was your teacher. Get to your feet!'

The ruler of Redana'a, who had (foolishly, as it turned out) emptied his city of anyone who might have helped him stand up to the Arrow-bearer, took the road to Prosopon with his hands bound behind his back, sitting uncomfortably on the back of a drab grey horse. His lieutenants were dismayed to see him a prisoner of the Arrow-bearer, but they could count, and did nothing to rescue their regent when faced with the knowledge that a great army lurked within a day's march. Instead, the Redana'a force withdrew with almost unseemly haste, leaving Leith to greet the latest additions to his army – and the two friends he dearly wanted to meet.

'Wiusago! Tua! How under the sky did you manage to arrive here before us? We did not see you on the road!'

He climbed down off his horse, and first Wiusago, then Te Tuahangata embraced him, both careless of the burning Arrow in his hand: Leith noted this, and it pleased him. 'We've been here for a week, Leith,' Prince Wiusago said. Beside him Te Tuahangata grumbled, 'Cooling our heels, waiting for you to rescue us,' but he smiled at Leith, taking the sting from his words. 'The brave prince here thought it best we not tear our captor's army apart; and, as I always do, I took his advice.'

Leith laughed, for the first time in years, it seemed to him.

'Let me guess. You've spent a solid week arguing what ought to be done, and no doubt we've interrupted another important debate. Should we wait in Kaskyne until you have resolved your differences?'

'Ah, now. The mighty Arrow-bearer jests with us!' Wiusago turned to his friend. 'Why should we listen to him? Unless you are impolite enough to point out I wear a scar from a wound healed by that very Arrow. You're not going to mention it, are you?'

Leith smiled again, an easing of the heart in the company of two people who did not yet hate him, who had not yet suffered at his hands, who had regard for him irrespective of the Jugom Ark. He dreaded the news he had in store for them, and knew Wiusago would be grieved to hear of the loss of so many Deruvian soldiers and of Sjenda the chatelaine. Resolved as he was to tell them of the disaster of Vulture's Craw immediately, once in the company of his friends he could not speak of it.

'We were less than a day behind you when you left Vindicare on the barges,' said Prince Wiusago. 'We could not follow you upriver, as it would have taken many days to build more barges.'

'And the Mist Children would not have travelled on them even if they sat in the river waiting for us!' Te Tuahangata added hotly. 'We will not float our way to war!'

Wiusago continued. 'So we struck out eastwards along the skirts of the Veridian Borders, hoping to join with you here. We heard the Taproot Hills were impossible to traverse in the winter, and Tua here took that as a personal challenge.' He laughed. 'To be fair, so did I. We have crossed the Valley of a Thousand Fires, and survived the *Khersos*, the Deep Desert of the Sanusi. What fears could a few hillocks hold?'

'I do believe you are being influenced by your bloodthirsty acquaintance,' Leith chided the Deruvian prince. 'But it appears he was right, or you would not be here.'

'He was right, but it was a near thing. We divided up our army and crossed the Taproot Hills by three separate passes, so we would not have warriors waiting for others to make way. It worked, except—'

'Except the Children were caught by snow in the northernmost pass,' said Te Tuahangata bitterly. 'We were not so foolish as to press on, but in the three days we huddled under the shoulder of a hill we lost fifty men. I do not blame anyone for this. Not the prince, who offered to take his soft Deruvians through the north pass, and not myself, who could not see the bad weather coming. But the fifty men we lost were all brave fighters, and not easily replaced.'

Wiusago turned to Leith. 'You came through Vulture's Craw,' he said. 'The snow must have been terrible there. How did you fare?'

Leith's good humour disappeared in an instant. *Just a few moments in which to forget myself – just a few moments, and then I must be the leader again.* He sighed. *Why must it always be so?*

It was a sombre group that rode into the Falthan camp late in the evening. A gentle rain fell, reflective of their mood. The loss of ten thousand men, including some Wiusago had known personally, stunned them, hardened soldiers though they were. Leith stripped off his cloak and made his way to the main pavilion, the Arrow banner hanging limp in the heavy air. He was followed by the prince and the Child of the Mist.

Pulling open the flap, he glanced around to see all the

Company assembled, along with his strategists and generals. Steeling himself for yet more silent recriminations, and maybe some not so silent, he was surprised when he was greeted with considerably more animation than he had for some time. They hadn't yet noticed his two companions, and already the Haufuth was on his feet. 'Leith, there is someone you need to hear. One of the scouts has returned.'

A pasty-faced young man was brought forward; he couldn't have been more than a teenager. He looked clearly nervous, brushing his long ginger hair out of his eyes and darting worried glances at the Arrow while he gave his report. Te Tuahangata and Wiusago sneaked into the tent as he spoke.

'My lord, I was sent east soon as Instruere fell to the northerners – the Arrow-bearers, begging your pardon. I was given a writ from the City to change to fresh horses whenever I needed 'em, so I made good time east. That's good time even for a horseman from the plains of Branca, and we're the best, no question.' His eyes flashed with pride. 'One month and twenty horses and I was through the Gap and into the Brown Lands. I stole a big-hearted grey stallion and took him right to the Bhrudwan army, high up on the Birinjh plateau, travelling by day and night. Best horses in the world, up on the Birinjh.'

'Well, son, what did you see?' Leith made his voice gentle.

'I stayed only long enough to count them, my lord. Horsemen count their herds on the hoof, so fifty thousand soldiers sitting around a thousand fires, fifty to a fire, were not difficult to number. They seemed well provisioned, and their horses are superior to anything we have in Faltha, certainly better than the donkeys I saw at the edge of this camp. Begging your pardon, my lord, but it's only the truth.'

'And how far away are they, man?' one of the Deuverran captains cried out, unable to contain himself. 'Tell him. How many days do we have left to secure the Gap?'

The young lad took a deep breath. 'Estimating walking distance from the saddle is hard, but we of the Branca grasslands are the ones to ask. One month is my guess. We have one month.'

Numbers, more numbers. 'Then we must reach our goal in thirty days, whatever it takes,' said Leith. 'The race for the Gap is on.'

CHAPTER 12

THE GAP

THE GENERALS LET THE Army of Faltha march hard for three days, every soldier at his own pace, until they were strung out along many leagues of the East Bank Road. 'Give them their heads,' had been the sage advice. 'Let them feel they are making up for the time we have lost.'

On the fourth day the pace slowed markedly. The generals re-formed their companies to allow a head count in the still hour before sunset.

Now we will find out what our losses truly are, Leith considered. The suggestion had come from the *losian* leaders, who argued that, in their experience, the losses of an army were often overestimated at first count. Injured, missing or otherwise engaged were often initially considered dead, a mistake usually not corrected until much later. If they were right, if the toll of death was less than first guesses had made it, the news would give the soldiers new heart. *Not just the soldiers*, reflected Leith. *I could do with some good news*.

He doubted there would be much chance for good news in the days ahead. Those few among the leaders who knew anything of the eastern roads were sceptical, even dismissive of the likelihood of such a large army making it to the Gap within a month. Four days into the journey, he could see their reasoning being borne out. The road, though running close by the River Aleinus where possible, was often forced to cut eastwards to avoid sheer cliffs, steep banks or ragged ridges of sharp black rock. There was no easier path further inland where, beyond a narrow strip inhabited by fisherfolk, the bitter, infertile ground gradually sloped upwards to a harsh upland, the dusty playground of capricious winds. The army travelled many more leagues than the map suggested, and at a pace far greater than any time on their journey east, yet their progress as recorded on the strategists' charts was less than before. Farriers reported thrown shoes; doctors talked of strains, tears and broken limbs; blisters and saddle sores were legion; and everyone suffered from a deep tiredness, whether they cared to admit it or not. Since the debacle at Vulture's Craw the *losian* Army of the North had stopped their nightly revelry, and apart from a few half-hearted attempts did not revive it, wisely conserving energy as their goal drew slowly nearer. Not a sound was heard from any other part of the army between sunset and sunrise. Leith's back and hindquarters ached, and his soul seemed wrapped in a weariness borne of months of sleeping in strange beds, walking under the stars and, latterly, the uncertainties that came from directing the lives of others. He had been told the great army would suffer on this march, but the reality still shocked him.

Soon the head counts began coming in. Some reported no losses at all; others numbered their deaths in the hundreds. The clerk who kept the tally sheet supplied the gathered commanders with a running total. Initially the count climbed but slowly: five hundred, eight hundred, one thousand, twelve hundred, fifteen hundred. Hope rose in the pavilion, but clearer heads pointed out that the larger sections, with the potential to have sustained greater losses, would take longer to count.

The mood deteriorated as the reports continued. Two, three, four, five thousand, all within a sobering ten-minute period. Silence descended as the numbers climbed. Six thousand was passed – and then the amounts being reported dried up. Leith watched the tent flap, and for many minutes it did not move.

'What is the final total?' he asked, hardly daring to hope.

The clerk took a deep breath. 'Six thousand, seven hundred and—'

The tent flap opened. In came an elderly man; surely a clerk, far too old to fight.

'I come to report on the losses of the Deruvian army,' he told them in tones from the grave itself. 'In the snows of Vulture's Craw we lost eighty wagons, over two hundred horse and one thousand five hundred and twenty souls, including our entire contingent of supply officers. We have less than three days' food left—'

'O Most High,' Leith groaned, cutting off the Deruvian clerk, who did not look impressed that a mere commander would interfere with the recitation of numbers. 'I forgot about Deruys. The total?'

'Eight thousand two hundred and ninety, my lord,' came the prompt reply. 'Far fewer than we feared.'

Excited talk broke out across the tent. Smiling commanders patted each other on the back. The self-congratulations made Leith feel sick.

'The total might be less than first thought, but I take no pleasure in these numbers.' He strode angrily across the cold earthen floor of the tent. 'How can I announce this dreadful news as though it was a triumph?'

'Because the men in your army wish to hear it,' Farr Storrsen retorted in heated tones. 'The count is nearly two thousand less than we thought. Is that not worth telling people about?'

'If I might suggest something, lord?' It was the old man from Treika, Jethart of Inch Chanter, the nearest they had to a real leader, Leith reflected. 'We have heard reports of great courage and bravery from those who survived the snows. There are rumours amongst the tents of some who made it through the Craw and all the way to Kaskyne on the northern road. With your permission, I would like to take such of these as can be verified with me on a tour of the soldiers' camps. Their stories might bring new heart to those who hear them.'

His idea was well received, and the old man was assigned helpers to uncover the tales of valour undoubtedly existing out there in the winter dusk.

The disaster had been enumerated, but Leith's heart felt heavier than ever. *Better when I didn't know*, he realised. Now he had eight thousand, two hundred and ninety more reasons to lie awake under the pale canvas of his tent.

Another day of white solitude ended as the litter jerked to a halt. Stella stretched her deadened limbs, and continued to nurse her anger, a great rage kindled by the Destroyer's cruel game. She knew he could force her to do anything he wanted, and she shuddered at the thought. But why did he not? Why did he insist on wearing her down? She had no powers with which to oppose him, apart from her own stubborn will. Why did he seek her surrender?

There can be only one reason: I have something he wants. But

I have nothing! At least, nothing I know about. Or perhaps there is something he wants me to do . . . Unbidden, her thoughts turned to the last time she had seen the Company, if only for a moment. Deorc had taken her out into Instruere, where he confronted the large crowd gathered in one of the squares. She could see it clearly in her mind's eye. Along the walls crept the Guard, ready to take the crowd and their leaders by surprise. She was forced to follow the guardsmen, gagged and in chains, pushed and shoved by Deorc himself, until the crowd opened before them . . . and there, at the head of the gathering, stood her friends.

She had not examined that moment since, finding the memory too painful to contemplate, but now she allowed the sights and sounds to flood back, while she searched for a clue. On her arm the rough grip of Deorc, his insane rage-smell in her nostrils. Directly in front of her the churning of the blue fire, eyes and mouth gaping horribly, ready to consume the world in hatred. On either side the murmuring and fear-cries of the crowd, men and women realising something frightening was happening. A short distance away stood the Company – *keep thinking! Don't turn from it!* – Mahnum and Indrett, Phemanderac, Kurr and the Haufuth, Hal a kind of blur, as though he was in two places at once, or somehow stretched between two places. Holding a bright object, which must be the Jugom Ark, was Leith. Oh, how she wished – she wished – it didn't matter what she wished.

The voice of the blue fire cried out to the crowd, and people screamed. Then a flash of blinding white light so intense everyone covered their eyes, everyone but Stella whose hands were bound, so she saw Leith leap on to a box and cry out to her:

'Stella!'

There was a world's weight in his cry, an intensity that seared her like nothing she had suffered under Deorc, like nothing she experienced even in the loathsome presence of the Destroyer. It was Leith, and the terrible depth of his need . . . and something even deeper, something else that burned . . .

. . . burned like a shaft of pure Fire that took her from the floor of Foilzie's basement back to her village in Loulea Vale, showing her what her friends thought of her . . . flames settling on her hand, burning up her arm, looking for an entry point . . .

. . . Kurr telling them stories as they rested on the Westway below Snaerfence, above the Torrelstrommen valley, telling them legends of the First Men . . . of the children from the Vale of Dona Mihst seeking the Fire of the Most High, learning the Way of Fire, the Fire set deep inside them . . .

. . . a cold concrete floor in the dark, her head spinning, a terrible vision of a haggard man healing himself, his cold, cruel voice . . . his searching, sifting, slicing violation of her mind in search of – in search of the Right Hand that held the Jugom Ark . . . and in the midst of the agony he pauses, staring at something set within her. The same flame.

The Jugom Ark, the Fire of her dream in the basement, the *Fuirfad* of Dona Mihst. The same flame. She knew the secret.

And now, if the Destroyer ever sifted through her mind again, he would know it too, and everything would be lost.

As if summoned by the thought, the silk curtains of her litter parted, framing his terrible face: she screamed and he laughed. 'Ah, Stella, am I so unhandsome? There are women in Bhrudwo who kill their husbands after a night in my presence, believing they gain a better chance of becoming my consort thereby. You will be the envy of every woman!' The smile left his face as though eaten by a cancer. 'Now, come. I have something I wish you to hear.'

Out in the dusky evening sat a circle of men surrounding the familiar blue fire. *No doubt contributing to its potency in ways they do not know*, Stella thought grimly.

'Make way for the Queen of Bhrudwo!' announced the Destroyer; and the men stood and bowed to her as he drew her close to the hungry flame.

'Speak!' he commanded it.

'O my lord,' came a distant voice. 'I present to you good news! We have lured the so-called Falthan army into a trap, and sent twenty thousand of them to their deaths!'

Stella screwed her eyes shut, but the man beside her held her shoulders in a tight grip, so she could not block her ears against the words.

'How many remain?' the Destroyer asked the flame, voice sharp as a needle.

'My landsmen estimate not more than thirty thousand survived, many of them in poor condition. They moved on towards Kaskyne, and we watched them until they crossed from Favony into Redana'a.'

The face turned to her. 'Do you hear that, Stella? Twenty thousand slain! We need hardly bother ourselves with Faltha at all. Our allies do the work for us!

'Well then, King of Favony: what do you claim as a reward?'

'A chance to serve you further,' said the voice promptly, and the fire burned with a red tinge. 'Your permission to send a force of men eastwards to Instruere, to finish the work your previous servants were unable to complete.'

The Undying Man stretched forth his one hand, and the

flame twisted as though in pain. 'Do you think to overreach yourself? Do you think to set yourself up as the ruler of Faltha?'

The voice that spoke was the same voice as before, but now it radiated waves of agony, as though caught in the grip of a huge fist. 'My lord, forgive me! I sought your favour so that I might rule under you!' The one hand opened wide, and the voice became a shriek, an unending shriek.

'That place is reserved for another,' announced the Destroyer, ignoring the suffering pouring from the flame and echoing through the oncoming darkness. 'You will content yourself with the lordship of Favony. I will soon walk beneath the Inna Gate in triumph. I have foreseen it.'

He withdrew his hand, and the fire shrank until it merely licked the embers. The screams stopped, and thick silence settled on the Bhrudwan camp.

'Do you see?' he said to Stella as he led her back to her litter. 'Do you finally understand? The army led by your villager friend is already decimated even before it meets mine. My plans are a thousand years in the making – and, thanks to you, I am aware of what my Enemy intends to do. His plans are set in motion. They are not easily changed, depending as they do on weak-willed mortals, whereas my plans are flexible. Now I have you here, I am ready to capture the Right Hand of the Most High for my own. I will have a hand in which to hold the Jugom Ark! And you,' his voice lowered to an intimate murmur as he turned to her, 'I have foreseen that you are the one who will bring him to me.'

Leith's army crossed the Aleinus for the last time at Turtu Donija, the chief city of Piskasia. The citizenry came out of their homes and down from the terraced fields to watch the soldiers make their way carefully over the narrow swingbridge.

The entertainment lasted all of the day, with the last of the wagons coaxed across the rickety structure just before true night settled on the wide valley.

The Falthan leaders did not make the journey across the bridge until early the next morning. Forewarned by Mahnum's knowledge, they expected stern resistance, or at the very least some sort of deceit or delaying tactic, from the Piskasian monarch named as traitor by the Destroyer, but there had been no opposition thus far to their journey through the Fisher-country. As far as they could tell, they had been observed by no one other than a few farmers and fishermen. They experienced no opposition even in the sprawling town itself. With a desire to dispense some justice, to avenge the martyr's death of the Arkhos of Piskasia – who had remained true even when his king played his country false – Leith took the time to bring his leaders and a small troop of mounted Instruian Guard to the main palace. They found it empty, deserted with signs of haste. Good. The king had heard of their coming, it seemed, and fled.

They stayed in the castle that night, eating what remained in the king's larder, and sitting up late beside a warm fire. And early next morning they woke to the sound of a crowd.

Five thousand men filled the city square, armed with every conceivable kind of crude implement that might be considered a weapon, and they uttered a thin cheer as the Company filed out of the palace gate. An obviously reluctant man, spokesman for this impromptu army, shuffled forward to meet them. The Company remained alert in case this was some kind of trick, though they thought it unlikely.

The greasy-haired man cleared his throat, glancing nervously at the flickering Arrow and at the swords of the mounted guardsmen. 'We hear about your army,' he said awkwardly, as if unfamiliar with the common Falthan tongue. 'You go to fight the Bhrudwans, people say. Well, we know about Bhrudwans here. They come through Piskasia on their way west to the slave-markets of Hamadabat. They lie, they steal, they treat us like dirt. Our king, he will not protect us, so we drive him away. Now we want to come with you and fight the Bhrudwans so they do not invade our lands.' Having said his piece, he stepped quickly back into the throng.

Leith turned to his generals. More soldiers would be a good thing – the number here in the square would come close to replacing the men lost in Vulture's Craw – but their attire and bearing did not inspire confidence. The Falthan leaders conferred and Jethart stepped forward.

He spoke quietly, but his voice carried all the way across the square. Someone must be enhancing. Automatically Leith searched behind him for Hal, but he had not accompanied them to the castle, and neither had his parents. He began to search his memory: when had he last seen any of them?

'If you go off to fight the Bhrudwans, one or two of you may be lucky enough to straggle back to your homes alive,' the old warrior said flatly. 'The rest won't. We would have to give you food and weapons, and spend much effort in trying to get you to the right place on the battlefield, yet you will still die.'

A few men in the crowd began to grumble angrily at these words.

'I do not doubt your courage. How could I? Here you are, ready to give your lives. But you would be far better remaining here, protecting your families, preparing your homes for winter, so that if a few Bhrudwans do eventually break through our lines, you will be ready for them.'

The muttering increased in volume, and it became apparent

the crowd had no mind to listen to craven, if sound, advice. Not wanting a conflict, and genuinely concerned about their ability to escape unscathed if they remained to debate the issue, the leaders of the Falthan army took to their horses and rode for the bridge.

A day north of Turtu Donija it became clear the Falthan army was being followed. A rag-tag collection of Piskasians, far more than had gathered in the square, pursued them on foot and by horse. 'We will have to feed them,' Leith was told; 'they will hold us up. This is a disaster.' But there appeared to be no Piskasian leaders to talk with, and no time to stop and talk to each one of the Piskasians individually.

Twenty-three days to go. The land either side of the much narrower, swifter Aleinus River looked desolate, empty of habitation, with few trees save the occasional gnarled survivor of better times. It began to rain lightly on the second day out of Turtu Donija; just a drizzle, but driven by an insistent east wind. The rain tasted stale, as though the water had been locked up in the clouds for years. Twenty-two days to go. On either bank of the Aleinus could be seen evidence of a huge flood that, according to locals they met, had torn through the area the previous spring. Trunks of huge trees, bleached by the sun, were strewn about like kindling wood, and large areas of raw earth exposed many spans above the river's dull surface. Anxiety rose within the leadership as for days the soldiers were forced to pick their way through veritable forests of driftwood as the cold rains fell. Eighteen days to go. The rains ceased on the same day a small town came into view on the opposite bank: someone told Leith it went by the name of Saumon, but he was so tired he hardly took it in. Up at dawn, pausing only for a hasty morning meal, riding from dawn to dusk, listening, consulting, counting and planning until his head swirled. Sixteen days to go. The informal Piskasian army had by now fallen some distance behind. On the advice of his generals Leith gave the order prohibiting the wagons from stopping for them. In this way, it was hoped, the Piskasians would be persuaded to return home. The snow-coated Wodranian Mountains that had overseen their progress all the way through the Fisher-lands now faded from view, drawing away leftwards from the river. Thirteen days to go. A small band of badly-equipped mercenaries came out of the Wodranian Mountains and offered their services to the Falthan army. Leith accepted despite the counsel of his generals: the Arrow had picked the Wodrani out, after all. Unity, he told his leaders. Finally they came to the end of the long Piskasian valley that ran south-west to north-east for nearly two hundred leagues. Nestled in a small hollow lay the tiny village of Adolina, a collection of low huts with tall chimneys, a league or so from the banks of the Aleinus. Leith's mighty army was exhausted, and there were still eleven days to go.

Wrapped in heavy robes to ward off the winter cold, the three conspirators met in an abandoned warehouse in the middle of the Granary district. Part of the roof was open to the grey sky, and the cold flagstoned floor bore scorchmarks from burned beams fallen from the ceiling. They circled the small table in the centre of the room, as though they held swords in their hands and looked for a chance to strike. There were no chairs, and no one would have sat if there had been.

'You owe me your loyalty,' the fat man wheezed, pointing a pudgy finger at the older, thinner man. 'I rescued you from that dungeon, where they left you to moulder. You are mine, and your people are mine.'

The bird-like man sputtered, the skin around his throat tightening as he tried to formulate a reply.

'Don't worry,' the big man laughed, the sound a rasp to their ears. 'My leadership will not be onerous. Your wants and my wants are the same, after all; to be rid of these cursed northerners, and to lead this addled City into a new Golden Age. Now the northerners are gone, the City is a ripe ear of wheat ready to be harvested.'

The third man, silent until now, raised his hand. Unlike his co-conspirators he had a fair face, a liquid voice and a serenity that lent his words extra power. Glimpses of his habitual blue robe could be seen underneath a nondescript brown cloak.

'We both acknowledge you as the leader here,' said the third man, his blond hair flicking across his forehead as he leaned forward. 'There is no issue about this. Neither the Escaignian nor I have the stomach for what must be done, and I do not want the guilt on my soul. The Most High has told me that the fire will come to Instruere; and although I have listened with all my might, cloistering myself so as to hear any whisper, He speaks to me no longer. This can only be because something has happened that does not meet with His approval, so He waits until the wrongs are put to rights. The northerners and that deceiver Tanghin are wrongs, and though Tanghin has burned, the northern peasants still survive. They also must burn.'

The circling around the table continued.

'And so they shall!' cried the huge man, his eyes black caverns into a realm of nothingness. 'And not them alone. All those who oppose our rule will pay.' His face hungered with a frightening intensity, like a starving man contemplating a banquet of the finest food.

'You will gather the remnants of your followers,' he said, stopping his circling long enough to fix each of them with his terrible eyes. 'We do not need many, so speak only to those whose loyalty is unquestionable. Bring them here: we will meet here two nights from now, and I will tell you what we must do.'

'And Instruere will be ours?' asked the thin man, his face full of hope.

'Not just Instruere.' The reply was breathy with desire. 'Who knows how much of Faltha will be given into our hands?'

Remembering her time of imprisonment by Deorc, and recognising that though the conditions were different, the powerlessness was much the same, Stella reinstituted her disciplines. She forced herself to take an interest in the lands they travelled through, in the people she could see, in those few she came in contact with; excepting the Destroyer, of course. She tried to glean any hints she could about the condition and location of the Falthan army. She stretched her muscles, aware her futile week on the run had revealed her lack of fitness. And she looked for any way to slow the progress of the Bhrudwans – not that she expected to get the opportunity.

Currently the eunuch shared her litter. He brought her some appalling gruel, salty and full of lumps. She had eaten as much as she could take, then offered the rest to her jailer, who ate eagerly. The plump man had said little since her recapture, but had obviously suffered some kind of punishment: his eyes had a haunted cast to them, and his cheeks were sunken in his sad face. Perhaps he accepted her scraps because he was being deprived of food.

'You won't talk about yourself,' she said to him, her voice coaxing. 'You are not just your master's tool. Where were you born?'

The unhappy cast to his face deepened. Stella sensed he both wanted and feared to speak. She watched while the warring within him went on. Finally he sighed, shrugged his shoulders and spoke.

'I may talk of nothing other than what is necessary to the execution of my duties,' he said in his singsong voice. 'I cannot talk to you of myself.' There was definite regret in his words.

'Telling me about yourself is part of your duty,' said Stella earnestly, searching her mind for any justification. 'I will be more likely to confide in your master if I have already confided in you.'

'You wish to confide in me?' The words were soft, human, underlined by need. What horrible things had been done to this man?

'I wish us to talk with each other. Was it beautiful, the place you were born?'

He nodded almost imperceptibly; then, as if emboldened by his own action, nodded again. 'Yes,' he whispered. 'It was beautiful.'

She watched his eyes, looking for any sign of the Destroyer's sudden possession, but there was none. 'How was it beautiful?'

'The sea there is a glorious eggshell blue, and the waters are warm. The sun plays on the sea like a happy child. If I could have any wish, I would return home to the sea just once before I die.'

'When were you last there?'

'Many years ago.' His eyes filmed over: for a moment Stella started in fright, but the eunuch merely shuffled through his memories. 'Jena and I swam in the pools below her house. I remember laughing with her, I remember holding her. Later that summer I was chosen by the recruiters, and I travelled north with them to Malayu.' His eyes were now closed, and his face wore a look of pain, as though the memories troubled him.

'Recruiters?' She knew she had to be delicate, but there was so much at stake.

'My master is always looking for people of outstanding intelligence to serve him in Andratan. My parents were so proud that I had been selected.' He paused, swallowed, then continued. 'I wonder if they are still alive.'

Stella began another question, but the eunuch continued on as though she had not spoken. 'At Andratan we were tested, and all but the most gifted were discarded. It is a place of unimaginable cruelty, my Lady; failure is never forgiven. They gelded me and shaved me, then brought me into the master's presence, where he bonded me to himself.' He opened his eyes. 'It was purest agony. He burns, he burns. Ah, Lady, kill yourself. Don't let him have you!'

A deep chill settled on her at these words. 'He has me already. Look at my prison!' She indicated the white lace and silk surrounding them.

'No, he has only imprisoned your body. Never let him trap your mind!'

Shocked, Stella reached out and took his fleshy hand in her own. 'I am so sorry. What can I do?'

The eunuch leaned forward so she could hear his tortured whisper. 'Kill me. Take my life! End my suffering. He has set a prohibition in my mind so I cannot lift a finger to harm myself. My only hope is to anger him enough that he will slay me.'

'What could you do?' she asked, horrified.

'What I have just done. Talked to you.'

'Will he kill you for talking to me?'

'He has dealt death to his servants for much less. Perhaps I will be fed to the fire. I would accept the pain if it will bring me release from his touch.'

Stella released his hand. 'And now he reaches out to touch the world. We must stop him.' She looked into his hopeless eyes. 'What is your name?'

For a moment he said nothing; then he spoke in a voice cracking with pain. 'I – I know it, Lady, but I may not say it. Should it pass my lips he would know, and there are many things he can do to increase suffering without extinguishing life. I have seen them all. I want to end my suffering, not prolong it. Forgive me.'

She nodded, and he put down her bowl. 'I must go,' he said. 'Look for me this evening. We will talk more, if he does not discover us.' He turned and struggled out of the litter.

'Goodbye,' Stella said quietly to his retreating back. 'Goodbye.' *Come back soon.*

Adolina was a beautiful place. Sheltered under the high plateau of the Nagorj, the northernmost town of Piskasia was a collection of steep-roofed homes separated by high hedges, of poplars and oaks, of gravelled roads and tree-lined lanes, all sparkling in the morning frost. A lump formed in Leith's throat as he rode up the wide road and into the village, at the head of a hundred horse. This looked so much, so very much like home.

Villagers came out of their homes to stare at the men and the horses. Leith stared back. That woman could be Merin, the Haufuth's wife – and the man at her side was large enough to be the Haufuth, if not so tall. There was Rauth from the village council; over here stood Stella's mother Herza. Those children playing around the feet of their elders, they could be Loulea's children.

Leith's gaze lifted from the village scene, following the spiralling chimney smoke up into the cold morning air, refocusing on the steel-blue slopes rising almost sheer behind the smoke, barren heights thrusting up until they met the overbright sky, their meeting a thin grey line.

Over that grey line the Bhrudwans will pour without warning. Down the slope they'll come shouting, obliterating anything not swift enough to get out of their way. Merin and Rauth and Herza will die, as will their children. Listen to them scream! The smoke turns thick and black, fire crackles at the base of the billowing clouds. The stony lanes run red. Then, suddenly, they are gone, as the Bhrudwans' grey shadow moves further down the valley. The village is quiet for a moment, save the groans of the dying and the sobbing of their children. The fires spread, shooting out from windows, licking at the eaves. Houses collapse in on themselves, timbers cracking, falling. Then silence. The snow begins, a light dusting as nature tries to bandage the wound.

It was a kind of double vision. Leith sat quietly on his horse and listened as Jethart spoke to the villagers, warning them of the trouble that might come; and at the same time, as though superimposed, he could see Loulea as well as Adolina and a hundred other villages, as though looking down a long tunnel, all burning, all overrun by the black tide.

The villagers would stay and fight, they informed the Falthans, and could not be deterred no matter what they were told. Some of the younger men had already run off, fetching rusty old swords which they now waved enthusiastically. On the brink of scolding them for their foolishness, Leith remembered the Company waving similarly rusty swords outside the Waybridge Inn at Mjolkbridge. Within a few days, he recalled, those swords were called on to defend against the men from Windrise.

But a few ragged bandits from Windrise cannot be compared to the Bhrudwan horde.

The Falthans were out of time: the difficult climb up the great Nagorj escarpment awaited them, and beyond it many days' hard slog to the Gap. They could debate with the Adolinan villagers no longer. Hopefully the Bhrudwans would never reach this gentle place.

The bulk of the great army passed to the west of the village, filing down narrow lanes or striking out across bare fields. They came together a league north of the town, at the very base of the escarpment, having replenished their wagons. Leith dearly wished he could protect this village, but he could not show favour even if he could afford to weaken his army. They left it behind, a group of homely dwellings in the wrong place.

The Falthan army travelled one of only two ways to enter Sna Vaztha, the largest and most isolated of the Sixteen Kingdoms, more isolated – by mountain and ice – than even desert-bound Sarista a thousand leagues to the south. The path zigzagged up the steep face of the escarpment, clinging on like a vine to a garden wall. The army halted for their midday meal facing the most staggering vista Leith had yet seen, the view owing as much to the crisp, cold air as to the scene itself. To their left the Aleinus River emerged from Sivera Alenskja, a sheer-sided, narrow-throated gorge cut into the escarpment, a jagged slash into blackness, while ahead and below them the wide Piskasian valley was laid out like the whole world in miniature. Sunlight and shadow picked out every fold of the land; and, if Leith concentrated, he could make out the thin ribbon of the Aleinus River winding away to the horizon.

All afternoon they climbed the road, spiralling upwards like smoke from a chimney. At the head of the army, Leith could look down and see his men spread out along the road, seemingly almost all the way back to Adolina, which from this height was no more than a tiny dark patch at the foot of the slope. Up and further up they climbed, and by dusk, after seven leagues of hard toil, the escarpment stretched as far above them as ever.

Ten days to go. After a bitterly cold dawn, the beginnings of a west wind began to swirl about them. Tents were packed in silence, whether in awe of the stupendous landscape on which they clung like flies or in trepidation of the prospect of another day's footslogging, Leith did not know. The leaders of the army set a fast pace, determined not to sleep a second night on the great slope, and within the hour fifty thousand men panted and gasped like new recruits on their first march. 'It is the height,' his generals told Leith. 'The air is thinner up here. We must not tax the men too greatly.' But he drove them on, turning right and then left up the escarpment, not allowing even a moment's respite for a midday meal. At last, at the bitter end of the afternoon and just as he was about to give up and call a halt, the road levelled out and deposited them on the Nagorj.

Up here on the wide, featureless tableland the west wind howled as though an army of wolves snapped at their heels. They tried setting up camp, but after the first three tents were carried off into the eastern gloom, it was decided to trek back down the road and shelter just below the level of the plateau. An unpleasant night followed. The constant howling on the tableland above them ensured none but the most exhausted soldiers found sleep. Most lay wide awake on their pallets, longing for the comparative comfort of Adolina two days' march back down the escarpment.

Nine days to go. The target they had set for themselves might not be accurate, but it was all they had until more of their scouts returned. The strategists sent more scouts ahead, to warn the main army in case the Bhrudwans had already won the passage of the Gap. Ninety-one days gone, nine to go. The time saved rafting up the Aleinus had been more than lost in Vulture's Craw, but they had clawed back a few precious days with their hurried journey through Piskasia. Now they were more or less back to their original schedule. The March of a Hundred Days would soon succeed – or fail.

The eunuch did not return that afternoon, nor the next. Food was thrust into the litter through the curtain by servants not seen before, and though Stella scanned the horizons from her confines she saw nothing of him.

The Bhrudwan army now marched through a truly otherworldly landscape. Whenever Stella peered from her litter it was to gaze out on a rocky, greyish plain. Some distance to her right a small stream twisted and turned its way across the rock like a snake in a hurry to get out of the cold wind. It had dug for itself a narrow channel perhaps ten bodylengths wide and five deep. Where the stream sliced into the rock it exposed virulent layers of poisonous-looking reds and ochres, quite unlike anything she had seen before, the stream a knife cutting through a rotten onion. With such inimical bedrock, it was no wonder little grew on the dry grey plain. No grass, no trees, nothing – except an extraordinary assortment of sharp-spined plants, some as high as trees, some low and spreading. Their browns and greens were the only relief from the grey tedium stretching into the distance, their spiky fingers thrusting upwards as though to pierce the iron-grey cloud canopy in their quest for water. In a few places rock and plant alike were overrun by what at first sight looked like sandhills, but were clearly made of pale flakes of some strange substance, as she discovered when they passed close enough for her to scoop some up in her hand. The flakes smelled faintly of – she struggled to remember – the sulphur on the slopes of Steffl mountain in Withwestwa Wood. She was about to discard the handful of flakes when they began to move – and a fat-legged spider bigger than her thumb emerged from under them, pincers clicking. With a convulsive jerk she sent it on its way back to its grey home, scattering flakes all through her litter.

A strong wind blew up from somewhere ahead of them, raising clouds of abrasive dust that stung the eyes. Within the hour progress slowed to little more than a child's crawl. The litter now shook in an alarming fashion. After a few minutes of worry about her own safety, Stella realised her four bearers undoubtedly suffered in the dust storm outside, but when she tried to see how they fared, the wind and the glass-like shards beat her back. The northern girl pulled her silken curtains tightly closed and prayed for the safety of her bearers, who were almost certainly victims of the Destroyer, undeserving of the treatment they received. Paradoxically, she prayed the wind would continue, even intensify. She didn't really believe in the Most High any more, not after the falsity of Tanghin of the Ecclesia, but she prayed nonetheless.

It felt to Leith like he travelled with a huge hand on his back, propelling him forward. The horses were restive, spooked by the howling wind, which was even greater today than on each of the preceding four days. According to his generals, his army had made over fifteen leagues on each of the last three days: indeed, they told him, it was almost impossible to make less progress, blown along before the wind like thousands of autumn leaves. *It should make things easier*, Leith considered, *but it has not*. The wild calling of the wind wore away at everyone, setting their teeth on edge, shoulders clenched as though warding off the attack of a dangerous beast.

The Nagorj sapped his army. Perhaps it might be a place of beauty in summer, albeit of a harsh, minimalistic kind, but in winter it became a soulless land, cold and cruel, empty of anything remotely human save the road stretching in front of them. Even the road seemed a bizarre artefact, made of crushed shells – *where had the builders gotten shells from with no ocean within five hundred leagues?* – and ran arrow-straight ahead of them. Some time in the last day it had turned, unnoticed, and now sped towards Sna Vaztha many days to the north. The land on either side of the road had been leached of all colour: some small, green and prickly bushes provided the only relief from a tombstone-like greyness matching the overhanging sky. *No wonder this place was known as the Eater of Travellers*.

'Leith, can you spare me a moment?' A polite but firm voice pulled him away from his thoughts.

'Farr! What is it? How do things go with the *losian* army? Do they think we're going to make it in time?'

The Vinkullen man laughed, but it sounded strained. 'The Fodhram are exhausted but aren't prepared to admit it. Otherwise, everything is fine – as fine as it can be up here on this awful place. Look, Leith, I haven't come to talk to you about the *losian*.'

'Oh? What is it then?'

'It's about your brother.' Farr thrust out his chin a fraction, no doubt unconsciously, but to Leith it seemed a prelude to him raising his fists.

'The talk around the campfires and in the tents is that you've treated him too harshly. He goes off by himself in the evenings – no one knows where – and often his bed is not slept in. His eyes are red and he avoids people. Leith . . . well, I can't put it any plainer than this. You spied on Wira and me when we argued over his drinking. No, don't deny it, I know it was you. No matter. You heard what was said. When he died, a heavy weight settled on my shoulders, a weight I can't shake off. Every day I wish I could speak to him, just a few moments would do, to tell him I loved him even though I didn't understand what he was doing.'

'Don't go on; I know what you're saying,' said Leith sourly. 'Who sent you? Kurr? The Haufuth?'

Farr shook the reins of his horse, which took a few nervous steps back. Dust blurred the mountain man's features, rendering him little more than a silhouette.

'You are mistaken if you think I could be ordered by any man,' he snapped. 'I came here at my own behest. I thought you were grown up enough to hear the truth, but I was wrong. Do you think it was easy telling you how I feel?' He sawed at the reins, jerking his mount away from Leith.

'Wait! Farr, wait! Why shouldn't he come to talk to me? Why do I have to be the one?' But the Mjolkbridge man had gone, and Leith's voice sounded petulant even to his own ears.

Jethart had told him about the loneliness of command. But Leith had not imagined it would mean the loss of his friends. He missed the old days of the Company, the evening campfires in Withwestwa Wood, the conversations on the Westway. So much lost already, and so much more at stake.

Five days to go. Leith peered ahead through the murk, as though he might see the Gap simply by concentrating hard enough. A few bushes, a few rocks. No, not rocks, horsemen! With a cry he pulled up his mount. Behind him the Falthan army began the slow process of drawing to a halt.

Leith lifted the Jugom Ark, but even the light of the Flaming Arrow could not fully penetrate the dust. The horsemen drew nearer. *Not enough to be an army, unless the army was hidden. Even if it was a minute's ride along the road, we wouldn't see it in this dust storm.*

'Arrow-bearer! Leith Mahnumsen! The Most High be praised!' The leading horseman reined in, leaned forward and extended a hand towards the youth with the Arrow, who responded with a shout.

'Modahl! Grandfather! I wondered if you had been successful!'

Quickly the leaders of the Falthan army gathered around. Those not of Instruere had heard Modahl had apparently returned from the dead, and all marvelled anew at his appearance here in the Nagorj. They had also heard he was Leith's father's father, and now the two were together, young and old, the resemblance was plain. The set of their eyes, the shape of their jaws, the stubborn thinness of their mouths.

It must be true! And if it was true that he lived, perhaps it was also true that he commanded the Sna Vazthan army.

'Have you brought us soldiers?' asked Wiusago bluntly. His fellow commanders leaned forward eagerly.

'The entire Sna Vazthan army march behind me,' he replied in his deep voice. 'We number thirty thousand.'

Thirty thousand? Could it be? The numbers flashed through Leith's head: *nearly one hundred thousand strong!*

'I offer my regret that we could not leave any earlier, but certain elements at court tried to impede our departure,' said Modahl. 'It seems the Destroyer anticipated this stroke against him, and so set snares to prevent our army leaving at all, or at least delay its departure. A number of courtiers we thought were loyal have lost their lives, but they partly succeeded: we would have been entrenched at the Gap by now if it were not for their interference.'

'But here you are!' Leith cried, taking his grandfather's hand and beaming all around him. 'And we might yet hold the Gap against our enemy!'

The old man pursed his lips as he gazed on his grandson. 'As to that, we have reports that the Bhrudwan army is a few days east of the Gap. Exactly how far we cannot be sure, as our scouts had to return into the teeth of this storm. Two days, possibly three. We may not make it in time.'

'Then we must ride on,' growled Leith. 'We cannot afford to wait.'

'First you must meet my monarch,' Modahl replied with slow dignity. 'She cannot merely join your army. Sna Vaztha must be acknowledged.'

From the rear of the gathered leaders a voice rang out. 'Not like Straux! My army was stripped from me by my liege lord' – he made the title sound like a curse – 'and I am little more than his prisoner!' The King of Straux pushed his way through the generals and advisers, his snarling face a counterpoint to the serenity of the Sna Vazthan general.

'My queen was never a traitor to Faltha,' Modahl replied simply. 'Be thankful you were not the monarch of Sna Vaztha, for by now your royal remains would be decorating the Inmennost Gate.'

'Why should we have anything to do with Sna Vazthans?' the King of Straux persisted. 'They invaded and destroyed Haurn, one of the Sixteen, and would eat us all up if we gave them a chance. We are employing a bear to drive out a rat!'

A pale shape beside Modahl drew a couple of steps closer, and lowered its travelling hood. 'This bear would happily take care of any rats the Arrow-bearer identifies for it,' came a woman's voice, and it was low, smooth as silk, but cold as ice. 'We seek nothing other than to protect ourselves, and all of Faltha, from the Bhrudwans.' She turned her large, flint-hard eyes on the King of Straux, who quailed at her stare. 'Who are you seeking to protect?'

Modahl spoke into the frigid silence that had formed between the two monarchs. 'Leith Mahnumsen, Bearer of the Jugom Ark and ruler of Instruere, may I present to you the Ice Queen of Sna Vaztha, the Spear of the North, the Diamond of her people, and the Mistress of our hearts.' Leith saw a swift look pass between Modahl and the queen, but could not interpret it. She held out her hand. Out of her view, Modahl motioned for him to take it in his; he did so, and raised it to his lips in imitation of his grandfather's gesture.

A coronet of gold nestled on her brow, set above an oval face, the palest Leith had ever seen. Unless it was painted to be white, Leith could believe her to have no warming blood at all. Yet her lips were full red, and her eyes warm, sparkling with something that faded even as he began to speak. Her hair was done in ringlets, gathered away from her neck. Peeping from under her travelling cloak was a jewel-encrusted robe. His cheeks coloured. Wasn't the Sna Vazthan queen supposed to be old? Hadn't she acceded to the throne at least twenty years ago?

'Your majesty, I bid you welcome to the Army of Faltha,' he replied, as formally as his under-utilised Master of Protocol could have desired. 'You are a guest as long as you wish to remain. My holding the Jugom Ark does not in any way imply my leadership over either you or your army.'

'Oh, but it does,' she replied coolly. 'And so it should. How could a mere queen take precedence over he who has been prophesied for a thousand years?' She laughed at his startled expression, the tinkling of ice falling from tree limbs. 'We might be many months' journey from the Great City of Instruere, but we are not provincials. We remember what makes us First Men. I make obeisance before the Fire of Life,' she said, and bowed to the Jugom Ark. Leith's cheeks reddened again.

'Will you ride with us?' Leith asked, blood singing in his ears. 'We still have a few leagues to travel before we can make camp.'

'Very well,' she replied, and smiled. 'We must leave the road here and strike out eastwards. Will you allow certain of my scouts to lead you? They were raised in the Nagorj and know its ways.'

People were raised here? Leith looked about him, at the dust overlaying the grey rock. *Where would they live? How could they survive?*

He nodded his assent to her in the way a king would

acknowledge an ally, graciously and with a degree of condescension, occasioning another unspoken exchange between the queen and the commander of her army. *He is everything you said he was*, Leith imagined she said. And his expression replied: *nevertheless, he will do well.*

The Bhrudwan army made camp amidst a broad stonefield. In many places the ground was arranged in regular patterns, a courtyard paved for a giant, but Stella could not imagine the effort the stone patterning must have taken. Surely it had not been done by humans? The ground radiated cold. Despite the trappings of her white cage, the girl from northern Firanes could feel the chill seeping into her skin.

But she was given little time to concern herself with stone patterns or the temperature. For the first time she had been commanded to the Destroyer's own tent, and she feared what she might find there. She had no illusions as to what awaited her, but had been able to hold the terror at arm's length as long as it was somewhere in the future. Now, however, the future had arrived.

'Welcome, Stella,' the Undying Man said pleasantly, as to a neighbour who had accepted an invitation to tea. 'Please, take a seat.' He indicated a leather-covered couch – which must have been hauled all the way here by some lackey, Stella reminded herself. *Don't be seduced by his cleverness. Resist him!*

He was appallingly hard to resist. After having demonstrated such unremitting cruelty, she could not help but be relieved when he granted the smallest of kindnesses. So she found herself taking a warm flask from him, and eating a sweet of some sort, before her resolution had time to harden.

A short, weather-beaten man came into the tent. He hadn't

announced his entry, so must have been expected. He muttered a few words to the Destroyer, who nodded; then the man withdrew.

'Forgive me a moment, pretty one,' the Lord of Bhrudwo said, spreading his hands. 'I have some business that must be attended to. You may wait for me in the annexe.'

Somewhat dazed, Stella went where he indicated, opening a small flap and taking a seat on a cane chair. The room was unfurnished save for her chair, a small pallet and an exquisite woven rug spread across the cold stone ground. It took her several moments to realise she sat in his bedroom.

Strange noises came from the main part of the tent. A cat? No, it sounded more like a wounded bird. She drew the flap aside . . .

It was a man – no, a boy. He lay face-up on the floor, back arched, limbs splayed out at unnatural angles, his matted ginger hair partly obscuring the many wounds on his face and scalp. This boy was the source of the noises she had heard.

'Were your forces still on the Sna Vazthan road when you left them?' asked the Destroyer in a voice no different to that which he had used on Stella. She could feel the compulsion in his words. The boy screwed his eyes closed and buried his hands in the rug, but words leaked out through clenched teeth: 'Yes . . . yes . . . still on . . . road . . .'

The grey-cloaked man bent over his victim. 'You've spied on us before. Did you report our position to your commanders?'

Grunts and squeaks came from the tortured throat, but the head nodded. Stella held her breath.

'You will return to the boy with the bright arrow and tell him we are holed up and unmoving, waiting out this windstorm. You will advise him that if he hurries he can be first to the Gap with his army.' The compulsion was unbreakable. Stella could feel the words burning themselves into her mind, and she was not the intended recipient. 'You will forget all about our meeting and the pain it has caused you. You believe you fell from your horse up in the rocks from where you spied upon us, and this fall caused your wounds.' He raised his hand. The boy screamed raggedly until Stella thought his throat must burst asunder, then swooned into unconsciousness.

The Destroyer turned to the annexe, and showed no surprise that Stella was watching. 'There are matters arising from this incident that I must see to. You will return to your litter and await my attendance on you.'

A few moments later Stella found herself stumbling unaccompanied across the stony ground, her feet steering her towards her hated silken home, without the slightest thought of resisting his awful compulsion. His power lasted until she drew the curtains closed, then she collapsed on to her bed, sobbing uncontrollably, the powerless plaything of a madman.

On the morning of the penultimate day the storm began to blow itself out, the sand settled from the air and Leith obtained his first look at their goal. Clouds like wet wool draped themselves over high mountains to the left and the right, but the way ahead remained clear, a narrow opening between the ranges with hazy greyness beyond. Still the wind blew from the west, driving them on; Kurr laconically described it as Bhrudwo sucking at them, occasioning a ragged laugh from the generals nearby.

'How far?' asked Leith, his Arrow blazing in anticipation. Beside him, the newly-returned scout rubbed the bandage on his head.

'A day and a half, lord,' he said quietly. 'If we hurry, we should be in the Gap by noon tomorrow, a full day ahead of our foe.'

'Thank you,' said Leith, genuinely grateful for the risks so many were taking in his name. 'Why don't you go and seek further treatment?'

'My wounds have been salved, my lord, but the doctors could do nothing for my headache.' A vein throbbed in his forehead as he spoke. 'Never have I been thrown from a horse that has been broken. I must have hit my head on a rock.'

Aware of the embarrassment this admission must have cost the red-haired lad, Leith waved him away and bade him find rest on one of the wagons.

Now the race entered its final frantic hours. The message flashed back through the ranks, rousing the late abed and setting the army marching a full half-hour earlier than usual. One or two sections of the vast army raised their voices in song, encouraging their fellows to expend their remaining energy. 'It does not matter what condition we arrive in, as long as we are the first there,' they told each other, and by mid-morning the officers and captains could do nothing to prevent the various factions competing against each other. Indeed, many of them condoned it. At the head of the army the generals despaired, and messages were passed seeking a more moderate pace but were misunderstood or simply not heeded. This was their one chance, after all, to establish a superior position, and every soldier knew how important that was. It might mean the difference between defeat and victory, life and death. By nightfall the chaos was complete. The army was mixed beyond sorting, and the ill and the lame lagged many leagues behind.

The Company spent the night talking with their strategists. The few men who had been through the Gap were summoned, and their wisdom compared. Leith thought of his father: Mahnum had been this way not much more than a year ago. But to his disappointment, his father could not be found. He was back with the wagons, some said. The young lord of the Falthan army forced down his unease, and concentrated on the advice being offered.

The floor of the Gap was paved with rough, stony ground, he was told. There were many places to hide an army, the best hidden under the banks of the River Aleinus, now incised in a stone valley to the north, and on the lower slopes of the mountains to the south. If they could occupy these vantages they could rush down upon their foe in a massive ambush that might end the conflict then and there. Some warned against this strategy as it involved dividing their forces, which was considered poor tactics, and others counselled against hiding on the slopes in case the weather turned to snow, trapping them there. On into the night the debate raged, but early on Leith made up his mind. The risk was worth it. Finally a consensus was reached. The majority of commanders agreed with Leith, to his relief. Instructions were prepared and runners sent to alert the hundreds of captains needed to implement their strategy. *One bold strike*, Leith thought, *and if our luck holds we break the Bhrudwans here on the Nagorj.*

Early next morning the white curtain twitched open, and Stella drew her sheets around her, the only defence she could mount. But it was not the Destroyer who entered her litter. She gasped with genuine delight. Her visitor was the round-faced eunuch, back after more than a week away. Though, as she looked more closely, he appeared to have been ill. His skin had a grey cast, and hung in folds from his cheeks and neck. 'What has happened to you?' she asked him.

He turned his eyes on her, twin vortices of despair, then opened his mouth. For a moment Stella did not understand. His throat worked up and down, and tears started from his sad eyes. Then she looked more closely, and her hands went to her face in shock. His tongue. Most High, O Most High! His tongue had been cut out.

Tongues wagged freely as the Falthan leaders directed their troops. The sun had risen on a clear sky, blue, remote and cold, and the breath of man and horse steamed in a crackling frost. The clouds had drawn back from the hills, exposing tall, snowcloaked spires, nameless peaks that together formed a forbidding wall stretching inward from the horizon to the left and the right, offering no way through other than the Gap. It was a scene of delicate beauty, like a glass sculpture.

'Not a place to fight a war, is it?' Modahl stood beside his grandson as all around them men from Instruere prepared for the final march. 'We've been lucky with the weather so far, but many of your men are not equipped for a northern winter. Let us pray the conflict is not prolonged, or you will be forced to spend your soldiers like fretas.'

Leith smiled at the old man. 'Is the queen well?' he asked shyly. The grizzled head bobbed in reply.

'Now for it, then,' said the young man to his grandfather. 'A journey begun nearly a year ago finishes here today. I just hope I know enough swordplay to keep alive.'

Modahl peered at him in surprise. 'Don't you know how to use the Arrow as a weapon? It's the talk of the camp: everyone expects you to wield that thing like a hero of legend. How can you not know?'

'He – I have spoken with someone who knows about the Jugom Ark,' he said, unwilling to betray his ambivalence about the bright thing in his hand. 'But he says there are limits to what I can do with it. Phemanderac promised to teach me more, but I haven't seen him in many days. I don't know what's happened to him.'

'Who have you seen?' the old man asked gently. 'Have you spoken to your friends? Your family?'

'Not you as well!' Leith growled. 'Why does everyone think my brother is more important than the coming battle? Can't I get on with the planning for this war?'

'Leith, I didn't say anything about—'

'And what of you?' All of Leith's tension on this day of days seemed to boil up to the surface. 'Isn't there someone you should be talking to? Have you even tried to speak to my father?' He could tell from the hurt on the old man's face that he had scored a telling blow, but he could summon up no joy at the sight.

The final march began, but the feet of the army did not carry them forward with the same swiftness as the previous day. Heads were raised, staring at the ever-widening opening in the mountain wall ahead of them, and many a man or horse stumbled on the stony ground as a result. The land became more and more broken, gentle slopes giving way to knife-edged ridges that had to be navigated around; then the badlands gave way to a grey rock plain. The Gap seemed so close in the clear morning air, but still tantalisingly far away.

Just before noon the vanguard of the Falthan army emerged from behind a ridge and found themselves at the foot of a shallow talus slope. Ahead lay the Gap, perhaps a third of a league away. Cheering broke out from those on horseback . . . but the sound died away to an echo, then to nothing.

Boiling down from the head of the slope came hundreds, thousands of small shapes, leaping lightly over the broken rocks, taking up positions of seeming impregnability all across the incline. Within moments it seemed that the whole slope seethed with them, as though someone had kicked over an ant's nest.

Emptied of all emotion, wrung out like a dirty cloth, devastated beyond belief, Leith sat on his horse and cried bitter tears as he watched the Bhrudwan army pour through the Gap and into Faltha.

CHAPTER 13

THE SIEGE OF SKULL ROCK

DOWN THE SLOPE POURED the Bhrudwan army, in almost complete silence. No yelling, no attempt to intimidate the Falthans. The Destroyer's army possessed a supernatural calmness, as if the Bhrudwans had practised for months for this moment, as if their victory was beyond doubt. As if they knew something. Their silence intimidated the Falthans more than any amount of screaming would have.

We've been tricked, Leith realised, *lured here like mice to a trap*. Somehow the Bhrudwans had known their army would arrive at the Gap first. How long had they been watching Leith struggling to form an army? Had spies reported on Falthan progress ever since his army left Instruere? Had they timed their own arrival to maximise Falthan exhaustion and despair? *If we had known we would lose the race, we would have taken the journey much more carefully*. The weight of over eight thousand dead settled even more heavily on Leith's shoulders, as it became clear they had died in vain. Had the misguidance of the Favonian landsman been a mistake, as his generals all assumed, or something more sinister?

'Get back from the slope!' a voice screamed in his ear, but it came to him as the crashing of waves on the shore, a noise without any meaning. 'They can roll rocks down on us! Back! Back to the plains!'

'I don't want to retreat,' Leith mumbled, his hands and feet numb, his shocked mind a blur. It was cold, so cold.

'Bring the Arrow-bearer! Take his bridle! We can't stay here a moment longer!'

Other voices, equally frantic, joined the shouting. 'Sound the retreat!' 'Send word to the wagons!' 'No! We must find high ground!' 'Look to the Arrow-bearer!'

The rattle of pebbles drew Leith's misting eyes back to the stony slope. The nearest Bhrudwan was no more than a minute's hard run from him, and still more warriors surged into view over the crown of the slope. His gaze lingered on the brown-cloaked warriors, and he finally realised in the pit of his soul that they were indeed real, not a figment of his father's imagination. The journey had been so long, he had forgotten that one day it would have an end. The Bhrudwans were real, they held the Gap, and their swords were out.

'Look down there,' said the Destroyer, his one hand gripping Stella's shoulder, fingers biting into her flesh. 'Witness the fruition of my plans!'

'I can see twice as many Falthans as Bhrudwans,' she spat back at him, heedless of the punishment she might receive. 'They may have prepared you a trap of their own.'

He laughed cruelly, a mockery of her brave words. 'They might have a hundred thousand fools on the field of battle, but they are untrained, exhausted by their hurried journey here. Dispirited, having lost the race to the Gap. My warriors are hungry for victory, while theirs are desperate to avoid defeat. They will not avoid it, this I prophesy. And you, my little tigress, will watch them die.'

He took his hand from her shoulder and something within her relaxed a little, as the trapped fly might relax when the spider turns his attention towards another victim in his web. 'Set the blue fire,' he commanded his servants. 'I must have contact with the *Maghdi Dasht*.'

Stella leaned out from their perch on top of a rocky outcrop, trying to see what happened below. Anything to distract her from the spider beside her. The Falthans were already in retreat, drawing back from the Bhrudwan advance even before they had engaged with their enemy, but even so the two armies were still closing. From where she stood the Falthans looked disorganised, the distant wagons still pressing forwards while the vanguard had turned back. The Bhrudwans pressed on unhurriedly.

It could all end right here, today. And with that chilling thought, she realised just how much she depended on a Falthan victory.

Leith came to himself. This was his army, and not all was yet lost. Perhaps, just perhaps, a victory won here today might lay eight thousand icy spectres to rest. His army's headlong retreat had nearly won them free of the treacherous, broken ground at the base of the slope. Before them lay a wide plain packed with Falthan soldiers, some unsheathing their swords, others nocking arrows to their bows. Horsemen, pikemen, footsoldiers, all competent, all ready to fight. The sight settled his nerves. Leith lifted the Arrow high and his army roared in response to the flash of flame.

'Turn!' came a cry from somewhere nearby. 'Turn and face!' It was Jethart. Leith swung his horse around to face the

Bhrudwans, and suddenly a great exhilaration rose within him. *Death. Death comes running towards us!* His heart hammered painfully at his ribcage. For a wild moment he went for his sword, desperate to strike a blow, then remembered the Jugom Ark. *No one will be able to stand against me while I have this!*

The first Bhrudwans came leaping over the last of the rocks and out on to the level ground. Just as they closed within reach, a volley of arrows arced down from behind them and thudded into the Falthans, who instinctively jerked their shields up to cover themselves. In many cases this proved fatal, as the Bhrudwans drove in with swords and pikes. Piercing death from above and ahead.

Leith endured a dreadful thirty seconds as the fighters directly in front of him absorbed the initial impact of the Bhrudwan assault. His hope that the first line of defence would hold them evaporated along with his men, as they melted away in the face of fierce swordplay.

There had been some talk about where he should be positioned when the battle began. Some of his generals had argued that he was too valuable to risk on the front line, while others, obviously in awe of the Arrow, saw his value to the morale of the Falthan fighters as outweighing any risk. But there had been little talk of it in the past week during the punishing sprint across the Nagorj, when their hopes of taking the Gap had been so high. Suddenly Leith felt awkward and out of place, and wondered where he should be: he spun around but couldn't see any of his friends. None of the Company, none of his family, and only a few of his generals. Up until now he had gone into battle with the Company at his side. What was he to do now? Where was he to go?

The Bhrudwans pressed closer. Leith saw a Falthan nearby

go down screaming with an arrow in his eye. His anger kindled, he raised the Arrow again and strode forward. His soldiers gave way before the fierceness of the blaze, and a path opened up to the Bhrudwan lines. From somewhere behind came the sound of his name, calling him back, but he ignored it. *Time to measure the worth of this weapon*, he decided.

Down came a volley of arrows, clattering off the shields of the Falthans – those fortunate enough to be carrying shields. Others cried in pain as they were struck. But not Leith: no arrows penetrated the bright flame of his own Arrow. In front of him men in brown cloaks rushed forward, then threw spears, twenty spears or more all aimed at him. They vanished in a crackle of flame, the spearheads falling hot to the ground. The Bhrudwans fled faster than they had advanced. Heartened, his men came up behind him. 'Follow!' he cried. 'Burn the enemy!'

'Burn them! Burn the enemy!' The cry echoed around the Gap. Leith pointed the Arrow, and willed flame: a jet of pure fire spat across the space between him and the fleeing Bhrudwans and enveloped a dozen or more browncloaks. A fierce yell erupted from behind him as the Falthans watched, exultant.

But their joy turned to terror as the flame winked out, revealing the Bhrudwans unscathed. Leith had only a moment to realise the truth of Belladonna's warning. The Jugom Ark was no weapon. It could not kill. No, more accurately it could not kill Bhrudwans, could not harm anyone not of the Fire. He could hurt his own people, but not the enemy.

For a moment the Bhrudwans stood frozen, clearly astonished, then with cries of glee they drew their swords and charged the bewildered Falthans. Men reprieved from death by fire, now seized by bloodlust. Behind Leith all but a few of the bravest of his men fled.

Cries of men and ringing of swords echoed across the valley. As yet only a small fraction of the two armies had engaged. The level ground was perhaps half a league in width, the northern third occupied by the swift-flowing Aleinus River. Phemanderac found a house-sized boulder, an erratic from one of the mountain ranges shaped eerily like a human skull, and clambered up the side of it for a better view of the battle. Surprisingly he felt exhilarated, not frightened, in spite of what Hauthius had written about wars. To watch this one at first-hand would surely earn him a scroll in the Hall of Lore in Dona Mihst.

There! A flash of light right where the armies had come together! Who was he fooling? He had not climbed this rock to watch the battle. He had taken this position to find Leith. Since the night west of Sivithar almost three months ago, Phemanderac had been afraid to speak to the Arrow-bearer, afraid of the feelings he carried for the clever, brave, naive fool who burned his heart like the Fire of Heaven. Jethart of Inch Chanter had taken the philosopher aside and charged him with telling Leith what he needed to know about the Jugom Ark, but he had not been able to do it. Every time he drew near . . . oh, it felt like a handful of hot stones churning in his stomach. He could not do it. And now Leith was out there, unaware of his danger.

Surely he knew? Surely he had been able to work it out? But deep in his heart Phemanderac knew that his stubborn northern friend would not have given it a moment's thought. Hurriedly the tall philosopher shrugged off his harp, placed it gently on the flat top of the boulder, then leaped to the ground.

The crash of the armies coming together shook Farr to the very core. He stood in the front line with the Fodhram, a place of honour given him by his laughing friends. They positioned themselves right in the path of the Bhrudwans clambering down the steepest part of the stone-slope. The advancing warriors, all of whom wore a red sash or bib, carried both sword and spear in addition to their shield; and just before they reached the Falthan lines they cast their spears down on the opposing army. But the Fodhram were ready for them. They knocked the spears away with their long-handled axes, then darted forward and began hewing at the arms and legs of their adversaries. Farr took his sword and, uttering a yell that would have turned every head in the Waybridge Inn back home, threw himself into the fray.

Immediately he was confronted by a squat man jabbing a curved sword in front of him as though poling a boat away from the shore. Farr fell back a step, drawing his man forward, then hacked at the sword hand, crushing his fingers against the hilt. As the man struggled to retrieve his blade, Farr struck at his unprotected neck. With a groan the Bhrudwan fell to the ground bonelessly, where he lay bleeding.

A great relief blossomed within the mountain man's chest. He had been afraid, he admitted to himself, deathly afraid he would find his courage lacking in the battle's fevered heart; afraid his skill would be found wanting; that at the crucial moment he would find himself unable to deliver the killing blow. Exhilarated, he cried out: 'Vinkullen! For Vinkullen and Wira Storrsen!' A few of the Fodhram rushed over to the fey foreigner, picked up his cry and began to lay about themselves in wide strokes, felling men wherever they swung, laughing and shouting all the while.

In the heart of the battle, Farr had come home.

Leith stood alone in the midst of a brown field, facing the oncoming Bhrudwans. His horse lay dead behind him, victim of a stray arrow from somewhere in the Falthan ranks. Sword in his shaking hand, he readied himself to strike and to die. He knew himself no swordsman. Everything had depended on the cruel, faithless Arrow. 'Why didn't you tell me!' he shouted at the useless object in his hand, but it did not reply.

Everything moved with a terrible sluggishness, as though mired in mud. On came the Bhrudwans, dozens of them, swords raised, spears out, cautious but no longer afraid. A strange silence descended, the noises of battle merging into a kind of background murmur, like a flock of crows in a distant forest. The world narrowed to a few paces.

With a cry a handful of Falthan soldiers burst past him and threw themselves at the Bhrudwans. The ringing of blade on blade echoed in Leith's ears and across the field. One snarling Falthan fell, three Bhrudwans on him, stabbing, thrusting, hacking long after there was no need, making sure of the kill. The other four Falthans formed a circle around Leith, blades out, deflecting the Bhrudwan charge, defending, playing for time. One man grunted as a spear laid open his sword arm.

These people are dying for me! If you ever want me to listen to you again, speak now!

<Don't waste time thinking about what the Arrow can't do,> came the calm voice. <Think about what it *can* do.>

Is that all? You owe me more than that! Another of his men was down, a spear in his side, death approaching, but still the man called out warnings to his fellows. Such courage! For a moment he considered letting the Arrow flame out – *maybe I could melt their swords and spears* – but his own men would burn as they tried to protect him.

'Get back! Get back!' he cried to his men. *I can't do anything to hurt the Bhrudwans – not directly, anyway. But they may still think I have power. So they might believe their swords and spears are too hot to hold on to.* He thrust aside his soldiers, bursting out of their protective ring with a roar. Immediately he let all his anger flow into the Jugom Ark, which went incandescent.

'You may not burn, but your weapons will!' he cried, even as he deflected a sword stroke. *Closer.* He pictured in his mind the blades melting, the handles heating – and as he imagined it, so it happened. *Illusion.*

<Yes. More powerful than reality.> The voice sounded smug. Leith watched the Bhrudwans throw down their weapons in pain, then run from the field.

Leith could not contain himself, 'Look around you!' he shouted at the voice. 'People died to protect me! Why didn't you tell me this before?'

No reply came, unsurprisingly. He could almost hear the voice giving him a Hal-like explanation: *I can only work through people. I sent my teachers to you, and you rejected every one. I wanted to tell you, but you were not willing to listen. So now people die.*

'I don't accept that,' Leith muttered. 'You don't care how many die, as long as you and your precious plan remain safe.'

<We'll see,> said the voice softly, and to Leith's dazed mind it sounded more like a lament than a promise.

As Stella watched, men died. The dun-cloaked Bhrudwans, with their bibs of various colours, rolled right over the greys and dark greens of the Falthan vanguard. There were few Bhrudwans among the fallen. To her left, near the base of the steepest part of the talus slope, the Falthans appeared to be doing a little better: the Bhrudwans had come down more carefully, and the defenders fought fiercely, with axes, bows and clubs as well as swords. Their numbers included some with bare chests and dark skins, she noted with surprise. But even they were suffering, mostly from the constant rain of arrows from archers carefully positioned at the top of the slope. Out near the centre of the battlefield the situation appeared far worse. Apart from little clusters of capable fighters, most of the leading Falthans fell within moments of their first engagement. Already the Bhrudwans had forced a wedge extending many paces into the lines of their foe, clambering over the bodies of the fallen in their haste to press home their advantage.

Her eye was taken by a flash of light somewhat to the right of the wedge's apex, standing out in the open. She looked more closely: there it was again. A man. No, a boy. Holding a burning torch.

Leith! With the Jugom Ark in his hand!

He had been seen by others far closer than she. A score of Bhrudwans, led by a man in a jet-black cloak, broke away from the wedge and began forcing their way towards the flashing light. *Leith! Watch out!* She did not realise she had spoken aloud until the figure beside her laughed.

'Don't worry, girl; unless he is very foolish or very unlucky he will not be killed. My *Maghdi Dasht* have strict orders to capture the bearer of the Jugom Ark alive. Soon he will stand at my right hand, as closely bound to me as you are.' And he laughed again, a hungry sound that seemed to suck light from the very sky. Beside his appalling darkness, the light of the Jugom Ark seemed very small and far away.

Jethart rallied his dismayed generals, calling them to his side. 'It is time to go to your own commands,' he said to them in a calm voice. 'Each of us will be most effective taking charge of his own people.' Without remaining to ensure his suggestion was being followed, he set spurs to his horse and made for the *losian* army, where the battle was thickest.

The man from Inch Chanter reached down and pulled his blade from its scabbard. He had not wanted this heirloom back. It reminded him of the evil times when his people and the Widuz fought incessantly, of the death of his elder son, of the disappearance of his only daughter, of the blood on his hands. Of the red harvest of unthinking deeds committed by a callow youth without regard for the ghosts that would come calling when finally he laid his weapon down. His broad blade and its jewelled scabbard had hung on the wall of the town's meeting house, a sort of shrine for the young men to gather around, but Jethart had not been back to see it in the years since he'd placed it there. Then the northern stranger Mahnum came to town, fleeing the Widuz, and miraculously restored his daughter to him. Mahnum Modahlsen was a name well known to one who watched the affairs of western Faltha from his humble cottage. The son of Modahl claimed the sword of Jethart for his own and escaped the Widuz under cover of night, in pursuit of his son. A son who now carried the Jugom Ark and was widely proclaimed as the fabled Right Hand of the Most High.

Jethart was inextricably bound in the greatest story of the age, a tale greater by far than the border conflicts in which he had fought with courage and renown; and when a messenger from his old friend Kroptur appeared on his doorstep, suggesting he organise an unlikely *losian* alliance and lead them eastwards, he could not remain aloof from it.

He couldn't help thinking how foolish his ornate scabbard looked slapping against his age-mottled leg. *Was I crazy to come all this way?* Of course he had been. He should be sitting by the fire with his daughter and grandson. Yet his had been the counsel sought by all the great generals of the land, and now his was the responsibility. Someone had to redeem the situation, someone had to devise new tactics to meet those of their enemy. There would be no opportunity to sit in a comfortable tent and debate at their leisure. He would rally the *losian* army, then find a way to turn this rout to their advantage.

Leith shook his head in weariness. He had entertained hopes of being a great warrior, striding across the battlefield, putting the enemy to flight. In his dreams the Destroyer burned as he wielded the fire of his Arrow, while his parents looked on. But quickly he discovered how difficult it was merely to stay alive.

He missed his horse. Down here on his own feet death hunted him from every direction. Spears, arrows, swords, clubs, axes. He couldn't keep the Arrow burning all the time: the protection it offered depended on his own energy, draining him as well as endangering his soldiers. Leith alternated between periods of euphoria, unable to believe he was still alive, and times of pure fear, ducking roundhouse swishes, dodging stabs, operating on instinct. At one point during that hectic first hour he fought side by side with Perdu. During a brief lull he sent Perdu off to look for a horse and a shield; a mistake, as the fighting redoubled around him after the man left.

There were heroes on the field that afternoon, Falthan and

Bhrudwan both. For a while Leith fought alongside a company from Straux, hardened warriors who asked him no questions about his powerless arrow. These men used staff and sword with the grace and efficiency of dancers. 'Left!' one shouted. The company swung left to meet a column of Bhrudwan pikemen, then dealt with them mercilessly. 'Right!' They engaged a troop of big men wielding broadswords, and in moments men from both sides littered the ground. In perhaps ten minutes of savagery they fought themselves to a standstill.

A huge Bhrudwan in an incongruous red bib barked a command, and the Bhrudwans withdrew. Too late for one. A smaller man, also with a red bib, found himself surrounded by Falthan swordsmen. He lurched first this way, then that, but his enemies would not give way. Spinning on his heels he tried to force a way through, but as he spun his sword was chopped from his hand.

With a wild yell the huge red-bibbed Bhrudwan barrelled into the Falthans, bringing half-a-dozen of them down on top of him. His compatriot dashed through the gap to freedom. Grunting with exertion, the huge man rose with three men still clinging to him, knives flashing. He made it all the way to his feet before slumping back to the hard earth.

The smaller man, rescued by this valour, shrieked as he saw his commander fall, and ran back into danger.

'Leave him!' Leith cried, realising what had happened. 'Leave the man alone!' Wordlessly the Straux warriors drew back, then turned in search of another battle, leaving the smaller Bhrudwan – a boy, really – to grieve over the body of his father.

And so the afternoon drew on. Leith had glanced up at the wan sun and found it had barely moved from when he'd last checked; then looked again a moment later and found it quartering towards the horizon. The smells and sounds were dreadful. Mass slaughter. Surely even surrender would be better than this. Even Perdu's return with a replacement horse did little to erase his horror.

An unsettling hum cut across the general noise of fighting, gradually resolving into a sort of low chanting, not quite sung, not quite spoken, a guttural rumbling that set Leith's teeth on edge. There! The strange chanting came from the weaponless man in the grey robe, cowled so his face was hidden, standing less than thirty paces away at the head of a column of Bhrudwan warriors. A raw, debilitating power lay hidden in the words; even though they were spoken in a language Leith did not understand, their intent was clear. Words of defeat, of despair. The words seemed to solidify on his skin, encumbering weights that made his progress seem as slow as swimming in mud.

A few Falthans threw down their weapons in the face of the strange assault: one such bowed his head as a spike-studded mace swung towards him. The crunching contact stove in the man's skull, and he fell to the ground, twitching out his life.

Whatever this is, it has to be stopped!

The Arrow in Leith's hand pulsed in time with the beating of his heart, weak and rapid. Just when it would have been most useful, there seemed no potency in it. Where was the anger he felt when last he was caught up in a battle? To his right a foot soldier went down with a spear through his stomach, collapsing on it, falling on the shaft so it drove through him, then rolling over on to his side in the throes of death. With wide, staring eyes the soldier looked up at the man who had slain him, his face contorted with pain, and lifted an arm in supplication as if calling on his adversary to undo what he had done. The Bhrudwan soldier reached out and took hold of the spear, then twisted it savagely: the resulting scream ended in a gurgle. A boot came down on to the man's torso, enabling the spear to be pulled out; then the boot kicked the body once and moved on. A man who had set out from Instruere, who had survived the journey through Vulture's Craw, had just become a body, a shell.

And now the hooded figure halted a few paces away. The incantation continued to roll from the man's tongue as he reached up and took hold of his hood, ready to lower it. The sense of menace sharpened.

At that moment someone leaped on to Leith's horse, landing behind him. Heart in his mouth, Leith turned to find Phemanderac. 'We leave this place now!' he cried in Leith's ear, reached forward, grabbed, then shook the reins and dug in his heels.

'Why? What happened?' Leith asked, rubbing his tingling arms through the sleeves of his cloak as they rode back through the ranks of his army. 'I should be seen where the fighting is fiercest!'

'No, Leith.' The philosopher's voice displayed an admirable firmness, betraying nothing. 'You think that you hold some kind of invincible weapon in your hand, but you do not. Yes, it will protect you from sword thrust or arrow shot, but you cannot use it against the Bhrudwans.'

'I know, Phemanderac,' he replied. 'I know!' *Why did you wait until now to talk about this?*

Phemanderac reined in beside a large rock, helped Leith to climb it, then carried on as though he'd not heard the Arrow-bearer's reply. 'The Bhrudwans are of Water, remember, not Fire like us. You will not be able to use the Jugom Ark to defeat your enemies.'

'I hadn't planned to, though Maendraga said the Destroyer—'

The philosopher kept talking, his voice urgent, his words

hot, his eyes fervid. 'The value of the Arrow was ever its ability to create unity. It does not need any special powers to do that. Without the Arrow of Yoke we would never have gathered this great army.'

'Which is dissolving away even as we speak!' cried Leith. *What is wrong with you, Phemanderac? Why can I see shame in your eyes?* 'How can I sit here on this rock and do nothing?'

'Because you have no choice; because I won't let you down. Yours are the only hands—'

'I know that! But we are losing! Mine might be the only hands left by day's end!' He shook the Jugom Ark in frustration, and it flared into sudden life, forcing Phemanderac to leap backwards.

'Can you not be more careful, Leith?' the tall philosopher complained as he clambered back up the rock. 'I might not be of the Sixteen Kingdoms, but I am of the Fire. The Jugom Ark will reduce me to a pile of ashes if I'm too close to you when you throw a tantrum.'

'You were supposed to teach me all about this Arrow.' Leith waved it in front of him, causing it to flame again, less violently this time. Still Phemanderac took a step backwards. 'Where have you been these last weeks?'

The Firanese youth and the Dhaurian scholar stood staring at each other on top of the rock, forgetting for the moment the battle raging below them. Falthan soldiers all around the battlefield looked up, saw the Jugom Ark uplifted high and took heart from it, throwing themselves back into the fight. By now all but the most rigorously trained and highly skilled warriors were exhausted, and most man-to-man encounters, if they were not resolved within the first few blows, degenerated into grappling matches; so that the living wrestled with each other amongst the broken bodies of the dead and the dying.

And all the while shrewd eyes watched the field of battle, waiting for the moment to put carefully-laid plans into action.

At some point in the battle Farr discarded his hopelessly notched sword. He now carried a long-handled axe in both hands, with which he hunted enemies. He had received a great deal of training in axe-handling in the past three months, occasioning much mirth, but had not felt comfortable with axes. No choice now. With a song of Vinkullen on his lips he ran from skirmish to skirmish, accompanied by a growing band of Fodhram, Fenni and Widuz warriors. They followed him in awe, recognising their friend was the most sainted of men, one who discovers what he has been born to do.

'*Skegox! Skegox!*' they cried approvingly as he swung the great blade at a mounted warrior, crashing through his armour and nearly cleaving the man in half. Axehaft assigned three men to keep spear-wielding Bhrudwans away from the battle-crazed northerner. Their task was necessary: a well-placed spear thrust could catch any two-handed axe where the blade joined the shaft, tearing it from its wielder's grip.

There is no prudence in the way he fights, Axehaft marvelled as he watched Farr Storrsen rain down a series of swift, uncultured blows on yet another hapless opponent. *And no tiredness in his arm.* It took only four blows this time for the courage to drain from the Bhrudwan lad. Two blows later the boy lay in a pool of blood, felled like a tree. *The axe was ever a weapon of passion, and Farr Storrsen fated to wield it.* The Fodhram leader hefted his own axe and met his next opponent. *Still a grim business, though.*

'*Skegox, skegox!*' The cries echoed around Farr as he laboured. A small part of his mind was in shock, having beheld the effects of his labour, carnage spattered on his cloak and over a wide area of stony ground. '*Skegox!*' His friends fought alongside him, he fought for them, every blow making him more worthy of their praise. '*Skegox!*'

Here came a nimble man with a broadsword in one hand and a knife in another. Farr read his intention before he even began. Two or three thrusts with the broadsword were supposed to distract him, leaving his left side open for the knife blade. Farr went along with it, but when the man drew back his arm for the throw, Farr hacked it off.

There came a huge man with a mace, whirling it around his head. Again, Farr read the nature of the attack from the way the man-mountain brandished his weapon. Before his opponent had a chance to close he thrust the axe-shaft forwards, upwards, tangling with the mace and jerking the man off balance. Once he was down, Farr buried the axe in his chest, then turned his back on the man and his bubbling cries of rage and frustration.

Here came a group of older warriors with pikes, and the Fodhram decimated them with throwing axes, then left Farr to harvest them like wheat. And there came another attack, rank after rank of soldiers ordered to the fray to take the place of those cut down. Farr's arms cried their pain, but he ignored them, knowing that a moment's relaxation would mean his doom. As the afternoon wore on so his weariness grew, adding a sharpness, a knowledge of mortality, to his exultation.

In the middle of the afternoon, two, perhaps three hours after the battle began, the Haufuth managed to find Jethart, who had set up his tent beside the wagons. Without waiting to be announced he entered the tent and confronted the Treikan general.

'What is going on?' he rasped. 'Hundreds – no, thousands – of men have died out there today. I have shouted myself hoarse trying to organise the ragged bunch of fighters I commanded, but still they run off and impale themselves on Bhrudwan pikes as though they could stop the Destroyer's advance by making a wall of their own bodies. I can't stand any more of it! Are we doing the right thing?'

Jethart turned from his hastily-drawn chart of the battlefield, his soft eyes sad and full of compassion. 'We are doing well, for the moment,' he said quietly. 'The large part of both armies has yet to fight, however. Look at this,' he said, beckoning the Haufuth over to the table. 'See here? The Gap is not wide enough to allow more than a few thousand men to engage at any one time. The rest wait their turn.'

'And our losses? I don't want to watch one more boy go down with a sword in his guts unless I can be assured that we are winning!'

'As to that, we have no real way of knowing. My tallymen suggest that we are losing two men to their one, which means, based on the numbers of the two armies, we are doing no more than holding our own.' The old man turned and gripped the Haufuth's forearms in his large, rough hands. 'What worries me is not the losses, though I am human enough to realise that each man lost is a tragedy. No, I am concerned that the Destroyer puts forth merely a show of his strength. Where are the dedicated warriors? Where are the fabled *Maghdi Dasht*? I know they exist, for I have heard tales of the prowess of the *Maghdi* attached to your own band. Where are the wizards, where is the magic? I don't understand what is happening. We should have paid for our failure to win the Gap with twenty thousand lives before the end of this day, and yet our death tally is as yet a mere tithe of that. What is the Destroyer preparing? When will he unleash it upon us?' Jethart banged his fist on the table, spilling a half-filled bottle of ink on the corner of his chart. 'Go and find that out for me. Then we can plan to counter him!'

Early in the battle Mahnum realised his place was not in the front lines. He was barely able to keep himself alive in the initial flurry of attacks, staving off a tall, broad-shouldered Bhrudwan only when the man twisted his ankle on a rock. *Why do they not attack in formation?* he kept asking himself all through the first hour of the fighting. *Why do they spend their men so wastefully?*

As soon as he was able he disengaged himself from the battle front and made his way back to the wagons, almost a league from the fighting. There a makeshift surgery had been set up, where the wounded were treated with whatever skill and kindness could be found. *Leith should have made more provision for dealing with the infirm,* Mahnum thought angrily as he surveyed the pitiful surgery. *Yet another reason why he should have involved Hal.* The Trader searched through the tents, knowing he would find his wife and elder son trying to help those who were suffering. *This is my place for now. Oh, Leith! Why did you turn from your family?*

The Lord of Bhrudwo lifted Stella to her feet, then took her chin in his hand. 'It is time for you to truly know the meaning of fear,' he announced, his lips peeling back from his teeth as though he prepared to savour a delicacy. 'The army of your peasant friend is thoroughly prepared. Now I will break them. And, as befits one who abandoned her friends, you will give the signal.'

His compulsion seized her. She called on every particle of

her will, but could not resist him even for a moment. It was as though she had not even tried, so easily was she ensnared. She took his arm and lifted it high; and trumpeters positioned all along the crest of the talus slope blew their horns in a braying that shook the earth, sending stones rattling down the slope in front of them. The Undying Man closed his eyes, focusing his enormous power; and behind him the blue flame roared into life, climbing higher and higher, the hungry eyes and mouth glowing red.

For a few moments nothing happened. Lips pressed together, knuckles white with anxiety for her friends, Stella watched the slaughterfield below, until eventually she discerned movement in the front lines. Grey-garbed figures drove into the Falthan lines in two places. Where they walked, the lines melted like summer snow. Slowly, deliberately, each of the two breaches filled with Bhrudwan warriors, following the grey men. Further and further into the Falthan army the figures penetrated, cutting down their opposition, forming two columns behind each of the breaches. They continued their grisly progress forward, still unimpeded despite the best efforts of those who died opposing them.

What was their objective? Stella searched the battleground in vain, until her eyes rested on a small rock some distance from the front lines, midway between the two pincers that drew around it, enclosing it in a ring of Bhrudwan steel. There were figures on the rock – two figures – and one held the Flaming Arrow in his hand.

For many minutes Phemanderac spoke, driving home point after point with a clarity he had thought beyond him. *A clarity born of desperation*, he acknowledged grimly. *If we are to ever see our homes again, this boy will have to learn how to control the fire in his hand.*

'The Jugom Ark is attuned to your emotions,' he repeated patiently. 'Whenever you feel something strongly it bursts into flame, as you have already discovered. But, if you don't mind me saying, of late your emotions have been centred around anger, from what I hear. We have yet to see how the Fire responds to other emotions: hope, joy, love.'

For a moment the philosopher fell silent, then he continued. 'I don't yet know why you can handle the Arrow.' He scratched his head, trying to crystallise his thoughts. 'My study tells me that no Falthan can hold the Jugom Ark unless they have received the Gift of Fire; and that Gift has not been given since the fall of Dona Mihst two thousand years ago. Withholding the Fire is part of the punishment the Most High meted to the First Men. So the records say.' He paused, thinking hard. 'Thus the Most High spoke to the exiles, as recorded in the *Domaz Skreud*: "You have forfeited your right to the Water of the Fountain, and the Fire of Life will die within you, to be given to another generation. You shall be banished from the Vale, and for many years will have to survive alone in the world ere I visit you again with My Presence." So, unless you are in reality of Bhrudwan or *losian* parentage, you ought to be susceptible to the heat of the Jugom Ark.'

He turned to the young Loulea peasant boy, the Bearer of the Arrow, with puzzlement on his face. 'Tell me, Leith: I've never understood how you knew you would not be harmed by the Jugom Ark. Whatever possessed you to reach out and pick it up, especially after seeing your Haufuth burn his hand?'

'Wait a moment,' said Leith sharply. 'Those words of the

Most High. I've heard them before. Kurr recited to us from them, I think. Doesn't it say there will come a time when the Fire will again be given to the First Men?'

'Most theologians believe that the Most High referred to the afterlife, where those who have remained faithful go to be with Him. Are you suggesting – do you think that the words might be taken literally?'

'Would the Gift of Fire somehow . . . speak to a person? In their thoughts, perhaps?' The question was asked with an undisguised intensity, drawing the tall man's attention.

'How do you mean?'

'For example, telling them that the Jugom Ark was hidden in a cave in an island in a lake? Telling them that it was safe to pick up the Arrow, as long as it was held tightly? Is that the sort of thing the Fire might say, or could it be the invention of – of a mind taken with madness?' The boy raised his face to meet his, his features filled with an uneasy mixture of hope and fear.

And with these words it became clear to Phemanderac, scholar of Dona Mihst, that the Gift of Fire had indeed fallen again. He had been there to witness it, but had thought it a dream. Obviously at least one of the people in the basement had opened himself enough to receive the Gift, and it had been speaking to him ever since. So. The Jugom Ark had attuned itself to the Fire within Leith. Others of the Company may also have received the Fire. Had he, Phemanderac of Dhauria? Could he reach out and take the Jugom Ark in his own hand?

'Phemanderac? Phemanderac!' The youth tugged at the sleeve of his coat. 'What is happening out there? Look!'

The tall scholar looked out from the rock, far too late, to see two columns of Bhrudwan wizard-warriors, one column to the left, the other to the right, both aimed at the rock on which he stood.

For the first time Phemanderac came face to face with the bane of Dhauria, the massed *Maghdi Dasht*, the Lords of Fear. And as he realised what was about to happen, terror turned his spine to ice.

The horns were heard everywhere across the field, announcing the arrival of that which Jethart feared. *The Bhrudwans are doing something*, he thought; and, abandoning his chart, he ran from the tent and called for his mount. *I do not remember my legs aching like this!* His aides struggled to keep up with him as he galloped towards the lines of battle.

Mahnum heard the horns, and at the same time felt something akin to a thickening of the air. At first he thought it might be the weather – a snowstorm, perhaps; it was certainly cold enough – but poking his head out of the tent revealed a high overcast sky, definitely lighter than earlier in the day. Yet the air continued to thicken, making it harder to move, harder to think. And with the thickening came a dread, unspecified but powerful and growing.

Maendraga and his daughter Belladonna laboured at the southern end of the front lines, alternating between the First Men of Deruys – who had taken a fearful battering, for all their undoubted skill and courage – and the *losian* Army of the North, who had done somewhat better. At the sound of the horn the magician jerked his head up, as though he smelled something in the air; a moment later, his daughter sensed it also. They abandoned their magics, and a whole troop of illusory soldiers disappeared, leaving a number of bemused Bhrudwan warriors searching for their enemies. The two former Guardians of the Arrow glanced at each other, then ran for their horses. And as they ran, the horns continued to sound.

Te Tuahangata of the Mist gave the horns no thought, so completely had the lust of battle taken him. Together with Wiusago of Deruys and Perdu of the Fenni he rushed to wherever the Falthan lines were thinnest, and many warriors followed them. He had slain dozens of the enemy through sheer speed and recklessness, allied with his skill with the warclub, and was pleased to observe that the enemy soldiers ran from him; though he was unaware that his blood-covered face under a shock of black hair made him look like nothing other than an avenging angel. Most of the blood was his own, flowing from a shallow wound on his left temple. He was also completely unaware that he laughed as he slew, a mirthless laugh filled with portents that drained courage from his adversaries. Even Wiusago and Perdu, professional soldiers who killed out of necessity, looked at him askance.

They heard the horns, they felt the air thicken, and their hearts seemed to grow smaller in their chests, troubled by doubts. But Te Tuahangata seemed untouchable as he laid about himself with a vicious extravagance, and those around him recovered some of their courage. Yet soon all heads turned towards the centre of the battlefield, drawn by some sense, as they realised something dreadful was happening.

Hal exchanged a quick glance with Achtal. There was no need for words. They had been expecting something like this, and had waited patiently, hidden in a rockfield some distance from the front line. No one would have understood this reluctance to fight, especially since Achtal would have been so valuable with his sword in hand; moreover Hal had been viewed with a strong degree of suspicion since the night Leith accused him of complicity with the Bhrudwan cause.

They bounded out from behind the rocks, Hal strangely lithe for one so crippled, and ran towards the place where the magic was being raised.

They were halfway there when the horns blew a second time.

Stella ground her teeth together in frustration as the twin Bhrudwan columns met on the far side of the rock upon which Leith was clearly trapped. Now the grey-cloaked men spread to the left and to the right, making space for more fighters to move forward. Perhaps five hundred Falthan soldiers were trapped within the narrowing inner circle: for a moment Stella held hopes they might resist, but they seemed to have been frozen into immobility, and were cruelly cut down. She wept where she stood, shaking with impotence as if she, too, were frozen, awaiting the fall of the axe. Beside her the awful figure breathed deeply, eating and drinking in the scene below them. She longed to hurt him somehow, as she had hurt Deorc, even if it cost her an eternity of pain.

Phemanderac finished his counting: thirteen thirteens. He knew what that meant, he could have given them a name even if their magic was not clearly evident. These were the *Maghdi Dasht*, the order that had invaded Dhauria a thousand years ago, laying siege to Dona Mihst, retreating only when word came to them of their master's defeat in Instruere at the hands of Conal Greatheart. Phemanderac had been instructed in their ways, as were all Dhaurian scholars, and knew what they were capable of.

What was I thinking, spending a comfortable session with the Arrow-bearer here on this rock in full view of the enemy? Why did I not sense the danger as it drew near?

He knew the answer, but he didn't want to examine it.

A second trumpet blast came from the top of the slope, instantly answered by action from the encircling Bhrudwans. The *Maghdi Dasht* stepped back, allowing sword-wielding soldiers to drive into the Falthans they had pinned down. So tightly had the binding magic pinned them that all the hundreds of Falthans could do was to stand in abject terror and await the blades that chopped and hacked their way towards them.

On the rock Leith roared with frustration. So his Arrow was not a weapon? It flamed high into the air, a light so strong it flickered along the base of the clouds above, a fire so fierce that Phemanderac cried out in pain as the hair on his face and forearms was singed. 'Leith!' he cried, sucking in a blast of hot air as he did so. 'Stop! You will slay me!'

The chanting continued, an abrasive sound that seemed to bore into the minds of all Falthans who heard it. Leith could still move: maybe the Jugom Ark provided a measure of protection against Bhrudwan magic, or – as was more likely – the Lords of Fear had yet to reveal their full strength. Slowly he stumbled from one end of the rock to the other, and all around him the same scene met his gaze. His soldiers stood like statues until they were felled with a series of pitiless blows, a field of precious grain harvested by a callous farmer. One by one they died. One by one. The numbers kept ticking over in his head; and the weight on his shoulders grew heavier and heavier. One by one. The slashing of swords, the droning of one hundred and sixty-nine throats, a dirge to accompany their deaths, numbers, numbers, numbers.

Leith thought he would go mad.

'Make a space!' Hal cried. 'Whatever you have to do, clear a space!' Taken aback, burdened with unnatural fear, the nearby

Falthan soldiers found something of courage in the words. For a moment they could move freely, and set about driving the Bhrudwans back. Within a few moments Hal and Achtal stood in the centre of an open space twenty paces wide. In answer to Achtal's quizzical look, Hal smiled tightly. 'They'll come.'

Within moments a horse burst into the clearing. 'The Destroyer isn't interested in defeating us!' cried the rider, who leaped from his mount like a young man. 'He's just holding us here until—'

'Until he can capture the Jugom Ark,' Hal finished.

'Who are you?' Jethart asked him. 'I'm sorry, but I do not have time for niceties.'

'Hal Mahnumsen, son of Mahnum and brother of the Arrow-bearer, who is in trouble. The Destroyer has sent the *Maghdi Dasht* after him.'

The old man nodded curtly. 'I'm sorry, I didn't recognise you. The help of any scion of Mahnum will be welcome. Tell me, how do you know of the *Maghdi Dasht*?'

'My knowledge of their existence matters less than my knowledge of what they are doing,' Hal replied curtly. 'They are imprisoning him with words of binding. If you are here—'

Maendraga and Belladonna appeared in the clearing as if by magic, followed by Modahl and a tall woman he had never seen before. A few moments later Mahnum stumbled his way in, clearly out of breath and bleeding from a gash to his arm: he glanced around the clearing, smiled at his son but took a pace backwards when he saw his father. Indrett followed him, a dazed look on her face. Soon a dozen or more people milled about in the clearing, protected from the Bhrudwan soldiers by the increasingly sluggish efforts of Falthan fighters.

'You are all here because something called you,' Hal told them, an urgency in his voice Indrett had never heard from him before. 'For a hundred days we have all been anticipating a physical battle, but that was never the real battle to be fought here. You feel the power being exerted by the servants of the Destroyer, but unlike those around you, you have been able to resist. You are the real warriors here today.' The Hal she had always known, the calm, serene child, had been broken by the accusations from his brother. What remained seemed more vulnerable, more human, but still had steel. 'There is something inside you that responds to the call, something that fights the magic of the *Maghdi Dasht*.' She shook her head, rubbing her temples, trying to clear the thickness that settled on her like the snow at Vulture's Craw.

'What is happening?' Modahl asked, his voice troubled.

'Leith and the Jugom Ark are surrounded by the Lords of Fear,' Jethart replied, pointing to the north where the sound of chanting continued to abrade across the battlefield. Hal nodded to him, then added: 'Phemanderac of Dona Mihst is trapped there with him. It is his call you feel.'

'Enough of the discussion,' Indrett cried. 'What are we to do?'

The Destroyer spun to his left, facing the girl he believed totally under his control. 'What are you doing?' he screamed at her. 'I can feel the power within you!'

Stella smiled through gritted teeth. She could not wipe the sweat from her face, could not control the way her body shook, but she could turn her head enough to see the face of her enemy.

'I'm fighting you, fool,' she whispered between clenched teeth.

* * *

A third trumpet volley rang out, heralding a change in the incantation that seemed to be winding cords of steel around Leith and Phemanderac. The philosopher had been driven to his knees, his voice little more than a whisper. 'Can't . . . breathe . . .'

Leith knelt beside him, taking his face in his hands. 'Phemanderac! If the Bhrudwans are of Water, how can they hurt us with their magic spells? They can't, can they?'

'It's an illusion,' Hal told them, 'though a very powerful one.'

'So it can be defeated,' Belladonna said confidently. 'Though it does not feel like any illusion I've ever encountered.'

'The horns were the key,' her father said. 'They convinced us something real was about to happen. We participated willingly in their illusion.'

'It can be defeated,' the cripple confirmed. 'Powerful resistance has already been raised against the Lords of Fear. Somewhere out on the field a great wizard opposes the Destroyer's plan.'

'Reject the binding, not those doing the binding,' Achtal said, and adopted a look of intense concentration. 'Pick on their weak place – right there.' He flung a muscled forearm towards a section of the Bhrudwan encirclement. 'We break it there.'

'We break it now,' said a figure that had just joined them. Casting aside her cloak, the Ice Queen of the Sna Vazthans added her will to that of the group. 'I have resisted his plans for years.'

'Come closer,' Hal called to them. 'Let me show you how.'

'Curse you!' the Destroyer shrieked at Stella. 'What have you done? From where do you get the strength?'

Her mouth was dry with the effort she had expended. Somehow she'd known to focus on just a few of the robed figures. Or, more accurately, on what they were doing, a binding akin to what the Destroyer had been doing to her since he had captured her. Stubbornness! Resist the binding! Months of pent-up fury, terror and frustration combined to give her a power she never knew she had. It felt as though a great flame surged up from deep within her. And down on the plain, just to the south of the rock, something happened in response to her efforts. Others – she could not see who – began to pour their resistance at the same figures she had chosen.

Her mouth was dry, but she still had saliva enough to spit in the Undying Man's face.

With a roar as deep as caverns the Destroyer struck out at her, his fist exploding on the back of her head, knocking her forward so that she pitched a few feet down the rocky slope. He cried something after her, but she did not hear it.

He's not breathing! Not breathing! Leith shook the blue-lipped form lying prone on the rock before him. *Breathe!*

<Use the Arrow.>

Sobbing with relief at the sound of the voice, Leith laid the Jugom Ark on Phemanderac's breast, then poured all his soul into the fire within. *Breathe!*

He was so filled with joy when the philosopher drew a ragged breath, he didn't notice the pressure around him decrease.

'Forward! Now!' Hal set off crabwise towards a narrow gap in the Bhrudwan ranks. At his side strode Achtal, who drew his sword and cleared a path for them. The others followed behind, not knowing where they were going, trusting in a cripple publicly spurned by the Bearer of the Jugom Ark. It seemed the height of foolishness, but they felt the call and knew they had no choice.

They came to the lines of *Maghdi Dasht*. Now Achtal smiled, and two of the figures turned to confront him, scarred faces confident despite losing command of their binding spell. Their confidence fell somewhat when they saw whom they were matched against; nevertheless, they drew their swords and stood shoulder to shoulder.

All around them the pressure in the air lessened noticeably.

I've seen this! Leith realised belatedly. *On the ceiling of the Hall of Conal Greatheart, as part of the prophecy of Sir Amasian.* Beside him Phemanderac grovelled on his hands and knees, coughing and trying to suck in enough air to take a breath, but for the moment Leith was transfixed. To the right and to the left a double circle of black-robed Lords of Fear wove a net over all those within their compass. In the image on the ceiling the net had been visible as strands of darkness. He remembered it clearly, one of twelve images in one of the twelve paths on the ceiling, all leading to the central image of Amasian's vision, Leith's victory over the Destroyer. All twelve paths were engraved on the roof of his mind, so long had he stared at them all, trying to glean knowledge from them of what was to come, of what he should do. What could he remember of the image? *Think!* Two figures standing on a rock shaped like a human skull, one holding up a burning arrow, surrounded by *Maghdi Dasht*. Behind them, at the top of the slope, stands the Destroyer, his fist raised in seeming triumph: Leith scanned the horizon and thought he could make out a figure on the rocky crest, but could not be sure. And in the foreground of the picture, opposite the slope leading to the Gap, had been a group of Falthan adepts breaking through the Bhrudwan lines, coming to save the Arrow. Leith spun on his heels.

The Destroyer screamed his anger to the skies. *How could I be baulked by such as her, even for a moment?* He looked down at her unmoving figure. *What are you? How can you have so much power and yet be unaware of it? I will tear you open, shred you, slice you into pieces, make you howl until I find out!*

He could sense the small knot of Falthan magicians, could weigh their strength, could estimate their chance of success. *Small enough, but I will not risk humiliation.* It had been only a momentary loss of concentration, but the northern girl had broken the binding spell and spoiled his triumph for the moment. *Delayed, but not denied,* he told himself. Slashing his arm in front of his chest, he motioned his trumpeters to give the signal.

The Falthan magicians fought valiantly against their opponents but, for all their efforts, they were about to be overwhelmed. More and more Bhrudwan soldiers poured from between the two lines of *Maghdi Dasht*, and Achtal held his own against his two opponents only by the most extreme effort. *He is an acolyte, after all,* Mahnum told himself as the renegade Bhrudwan barely avoided another lethal swipe, flowing between the two men as though he danced with them both. The sight of their arrogant, power-limned faces brought back chilling memories of months of riding to escape, and further months of captivity at their hands. *If I could just slay even one of them, perhaps I might lay my nightmares to rest.*

The trumpets rang out again, splitting the sky with their cry. *What new magic are they calling down on us?* Mahnum wondered, but to his amazement the Lords of Fear turned and marched from the field, back towards the rocky slope. The thickness in the air vanished a moment later.

We've beaten them! the Trader crowed. *I don't know how we've done it, but we've defeated them!* His spirit surged within him, and he joined the others in forcing their way through the few remaining Bhrudwan warriors and towards the skull-shaped rock where his son waited for them.

The rage of the Destroyer could not be measured or contained. His aides sheltered behind the nearest cover as their master strode back and forth along the crest of the slope. Already he had struck down two of their number as well as the girl, sending one of them falling into the blue fire, which roared as it accepted the sacrifice.

Finally he came to a halt, and turned his face to the battle below. 'I will not allow them time to celebrate their supposed victory,' they heard him say. 'I will crush their army! I will walk to Instruere over a carpet of their slain! No one will remain alive who has opposed me! NO ONE!'

He signalled again. This time the trumpets let out a prolonged blast, calling forth the hidden reserves of elite warriors from their places at either end of the Gap. The sun sent a single gleam down through the low clouds, picking out for a brief moment the paralysed heart of the Falthan army, and the Bhrudwans set their sights on the place the beam had illuminated.

They saw the Lord of Bhrudwo cast a glance down the slope at the broken remains of the Falthan girl, his plaything. 'No one,' a few of them heard him whisper.

CHAPTER 14

IN SEARCH OF A VISION

ANOTHER COLD, GREY DAWN, another bowl of stew to look forward to, as if that would do more than stave off for an hour or so the hunger hollowing out his insides. Another meeting in the striped tent, another calm recitation from his clerk of the previous day's losses. Another grave to visit, to pay respects to yet another hero whose fall could not be borne. Another in the month of days that had passed since the Destroyer sprung his trap. Except that today the grave they would visit was that of Jethart, the leader of the Falthan armies.

The hero from Inch Chanter had been caught in a small ambush just off the Sna Vazthan road as he went about his daily inspection. His route was changed every day to avoid such an ambush, so he had either been extremely unlucky or he had been betrayed. They killed his escort outright, then tortured the old man in sight of the Falthan army, finally casting his desecrated remains at them with contempt, along with his sword, broken at blade and hilt.

Mahnum reacted with an extravagant fury, and would have rushed out to confront the entire Bhrudwan force if not immediately restrained. For the rest of the day he insisted on fighting in the front line, and none of the enemy had been able to withstand his white-hot wrath: already the whispers throughout the camp were being converted into song.

Leith sighed, rubbed his aching back and picked up the Jugom Ark. It seemed like the main benefit the Arrow conferred was keeping his sleeping tent warm while everyone else suffered from the cold. He pulled back the tent flap and stepped out on to the snow-covered ground.

A month of horror, a month of futility. On that first afternoon, when he and Phemanderac were so dramatically rescued from the clutches of the Lords of Fear, the whole war might have ended. The Destroyer had loosed his shock troops on them, fierce, savage men who had cut down thousands of Falthans on that terrible afternoon, and for a time all seemed lost. Only the coming of darkness had saved them that day.

Yet the Falthans demonstrated a courage far beyond that which Leith could possibly have guessed. Perhaps they knew the only way down from this accursed plateau was through the Bhrudwan army, or perhaps the image of what would happen to the towns and villages of Faltha was fixed in their minds. Whatever the reason, they fought with a stubborn determination, holding off even the most skilled of the Destroyer's fighting men, though with terrible losses. All the first week they were driven slowly backwards across the grey stone of the Nagorj, giving ground only with the greatest reluctance, retreating only when the sternest of orders from their commanders made it plain they had no option.

By the end of that week the Falthan army had lost three leagues, and were fighting along a greatly extended front in a much wider part of the plateau. They had lost seventeen thousand men, a figure so dreadful that when it was pointed out to Leith that this figure included the wounded as well as the dead, he hardly heard the good news. The Bhrudwans had lost perhaps a third of that number, no doubt their weakest and least competent fighters.

Then the snows came, and for two weeks there was little or no conflict as both armies settled down to the business of survival. Dry snow, hissing down day after day, piling up in drifts, engulfing tents and making life miserable – and in some cases impossible – for the horses and other beasts accompanying the Falthan army. Only the aurochs, which the Fenni clan chief had so far kept in reserve, seemed to thrive in the cold weather.

Leith spent the two weeks close to the apothecaries' tents, employing his Arrow to warm the cold and heal the wounded. The Jugom Ark neither harmed nor healed the *losian*: the only help he could offer his allies was to lift their morale. He tried to inure himself to the awful sights inside the tents of healing, but could not ignore the hundreds of men and boys, and a few women, who had sustained terrible wounds in his name. He wanted to beg their forgiveness, to seek their absolution. Agonisingly, all but the most sorely wounded tried to wish him well, expending freely of the energy they had left to reaffirm their support, their belief in him, their next-to-worship of the Jugom Ark. He would have been less troubled had they reviled him.

In all that time Leith did not see his brother. He had assumed that Hal would be working in the tents with his parents, but his family was somewhere else in the vast spread of the Falthan encampment. He missed them terribly, but never had a moment to seek them out: there was always someone else to heal, always another meeting to attend.

He remembered the moment on that first day when the Lords of Fear left the battlefield, and the little group of Falthan magicians had come to his rescue. So much that was surprising! Apparently his mother, his father and his grandfather possessed some ability in that area, just as did his brother. There were others, too, to whom he owed his life: even Phemanderac had helped dampen the attack of the *Maghdi Dasht*, though the lean philosopher denied it. Certainly some mighty magician exerted a great power on his behalf well before the group joined together to rescue him, though no one was sure who it had been. Leith and Phemanderac had embraced each of their rescuers in turn, thanking them profusely, and there had been an awkward moment with Hal.

'Hal led us,' his mother said, voice hard, searching, demanding. 'He drew us together and showed us how to combat the magic of the Lords of Fear. Without him you would be dead by now.'

'I'm sure he had his reasons,' Leith retorted, and walked away, ignoring the gasps behind him.

Perhaps he did owe his brother an apology, but short of an organised search Hal simply could not be found. It couldn't be helped: there were more immediate issues to be dealt with, such as a dire food shortage. The wagons from Adolina and Sna Vaztha grew much less frequent, for even the enticement of Instruian gold could not overcome the snowdrifts and frozen roads that made travelling a treacherous business. The few animals imprudent enough to show themselves on the Nagorj were bagged by the soldiers. *How were the Bhrudwan army kept in food and supplies? It must be much further to the nearest source of food for them.*

As he walked towards the striped tent that until yesterday

was Jethart's domain, Leith struggled to keep the cloying despair from clouding his features. *Can't have the soldiers thinking we're giving up!* He waved to them cheerily, and they applauded him as he walked by: each smiling face another nail in his chest. If he was hungry, having been supplied with the best of the food, how much must his soldiers be suffering? He scowled at the Jugom Ark, flickering quietly in his right hand: *for all your healing power, you can't make food magically appear or take hunger pangs away.*

Leith entered the tent and found he was the last to arrive, so took a seat at the back of the room. *What will we do without Jethart?* he wondered emptily. *Who else will we lose during this cursed war? And who will replace Jethart? Who can bring even half of his wisdom and good counsel to the table?*

The latter question was answered almost immediately. Apparently he was even later than he thought: there had already been a discussion, and the new commander stood to address them. Leith squinted through the misty air in puzzlement, then disbelief. The woman standing in front of them all was his mother Indrett.

'Well then, we have much to consider,' she said, voice clipped and competent in the way Leith had heard her conduct herself both in Loulea and in the markets of Instruere. 'We have lost a great man, and it is our task to ensure that we do not lose too many more. The Bhrudwans have shown they are preparing to re-ignite the conflict. But before we rush away to our companies and prepare for battle, we must think carefully. What does the Destroyer hope to accomplish?'

Judging by the amount of muttering as she spoke, not all of the generals and strategists were comfortable with a woman leading them, however tactically gifted she had shown herself, irrespective of whose mother she was. For a moment they assumed that she asked a rhetorical question; but when she did not continue, merely waiting, holding them with her fierce eyes, the answers began coming.

'The total destruction of our army,' offered Axehaft the Warden.

'No! They will try to capture the Jugom Ark once more. We must protect the Bearer of the Arrow at all costs!' cried the Captain of the Instruian Guard.

Modahl's deep voice cut across the speculation of others. 'The Destroyer wants one thing above all others: to stand acclaimed in Instruere as the ruler of Faltha.'

Indrett nodded. 'That is what I think also,' she said, smiling slightly. 'He will bypass our army completely if it means he gains Instruere. If it were summer, I believe he would already have struck out along the Sna Vazthan road, looking to travel across the southern province of Am'ainik and through the lands of Pereval and Haurn, then down the Branca through Asgowan and Deuverre. But his way is undoubtedly blocked by snow and ice, so he has no choice of route. He will go through us, but at as little cost as possible, for he will need many men to control Faltha. Each of the Sixteen Kingdoms will oppose him, and he will have to reduce them one by one—'

'Though there are some kings who will open their cities to him,' Mahnum offered. Indrett nodded to him in acknowledgment.

'True. But he does not want a long war, of that I am certain. He will try something as soon as the weather clears, something of trickery or magic, or perhaps both.'

Most of those in the tent nodded, and the conversation began to revolve around their movements. Should they abandon the Nagorj at a time of their own choosing, or should they hold on until they were driven from it like a dog from a tabletop? What would happen once they descended into habitable lands? How many innocents would suffer as the war moved west? Was there any way they could use magic themselves to strike at the Destroyer?

Leith, who was finding the discussion uncannily reflective of the thinking that kept him awake through the bitter nights, said nothing but listened intently. These people had so little on which to base their decisions, and knew that wrong choices would result in thousands of deaths, but they sought a decision anyway, prepared to accept the consequences. *How can they sleep at night? Don't they hear the fading cries in the snow?*

The girl lay cold and unmoving on the pallet while steel-shod boots paced back and forth across the beautifully patterned rug. Life flickered in the ruined figure, a faint ember that teetered on the edge of going out. The man wearing the boots had for two thousand years practised the art of keeping broken bodies alive that otherwise could not hold on to life: only by the most extreme exercise of his art had the girl not died. She must have suffered indescribably from the measures he was forced to use. *I will not give her up*, he told himself. *I must have that flicker alive to study. I must learn how she came by the Fire.*

He could see right into the girl's deepest places. Her dreams were filled with colour, but not the fresh, clean colour of spring. Rather, she endured the pale ghosts of winter, the spiral towards darkness she had always hated, the cruel greys and drab browns that beckoned her onwards through the pain to sleep and oblivion. Yet at the heart of her dreams burned a small flame. From time to time it talked to her, telling her not to go to sleep but to stay awake, that she still had something precious to share. At those times the flame burned with a blue tinge, and the girl loved the voice, but knew it lied to her even as it seared her with a pain so far beyond pain that it made mere agony seem like surcease. Sometimes it whispered to her in sounds too fundamental for words, sounds that reminded her of the cooing a mother made to her child. As the voice whispered the flame burned yellow: the girl feared the voice but knew it sustained her, enabling her somehow to bear the pain that ought to have driven her down the spiral and into the darkness.

The day came when the girl could breathe freely without choking on her own blood, and the man with the boots finally relaxed. He emerged from his tent for the first time in a month, a haggard figure with the bearing of an old man, and finally gave orders to his perplexed commanders who had thought him insane if not dead. The battle for the girl's life was over; now the battle for Faltha could recommence.

The Falthan scouts should have delivered warning of the Bhrudwan offensive, but to a man they were slain by expert trackers who had followed them virtually from the outskirts of the Falthan encampment. Thus the first the assembled captains knew of the attack was the sound of distant screaming intruding on their meeting.

Instantly Indrett leaped to her feet, abandoning the chart they had been poring over. 'Out!' she cried. 'Out! Each to his command! We will not survive long at such a disadvantage as we must now be facing. Take your charges down the escarpment as soon as you can disengage. We will reassemble on the river flats near Adolina!'

In that first hour the camp was nearly overrun. Bhrudwan

warriors made it as far as the striped tent, which had been abandoned only minutes earlier: they hacked at the incomprehensible charts until their officers told them to desist, but little remained to betray Falthan thinking. Some of the Falthan wagons were captured, but the food remaining in them had long gone rotten.

The fighting was quite unlike that which had taken place a month earlier. So completely had the Bhrudwans taken the Falthans by surprise that small knots of attackers and defenders fought all over the field: the Falthans had not been able to form a defensive line capable of holding the Bhrudwans back. As much as they wanted to remain and fight, as unhappy as they were to finally give up the Nagorj which so many of their fellows had given their lives to defend, the Falthan commanders realised that their only hope was to retreat and regroup. How had the woman seen it so early, so clearly? Those Firanese were witchy, none more than the family of the Arrow-bearer. Perhaps she too had powers beyond those of ordinary mortals. Perhaps the Jugom Ark told her what to do. It was against everything they believed to have a woman leading the army, but if she could somehow deliver them, her sex could be forgiven her.

So long had the Deruvians and the Children of the Mist fought side by side, there was now little thought of them as separate forces. Their leaders were seldom seen apart, and this morning they fought back to back, together the match of anyone on the field. Te Tuahangata again wore no cloak, even in this heartless cold, and his torso rippled as he swung and ducked, avoiding a spear thrust with ease, then stepping forward and clubbing his foolish adversary. Prince Wiusago muttered curses under his breath: the men coming against them were Red-bibs, part of the well-trained unit that had fought them on that very first day an impossibly long time ago. The man he fought relied on brute strength rather than finesse, but had technique enough to avoid Wiusago's best sallies: the match would not remain a stalemate for long. The curses grew louder. He would soon have to ask Tua's help yet again.

A groan told him the fate of the fight behind him. A moment later the incautious Bhrudwan opposite him jerked up his head as a giant green club whistled through the air towards him, a movement that exposed his breast to Wiusago's sword thrust.

'Once again, friend,' the prince said wryly, flicking his hair out of his eyes. 'Much more of this and I'll not be able to repay the debt.'

'I own you now, skinny man,' Tua replied easily. 'You coast-landers should not be allowed out of doors without an escort.'

'We must abandon this place, and quickly. Look: more of the Bhrudwans come to the battle. We are not enough to keep them at bay.'

'We are twice as many as they! How can we not resist them? We should stay and fight!' The words were belligerent, but spoken for the sake of form.

'Very well. I'll come back tomorrow and rescue you, as I have had to do so many times already. One more time will make no odds.' He laughed, removing any sting his words might have had.

'So we run like cowards and bring the Bhrudwans nearer to our lands and our homes. That is the good sense of the First Men.' His voice flat, Tuahangata signalled his men to begin the retreat.

'It does not matter how many times we retreat, old friend, as long as at the end we advance,' Wiusago commented; then he, too, gave his soldiers the signal to abandon the field. 'And as long as we are alive to see the Destroyer brought down.'

By nightfall the bulk of the Falthan army had reassembled in northern Piskasia, though men and wagons still streamed down the winding path from the plateau high above. A count was ordered, sending officials scurrying around the encampment; by dawn the next morning the best estimate was that there were less than fifty thousand Falthans camped on the river flats beside Adolina.

'So what do we do?' the generals and tacticians asked each other. 'Where can we hold them?'

They called in villagers from the town, who advised them that there were many paths through the foothills of the Wodranian Mountains to their west which would allow the Bhrudwans access past the Falthan army. The debate that followed was hurried, with so little time before the inevitable assault from their enemy, and conclusions were rushed and often went unheard. A short distance away, soldiers assembled a hasty barricade at the bottom of the escarpment, knowing it was a futile gesture, but knowing also there was little else they could do. Swords were cleaned, damaged spear-shafts replaced with the last of the surplus from the wagons, and many warriors had to fossick down by the river, picking over driftwood to find a shaft long and straight enough that might do to protect their lives for another day.

'We're in a bad way,' Indrett told her commanders. 'This place is indefensible, and the valley behind us is broad. I know of no place between here and Redana'a that might serve for us to make our stand.'

'There is one place.' A thin, patient voice cut through the murmuring that followed the woman's pronouncement.

'Unless they are prepared to wait until summer's heat, anyone who wishes to pass through to the rich plains of Straux and Deuverre, and ultimately to Instruere, must pass through Vulture's Craw. I have seen it! There the final conflict will be decided: there the Jugom Ark will be matched against the wiles of the Destroyer!'

Leith stood up, knocking his chair over. Sir Amasian! He'd assumed the man had remained behind in Fealty. He had so much to ask him!

'You have seen it? What nonsense is this?' Many of the commanders had little patience left, worn down by a month of uncertainty and fear, and were conscious that precious moments sped past without any decision.

'Not nonsense,' came a clipped voice, and Sir Chalcis stepped forward. 'We are the Knights of Fealty, the heirs of Conal Greatheart, he who drove the Destroyer from Faltha a thousand years ago. To us are regularly vouchsafed visions of what is to come. Who better to carry the promises of the Most High?'

More argument followed this pronouncement. Phemanderac quieted them with outspread arms. 'Do not dismiss such things lightly. I am Phemanderac of Dhauria. I make my home in the lost city of Dona Mihst. Enough of you know me to attest to my reliability. I have been a member of the Company and a companion of the Arrow-bearer since before we arrived at Instruere, and I was one of those who found the Jugom Ark. Legend and fact have become inextricably mixed in these days. Do you who doubt Sir Amasian's visions – which I beheld on the ceiling of Fealty's Great Hall – also wish to doubt the miracle of the Jugom Ark burning under your very noses? Sir Amasian foresaw the attack by the Lords of Fear on the Arrow-bearer: I was there, I saw the vision come true, though I did not remember it until afterwards. I think perhaps we should listen to what Amasian has to say.'

Indrett went over to the old man, and raised him from his seat. 'What do you have to tell us, Sir Amasian? What have you seen?'

'I have seen far too much to speak of it at such a time as this,' he said simply. 'Nevertheless, I have been shown visions regarding the Jugom Ark. Twelve souls were called by the Most High to recover the mighty Arrow from its resting place and restore it to true Falthans. I saw the possible paths of these twelve faithful ones, the roads that would bring them to the place of final confrontation, and I drew these paths on the ceiling of Conal's Great Hall. One by one these souls abandoned their quest, most not making it past the borders of their own lands, and their paths have faded in my mind. But one path is still clear. It is the path of Leith Mahnumsen, who with his companions solved the riddle, found the Jugom Ark and now lead us in defence of our lands and people. I stood in the darkness and watched him study the prophecy, so I know that he knows what I say is true. Is that not so, Arrow-bearer?'

All eyes swung across the open space to where Leith sat, the Jugom Ark warm in his hand. 'It is true,' he responded, standing as he spoke. 'But, Sir Amasian, if you knew that the final confrontation, as you put it, will take place at Vulture's Craw, why did you not say so? Why did you let us pass by on our way to confront the Destroyer at the Gap? How many lives might have been saved if we had remained in the correct place?'

As he waited for a reply, Leith harboured a shameful secret hope: *perhaps if it is his fault, this weight will lift from my shoulders . . .*

'Truly, I did not know until we passed through. I have never been there before, you see.' He did sound apologetic. 'And should I have taken you aside at that moment, assuming that I could have found you in the snow, and suggested that we somehow miss out the scenes to come? Is there a shorter path to victory than the one shown to me by the Most High?'

Leith nodded sadly. He had suspected that it would not have been as easy as that. 'Are you therefore saying that we should make for Vulture's Craw now?'

'It makes good sense from a tactical point of view,' Indrett answered. 'We can choose our place of defence, and the valley there is narrower even than the Gap. If we can hold our lines with fewer soldiers, then fewer will die, and our warriors will have time to rest and recover from their wounds.'

'What do we need to do in order to—' began the captain of Deuverre's forces, but he was interrupted by a series of horn-blasts sounding from several different directions.

'Come, now!' Leith cried, filled with anger and a desperate weariness. 'Let us fight with whatever strength remains, so we can win ourselves time to retreat!' And with the decision made, the commanders of the Falthan army ran for their horses.

Later that day Leith found himself riding southwards, his horse stumbling with tiredness, the Jugom Ark barely flickering. It had been a day filled with horrible surprises. The Bhrudwans had changed their tactics, so that instead of meeting the Falthans on a broad front, they sent their most potent warriors against one small section of the Falthan lines, driving through at an angle, then turning further to their right and driving through the ranks of unengaged soldiers and out to the west. A full tenth of Leith's army was cut off before anyone realised what was happening, and though his forces made a number of attempts to rescue their comrades, the captured salient had eventually been engulfed by the Bhrudwans. Of their fate, no one could say. Another five thousand, his mind noted, adding them to the total.

Then there were the fire-tipped arrows. Legions of archers had come in close to the Falthan lines, exactly where the front lines were closest to the supply wagons and the command tents, and fired arrow after arrow, continuing long after they were surrounded. The archers made no effort to defend themselves: in fact, they were armed with nothing other than the longbows they used to loose havoc on their opponents. Leith wanted them held captive, but did not arrive in time to prevent the archers being hacked to pieces by a vengeful army, frustrated at having to watch their friends and countrymen methodically obliterated just out of their reach. The fires were difficult to put out, as the river was nearly a league away. According to the Chief Clerk of Instruere, nearly half the wagons were destroyed.

Yet there seemed as many Bhrudwans as ever. His strategists assured him that it was not so; that they suffered grievous losses, that they were only two-thirds of what they had been. His mind processed the numbers without his volition: perhaps thirty-five thousand Bhrudwans still remained – if they had not received reinforcements, his constant worry. Until his army was some distance further down the valley, he could not send spies to report to him about Bhrudwan supply lines and possible reinforcements.

Certainly the Falthans had received no extra soldiers, and might not receive any for some time. The Saristrians would come, he had been assured, but they would either have to cross the formidable Deep Desert or sail to Instruere. Even if their loyal king had raised an army as soon as he'd received news of the Jugom Ark, it would be many months before they were seen on the field of battle. Nemohaim would send no soldiers; neither would Firanes. Anyway, both places were still too far away to make a difference, as was Plonya, from whom some help might be expected. What of the *losian?* Were the Wodrani likely to descend in their thousands from the hills to the west and fall upon the Bhrudwan army? Those who knew of them said they were very few, and not much interested in the affairs of the First Men, secure in their mountain fastnesses. Who else? Possibly the Pei-ra . . .

Leith pulled his mount up, sickened. After slowly climbing for a few minutes, the road had been about to descend a steep slope. For a moment the horse fought him, but then halted on the crest of the ridge. O Most High! The Pei-ran navigator had promised him a thousand warriors in exchange for free access to Astraea, and Leith had committed himself to sealing the bargain over a meal. The meal had never taken place. How could he have been guilty of such an oversight? He could see it now: the navigator waiting patiently, denied access to Instruere until finally being told that Leith had departed – or perhaps even standing sadly in the crowd that cheered their departure. The thousand warriors would remain on their islands, and the Pei-rans would never return to Astraea.

At that moment the Knights of Fealty began to file past, now numbering less than eighty riders on starving mounts and perhaps fifty pages. At a sign from Leith they halted.

'Is Sir Amasian among you?' Leith called to them. It would be just his luck if the seer had been slain that very day.

'I am,' came the reply, and a horse and rider emerged from the group.

'I wish to have words with you, Seer of Fealty,' Leith said

politely. Sir Chalcis nodded, and shook Amasian's gauntleted hand. Within moments the Knights of Fealty had ridden off into the half-light.

'I will rejoin them later,' the knight said quietly. He looked beyond exhaustion.

'How fares the battle?' inquired Leith gently, his head still filled with his blunder.

'The battle is a terrifying place,' the old man replied, his faceplate open, his breathing laboured. 'I am shocked and upset by every death, whether 'tis friend or foe. I cannot see how this is the wish of the Most High. Better to let the Bhrudwans have what they want. Yet I know that this is not so, and that many valiant deeds are done daily on the battlefield. Ah, Arrow-bearer, I was not made for this! I should have remained in my tower, seeking wisdom and insight at the hand of the Most High!'

'Yet you are here, and you might be of assistance to me.' Leith's words trailed off, and he turned to the north, where the knight's attention had suddenly been taken. From their vantage point on the ridgetop they could see back across the wide valley towards Adolina, perhaps half a league in the distance. The setting sun sent her last rays to illuminate the town . . . Leith and Amasian the Seer gasped together. Both knew what they were seeing.

Smoke rose from the village. Down the slope behind the town swarmed the Bhrudwan army. Flames burst forth from the base of the smoky columns. Dark figures moved along the lanes, climbed over hedges, many carrying torches. The flames reached into the darkening sky. Now the two men could hear screams.

'I didn't think they would bother with the village,' Leith whispered. 'We warned them, begged them to leave.'

'Perhaps they have,' the old man replied. 'Perhaps we hear the Bhrudwans dying in traps left for them.' But his voice was hesitant, filled with doubt.

'This is – this is on the ceiling. Next to the Skull Rock picture. This is one of your visions.'

'It is,' said Sir Amasian, entranced. 'The first one I have seen in reality.'

'Oh, Sir Amasian, why did my path have to include this?' Leith cried. 'Why do I have to preside over so much suffering? Why is it all being charged to my account?'

The old knight did not answer, but his presence comforted Leith. They stood there together as the sun set behind them and watched as the fires raged, then died down. A light snow began to fall, a forlorn attempt to cover the desecration. The vanguard of the Bhrudwan army approached them, a grey, shapeless mass spread across the valley, a swarm of parasitic insects feeding on the corpse of Faltha. The two men watched until the last possible moment, then urged their horses down the road and back to the Falthan army some distance ahead.

'Stay with me,' Leith asked the old man. 'Remain by my side. Perhaps the key to our victory might lie in your second sight.'

'Certainly, my lord,' Sir Amasian replied. 'Certainly.' And he smiled at the boy: so young, so brave, and with so little faith. Such a fragile vessel for the will of the Most High.

The Falthans adopted a strategy of deceit and subterfuge to disguise their purposeful retreat. They put forth a show of force, rotating their army to expose fresh troops every few days, alternately holding the Bhrudwans up and then drawing them onwards. Twice they drew numbers of their enemy forward, away from their main force; and these they utterly destroyed in the manner learned from the Bhrudwans themselves – but their grim harvest totalled in the hundreds, not in the thousands. They looked to manoeuvre the brown army away from populated areas, sometimes abandoning the highway to divert their pursuers around towns and cities. In these cases they spent time digging up the road and disguising it with hedges transplanted whole from nearby farms. The citizens of Saumon, safe on the far side of the river, stood on the banks and called encouragement to the Falthans as they trudged past, then hid in their homes as soon as the Bhrudwans came within bowshot, having heard the tales of what had happened to pretty Adolina. Further south the leaders of Turtu Donija threw down their bridge before the Falthans arrived. Indrett and her fellow strategists cursed their cowardice, having planned to cross the river before casting the bridge into the swift-flowing waters, but Leith understood. *We of Loulea surely would have done the same.* And it meant that another number was not added to the hideous total.

So the weeks passed, and the Falthans led the Bhrudwan army south through Piskasia, then west past Kaskyne. Some thought was given to crossing the bridge and seeking the much narrower (and therefore more defensible) southern path through Vulture's Craw, but the capital city of Redana'a had perhaps twenty thousand people, and Leith was not the only one who objected to their sacrifice.

Some time during the interminable journey back through Faltha, the army – or at least that part of the army whose homes were in northern lands – celebrated Midwinter's Day. *One year ago*, Leith remembered, *this all began*. The Midwinter Play had featured himself and Stella, and then later that night his parents had been snatched away from Loulea. His mother and father had been rescued, but Stella was lost. Leith celebrated with his Loulea friends and family but, like them, his heart was heavy and little was said.

Late one night a figure crept closer to the tent of the Arrow-bearer. Servants waited outside the entrance to the tent, ready to do the will of their master, but he wanted nothing to do with them. It should be easy enough.

No moonlight, no starlight, only the flickering of firelight from the various watch-fires set around the camp. The flickering helped the man escape detection, as it was much easier to conceal movement in moving light. He would move slowly, taking as long as was necessary, for what he had to do tonight was crucial to the success of his army.

Perhaps half an hour later he stood beside the tent he had been so patiently moving towards. Through the thin tent-skin he could see that the boy was awake, reading some document by the light of the legendary Jugom Ark as if it was a mere torch. Good. He did not want to have to wake the boy up. He eased the tent wall up, then slid underneath.

The boy heard something and swung around on his pallet, hand grasping the Arrow. The man put his finger to his lips and the boy nodded, then indicated that his unexpected visitor should find himself a seat. The man sat on the edge of the boy's pallet.

'Son, I've been sent to talk to you,' said Kurr, the old farmer. 'I've come late at night and unannounced to spare you any embarrassment.'

'Embarrassment?' Leith responded, puzzled. 'How so? Why would I be embarrassed to have you visit me?' Then, as the import of the words hit home: 'What do you mean, "sent"?'

'From the look of it, you seem not to want to associate with your friends or your family,' said the old man testily. He held up his arms, cutting off Leith's retort. 'Just listen, boy. See it our way. You haven't spoken with your brother since the night you questioned him – I don't criticise you for questioning him; I have some of the same concerns. You avoid your father and mother, choosing to speak to your mother only as much as is necessary even though she is now in a position where your close cooperation is needed. Don't you know that they are sick with worry over you? Trouble with you, boy, is you've grown up too quick. Think you're above dealing with the people you once depended on. We know you have an intolerable burden to bear. We can't hold the Arrow for you, so we want to do the next best thing, and hold you up against the forces that seek to destroy you. But we can't do that, boy, if you won't let us near.'

Leith shook his head at the unfairness of it all, and he could not keep the tension from saturating his voice as he explained things to the old farmer. Avoiding his parents? He'd looked for them time and again, only to be drawn back into the responsibilities of command. Avoiding his friends? Phemanderac continued to avoid him, and a look of shame in his eyes whenever Leith cornered him drew their conversations to a swift end. He would have loved nothing more than to confide in them, but he thought they expected him to bear up without their help. How could they understand the burdens he carried? Did they carry a tally around in their heads, one which grew every day? Did they carry in their hand the Hope of Faltha, a weapon that was no weapon? Did they carry on their faces a false smile, placed there to keep the Falthans in good heart?

The old man listened to the boy's litany of complaints,

then stood. 'It comes down to this. You let go the people that matter most in the quest to protect them, and you wind up losing even when you win. Numbers are deceitful things, boy. Fifty thousand able-bodied men, fifty thousand dead or injured: in the end not as important as one Company, a handful of friends, one family. One brother. Go and make your peace with him, Leith, and everything else will fall into place.'

'Hal sent you, didn't he,' said Leith flatly.

Kurr looked at the boy, his eyes narrowed. It was as well to remember that he was clever, much cleverer than he appeared. Truly the son of his father. 'Yes, the cripple sent me. He warned you about this. You need to keep the love of your family close to your heart and always in your thoughts at times like this. Come and visit your friends, son, come and call on your family. There'll be no recriminations.'

'You can tell Hal you delivered his message like a good delivery boy,' Leith said, intending the insult, and was savagely glad – and bitterly hurt – to see the old man's face harden. 'Leave me to think on what you have said. Go out the door, go past the guards. I am not ashamed of you.'

'But *I* am ashamed of *you*,' the old man growled. 'A boy called to be a man, but who insists on acting like a boy. Well, boy, I am leaving. But remember that a boy needs his friends and family if he doesn't want to grow up into a lonely and bitter old man.' The old eyes fixed on the young man's pale face, holding his gaze. After a few moments, Leith dropped his head.

Without another word Kurr turned on his heel and left the tent, occasioning grunts of surprise from the guards outside. For a long time after the flap had closed Leith lay unmoving in his pallet, staring at the play of light on the ceiling. Finally he rubbed his eyes and turned away from the light, seeking the questionable solace of sleep.

The Lord of Bhrudwo understood his enemies and knew what motivated them. Constantly they underestimated him, thinking him mortal like them, limited as they were limited. How could they know that at various times in the last hundred years he had travelled to Faltha, had lived and walked in their towns and cities? How could they even suspect his planning would be so meticulous? He learned so much and forgot nothing, his disciplined mind a repository of transcendent wisdom. As a consequence he knew that uppermost in their minds would be concern over the numbers of dead and wounded – in particular of those whose misfortune it was to live in the path of the conflict. Bizarrely shortsighted or simply sentimental, they would protect these people even at the risk of losing the war. He challenged them at every opportunity by sending men to destroy the villages the Falthans tried to save, on occasion having some of the inhabitants publicly tortured, so as to unsettle them.

Moreover, he knew the lie of the land far better than any of them. Did they think they had deceived him with this clumsy attempt to lure him towards Vulture's Craw? It was the only defensible place west of the Gap, and would suit his purposes admirably. Indeed, the Undying Man had once spent a year living in Aleinus Gates, acting as a river guide, studying the Gates and the country behind them. It had then been his thought to engineer this as the place of the final battle. His decision had been confirmed by what he had learned in the two following years, which he spent in the far west shadowing an elusive prophecy he'd heard from a Dhaurian's dying lips. The blind Falthans believed they could spy out his land with impunity, and never for a moment thought that he might come to Faltha to learn what he needed to know. And since that time everything that happened was according to his plan.

Looking through the eyes of the eunuch, he smiled down at the face of the girl sleeping uneasily in her litter, and was content.

Once things were organised, the right people paid and other people intimidated or eliminated, it took a surprisingly short time for the City to fall into his hands. Yes, *his* hands, even though his would not be the hands everyone saw. The citizenry still thought the City governed by the collective of business leaders and worthies appointed by the northerners; but unknown to all but a few, the Guard and the warehouse owners took their orders from him. Soon two of the appointed leaders would suffer tragic accidents, allowing the Escaignian and the Mystic to step in. They, too, would follow his orders, though they did not know it yet, and thus he would control their followers.

The Arkhos of Nemohaim stretched languidly, eyeing the shivering figure in the corner of the well-furnished room. His old room, in fact; the symmetry pleased him. He pursed his lips. Pleasure could wait. Clasping the vial in his left hand, still unable to use his right – curse the northerners! – he motioned his servants to prepare the blue fire. His old master would be surprised.

The snow lay heavy on Vulture's Craw, deep but frozen, and the Army of Faltha forced themselves a path, after a fashion.

There was no helping the fact this would make it easier for the following Bhrudwans. It had been nearly two months since the loss of the Nagorj. Their strength and conditioning had recovered somewhat, so now was the time to test themselves by an all-out sprint to the narrowest part of the steep-sided valley. They had no time to lay obstacles in the path of their pursuers. The weather offered them no assistance, for it was as settled now as it had been wild when last they had come this way.

Gradually the hills became familiar to Leith. *Here is how far east we came on the southern path.* The snow here was at its thickest, and occasionally the marchers came across sad reminders of the disaster a season ago: a discarded shield, the carcass of a horse, an abandoned wagon. Leith did not look too hard, so as not to see any frozen bodies, although he heard the talk. His men were unsettled, but he had no choice. This was where he had to be. They pressed on, perhaps a day's march ahead of the Bhrudwan outriders.

There came a morning when the forward riders, including Leith and Sir Amasian, his ever-present shadow, passed under a high bluff, and the Loulean youth realised that under this cliff Sjenda and the wagoneers had perished. And around the corner the valley opened up a little, revealing the place where the Falthan army had recovered from the untimely snowstorm.

'We have one day,' he said to his generals. 'One day to prepare a defence. We will keep the Bhrudwans from passing this bluff. They must not enter the valley downriver.'

His mother Indrett stared at him. Of late she had been doing a great deal of that. The chief strategist she might be, but he was the Bearer of the Arrow. There could be no argument on this point, for Amasian had been quite specific.

This was the place he had seen. Leith glanced across the river, and noted the presence of a bluff that might have been the twin of that which they stood under. *Yes*, he thought, the image on the ceiling shining brightly in his mind. *This is the place*.

CHAPTER 15

RAINBOW FALLING

THE HUGE GORGE OF the Aleinus River narrowed until the winter sun could not penetrate, not unless it was directly overhead. *And cloud-free, of course*, the tall, grey-robed man thought as he stood at the head of his army. *This place is never cloud-free.* He remembered his days as a guide on this river, Faltha's artery of trade and commerce. Boats going east and west, traders making profit from Favony and Redana'a, bringing fish downriver from Turtu Donija and even further north, and sometimes illegal goods traded from the Wodrani: exotic powders or liquor. The shouting of boatsmen echoing from the cliff walls, all quiet now in winter. There were always clouds above the narrow-throated gorge, whipped up by the relentless winds or driven south from the Wodranian Mountains. *The river sometimes seemed to breathe the clinging valley mist into existence*, he recalled. *There was a bluff some distance ahead which used to have every kind of moss growing on its sheer-sided walls.*

It would be the place chosen by the Falthans to mount their final defence. The valley widened out downriver, and perhaps a day's ride west of the bluff a bridge crossed the

Aleinus. *They will not want us to get near the bridge. The valley is perhaps two hundred yards wide by Moss Bluff, and they will wall it off. Perhaps we should approach more slowly, to give them time to complete their construction. Or would that be too obvious?* No: the Lord of Bhrudwo knew nothing could be too obvious for those who had charge of the Falthan army. *Not like Conal. That one was clever, cunning and patient.* He laughed quietly. *But over nine hundred and fifty years dead. Safe in the arms of oblivion . . .*

. . . the huge figure shadowed against the sun . . . the indrawn gasp of the crowd in the Square of Rainbows . . . the *swish* of the arrow as it flew towards him . . . the *thunk* as it sliced through his wrist and lodged in the Rock of the Fountain. But above all the burning of the Water as it travelled down his throat! *Aaah! The burning!* The agony as it touched the place where the embers of the Gift of Fire still lodged, the agony that spread through every joint in his body . . .

. . . these had been his dreams for two thousand years. Two thousand years and never a moment of oblivion! Always the same dream! But the last two months had been different. He would have brought down the Citadel of the Most High himself, were it accessible to one who was not dead, for one dreamless night's sleep. But for two months! No price would have been too high to pay.

He glanced at the litter beside him and at the four plump figures that bore it. The person in the litter had been responsible. Just seeing the litter reminded him of the nightmares that had finally passed. It was difficult not to feel gratitude.

She had spat in his face, and he struck her an instinctive blow with all of his pent-up power and rage behind it, knocking her some way down the slope. It had been the blow, not the fall, that had almost killed her, but the fall had done further damage, if it was possible to further damage someone who was so close to death. In his fury he had taken her up to his own tent, intent on breathing some life back into her, if only to crush it out of her again, slowly.

But she had been a challenge he could not resist. Her life had been all but extinguished, the merest spark remaining to taunt him, as a challenge to his limitless power. Could he draw her back from the arms of oblivion? Could he let her escape so easily?

He tried everything he knew, reaching for vials and ointments he seldom used outside of Andratan's cruel confines, but the best of them merely kept death waiting at the door. Finally he had resorted to the most extreme measure of all. To his surprise, it had worked. The cost to her, however, would be enormous.

He had been there when she awakened; not through the eyes and ears of his foolish servant, but in the flesh. He sat there in the shadows of his own tent as she babbled and groaned, as she finally found the strength to run her hands over her numerous wounds, as she rose from the bed and saw herself in the mirror, as she saw what she had become.

Aaah, the screams had been worthy of Andratan. A soul that knew it was truly lost, that it was worse than dead, bound forever to one who would not die. The eunuch had warned her, for which he'd had his tongue cut from his pleading mouth, so she knew what had happened. She knew what he could now do to her.

But she suffered a greater agony still, about which none of his other unwilling servants knew. Unlike them, she had already acquired the Gift of Fire. And now, because of what he had done, she would know unremitting pain for the rest of her life.

The *rest* of? How could the unrelenting span of eternity be called 'the rest'? Soon she would know the truth of the Most High's curse of Life, just as he knew it.

Inside the litter Stella tensed. She could sense the Destroyer close by. Part of what he had done to her had tied them together, as though they were attached by some sort of cord. For the thousandth time she railed at her fate. *Why didn't he let me die! How could anything I have done, including running from the Company, merit this punishment?*

She had awoken from a sleeping nightmare to a waking horror. Skin broken, body twisted near to ruin all down her right side, it had been all she could do to walk the few steps from the bed to the mirror on the wall, where she beheld what had been done to her, the remaking of Stella in her new master's own dark image. The waxen face staring back at her drooped on one side, lips slack, grey skin hanging loose on her thin neck. Her right hand was a claw, fingers twisted in on themselves, unresponsive to her efforts at straightening them. Her insides seemed to boil as though they had been set afire. Several times since waking she had checked herself, fully expecting to see gouts of flame emerge from her arms and legs.

Over the weeks that followed, she pieced together what had been done to her. Some of the pieces were given to her by the Destroyer himself, who spoke of the lengths he had gone to in order to keep her alive. She had new gifts, he told her, as if he thought she would be grateful for the constant torture her life had become. 'You and I, we are the only ones in the world with both Gifts, Fire and Water,' he said to her. 'You know what that means, don't you?'

He had infused her with the water of the Fountain, for the drinking of which he was cursed by the Most High, driven out of Dona Mihst and rejected by the First Men. There was only one source for such an infusion.

His desperate remedy for her injuries had been to *give her some of his own blood.*

She felt him draw nearer, then the white curtain opened and the Undying Man entered the litter. She turned her hideous face on him and he laughed. 'Now, now, you have all the time in the world to become used to your new looks. Surely you cannot be vain, not after all that has happened to you? All I saved you from?'

No, not vain. I don't care how I look. I'm sick of being saved. Just let me go. Let me crawl off somewhere to die.

'Come with me, Jewel of the North, and watch the destruction of the Falthan army,' he said gaily, as though inviting her to an afternoon's picnicking.

'An invitation you issued months ago, but have not been able to deliver on yet. Can your powers be so limited?'

His eyes flashed momentarily, then a broad smile spread over his false features. She knew what was hidden beneath; she had seen it the day she was taken by the blue flame. The ancient features of a two-thousand-year-old man. She fixed those features in her mind, the better to take the sting from his jibes.

'Still putting up token resistance? You are just like your foolish Falthan friends. They resist long past the time they should sue for peace. What of you, Stella? When will you surrender?'

'Surrender?' She spat the word back in his face. 'Why must you have me surrender?'

The Lord of the Brownlands chose not to answer her, instead extending his hand and his coercion at the same time. She took his arm – not by choice, oh not by choice – and he guided her out into the daylight, where the Falthan sun broke through for a moment, sending a few weak rays of light to illuminate Falthan rocks and scraggly Falthan soil. Stella's heart nearly burst at the purity, the beauty of it. The world outside her litter was so glorious in comparison to the world within.

'Here is why,' he said to her, and extended his handless arm westward. From the slightly elevated vantage point the valley spread in front of them, framed by tall mountains. The River Aleinus ran past them to their left, hugging the southern cliffs: above it a narrow path had been cut into the rock. On it, Stella noted with a frisson of fear, marched company after company of Bhrudwan warriors.

'Bhrudwans are not clever enough to capture boats as they march, according to Falthan wisdom. They would not think of dividing their force and trapping their enemy in the very place he thinks he is strong. They think Bhrudwans are brutes, and so assume we will use brute force.' The Destroyer slammed a boot down on the stony ground. 'They will learn!'

In the distance lay the Falthan encampment. Activity raged all around the tents, Stella noted. Small figures carried things here and there, while others dug trenches and still others built walls out of whatever they could find.

'I do not want to destroy them, not utterly,' the voice at her side continued. 'I do not wish to rule over a land empty of subjects. I have set myself the much more difficult task of convincing them to surrender.'

'Never!' the girl snarled through her ever-present pain. 'They will never surrender to you!'

'They will be just like you, is that it? They will hold out even though every breath is torture?' He gazed on her, and for the first time allowed the full force of his power to pour through his eyes, binding her utterly, wiping the slate of her will clean of resistance. 'You surrendered to me a long time ago! You were mine the moment you saw me. It was confirmed when I tricked you into thinking you had escaped me. The only reason you continue to defy me with your lips is as a sop to your own pride. You are mine more completely than anyone else who has ever lived!

'Yet there is room at my right hand for another. I will have the chosen weapon of the Most High as my own talisman, and it will be brought to me by the boy from your own village. Ah, how this simple plot you are all part of reeks of the Most High! How foolish he is to entrust his will to such as you! The boy is the Right Hand of the Most High, as evidenced by his possession of the Jugom Ark. Soon the circle will be complete; soon he will be mine.'

'How?' Stella whispered as soon as his enormous, irresistible will withdrew. 'How will you do this?'

The Destroyer smiled. Surrender, whether she recognised it or not. 'Come with me: we have a hill to climb. Then you will watch, and you will see.'

The Bhrudwans were perhaps two hours' march from the Falthan walls and trenches. By rights Leith should have been riding among his soldiers, reminding them of the promise of the Most High by lifting high the Jugom Ark, granting them a little courage in the face of what was to come. But his thoughts had turned to his family, and he found himself powerless to prevent his feet taking him to where they were gathered. It was past time, he'd held out too long, hurt and misunderstood, but no time remained.

They were all there, his family and the others of the original Company, taking their midday meal in a green-sided tent capped with the standard of the Jugom Ark fluttering in a rising breeze. Voices were quiet and people moved slowly, as though savouring the food and the company. Instructing his guards to remain outside, Leith stepped into the tent, and silence fell.

Kurr nodded to him, then took the Haufuth's arm and motioned him to follow. For a moment the big man looked longingly at the food spread on the board. *Not a snack for the man we knew as our village headman*, Leith reflected as he followed the Haufuth's eyes to such poor fare. *How has it come to this?* But he could not ask the question, so admissive of their perilous state would it have been; and the two men left the tent, leaving Leith alone with his family.

Three figures waited patiently for him to approach the table. 'What will you have, son?' Mahnum asked him, indicating the food.

'I will have peace between us,' said Leith formally, trying to hold in a whole world of hurts. 'I will have understanding and respect, even if we can never have what we once had.'

'You might be surprised what can be reclaimed from the ashes of misunderstanding,' Modahl said quietly, his arm resting lightly on Mahnum's shoulder. *Modahl?* Leith had been sure up until the moment the man spoke that it had been Hal standing there, not his grandfather.

'What do you want, son?' his mother asked him, and at the sound of her voice he could no longer keep the tears inside.

'I want you to be my mother and not the commander of the Falthan army,' he sobbed as she held him tight. 'I want Mahnum to be my father and not the Trader of Firanes, always ready to leave his family in the service of his king. I want Modahl to be my grandfather and not the famous Arkhos of Sna Vaztha.' He took a deep breath and wiped his nose on his sleeve. 'I want Hal to be my brother and not some wild magician with terrible powers who might betray us at any moment. And I want to be Leith, and not the Bearer of the Jugom Ark! I wish I was home in Loulea, not here awaiting the slaughter that will come today, whether or not we win the battle. Isn't that what you wish too?'

His family were all around him, saying things he could not hear through the pounding of his heart in his ears, hugging him tight, reassuring him.

'Go and find Hal,' his mother whispered to him. 'Speak these words to your brother.'

'Where is he?' Leith asked them. They did not know: his brother had left some time earlier. 'He spends a lot of time on his own, since . . .' His father did not finish, but Leith knew what he referred to.

'I will find him,' Leith said, and left the tent less burdened than when he had entered it.

Somehow he knew where Hal would be. The Falthan army had camped in much the same place they had used when recovering from the snowstorm nearly four months earlier, and the dell in the centre of the camp was as unoccupied now as it had been then. His crippled brother was there, sitting as still as a statue at the bottom of the depression, and did not move when Leith cried his name. Finally his brother raised his head and looked at Leith with red-rimmed eyes.

'Hal, I. . .' Leith began, his mouth dry and his heart on fire. He had seen much during their journey. He'd witnessed his brother become a stinging insect, inflicting illness on an innocent man; he had heard Hal's voice offering him counsel – not only since they had left Loulea, but all through his life.

'Hal, why is it always me that has to say sorry?' It was not the question he had intended to ask, and he saw his brother's face close up as soon as the words left his lips. He wished he could call them back, but they sped towards their target like arrows from a bow, and with as devastating an effect.

It used to be that I couldn't hurt him, no matter what I said.

Hal took a deep, settling breath. 'I have cried with you many times, Leith. I nursed you when you were sick, I defended you when others tried to hurt you, I offered you words of comfort and support whenever I could, and received little in return. What have I done to apologise for?'

His brother's voice was thinner somehow, his cheeks hollower than Leith remembered. He drank in the sight of him nevertheless, the one person who had remained steadfast and true when his father was gone and his mother didn't understand. *How could I have done anything other than love him?*

And yet . . .

'You should apologise for all those things you did!' Leith cried, his shameful, secret self finally exposed. 'For always being right! For always being the voice of reason! For the guilt I cannot shake off! The Most High curse you, Hal! The number of people I have lost since all this began burns in my head, and the very first number is YOU!'

Hal held out his crippled hand. Leith could see what an

effort it was. Had his brother been eating? Had he wounded him so deeply that he refused food?

In an agony of indecision, his own need for release finely balanced against the needs of his brother, he reached out his own hand. Their fingers came close together, touched. Forgiveness, understanding, love; all in that touch.

A hundred horns rang out, swamping the valley in noise. Both Leith and Hal clapped their hands to their ears as the echoes beset them. Again the horns blew, and Leith knew, without being told, the assault had begun. *Later: we can finish talking later*. He turned and ran up the sides of the dell, emerging into the central scene from the ceiling of Greatheart's hall.

The Falthans knew the horns would blow to signal a Bhrudwan attack, but the horns had blown far earlier than they expected. Though there was a rearguard, no one seriously thought the Bhrudwans would attack them from behind – but somehow they had appeared in great numbers on the downvalley side. All over the valley companies fought with each other, engaged past extrication. There was no doubt in anyone's mind that the final battle had come, and victory would go to the army that avoided total destruction.

An arrow hissed past Leith and struck a soldier just to his left. The man went down with the shaft lodged in his throat, his hands scrabbling at the thing killing him. Leith poured himself into the Jugom Ark, but even as the Arrow flared into life he knew that it was too late for the man lying dead on the muddy ground. The field of battle rapidly became a confusion of grunts, shouts and cries; and Leith seemed to be cursed, arriving just too late time after time.

There came a tug on the sleeve of his cloak, and he shook

it off in his frustration and anger. The tug came again, and with it a voice: 'My lord? My lord! It is time! The prophecy, my lord!'

The man with his hand on his sleeve was Sir Amasian. Leith shook his head, but did not succeed in clearing it. All around him the screams of the dying continued to steal whatever clarity he strove for.

'The knights will help us,' the old seer continued, as though Leith had understood him. 'The Knights of Fealty will cut a path to where you must stand. They are ready for this task; it is what they have prepared for ever since the vision came.'

Numbers. The numbers rustled in his head like sheaves of paper falling one on top of the other. Every dead warrior was another number. Where better to count from than one of the hills? In a kind of madness, overwhelmed by events, he pulled away from the knight, but apparently had struck out in the direction they wanted him to go. They rode ahead of him without a backward glance. His guards followed the mounted troop, unsure of their role. Left and right the armoured figures swung their heavy blades, driving the enemy before them, parting the massed Bhrudwan ranks, clearing a path for the Arrow-bearer to meet his appointed destiny.

Soon they came to a narrow path, and here the Knights of Fealty formed a line, parting momentarily for Leith and the seer to pass through. 'Up the path,' Sir Amasian said, wheezing slightly.

'Are you sure you can make it?' Leith asked. The bluff towered above them, its crown perhaps a thousand feet above the valley floor.

'I see myself standing beside you. I behold your victory. I will survive the climb.'

The guards made to follow, but found their way barred by the Knights of Fealty.

Phemanderac ran to and fro on the battlefield, searching for Leith. Something was amiss, something clearly wrong. It hovered on the edge of his mind. Something to do with the old man's vision. The Dhaurian scholar had studied the ceiling of the Great Hall of Fealty for a time that evening, had memorised the images, and knew that what he beheld on the field this afternoon was but one image from the centre. Though they seemed to be heading towards defeat, the prophecy told of imminent victory. His mind could find no flaw, but his heart misgave him. His heart misgave him, and he knew that in this matter, if in no other in these days of confusion, he could trust his heart. His heart misgave him, and he could not find Leith to warn him.

The view from the top of the crag was one to rend the heart. The two armies were completely engaged for the first time since the bitter campaign had started, and the restorative power of two months without fighting meant, paradoxically, both forces had energy enough to slay each other more effectively. As the minutes passed, Leith counted the fallen. Already they numbered in the thousands.

He raised his eyes from the scene of death below. From this height he could see along the Aleinus valley. He looked out from the throat of Vulture's Craw, past Aleinus Gates and into the soft distance, where lay the rich heartland of Faltha. To his right rose the rocky heights of the Wodranian Mountains, shoulders thrusting into the grey clouds. Similar hills marched into the distance on the other side of the gut: the Taproot Hills, part of the country of Redana'a. He had seen them before; they formed the backdrop to the central image of the prophecy. Beside him Sir Amasian stood, wild-eyed and fey as his life folded back on him.

Opposite the bluff on which they stood rose another of similar height, and on the crest of this hill Leith could make out a figure. Two figures. Good. These had also been depicted on the hall's ceiling.

As he turned his attention back to the battle, as he began to wonder what part he would play, how exactly he would summon the efficacy of the Jugom Ark to their advantage, the singing began.

It was harsh, it was bitter; it was sonorous, it was bewitching. It echoed across the valley, swelling well beyond normal volume, sound multiplying on sound until to Leith it might have come from ten thousand throats. It was undoubtedly magical, and it was not of Falthan origin.

Then the singers came into view, marching left to right across the field of battle. Leith counted them without thinking. Thirteen times thirteen was their number, one hundred and sixty-nine grey-coated Lords of Fear finally revealed in all their terrible power. Each a magician of note, and a large part of the strength of their master lay in them. No mere acolytes, these: they were warriors, scholars, wizards all, mercilessly trained, inured to suffering. On they came, passing through the battle as though it did not exist, and their song rose up the valley wall, magnified beyond imagining. Above Leith the very sky groaned in pain with the sound.

Beside Leith, the old knight's hands dropped to his sides and his mouth fell open. 'No,' he whispered. 'It cannot be.'

Achtal fought at the edges of the wagons, as close to Hal as he could be while still remaining in the battle. As the sound of the *Maghdi Dasht* reached him, his face turned pale and his great sword fell from his fingers.

Stella lay grovelling on the hilltop, heedless of any danger to herself. The singing touched the pain locked inside her, sending it searing across her body as though skinning her alive. Beside her the Undying Man put forth even more of his power, and the magic that hid his ravaged face fell away, unable to be sustained. He knew this, and yet continued to draw on the combined will of his servants in the cauldron below, sending it up into the clouds.

'Water to quench the Fire!' the Undying Man cried in a terrible voice, his arm slashing downwards.

A few scant moments ago the cloud base had been an unmoving layer of grey; now it roiled and spun like the Maelstrom of the Kljufa River. From the vortex came lightning, crashing to earth with a roar, claiming Bhrudwan and Falthan alike indiscriminately. A heartbeat later came the rain, cascading down on Vulture's Craw in torrents, driven into the faces of the warriors by a sudden wind from the east, blinding them all in a stinging fury.

Hal stood alone at the edge of the dell, perhaps a hundred paces from the ranks of the *Maghdi Dasht*. Down in the valley bottom their song drowned out even the sounds of thunder and driving rain. It was not a binding like last time, Hal knew; they were creating something with this, something more than an illusion. This was real power, sourced from within the Lords of Fear, who willingly drained their own lives in the service of their master. Their power could not be used directly on the Falthans, but they could shape a weapon that might bring about a victory for the

Destroyer. He could feel the magic building, and made ready to oppose it.

As did others. The Lords of Fear continued their chilling song; and as they did so, many Falthans were drawn to this place, the centre of resistance. All those who had previously fought the *Maghdi Dasht* made their way to Hal's side, all except Jethart who was a grievous loss. He alone of the strategists might have warned against being confined in such a place, of fighting a battle where there was only one way of escape, vision or no vision.

Others were drawn to the scene. Common soldiers who knew nothing of magic, but felt an intense anger against the song, obeyed the inner prompting and came to oppose the singers. A number of the *losian* came, though their fellows were still heavily engaged on the far western edge of the battlefield. Even a few of the servants and wagoneers found themselves standing with Hal on the lip of the dell, facing the Lords of Fear, wondering why they had been so foolhardy.

Leith looked down into the cauldron, a blue-grey swirling pattern of rain and wind, running and falling figures, punctuated by lightning lances hurled down into the chaos. *This is not what I saw!* Sir Amasian was on his knees, his face lifted into the storm, eyes wide open and staring at something not of this world. 'It is all . . . running backwards!' he screamed.

Down on the plain a small group stood in opposition to the *Maghdi Dasht*. Leith's gaze was drawn to this stalwart group. As he watched they appeared to ripple for a moment, as though suddenly heated by a smith's furnace, and began to glow faintly. At the same time the Lords of Fear seemed to solidify. The gaps between the individual warriors vanished. One body, one throat, one song.

Raise the Arrow, came a voice into his mind. *Raise the Arrow!*

For a moment Leith hesitated. Was this the voice he knew? In the midst of the wind and the rain, the fire and the water, he could not think. Below him the Falthan group pulsed orange and yellow.

Raise the Arrow!

Something within him wanted to resist the command. Why should he obey? But he had been too stubborn for too long, and his own reckless decisions had cost thousands of lives. Time to stop questioning, to put doubt aside. He raised the Jugom Ark.

Instantly a surge of raw energy burst from the glowing group below, rushing up the wall of the bluff. Before Leith could react, the Arrow in his hand flared white-hot, the two flames combined into one immense conflagration, and raced into the sky, finally detonating against the base of the cloud vortex with a huge explosion. The sky flashed white, then black as the two powers met, and Leith expected the world to start coming apart, so incredible was the blast.

The noise rumbled around Vulture's Craw for a minute or so, then faded into silence. Leith opened his eyes to see the maelstrom above him gone, the tattered edges of cloud fluttering like shredded cloth as a rising west wind dispersed them. Beside him Sir Amasian lay on the ground, hands over his eyes, groaning as though in the throes of death: 'No, no, no . . .'

Did I burn him with the Arrow? Leith wondered, and went to check, but a flash of colour caught his eye. He straightened and looked out over the valley.

There it was.

There hung the vision, the prophecy, the image on the ceiling of the hall of Conal Greatheart. Behind him the Destroyer's storm fizzled and flickered, driven away eastwards by the power of the Arrow. Below him men and beasts struggled to rise from where they had fallen, but already cheers rang out from Falthan throats, eyes raised to the heavens, arms pointing to the sign hanging in the sky.

Over the valley of Vulture's Craw hung a great rainbow, a many-coloured arch anchored on the hills right and left. It was so close Leith imagined he could reach out and touch it. The colours shone with a bright-washed joy, a symbol of victory. The Bhrudwans seemed to be running, all fleeing to the western end of the field. A fierce exultation sprang up in Leith's heart. It has all been worth it! The many deaths were not in vain!

'Behold!' he cried, and his voice carried across the valley, magnified by the magic that still hung in the air. Every eye looked skywards, every man and woman on the field of battle saw the figure holding the blazing Arrow. 'Behold the victory of the Most High!' And the Falthans cheered.

A gasping voice from the ground at his feet spoke into the silence that followed the joyous shouts. Each word seemed purest agony.

'What . . . happened . . . to the fist?'

Phemanderac ignored the cheering. His feeling of unease had been growing all day. For a while he thought it was just because Leith had spurned him, having not sought his counsel or teachings since the siege on the rock, but the tension continued to grow in that still place he had created long ago, the place he had learned to trust. Though he had no idea what might be amiss, and little hope that the Arrowbearer might listen to him, he sought Leith – but had not been able to find him.

His eyes were drawn upwards by the rainbow, and for a heartbeat his spirits lifted: perhaps he had been wrong! But then he heard Leith's cry of triumph, and in that instant he knew. He had studied the prophecy, and he knew.

The path to the top of the bluff was guarded by the Knights of Fealty, and they barred his way with their swords as he approached. He begged and pleaded with them, but they would not hear his arguments. *There is no time for this!* he thought, and fashioned the most frightening illusion he could remember from the teachings of his Dhaurian master. Snakelike, the wide-mouthed apparition snapped at the knights, who scattered in confusion. Phemanderac darted between two of the armoured figures and along the path, but staggered; and as he lurched to his feet he felt a blow across his shoulders, accompanied by sharp pain. *Can't stop!* Forcing himself onwards, he stumbled up the steep path. But before he had gone more than halfway he knew he was too late.

The rainbow hung in the sky, a banner of light. Then, like a desecration in a temple, the singing began again.

Immediately Leith's eyes flashed down to the battlefield below, but the thirteen ranks of *Maghdi Dasht* were no longer visible, having scattered all across the valley floor. Yet the song swelled anew. *No! Be quiet! We have won!*

Rasping laughter reached his ears. The figure across the river stood facing him, his right arm held aloft by the second, smaller figure. Leith could feel the evil in them both. They were more than a league away, yet the laughter continued to echo in his head.

Groans of dismay floated up from below, mixing with the *Maghdi* song to create a dissonance like the swirling of ravens in a farmer's field. Leith was held a moment longer by the Destroyer's laughter, then jerked free and turned to the battle . . .

. . . where a giant fist rose high into the sky, solidifying by the second.

Dumbfounded, the Falthans watched as the vast hand opened, the gnarled fingers extended, with nails as long as claws, ready for rending. Groans turned to shrieks of fear as for a moment it appeared that the hand was about to reach down and scoop them all up: instead, it moved up the valley until it hovered next to the rainbow.

The singing changed, taking on a deeper timbre, and the ground shook. With incredible slowness the hand closed around the rainbow, squeezing it, squeezing it tight. Then, accompanied by an earth-shattering shout, the hand tore the rainbow loose from the hills and crumpled it in its fist like a piece of multicoloured parchment. Shards of colour and light spiralled downwards towards the upturned faces.

The singing stopped, the fist disappeared; the broken shards of the rainbow hung in the air a moment longer, then they, too, vanished.

A few seconds later Phemanderac arrived at the top of the pinnacle. There Leith knelt, face drained of all colour, breathing heavily. Beside him lay the body of the seer, slain by the vision he had misinterpreted. A profane laughter swirled all around them.

'Behold!' a great voice boomed, filled with inhuman glee. 'Behold the victory of the Undying Man!'

Leith pulled himself to his feet, his heart still beating, his mind still spinning, unsure as to why the Destroyer's power had not ended his life. Phemanderac placed a hand on his shoulder, a support for the unsteady youth. Within the philosopher rose a genuine fear that Leith might fall from the bluff, so badly was the boy disoriented.

Below, on the field of battle, everything had changed. Many of the Falthans cast down their weapons in fear and stood with lowered heads, uncaring of their fate. Others ran blindly, overwhelmed by panic; a number of these blundered into the river. The Bhrudwans recovered more quickly, and made short work of any Falthan who stood fast.

'All is lost,' Leith whispered, and the despair in his voice hammered into Phemanderac like a blow. 'My army is no more. The way to Instruere is open. We are defeated.'

'Not so!' the tall scholar argued. Taking Leith's hand, he pointed into the distance. There, on two low hills, perhaps ten thousand Falthan warriors fought with the bulk of the Bhrudwan army. 'They fight still! Take heart!'

But Leith could think of nothing except the destruction of the vision. 'What went wrong?' Leith groaned. 'What happened to the prophecy? How could we have been dealt such a blow?'

Phemanderac ran his hands through his hair. Just when he needed the soothing tones of his harp the most, he'd left it behind. Lost now, no doubt. 'Leith, the vision of Sir Amasian was flawed. He saw truly up until—'

'Son of Mahnum!' called the voice of the Destroyer from across the gorge. 'Son of Mahnum! Lay down your Arrow! Surrender to me and I will guarantee the safety of your warriors. Your friends and family will be allowed to go free!'

The words battered at Leith like hammers. *The Wordweave*,

he thought. *He is using his power to strike at my despair.* Yet even with this knowledge, the words were difficult to resist. *So easy, so easy to put down the Jugom Ark. All this time I've wanted to – and now no one would blame me if I did . . .*

'Are you watching, Son of Mahnum? Do you see what happens below? With every moment that you delay the inevitable decision, you take more of your countrymen's lives! Can you count to ten thousand? Twenty thousand?'

The Falthan soldiers on the two hills were now hemmed in by Bhrudwans. The Destroyer's men had finally been joined by the *Maghdi Dasht*, fighting as warriors and not as magicians, each Lord of Fear worth a hundred men. Leith could make out a group of barechested warriors in the midst of the fighting. His heart fell as he realised that the Children of the Mist were trapped along with the rest. *Where Tua is, Wiusago will not be far away*. Sure enough, there fluttered the Deruvian banner, green against a sea of brown.

'Phemanderac!' Leith groaned. 'Surely that cannot be all who remain? I do not see the Instruian Guard, nor the *losian* Army of the North. Have they escaped? Are they destroyed? Do they fight on still?' The philosopher's grip on Leith's hand tightened until the youth cried out with the pain of it.

They watched as the battle raged across the twin hillocks below, trying to ignore the taunts coming from the southern bluff. At one stage it seemed the Falthans might break free: indeed, a few score warriors drove through the Bhrudwan ranks, having chosen a place where no *Maghdi Dasht* fought, and might have escaped had there not been a company of Bhrudwans patrolling behind their own lines, waiting for just such an occurrence. They were cut down within minutes, and their piteous cries echoed in the ears of the Arrow-bearer and his friend.

The voice across the gorge fell silent, and Leith glanced at the far bluff. There seemed to be some sort of struggle on top of the pinnacle, as if the smaller figure battled the larger. But it could not be, could it? Would the Destroyer have brought an enemy to watch the battle with him, one with power enough to challenge him? The bright southern sky made silhouettes of the figures, rendering them difficult to see.

When Leith's attention returned to the battle below he was shocked to see how quickly the Falthan numbers had dwindled. Perhaps half the force remained, clearly without hope of escape or rescue.

'I cannot watch this,' Leith said, but he did not move. To his left the sun admitted defeat and sank towards the Taproot Hills, while below him the remnants of the Falthan army were systematically destroyed.

Prince Wiusago lowered his bruised and battered shield arm. *For just a moment*, he told himself, trying to catch his breath. It took the next challenger a few precious seconds to clamber over the bodies piled up in front of him, enough time for the Prince of Deruys to cast a hopeful glance around the battlefield.

'We Deruvians and Children are the last of them, Tua,' he said grimly to the man standing behind him. 'There is no other fighting anywhere on the battlefield.'

Te Tuahangata swung his mighty club with as much vigour as ever, catching a skilled Bhrudwan fighter behind the knee. 'It is fitting that we are the last,' he replied. 'We may die, but we are not disgraced.'

'Defeated only by weight of numbers,' Wiusago agreed, laughing despite himself. 'Ah, Tua, I am glad it is you I fight alongside. I am proud to call you my friend.'

The next opponent finally reached him, and for a few moments Prince Wiusago struggled to stay alive against a man at least his equal in skill, and much less weary. Not a Lord of Fear, as none of the *Maghdi Dasht* had come their way, much to Tua's disappointment. The Mist-man had even tried to attract their attention. The Deruvian's only advantage against his current opponent was a hard-earned one: the Bhrudwan had to be careful where he placed his feet, for fear of stumbling over his dead comrades. This one really was very good, light on his feet and with a sword that flicked in and out more quickly than the blond-haired man could match.

'Friend Tua, I might need help with this one.'

'Friend, is it?' the Mist-child growled from behind him. 'Friend?' he repeated, as though running the word across his tongue, checking to see if he liked the taste. 'More of a friend if you were a better warrior.'

Wiusago laughed again, so unexpected a sound in such a dark corner that his opponent jerked up his head – right into the path of the prince's tired and ill-timed stroke.

'More luck!' Tua said. 'But it will not last. We die here.'

'Yes,' the Deruvian said sadly. 'Here we die. But not yet!'

Despite his bravado, the Prince of Deruys groaned inwardly. Their enemy numbered so many – or, more accurately, their own numbers were so few – that now two warriors climbed the hill of the slain to match swords with him.

'You are not a friend,' came the voice from over his shoulder, and for the first time Wiusago could hear the exhaustion in it. 'You are a brother. You are my brother! I name you husband to my sister, and one day we three will walk in the Glade of True Sight and talk with our ancestors.'

Perhaps it was the tears filling his eyes, or the sound of laboured breathing behind him signalling that Te Tuahangata had taken a hurt, but the prince could not avoid the stroke that came without warning from his left. It glanced off his shield and crashed into his upper arm, opening a horrific wound. One final, futile parry . . . Prince Wiusago did not see the slashing blow that took his head from his body.

Tua gave a great cry of anguish, threw down the three men opposing him, and turned to his brother's slayers – but spun too quickly and tripped, ending on his back with three blades at his neck. One of the men lifted the visor on his helmet, and a muffled voice spoke, the common tongue harsh but identifiable: 'We honour you. You are a mighty warrior!' His arm drew back for the final thrust.

Te Tuahangata closed his eyes, content.

'They are down . . . the last of them is down. There, the standard is captured. It is over.' The philosopher's voice sounded hollow. 'It is over.' The voice of the Destroyer drifted over from the far side of Vulture's Craw, offering the use of some of the Bhrudwan warriors, since their own had proven so inadequate.

'What now?' Leith said quietly, ignoring the gloating. 'Should we try to escape, hide somewhere, and maybe one day raise another army to drive the Destroyer out of Faltha? Or do we simply surrender?' He could not imagine handing the Jugom Ark over to the owner of the smug voice. He would die first.

'We do not surrender!' came a voice, one he knew well. Leith spun around and there, at the top of the path, stood his mother.

'We are bested today,' Indrett said, steel in her voice, 'but we are not defeated. Things have happened even the Destroyer does not know about.'

The young man regarded his mother, but did not allow hope to stir, not yet. 'What things?'

'We will talk as we go,' she replied, 'for we are not safe here. But one thing I will tell you. More than half our army remains alive, and is hidden from our enemy's sharpest eyes.'

CHAPTER 16

SINGLE COMBAT

TAKING GREAT GULPS OF air, Stella tried to find some way of getting to her feet without using her ruined hands. The skin on her fingers bubbled like boiling fudge where she had touched him, yet he had been the one to cry out in pain. A reckless impulse, a desperate reaction to the slaughter below and the final ruination of her last hopes, had driven her to try to cast the Destroyer from the top of the bluff. It had come so close to working! She waited until he had his full attention on the battle, then lunged for him, hands and arms first but with all the weight of her body, hoping to carry him into the depths; and hoping that she might fall with him. Oblivion was the best she could hope for now.

But it seemed the gods had not yet finished punishing her. If she understood correctly the forces at work, she should have been able to at least touch him without harm, perhaps the only person alive who could do so if he did not wish it. But he burned her, the excess of power he contained almost consuming her as she tried to make him fall. For a blessed moment he had stumbled, dislodging a rock which tumbled into the gorge below; but then he turned and, with a snarl, cast her backwards to the ground. She tried to move, to continue her attack, only to discover the Destroyer had pinned her to the ground, though she could see nothing holding her down.

In her mind she followed the imagined progress of the rock as it spun slowly towards the waiting river. Rock-face, sky, ground, river; all tumbled through her mind as she visualised herself falling. Her arms spread wide, hungrily seeking the finality. A moment of pain, then bliss . . .

She managed to get herself into a sitting position by using her knees and elbows, scraping the skin raw as she tried to deal with the blisters and the still-awkward misshapenness of her right side. When finally she could raise her head to see what had happened, the Undying Man stood over her.

Stella braced herself for pain . . .

'You continue to amaze me,' the Destroyer said lightly, as though discussing the ability of a child to cause trouble. 'Your power is walled off where you cannot use it even if you knew how, you are bound to me so tightly I should be able to read your every thought, you are in so much pain you ought not to be thinking of anything else – yet you can still take me by surprise. Do you know, girl, that I came closer to failing just then than at any time since I wrested the Water of Life from the Most High?'

He jerked his hand, and she sprang to her feet under the influence of his power. His eyes were perhaps a hand's-breadth from her own. 'There is something about you, Stella, that remains a mystery. I am not angry with you. How could I be angry when you have already provided me with so much – and with so much more left to discover? I may revise my plans for you after all, particularly if the boy with the arrow continues to walk into my traps. He may govern Faltha in my stead, while you rule as queen in Andratan, enthroned beside your eternal king!'

Then he closed his fist, and her mind burst into multicoloured shards of pain. 'But don't touch me again,' he hissed. 'Not until I find out how you resist my will.' She nodded, eyes filled with proper fear, and he grunted his satisfaction.

'We will return to our army, O queen,' he said. 'Now the destruction of the Falthan army is complete, we will receive their surrender. The boy will place the arrow into the hands of my representative. Assuming her hands are not too troubled by pain, that is,' he added, and laughed. 'Come on!' His power compelled her forward. 'I have a triumph to share with you.'

'Half our army remains alive?' Leith regarded his mother with scepticism. 'Is this real? From this place I saw the whole battle. No one escaped. They all died. Where is this army? How is it hidden?'

'Alive and uncaptured,' Indrett told her son as they made their slow, careful way down the hill. 'We could see that the forces of Deruys and the Mist were surrounded, as were many soldiers from Straux and Deuverre, but we could not help them. There were far too many Bhrudwans between us and them.'

'Deruys and The Mist were destroyed,' Leith said bitterly. 'We watched them die. Wiusago and Tua were there, I saw the prince's standard fall. They must be dead.'

'But some survived,' Phemanderac added gently. 'Look. The Bhrudwans have many thousand captives.' And indeed, illuminated by the dying sun Leith could make out the enemy's brown horde encircling perhaps five thousand of his soldiers. 'Straux and Deuverran, mostly,' the tall philosopher added, his sharper eyes able to pick out their colours. 'No doubt they have surrendered.'

Anyone alive is a victory, Leith told himself, but his mind counted the numbers. Fifteen thousand lost in today's battle. The total was – the total was unthinkable. How many children would never see their mother or father again? How many families would soon be so devastated by the news that the identity of the ruler of Faltha would make little difference to them? He knew how many, but would not think it.

'And the others? My father and grandfather? The Company? Who remains?'

'Your family is safe, thanks to Achtal who hacked a path to safety for us. We were drawn to confront the singing men, and somehow Hal took our resistance and fashioned it into a weapon against the unnatural storm they sang into being. Then Achtal made a way of escape, though he was wounded for it.' Indrett drew a shuddering breath. 'In my youth I watched many a duel where money changed hands on the outcome. Such things are common in the Court of the Firanese king. Nothing I saw there prepared me for the power and grace of Hal's Bhrudwan protector. It was like – like he instinctively knew at what tempo to fight; a speed, fast or slow, that defeated his opponent. No matter.' Indrett shook off the effects of an event that had obviously marked her. 'What he might have done to us on the Westway if Hal had not befriended him!

'So we escaped,' she continued. 'We stood in wonder and marvelled at the rainbow in the sky above us, and it seemed to signal the end of the conflict, although why we thought this way when the Bhrudwan army remained undefeated, a goodly portion of our own army was under siege, the *Maghdi Dasht* had yet to be seriously challenged and the Destroyer stood on a hill high above, I do not know. But we celebrated nonetheless. We then realised that much of the Falthan army had been scattered by the rain and the lightning, and began to gather them together, with the aim of setting the trapped Falthan soldiers free. Before we made any real progress, however, the singing began again and the great hand formed in the sky. After that . . . for a while few of us could think clearly, so great was our sorrow. Again, I don't know why we felt this way. We were not completely defeated, the Jugom Ark did not lie in the hands of the Destroyer, and with care we could conserve our forces, the better to fight another day; yet we despaired. Hal cried out that it was magic, that the Destroyer poisoned our hope, but we could not hear him for a time.

'By the time we recovered our senses, the Bhrudwan army had been bolstered by the return of many warriors scattered by the rain and the lightning. Kurr exhorted us to rescue those trapped by the Bhrudwans, but Hal counselled another way. He spoke to certain of the magicians in our party – there are many more than we thought, and some did not know themselves that they held the power until today – and together they wove a magical net of some kind, one which hid us from the eyes of the Bhrudwans.'

Phemanderac took a pace forward, eyes large. 'A Net of Vanishing? You were hidden under a Net of Vanishing? Hauthius wrote about such a thing, but no one in Dhauria took his words seriously!' Then his eyes narrowed. 'But – such a net must surely have been visible to the Destroyer, whose eyes will pierce any illusion of Fire or Water?'

Indrett laughed, a fresh, clean sound. 'Yes, you are right, and so Hal reasoned. But the magicians he employed to construct the net were of the Fenni, the Fodhram and the Widuz, and these peoples are of Earth and Air. The Destroyer evidently cannot sense such magic, and has forgotten to take it into account. Thus it may be that Hal has provided us with a key to victory – and might have done so much earlier had he been consulted.' Indrett very pointedly did not look at her son.

'Where is the army now?' Leith asked, more bluntly than he intended. *He could have come and offered his insight. There was nothing to prevent him. How many lives might have been saved? How many surprise attacks could we have launched?* His suspicion of his brother flared again: why could the others not see it?

'Still under the net, awaiting our next strategy,' his mother replied. 'I will take you to them. On the way we will give thought to how we might best use this new weapon to our advantage.'

One hundred and sixty-nine heads bowed as one when the Lord of Bhrudwo, supported by his servant-girl, stepped ashore. Utter silence spread across the battlefield, the place known by locals as The Cauldron, as the black-booted figure trod across the muddy, body-strewn ground. He approached his army in an atmosphere which might have been mistaken for reverence by some of the captive Falthans, if they had been able to think of anything other than their growing terror, but was in fact part awe at the power they had just witnessed, and part fear at what might happen now. The servant-girl followed along behind, limbs working awkwardly, obviously a cripple, struggling to keep up.

The Undying Man raised his hand to the commander of the Lords of Fear, acknowledging their efforts with a salute. Then his army roared his name, and he permitted himself a small smile.

'Flatterers,' a voice hissed from behind him. 'They fear your shadow!'

He laughed richly, then said: 'I am more and more certain that I made the right decision to keep you, Jewel of the North. You add a piquancy to everything!' Nevertheless he clenched his fist, and the girl fell to the ground and writhed in the mud.

The Destroyer addressed his warriors, congratulating them on their courage in overwhelming superior odds. He spent some time describing the lands to the west, explaining to them that they could claim the lands of anyone who had fought against them thus far, or who resisted them in the future. They would leave this valley soon to commence the march to Instruere, which city would be wholly Bhrudwan from the moment the gates were opened to them; but first they would assemble to witness a number of executions and the acceptance of the Falthan surrender.

As night fell, the Bhrudwans moved their camp from around the two hillocks to the centre of the battleground. Soldiers were dispatched to bury the Bhrudwan dead, leaving two hillsides strewn with Falthan corpses. Six far more sinister holes were dug just outside the Bhrudwan encampment, six thick posts driven into them, and limbs hacked from the nearest tree, a bare oak growing in the centre of a small depression perhaps a hundred paces in front of the camp.

Later that evening, after a very poor meal made from the little that remained to them, just over twenty thousand Falthan soldiers began to march westwards from the mouth of a small valley perhaps a league east of the northern bluff upon which Leith had stood. Slowly, so slowly they moved, knowing the net that covered them would not prevent any sound they made from carrying down the valley. All during the long night they crept forward, rank after rank of Instruian Guard led by their incredulous captain, followed by the *losian* Army of the North – still over five thousand strong, and including almost all the aurochs – with the remnants of the Sna Vazthan army occupying the rear. Occasionally they encountered a Bhrudwan patrol, which they destroyed with ruthless efficiency: they could not afford rumour of an unseen army reaching the ears of the Bhrudwan command.

Just before dawn Leith and the commanders of his army moved forward and out of the cover of the Net of Vanishing. 'We will approach the Bhrudwans as though offering to surrender,' Indrett explained, outlining her risky idea. 'They will assume we are all that remains: they may have doubts, particularly if they have closely examined the field, but it is unlikely they will anticipate the trick we are playing on them.'

Within minutes they were seen. A swarthy officer rode up, followed by a troop of archers, arrows nocked to bows. 'We are the Army of Faltha,' Leith announced, holding the Jugom Ark up for inspection: the man's narrow eyes widened considerably. 'We have come to discuss terms with your master.'

A man was found who understood the Falthan common tongue, and the officer sent one of his men running towards the large spread of tents they could all see in the distance. Behind Leith his hidden army waited, tense but completely silent. To cover any inadvertent noise, Leith and his commanders sang quietly, as though offering each other solace.

Soon a tall man in a black robe came striding across the open field. Was this the one? Could this be the Destroyer? No, the man was in possession of two hands.

'The Lord of Faltha and Bhrudwo will receive your surrender now,' the man rasped. 'There will be no terms other than those he dictates. Accept this now or be slain where you stand.' His eyes narrowed in sudden suspicion, and his head jerked left and right. There had been no noise Leith had heard, but perhaps this man had special powers, or they had given themselves away in some other fashion. They stood perfectly still, hardly able to breathe . . . but the tall man could not afford to keep his master waiting.

'We will listen to what your master has to say,' Leith replied carefully. The response was a jerk of the tall man's arm, indicating that they should follow him.

Now was the time of greatest risk. Should anyone try to walk behind Leith's small party, the ruse would be defeated. The Falthan army had to inch its way forward. Wagons had been greased, animals muzzled, and in some cases boots removed, yet the army still feared the slightest sound. Many of the soldiers feared that the beating of their collective hearts would be heard. Stomachs rumbled, and one or two sneezes had to be repressed. Near the rear a man collapsed, wounded the previous afternoon but too proud to admit his hurt, and two others tumbled over his body: the resulting noise sounded deafening in the morning stillness, but their escort did not turn.

Finally Leith and his band stood in the centre of The Cauldron. The Bhrudwan camp occupied a surprisingly small space, but contained many times enough men to wipe out his small group of commanders. One large tent had been pegged a little way in front of the others, and just in front of this tent six stakes had been erected, three to the left, three to the right. The Falthans waited quietly, aware that their army had halted a few hundred paces behind them, just out of arrow-shot.

The shadows slowly crept away from them as the sun rose, and they waited still. The Bhrudwan army emerged from their tents, then began to strike camp. Brown-cloaked soldiers with bibs of various colours gathered from all over the plain, forming ranks stretching left and right behind the large tent. Each warrior found a place amongst his fellows of the same bib colour, then settled down to wait patiently. Morning mist cleared from around the valley rim, and Indrett savoured the warm rays of the sun on her back even as she cursed the weariness in her legs. Finally, she thought ironically, the days of standing in the Firanese Court at Rammr pay off: she could imagine the cramping going on in the hidden army behind her, and hoped fervently that whatever was to happen would not be delayed much longer. *Should we simply attack without regard for what the Destroyer might say?* As soon as the thought had flickered through her mind, the tent flap parted and six chained figures were led out to stand before them, one in front of each stake.

'The cruel, cruel man,' she hissed in her husband's ear. Behind her Modahl responded: 'He does this to break us. We can do nothing without showing our strength. Do not let this goad us into revealing our weapon untimely. We will weep for them later.'

Indrett did not recognise the six men, though by their dress they appeared to be from Straux and Deuverre. The commander of the Army of Faltha bit her lip in frustration, knowing that by this act the Destroyer wished to emphasise their powerlessness. She sincerely hoped that the King of Straux, who had been forced to remain with the hidden army, would not react to what was about to happen.

The tent flap swung open again, and this time a thin but dignified figure emerged, followed by a much smaller servant.

All eyes were drawn to the man who stood before them, and they did not need to see the handless arm to know who it was.

His face was longer than the Falthan norm, elegant without being truly handsome, with a fine jaw and thin lips. *He reminds me of Phemanderac,* Indrett thought, and a moment later remembered that the Destroyer had once lived in the philosopher's home town. *He looks like Phemanderac, but he feels . . . cold, somehow; aloof, as though he was a glacier hanging over a small village, ready to grind it into pulp.*

One hand. The missing hand had been hewn from his arm by the very Arrow in her son Leith's right hand. Did the Jugom Ark behave differently in the presence of its ancient victim? It still burned, flames running up and down the shaft, but seemed not to know who stood close by.

'Welcome, men and women of Faltha,' the man said in a deep, cultured voice. *Laced with Wordweave, of course,* Indrett realised; but they had all prepared for that with Modahl's assistance. *Don't resist it directly. Let it slide past you.* 'In a moment you will present me with the arrow in your possession, which from this day shall be the symbol of my conquest over the plans of the Most High. You will then be taken into captivity, where your suitability for life in the new Faltha will be assessed. Most of you, I am sure, will be able to persuade me that you can abide by my simple requirements.'

Indrett took a step forward, bringing a momentary frown to the brow of the Undying Man, who would surely have expected the Arrow-bearer to speak for the Falthans. 'And if we refuse?' she asked, the words barely emerging from her throat. *Speaking to the Undying Man! How can I dare it?* 'What then?'

The Destroyer laughed – and, just behind him, his

servant-girl put her fist to her mouth. It was an action that should have given her identity away to the Falthans, had they been watching anything but the man in front of her.

'What then? After I have whittled you away into a nub of pure pain, I will do the same right across Faltha,' he ground out in a voice of ice, then his face changed. 'Do not be mistaken!' he roared suddenly. 'I can choose to unleash such destruction that future travellers will never suspect people once lived in this land! Or,' he continued, his voice now level again, 'I can place Falthans to rule benevolently in my stead, and return to Bhrudwo happy in the knowledge I have achieved all I needed to, having proved to two continents that I, not the Most High, am the supreme authority in the world. Which of these courses I take will depend in large measure on the cooperation I receive today. Now, do you surrender the Jugom Ark to me, and with that act gift me Lordship of Faltha?'

Indrett took a pace forwards. It was as difficult as walking into a huge wave. 'We could fight you for it,' she said quietly.

Instantly the Net of Vanishing disappeared, and forty thousand Falthan warriors suddenly materialised in the middle of the valley. The *losian* magicians sustained an illusion which duplicated the entire army, which, it was hoped, would fool even the sharp eyes of their foe. Most gratifyingly, groans of dismay rumbled across the plain, involuntarily forced from thousands of Bhrudwan throats: men who thought their fighting was over now faced an army which once again overmatched them. A burst of cheering arose from the Falthan prisoners penned by guards some distance away.

At the moment of her pronouncement Indrett locked her eyes on those of the Lord of Bhrudwo. His face showed no visible change. Surely he must have been taken by surprise?

Unless he already knew of their deceit and had made plans to counter it. Or . . . a new thought entered her mind. *Are we the only ones to use illusion? Maybe he does not show his true face to us.*

'As you can see, we are not quite ready to surrender just yet,' she said in the voice of a northern peasant, all the better to irritate the man. 'Perhaps you have another proposal to set before us. Otherwise, we will ready ourselves for another battle with your army, the outcome of which is less certain than you would like it to be.' She smiled; then, as an afterthought, she added: 'And you can take those silly posts down. You're not impressing anyone with your absurd ruthlessness.' She folded her arms, having finished her scolding of an errant child.

Still not a flicker: the man must have incredible self-control. *Well, he's had two thousand years to practise.*

'So, an impasse,' he said in a voice of stone. *His voice betrays him*, Indrett thought. 'What, then, is to stop me ordering my army to drive your ragged remnants right across the valley and into the river? Or,' he added, a new thought coming to him, 'threatening to put to death six thousand prisoners unless you withdraw? Surely you wish to leave the field with at least a small portion of your pride intact?'

Indrett smiled at him, endeavouring to keep her demeanour ironic, her tone light. 'If I was the cruel and pitiless leader of a ravening horde gathered and trained to sweep across Faltha, I think I'd ensure that I had enough soldiers left to complete the job,' she said. 'You attack us now, and the likelihood is that you will eventually emerge victorious. But I imagine the few hundred battered and bleeding survivors that remained to you would be defeated by the next fighting force you came across. Or did you think we were all that could be raised against you? No, we are but the first wave. Even as I speak to you, armies prepare to march eastwards, and ships from the Southern Kingdoms put into Instruere's docks. Weigh my words and know them for true! Your only hope of final victory is to leave here with your entire force intact, which you will find difficult to do, as you are a man who has not yet mastered his pride.' She smiled sunnily at him, still watching his eyes, which glittered with malevolence at her. *He wants to tear out my heart*, she realised.

'So, man of ancient wisdom, hear the counsel of a peasant woman of forty summers. Gather the tired remains of your army, along with your badly bruised reputation, and take the eastward road. Perhaps we might entertain you again after you've thought things through more completely.'

The only sign that her words had impacted on him was a slight thinning of the lips. *Someone will suffer for this*, Indrett thought ruefully. *I only hope it's not us.*

'As I said, an impasse,' he said companionably. 'I have made my offer, and you have countered with yours. Go back to your counsellors and consider my terms. I will not wait long.'

He has some other plan in mind, Indrett knew. *As much as we have discomfited him, he still has the power here. We will have to await his next move.*

That move was not long in coming.

'Son of Mahnum! Son of Mahnum!' a voice boomed across the valley, drawing the Falthan leaders from their hastily-erected tent. 'Come and face me, Son of Mahnum!'

The Destroyer stood alone at the far edge of a small depression, some distance from his own tent. As the Falthans drew nearer they could see he no longer wore his grey cloak.

Instead, he was garbed in armour, and wore a broad helm on his head. Against his right hip hung a silver scabbard, from which he drew a long sword with a curve near the point.

'What is he doing?' Leith asked.

His father put a hand on his shoulder. 'Unless I'm mistaken, your mother has done her job far more effectively than we might have wished.'

'Is that good?' asked Leith, thoroughly confused. His father regarded him for a moment, then squeezed his shoulder.

'No, Leith,' he said gravely. 'It is not good.'

'Son of Mahnum!' cried the Destroyer yet again as he handed his helm to his ever-present serving girl, who placed it quickly on the ground as if it burned her. 'Son of Mahnum! Heed my challenge or forever be known as craven!'

'Go forward and listen to what he has to say,' Kurr whispered in his ear. 'But be careful. Though we have magicians ready to act, it may be at the cost of losing our phantom army.'

Leith moved out from behind his leaders and stood in the open, knees shaking, the flame in his hand pulsing with the rhythm of his heart. 'What is it you want?' he replied, his voice husky with fear.

'This is what I propose, to preserve honour and to bring this war to a close. Listen to me, champion of Faltha, for I will make this offer only the once.' He raised his voice, and his magic carried his words to both armies: to the Bhrudwans with their Falthan captives, and to the Falthans themselves, the Instruians, the *losian* army, and all Leith's other allies.

'Hear me! The Undying Man, the Lord of Bhrudwo, offers challenge in single combat to the son of Mahnum, Trader of Faltha and sometime visitor to Andratan, thereby to prove upon his body the right and wrong of the present conflict!

A Truthspell will be spoken, and both armies will be bound by the result of the combat. Should victory go to the son of Mahnum, the forces of Bhrudwo will renounce their claim to Falthan lands, both now and at any future time, and will set out on the eastward road before nightfall this day. A Declaration of Withdrawal will then be signed by the Chief of the *Maghdi Dasht* and the Bearer of the Arrow, and thus the Truthspell shall be sealed. But should the Lord of Bhrudwo prove the stronger, the Falthan army will surrender and disperse to their homes, except for their commanders who will be held captive by Bhrudwo. Upon the signing of the Declaration of Surrender by the Undying Man and by whomever commands the Falthan army, the Truthspell shall be sealed; and he shall be given lordship of Instruere, and shall claim tribute from any other lands whose people are represented here. Thus shall the war be decided in favour of one side or the other!'

The magic faded, and the Destroyer brought the full force of his gaze to bear on them all. 'Should I defeat you, son of Mahnum, I will take the woman who spoke for you this morning and make her my personal servant, replacing the present holder of this position who has outlived her usefulness.' Again the hand in the mouth, and this time the Haufuth saw the servant-girl for who she was, and what had been done to her, but managed somehow to stifle his shout of grief.

The hateful figure drew himself up to his full height. 'You may use any weapon you wish, including the arrow you hold in your hand. And I will use whatever weapon I choose.' He paused, and again Leith felt magic ripple through the air. 'Now, do you accept? Or will you flee from this as you have fled from my army? What is it to be, son of Mahnum?'

'I – I . . .' His stuttering reply rang across The Cauldron, and a raven that had set down on the tree in the dell between them burst into startled flight. Forty thousand ears and more listened for his answer.

'I – I will consider your challenge,' he got out at last. 'You will have my reply within one hour.'

'Good,' replied the Destroyer, laughter playing around the edges of the word. 'As one warrior to another, I offer you advice. Do not wait too long to bring me your answer, for the delay will sap whatever little courage you possess.' And the laughter rang out then, loud and long, and the raven gave a squawk of fright, took to its wings and vanished among the hills.

Leith looked longingly after it, wishing that he, too, could fly away so easily.

'I'm going for a walk,' the Arrow-bearer insisted over the storm of protest. 'Can't I have some time to think about it?'

'It is a trap,' Farr argued. 'Do you think the Destroyer would propose a challenge that he was in danger of losing?'

'It's not like you to step back from a fight,' Leith replied sullenly. 'How is it that you offer me such counsel now?'

The acknowledged hero of the Gap frowned at him. 'But I would never take on impossible odds . . .' His voice trailed to a halt amongst nervous laughter. That was, of course, exactly what he had done, to great renown, in the first battle against the Bhrudwans.

'He should fight,' Kurr said. 'For what other reason was his the hand into which the Jugom Ark was given?'

'Are you saying that we should put our faith in the Most High?' snapped the Haufuth angrily. 'I see scant evidence of his assistance up to now, and much evidence suggesting the contrary.' He bit his lip, on the point of telling them what he had seen.

'We must be realistic. It might be a choice between one man and us all. I fear that we will not survive another battle.' The Captain of the Guard passed a weary hand across his face. 'And I have seen many great things done by the hand of this boy. The parting of the Aleinus River, the discovery of the Jugom Ark, the ending of the Battle of the Four Halls. I am willing to put my trust in the strength provided us.'

'What does Hal say?' Phemanderac said. 'He was one of the original Company, and he often sees truly. His advice here would be of much interest.'

'He is not here,' his mother said, troubled, 'and he cannot be found.' She sighed. 'I fear my clever words have led us to this place. If it were any other hands holding the Arrow I would counsel them to take the risk. But since his hands carry my blood, I do not want him to do this thing.'

'I thank you for your thoughts,' Leith told them politely, his face white, 'but I wish to make up my own mind. I am going away somewhere I can be alone so I can think about this. I will trust the Jugom Ark to protect me.'

'But what if this whole thing was designed to draw you out in just such a solitary walk?' the Fodhram leader asked. 'Is it not folly to wander unprotected on paths that may be patrolled by the enemy?'

'I am not unprotected,' Leith responded, and the Arrow roared briefly into flame, driving his friends away from him. 'Very well, I will take one guard, of the *losian*, so that if I fall, there might still be a hand to pick up the Jugom Ark.'

Axehaft stepped forward. 'I will accompany you,' he said stoutly. 'Any Bhrudwan ambushers will need to wear knee-length armour.' And he laughed, a refreshing sound that, for a moment at least, eased the tension among the Falthan commanders.

'It is difficult, this,' reflected the leader of the Widuz, as the tent flap closed behind Leith and the small Fodhram warrior. 'Months of fighting, and it all comes down to a moment like this. We are uneasy because we can do nothing.' Heads nodded all around him. 'He will choose to fight, because he has gone to find his courage. He will fight well. I have heard the tales of how he survived Wambakalven, and know the measure of his courage. He will fight well.'

His feet led him to the top of the bluff. Up here the breeze blew, and it was much colder than the early spring warmth down below. For a moment he closed his eyes, and again he could see the rainbow stretched across Vulture's Craw, again he could hear the groaning of Sir Amasian. Again he saw the vast hand rise up and snatch the rainbow from the sky.

Always our enemy will counter our best efforts, Leith realised. *Always he has out-thought us. Perhaps it is time to risk all.*

He held the cursed Arrow in front of him. *Just over two feet long . . .* He wondered how, if the Most High had towered over Kannwar of Dona Mihst in the moment he partook of the Fountain of Life, the Jugom Ark was so small. *Isn't the scale all wrong?*

The flames burned merrily, seeming not to reflect his anguished state of mind. Was it like Phemanderac said? Did the Arrow respond to his emotions? Or did he respond to the wishes of the Arrow? For a moment Leith considered asking the voice to speak to him.

Was this truly a decision he was free to make? Or, like every other moment since he had begun this preposterous journey, was his path already mapped out? For a moment he rebelled: *if the voice wants me to fight the Destroyer, then I will run and run and run and run.*

But that was the path of madness. To flee from what a voice might ask him to do, a voice that no one else heard, a voice that now, in his time of need, remained steadfastly silent.

No. It was courage he needed, not advice. His life had been shaped, he could not deny it. He had been brought to this moment, and he could not avoid it. *Perhaps if I get through*, he told himself, *I will make some choices for myself*. Then he laughed. *If I get through?* He could not fool himself: today was likely the last day of his life.

He would fight.

A crunching of gravel wrested him from his thoughts: someone approached along the path. Axehaft had his weapon ready to strike, and Leith realised how truly grateful he was for all the people who had guarded him.

'It is only me, your village Haufuth!' came a voice, distinctly short of breath. 'Leith, will you allow me to speak to you for a moment?'

'If you wish to give me advice as to what to do about the Destroyer's challenge, you are too late,' Leith said. 'I have decided.'

The Haufuth struggled up the last few steps and promptly sat down on the stony ground. 'I know you have,' he said gently. 'But there is something you must know now, for I fear that the Destroyer means to taunt you with it at some stage during your encounter.'

Leith looked on the Haufuth, a patient, compassionate man. 'What is it?'

The village headman told Leith what he had seen – *who* he had seen – and the bright flash that followed his dreadful words eclipsed for a moment the light of the sun.

* * *

Leith came to himself a moment later, unable for the present to think beyond the fact that Stella was alive, but in the hands of the Destroyer. Even as the news sank in, his attention was drawn to the battleground. Some sort of ceremony was beginning, judging by the noise filtering up from below. He wiped the tears from his eyes and tried to find the cause. For a moment he simply could not believe what he was seeing. When his brain finally registered what his eyes beheld, the Jugom Ark flashed incandescent for a second time, fit to burn the world to cinders.

And in the midst of the great light, one word reverberated through the sky, crashing from cliff to cliff, setting the trees to groaning.

'HAAAAAAAL!'

The Destroyer stood on the lip of the dell, the tip of his tall sword planted in the ground between his booted feet. He was prepared to be patient, for he knew the Right Hand of the Most High would be drawn to the challenge. For what other reason did he exist?

But there were things these northern peasants did not know about conflicts such as these. The Undying Man remembered the first hundred years of his own reign in Bhrudwo, when his authority was challenged again and again by the most powerful thaumaturges of the land. He had beaten the best of them, and remembered every lesson he been taught. There had been surprises then, but now the tricks and stratagems of a score or more wielders of magic resided in his awesome memory. None had ever come close to overcoming him, and this untutored rustic would not do so now. Yes, he had the Jugom Ark, but that had been effective only in the hands of the Most High himself. It was a risk, but because of the words of that cursed woman spoken in front of his own army, he could not abandon the field of battle. There was no other way to achieve his objective.

I am immortal, he reminded himself. *I have been gifted with life. I cannot taste death. The bargain was made at the cost of my own right hand.*

He remembered the years spent growing up in Dona Mihst, and his dissatisfaction with the way in which the First Men acquiesced to every requirement of the law. *Why were we given the Fire of Life, and all the wisdom attending on it, if not to make our own laws?* No one could give him a satisfactory reply. Then had come the years of searching, when he wandered the wide world in a vain quest for answers, only to find them in himself. Such risks he had taken then, so desirous was he of knowledge, and the stand he took eventually cost him his hand.

More recently he had begun to wonder whether he was settling into exactly the same sort of complacency he had once found so distasteful in the citizens of Dona Mihst. Would the day come when, for all his care, he would be driven out of Andratan by some young risk-taker, left to lick his wounds and dream of his days of glory in some forgotten cave?

No, it was time to take a risk. But just to be certain of success, he began to wrap himself in spells, muttering to himself in a barely audible voice . . .

. . . which is why he did not hear the approach of booted feet until the voice called to him from across the dell.

'Undying Man, do you wish to challenge the son of Mahnum?'

His proud head jerked upwards, where he saw a solitary figure on the other side of the shallow depression.

'What is it you want of me?' he growled, angry to have

been interrupted. He thought to put this man to death, but decided to wait. Perhaps he was an emissary.

'I asked you if you were prepared to challenge the son of Mahnum. I am Hal Mahnumsen, older brother to the Arrow-bearer; and, by right of law, the proper recipient of your challenge. By the ancient law of primogeniture you cannot fight Leith until you have defeated me. I know the magics you have used in issuing the challenge, and know that it cannot be withdrawn or changed, only refused. And, as you can see, I do not refuse it.'

What trick was this? But then he remembered how he had phrased his challenge, and exactly what Words of Binding he had spoken into the air. The man was right.

'But I am at a disadvantage,' the Destroyer said smoothly. 'I have but one hand, and I see that you have two.'

'My brother also has two hands, and it was him you intended to fight. But even now you reach out to me, trying to gain a measure of my strength. Does it surprise you to learn that I am strong?' He waited, and saw the Destroyer's eyes widen in surprise.

'Strong in Fire and in Water,' the Undying Man breathed, the thin tendrils of doubt searching for purchase in his soul. *How could this be?* He kept the doubt at bay. 'But you are a cripple.'

'I am. It will be an even contest.' The young man's voice was firm, with no wavering, no hint of fear. Nothing for the Destroyer's magic to take root in. His spells had been woven across the dell, ready to entrap anyone who expressed even the slightest fear or doubt.

'Very well, then. We will fight, then I will take your brother and make him my right hand, as has been fated for a thousand years. I have studied the prophecies, obviously more closely than the sages of Faltha, judging by the recent premature proclamation of victory we all witnessed yesterday. I will turn him, and he will serve me gladly. Now: are your fellows coming to watch you die – or do they even know of your challenge?' He laughed then, recognising the last desperate gambit of an army on the brink of defeat, and shook off any doubt. 'You will die alone and unmourned, and the birds will fight over your carcass!'

'I accept your challenge,' Hal declared, then exerted his power so that the words were binding. 'As the rightful elder son of Mahnum and his legal heir, I accept the challenge issued by the Undying Man, including the terms as they were spoken,' he intoned. 'By this Truthspell are they sealed!'

As soon as he uttered the words, he strode forward into the dell. The Destroyer matched him stride for stride.

'You do not walk like a cripple,' the Undying Man remarked as they drew nearer to each other.

'Not today,' said Hal grimly.

A great shout came from somewhere behind him, beyond the rim of the small dell. Achtal had uncovered his master's deception, but it was now too late for anyone to do anything about what was going to happen.

The discussion in the Falthan tent had come around to the length of time Leith was taking. The Haufuth had gone to inform the Arrow-bearer the hour was nearly up, and that he would soon be required to answer the challenge, and others in the tent were becoming impatient, unable to deal with their tension.

Suddenly one whole side of the tent caved in, and a deep, accented voice cried: 'Hal! Hal fights the Destroyer!' Achtal extricated himself from the tangle of cloth and animal skin, then repeated his cry to a stunned group. 'Come! Come quickly! He will die!'

Within moments the Falthan command stood at the edge of the small dell. Stretched tight across it, like the skin across the top of a storage jar, was a shimmering layer of light made of yellow and blue strands. Twice already Achtal had thrown himself at it, and twice he had been repulsed.

'It is the Truthspell,' Phemanderac said. 'Halkonis wrote about this. It seals the fighters together in single combat, ensuring they receive no outside help, until the challenge is completed. In this case, that will come with the surrender or death of one of the contestants.' He sighed, then turned sorrowfully to Achtal. 'I think the Destroyer would have accepted Leith's surrender,' he said. 'But I think he will kill Hal.'

Nearby stood Mahnum and Indrett, in each other's arms. 'Stubborn Hal! Thus he seeks to redeem himself in his brother's eyes!' Mahnum shook his head.

'There is more to it than that,' his wife replied. 'He wishes to . . .' Her voice faded to silence, and a great hush fell all around the rim of the depression. Hal and the Destroyer now stood face to face, weapons drawn.

The Undying Man held his sword with the aplomb of a seasoned fighter, but knew that his stance, designed to impress a gifted opponent, was wasted on the youth standing in front of him. His two-footed stance, the way he held his short blade far too tightly, even the choice of blade – surely they had better weapons in Faltha, he wondered – all told the Lord of Bhrudwo he was dealing with an unskilled adversary.

He stood unmoving for a moment, reinforcing the link between his sword and his will. That was all that really mattered. The stance and even the armour were merely for show. Then he opened his mouth as if to talk, and struck with his blade, heavy with purpose. It should have been enough, but the Falthan deflected it with a perfectly placed block. Thrown off balance, the Undying Man barely recovered before the counter-thrust whistled in front of his face.

Thus chastened, he settled down to fight in earnest. There were no accompanying bursts of magic power, as all their art was focused on the blades they wielded. Even so, both men moved more swiftly than ought to have been possible, limbs unencumbered by the doubt and fear that slows the merely mortal fighter. Back and forth across the dell they danced, thrust and parry, combinations of blows endured patiently, eyes searching for the opening that surely must come.

Eventually the two combatants sprang apart. 'Who taught you to fight, boy?' the Destroyer rasped, striving to keep weariness from showing in his voice. 'You have a style that reminds me of the swordsmen of Birinjh. Where do you come from?'

Hal laughed. 'My teacher is a *Maghdi Dasht* from a village on the High Plateau,' he said.

'Impossible!'

'Nevertheless,' came the reply, 'it would take far longer than two thousand years to be aware of everything happening in your domain even at one moment. What conceit leads you to think that you can trust your own knowledge, when it has proved to be so partial?'

He knows the magic, the Undying Man reminded himself. *He's trying to sow doubt*. In answer he hurled himself at the Falthan, raining blows on him from every direction; and could feel the youth faltering.

'Knowledge isn't everything, youngling,' he panted. 'Sometimes strength and desire are what count in the end.'

The two armies crept closer to the bowl, knowing their fates were bound up in the conflict being played out below them. Each small advantage was cheered, each step backwards greeted with a groan of concern.

'How is he doing this?' Modahl asked his son and his daughter. 'From where does he draw the power? How can he stand against the Destroyer?'

'There is more to Hal than anyone knows,' Kurr replied, and many nearby heard his words. 'It is not my story to tell, but the Most High made no mistake when selecting him as one of the Arkhimm.'

'I thought it was a brave but foolish gesture!' Farr said in genuine wonderment. The swordplay was so crisp, so fluid, so beautiful. 'Had he fought this way in the Battle of The Gap, we might have driven them back to their own lands!'

'I do not think he could have,' said the Ice Queen of Sna Vaztha. 'He uses his life-strength to do what he does.'

'He fights like his teacher,' Kurr remarked, indicating the Bhrudwan acolyte standing on the lip of the dell, eyes empty like a lightless room. 'But there must be something more, for even Achtal could not stand against the best of the *Maghdi Dasht*, and surely they are but shadows of their master.'

'There is power enough down there to reshape the world,' Phemanderac gasped. 'The Destroyer draws on reservoirs of power laid aside over millennia. But upon what does Hal draw?'

Down in the dell the two combatants closed yet again. Without warning, a light brighter than the sun seared across the vision of everyone there; then, just as they were able to open their eyes, the light exploded again, this time accompanied by a shout.

'HAL!'

The first flash of light momentarily blinded them both, but they recovered in seconds. The Destroyer came forward swinging, trusting senses other than sight. Hal was ready for him, and struck a blow across the Undying Man's right side, opening up a wound at least a forearm-span in length.

But the Lord of Bhrudwo did not slow down, and instead revealed his great advantage. As Hal watched, the wound healed itself. 'Did you think that you struck at anything but illusion?' the Destroyer mocked. 'Perhaps two thousand years of life is not sufficient to know everything. But twenty years is barely enough time to learn how to stand upright!'

'But – your body is there,' Hal gasped, on the edge of exhaustion.

'Wrapped in illusion. You may strike me, but only if you are lucky. You, on the other hand, are about to be—'

The light flashed again, and both men knew it to be the Jugom Ark. Hal heard his name shouted in anguish, and for an instant he turned in the direction of the one who called his name, feeling the intense need in the cry.

The opening was small, but it was enough. Though he was half-blinded by the light, though he had been driven further into his hard-won supply of strength than ever before, the Undying Man still had enough energy remaining to drive his blade forward and into the breast of his opponent.

Hal cried out, his voice bubbling into silence as he fell to the ground.

* * *

Leith came flying down the path. 'Hal! Hal! What are you doing?' he cried as he smashed through bushes and knocked aside boulders in his haste to reach his brother. 'What are you doing?'

<What I must,> said a voice in his mind; and then: <Goodbye.>

The Arrow-bearer reached the bottom of the path and hurled himself across the muddy field of The Cauldron. 'No, Hal! No! NO!'

There were the two armies standing strangely silent as they faced each other. There was the dell where he had spied on his brother. There was the barrier of shimmering light, which faded even as he approached it. There were the two figures at the bottom of the dell, one with his arm raised in triumph, one lying prone on the ground. He threw himself down the slope, his legs barely able to keep up with his body, and neither able to keep pace with his will. 'Hal! HAL! No, Hal!'

He cast himself on the body of his brother, taken by a madness that drove him into a black pit of despair from which there seemed no escape. Blood, his brother's blood, soaked into his robe.

'Please, Hal,' he whispered. 'Please don't die.' But his brother was beyond listening.

'I love you, Hal,' Leith rasped brokenly, too late.

Discarded carelessly on the ground beside him, the Jugom Ark flickered one last time, and went out.

CHAPTER 17

THE RIGHT HAND OF GOD

THE CEREMONY OF SURRENDER, effectively handing control of the Falthan army over to the Destroyer, took place just before sunset. Leith Mahnumsen did not attend, nor was his absence questioned. His mother was there, though his father was not. Throughout the short ceremony Indrett seemed to be having difficulty standing, and leaned heavily on the arm of Modahl of Sna Vaztha. Forty or so Falthan commanders stood in front of the Bhrudwan tents, representing the defeated force, trying to keep the desolation from showing on their faces. On the far side of the depression waited the remnant of the Falthan army, now its true size with the illusory extra warriors removed.

Earlier the commanders had been sent to explain the terms of their defeat to the Army of Faltha. The combat between the son of Mahnum and the Destroyer had been hedged about with spells, they explained. The loser's army was now bound by a Truthspell, and could no longer oppose or deceive their adversaries. When the Declaration of Surrender was signed, the magic would become binding for all time.

'The Sixteen Kingdoms will resist him, each one,' said an

Instruian soldier to the man standing next to him, who happened to be of the Instruian Guard. 'There is hope yet.' He kept his eyes on the open space in front of the Bhrudwan encampment, where the ceremony was being held.

'Aye, there is hope,' came the gruff response. 'But not much. You have heard the rumours that half the kingdoms have already gone over to the Destroyer?' The soldier nodded eagerly; he always kept an ear open for rumour. 'The tales are true, and more. There are many as would welcome the Bhrudwans with open arms,' said the Guard, and waited for the reaction.

'Are you saying you know guardsmen who would betray Faltha? That you are a traitor yourself?' The words were offered in a shocked undertone.

'I'm sayin' nothing of the kind,' said the guard, 'but how could the Bhrudwans be worse than the Arkhoi we've had running Instruere?' Seeing the doubt on the other man's face, he continued. 'I've done service in the Hall of Lore, and I've seen things that would turn your stomach.'

'But what about the burnings this afternoon? Those soldiers surrendered properly. They shouldn't have been executed for it.'

'That's what the army needs, a little more discipline,' the guard said, running his tongue over his lips. 'How else did fifty thousand of them defeat a hundred thousand of us? Faltha is soft, mark my words; soft and weak. This war has weeded out the weaklings, and only the strong like us remain. We'll be wanted in the new set-up, no question.'

The soldier shook his head and moved on, trying to get a better view of the ceremony, but the words of the guard stayed in his head.

Trumpets blared, and the Destroyer – *the Undying Man*,

we have to call him now, Kurr remembered bitterly – strode forward, resplendent in his black robe, a silver crown on his brow, his sword resting on his hip. As they had been instructed, the Falthan commanders fell to their knees and pressed their foreheads to the dirt. The *losian* commanders had refused to consider this demand when the details of the ceremony were relayed to them, and some even spoke of killing themselves before acquiescing, but the Haufuth suggested quietly substituting First Men for their absent allies. So far it seemed to have worked.

Kurr remained kneeling along with the others, watching out of the corner of his eye as Indrett stood, then approached the slayer of her son. *So hard*, the old farmer thought; *so cruel to ask her to do this*. Yet she knelt on one knee in front of the Undying Man, and spoke the words of surrender in a strong, clear voice. *So much courage*.

All felt the magic of it pull tight around them. Perhaps other people at other times would be able to resist the Lord of Bhrudwo, but not them, not now, not for as long as the Binding lasted. And when the Declaration was signed, the Binding would become immutable, lasting forever. A dreadful fate, they realised; but they had entered into this agreement freely, they had accepted his challenge, they had brought this on themselves.

Stella stood beside the Destroyer, her body aflame with pain as always, but sustained by his will so that she could not even move a muscle in relief unless he wished it – and he never wished it. *As I am bound, so Faltha is bound*. She considered the irony, but even thinking gave her pain. There seemed little of herself left apart from the hurting.

She had heard the Destroyer issue his challenge, and hope

had risen within her despite the evidence she had of his duplicity. When Hal and not Leith accepted the challenge, hope had evaporated. But with surprised eyes she had witnessed the cripple fight with astonishing skill, and all through the match she had begged the Most High for Hal to emerge victorious. She poured out her soul to the boy from her own village, and had felt the same drawing she had experienced the day when Leith had been under attack by the *Maghdi Dasht*. *The Fire that burns in me is somehow being used by Hal*, she realised, even though the Destroyer continually taunted her by telling her that it was locked away beyond her capacity to use. With every blow she willed Hal on: it needed just one stroke of luck and she would be set free! It was so close she could almost feel the shape of freedom. But that blow never came, and in a moment of horror she watched the Destroyer strike Hal down, saw him die. Hal, loving Hal, friend and companion, dying at the end of an evil blade. She had closed her eyes and resolved never to open them again, so deep was her sorrow.

But in spite of herself she had opened them, if only to avoid falling in the dirt as his irresistible will dragged at her. She saw Leith embracing his brother's body, heard his cries of anguish and the low moans of fear that rippled through the Falthan army as they realised the war was over, that they had lost. She beheld the smile on her master's face, and wished she had the power to spit on him as she had done once before. She watched him wipe his blade clean of Hal's blood, foulness cleansing himself of purity.

The Destroyer seemed to give her no more thought after locking her into position just before the ceremony of surrender began. He had spent the afternoon using the blue fire to communicate with various of his traitorous allies – Stella was too weary and heartsick to note whom he had spoken to – and later the husks of the six Falthans he had drained of life for the fire were taken to the poles and burned there. In some fashion this had refreshed him, and the ceremony had begun soon after.

She wondered if the Falthans realised just how close the Destroyer had come to losing everything. His blood burned in her veins; thus she could sense his extremity. His illusory skin had faded as he expended all his energy on keeping Hal's sword at bay, and for a few moments all saw him as he really was, a wreck of a man, tormented by the contradictory powers running through him. But perhaps they thought this ghastly apparition was the illusion, designed to frighten Hal. *So close!* He would not have died, of course, but he would certainly have been stripped of his powers, freeing her and so many others. For a moment she thought of a man without a tongue. *So close.*

Helpless and hopeless, she watched the ceremony take place. The trumpets and the obeisance and the words of surrender were spoken by a woman from her own beloved village of Loulea. Stella stood no more than a few feet away from them, but was not surprised that no one recognised her broken body as that of one of their former companions. At least, almost no one: the Haufuth occasionally cast glances in her direction, though since he had his forehead pressed to the ground it was difficult to tell exactly what he was thinking.

There was a document to sign, apparently, but the Destroyer did not intend to sign it here in Vulture's Craw. 'I will have the signatures of the leaders of Faltha from their own hands, as they grovel before me in the Hall of Meeting at Instruere,' he said, savouring the coming delight as though he experienced their humiliation and his glory already. The servant-girl could feel his eagerness, his vast hunger, his insatiable desire for revenge on anyone associated with the Most High. For him, the true moment of surrender would come when the Sixteen Kingdoms bowed before him. In spite of his longing, he was prepared to wait until then.

Now the ceremony was over and the Falthans left, each commander accompanied by a *Maghdi Dasht* to ensure obedience. Stella watched them leave without experiencing the feelings of abandonment and loneliness she might have expected. Instead, she realised that they had become just like her, each with a black shadow. Or, perhaps each of them now a pale shadow to a black-cloaked reality. This should not have consoled her, she knew, but it did.

They came for Leith after dark. Phemanderac made his way down into the dell, followed by two menacing Lords of Fear. The Bhrudwans seemed to have identified everyone who could operate in the realm of Fire, and had assigned each one a sinister guardian. Leith's jailer, the chief of the *Maghdi Dasht* and the most powerful of the Bhrudwans save the Destroyer himself, would hardly be necessary, Phemanderac thought as he lifted the insensible youth to his feet. Grief already held him prisoner.

Phemanderac himself was in mourning, and over such a trivial thing. They had taken his harp and smashed it, and the sound of the rosewood breaking was more than he could bear. It seemed to signify every fine thing that had been lost. *Crafted by Mandaramus himself*, he thought as he grieved; *possibly the last of its kind*, and he let the tears fall. As Hal was, as Wiusago and Te Tuahangata were, as many others had been. He wept for them all.

'Come, Leith,' he said gently, knowing that if the youth didn't respond, he would be made to obey. 'Time to let him go.'

The boy's hand slipped out of his brother's cold fingers. For as long as he dared Phemanderac stared at the features of the cripple, which registered no more than a mild surprise. The sword had been taken from the body, but the small entry wound was still visible, just below his heart. His face and hands were white as alabaster, as though he was a broken statue. *Smashed like a harp*, the Dhaurian scholar mused. *He will be missed.*

'Phemanderac? What did we do wrong?' The voice was hoarse, ragged.

He turned away from the body and towards the deep, wounded eyes of Hal's brother. 'Do wrong?' he echoed, unsure of the question, surprised that Leith could ask it so soon.

'Yes. Was it tactical? Should we have waited to gather a larger army? Or was it because we put our trust in magic and not in our own strength? That we trusted the arrow of unity more than the strength unity would bring?' The eyes were overbright, the face flushed.

'Leith, it is not a good time—'

'Or was it what Kroptur said? Did I somehow bring this down on all our heads because I didn't love my brother when it mattered?'

'No more talk!' snapped a voice, and both Phemanderac and Leith found themselves carried out of the dell, slung over broad shoulders.

'What about the Jugom Ark?' Phemanderac asked their captors.

'Just another arrow now,' came the harsh reply. 'Leave it where it lies.'

'And Hal? Surely he at least will receive the honourable burial his skill and valour deserve?'

'He is carrion. He will feed the birds.' The two *Maghdi Dasht* reached out with their coercion, and Leith and Phemanderac were given no further opportunity to ask questions.

Over the next few weeks winter turned to spring. Few of the beaten Falthan army had the heart to see the new blossoms on the trees by their path, or the renewed activity in the sky above the great plains of central Faltha, or on the never-ending grasslands themselves. They learned instead to obey the severe discipline of their new masters, to live with hunger and cold as the best was taken by the Bhrudwan army, and to cope daily with humiliation. Even the discontents within the Falthan ranks were unsettled by the capriciousness of their captors, who seemed to take great delight in punishing their charges for the most minor deviation from the rules – but only after ignoring these infractions for days or longer, and sometimes taking one man and leaving unpunished another who committed the same offence. And the punishments were brutal. One man, driven beyond endurance, lost a hand for striking a Bhrudwan officer, while another suffered the same fate for respectfully asking for a misheard order to be repeated. The taking of a hand seemed to be their standard punishment. Worse, the punishments were public, and all close by were required to witness the swift and terrible judgments of the *Maghdi Dasht*, and learn thereby.

They learned to hate.

Graig and his father Geinor walked into chaos, there was no other word for it. Graig was especially anxious to be reunited with Leith, the mighty and magical Arrow-bearer, who paid him such respect when first they had met. He had begged to be allowed to remain at Leith's side, but reluctantly saw the sense of travelling south with his father and the other messengers in search of support for the coming war against Bhrudwo.

Every day on the southern journey he took time to practise with the sword, remembering the jibes of the Arkhos of Nemohaim, and was determined to be accepted into the service of the Arrow-bearer. Geinor tried to speak to him of diplomacy and the workings of a king's court, knowing that this would be of more use to his son, but Graig had seen action in the Battle of the Four Halls and again on the dreadful night when the Ecclesia had been betrayed, and for now the glory of the swordsman closed his mind to everything else.

After four weeks of hard riding they reached the Bay of Bewray, to find the land in an uproar. The humiliated King of Nemohaim had stepped aside a matter of days after Leith had spoken with him, and contention over the throne had swept across the country in waves of killing. This dreadful chance meant that most of the soldiery in Nemohaim was otherwise engaged, and so Geinor and Graig had no king to entreat.

The two men spent fruitless weeks trying to enlist support for an eastern war, but such a nebulous prospect drew few away from the war of succession. Until the day, that is, when a fleet of tall ships under full sail ghosted up the Bay of Bewray and succeeded in gaining everyone's attention. Fifty ships with five hundred swarthy southerners in each, men with long dark hair and broad moustaches from ports such as Silsilesi, Kauma, Jardin and the pirate island of Corrigia. Sarista and Vertensia had thrown themselves behind the Jugom Ark: every seaworthy vessel they could call on now sailed the perilous winter seas for Instruere.

Geinor and his son rode down to the wharves to meet them. The admiral of the fleet, a small, effete man with a stammer, belied the image of a southern pirate so feared in Nemohaim, but his mind was sharp and his commission clear.

'We sail north tomorrow with as many Nemohaimians as we can raise,' the admiral stated in his lisping way. 'I would have expected the king himself to meet us. Are the men of Nemohaim so inured to the presence of southern ships that they care not we fill their harbour?' Geinor explained the situation, and the admiral cursed loudly, sending the seagulls to flight. 'What sort of place is this?' he railed, then apologised when he saw that the aged courtier had taken offence.

'May I ask when you put to sea?' Graig asked him respectfully.

'The first ships left Morneshade, two days east of Kauma, nigh on a month ago. We've stopped at most ports on the way, gathering support for my king's quest.'

'A month ago?' Geinor responded quizzically, realising that his lessons had not been entirely wasted on his son. 'Then you cannot have set sail because of our emissaries.'

'Indeed not! And why would Nemohaim send emissaries to Sarista?'

Geinor's brow furrowed, then cleared. 'Not Nemohaim, but Instruere. I am one of the Arrow-bearer's men, sent south to raise an army to help oppose the Bhrudwan force we feel sure is coming west.'

Now the admiral wore a broad smile, and invited the men on board. There they ate and drank of the legendary Saristrian fare, and explained all about Leith Mahnumsen and the Jugom Ark; and how they had been written right into the heart of the story.

'My king heard about the coming invasion through his brave Arkhos, struck down by the evil now abroad in

Instruere,' said the admiral. 'We come north to cleanse the Great City of that evil.'

'Then you travel north in vain,' said Graig stoutly. 'Leith has already cleansed the City with the Jugom Ark. But you can come north anyway, just in case, through some foul wizardry, the Bhrudwans passed through the Gap before the Falthan army arrived.' He supplied the admiral with the numbers he asked for: the date the army had most likely left Instruere, and the probable numbers it comprised.

'Your friend's army will be too late,' said the admiral shortly. 'We sent our own spies north many months ago, using a little-known path along the eastern edge of the Idehan Kahal, the Deep Desert as it is known in the north. Lately they have returned, and reported to the king of a large Bhrudwan force that was even then high up on the high plains of Birinjh, and would have made the Gap ere our spies returned home.'

'So they will be fighting now? Even as we speak?' Graig asked, his eyes sparkling.

'Aye, they will be fighting,' growled the small man, tugging at his moustache irritably. 'They will be fighting, and they will be dying like flies in winter. I would not expect more than a quarter of the victorious army to march back home. Think on it, lad: three chances out of four that you would be left lying unburied on some rocky field, a cast-off of an ill-conceived war.'

Graig was not sure he liked this man, but he and his father gathered as many countrymen as they could and accepted passage on one of the great southern galleons. The fleet passed northwards through dark, cold waters, landing once at Lindholm, the westernmost city of Deruys, to take on provisions. There they were joined by a few eager Deruvians who had been left behind by the main army. Somewhere north of Te One-tahua, an island at the northern extremity of the Pei-ra Archipelago, the fleet was hit by a huge winter gale from the Wodhaitic Sea, and the huge ships were scattered like seeds, driven towards the Deruvian coast near Derningen. One of the smaller ships foundered and sank before anyone could get near it, and two others were crippled to the extent that they were forced to make for the small harbour at Brunhaven. The normally carefully-composed admiral threw curses at the wind and the sea for a week, stopping only when the last of his seaworthy vessels was accounted for. Then, running before a flagging breeze, the southern army sailed east until finally the vast delta of the great river came into view, a brown stain on the pure blue sea.

The shocking news of the defeat of the vaunted Army of Faltha spread quickly across the wide plains of central Faltha, as bad news is wont to do. It was whispered that the Jugom Ark had been lost, and the favour of the Most High had been withdrawn, because the Arrow-bearer had refused a challenge from the Destroyer. This could scarcely be believed, but many people were prepared to take the risk to find out for themselves. Initially, farmers and town-dwellers lined the route as the captive army and their conquerors made their way west from Vulture's Craw. Some of those who gathered decried their own soldiers, hurling abuse and sometimes stones at the ones whose failure had consigned them to Bhrudwan rule. These were the same people who had cheered them on their eastward journey, reflected many of the captives angrily. With typical inconstancy the Bhrudwans left this disrespectful behaviour unpunished, except on occasion when they would drag some white-faced peasant out from behind whatever hedge he had hidden, and give him or her the standard punishment. The hand would be left behind in the road, and the local populace would be forbidden to touch it.

At Ehrenmal, the largest Favonian city save the capital Sturrenkol, the Destroyer and his retinue were received by the King of Favony and his court, who begged to be allowed to accompany their new master westwards to Instruere. Their request was granted, they were told, but they would not be given the City. That gift was to be given to another. The king waited too long to offer his thanks for this favour granted him, and to him, also, was given the standard punishment. Or, at least, that was the rumour that made its way around the Falthan camp.

Leith and Phemanderac were not free to join the others, but were afraid to ask why. They were kept apart in a small tent and forced to eat, make their ablutions and sleep in the company of their two *Maghdi Dasht* captors. Sometimes they were allowed to speak to each other, and the long days and weeks of desolation were whiled away with small talk: of the trees that grew on the hills above Dona Mihst and what animals might be found in them, of the huntsmen of the Great North Woods, some of whom occasionally visited Loulea; of the singing in the Hall of Worship, where the Dhaurians gathered to worship the Most High, and of the rolling breakers that surged along the cold grey coasts of the North March. Things of value, things enjoyed without a thought for the future, things they might never experience again.

'Amasian was almost right, Leith,' Phemanderac said one afternoon as they drew close to Sivithar. The boy turned his head to stare blankly at the philosopher.

'Who?'

'Have you forgotten the prophecy on the ceiling of the

Hall of Conal Greatheart?' He kept his voice low, knowing that the name of Conal might earn them a reprimand.

'Oh,' Leith responded, then turned his head away, clearly discomfited.

Phemanderac let the subject drop, but began again early the next morning. 'Sir Amasian saw truly, Leith. But his mind rebelled against what he saw. I have no doubt that in his vision he beheld the rainbow broken by the hand of the Destroyer. After all, the rainbow was the after-effect of the storm sung into being by the *Maghdi Dasht*. Amasian was unable to conceive of a prophecy of doom, so he turned defeat into victory by turning the two parts of the vision around.'

'He said something about the vision running backwards,' the youth acknowledged. 'But why was he granted a vision that predicted our defeat?'

'Perhaps it was a warning, or maybe we were supposed to accept it and not fight it.' The tall philosopher had no clear answers. So much of what had happened in the war against Bhrudwo was a mystery. For a long time they walked on, their grey shadows marching right behind them.

'My head is full of numbers,' Leith said suddenly, earning him a grunt from the powerful figure assigned to him. The youth repeated the words, this time in a much quieter voice, then added: 'Over seventy thousand Falthans dead. Thirty thousand Bhrudwans slain. One hundred thousand people gone, mostly good people, few who deserved to die. Perhaps three or four hundred thousand people who are grieving or who will grieve. Wiusago and Te Tuahangata slain. Jethart ambushed and tortured. Hundreds killed in Instruere as we fought over the city. Wira killed! Stella gone! Hal dead! I have no more room in my mind! Thousands of feet walk through my head, their owners crying out for rest or revenge!

'Phemanderac, I have a question. To what extent am I responsible for the size of the numbers? Would the numbers be much smaller if I had remained in Loulea?'

His friend looked with great pity on Leith's stricken face, and he shaped first one, then another answer in his mind. Rejecting them all, he gave the boy the truth, as far as he understood it.

'You are responsible for every one who died,' he said quietly, and winced at the youth's agonised indrawing of breath. 'But,' he added, 'the numbers would have been far greater had you remained in your village. Try to count the numbers you saved, not the numbers who died. Promise me you will try!'

The boy nodded, wiping his nose on his sleeve as he cried. Phemanderac gazed with love on the youth who had been destroyed by his willingness to follow the Most High, and found that he had a hitherto unacknowledged anger buried deep in his heart.

It ought not to have turned out like this, he thought.

He had occasion to repeat this thought during the weeks of their journey of disgrace, the long defeat, as they were marched towards Instruere and the sealing of their servitude to the Undying Man. Again the crowds came, and this time the Bhrudwans let their derision go unchecked. Even worse were the towns where the local burghers encouraged the citizens to cheer the Bhrudwan army, or to throw spring blossoms in front of their cruel feet. Men shouted their praise, and women offered their bodies.

It ought not to be like this.

The random punishments continued, and one afternoon, not long after they had crossed to the north bank of the Aleinus at Sivithar, the whole army halted to watch three executions. There had been a minor revolt within the volatile *losian* camp, and two Fodhram and a Widuz were burned at the stake. The Destroyer himself set the fire, and it burned blue, licking their struggling limbs with a hungry flame. One of the men looked like Shabby, the man introduced to Phemanderac as one of the Company's four companions during the southern run a year ago; but Leith watched the burnings along with all the others and did not seem to recognise any of the luckless men. Or, if he did, he did not acknowledge it.

Things should not have turned out this way.

Phemanderac was forced to admit that the life had gone from his friend. Where there had been inquisitiveness, a quick understanding and a naive, wholesome love, there was now only a void, a blankness slowly filling with guilt and self-recrimination. So much had been ripped from him: his brother, his arrow, his pride. And perhaps the boy imagined that he had lost much more. It might be that he thought he was despised, blamed for the failure of the Jugom Ark and the fact that the Destroyer stood less than a week's march east of Instruere.

Perhaps everybody does blame him, the philosopher admitted. *Perhaps he is responsible. Perhaps he was at fault.*

It was all so terribly unfair. *How could it have come to this?*

The Destroyer would have come to claim a city set against him, had it not been for my intervention, the Arkhos of Nemohaim reflected as he busied himself with the buttons on his red robe. Larger than ever, he had been forced to obtain a new robe from one of the markets. That and the unexplained loss of his favourite chair irritated him, though in truth very little could upset him in these exciting days. The Undying Man had been agreeably surprised to find his old ally in charge of Instruere, and had agreed to the broad sweep of his plan for the City's defence against anyone looking to support the Falthans against Bhrudwo. It had been hinted that a great reward lay in store for him, and it was mentioned in passing that the Destroyer might leave a regent to rule in his stead. Everything he had planned for. *Deorc!* The black voice inside him howled. *Where are you now?*

Correctly predicting that the callow, conservative southern kingdoms of Sarista, Tabul and Vertensia would offer their support to the Bearer of the Jugom Ark, the Arkhos of Nemohaim concentrated his defences on the place a few miles downstream where the great river divided into many navigable channels. Here he built two giant towers, from which arrows and rocks could be hurled at any ships foolish enough to brave the river. Just seaward of the towers he organised a blockade, hiring mercenaries and seamen skilled in ship-fighting, supplementing their numbers with those who had lost their source of income now that no trade came up the Aleinus.

And, as he had predicted, the allies of the Arrow-bearer had come. *Where would the Destroyer's plans be if it hadn't been for me?* First to attempt the blockade was a ragged collection of canoes bearing strange men from the outer islands, but they were beaten back. More recently they had been joined by the tall ships of the south. 'I cannot destroy them, my lord,' the Arkhos reported through the blue fire. 'They are too many, and it would not be prudent to leave the walls of the City unmanned in order to grapple in earnest with them. But I can hold them where they are. Would this be in line with your will?'

Yes, the blue fire had replied. *Hold them until I come, then together we will sweep them into the sea.*

Together, the Arkhos remembered as he fastened the last button on his robe. He liked the sound of that.

* * *

The Hermit and the Presiding Elder waited nervously in the corridor, and both greeted him effusively when he finally emerged. 'Latest reports have them two hours' walk from Longbridge,' the thin-necked Presiding Elder informed him with all the officiousness of a secretary.

'Then we'd best make ourselves ready,' he snarled at them. 'I trust your followers are well presented and have been briefed on what is required?'

'Most certainly,' the Hermit replied. 'This day the Fire will finally fall on the city of iniquity, and all evil, all worldliness, will be purged away.' His words sounded reasonable, delivered in a level tone, but in his eyes madness burned. 'His chosen instrument will bring low the wise and elevate the humble. My prophetic vision will be confirmed when fire burns on the hand of the Servant of God!'

Something settled on the Arkhos as the words were spoken. He'd felt similarly uncomfortable on his last sojourn in Andratan, but he had expected magic there, and had not been disappointed. *Just superstition*, he told himself. *This fool cannot know the secrets of the Wordweave.*

'Yes, yes,' he said irritably, waving his hand to indicate that the others should follow him. 'We've heard it all before.' *And soon we will have heard it for the last time.*

The three men emerged from the Hall of Lore to the cheers of the gathered crowd. *They think they come to see the triumphant return of their army*, the Arkhos told himself, and suppressed a chuckle. *They are in for a surprise.*

Today was the day the great Army of Faltha returned to Instruere, the people had been told. Eager to welcome their heroes home, citizens lined the Vitulian Way, dressed in their most colourful spring clothes. The rich rubbed shoulders with the poor; babies and their great-grandmothers, equally unaware of the day's importance but keyed up by the general excitement, had been carried outdoors to various vantage points. Bright banners were readied, and those without banners brought strips of cloth in yellow and orange to honour the Bearer of the Arrow.

It had been an almost impossible task to keep the citizens of Instruere ignorant of the true result of the war between Faltha and Bhrudwo, but it had been achieved through a combination of control of the bridges and judicious misinformation fed at intervals to certain key people in Instruere. Once or twice someone slipped through the net, but the Arkhos knew where assassins could be hired. A rumour that the Arrow-bearer had been slain took hold in the poor district, so the Arkhos of Nemohaim put his second plan into action, and paid people to exaggerate the rumour until even the most credulous of citizens scoffed at it. Within days the rumour had disappeared, and eventually everyone believed a great victory had been won 'out east'. Not without cost, they were told, and many of those in the crowd waited with nervousness and fear lest their loved ones did not walk through the Inna Gate with the other conquering heroes. Mid-morning came and went, and the muttering increased. Just before noon a shout went up: someone had seen a cloud of dust from the wall, and for a while it was thought the army was here at last; but it was soon pointed out that the man who had seen the dust was stationed on the west wall, and so could not have seen them.

Noon passed, and still the restive crowd waited.

The troops promised to the defenders of the Aleinus Delta by the Arkhos of Nemohaim had not come, and their latest rider had returned from Instruere with yet another refusal. Instead the southerners had renewed their attack, driving through the blockade with their tall ships. They had still not found a way past the siege towers, but the remaining Instruian soldiers now knew they did not have long to live. Anger spread through the camp. Why should they lay down their lives in the service of one who refused to supply them with the arms and people they needed?

It did not take long for the Instruians to decide on surrender as their most prudent course. One by one they clambered down the long ladders and made their way along the reed-lined river bank, hands in the air, hoping for mercy. They halted by the blockade. A hundred fishing boats, half of which were now sunk, had been stretched across the only navigable river channel, so that the entrance to the Aleinus River could be held against the armies of the south. But now the boats were empty, the mercenaries hired to man them having been slain, taken captive or perhaps run off – the latter the most likely, the soldiers from the siege towers considered. There were no bodies visible, and little blood to be found on the boats or in the water.

No defenders, but neither were there attackers. No one remained to surrender to. The tall ships stood at anchor, and a number of small boats had been beached some distance downstream of the blockade. Had the southerners taken the risk of trying to find a way through the pathless swamps of the river delta? Or had they found a guide who, willing or unwilling, would lead them to dry ground and ultimately to Instruere?

'Well, boys, we could have stayed in our towers after all,' said the commander of the Arkhos's western force. 'It seems our southern friends have found another path to their goal. Any of you have kin in Instruere?' The majority of the Arkhos's recruits were from Mercium, but a very few men put up nervous hands. 'Then you take the horses and ride,' the hoary old veteran told them. 'We will follow more discreetly.' It was not their city; the likelihood of anyone getting paid for this had just vanished; and so there appeared to be no compelling reason to rush east, particularly since they might overtake the army they had tried to delay. The men settled down for a good meal.

The thousands of captive Falthan soldiers were finally halted a league north of Longbridge and waited in trepidation as the Bhrudwans bound them hand and foot. The Instruians among them could see their city wall and, knowing that their families were within, wondered if they would ever see them. Some among them thought they were being bound in preparation for a slaughter, and their cries of fear were heard by their commanders, themselves captive.

The Destroyer mounted a tall white stallion, which tossed his head nervously and stamped at the ground, as if reluctant to have such a rider on his back. The Falthan commanders were forced to line up two abreast behind him, along with their *Maghdi Dasht* minders, and begin a slow procession southwards to the City.

Leith was placed at the head of the Falthans, with Phemanderac at his side. Directly behind him was his mother, and they embraced in the few moments they had together, both running their eyes over each other to check for mistreatment. Watching, Phemanderac shed a tear at their bitter loss, and noted that Indrett's face was marked by it as deeply as was his. *She has both hands, at least*, the philosopher saw, relieved. *And she seems to be otherwise uninjured.* Then he laughed sourly at himself. *How could she be without injury? She has seen her son struck down in a gamble she precipitated.*

Two people destroyed by guilt, trying to gain comfort from each other. He was not close enough to hear the hurried words they exchanged before a barked reprimand from the *Maghdi Dasht* jerked them apart.

It was that moment, witnessing two strong and proud people so swiftly obedient to the wishes of their enemy, that finally convinced the Dhaurian that Faltha had been defeated.

On they marched, and the *Maghdi Dasht* began to sing. The words were indecipherable – undoubtedly in a Bhrudwan ceremonial tongue of some kind, the scholar Phemanderac reasoned – but the sentiment was plain. This was a song of victory, and it swelled on the breeze that bore it south towards the largest city in Faltha.

The procession clattered across Longbridge, and the people gathered there gasped as they realised that the supposedly victorious Falthan army was being led by a figure the like of whom they had never seen. A few dived into the river to escape the whips that were already being plied about, clearing the environs of those who might interfere with the vanguard of the Destroyer's triumphal entry.

The grey-robed figure halted at the southern end of the bridge. A deep silence fell. *He stands only a few paces from where Parlevaag fell*, Phemanderac realised, and the anger he held back fought to escape him. *Careful . . . one foolish action and many others might pay the cost of it.* Then the silence was ripped apart by the sounding of brazen trumpets, and the Gate began slowly to open.

In through the Inna Gate rode the Destroyer to shouts of acclamation, and he stood up in his stirrups, raised his sword and cried a word of victory. Answering cries came from the *Maghdi Dasht* following in behind him. Banners waved, pieces of cloth floated across the road in front of him, and for a few moments the City of Instruere celebrated the return of their conquering heroes.

This is carefully orchestrated acclamation from well-coached sections of the crowd, Phemanderac told himself. *Most of the people here don't yet realise they have been tricked, that they are welcoming the one who will make their lives miserable and short. They just don't realise.* His rationalising, however, could not temper the depression swamping his normally indomitable soul.

Soon the thousands of people gathered on either side of the road began to realise something was wrong. 'Where is the Arrow?' some asked. 'Who is the man in grey?' Then, as the gate closed far too soon behind the last of the Falthan captives and their attendant *Maghdi Dasht*, they asked: 'Where is the army we sent?' The cheering died away into an uneasy, murmuring quietness.

'Render praise to the Lord of Faltha and Bhrudwo!' cried the Destroyer, and one hundred and sixty-nine throats echoed: 'Praise him!' Their combined words, laced with a powerful Wordweave, placed hooks in the watching crowd, pulling them to their feet, prising open their mouths, dragging their reluctant voices up from their throats: 'Praise him!' cried the crowd, all the while struggling against a power they never thought would touch them. Some among them resisted the Wordweave; those strong or gifted people sprang to their feet and ran for any hiding place that might offer them shelter. A few others were completely overcome by the power and fell to the ground clutching their heads as though taken by madness or death.

'I am the new Lord of Instruere!' cried the grey figure on the white horse, and the crowd groaned. 'After an absence of a thousand years I return to take up my rightful lordship!'

There was now little doubt who addressed them, and many began to weep for how they had been deceived, what they had lost, and for what would soon happen to them. 'You are my subjects!' he continued. 'You will show me absolute loyalty, or you will die – like this one here!' He pointed his sword to one part of the crowd, and a woman who somehow had contrived to find a bow and a few arrows found herself lifted in the air, higher and higher, screaming, to the height of the tallest tenement on the street . . . and then, released by the Destroyer, she fell. As she hit the ground a gasp of fear rippled through the watchers, and many cried in dismay and terror, turning away from what they saw; but none could leave.

'My servants can sense rebellion as clearly as I, and will deal with it as ruthlessly. Obey my every wish and you will live. Withhold anything from me, baulk me at any moment, and you will know death. And know this: it will not be as quick as the death you have just witnessed.'

Stunned silence fell, save for the cries of frightened children, who knew only that the celebrations had gone wrong.

'Now, come with me to the Hall of Meeting and witness the moment when the documents of surrender are signed, and I claim this place in law as well as in fact!'

The Undying Man shucked the reins of his horse, which stepped forward slowly in response. Now the crowd could see the captives, and some recognised the northerners who had been so kind to them after the fires; many more saw the face of the Bearer of the Arrow and knew him. All these people realised that the Jugom Ark had somehow failed them, and the mutterings started.

Let this charade be over, Phemanderac thought bitterly. *Why did he not sign this document back at Vulture's Craw?* And his knowledge of the *Fuirfad* answered him: *the efficacy of the*

Truthspell that bound them all to him will be greatly increased if he signs the document here. Further, he didn't need to be a loremaster to know that this march through Instruere had been uppermost in the Destroyer's thoughts for a thousand years. It would be signed here, and then . . .

. . . would they be permitted to live? Sooner or later the *Maghdi Dasht* would interrogate them all, all the Falthan leaders, to prise out anything of use. They would discover they had a Dhaurian in their hands, one of those whom the Destroyer hated with a passion far in excess even of that he felt for the Falthans. He would be confined, then tortured and stripped of everything: his knowledge, his memories, his identity. He would be killed, and by then he would be begging for death.

Would any of those walking behind him survive? Leith – his heart contracted in fear – might be kept as a servant to the Destroyer's court, but would probably be put to death eventually. The Undying Man had already hinted at the dire fate in store for Indrett. As for the others, few of the Company would survive. Few of them would want to.

The awful truth was that few of the captives and fewer of the crowd yet realised how bad things would get.

The reluctant Instruians followed the Destroyer along the wide street. In the distance, drawing ever closer, stood the Hall of Meeting. The Lords of Fear began to sing again, and this time their Wordweave was designed to drain the City of its will to resist.

Phemanderac narrowed his eyes, peering into the distance, trying to guess the identities of the three figures who waited by the door to the Hall of Meeting, ready to greet their new master. A huge man in red, a tall, blond-haired man in a blue robe, and a thin, balding man in a brown cloak. The three names of their latest betrayers assembled themselves in his mind: the Presiding Elder of Escaigne, the Hermit of the Ecclesia, and the Arkhos of Nemohaim.

The Destroyer halted, and dismounted from his horse. 'My lord,' the Arkhos of Nemohaim wheezed. 'I give the City into your hands, and await your instructions as your ever-faithful servant.' He bowed, an impressive feat for one of his bulk.

'Ever-faithful?' mused the Undying Man. 'Ever-faithful? You might have chosen better words to describe yourself in the hour when a Truthspell is about to be sealed!'

'My lord? How have I displeased you?' A note of fear edged the big man's voice.

The Destroyer turned to his servants and the crowds who spilled out behind them. 'Here stands a man who sought to overthrow my appointed servant, Deorc of Andratan,' he said, his voice menacing.

Nemohaim took an unwise step forward. 'But Deorc was an incompetent—'

'He was a renegade, ultimately playing me false, but you still should have served him with all your heart. Would you also betray me, looking for a way to reclaim this City for yourself, if you found my orders disagreeable?' The fingers of his one hand extended, then closed into a fist, and the terrified Arkhos felt the net of truth burn into his skin. He opened his mouth to deny the accusation . . .

'Yes I would,' his voice said. 'I want dominion over Instruere, then all of Faltha.' His black voice had betrayed him at last, and it howled for death. 'I want dominion over you and all your followers! I want to swallow the world!'

As his voice condemned him, the Arkhos's boots began to smoke. 'A laudable ambition,' the Destroyer laughed, as flames played up and down the obese man's legs. 'But if one does not have the ability to bring the vision to pass, then one must suffer the consequences.' Now blue fire wrapped itself around the figure, who bellowed his rage and torment as his body began to melt.

But deep inside him, unheard by anyone watching the grotesque scene, the black voice cried out in final triumph.

'Does anybody else wish to profess their faithfulness?' the grey-cloaked figure asked them. He waited, though he and everyone else there knew no one would respond. One look at the smoking ruin that had been the Arkhos of Nemohaim was enough.

Finally, after a thousand years of patience, the Lord of Bhrudwo faced the Iron Door of the Outer Chamber. It had obviously met with some mishap, or perhaps had simply decayed in the same fashion as this backward land. For a few short years a millennia ago he had ruled this City when it had been at the zenith of its power and glory. Now, like the door in front of him, Instruere seemed on the verge of falling apart. How could his victory be properly savoured when the once-proud City was reduced to this?

No matter. The Iron Door was a powerful symbol yet, and it was important to bring it down so there could be no doubt among the Falthans that he would destroy any barrier in his way. He raised his hand, the open palm facing the indomitable door, then spoke a single word.

Instantly the huge iron mass jerked left and right, again and again, until somewhere deep inside the wall a mechanism groaned, then snapped. The great slab came rushing down, slamming into the floor, bursting through the containing wall; then it fell forward with a crash, bringing with it the accumulated dust of a thousand years and more.

The Destroyer stepped on to the metal ruin and turned to face the Falthan captives.

'And so falls your last defence against me,' he intoned, and his voice scoured away their remaining hope. Gathering up his cloak he turned and strode across the door and into the Outer Chamber. The hollow echo of his boots rang in the Falthans' ears.

Leith followed the Destroyer into the Outer Chamber. Behind him came his fellow Falthans, first the commanders, then the citizens. Those unfortunate enough to have found themselves at the head of the crowd were shepherded into the building, and after a period of shuffling they sat on the benches, rows and rows of round-eyed faces staring at the empty platform, the smell of fear thickening the air, mouths firmly closed lest any undue attention be drawn to their owners who clearly wished to be anywhere other than where they were. The Destroyer waited until they were all seated, then set out for the platform. The click-click-click of the steel-shod boots pulled Leith onwards past the white faces, up the steps and on to the platform. His minder indicated curtly where he should sit.

Time seemed to fold back in on itself. Here he was on the platform with members of the Company, in the presence of Instruians, just as he had been a few months earlier when, against all expectations, he had been acclaimed Lord of Instruere. On top of this image lay the present reality, where in a few moments the Destroyer would take that title from him. *Why not? He's taken everything else: the Arrow, my brother, Stella . . .* The hollow place inside him seemed to grow every time he thought about them. He had not realised – had never considered the possibility – that he loved Hal until he was taken from them. *No! Don't think about him!*

He looked out over the crowd, and a thousand Hals stared back at him. *I loved you! I killed you!*

Mercifully, his thoughts were cut short by the Destroyer, who stood beside the table. 'Bring forth the Declaration!' he cried, and the crippled servant-girl, whom Leith had not seen since the day everything had fallen apart, stepped forward from the shadows and slowly, achingly slowly, fought her way up the stairs.

Every vestige of breath in his body disappeared as he watched her. A slow scream began to build up inside him, gathering up everything he had.

He knew who she was.

Step, drag. He could hear her breathing, panting like a cornered animal, wounded and suffering. Step, drag. He remembered her face in the moonlight, as it had been on Lake Cotyledon. Step, drag. Her face had been twisted by some awful torture and now one side hung slack, drool running unchecked from the corner of her mouth. *Still beautiful!* Step, drag. Her eyes were wells of sorrow, and as she raised them to meet his, the scream built until he thought he would not be able to contain it. *Stella, oh Stella!* She knew him, he could see it, and her eyes roamed across the platform, finding the others: registering those present and those absent. Step, drag. She reached the top of the stairs and rested there a moment, fighting to regain her breath. *What has he done to you?* The Destroyer beckoned to her and she stumbled forward, clearly exhausted but unable to resist the spell he held her under.

An age to walk the ten paces to the table, then her eyes closed as she held out the parchment. His foul hand touched hers, and she shuddered. He took the Declaration and placed it on the table. Stella collapsed in a heap, unregarded by any of the Bhrudwans. Beside Leith, Indrett wept openly, and there was not a member of the Company present who did not have red eyes and a heavy heart.

'The so-called Commander of the Falthan army will stand and sign the document,' announced the chief of the *Maghdi Dasht*. Leith could feel the power in the command – but, amazingly, his mother fought it. Slowly she rose, shaking with effort, the power of magic gradually overcoming her sheer stubbornness. In a series of jerks Indrett moved across the stage to the table, fighting all the way. Leith's heart filled with pride: he had felt the bludgeoning force of their magic, and knew he could not have resisted as she did.

The Destroyer laughed, a mocking sound, and idly he flicked his arm in her direction. With a shriek her struggles ceased, and she took up the pen and signed her name as though it was the key to their victory.

'Now, the former Lord of Faltha and Bearer of the Jugom Ark will affix his name to the document,' the voice intoned, and without warning Leith was jerked out of his seat and across the platform. He could not even think of resisting. His face burned with shame as he signed his name under that of his mother. *They all saw my inability to resist? What will they think of me?* And he answered himself: *they are far too busy worrying about themselves*.

As Kannwar the Destroyer prepared to sign the terms of surrender, Leith's attention was again drawn to the crowd, their helpless eyes fixed on him as his were on them. He refused to watch the pen move across the paper. He could not bear to see the moment of his final defeat, the moment when his true life would end. There would be time left to him, he knew; but it would be a life of torment. He knew the Destroyer better than to hope for a quick death. He had seen what had been done to Stella.

A tomb-like silence enfolded the Hall of Meeting as at last Kannwar savoured his triumph. Leith's eyes were drawn upwards, following a delicately-carved column up, up to the great row of carvings depicting the Vale of Dona Mihst. He had seen them many times since the day he had first been admitted beyond the Iron Door, the day the corrupt Council of Faltha rejected the warning so hard-won by his father. There among the carvings high on the wall, just as down below in the hall, Kannwar took centre stage, kneeling to drink from the forbidden fountain, carven in jet-black stone at the moment of his triumph; there the Most High waited to loose the arrow – the Jugom Ark, Leith remembered poignantly – against he who would one day be named Destroyer. A slight breeze stirred the feathers of the arrow; its stone tip pointed at the grey figure who prepared to drink, unaware of his imminent doom.

Below, the Destroyer dipped his pen in the ink and lifted his good hand.

And then Leith froze, his skin tingling with fear, awe, wonder. It had taken him a moment to register what he had seen.

Mariswan feathers stirring in the breeze . . .

. . . yet the feathers were carved from stone.

Below the carvings, Kannwar put pen to parchment.

Stunned, Leith stared at the great carving. For the first time the Most High had a face, and alone of all the people in the hall, Leith knew whose face it was. A fragmentary glimpse, a moment forever graven on his memory. A face of alabaster, just as he had last seen it. The Right Hand of God revealed.

No spell could keep him silent; the scream had finally found an outlet. 'HAAAAAL!' he cried at the top of his voice.

The crowd turned; the Destroyer looked up, momentarily distracted.

At that moment the stone figure loosed the arrow in a

graceful, fluid motion. It flamed as it flew, remorselessly seeking its target. With a hollow thud it severed the Destroyer's one good hand cleanly from his arm, then slammed into the signing table and burst into incandescent brightness.

'No!' The Destroyer's howl cut through the shocked silence. Pain, fear and frustration intermixed. 'NO!'

Instantly a great clamour arose in the hall. Bhrudwan and Falthan alike were loosed from their momentary stasis by the cries of the world's conqueror. Confusion descended upon the place. People surged towards the signing table. Others, who had not seen what had happened, cried out in bewilderment. Panicked *Maghdi Dasht* laid about themselves, striking down anyone who moved. The Destroyer continued to bellow like a wounded animal.

Leith did not move. He remained transfixed, staring at the Jugom Ark embedded in the table, flaming as it always had, its feathers moving slightly. His hand tingled with the memory, and the Arrow glowed brighter still.

Hal.

CHAPTER 18

FIRE IN INSTRUERE

THE MOMENT STRETCHED OUT until Leith was sure time itself had been halted. And perhaps it had. If Hal could return from death itself to defeat the Destroyer, what was he not capable of?

<Pick it up.> The voice slammed back into his mind.

Hal! Hal, is that you? Hal, I'm so sorry! I should have spoken to you.

<Not quite Hal, but close enough for now. You'll understand later what has happened. You did try to talk to me; I haven't made it easy for you.>

Hal, what happened?

<Again, that's something for the future. For now, just pick up the Arrow – unless you want to take this moment to have one of our interesting debates.>

Leith laughed, the sound passing the sudden constriction in his throat with difficulty. *Once again, we'll leave that for the future*, he said to the voice, hardly able to contain his joy, and the voice laughed in response.

He took a pace forwards and the moment shattered. Cries and screams swirled around him, and a great booming explosion shook the hall at the exact moment a grey figure flashed past his eyes. Within moments he stood by the table, then reached out his hand . . .

. . . and time seemed to pause again.

I'm choosing to pick up this Arrow because I want to, he indicated defiantly, with a hint of self-mockery. *Not because anyone's making me, or from some sense of duty. Is that clear?*

<Very clear,> the voice said dryly. <But would you mind picking it up quickly?>

There it was. Leith had held it in his hand during his waking hours for more than half a year, and he could tell beyond doubt that it was the very same Arrow he had left lying in The Cauldron – just as the face he had seen on the carved wall was the same face he had left lying by the Arrow. And there beside the Arrow was a severed hand. Ancient and scarred, it looked more pitiable than terrible. *Get what you came for*, he told himself, and reached out before any doubt, any question of his worthiness could take hold. The Jugom Ark settled into his hand as easily as its voice had settled into his head.

'I'm sorry,' Leith said aloud. 'I'm so sorry.'

<I speak with the voice of a prophet,> the voice said. <This is my prophecy: that won't be the last time you apologise to me.>

I'm sure it won't be, his brother replied, amused. *So, what now?*

<That is up to you. I would add two cautions, however. Don't be surprised if not everyone here accepts your version of events. Few saw what you saw, and almost no one else here hears what you hear. And don't pursue your enemy to the death. Remember that his curse is to live, and not even the Jugom Ark can undo that.>

But there is someone . . .

<Of course. But that is up to you – and her. Just like you, her journey is not yet finished.>

Again the moment ended with a sudden surge of sound and movement. It took Leith a while to orient himself.

'Leith! Leith! What happened?' His mother took his arm, her tear-smeared face a mixture of shock and elation.

'That's something to be talked about later,' the Arrow-bearer answered calmly, unconsciously echoing the voice he had just spoken with. 'Is everyone safe?'

'We're not sure. Mahnum rounds them up even as we speak, but some have gone in pursuit of the Destroyer.'

'The Destroyer?' Leith had almost forgotten him. 'He will have found some way to use his magic to escape, surely?'

'We don't think so. We think the loss of his hand might have limited him. Most of his power was exercised through his hand. Remember?'

'If that is so, where is he?' Then he added, as his mind continued to clear: 'And where is Stella? Is she safe?'

'We have seen neither him nor her since the Arrow was loosed. We think she remains his hostage still.'

Mahnum put a hand on his son's shoulder. 'Something must be done about the enemies that remain,' he said, thinking things through as he spoke. 'The Destroyer appears to have allies in Instruere, and it would not surprise me to find him sheltering in their midst. However, you also have a City to speak to. The people of Instruere are no doubt frightened, and the sound of your words and the sight of the Jugom Ark will do much to comfort them. I do not know which you should do first, but if I was to advise you I would suggest that your prime responsibility is to speak to your people. Go to them, Leith, and leave the search for the Destroyer to others.'

Leith nodded, still half-dazed, but he recognised the wisdom of the counsel, even if it came from a father keen to keep alive the one son remaining to him. Already some of the commanders were running in pursuit of their enemies. As much as he wanted to find Stella, the Arrow burned in his hand. The Jugom Ark: the Arrow of Unity. Of responsibility.

His father leaned closer. 'And now I have a question for you, my son. I saw you talking to the Jugom Ark, and I swear I could almost hear it talk back to you. Would you tell me about it as we go? After the events we have just witnessed, I am prepared to believe anything, so make it as fanciful as you like.'

The southern Army had not expected to be opposed in their landing, so were taken by surprise by the blockade and the two siege towers. They had to endure another slow, frustrating week until the opposition could be assessed and worn down. Again the Saristrian admiral wore his discomfiture poorly, constantly cursing these ill-favoured lands for providing no true harbour. His men were harassed by a flotilla of small boats, and had to be constantly on their guard against poorly equipped but fiercely determined raiding parties. Reluctantly – for these were Falthans who opposed him – he allowed the Corrigians among his crew to deal with this threat in their own ruthless manner. Raiding parties were much more reluctant to try to scale a ship's side when one of their fellows could be seen hanging over the side from a makeshift gibbet at deck level.

One of the ruffians was eventually caught, and under duress agreed to show them a way around the blockade. The admiral had been told that the swampland of the delta was impenetrable to anyone not familiar with it, but sent men anyway, none of whom had returned; so he was delighted at his good fortune. But first, at the cost of a precious extra day, he sent the man out with three of his best officers, just in case the whole thing was a carefully planned ambush.

Finally the route was mapped. The mercenary revealed the existence of a southern path which the admiral decided to take on trust. He divided his forces: nine-tenths of the men would cross the northern delta and make for Instruere and the Inna Gate through Deuverre, while a much smaller force of less than three thousand men would use the southern path and look to enter Instruere by the Struere Gate. The ships would be left to fend for themselves. This last was a grievous situation, but since there was no telling whether Instruere was already occupied by the Destroyer – and the presence of a blockade indicated this might be the case, and, further, that they were expected – the Saristrian admiral considered he had no choice.

By dawn the divided southern forces were well on their way across the swamps, north and south. Two days of stiff walking enabled Graig to regain his land-legs, and just before sunset on the second day he and the rest of the northern force could see Instruere's walls in the southern distance. And they could see something else: from a dozen places behind the wall rose plumes of black or grey smoke. The town had clearly been the site of a great battle.

The cautious admiral, the greatest tactician of his generation according to his king, sent out spies. And not just to Instruere: north and south he sent them, looking to find the trail left by the passing army, thus to estimate the force he might be contending with. Within half an hour one of his spies came sprinting back to camp with the surprising news that a large Bhrudwan force was camped less than a league east of them.

'I guess around fifty thousand souls,' the spy gasped out. 'We would have run into them had we continued on our course.' Graig sighed heavily: if that number were left outside the City, how many more might be hidden within?

'Possibly none at all,' the admiral replied with a frown, and the young Nemohaimian was mortified to realise that he must have spoken aloud. 'The reports my king received suggested no more than that number were in the original Bhrudwan army. So,' the man continued, counting off the possibilities on his carefully manicured fingers, 'the Bhrudwans might have done some forced recruiting.' He turned to his spy. 'Did you see any evidence of Falthans among the Bhrudwans?'

'Sir, there were a large number of men – perhaps two-fifths of the army – sitting on the ground without cover. I did not think to look more closely, but they could have been captives.'

The admiral went back to his fingers. 'Might the whole Falthan army have surrendered? That is another possibility, though unlikely in my opinion. More likely is that the Bhrudwans have yet to lay a proper siege to Instruere, and that the fires within are the result of some sort of incendiary missile used in an initial assault.'

He paced about for a moment, then stopped, legs wide apart as though he stood on the deck of a ship. First he addressed the spy. 'You will return to the Bhrudwan camp at dawn tomorrow, and this time make a full observation. I expect your report an hour after sunrise.' Then he turned to Graig and Geinor, who stood with the officers of the southern force. 'Meanwhile I will send some men to knock at the gate of this City. Let us see exactly what condition it is in, and who rules it, before we decide what to do. Graig, at first light I want you to take your father and ten thousand of my men. Go and make it a loud knock.'

It took even the Lords of Fear a few seconds to react when the Arrow of the Most High struck their lord. They all felt the enormous power of it lacerate their souls, and grovelled witless where they stood as the Jugom Ark burned beside their master's hand. The crushing power eased when the Falthan boy picked it up, but access to their inner powers still proved impossible. Fortunately, they possessed many other abilities in no way limited by the burning of an arrow, however magical.

Swords out, they summoned up all their hard-earned discipline and locked their pain behind walls of their iron wills, as taught them by the ancient practice of *Mul*. A signal from their leader sent all those who had recovered sprinting towards the rear of the hall, where their lord had sought temporary safety in a small annexe. By day's end they would undoubtedly be far fewer than thirteen thirteens, but such losses were acceptable if they could bring their master through the snares of the enemy.

They moved swiftly, with an unmatched grace, only to find the way to the annexe held against them.

'*Nu Achtal ennach tupic!*' their leader cried to the figure who barred their way. '*Nu Achtal tupic!*' But the man did not move, instead slowly raising a sword he'd found somewhere and readying himself for combat.

This man was one of theirs. They had heard rumours. It was known that Deorc of Andratan was himself an adept. Though rejected for *Dasht* training, he found himself another path into the Undying Man's service, and had given four *Maghdi* orders to pursue a man westwards into Faltha. It was assumed these orders came from the Lord of Bhrudwo, but it transpired this was not so: Deorc wanted news of the Right Hand for his own purposes. It was believed the four men had met dishonourable deaths at the hands of mere peasants, failing to carry out the orders they had been given. Now it appeared that one of the men lived, and to his shame he would be forever branded *ennach*, an outcast no longer of the order. But, impossible as it seemed, the man had been turned, and now set his will against theirs.

He would not survive, of course. He was a mere acolyte, not yet one of the thirteen thirteens, and the sword was clearly not his own. Nevertheless, because the *Maghdi Dasht* seldom fought each other in earnest, there was keen interest in who would be given the chance to match with him. The chief of their order, a man from whom many had received their first scars in training, had killing rights. He unlimbered his own sword and beckoned the others to step back. His opponent would not be allowed to use the onlookers to cramp him.

The two men came together with a crash that sounded like an explosion. For Achtal the encounter was pure joy. He watched the chief of the *Maghdi Dasht* look in vain for fear in the eyes of his adversary. Left and right he pivoted, now blocking, now sending his weapon forward like a snake seeking its prey. He was at a disadvantage, he knew, as he did not want to move aside from the opening and allow his brothers to help their master.

Not my brothers, he told himself. *Hal is my brother*. He had heard Hal's voice when the burning dart landed on the signing table, and had not been surprised.

His opponent swung vigorously at his front foot. Instead

of jerking back Achtal moved only fractionally, then followed the blade with his own, pinning it to the stone wall. It burst from its wielder's fingers and fell to the floor with a clatter. A deadly silence descended as the renegade Bhrudwan pressed his sword-tip against the throat of the Lord of Fear.

'Hal died but I still hear his voice. I die and I meet him again,' Achtal said to the head of his order. 'Who will you meet?'

In went the blade and with a great sigh the chief of the *Maghdi Dasht* fell.

Angered beyond reason, another black-cloaked warrior threw himself at this traitor to their brotherhood. After a period of furious fighting four bodies lay at Achtal's feet, but they all knew he had been fortunate in at least two matches. They could see that he was tiring, yet still approached him one at a time.

Farr grabbed the arm of Axehaft, the Warden of the Fodhram, drawing his attention to the fighting at the far end of the hall. 'The Destroyer has escaped into the Inner Chamber, by the look of it. Hal's pet Bhrudwan is besieged by the *Maghdi Dasht*. Have you ever wondered what it would be like to cross swords with them?'

'Ever since one of the Fear-Lords took Mulberry's hand for nothing more than sharing a joke, I have not wanted anything else,' the small man said grimly. 'But we have no weapons.'

'No; but I can see four Lords of Fear who won't be needing theirs. If we are very careful, we might be able to snatch them up before their fellows know we're there. Then Achtal would have a chance.'

'Four swords? Why don't we find two more sword-arms? I know just who to ask!' he cried, and hurried off towards the Iron Door.

A few moments later he returned with three other men. Two were Widuz, the third an enormous Fenni who was easily the biggest man Farr had ever seen, and who carried a pole he had found somewhere like it was a twig. Together the five of them crept towards the massed *Maghdi Dasht*, the lust of battle in their blood, uncaring of the outcome.

Her simple spun cloth dress turned red from the blood, but his twinned forearm grip was unrelenting. He stood close behind her, with her head wedged between his forearms, and the two stumps – one old, the other new – jutted out either side of her head. His touch burned her just as it always had, and she struggled in his grip.

'Stay still, wretch!' he hissed, and each breath he took seemed to her to be paining him as though he had a throat full of knives. He was drawing on her somehow, taking advantage of the link he had forged between them with his blood. *He must have lost his magic!* she realised, but once again she could do nothing to free herself. The old frustration washed over her: she had been within feet of them all, had so nearly freed herself from his compulsion in the moments after the blessed Arrow had struck him down – *but why, why, why couldn't it have taken him in the chest!* – only to be dragged by pure force down the hall, past frightened people who did nothing to help her, and into the Inner Chamber, where the Company had met the Council of Faltha.

He began drawing on her as soon as he wedged the door closed. Some sort of spell to prevent the door being opened, no doubt. Now he worked at the shuttered and barred window, trying to force it open. 'It is just a window!' he growled at one point, frustrated at his lack of power. His sweat ran down the back of her neck. Again and again he bent his will, and hers, on the metal bars, until he stepped back with a gasp of satisfaction.

'Ah, Stella,' he said fondly, turning his ruined face towards hers. 'What would I do without you?' And with no warning he heaved her forward into the window, which collapsed outwards and downwards on to the sunlit lawn. She was unconscious before she hit the ground.

The crash echoed through the locked door. Achtal jerked slightly, and rather than sliding inside a ferocious blow from his sixth opponent, he caught it on his left shoulder. A roar went up from the gathered throats.

At that moment four figures rushed from right and left, dived at the dead warriors and claimed their swords. One of them, clipped by a blow from one of the *Maghdi Dasht* somewhat more alert than his fellows, crashed to the floor and did not move. The other three stood facing the assembled might of Bhrudwo's warrior cadre, and to Farr at least the idea of facing the Lords of Fear suddenly seemed less sensible than when he had first suggested it.

The warrior who had just dealt Achtal his first wound held up his hand, then cried something in their language. Instantly the entire group pivoted as one and sprinted away down the hall, knocking people over left and right as they went. Achtal slumped to the floor, absolutely spent, his broad hand pinching the shoulder wound closed.

Farr turned to his fellows. 'One of you see to this man. He is a hero.' He then instructed the big Fenni warrior to break down the door, which he did with little difficulty. 'Closing spell gone,' mumbled the Bhrudwan warrior. 'Lord of Bhrudwo gone also. *Maghdi Dasht* seek him.'

'Then they had better not find him,' Farr said, and dashed

into the Inner Chamber. 'This way!' he called. 'He can't be far ahead!'

Leith wanted to find Stella with all his heart. *Too many lost,* his soul cried at him, ready to provide the numerical evidence. *No more!* However, the hand of duty rested heavily on his shoulders. Once again the Jugom Ark laid claim to him. He ran lightly over the ruins of the Iron Door, then negotiated the corridor and burst out into the open.

Thousands of confused and frightened people had gathered there. Many more would even now be seeking any way they could find out of the City. He could imagine the chaos down at the Docks and at Struere Gate. But these citizens stayed to find out what their City's fate would be. He had no great speech to offer them, drained as he was. Instead, he pushed into their midst and held the Jugom Ark above his head.

'Behold!' he cried, and the Arrow amplified his voice. 'The Destroyer is defeated! The surrender remains unsigned, and he binds us no longer!' His words brought a cheer, but not as great as he expected. *Some of these may be the people who cheered the Destroyer, and others may be too stunned to receive the news.*

'The Destroyer lives still, and is at large in the City,' he warned them. 'We will find him and drive him out! Return to your homes and do not venture out until morning. And another warning: if you are one of those who chose to cheer the arrival of our great enemy, consider your options. There will be no place in this City for you unless you change your allegiance. Or do you think you can hide from the all-consuming Arrow?'

Unbidden, his mind flashed back to when last he had

addressed an Instruian crowd. Then there had also been fear, but that fear had been held in check by optimism: the battle was to be fought so far away, and they believed in the Jugom Ark. Now the reality visited them all in its full terror, and numbness replaced hope. The great Falthan army was somehow lost, and they did not yet know what had happened to their soldiers. Apparently even the burning Arrow could not bring them much cheer.

Leith told them about the battles at the Gap and Vulture's Craw, finishing by explaining where the army was now held. Some of his hearers were encouraged by the news, but not many. Most figured the odds, and realised the chances of seeing their loved ones again were less than even.

Gradually the crowd scattered, many heading to the northern walls to maybe catch a glimpse of the captive Falthan army. Leith turned to go back to the Hall of Meeting, and was startled to find the Falthan leaders standing behind him. Before he could open his mouth the questions came, all variants on 'What are we to do now?'

'Too many things,' Leith said sharply. 'The Great Enemy is loose in Instruere, and may have already escaped—'

'Is that not what we want him to do?' asked the Captain of the Instruian Guard.

'Not while he has Stella!' Leith said, and the Haufuth shouted his agreement. 'We must find him and make him give her up!'

Some of his allies knew nothing about whom they referred to. 'We must drive him out or, better, see him dead,' the Ice Queen of Sna Vaztha said with feeling. 'We gain nothing if he remains alive.'

The Arrow-bearer turned wearily to Kurr. 'Old friend, would you organise a group to track the Destroyer?'

To his surprise, the old farmer shook his head. 'Farr Storrsen has already left in pursuit of the Dark One, taking strength of arms with him. Farr will find him, if he can be found at all.

'I must speak with you, Leith,' Kurr said, with gentler speech than the boy had ever heard him use. 'Please. I have . . . not told you all the truth about myself. There are things that you must hear, so you will understand what has happened.' Leith looked at the old man more closely. Grey and tired, the farmer looked his age and more for the first time Leith could remember.

'Yes, of course,' he replied. 'Just as soon as we find the Destroyer—'

'You are wasting your time if you think to corner and kill him,' Kurr continued, voice low enough that even those nearest to them could not hear clearly. 'You heard the voice; you heard him tell us that the Destroyer cannot be killed.'

'That doesn't mean we shouldn't—' Leith stopped and stared at the old farmer. 'How do you know? How did you hear the voice? Do you know who it is?' Leith's mouth remained open in surprise.

'It took me a while,' said the old man sadly. 'But yes, I know who it is. You see, in a way, I was his father.'

The *Maghdi Dasht* found their master staggering along an open sewer with his servant-girl slung over his shoulder, clearly near the end of his strength. It was an indication of just how thoroughly he had them in thrall that none of them thought to seize the moment and supplant him. Instead they emerged from the shadows on either side of the street and surrounded their lord.

A dozen of them knelt before him and offered their lives. Their master knew spells to sustain him, maybe even to break through the grip of the Truthspell that had rebounded on its caster, and perhaps set him free to reclaim all his old power. But the spells would require strength from somewhere. The Destroyer considered a moment, then nodded; and in the middle of a narrow Instruian street he drained dry three of his most loyal servants in an attempt to regain his strength, and left their bodies lying by the sewer.

He failed to break the Truthspell, as he had known he would – hadn't he himself woven it? – yet enough power was made available to spin an illusion of invisibility, which he cast over himself and his Lords of Fear. One of his warrior-servants reached out to take the burden from him, but he shook his head and held on to her legs, even though the effort clearly took a severe toll on him. 'No one touches her but me,' he spat. They backed away from him, in awe of his fierce pride.

'Take me to the nearest section of the wall,' he commanded. His *Maghdi Dasht* began a slow walk down the street, heading eastwards. 'You can go faster than that!' he hissed at them, and they broke into a trot. Stumbling and bent, but not broken, the Lord of Bhrudwo struggled along with his men. *Not broken.*

Down street after street, keeping to the narrow alleys and avoiding open spaces. Hurrying to beat the onset of evening. Dragging himself across the last square before the wall. Too tired to sustain the Net of Vanishing. Up the stairway that led to the path along the top. Along the wall to where he could see the Aleinus River. 'Now, each of you put forth your power,' he told them. 'I hear the Arrow-bearer caused the river to run dry. We will do better. Then when we reach the far side, we can begin to plan our revenge!'

* * *

Farr and his companions clattered across the square. Their quarry were silhouetted against the darkening sky, clearly visible as they moved along the battlements. Amazingly, Achtal rejoined them as they ran across the City, bringing all the *losian* leaders with him. His wound was closed, though the jagged tear in his cloak remained. To Farr it seemed as though the Bhrudwan had emerged fresh from days of rest, rather than having just been involved in a series of duels with the most deadly warriors in the world. When Achtal saw his former master he cried out like a hound on the scent of a fox.

With a gesture the Vinkullen man divided his force in half, sending one group to the left to find a way up the wall behind the *Maghdi Dasht*, while he took the rest to the right, meaning to appear on the wall ahead of them. He could not tell if those on the wall had seen their approach: he assumed they had. There would be no surprise attack, and the inevitable confrontation would undoubtedly cost many of them their lives.

Up the stairs they pounded, and then along the wall. But where had the enemy gone? One black figure remained: as they watched, it leaped from the battlement out into space. Farr rushed to the nearest crenellation, to see the figure slow somehow in the air, then settle down on the grass as though he had simply stepped off a stair.

'Magic,' a voice behind him breathed.

'Yes,' said Achtal, dragging a limp body with him and dumping it in front of Farr. 'Magic costs them much.' Horribly fascinated, Farr stared at the corpse, which looked as though someone had sucked out its bones and innards, leaving little more than a skin. The eyes were blank, windows into emptiness.

Down by the river's edge the remaining *Maghdi Dasht* were doing something. Their eerie chant rose up to the ears of those watching impotently, unable to jump the many feet to the ground and knowing that the nearest gate was much too far away. And as they watched, the river began to solidify in a line stretching from where the Lords of Fear stood across to the far bank.

'They make a bridge of water,' Achtal commented, listening to the song. 'They freeze the water and will walk across on the ice.'

'How do they have the power, when their master is injured so badly?' Farr asked him.

'They are of water, so work it more easily,' came the reply. 'But look! They still die to feed the bridge.'

It took everything they had. One by one the *Maghdi Dasht* collapsed, falling into the river from the fragile bridge they had conjured. Less than a hundred remained when finally the Destroyer stood safely on the southern shore.

He turned then and raised both his arms, facing the city that had once again bested him. Fires glowed in the darkness, making the water shimmer at his feet. 'I curse you, City of Faltha!' he cried, pouring two thousand years of poison into the words. 'May your rulers never find peace, and may your people die unsatisfied!' Then the Lord of Bhrudwo, still with Stella on his shoulder, spun on his heel and set out, no doubt to try to find what was left of his army.

The Hermit of Bandits' Cave sat down on a box marked 'Dates/Sarista/17 Days' and took stock as he tried to regain his breath. The sound of pursuit had lessened out here in the Docks: people seemed to have taken refuge in their homes, and his pursuers were obviously content to have driven him and his followers away from the houses and tenements of Instruere.

Burn! They will all burn! The word of knowledge must be fulfilled!

<Oh, but it has, and you did not see it.>

No! The Hermit fell to the floor of the storage shed, clutching his head in his hands. *No! Get out of my head!*

<When was the first time you put aside my voice for your own, yet claimed it was me you heard? Why did you not heed my warning when I came to you in your cave?>

The blue-robed body jerked across the dirty floor as the inner battle raged. *When did you come?*

<You would not accept my rebuke, and you will not accept it now. Thus you will be destroyed by that which might have saved you.>

You never came! Get out of my head! I never saw you! Don't leave me!

The Hermit rolled on the floor, trying to shake the voice from his mind. He crashed into a small table on which a trader's accounts were kept, knocking over the torch with which he had fired all those houses in the City . . .

He and his few remaining followers had run from the Destroyer's fall, snatching up burning brands and seeking places to set alight in fulfilment of their vision. Instruere must be cleansed; the corrupt rulers and evil-doers must be driven out. Somewhere on their flight from the Hall of Meeting a mob gathered, trying to stop them from their fanatical task. The Presiding Elder fell to them, unable to keep up, and was crushed under their feet. Across the City the Ecclesia had run, heading west towards the Docks, stopping whenever the pursuit dropped back to put their torches to another tenement. The shrieks of those trapped by their flames seemed to them the cries of the wicked, and the smoke and flames the evidence of judgment.

One by one his followers had been taken by the howling mob, until he was the only one left. Through the unguarded Dock Gate he had run with a torch in each hand, barely twenty paces ahead of his chasers. Ahead was a maze of small buildings and narrow, dead-end alleys; but he could not stop to consider his path. Could not stop . . . *my path had long ago been set before me.* He laughed raggedly, then turned and pitched one of the torches into the following crowd, dragging more shrieks from the throats of the unclean, seeing once again the bright, clean flame blossom like a spring flower in freshly ploughed ground . . .

For a moment he came to himself. The wicked voice had left him weak and shaking: he pressed his eyes tightly shut until the words it had spoken faded from his mind. Eventually he rolled over on to his side and manoeuvred himself into a sitting position, then opened his eyes. Immediately he shaded them against the flickering light that seemed to surround him.

I was faithful! he raged. *I spoke only the words I heard! Hundreds came to hear me speak the words of the Most High. But few would heed my warnings, and so their punishment is just! I am the Anointed One! The Fire falls at my command!*

Behind him came the crash of timbers as the small shed began to collapse, consumed by the flames from the Hermit's torch. His eyes came wide open, and he realised the peril he was in. His robe caught fire, and flames dripped down on him from the thatched roof above . . . already his hair was alight . . .

The vengeful citizens of Instruere who had been attacked

by flame-wielding men – Bhrudwans, they assumed – were drawn to the screams, initially thinking that yet another innocent had been taken by the fire. A figure of flame staggered to the door of the shed, arms wide, mouth open. Then they recognised their tormentor, and watched in silence as he enacted some crazy rite of self-immolation, clutching the door-frame with weakening fingers until finally the shed came crashing down on top of him.

The Falthan commanders were clearly desperate to leave the City and go north to where their army was still – for all they knew – held by the Bhrudwan force. Perhaps the *Maghdi Dasht* had made their way north to their army. If they could make a bridge across the river in one direction, why not in the other? It might be that, even as they waited in frustration, their soldiers were being executed, one by one. It was their duty, they had to go.

But clearly they could not. Fires had taken hold all through the western part of the City, and the Arrow-bearer had commanded them to help put them out. No one thought to disobey the man. It was through him, after all, and the trick he had played on the Undying Man, they had gained their own freedom. Few people were entirely clear what had happened that afternoon, and they discussed it as they handed buckets to each other.

'I saw the Jugom Ark flash across the hall and strike the Destroyer,' said the Captain of the Instruian Guard. 'The wielder of the Arrow is a magician of rare power! I witnessed him dry up the Aleinus River to make his escape from Instruere.'

'But why did he wait so long to strike?' one of the Fodhram asked. 'If he had the power to defeat the Destroyer, why did he not do so much earlier? Why did he refuse the single combat offered him?'

'Yes!' another of the Instruians agreed, then paused a moment to pass his bucket on to a man who dashed into the burning tenement. 'I saw hundreds of those under my command slain. Why didn't he do something about it?'

Perdu clapped the Instruian on the shoulder, turning him half-around. 'I might as well ask you why you let this building catch alight. Why didn't you prevent it catching fire?'

'Because I was too busy with another fire!' came the indignant response. 'How could I prevent it when I was not here?'

'Exactly,' said Perdu. 'Leith is a young man, not a god. He could not foresee what the Destroyer would do.'

'But he refused the combat,' said a Deuverran officer. 'I was there. You can't tell me otherwise. The Destroyer challenged him and the Arrow-bearer just walked away.'

Perdu spread his arms. His wife and children were somewhere in this City, along with other Fenni who had not made the journey east, but as yet he had not found them. They could be anywhere, even in this tenement. 'I don't know why he refused!' he said irritably. 'Perhaps his courage failed him. At least he did something about it when it mattered!'

'It mattered to my brother,' growled a youth from Straux. 'He was caught up in the fighting on the two hills west of The Cauldron. Dead or captive, I don't know. Will he bring the dead back to life with that arrow of his?'

The adopted Fenni put down his bucket and stared at the youth. 'I'm sorry to hear of your loss,' he said softly. 'But I saw the boy you rail against suffer under the weight of our expectations. You had better pray that you are not chosen one day to be the instrument of our rescue. I doubt that you would fare as well as Leith!' He kicked his bucket over and stalked away.

'What ails that one?' the boy from Straux asked those around him. 'Why did he take it so personally? I just wanted some answers!'

'Because he was one of the northern Company, that's why,' said the Captain of the Guard. 'He's seen more in the last year than you will ever see in your life. I would keep my mouth closed in future, if I were you. Such criticism may not prove all that popular in the new Faltha.'

The boy grunted and picked up the overturned bucket. Around them the City glowed orange, slowly fading as the night drew on and one by one the many tenement fires were doused.

It was not until the hours before dawn that the hundreds of firefighters were able to draw breath. Leith, his Arrow but one flame among many, sent messengers to fetch his commanders to a meeting. It took more than an hour before the last of his captains made his way to the Hall of Meeting, stumbling with weariness.

'The fires are still burning, but everyone who was in danger has been rescued,' his chief clerk told them in a tired voice. 'My lords, the City has been searched extensively, and no sign remains of those who started the fires, save a score or more bodies.'

'And the *Maghdi Dasht?*' Modahl inquired in his deep voice. 'Any reports of them still within the walls?'

'No, my lord. It appears that they all escaped over the wall and across the river, just as we were told.' Here he indicated Farr, who grunted at the man's sceptical tone.

'We heard it was they that started the fires,' said Sir Chalcis of the Knights of Fealty. 'We searched the streets and alleys, but did not find any evidence of their passage.' His voice was softer than was his habit: he had seen too much, and it had been one of his knights who had falsely interpreted his vision. The deaths of so many knights, and the failure of their order to live up to the ideals of Conal Greatheart their founder, weighed heavily on him.

'No,' said the Haufuth. 'It was the followers of one of our former companions, a man we befriended. He claimed to hear the words of the Most High. Perhaps he did; I half thought he did. He formed the Ecclesia, and for a while it seemed that he and his followers were a force for good—'

Someone in the group snorted derisively: the sound echoed in the huge chamber.

'Whatever his intentions,' the Haufuth continued, 'it is clear they were corrupted somehow, driven by a vision of good and evil that, if fulfilled, would have seen the deaths of many people. He made alliances with the remnants of Escaigne, and then with the Arkhos of Nemohaim.'

At least four members of the group shuddered, remembering their former association with the traitorous Arkhos. Former Arkhoi themselves, they knew they had been lucky to escape with their lives when so many of their fellows were dead. They glanced around the group who sat on the front benches, their eyes on a level with the platform on which the signing table still stood. Someone had disposed of the hand. What might have become of them had the Destroyer gained control of Instruere?

'How many people have we lost today?' Leith asked, trying to suppress the dispassionate voice in his mind already beginning to recite the numbers.

'Well, my lord, we rescued many citizens from the fires, but perhaps a hundred people were unluckily consumed before we could get to them—'

Farr Storrsen had heard enough. 'We can hear the death count later. What won't wait are the questions, and I have two. First, what happened yesterday afternoon? And second, how can we relieve our soldiers out there on the plain?'

It was late – or early, depending on how one looked at it – and there were things Leith did not want to examine too closely. Not yet. Not when he didn't have any clear thoughts. However, there was a high degree of agreement with Farr's sentiment, and as the demands for answers became more strident, the Arrow-bearer nodded wearily; but before he could begin, Modahl stood and motioned for silence.

'There is a misconception abroad that must be cleared up now,' he said forcefully. 'I have heard talk that my grandson, the Bearer of the Arrow, refused to face the Destroyer in single combat. Further, I have heard it said we were betrayed by his brother, who took up the challenge in the name of the Arrow-bearer with no expectation of winning, thereby placing us in his hand. Now, Hal Mahnumsen cannot defend himself, as he is dead; and Leith Mahnumsen will not speak in his own defence, as he does not consider the ignorant criticisms of others worth answering. So I will speak on their behalf.

'Such a challenge as Leith received would no doubt have broken many of you by sheer force. Some of you may not know about the magic of the Wordweave, with which the Destroyer fortified his words. The Destroyer bound himself with the challenge, and had Leith accepted it without thought, would have bound us also. However, he took some time to consider it. To sift the task from the trap. Where is the shame in that?' He gazed at those around him, many of whom still looked mystified.

Leith got to his feet. 'No, grandfather; that will not do,' he said. 'The truth must be told. I've held the Jugom Ark in my hand for many months, but I didn't want to find out the truth about it. I was afraid, you see,' he said, trying to hold back the tears of shame. 'I thought the destiny I was being pushed into was stealing away my life. I didn't listen carefully enough to those who tried to instruct me in what they knew about the Arrow. So when the Destroyer challenged me, I couldn't see how it would help me defeat him.'

'Leith, you don't have to do this,' Indrett said to him, tugging at his cloak, but he shook off her hand.

'Some of you know that I was very angry with Hal, my brother. Hal has always been magical, has always been able to see further into the realm of the unseen than anyone I know. It's so hard to live with someone like that; always his advice proved right, and I seemed useless beside him. In my anger it seemed to me that he constantly sabotaged my efforts to save Faltha from the Destroyer, and so I – I turned my back on him.' The tears were coming now, there was nothing he could do to stop them. 'I hurt him deeply, more deeply than I think anyone realised. So when the challenge was issued and I did not take it up, he sought to fight on my behalf, I guess to save me from dying at the Destroyer's hand.

'It should have been me lying on the ground with the sword in my chest. That, I think, was the fate destined for the Bearer of the Arrow. Had I accepted my fate, then perhaps many others might have lived. Certainly Hal would have lived, and I would be dead, not alive with this huge weight of guilt pressing in on me.' He stood there, alone and forlorn, speaking as though separated by a great distance from the rest of humanity.

Kurr left his chair and walked out in front of them, his face carved from stone. 'Sit down, boy, and listen to what I have to say. When you have heard me out, then you can decide whether you are to blame for what has happened.'

He sighed deeply, then stepped back a pace so his old frame leaned on the platform. 'I would have preferred this story to have been for Leith's ears only, but I suppose it is more than time to pay for my old sins.' He cleared his throat nervously. 'Nearly fifty years ago I left these parts and travelled north to Firanes, trying to escape my past. I did many things during those battles that I'm ashamed of, but we had to survive. I'd seen too many of my friends and family die in the battles of Sivithar, and despite my rank as a Watcher, I wanted no more to do with the politics of Faltha.

'For many years I lived a solitary life in a small cottage on Swill Down, a place not far from Loulea, the village where the Arrow-bearer comes from. Then, about twenty years ago, a number of strange things began to happen in the district. For no good reason healthy people became sick overnight and died, and others were found dead of dreadful wounds. For a year Loulea Vale became a place of nightly fear. Few people now remember those times.

'During those days I met a young woman and we fell in love. She lived in Vapnatak, a town a day's walk east of Loulea, and I would happily walk there to pay her court. On one such day I surprised a dark figure leaning over something by the side of the road: I shouted and waved my quarterstaff, driving him off. When I reached the place he had stood, I discovered two bodies. They had been ripped apart.

'From that day on I knew something unholy had made its home in Loulea Vale. However, I remembered the months of struggle and the things I was forced to do in Sivithar, evil things in the name of good, so I said nothing. Keeping out of the public eye was more important to me than warning the Vale. May the Most High forgive me!'

'Carry on, old man! Explain what this has to do with the defeat of the Destroyer!'

The old farmer laughed. 'Oh, Farr! You remind me so much of a young man I used to know, one who should have died in Sivithar all those years ago, one who stands before you now. I will explain all, if you will but retain your patience.

'Many weeks and many deaths later, I came one day to Vapnatak to find my Tinei's parents distraught. Someone – or something – had spirited her away during the night. For months I searched, but found nothing.

'Then one day I saw a woman walking up the path to my cottage. I looked more closely, and saw it was Tinei, my intended. Something dreadful had been done to her in the intervening months. Her face was thin and ragged from abuse, and she limped, crippled down one side. She was also with child.

'Listen to me, and please do not question my words, not yet, not until I've finished. For days she could not speak to me at all, but when she could finally talk, she told me that she had been made the slave of the Destroyer, the Undying Man himself. I did not believe her, of course. How could the Destroyer be there in Firanes, when his ancient home was in Andratan at the other end of the world? Yet obviously something had hurt her, and any man with courage should have sought that something out and confronted it. I did not. I told her parents I had found her wandering witless, and that her child was mine. I doubt they believed me, but they would have nothing further to do with me, accusing me of abducting her myself.

'Eventually her child was born, and it was poorly formed, a cripple down its right side. Tinei would have nothing to do with it, and shrieked when I tried to place it in her arms. I tried to raise the child, but I would not have made a good father. Tinei refused even to sit in the same room as the infant. So I took the child to the village, waited until a childless couple I knew were walking along the road, and left it where they might find it.'

White-faced, Leith turned to his parents. They both sat bolt upright, clutching at each other as though buffeted by a strong wind.

'Tinei never fully recovered from what was done to her. We did not have children of our own. Then just after the Midwinter's Day before last, she died. That chapter of my shameful life was over, I thought.

'Yet it was not. I learned that the man and woman who had adopted my wife's child had been abducted by Bhrudwans, and the awful truth began to work its way down into my heart. Why would the Bhrudwans be interested in Mahnum and Indrett? Yes, Mahnum had knowledge the Destroyer wanted to suppress, but would that knowledge have been enough to prevent his army attacking Faltha? As we have seen, it was not. No, there must have been some other reason the Destroyer was interested, and I could think of nothing else than the crippled son of Tinei, Hal Mahnumsen. Hal and his brother left with myself and the village Haufuth as we set out to rescue their parents. But, as you know, we soon became part of a much larger story.'

Indrett stood, and she shook from head to foot. 'You – you – why did you say nothing? We wanted to know! Tinei's child? Who was the father?'

'I did not find out who the father was, girl,' he said gently.

'But the evidence points in one direction. He must have been someone steeped in magic, if Hal's powers are any guide. Moreover, he was an evil man. I am sure he was responsible for the awful things that happened in Loulea Vale. Did you think I would ruin your life with news such as this?'

'Are you saying . . . do you think his father was Bhrudwan?' Mahnum stood at his wife's side, hands clenched.

Kurr sighed. 'If we have learned anything, it is that the Bhrudwans are people just like us. You of anyone should know this, Trader, since you lived among them. No, I do not think his father was a mere Bhrudwan.'

'A Lord of Fear?'

'Undoubtedly,' Kurr said, firing the affirmation at them. 'Who knows how long the Vale was spied upon? How long the Destroyer has known that someone he fears would come from Loulea? Otherwise why would he send such a one to spy on us?'

'Hold!' Phemanderac fairly leaped into the air. 'What you are saying cannot be! Listen, man: are you suggesting the Destroyer *knew* the Right Hand of the Most High was to be found in Loulea Vale, and that he sent a *Maghdi Dasht to bring him into being?* Why would the Undying Man want a challenger, long prophesied, to rise up against him? No, we are still missing something. It all comes down to the identity of the Right Hand of the Most High. Who is he?'

'Perhaps that will become clear if we examine the Destroyer's desperate ploy at the height of the war,' Kurr said, silencing the philosopher. 'After the Battle of The Cauldron he thinks he has us beaten. Then he discovers that we have another twenty thousand men still on the battlefield; which, through trickery and magic, he thinks is twice that. He is pinned and in danger of defeat. So he proposes single combat, and prepares binding magic in the event of his victory. Hal fights him, and holds his own until – well, from what I saw, he allowed the thrust that killed him. I don't expect anyone to agree with me, but that's what I saw.

'Now the magic binds us, and will be sealed at the Hall of Meeting. For me the crucial piece of knowledge is whether Hal knew that the Truthspell could be broken if the Destroyer could not sign the surrender document. We will never know for sure, but I ask you this: who amongst us knew more about magic than Hal? If anyone would have known that we still had a chance, even if we lost the single combat, it was he. I think he planned on it. I think he used the Destroyer's power against him. So, now for it: what happened yesterday?

'Let me tell you what I saw. The commander of our army and the Arrow-bearer both signed the document, then made way for the Destroyer. I watched with a heavy heart, but . . . I realise how easy this is to say . . . I thought something might happen. I heard a noise, looked up and saw the Arrow coming down from the ceiling to strike the Destroyer. The spell broke, and chaos erupted as we were set free from the spell, able to oppose our conquerors.'

'But – who loosed the Arrow?' The question came from a dozen throats. Leith held his tongue: *not yet.*

'I saw who fired the Jugom Ark,' said the Haufuth. 'It came from the great carving above us. Look! Is there not supposed to be an arrow in the bow of the Most High?'

They followed his outstretched arm with their gaze. There, high above them, stood the carven figure of the Most High, bow tightly drawn – but with no arrow.

Leith clapped his hands, and instantly all eyes were on him. He took a deep breath, then told them what he had seen and heard. In complete silence he explained to them about the voice, and told them that it continued still. Mahnum and Indrett wept openly, his mother sobbing with joy and with sorrow.

'It was Hal's face I saw, Hal's voice I heard,' Leith summarised. 'I think Kurr is right. He planned this all along.'

'Then we were rescued by the deliberate sacrifice of your brother,' said Phemanderac. 'Loosing the Jugom Ark against the Destroyer could be seen as the last stroke of the single combat. Hal died knowing that somehow he could come back long enough to shoot the Arrow.'

'As he had done once before,' Leith said.

It took even the Dhaurian scholar a minute to work out what Leith suggested. 'Are you saying that Hal . . . that Hal and the Most High . . .'

'Does it really matter?' Leith countered. 'But how else could my brother have worn the face of the carving? Look closely, those of you who know Hal. Is that not his face still?' They moved as a group over to the far wall, and stared up at the white face, featureless no longer. Not Hal exactly, but a face that might possibly have been Hal in the full maturity of manhood.

'A problem, young sirs,' spoke Sir Chalcis in an agitated voice. 'Suggesting that a crippled boy was in fact the Most High incarnate is bad enough, but you now claim that he was also the son of an evil Bhrudwan lord! This discussion sails too close to blasphemy for my taste.' He stood stiffly and pulled on his gauntlets. 'If you are in fact a Dhaurian,' he said, addressing Phemanderac, 'you should know the error you commit. The Knights of Fealty will now withdraw from this alliance and return to their castle. The vision of Sir Amasian has yet to be fulfilled.' He nodded once as if underlining his pronouncement, and left the hall.

Leith shrugged his shoulders, and looked around the hall for help or inspiration, but there was none forthcoming.

'He makes a good point about the mystery of Hal's birth,' Phemanderac conceded finally. 'But what we believe about Hal makes no difference to our material condition now. We still have to rescue the remains of our army.'

At this the *losian* commanders, to whom this theological discussion held little interest, began to take notice. Dawn came with the commanders deep in discussion, proposing and rejecting idea after idea, with only the occasional nervous or awed glance up at the silent and still carving above them, or at the blazing Arrow in the young man's hand.

Somewhere in the distance a horn blew, then another and still more. One by one the heads of the strategists and commanders came up, wondering what else could possibly happen. A short time later a man came running into the chamber.

'My lords!' he cried. 'There is a great army at the Inna Gate!'

Barely had the words been uttered when another messenger came in, this time still on his horse, which he had ridden right into the building. 'My lords! A force of men are gathered at the Struere Gate!'

Bewildered, the Falthan leaders looked to each other for inspiration. Gradually the noise died down, all except the mad laughter of the Arrow-bearer.

CHAPTER 19

INSIDE THE ENEMY CAMP

GRADUALLY THE DARKNESS TURNED into light, and with it the tortures began anew. Newly added to her catalogue of hurt was a throbbing pain in the area of her right cheek. Without thinking, she lifted a hand to feel for damage, but found she could not make it work properly. Then the realisation that she was a cripple hit her again, as it did every morning.

She hung over someone's shoulder, her head resting in the small of his back. It was not the Destroyer who carried her. She could see him walking behind her if she lifted her head slightly, though the increase in pain dissuaded her from repeating the exercise. Two handless arms, one heavily bandaged, reminded her of yesterday's events; though the recollection of the Destroyer's defeat could do little to penetrate the darkness enveloping her.

Even the ambush some time during the night failed to rouse her from her torpor. She had regained consciousness with a cry of anguish on her lips, finding herself lying in the bottom of a small boat poled by two shadowy figures, with fearsome cries and the ring of steel on steel all around her. A frighteningly familiar sound. She tried to manoeuvre herself up on to a bench to see what was happening – and to stop an arrow if she was lucky. But there were no arrows, only men in canoes paddling vigorously around a number of rowboats. Confused by her sudden awakening, driven to the point of madness by her never-ending pain, Stella could not be sure even of which force – canoes or rowboats – she was attached to. A sudden movement of the boat sent her head banging against the gunwale, and she fell back into the boat with a moan. Above her two figures grappled together for a moment, then toppled into the water. She could dimly hear their thrashing next to the boat, then even that noise stopped and she was left in blessed silence.

Now she had awoken again. Unable to lift her head, she could still count pairs of feet, though it took her a long time. Twelve. For a while she fell asleep, then awoke again with the number in her mind, but was unable to remember what it meant. Eventually she was lowered to the floor of a tent, her back against the cool rug, and gentle hands fed her.

'Twelve,' she mumbled, as if this information was important somehow. No answer came from the person spooning small morsels of broth into her mouth, but a sudden splash of wetness landed on her forehead, then another. She forced her eyes open, forced them to focus on the round face, the poached-egg eyes brimming with tears, on the sad mouth from which would never come another word. With her good hand she reached up and caressed his face: with the touch her soul convulsed, and the inarticulate cry that had been held back for so long, reluctant to admit weakness or acknowledge defeat, finally found expression in a storm of weeping.

'Twelve,' she said again when the storm petered out. 'Twelve left, and no hands.' This seemed to make perfect sense to the eunuch, who nodded, his eyes sparkling with a dangerous light, as though he had been personally responsible for the reduction of the Undying Man and the destruction of the *Maghdi Dasht*. Twelve. She would keep count until there were none.

Leith and Graig embraced in the shadow of Inna Gate as the spring sun rose behind the City. The Arrow-bearer explained briefly what had transpired, a bittersweet tale. Leith clasped the hands of his friend, and said with all his soul: 'How can such a victory feel so much like defeat?'

The young Nemohaimian swordsman had no answer, but his joy at finding his liege-lord alive was clear for all to see.

Geinor told them the story of the Southern army, and the captains of Faltha exclaimed in surprise when they heard how near to the Bhrudwans the southerners had made camp. 'They may not yet know of our presence,' Geinor added, 'as we are separated from them by a small rise. However, they will surely be expecting an attack this morning from some quarter or other.'

'As to that, how might we attack them?' said the Captain of the Instruian Guard. 'They hold our fighters hostage, and though we might regard the deaths of both captors and captives a good exchange if it rids Faltha of the Bhrudwan menace, I am reluctant to support any plan that sees defenceless prisoners cut down.'

'They are captives, defeated in battle,' said the Fenni clan chief through his interpreter-priest. 'They will have to take their chances.'

'Not while I give the orders,' said Leith firmly. 'This needs to be considered carefully.'

'But swiftly!' Geinor added. 'Be assured that the Bhrudwans will be preparing for our offensive, or readying one of their own.'

Graig spoke up. 'Then I suggest the Falthan captains come back to the camp with us, and meet the Saristrian admiral. He is a clever man, and might have devised a way to bring this stand-off to an end.' Leith smiled at the young man, still flushed with excitement at being given command of such a large force.

'The southern contingent now outside the Struere Gate can keep watch over Instruere while we are gone,' said Farr eagerly. 'We should strike now before our enemy has time to regain his strength. If we do not, we may end up little better off than when we first arrived at the Gap.'

'Well said!' cried Axehaft. 'And we have many deaths to avenge!' At this the *losian* generals let out a shout of agreement.

'Very well, then,' said Leith. 'Go and tell my mother and father we have gone to speak with the southern generals,' he told one of his messengers. 'We will be back some time later today, I have no doubt.'

An hour later the Bearer of the Jugom Ark was introduced to the Lord Admiral of the Saristrian Fleet, and they warmed to each other immediately. The admiral offered Leith the alliegance of his king and placed the Southern army at his disposal. Leith accepted, then promptly installed the admiral as its leader, thanking him for his heroic efforts. Accompanied by a few of their officers, the two men sat down to a late breakfast and spoke of their adventures, filling in time before the latest spies returned with further reports.

Soon they came to the nub of their meeting. 'I do not believe it will be possible to rescue so many prisoners without a full-scale engagement,' the admiral told Leith. 'If the battle goes against them, they will kill, or threaten to kill, their captives. It is certainly what I would do in their place.' Leith's eyes opened wider at the strong sentiment from this mild-mannered man. 'We may have to negotiate with them,' he concluded.

'But we have nothing they want!' Graig protested, then immediately corrected himself. 'I suppose that refraining from slaughtering them is a bargaining position of some kind.'

'I will not bargain with the man who slew my brother,' said Leith flatly.

'Not even to rescue many thousands of captives?' Geinor asked him gently.

'Not for any reason!'

The Haufuth stood, came over to Leith and put a hand on his shoulder. 'They do have something we want,' he said quietly. 'What would you grant them in exchange for Stella?'

At the mention of her name Leith went pale. 'I don't know, I don't know! Don't ask me to weigh her life against that of twenty thousand!'

'Perhaps the answer might come to us if we ourselves go to spy out their camp,' said the admiral thoughtfully. 'Oftentimes a sight of the battleground brings counsel when planning fails.'

The urge to do something, rather than just be an observer of events over which he had no power, began to take hold of Leith. 'Yes,' he said. 'We will go and look at their camp.'

Seven men lay hidden behind a clump of spring-green broom standing in isolation halfway down a bare slope. At the base of the slope, perhaps five hundred paces from the broom, lay the Bhrudwan encampment, tents laid out in a series of concentric circles centred around their shelterless, still-bound captives. As the seven men watched, a group of a dozen or so grey-cloaked men shuffled across the wide plain from the south, heading towards the camp. Eventually they were absorbed into the morass of activity at the southern margin of the encampment.

The Bhrudwan sentries were clearly alert, and the Falthan captives well guarded. Foraging parties came and went from the camp, giving Leith some unease about their own position. Adding to the disconcerting mixture of feelings brewing within him was the sight of a number of poles standing in the centre of the camp. Two of them seemed to have bodies bound to them.

'Let us assume we have no choice but to attack them,' whispered the admiral. 'What is the best way to go about it?'

'We charge straight down the hillside,' Farr replied promptly. 'If we concentrate our attack in one place, we can drive right through the camp and make a way for the captives to escape. Given some good fortune I believe we could save most of them.'

'And if we are given bad fortune?' asked the admiral. 'What then?'

Farr pressed his lips together, refraining from an acerbic comment. Leith could predict the result of this strategy. A prolonged battle against a numerous and well-trained army. The death of all the captives, including executions staged to intimidate and dishearten the attackers. And no final resolution, unless the Destroyer had time enough to regain his strength.

Geinor cleared his throat. 'I would suggest a different course. We can take advantage of the cover this hill offers, and bring our force very close. Then we quickly encircle the Bhrudwans, cutting off their supply of provisions. In effect, we conduct a siege. Eventually they will be forced to meet our terms.'

'Tell me, Father,' said Graig, 'who will be the first to starve? Will the Bhrudwans keep the Falthan captives well fed while they themselves starve? It seems that your strategy is merely a slower version of that Farr Storrsen offers us.' Rather than taking offence, the old courtier smiled widely at his son.

'Is negotiation the only way, then?' said Axehaft the Fodhram plaintively. 'Will we end up bartering safe passage east in exchange for a portion of the captives, or might we be forced to give away some of our lands to them?'

'It seems we will have to assemble a delegation.' The southern admiral frowned, then shook his head. 'Either that or we wait to see what happens.' He began to talk over this possibility with the men from Nemohaim.

Leith leaned over and whispered in Farr's ear. 'What languages do the Bhrudwans speak?' he asked casually.

The Vinkullen man tilted his head, puzzled at the request. 'Well, the warriors we fought spoke in their own languages to each other; it all sounded like jabber to me. But I did notice that when soldiers wearing different coloured bibs came together, they used a variant of our common tongue. Why? What is important about how they spoke?'

But Leith had already turned away. 'Hold this for me,' he said quietly to Axehaft, and placed the Jugom Ark in the startled man's hands. Then, before any of them could ask him what he was doing, he broke cover and began to walk down the hill straight towards the Bhrudwan camp.

'Leith!' Graig hissed. 'Leith!' But the Loulean youth was either already too far down the slope to hear the words, or chose to ignore them. Consternation grew into panic behind the stand of broom: was the boy mad, or had he been compelled to reveal himself by some powerful spell? Or did he have some grand plan, as yet unrevealed? Whatever the reason for his rash act, there was nothing the six remaining watchers could do. They dared not come out from behind their cover.

The Haufuth passed his hand over his sweating face. 'Don't any of you know what he's doing?' He looked at their blank faces. 'He's going to exchange himself for the captives, that's what.'

'Then he goes to his death,' said the admiral sadly.

'Yes,' said the headman of Loulea in agreement. 'But I think that is exactly what he wants.'

Too long tossed by events, too much responsibility with no real power, far too long following the paths set before him by others. As they had lain there talking of more waiting, something within Leith rebelled. He longed for a pure, clean, simple act rather than the complicated swirl of politics and armies that had taken him across the world and back. An act that might redeem all the mistakes he had made and somehow set him free for the continued guilt of all the numbers in his head. *If I can just rescue one, if I can reduce the tally by one, then I'll feel better.*

A plan sprouted like a spring flower in his mind as he had listened to the discussion, and he acted on it without waiting for common sense – a cloak for cowardice – to crush its tender leaves. An enormous wave of relief swept over him as he picked his way down the slope. Finally! To do something only he was responsible for, and that only he would suffer for if he got it wrong! And as the marred but still-beautiful face flashed in front of his eyes, the face of the one he sought to rescue, his stride lengthened.

'Halt!' cried a green-sashed guard. 'Identify yourself!' The man held a tall pike in both hands, and frowned down his long nose at the stranger who had approached the camp. The guard's partner leaned forward for a better look.

'Sorry,' the stranger said in an abominable corruption of the standard speech. 'Separated from my own troop. Lost in a thicket my bib of red. Seek permission to rejoin them—'

'Rejoin them? You'll be thrashed for this, or worse! Better you had run off than return with neither sword nor bib. Just because Roudhos got himself burned doesn't mean discipline is any less stringent!' His partner laughed as the guard began to paint a picture of what would happen to the stranger when he finally reported to his captain. Leith waited patiently for the lurid descriptions to finish.

'Away with you, then! And mark this! The Undying One has returned with only a few of his precious Lords. I think something has gone wrong. If it has, the gods help anyone caught not in the right place, or not wearing the right attire!'

The willowy stranger thanked them in his awkward way, then scuttled off in the opposite direction to where the Red-bibs had set up their tents. About to shout after him, the guard was restrained by his fellow, who pointed out what a splendid story the fool's eventual punishment would be. 'Perhaps we'll see him decorating one of the posts like his master did.' And they laughed together before resuming their surveillance of the green fields and rolling slopes to the west.

Leith knew his survival depended on finding a bib, and then a job to do, in some other area of the camp, where he would be expected to speak in the common speech. He searched frantically among the ordered tent-streets until he came across a row of yellow bibs ready for washing, most covered in blood. Glancing around, he waited until there was no one in sight, then grabbed the least soiled bib, setting it over his shoulder and across his chest. *What was the name of the man whose blood decorates this bib?* he wondered. Just one of those whose number filled his head . . .

Now, to find a place where he could make himself inconspicuous . . .

'You!' a voice cracked like a whip. 'Yellow-bib! What are you doing outside your area?'

Leith spun towards the owner of the voice, a broad-shouldered man wearing a blue sash, who looked for all the world like the Captain of the Instruian Guard. His manner, however, was much more peremptory. 'Well? Do you have an explanation?'

His mind a blank, Leith sputtered: 'I was sent—'

'No matter! Unless your orders came from the Lord of Bhrudwo himself, you can forget them and come with me. The cursed clerks haven't given me enough prisoners, and the two I had digging the latrines are too bruised to carry on. Carrion!' He laughed at his joke, then poked a finger in Leith's chest. 'So guess what you'll be doing for the rest of the day, my boy!' And he hooked a broad finger in the top of Leith's jerkin and dragged him along the grassy path after him.

Thus the Bearer of the Arrow spent his imperilled afternoon alone in the Bhrudwan camp disposing of their waste. Though it was possibly the most unpleasant task he had ever done, he silently gave thanks for his luck, for none would approach him. His bib was no longer yellow, and his boots, well . . . From time to time his overseer came to check on his progress, and after the obligatory grumbling and stick-waving would move off to attend to other business. Leith's hands blistered, but he remembered the image of Stella attempting to climb the stairs in the Hall of Meeting and tried to disregard his pain.

Just before sunset Blue-sash the overseer came over to where Leith had started yet another hole. 'Time for you to go,' he growled, but there was a degree of respect in the voice. 'You've been a good worker. Would you like me to sign your form?'

'No!' Leith said sharply. *What form?* He forced himself to relax. 'No – I come for you to sign later. First this hole I finish, then sign form.'

The overseer shook his head at this stupidity, but what happened to the fellow if he was outside his area after curfew was none of his concern. 'Very well; come and see me when you are ready. There'll be extra pay for you.'

Leith smiled at the man until he had seen him off, then lowered himself into an extra hole he had dug, and pulled the cover over it. Noisome as it was, he would remain undetected until it was no longer necessary.

He waited patiently until night set in, spending the time wondering how his disappearance had been received. He'd not thought that part of it through. He only hoped that no one would decide to invade the Bhrudwan encampment for his sake. Then there would be more numbers . . .

And his parents would worry. He had not thought about them either. Already they had suffered far too much, with the loss of their elder son. As had Kurr.

He needed more time to reflect on the old farmer's story. As incredible as it sounded, it rang true. Hal's feyness, his giftedness, had come from somewhere other than the unremarkable North March of Firanes. Just who could the father have been?

As he began to think, an image, two images, flashed through his mind.

He handled this new piece of the vast puzzle with fear and trembling. Twin images: Stella limping up the stairs, crippled down her right side, no doubt as a result of the mistreatment dealt her by the Destroyer. Hal limping across a stonefield, crippled down his right side.

Could it be? But what had Kurr said about Tinei? She had been mistreated also. What had he said? Leith couldn't remember, though something told him the knowledge was vital. *One piece more and I'll unlock everything.*

He pulled his mind back from the brink. It was time to try out the idea that had been taking shape ever since the evening he spent in the Hall of Conal Greatheart. If the idea did not work, well, it was a long walk back to camp, and this fearful risk had been all for nothing. He took a deep breath, and was unable to stop himself glancing at his right hand, empty as it was. Tonight he was not the Arrow-bearer. Tonight, if he was right, he did not need to be.

You spoke to me in the Great Hall of Fealty, he said to the voice in his mind. *I didn't have the Jugom Ark with me then.*

<True. And I spoke to you many times before you found the Jugom Ark in the first place.>

So the fire-dream I had in Foilzie's basement?

<Was not just a dream.>

I suppose I should thank you. Though I'm not sure what I'm thanking you for.

<As for that, think carefully on what you dreamed about.>

Fire? I didn't realise the Gift of Fire would be packaged in a vision like that. Tell me, how many people might have been saved if I'd learned to harness it earlier?

<You're not thinking carefully enough. What does fire do?>

It burns . . . oh.

<Yes. The Fire of Life burns away the accumulated hurts and habits that stop people living. It doesn't add anything; it subtracts. It heals by drawing out poison. It is not a weapon. No one could have taught you to use the Arrow as a weapon.>

But – surely the Most High used it as a weapon!

You, of anyone, should know the Most High can use anything. But even the Destroyer could use the Fire to heal himself, if that was his true desire.

But why didn't the Fire heal me?

<Remember when you and your brother used to play in the bedroom back in Loulea? You shut the door so you could immerse yourselves in your private world. It didn't take long for the room to grow cold, did it? In the same way, the Fire burns brightly in one room of your mind, giving you the strength, for example, to command others. Would the Leith I knew a year ago have been able to do this? Yet some of your other rooms are still cold.>

Leith laughed, an incongruous sound in such a place. *Still the same old Hal. Still speaking with the voice of truth, still always right.*

<So you have realised that the voice is of the Fire, not the Arrow. What else have you realised?>

That I don't need the Jugom Ark to operate in the realm of Fire. That those not of the Fire can hold the Jugom Ark, though they cannot use it, because they do not have the inner flame. That they no doubt have their own inner strength, based on some other element. That the Arrow burns people of the Fire, those who have not received the Fire of Life, because it is like the Fire falling, burning away the realm of the flesh, as Kroptur would say. That the Jugom Ark is as Phemanderac said in the beginning: just a symbol. That I have been doing the healing, the illusions and all the rest by myself from the beginning. That I can continue doing them even without the Arrow.

<And so?>

And so I can press ahead with what I plan to do without the Jugom Ark.

The voice laughed. <You've been listening too long to your brother. We'll make a mystic out of you yet. Now go to it! You don't have much time remaining. And here's a word for you: do not be surprised if it turns out a little different than you envisage. More than one person stands to gain – or to lose – from what you do tonight.>

Must words of the future always be cryptic?

<They are as clear as any other words, but only with hindsight. Go, Leith!>

There is never enough time to ask you about everything I want to know, Leith sighed as he pushed the cover away and eased himself out of the hole.

Full night lay on the Bhrudwan camp. The overcast above glowed silver where the moon-sliver hid. A few torches marked the entrances of officer tents, and in the distance the camp was ringed with watch-fires. That, and the pale glow from within an occasional tent, was the sum of light for Leith to avoid. He focused his mind, imagining he reached out for the Jugom Ark—

—and immediately he could feel, as he had known he would, two other sources of Fire in the encampment. One large, burning with a flame at least the equivalent of the Jugom Ark, the other much smaller, enclosed somehow as though fenced by pain. He smiled with satisfaction, then turned to face the flames, which both lay in the one direction. *O Most High, what if they're together?*

He set off through the camp. The sources of the Fire were at the southern end, fine for their escape but dangerous now. How had Hal made the net he'd used to cover the Falthan army? No matter. He didn't need it; he was practically invisible. The danger was in the noise he might make, not in being seen.

He stepped lightly across the cool grass, already coated with the dew of a spring night. Off to his right stood a large tent: flickering light inside projected grotesque silhouettes on to the woven walls, and the murmur of conversation came clearly across the intervening space, punctuated by gusts of laughter. Not there, no Fire there. Beyond the large tent he crept, slinking from darkness to darkness, making no noise. It was like being back in the Great North Woods, hunting foxes with his father; mustn't make noise, mustn't be seen. Down another long path, small tents to the left and right, gentle snoring coming from some, no sound at all from others. Make a deviation to avoid two men sitting outside their tent by a small fire, dicing and drinking together. Head for the tent at the end of the path. Draw nearer, nearer, still nearer: this is the one!

A thought crossed his mind. *If I can sense the Destroyer, can he sense me?* He hoped the Undying man was not also unsleeping.

Leith flitted across an open space in front of the tent, looking left and right in case someone approached – and almost ran straight into a black figure standing impassively, arms folded, as though waiting for someone. At the very last moment he threw himself to the side, landing heavily on the ground and winding himself on a tent peg. Glancing up, his heart seemed to lodge in his throat. The black figure had turned to face him, arms still folded.

'I can hear you,' growled a voice, 'but I can neither see you nor sense you. Come out, that I may determine your kind.' The head seemed to be focused on a point somewhere behind him. The feet moved slowly forward: they came to within two paces of where Leith lay trying to pant out his hurt without making a sound.

He cannot see me. Why? Is he blind? Are the shadows too deep? But the edges of Leith's cloak gave a faint silver gleam. *Why can't he see me?*

Gradually the youth edged his body away from the black figure, crawling spider-like on hands and feet, his back just off the ground. Fast enough to avoid the feet still moving forward, slow enough not to make noise.

'Why can I not sense you?' the man said in the sort of snarl that Leith associated with the *Maghdi Dasht*. But this man sounded too frightened to be a Lord of Fear. 'What manner of man are you? Where have you gone?' He turned to face Leith again, but seemed not to know he was there. Pale moonlight illuminated his cruel features, now distorted by panic. What had happened to make them so frightened? As he watched, the features composed themselves and the figure stepped back to where he had been standing.

He thinks he imagined hearing me, Leith realised.

An hour passed before Leith was able to fully compose himself. The tent peg had drawn blood, leaving a bruise just under his ribs. He was dizzy with relief that he had escaped, but his head filled with questions, confusing him. Finally he felt ready to examine the tent, and this time he watched carefully for any other guards.

It was without doubt the tent of the Destroyer. He remembered it clearly from the surrender at Vulture's Craw: the silver-on-sable device, the silk sides, the elaborate flaps now closed. He circled around it. One source of the Fire – by far the greater – he found in the main part of the tent, with the smaller source in a small annexe. Clearly Stella was housed in the annexe, but he would have to pass by the Destroyer to rescue her.

The probability he would be caught became a certainty

in his mind. The Undying Man would know what he had in his possession, would squeeze what knowledge he had out of his head, would harm him like he had harmed Stella. He had watched her try to climb the stairs . . . Nearly his heart failed him, and nearly he turned and made his way quietly out of the camp. But she climbed the stairs in his mind still, and he could not leave her here if there was even the smallest chance she could be rescued.

Breathing shallowly – to reduce noise, Leith told himself, and not because he was afraid – he approached the door of the tent. The black figure stood not ten paces away, looking down the grassy path that led into the centre of the Bhrudwan encampment. *He can't see me, he can't see me*, Leith repeated under his breath, trying to make it true. Cautiously he opened the flap and slipped through.

Farr delivered the news of Leith's folly to his parents as soon as they returned to Instruere. Mahnum simply closed his eyes and sighed once, but his face seemed to close up as though he had reached some kind of limit and wanted to receive no more bad news. Indrett staggered, dropping to one knee, and her eyes filled with tears. 'Why?' she sobbed. 'Why would he do such a thing?'

The Haufuth told them what he thought Leith was doing. Kurr nodded his head in agreement, but Indrett stepped right up to the old farmer as though she wanted to strike him. 'No!' she declared. 'He has accepted his responsibility as the Arrow-bearer. He would not leave us here so lightly!'

Axehaft held out the Jugom Ark, which burned brightly. 'He is alive still. Look! If he were to die, the flame would die with him.'

Phemanderac had said nothing, but his pallor had changed

to grey. 'Right, you are right,' he said quickly, trying to persuade himself. 'The Jugom Ark is linked to him. We will know if he is killed or captured by the nature of the flame.'

'But what can we do?' Indrett cried, her anguish undisguised. 'We could – we could take the Southern army and break him free!'

'No, we could not.' The Saristrian admiral was firm. 'The risk of defeat is too great if we act without careful planning. We could end up leaving Instruere, and therefore all of Faltha, exposed to the Destroyer. Are you suggesting that we gamble thousands of lives to save one?'

'Yes!' Beside herself with grief, Indrett ground out her reply. 'Yes! He gambled his life to save ours!' But those gathered around her bowed their heads, and she knew no attempt would be made to rescue her son.

'Curse the day you were ever found!' she screamed, then snatched the Arrow from the hand of the startled Fodhram leader and slammed it point-first into the table. There it stood, quivering slightly, flame burning as brightly as ever. A dozen faces turned to Leith's mother, whose own face registered the enormity of what she had done. Then all eyes went to her hand, which she held out, palm up, to reveal no burn.

'Oh,' she said softly.

The thin Dhaurian philosopher put a hand to his forehead as he finally realised how much he had not known. Kurr nodded, his own suspicions confirmed. The others wore masks of disbelief and incredulity.

'I can feel him,' Indrett whispered. 'He is out there, somewhere to the north, and he is frightened, but he is still alive. I can feel it!'

Slowly the small group found their seats and leaned forward, all drawn to the Jugom Ark. The flame continued to flicker unconcernedly in their midst as the night drew close around them.

Only the faintest of light penetrated the tent walls, but it was enough to give shape to a low pallet perhaps three paces from where he stood. A blanketed form twitched and turned on the pallet, asleep but perhaps precariously so. Knowing that any careless movement would waken the Undying Man, Leith began to edge to his left, making for the small annexe where Stella would be found. Step, listen; step, listen . . .

Without warning a huge white shape reared up in front of him, arms wide and grappling, mouth wide open in a soundless cry. Before he could react, Leith found himself crushed in an unbreakable grip which took the wind out of his chest: he could not scream, he could not breathe. He tried to summon up thoughts of Fire, but no clear image could penetrate the haze of panic that built up inside him. The arms lifted him off the floor and over to the pallet, and even in his extremity Leith could feel the enormous power of the man lying there.

His captor loosened one arm, and Leith was able to take a shallow breath, but even with only one arm he was securely held. The other arm reached out to the head of the pallet, twitched aside a blanket, touched the exposed cheek of the sleeping one with a gentle, almost reverential caress . . . and placed a finger on the lips. The figure groaned, the head turned, the eyes came open, then widened until they seemed to fill the beautiful, ravaged face.

'Leith,' said Stella sleepily. 'How did you break into my dream?'

The captor placed a chubby finger firmly on Leith's lips, and withdrew his other arm. Even had the warning not been given, however, the boy from Loulea could not have spoken, such was his shock.

'Leith?' came the soft voice, full of wonder. 'You are here. Really here! Are you his prisoner too?'

'No, Stella. At least, I don't think so.' He turned to the big man who now stood beside him, one hand on Leith's shoulder, one hand on Stella's. The round head shook back and forth. 'No, I am not a prisoner. I have come to rescue you.' *But with such Fire inside you, why should you need rescuing? Why have you not already escaped?*

Stella sat up on her pallet. Leith could clearly see the deep scars on her face and neck, and his anger began to burn. He reached out for her, took her arm and began to draw her to her feet. 'Come on,' he said, his eyes brimming. 'Let's go home.'

'No!' she said, and he let her arm go in surprise, though he could still feel her coolness on his palm. 'No. I will not leave while my friend remains.' She indicated the huge man beside him, who looked on them both with his sad brown eyes.

'Then we will take him with us!' Leith said, reaching for her again. Maybe they could make it even with this man with them.

'No!' she said again. 'He is tied to this place and cannot leave it. He is bound to the Destroyer, and would die if he passed beyond the boundary of the camp. I can't leave him alone.'

'Stella, oh Stella,' said Leith desperately, unbelieving. 'Not even for me? Not for your friends who wait in Instruere? I cannot bear it! To have come so close – and you would send me away?'

'I want to come with you more than anything in my life,' she said simply, and he knew it for the truth. 'But I cannot abandon my friend now. If the Destroyer should awake to find me gone, he would punish him in ways you cannot begin to imagine. I can't, I can't let that happen. He's already lost his tongue for me.' And for an instant her eyes darkened, and in them Leith read a bleakness beyond anything he had ever known. 'Leith, go back to your friends. I saw their faces in the Hall of Meeting, I know how much they love you. No one will miss me, but your death would be too much for them to take. Please, Leith.' She reached up with her crippled hand and touched his cheek, tracing the path of his tears. 'I love you. Take my love back with you. My life will be more bearable knowing that you live.'

'Oh no, Stella, please . . .' Leith sobbed, but nothing he said could move her. 'You don't love me,' he said through his tears, but he knew the accusation was false even as he said it. She had decided what she must do, and Leith himself was aware of what it was like to carry guilt for the suffering and death of others. Would he not return to Vulture's Craw if it meant he could rescue some of those who had died in the snows? Was his guilt not the very reason he had taken this mad risk?

The next words he said were the most difficult he had ever made himself speak.

'I love you, Stella; I love you so much more now than ever I did. I want to drag you away from here, but I know that I would destroy whatever might grow between us. I will return to Instruere and tell all who love you of your courage and your beauty.' His voice was fierce.

She smiled weakly. 'Beauty? Leith, I have been marred by my own foolishness and the evil of my possessor. I am no longer beautiful, if ever I was.'

'You *are* beautiful, and you are powerful. I can feel the Fire burning within you. Harness it, Stella. Perhaps you might be able to challenge the evil that holds you here.'

Her face changed suddenly, and it became suffused with panic. 'Go, Leith! He wakes! Go now!' And Leith heard a stirring from the annexe.

He jerked back in fear, but forced himself back to the small form on the pallet; then bent down and kissed her on the cheek. His tears fell on to her ravaged skin. 'Goodbye, Stella,' he whispered. 'Goodbye.'

She touched her lips to his, then pushed him away with her good arm. 'Go!'

Heartsick and unheeding, the youth from Loulea slipped through the opening and out into the night. He could see nothing in front of him but her face, and did not step aside to avoid the dark figure standing guard. Instead he struck at it with all his might, his arm guided by fate or desperation, and knocked the Lord of Fear senseless to the ground.

A roar came from behind him, from somewhere in the tent, and the sound spurred him on into a dead run. Down the path he ran, careless of those who might be abroad, not looking back to see whether he was pursued, running from the roar but running also from the face and the whispered words and the cool lips and the glistening tears.

The perimeter guards heard him coming, but could see nothing. Expecting any attack to come from outside the camp, they were slow to react, and their pikes came around too late. The pounding of feet, the sound of laboured breathing, a gust of wind and he was gone.

Indrett looked up at those who sat around her. The Arrow had dimmed for a time, and all hope had failed, but now it blazed brightly. 'He is coming home,' she said, and smiled.

CHAPTER 20

CEREMONY

IT WAS MIDWINTER'S DAY, and all over the frozen North people gathered to celebrate the shortest day and the promise of spring to come. Here in Instruere the mild weather continued, though a light rain marred the perfection of the day. Those fortunate enough to be attending the day's big event held brightly-coloured parasols above their heads as they streamed down the Vitulian Way and across the close-cut lawns towards the Hall of Meeting. Inside the hall Leith Mahnumsen, Lord of Instruere, fiddled nervously with the silver buckles on his boots as he sat and waited for the ceremony to begin.

Nine months had passed since the surrender of the Bhrudwan army, nine long months in which the city of Instruere had been reborn. Fire-damaged tenements were torn down and rebuilt, funded by the little gold remaining in the City's coffers and a great deal of borrowing, and all the damage done by the Ecclesia in pursuit of their wayward vision was put right. Lest the City come to think of the Ecclesians only as misguided fanatics, Leith caused the lawn before the door to the Hall of Lore to be dug up and planted with seedlings from the northern forests in remembrance of the many people betrayed by Tanghin-Deorc and cut down by his guardsmen. Craftsmen from the capital city of Straux were summoned to Instruere to rebuild the Struere Gate, which was renamed Mercium Gate in honour of the rebuilders. Thus were the suspicions and resentments of the King of Straux at least partly assuaged. The one truly unpleasant task had been the dismantling of The Pinion, with the attendant draining and filling of the dungeon below. Leith seriously considered erecting a memorial to those drowned there, with the names of those unlucky enough to have found themselves dismantling it also listed, but decided that there were some things the City did not want to be reminded of.

Today the Hall of Meeting was filled with the citizens of Instruere. Leith had worked hard to ensure that not only the business leaders and the wealthy found seats: a whole section of the hall was reserved for those who came from the poorer areas of the City, including the poverty-stricken Granary district, still struggling to recover from the sabotage of the Escaignians. There they sat, eyes bright, some of them having waited in a long queue since the previous evening, under cover in the Hall of Appellants but nonetheless cold. Against the advice of their officials, who worried about the propriety of such things, Leith and the Company had brought soup to those who waited early in the morning.

Leith himself sat on a low chair positioned at the base of a marble stair, newly-made for the ceremony. At the top of the stair was another chair, far more decorative. A throne of gold leaf and red velvet, impossibly elaborate, which the people of the City had made for him. Behind the stair lay the Inner Chamber, now unused; indeed, it had been decided to wall it off, the better to encourage people to forget the old Council of Faltha.

There had been other changes made in the Hall of Meeting. The Iron Door had been cut up for scrap, its wondrous engineering now forgotten, the great expanse of steel propping up some of the damaged warehouses in the Granary district. In its place stood magnificent wooden doors, carved by men from the Mist with a variety of fantastic motifs: it served as a memorial to their brave warriors. The signing table, on which the Destroyer's severed hand had lain, was now repositioned directly under the huge carvings on the west wall.

The carvings themselves had been left untouched. Leith allowed a scaffold to be erected so that men of lore could study them. Phemanderac had not long returned from Dhauria, where he had gone to bring back with him the best scholars of his land. Two men and three women had come, and strange and secretive they were, shocked by much around them; but none of the loremasters could explain the face on the carving of the Most High, the face that looked so much like Hal, nor could they offer an explanation for the absence of the Jugom Ark from the wall carving. The scaffolding had been taken down the previous day, and now the carvings looked down on the gathering with the same patience they always had.

An expectant hush fell. Leith stopped his absent-minded fiddling and looked up to the musicians' balcony. A herald flung open a window, and a single trumpeter stepped forth, then set his instrument to his lips and blew a sweet fanfare, a call to celebration that lifted the heart. Perhaps twenty seconds only did it last, with the final note ringing in the ears and then fading, to be replaced by a timpanist quietly repeating the rhythm set by the trumpet. Again the instrument played for a few seconds, with the following silence filled by the swelling of strings.

'The first part of the piece is a celebration,' Phemanderac had told him proudly. The musicians had been practising the philosopher's piece for weeks, and the addition of five skilled Dhaurians had given the music an added life. The strings settled into a sedate melody, a calm assertion of the continuation of Faltha no matter what was brought to bear against it.

Leith was borne away on the wings of the music. Yes, he was prepared to concede, they had been victorious. A few days after he returned from his unsuccessful attempt to rescue Stella, the Bhrudwan army suddenly, inexplicably, surrendered. When questioned by the surprised Falthan captains, the Bhrudwan officers spoke of unrest and insubordination in the ranks, of no orders from their superiors, of the absence of the Undying Man and his *Maghdi Dasht*. The entire encampment was searched, but no sign of the Destroyer or his retinue could be found, and no one would admit to having seen them leave the camp. Though someone must have been concealing the knowledge that might have enabled Leith to track his enemy, no amount of questioning could uncover any information. Despite this, the surrender was counted by most as a great victory, and the end of the war with Bhrudwo.

Now the strings echoed the theme first announced by the trumpeter. Stella had not been found, of course, and Leith could not conceive of calling such loss a victory. Nevertheless, the numbers had begun to fade from his mind in a way he knew they would not have, had he forced her to accompany him back to Instruere. If he had been able to. Where was she now? What indignities did she suffer? What new kinds of courage would she author as she tried to survive? The great Hall filled with the soaring sound of Phemanderac's composition, and the strings again recapitulated the main theme, this time accompanied by the original trumpeter. Who could not fail to be moved by such music?

Sixteen richly-dressed figures marched down the double-width aisle towards the stairs by which Leith sat. Each of the figures wore a crown. Fifteen men and one woman, four of them newly sworn to Faltha after renouncing their alliegance to Bhrudwo, a further five only a few months into their reign, replacing monarchs who chose death rather than repentance. The King of Favony had hanged himself, leaving a letter detailing his delight at the effects of his treachery, expressing regret that any of the Falthans survived the snows of Vulture's Craw. The letter horrified the Captains of Faltha, but strangely it had lightened Leith's heart to know that yet another shared the blame. The sixteen figures maintained a stately walk, and Instruians both noble and common marvelled at the power and dignity that descended upon them, come to pay homage to their new leader.

Leith took his eyes off the sixteen kings and instead surveyed the first row of seats. Sitting there were the people now collectively known as the Captains of Faltha: the surviving members of the Company, the leaders of the *losian* Army of the North, the admiral of the Southern army and other leaders of the Falthan army.

Near the aisle sat his parents. His mother's eyes were clear in a way they had not been since the death of her elder son, but even as Leith looked on her, he saw her glance up to her right, to where Hal watched over them all.

Modahl had taken the seat next to his son, whose bitter anger at his abandonment by the famous Trader had moderated. They seemed at least to be talking, and Mahnum had willingly acted as his father's second at the grizzled old man's recent wedding to the Ice Queen of Sna Vaztha. Indeed,

Mahnum seemed proud that he would have kings for both father and son.

The music gentled, the strings softened, the trumpeters took their seats and were replaced by flutes and recorders, supported by the plucked strings of Phemanderac's new harp, of Dhaurian make.

Leith gazed at the people he loved. Farr would leave in the morning, accompanying the remaining commanders of the *losian* Army of the North on their homeward journey. He had stated his intention to visit Mjolkbridge to report the death of his brother and how he was avenged, but then he would return to Vindstrop House to take over the trading post recently left empty by the death of its proprietor. Maendraga and his daughter Belladonna had made their home in Old Struere, in the heart of the poor district, having taken lodgings with Foilzie who had used the money given her by her Escaignian friend to purchase one of the rebuilt tenements. Bella had made clear her affection for Phemanderac, and struggled to accept the friendship that was the best the Dhaurian could offer. Nevertheless, her laughter could often be heard echoing along the corridors of the Hall of Lore, overlaying his mock exasperation at her antics as they rummaged through the archives of Instruere. As the harp rang clear through the hall, her face lifted towards the musicians' balcony, her rapt intensity a clear message of the feelings beneath. And beside her Perdu sat with his family, his girls giggling at some joke, or perhaps at the bright clothing worn by the monarchs who now stood unmoving at the base of the stairs, clothing so unlike the plain but serviceable garments of the Fenni. They were to return to the vidda, and Leith would be sorry to see them leave.

The sixteen sovereigns turned and faced the gathered

crowd, and the music mellowed, transmuting to a sedate waltz. As if conjured by magic, thirty-two costumed dancers sprang down the aisle on light feet, dresses and capes swirling as the music settled, then began to build. The celebration was drawing to a climax.

Leith had listened to Phemanderac's piece many times, had even offered untutored suggestions during its composition. But he had never heard it like it was being played today. The dancers were being drawn up into the music as the notes ran together and climbed the scale, suddenly and unexpectedly to repeat the main theme in a glorious acclamation, this time with ten trumpets swelling the call to celebrate. Recognising his cue, he stood and ascended the stair as the music itself ascended, and took his seat on the great throne of Faltha as the trumpet-call rang out. He could no more keep the tears from his eyes than he could prevent the chills of awe from running down his spine. The orchestra came down from the heights, bringing their heavenly theme back to earth as they signalled the end of celebration and the beginning of Phemanderac's lament.

The King-designate of Faltha looked out over his subjects from the vantage point of his throne. Beyond the Captains of Faltha he could see a number of Pei-ratin, and recalled their story, perhaps the strangest of all. Forgotten by the Arrow-bearer, they had come still to offer their services in the hope that the kai-nan would be honoured, but had been held up by the blockade instituted by the Arkhos of Nemohaim. Finally they had broken through, and after resting for a day they had paddled up the Aleinus River until, some time after nightfall, they literally collided with a small flotilla of rowboats manned by the Lords of Fear, shepherding the Destroyer back to his army. The fighting had been short but vicious, and both sides had taken many casualties. In their magic-weakened state, and with a disabled master to protect, the *Maghdi Dasht* suffered their worst ever defeat, losing more than eighty warriors to the river-craftiness of their foe. A small graveyard had been laid out on the northern bank, and it was visited by the Pei-ratin when they returned from burying the names of their friends. The treaty had been concluded with the long-delayed meal, and Leith hoped that soon Astraea would be inhabited once again – though if the rain that had fallen when he had passed through it was the norm, his visits might be infrequent.

Near the Pei-ratin sat a lissom, brown-skinned woman and her father, chief and princess of the Mist, both in mourning dress. The bodies of Te Tuahangata and Prince Wiusago had been found side by side on the fields of Vulture's Craw, surrounded by the many husks of their enemies. The stern face of the chief had not been softened by news of his son's heroism, and he had refused to talk to anyone until the proper rites of passage had been performed. Leith still held hope that the conflict between Deruys and the Mist might be resolved, but any such resolution had been dealt a severe blow by the deaths of the two young men. Leith's heart ached whenever he thought of them. He missed their arguing and their passion, two men trying to make sense of the complex grievances handed them by their fathers. For such things as these the Destroyer should be required to pay.

Now the Lament of Phemanderac took hold of all those gathered in the hall. The strings slowed, and their melody settled into a haunting melancholy. Leith took the time to remember those who had given their lives in his quest. Wira, Parlevaag, the unnamed Escaignian, Sjenda of Deruys, Jethart, Shabby the Fodhram – and Hal.

One further name he would not add to the sombre list. He would not. She had not died. He would mourn for the others, but not for her.

Other names rose to the surface of his mind. The blue-robed Hermit had died a madman, but for a time had served the Company well. His Ecclesia was disbanded, and all but a few of the fire-raisers dealt with according to the City's justice: less harsh than that dealt out by the chasing mob on the night Instruere burned, but still firm. Disturbingly, Leith had heard rumours in the last few weeks of small cadres of worshippers reviving the Ecclesian fanaticism, this time under the name of Hal Mahnumsen. Something would have to be done about them.

The Presiding Elder of Escaigne had met with the fate his actions deserved, crushed under the feet of the citizens he despised. Leith felt no pity for him, but had expended much effort to integrate the surviving Escaignians into Instruian society. True-hearted Foilzie and her bald-headed friend from Escaigne devoted themselves to this cause.

No one spared a thought for their erstwhile ally, the Arkhos of Nemohaim, who even after his death continued to haunt those trying to repair the damage he had done to the great City. The Instruian Guard was subjected to intense scrutiny, and a number of recalcitrants exiled. Two men who were demonstrably involved in the killing of unarmed Ecclesians were hanged, and others accepted back into the Guard on probation. The Captain of the Instruian Guard reported some remaining animosity against what was seen as the usurping of the old Council of Faltha, and indicated he still had some work to do.

The threnody continued, a minor-key echo of the celebration, reminding those gathered there that victory and loss were inextricably entwined. Such a bittersweet moment it was, the loss of friends like the loss of limbs, but knowing that at least some remained alive to feel the loss. Joy and sorrow wounded and healed them all at once, as the music enfolded them like the consoling arms of a friend.

The strings and the trumpets united in a final extended fanfare, and the Raving King of Deruys stepped forward, mounting the marble stairs with a golden crown in his hands. Silent for once, and with tears streaking both cheeks, he stood beside the throne and waited for the final consummation of lament and celebration when, as agreed by the Sixteen Kingdoms, he would crown Leith the first King of Faltha.

The notes rang out, the Raving King lowered the crown – and just before the glittering assemblage of gold and jewels settled on Leith's head a shaft of light appeared in the middle of the aisle below, catching his eye. The light came from the place where the double wooden doors had just been opened; where, as the music reached its final crescendo, a small figure limped into the vast hall, a walking-stick in one hand.

'Two rotting salmon and five stale loaves of bread,' said the grass-stained man nervously in the tongue of Andratan. 'The villagers would not part with more. It has been a hard summer, my lord, and the harvest will be poor.'

The ravaged face looked up from the filthy cot. 'Feed me,' said the mouth.

The voice could not be disobeyed. The servant ripped a hunk of bread from the end of a loaf, placed it in his own mouth and chewed vigorously, then spat it out and fed it to the hideous man. At least water was in plentiful supply. It was a wet autumn, certainly by Bhrudwan standards, and they continued to drink their fill at the nearest stream even after Lord Uchtana had died from the gripes. Water followed bread, nervous fingers holding the cup for the one who could not, and eventually the tortured face signalled satisfaction and sank back into its torpor.

Five months of continual hiding, of begging for bread, of rejection by the people he aspired to conquer, had turned the Lord of Bhrudwo into a spitting, whining animal. These days he had little to say that could be considered intelligible. The loss of a large part of his former power had robbed him of the personable façade he had formerly employed when it suited him: his anger was capricious and spiteful, and his attendants kept him hidden whenever they were forced to have dealings with the locals of whatever land they were currently passing through. Although the Destroyer had folded in on himself, noticing little beyond his limited reach, his retinue remained faithful. Such as they were. Seven Lords of Fear and four servants – including the tongueless eunuch – accompanied Stella and the Undying Man on their agonising journey eastwards through the heart of Faltha.

For the first few weeks of his journey the Lord of Bhrudwo seemed largely unchanged, outwardly at least, apart from his handless arms, of course. His power had diminished somewhat, they were all aware of that, but his continued command of magic was attested to by the compulsion that sat heavily on their shoulders. This compulsion roused them from their beds late on the night after everything went wrong in Instruere, had closed their mouths but made it clear what was expected of them, had cloaked them in invisibility and enabled them to flee from the safety of their own camp. None of his servants, save the Falthan girl, who would not say, understood why their master had suddenly abandoned their camp, and the two who had asked had paid for their temerity with their lives.

For many days they hustled north-eastwards across the wheatfields of Deuverre, stealing and coercing food from those around them, leaving a trail of misery and death in their wake. Then their lord faltered, and only Stella guessed he had drained dry his reservoir of magical power. His face grew older and more haggard by the hour, just as it had done when almost overmatched by Hal in the single combat; in the course of one afternoon he became a walking cadaver, parchment-thin skin stretched over ancient bones, but pulling away from his pain-encircled eyes.

He could not spare any energy to maintain his bodily illusion, but he still exercised enough power to hold his servants in thrall. For a wild moment Stella had thought her chance had come, that his vigilance might fail and that she and the eunuch might escape, but the tie between herself and the dreadful figure remained intact, though she could feel the strain. Or, more correctly, she could feel the link between them draining her strength, as though he drank from the well of her spirit.

They struggled eastwards for four more months. At Barathea they crossed the deep blue Branca, of all Falthan rivers the largest save the Aleinus, then struck out across the pathless plains for the town of Bis, which liked to claim it was part of none of the Sixteen Kingdoms, but in fact lay on the border of Asgowan and Favony. That they eventually made it to Bis with the loss of only two Lords of Fear and one servant was due more to good fortune than to their own survival skills. Food was scarce out on the pampas, where trees would not grow and the ferocious west wind would come sweeping down from the Remparer Mountains a hundred leagues to the east. The Bhrudwans lived on horsemeat and wild vegetable roots from Barathea all the way to Ehrenmal, where they finally found a family who took pity on them. After disposing of their bodies in the Aleinus, they crossed the great river by boat and made their way east on the southern shore.

And now they huddled, hungry and drained, in their one remaining tent and gazed eastward at the towering Aleinus Gates. Wreathed in stormclouds, the huge cliffs seemed to lean towards them like a warning carved in rock. Below the cliffs stood something equally forbidding: a contingent of armoured men in Instruian livery. *Naturally they would be here*, thought Stella. *Let the Destroyer find his way across the vast plains of central Faltha, waste no time looking for him there, but wait at the entrance to Vulture's Craw, where all eastward travellers were bound to come eventually.*

'Go . . . and count them,' the Undying Man rasped, saliva running down his chin. 'Find a way . . . past them.' His Lords of Fear bowed, then left the tent.

'Ah, Stella,' he said fondly when they had gone. 'What would I . . . do without you?' She said nothing in response, she never did, but as always he could read her. 'You . . . think I am horrible. And so I am! But I have . . . been this way before. The cursed Arrow . . . affected me this way the first time.' He cleared his throat, then was taken by a fit of coughing that subsided only when it seemed something inside him was about to break. Again Stella felt the pull on her soul. 'Back then . . . I had no one to help me. Now . . . I have you.' He smiled, a skull-grin that made her sick to her stomach at the same time as it raised a strange pity in her breast. 'Dear Stella.'

He bowed his head and closed his eyes, exhausted by his speech and the racking coughs.

'You'll not have her any longer,' said a voice.

The head jerked up, the eyes sprang open, and beheld the eunuch standing beside his servant-girl, his love, his life . . . *Another hallucination. The man cannot talk. I have his tongue.*

'You may have his tongue, but I have given his heart a voice,' said the eunuch, his tongueless mouth opening and closing as though he made the words. 'You are weak enough now that he can break free of your hold on him, and take the girl with him. It is time to live the life you chose for yourself without stealing from the lives of others.'

The Undying Man found his feet. 'You!' he screamed. 'You have taken both my hands. You cannot have my heart! Take the man, he is carrion; I ask you to leave me the girl!'

'The girl herself will decide,' said the voice.

Hal's voice? How can it be? I saw him die!

'Well, Stella? Will you come west with the man you rescued from death with your care, or will you remain with the one who claims to love you, yet feeds on you?' The eunuch's mouth closed, but his eyes still burned with a brightness beyond imagining.

Of course the choice was easy. *There is no choice!* she told herself. Yet the bond between her and the awful wreck of a man was as strong as ever, and some of it, she was horrified to realise, was of her own making. 'Queen of Bhrudwo!' the Destroyer cried, holding his outstretched arms to her, his stumps a mute testimony to his need. 'You will live forever! Come and live with the only one who will never leave your side!'

<The Fire of Life burns within you,> the voice said in her mind. <Take it and set flame to the cords that bind you. Then you will be free to choose.>

I didn't leave the eunuch when he needed me, she replied. *Should I leave the Destroyer? He needs me too.*

<That is your choice. But heed this: I testify to you that it is hard to withhold aid from those that need it, yet sometimes it is the only way they can be helped. Many times I could have assisted the Company on their journeys, but had I done so none of them would be fit for the responsibilities they now hold. Make your choice with haste: the Lords of Fear return.>

Leith told me about your views. He didn't like them and neither do I. Abandon those in need and call it a kindness? There are too many selfish people who would use that kind of thinking as an excuse for inaction.

<But not you, Stella, which is why for you that kind of thinking is possible. Please, take the Fire and burn your bondage away. Only seconds remain.>

She took one more look at each man, then made her decision.

The seven Lords of Fear entered the tent a few moments later to find the Lord of Bhrudwo on all fours, mouth wide open, screaming words of loss in a ragged, soul-wrenching voice. The servant-girl and the eunuch were gone. No trace of them could be found, no matter how hard the *Maghdi Dasht* searched – and they searched long, trying to escape the screams that continued for hours.

Never again did the eunuch speak with the voice of Leith's dead brother, and neither did Stella hear the mind-voice at any point on their long journey west. Kindness and pity the cripple and the eunuch found in great measure, and of even greater value was the unexpected gift of passage with a company of soldiers encountered a day east of Ehrenmal. They were bound for Instruere, they said, where the King of Faltha was soon to be crowned: a man of surpassing wisdom and courage, to whom all Sixteen Kingdoms had sworn fealty. There was some concern expressed over his links to the *losian*, against whom some of them had spent many years fighting, but others argued that the *losian* had proven their worth in the Great War.

'Is it truly over?' she asked them, and they laughed. 'Truly over? Yes! There are no enemies left in Faltha!' A great age of peace was coming, they told her, in which all Faltha would prosper. She joined in their laughter, and was delighted when they offered her and her silent companion passage on their river-boat from Ehrenmal to Vindicare. 'Got to be at Instruere when the new king is crowned!' they said.

'I'd like that,' she replied, and smiled.

Yet she saw the glances they gave her when they thought she wasn't looking, glances of pity, with none of the concupiscence she might have expected from soldiers. They appreciated her wit, but did not think of her as a woman. For a time she could not bear to look in a mirror, so ashamed was she of her marred beauty. *He said I was beautiful*, she reminded herself, but at times she could not remember which man had spoken the words, Leith or the Destroyer.

As winter wrapped its cold arms around the world they made their way across the plains of Straux, passing under the great Keep of Fealty, drawing ever closer to Instruere – and the moment she had begun to dread. Would her friends see her as a traitor, a servant of the enemy? What would they say to her? Was there any chance they might make a place for her at their side? Her heart ached with worry, and the eunuch could offer her no words of consolation.

Finally the day came when the soldiers marched through the Gates of Instruere, and bade her farewell with a laugh, their captain even issuing her an invitation to join them for a meal at their barracks. Stella smiled and thanked them, trying not to show how much they wounded her even as they helped her. She stood in the middle of the street and watched them march off, coming to herself only when they vanished from sight.

The streets were strangely deserted, the City oddly quiet. The only sound was a light shower of rain pattering on the cobbled street. Surely there was nothing wrong? Surely on their travels they would have heard news of anything untoward happening here? Taking the big man's hand, Stella began to walk slowly down the road. Someone would know where he could be found.

Her damaged leg cried out in pain; and, without having to be asked, her protector halted at a small market and begged a stout walking stick. Stella asked the stall-owner where the people had gone, and was told that the new King of Faltha was being crowned today, even as they spoke, and didn't everyone know that? And wasn't it unfair that there was room only for a thousand in the Hall of Meeting, otherwise he would have gone, but there was a great gathering outside the hall on the wide lawns, and what had happened to her leg? She thanked the man breathlessly, and redoubled her pace.

There it was: the hall, surrounded by thousands upon thousands of people. As they came up to the great building, she could hear the music – a lament, it sounded like, one fit to scour the soul to the very depths. Would she wait? Would there ever be a time when she could speak to those she had abandoned in her selfishness?

Do not wait, something whispered in the depths of her mind; *you have atoned*.

She entered the building, and walked slowly down the Corridor of Appellants towards the entrance to the Outer Chamber, her stick clicking on the marble floor.

The eunuch stood back a few paces from the wooden doors, smiling, his arms folded over his stomach. *Go on*, his eyes told her. *Open the door. Go to your friends*.

She put her hand to the door, and the music swelled into a thundering climax. *At least no one will notice me*, she thought, and pushed open the door.

A thousand heads turned towards her, but she saw only one. Stella smiled as the boy on the throne cried out, leaped forward and promptly tripped over his boots as the music came to an end. In perfect silence he picked himself up, descended the stairs and walked towards her.

'Stella,' said the newly-crowned King of Faltha in a choked voice. 'I knew you would come back.'

'Liar,' she said, and took his right hand.

GLOSSARY

AS = Ancient Straux
CT = Common Tongue
D = Deruvian
FA = Favonian
FI = Firanese
FM = First Men
FN = Fenni
JS = Jasweyan
M = Mist
MB = Middle Bhrudwan
NM = Nemohaimian
OB = Old Bhrudwan
OD = Old Deruvian
OF = Old Falthan
OSV = Old Sna Vazthan
OT = Old Treikan
P = Pei-ran
S = Sanusi
SA = Saristrian
ST = Straux
SVZ = Sna Vazthan
WZ = Widuz

Achtal (**Arck**-tahl) aka the Acolyte: Personal name of the young Bhrudwan acolyte, a Lord of Fear [OB *death dealer*]
Adolina (A-doh-**lee**-nuh): A small town at the western end of Sivera Alenskja, the great gorge of the Aleinus River; first dwelling place in Faltha of the First Men [FM *idyll*]
Adrar, Pass of (**Add**-rar): Westernmost pass over Veridian Borders, seldom used by slavers seeking passage from Ghadir Massab to Bhrudwo [OB *lion*]
Adunlok (Ah-**doon**-lock): Fortress of the Widuz, built around a deep sinkhole just south of Cloventop [WZ *down look*]
Aldhras Mountains (**Ell**-drass): High mountains on the border between Faltha and Bhrudwo [FM *old head*]
Aleinus (Ar-lay-**ee**-niss): Great River of Faltha with headwaters in the Aldhras Mountains, then flows through central Faltha [FM *barrier*]
Aleinus Delta (Ar-lay-**ee**-niss): Wide area of swamp, forest and fen where the Aleinus River discharges into the Wodhaitic Sea [FM *barrier*]
Aleinus Gates (Ar-lay-**ee**-niss): Place where Aleinus River emerges from Vulture's Craw, surrounded by high cliffs [FM *barrier*]
Almucantaran Mountains (Ell-moo-kan-**tah**-ran): A dense knot of high mountains in eastern and southern Nemohaim [FM *mountains of the dream*]
Am'ainik (Arm-**eye**-nick): Southern and least populous province of Sna Vaztha [SVZ *shoulder*]
Amare, Plains of (Ah-**mar**-ay): Densely populated lowland to the west of Bewray in Nemohaim, site of many battles [NM *wind*]
Amasian, Sir (Ah-**may**-see-in): Seer of Fealty. One of the Knights of Fealty, given a vision by the Most High [FM *majesty*]

Andratan Island, keep (Ann-druh-tan): Island off the coast of Bhrudwo, home of the Destroyer [OB *dead*]
Appellants' Hall: Corridor in the Hall of Meeting where those seeking a ruling from the Council of Faltha gather to wait their turn
Arkhimm, the (Ar-kim): The five members of the Company who set out to retrieve the Jugom Ark [FM *five of the arrow*]
Arkhos (Ar-coss): Leader of a clan in the Vale of Youth; later coming to mean an ambassador to the Council of Faltha [FM *arrow-bearer*]
Armatura, the (Ar-muh-**too**-ruh): Lofty and impenetrable mountain range separating Faltha from Bhrudwo, runs between the Gap and Dhauria along an ancient fault [FM *armoured hills*]
Arrow of Yoke: Alternative name and literal translation of the Jugom Ark
Asgowan (Az-**gouw**-in): One of the Sixteen Kingdoms of Faltha, located north of Deuverre [FM *horse country*]
Aslama (**Az**-la-muh): Nemohaimian name for Rehu Archipelago, an extensive island chain to the north of Nemohaim and Deruys [NM *spoiled islands*]
Aslaman (**Ass**-la-muhn): Nemohaimian name for the inhabitants of Aslama [NM *spoiled men*]
Astraea (Az-**tray**-uh): Nemohaimian name for an old *losian* kingdom, home of the Pei-ra until they were driven out by Nemohaim [NM *spoils of war*]
Aurochs (**Or**-rocks): Legendary wild ox, found only on the inland moors of Firanes [FN *urus*]
Austrau (**Orst**-rouw): Eastern and less populous of the two provinces of Straux [FM *east wheat field*]
Axehaft aka Leader: The Warden of the Fodhram, from Fernthicket

Badiyat (Bard-i-**yat)**: Eastern province of the Sanusi [S *scorpion sand*]
Bandits' Cave: Limestone formation in Withwestwa Wood, formerly a base for robbers, now the abode of the Hermit
Bannire (Bann-ire): Borderlands south of Treika, once inhabited by warring *losian* tribes [FM *banner*]
Barathea (Barr-uh-**thee**-uh): Deuverran town at the confluence of the Aleinus River and its largest tributary, the Branca River [FM *house of God*]
Basement, The: Remnant of Foilzie's burned tenement in Instruere, gathering place for the Ecclesia
Belladonna: A young woman of the Vale of Neume, daughter of the Guardian of the Arrow; her name comes from the tradition of naming guardians after species of plants found in the Vale
Bewray (Bee-**ray**): Arkhos of Saiwiz, entrusted with the Jugom Ark by the Council of Leaders. Founded Nemohaim and hid the Jugom Ark [FM *to reveal involuntarily*]; also capital city of Nemohaim
Bhrudwo (Brood-woe): Continent covering the north-eastern hemisphere, a federation of provinces ruled by the Destroyer [OB *brown land*]
B'ir Birkat (Buh-**air** Bear-cat): Vast province of Bhrudwo, located in the north-western interior, a land of desert and plateau [S *golden lake*]
Birinjh (Bear-**arnge**): Vast province of Bhrudwo, located in the north-western interior, a land of desert and plateau [OB *tableland*]
Bis (Biss): Village of Asgowan, situated on the pampas plains of central Faltha. The name is probably onomatopoeic for the sound of wind in the long pampas grass
Branca (Bran-kuh): Large northern river draining Asgowan,

Haurn and the far north borders; a tributary of the Aleinus [OF *river*]

Breidhan Moor (**Bray**-than): Westernmost highlands of inland Firanes, considered part of the Myrevidda [OF *white lands*]

Brown Army: Colloquial term for the Bhrudwan army which overran Faltha at the end of the Golden Age

Brunhaven (**Brohn**-hay-vin): Coastal city and capital of Deruys, one of the Sixteen Kingdoms; home of the Raving King [FM *last home*]

Cachoeira (Cash-oh-**ay**-rah): Coast of south-western Faltha most vulnerable to pirate raids from Corrigia; leaving place of the Pei-ratin when they abandoned Astraea [NM *store-house*]

Captain of the Guard: Leader of the Instruian Guard, answerable to the Council of Faltha; currrently under orders of the Arkhos of Nemohaim

Cauldron, The: basin east of Aleinus Gates, part of Vulture's Craw. Named for its swirling winds

Ceau (Say-ow) aka Bright-Eyes: Escaignian who helps rescue the Company, accompanies the Arkhimm southwards [ST *abrupt*]

Central Plains: Vast lowlands of central Faltha, a hundred and fifty leagues from north to south and three hundred from east to west

Chalcis, Sir (**Chall**-sis): Chief knight of Fealty, an old but hale warrior-priest [FM *cleansing vessel*]

Children of the Mist: The *losian* who dwell in the land of the Mist, forced there by the First Men

Claws of Adrar: Claw-shaped formations near the summit of the Pass of Adrar. Part of the large feature known as the Golden Lion

Company, the: The group of northerners who came south attempting to warn Faltha of the coming Bhrudwan incursion
Conal Greatheart (**Conn**-arl): man of Instruere who rose up against the rule of the Destroyer. Aided by a band of warriors (some historians say criminals) he drove the Destroyer from Instruere and set up the Knightly order of Fealty [FM *spike*]
Corrigia (Coh-**rigg**-ee-yah): Pirate-infested island off the coast of south-western Faltha. The pirates of Corrigia harass shipping and coast-dwellers in southern Nemohaim and western Vertensia [NM *boat*]
Cotyledon, Lake (**Cott**-ee-**lee**-din): Large lake on the Mossbank River [FD *pennywort*, sense of meaning from FD *cup-shaped depression*]
Council of Faltha: Ruling council of ambassadors from the Sixteen Kingdoms of Faltha, based in Instruere
Cuantha, King (Koo-**ann**-thah): King of Favony, traitor to Faltha [FM *antlered stag*]
Culmea, the (**Kull**-me-ah): Hill country to the south-east of Bewray in Nemohaim, heavily populated [FM *pasture*]
Deorc (**Dee-york**): Lieutenant to the Destroyer, Keeper of Andratan [JS *spearhead*]
Deningen (**Den**-ing-in): coastal fishing village of central Deruys [D *fish bucket*]
Deruys (Dee-**roys**): One of the Sixteen Kingdoms of Faltha, a coastal land south of Straux [FM *no regard*]
Dessica (**Dess**-ih-cuh) aka Khersos, the Great Desert: Desert land extending over southern Faltha [FM *to dry out*]
Destroyer, the aka Undying Man, Lord of Bhrudwo, Lord of Andratan, Kannwar: Rebel against the Most High, cursed with immortality and now makes his home in Bhrudwo. Rules from his fortress of Andratan
Deuverre (Doo-**vair**): One of the Sixteen Kingdoms of Faltha,

located north of Straux in central Faltha; rich, densely populated farmland [FM *twin rivers*]
Dhaur Bitan **(Dour** Bit-**arn)** aka The Poisoning: Story of the fall of Kannwar and exile from the Vale, contained in the Domaz Skreud [FM *death bite*]
Dhauria (Dau-ree-yah) aka the Drowned Land: Names for the Vale of Youth after it was drowned by the sea [FM *death estuary*]
Diamant River (Die-ah-**mant)**: Broad river draining the western flanks of the Aldhras Mountains, cutting a deep valley into their unexplored heart. Said to be a sacred valley [SVZ *precious metal*]
Docks, the: Warehouse and shipping district of Instruere, outside the main wall of the city
Domaz Skreud **(Doh**-marz **Scroyd)**: The Scroll which recounts the rise of the Destroyer and the fall of the Vale of Youth [FM *doom scroll*]
Dona Mihst (Doh-na **Mist)**: City built on the site of the Rock of the Fountain in the Vale of Youth [FM *misty down*, later corrupted to dunamis, FM *power*]
Donu River (Doh-nu): River draining the southern Wodranian Mountains, emptying into the Aleinus River [FM *hillwater*]
Druin (Drew-in): Youth of Loulea, large boy who bullies others and is keen on Stella [FI *brown*]
Dukhobor (Dook-oh-bore): Gathering place of the Haukl, a city supposedly never seen by mortal eyes [FM *city of monsters*]
East Bank Road: Road running through the eastern provinces of Redana'a and Piskasia, parallel to the main road to The Gap
Ecclesia (E-**kle**-zyuh): Name given to the group who began meeting at Foilzie's basement [ST *called out*]
Ehrenmal (Air-en-mall): Town in western Favony on the north bank of the Aleinus River [FM *bad blood*]

Elders: Rulers of Escaigne, once high-ranking members of the Watchers

Escaigne (Ess-kane): Hidden kingdom in rebellion against Instruere [FM *entangled*]; Escaignians are also known as Cachedwellers

Faltha (Fal-thuh): Continent of north-western hemisphere, an alliance of sixteen independent kingdoms [CT contraction of *Falthwaite*, itself a corruption of *Withwestwa*]

Falthan Patriots: Name given by Arkhos of Nemohaim to those who joined him in treason against Faltha

Farr Storrsen (Far Store-sin): Elder son of Storr of Vinkullen, a thin, angular man [FI *far*]

Favony (Fah-vone-ee): One of the Sixteen Kingdoms of Faltha, located on the central Falthan plains north of Straux [FM *hot wind*)

Fealty, Knights of: Knights said to have driven the Destroyer out of Faltha a thousand years ago, led by Conal Greatheart

Fealty, Treaty of: Treaty signed by the kings of the Sixteen Kingdoms at the home of Conal Greatheart, establishing the Council of Faltha

Feerik (Fee-rick): Man of Sivithar in northern Straux, now the Presiding Elder of Escaigne [ST *foeman*]

Fenni, the (Fen-ny): Race of *losian* dwelling on the moors of inland Firanes [FN *ancient people*]

Firanes (Firr-uh-**ness**): Westernmost of the Sixteen Kingdoms of Faltha. Named for the sunrise on the heights of the Jawbone Mountains [FM *Fire Cape*]

Firefall, the: The moment in the Vale when the Most High came to the First Men with fire; also applied to subsequent visitations to individuals and groups

First Men, the: Those called north from Jangela by the Most

High to live in the Vale of Youth; name also applies to those exiled from the Vale who settled in Faltha, and to their descendants

Fisher Country: Colloquial name for Piskasia

Fodhram (Fodd-rum): A short-statured *losian* race dwelling in the forests of Withwestwa [FD *woodsman*]

Foilzie (Foyl-zee): Widow from Instruere, tenement-owner, shoemaker and stall-holder [FM *help mate*]

Fountain, Rock of the: Place in the Vale of Youth where the Most High set the fountain of eternal life

Fountain of Diamonds: Once the most famous of Sivithar's many fountains, now destroyed

Four Halls, Battle of the: General (and somewhat erroneous) name given to the struggle for control of Instruere

Frerlok (Frer-lock): Fortress of the Widuz, south of the Sagon River, built entirely of marble slabs [W *lookout*]

Frinwald (Frinn-wold): Messenger for the King of Straux [FM *harefoot*]

Fuir af Himmin (**Foo**-ir Ahf **Him**-min): Affirmation of the Watchers, used as a greeting [FM *Fire of Heaven*]

Fuirfad (Foo-ir-**fadd**) aka Realm of Fire, Way of Fire: The lore and religion of the First Men, teachings which enabled them to follow the Most High [FM *fire path*]

Furist (Few-rist): Arkhos (leader) of the House of Landam in exile, founder of Sarista [FM *to be admired*]

Furoman (Foo-row-man): Personal secretary to the Appellant Division of the Council of Faltha, headed by Saraskar of Sarista [ST *tight grasp*]

Galen (Gay-linn): servant in the employ of the Council of Faltha, works in the Hall of Meeting [ST *ruddy*]

Gap, the: Narrow pass between Aldhras Mountains and The Armatura, linking Faltha and Bhrudwo

Geinor (**Gay**-nor): Adviser to the king of Nemohaim, one of his oldest counsellors; father of Graig [NM *charity*]
Ghadir Massab: City of the Sanusi, fabled city of gold, a trading centre and slave market on the shores of B'ir Birkat in the Deep Desert [S *oasis at the river mouth*]
Glade of True Sight: Small clearing in Hinepukohurangi, the land of the Mist, where the fortunate men or women might meet their ancestors. The Glade is seldom found in the same place twice
Golden Lion: Large rock formation near the summit of the Pass of Adrar; once the site of bandit ambushes
Graig (Grayg): Soldier in the Nemohaimian army, son of Geinor the counsellor [NM *spear*]
Granaries, The: Suburb of Instruere made of warehouses, many for the storing of grain
Great Harlot: Perjorative Escaignian name for Instruere
Great North Woods: Boreal forest of northern Firanes, part of a much larger forest encompassing northern Faltha
Great South Road: The Straux section of the road between Instruere and Bewray, the major road to the south-western kingdoms
Great Southern Mountains: Wide mountain chain separating southern Bhrudwo from unknown lands
Hal Mahnumsen (Hell): Youth of Loulea, adopted older son of Mahnum and Indrett. A cripple whose name is seemingly ironic [FI *whole, hale*]
Haldemar (**Hall**-da-marr): Fenni wife of Perdu, the adopted Fenni [FN *wholesome*]
Halkonis (Hall-**koe**-niss): Dhaurian scholar, expert on spells of all kinds [FM *whole-hearted*]
Hall of Lore: One of the four halls of Instruere, modelled on the halls of Dona Mihst. Here are housed the Archives,

and many of the Councilmen live in the annexe to this hall

Hall of Meeting: One of the four halls of Instruere, modelled on the halls of Dona Mihst. Behind the Iron Door is the large Outer Chamber, where important city meetings are held; the Council of Faltha meet in the Inner Chamber

Hamadabat (Har-**mard**-ah-bat): Northern province of the Sanusi, between B'ir Birkat and the Veridian Borders [S *stinging sand*]

Hauberk Wall (Haw-berk): Tall peaks of the Aldhras Mountains, located at the head of the valley of the Daimant River [SVZ *mail-coat*]

Haufuth, the (How-footh): Title of village headmen in northern Firanes [FI *head*]

Haukl (How-kill): Legendary race who dwell in the Aldhras Mountains, supposedly a contemplative people who avoid contact with men [*meaning unknown*]

Haurn (Hown): One of the Sixteen Kingdoms of Faltha, located north of Asgowan. Annexed by Sna Vaztha in 1006 [FM *horn*]

Hauthius (How-thee-yoos): Scholar of Dhauria, author of the *Sayings of Hauthius* [FM *head scholar*]

Hauthra (How-thruh): Capital city of Haurn, sacked by Sna Vaztha in 1006 [FM *head*]

Helig Holth (Hay-ligg **Holth**): Huge sinkhole on the edge of Clovenhill, on which the fortress of Adunlok is built. Venerated by the Widuz as the mouth of Mother Earth [WZ *holy mouth*]

Hermit, the: Man of Bandits' Cave, drawn south with the Company

Herza (Her-zuh): Mother of Stella, wife of Pell, woman of Loulea Vale [FI *choice*]

Hinerangi (Hi-nay-rang-ee): Daughter of the paramount

chief of the Children of the Mist, brother of Te Tuahangata [M *skysong*]
Idehan Kahal (Eye-dih-harn Kar-**harl)**: Sanusi and Saristrian name for the Khersos, the Deep Desert of southern Faltha [S *killing fields*]
Illyon (Ill-yon) aka Freckle: Escaignian woman who helps rescue the Company, and accompanies the Arkhimm southwards [ST *harbinger*]
Inch Chanter (Inch Charn-tuh): Treikan walled town, hunting and farming community in Old Deer [OT *small song*]
Indrett (Inn-dritt): Woman of Loulea, formerly of Rammr, married to Mahnum [FI *right hand*]
Inmennost (In-men-ost): Capital city of Sna Vaztha and seat of the descendants of Raupa, Arkhos of Leuktom. Greatest of the northern cities of Faltha [of uncertain origin]
Inna (In-nuh): Northern of two villages founded on an island in the Aleinus River, coalescing into Instruere; also one of the three main gates to the Great City [FM *within*]
Inner Chamber aka Chamber of Debate: Small meeting hall, an annexe of the Hall of Meeting, where the Council of Faltha meet
Instruere (In-strew-**ear**) aka Great City: Largest city in Faltha and seat of the Council of Faltha [combination of Inna and Struere, together forming the OF word meaning to *instruct*]
Instruian Guard: Soldiers under the control of the Council of Faltha, charged with keeping the peace in Instruere
Inverlaw Eich (Inn-vuh-lore **Aick)**: Town on a terrace above the Lavera River, destroyed in 979, replaced by Ashdown [WZ *between hill place*]
Iron Door: Door guarding the entrance to the Outer Chamber of the Hall of Meeting in Instruere, where the Council of Faltha meet

Iskelsee (Iss-kill-see): Ice-bound bay in the remote north of Firanes, a place where seals gather. A favourite of Firanese, Halvoyan, Scymrian and Fenni hunters [FI *ice sea*]
Jangela (Yun-**gella**): Land to the south of Faltha, supposedly impenetrable jungle, beyond which the rich and exotic Southlands are said to be [FM *jungle*]
Jardin (Jar-**dinn**): Capital of Vertensia, a small city at the centre of a horticultural region favoured by seasonal rains [FM *garden*]
Jasweyah (Jarss-**way**-uh): Mountainous kingdom in southern Bhrudwo, formerly Deorc's kingdom [OB *look over*]
Jawbone Mountains aka Tanthussa: Main mountain chain of Firanes (rare form Tanthussa derived from FM *teeth*)
Jena (Jenn-uh): Former friend of the Destroyer's eunuch, lived on the Fisher Coast in the south of Bhrudwo [OB *sweet one*]
Jethart (Jeh-thirt): Heroic figure of western Treika, hated foe of the Widuz, now an old man [OT *bright hunter*]
Joram Basin (Jaw-im): Deep cirque-like basin set between the Sentinella at the head of the Vale of Neume [FM *jewel*]
Jugom Ark (Yu-gum **Ark**) aka Arrow of Yoke: Flaming arrow loosed by Most High at Kannwar, severing his right hand and sealing his doom. Symbol of unity for Faltha. Name derives from 'yoking together' like oxen [FM *yoke arrow*]
Kanabar (Can-a-barr): Wide inland steppes in southern Birinjh, a province of Bhrudwo [OB *sulphur brown*]
Kannwar (Cann-wah) aka the Destroyer: Original name of Destroyer, means Guardian of Knowledge [FM *ken-ward*]
Kantara (Can-**tah**-ruh): Legendary castle in the sky which comes down to earth once in a thousand years [FM *thousand*]
Kaskyne (Kass-kine): Capital and largest city of Redana'a. One of the Sixteen Kingdoms; situated on a hill above the southern banks of the Aleinus River at the head of Vulture's Craw [FM *short rapids*]

Kauma (Cow-muh): Capital city of Sarista, at the mouth of the Lifeblood River [FM *calm*]
Kljufa River (Clue-fah): Largest river in Firanes, carving a path through the Jawbone Mountains [FM *to cleave*]
Kroptur (Crop-tuh): Seer and Watcher of the seventh rank, lives on Watch Hill near Vapnatak [FM *spell-caster*]
Kula (Koo-lah): Old Widuz warrior, experienced in border campaigns [W *axeman*]
Kurr (Cur) aka Kurnath: Man of Loulea, formerly from the south. Reflects ironic naming practices of Straux [OF *ill-bred dog*, perh. from FM *grumbler*]
Landam, House of (Lan-dam): One of the four great houses of the First Men [FM *house of earth*]
Lankangas, the (Lan-**kan**-guz): Ten feudal cities of south-eastern Firanes unwilling to accept leadership of King of Firanes [FI *long plain*]
Laya (Lay-uh): Pei-ratin girl who died of a sickness in her bones [P *frond*]
Leith Mahnumsen (Leeth): Younger son of Mahnum of Loulea and Indrett of Rammr. Name carries sense of putting aside the past [CT *forgetful, lethargic*]
Lessep: (Less-ip): Young rascal from the streets of Instruere, of indeterminate origin [FM *close-mouthed*]
Lifeblood River: River of southern Faltha whose headwaters are the Thousand Springs. Flows through the Deep Desert and into Sarista
Lindholm (Lind-home): City of western Deruys, near border with Nemohaim [OD *flower hill*]
Longbridge: The mile-long bridge connecting Instruere with Deuverre. Its southern counterpart is Southbridge
Lore, Hall of: Centre of learning in Dona Mihst; latterly a major building in Instruere

Lore Market: One of sixteen official markets in Instruere, sited near the Hall of Lore
***Losian* (low-si-yin)**: Properly those who left the Vale of Youth before the fall, forsaking the Most High; popularly, all those races of Faltha who are not First Men [FM *the lost*]
Loulea, village, Vale (Low-lee) aka Louleij: Small coastal village in North March of Firanes, set in vale of same name [CT *low lea*]
Mablas (Mah-blass): Scholar of Dhauria, expert on the Maghdi Dasht [FM *parchment*]
Maelstrom, the (Mal-strom): Whirlpool in the Lower Clough of the Kljufa River, below which the river runs underground until surfacing downstream [FM *whirling stream*]
Maendraga (Mah-enn-**drar**-gah): A middle-aged man from the Vale of Neume, the Guardian of the Arrow; his name follows the tradition of naming guardians after species of plants found in the Vale [FM *mandrake*]
***Maghdi Dasht* (Marg-dee Darshht)** aka Lords of Fear: One hundred and sixty-nine feared Bhrudwan warrior-wizards [OB *Heart of the Desert*]
Mahnum (Marr-num): Trader of Loulea, son of Modahl, married to Indrett [FI *man, human*]
Malayu (Mah-lah-**you**): Chief city of province of Malayu, most populous city in Bhrudwo [OB *corruption*]
Malos (Mar-loss): Loulea villager, small in stature [MF *gentleman*]
Mandaramus (Man-da-**rah**-muss): Dhaurian harp-maker and master harpist [FM *gifted man*]
Maremma (Muh-**rem**-muh): A vast low-lying area in the Central Plains of Faltha, in the countries of Straux, Deuverre and Asgowan [FM *death swamps*]
***Mariswan* (marr-ih-swan)**: Huge birds now extinct. The

Jugom Ark is fletched with *mariswan* feathers [FM *majestic fowl*]
Maufus (**Marw**-foos): Dhaurian, contemporary of Phemanderac, elevated to Dhaurian Congress while young [FM *steady, stable*]
Meeting, Hall of: Largest building in Faltha, the place of public gatherings in Instruere; latterly the home of the Council of Faltha
Mercium (**Merr**-see-um): Capital city of Straux, the second-largest city in Faltha, on the inland edge of the Aleinus Delta [AS *merchant*]
Merin (Mair-in): Wife of the Loulea village Haufuth [FI *laughter*]
Midwinters' Day: Midwinter celebrations, held in northern Faltha, asserting the coming of spring
Mist, The, aka Hinepukohurangi: Forested lands between Deruys and the Valley of a Thousand Fires, often cloaked in mist; home to the Children of the Mist, considered *losian* by the First Men
Mjolkbridge (**Myoulk**-bridge): Town in inland Firanes, on the southern bank of Mjolk River. Site of the last bridge across the river [OF *milk*]
Modahl (Mow-**darl**): Legendary Trader of Firanes, father of Mahnum and grandfather of Leith and Hal [FM *manservant*]
Morneshade (**Morn**-shayd): City of Sarista, on the eastern desert coast
Most High: Supreme god of the First Men
Motu-tapu (moh-too-tah-poo): Sacred island of the Pei-ra, part of the Rehu Archipelago [M *sacred place*]
Nagorj (Nah-**gorge**): Southern upland province of Sna Vaztha immediately west of the Gap [OSV *north gorge*]
Nemohaim (**Nee**-moh-haym): One of the Sixteen Kingdoms

of Faltha, set on the southern Bay of Bewray. Once home to Bewray, guardian of the Jugom Ark [FM *new home*]
Nena (Nen-ya): Wife of Mandrake the Guardian, originally an Aslaman but was exiled [P *blossom*]
Nentachki (Nenn-**tach**-key): Unit of currency used by the Sanusi; roughly equivalent to a month's wages [S *cold month*]
Net of Vanishing: An Illusion designed to make a person or thing invisible. The Net of Vanishing requires considerable power
Neume, Vale of (Noome): Valley in the Almucantaran Mountains, in southern Nemohaim; supposed location of Kantara [FM *numinous*]
New Age: Calendar of Faltha, the first year of which was the Destroyer's supposed defeat by Conal Greatheart
North March: Area of Firanes bounded by Iskelsee to the north, Wodhaitic Sea to the west, the Fells to the east and the Innerlie Plains to the south
Northern Escarpment: Southern edge of the Sna Vazthan tableland, scaled by the road to The Gap
Outer Chamber: Main meeting hall in the Hall of Meeting, site of public gatherings in Instruere
Parlevaag (Parl-ih-vagg): Fenni woman captured by Bhrudwans, slain by Widuz warriors [FN *storyteller*]
Pei-ra, the (Pay-rah): A *losian* race from the mountains of south-western Faltha, driven out of their home of Astraea by the First Men [P *the people*]
Pelasia (Peh-**lay**-see-ah): Woman of Instruere, one of the Ecclesia, slain by the Instruian Guard [CT *precious one*]
Perdu (Purr-do): Mjolkbridge hunter rescued from death by the Fenni, now serving them as interpreter [FI *in hiding*]
Pereval (Peh-reh-varl): Disputed province between Haurn

and Sna Vaztha, currently under Sna Vazthan jurisdiction [SVZ *plainland*]

Petara (Peh-**tar**-uh): Elder from Escaigne, one who helped plan the overthrow of Instruere [FM *small*]

Phemanderac (Fee-**man**-duh-**rack**): Scholar of Dhauria who leaves his homeland to learn the whereabouts of the Right Hand [FM *the mandate*]

Philosophers, the: The senior members of the School of the Prophets in Dhauria

Pinion, The: Longhouse in Instruere, houses the Instruian Guard. Notorious for its dungeon, known ironically as the Pinion Inn

Piskasia (Pisk-**ay**-zha): One of the Sixteen Kingdoms of Faltha, located south of Sna Vaztha along the banks of the Aleinus [FM *fish land*]

Plafond (Pluh-**fonnd**): Capital city of Deuverre, at the western end of the basin formed by the Central Plains of Faltha [FM *plate lip*]

Plonya (Plonn-yuh): One of the Sixteen Kingdoms of Faltha, located between Firanes and the wild Widuz country [FM *floodplain*]

Porveiir, Mount (Pour-vay-**er**): Huge volcanic dome, intermittently active, on the western margins of the Wodranian Mountains in Favony [FA *pourer*]

Presiding Elder: The head Elder and ruler of Escaigne; formerly a high-ranking Watcher. The current Presiding Elder is named Feerik

Preuse River (Proyse) Major river of Sna Vaztha, draining the northern marches of the Wodranian Mountains and crossing the Fruesan Plains [SVZ *ice*]

Prosopon (Proh-soh-pon): Second city of Redana'a, located at the feet of the Taproot Hills [FM *promise of prosperity*]

Pylorus, Sir (Pie-**lore**-us): One of the Knights of Fealty, keeper of the Hall of Conal Greatheart [FM *faithful*]
Pyrinius (Pie-**rinn**-ee-yoos): Dominie (teacher) of Phemanderac, expert harpist and scholar of Dhauria [FM *fire servant*]
Raupa (**Rau**-puh): Arkhos of the House of Leuktom in exile, founder of Sna Vaztha [FM *royal one*]
Rauth (Rowth): Loulea village elder, red-haired. Likely a nickname [CT *red*]
Raving King of Deruys: Nickname by which the king of Deruys is widely known, attributed to his cryptic speech
Reaf (Reef): Deruvian general, perished in the snows of Vulture's Craw [FM *to hold back*]
Redana'a (Re-**dar**-na-ah): One of the Sixteen Kingdoms of Faltha, an inland country on the southern bank of the Aleinus River, hemmed in by the Taproot Hills [FM *red roots*]
Remparer Mountains (Remm-pa-**rair**) aka Ramparts of Faltha, Manu Irion, Man-Eaters: Continental mountain range dividing western from central Faltha [FM *the ramparts*]
Rhinn na Torridon (**Rinn** nar **toh**-rih-don) aka Tarradale Broads: Coastlands south of Remparer Mountains [WZ *rack of gentle valleys*]
Rhynn (**Rinn**): Arkhos of Asgowan, one of the Council of Faltha [FM *rack*]
Right Hand: Mysterious weapon, person or organisation mentioned in prophecy as overcoming the Destroyer
Robber of Firanes: Perjorative name for Modahl, given by his Sna Vazthan enemies
Roleystone Bridge: Stone arch over the Kljufa River at the head of the Upper Clough, the only bridge north of the Trow of Kljufa
Room of Four Windows: Viewing room at the top of the

Tower of Worship in Instruere. Each window faces a cardinal point of the compass

Roudhos, Duke of (Raud-hoss): Leader of Neheria, one of the most prominent provinces of southern Bhrudwo. Of an ancient and proud lineage, Roudhos was an unwilling servant of the Destroyer [OB *Red Duke*]

Ruben-rammen (Roo-bin-**ramm**-in): Landsman of Favony, in league with the King of Favony to deceive the Army of Faltha [CT *prevaricator, lit. here and there*]

Saiwiz, House of (Sigh-wizz): One of the four great houses of the First Men [FM *house of the sea*]

Salentia (Suh-**lent**-ee-yuh): Independent city on the border between Piskasia and Favony, but owing allegiance to neither. It occupies flat land on the northern bank of the Aleinus River [FM *time of peace*]

Sanusi (Sar-**noo**-see): A desert people who dwell in Dessica, the Deep Desert. Scholars are unsure as to whether they are *losian* or have come west from Bhrudwo [S *sand men*]

Saraskar (Sah-ra-**scar**): The Arkhos of Sarista, and head of the Appellant Division of the Council of Faltha [FM *sun child*]

Sarista (Sah-ris-**tah**): Southernmost of the Sixteen Kingdoms of Faltha and the last to be settled. Saristrians are dark-skinned [FM *sunlands*]

Saumon (Sau-monn): Fishing village in Piskasia, on the eastern bank of the Aleinus River [FM *rainbow fish*]

School of the Prophets: The University of Dhauria, in which young men are trained in magic and scholarly arts

Sentinels, The aka Sentinella: Twin peaks of the Almucantaran Mountains in southern Nemohaim, guardians of the Jugom Ark

Silsilesi (Sill-sill-**ay**-see): Mining district of Sarista, providing much of Sarista's wealth and exports [FM *iron ore*]

Sivera Alenskja (Siv-**er**-ah Al-**enn**-skyah): Steep-sided gorge of the upper Aleinus River, south of Sna Vaztha, west of The Gap [OSV *deep sky rapids*]
Sivithar (**Sih**-vih-thar): City on the southern bank of the Aleinus River, in northern Straux, a river port [AS *silver thread*]
Sjenda (Si-**yen**-duh): Chatelaine of the Deruvian palace, serves Leith as procurer of provisions. Lost in the snows of Vulture's Craw [OD *settler*]
Sna Vaztha (Snarr **Vazz**-thuh): One of the Sixteen Kingdoms of Faltha, located to the north-east of Faltha [FM *frozen snow*]
Southbridge aka Straux Bridge: The bridge connecting Instruere with Straux. Its northern counterpart is Longbridge
Steffl (**Stef**-fill) aka Meall Gorm: Active volcano in Withwestwa Wood, a well-known landmark by the Westway. Place where the Company rescued Leith and Hal's parents [FM *the hood*]
Stella Pellwen (**Stell**-ah **Pell**-win): Youth of Loulea, daughter of Pell and Herza of Loulea [CT *from the stars*]
Sthane (Sthayn): Leader of the smallest clan and member of the Council of Leaders in the Vale of Youth; opposes Kannwar [FM *spine*]
Stibbourne Farm (Stib-**born**): Farm of Kurr, located on Swill Down, possibly named after corn stubble, or less likely an FM word (*stiborn*) meaning stubborn
Straux (Strouw): Most populous of the Sixteen Kingdoms of Faltha, located south of Aleinus River on the Central Plains [FM *wheat field*]
Struere (Strew-**ear**): Southern and larger of two villages founded on an island in the Aleinus River, coalescing into Instruere; also the name of the southern gate of Instruere [FM *instruct*]

Swill Down: Hill forming the southern boundary of Loulea Vale. Location of Stibbourne Farm
Tabul (Tah-**bull**): One of the Sixteen Kingdoms of Faltha, a southern inland kingdom with great mineral resources [FM *table land*]
Tanama (Ta-**nah**-ma): Widuz chieftain, from a village just north of Tolmen [W *second chance*]
Tanghin (**Tang**-in): Man from Bhrudwo who joins the Ecclesia; rapidly promoted to one of the Blessed [JS *torment*]
Taproot Hills: Mountain range of Redana'a; southern continuation of the Wodranian Mountains. Forms the southern part of Vulture's Craw
Te Tuahangata (Tay Too-ah-hung-ar-tah): Man of The Mist, son of the paramount chief, accompanies the Arkhimm on their journey southward [M *man who journeys*]
Thraell River (**Thray**-ell): River draining the eastern part of Breidhan Moor, flowing into Kljufa River [FM *in thrall*]
Tinei (Tin-**ay**): Wife to Kurr of Loulea [OF *twist*]
Tor Hailan (**Tor-Hi**-lan): City of Pereval province, built on the mountain of the same name. The battle between Sna Vaztha and Haurn was fought here [SVZ *high bare hill*]
Treika (**Tree**-kuh): One of the Sixteen Kingdoms of Faltha, located between Widuz lands and the Remparer Mountains [FM *forest land*]
Tructa (**Truk**-tuh): Town in southern Piskasia, on the west bank of the Aleinus River [FM *grey fish*]
Truthspell: aspect of spoken magic allowing the speaker to trap anyone who responds to the truth woven into the words
Turtu Donija (**Tur**-too-Doh-**nee**-juh): capital and largest city of Piskasia, on west bank of Aleinus River [FM *city of rest*]
Uchtana, Lord (Uck-**tar**-na): A Lord of Fear [OB *to take forcibly*]

Uflok (**Ouf**-lock): Widuz town on the banks of the Sagon, where the families of the warriors of Adunlok make their homes [WD *up look*]
Valley of a Thousand Fires: long, narrow land between the mountains of south-western Faltha and the Deep Desert; hot, arid and filled with volcanic activity
Vaniyo (**Var**-nee-yoh): Bhrudwan Trader [MB *subtle hands*]
Vapnatak (**Vapp**-nuh-tack): Largest town in the North March of Firanes. Named after the annual weapontake that took place here in the years of the Halvoyan incursions [OF *weapontake*]
Vassilian (Vass-**ill**-ee-yin): Town on the Plains of Amare where a battle was fought between Nemohaim and Pei-ra; neither side claimed victory [NM *valiant struggle*]
Verenum Spire (**Veh**-reh-nim): Active volcanic cone, constantly erupting. Located in central Haum [FM *green mountain*]
Veridian Borders: Mountain range on the southern border of Straux, separating the fertile Central Plains from the arid lands to the south
Vertensia (Verr-**ten**-see-yuh): One of the southern Sixteen Kingdoms of Faltha, a land of coastal gardens and severe highlands [FM *garden land*]
Vindicare (**Vin**-di-care): major city of Austrau province, Straux. Located on southern bank of Aleinus River, deep-water port and trading centre [FM *triumph*]
Vindstrop House (**Vinnd**-strop): Main town of the Fodhram, a trading post on the Mossbank River [MT *wind drop*]
Vinkullen Hills (Vinn-**cull**-in): Hills to the north of Mjolkbridge, Firanes [FI *shield hills*]
Vitulian Way (Vih-**too**-lee-in): Main street in Instruere, connects the Inna (northern) Gate and Struere (southern) Gate [ST *straightway*]

Vithrain Uftan (Vith-**rayn Ouf**-tan) aka Valley of Respite: Middle valley of the Torrelstrommen, broad and straight [FI *valley of ease*]
Voiceskill aka Wordweave: The magical ability to weave different meanings into the words one speaks, thereby affecting the behaviour of others
Vulture's Craw: Central gorge of the Aleinus River through the Wodranian Mountains, dividing Piskasia and Redana'a
Wambakalven (Wumm-buh-cal-vin) aka Womb Cavern: Large cave directly below Adunlok, part of Adunlok cave system [WZ *womb cavern*]
Watchers, the: Secret organisation dedicated to protecting Faltha from invasion
Westrau (Wesst-rouw): One of the two large provinces of Straux, the westernmost and most populous [AS *west wheat field*]
Westway, the: Former main highway east from Firanes to Instruere, now superseded
Whitefang Pass: One of only two routes through the Remparer Mountains, a dangerous pass that regularly claims lives
Widuz (Vi-**dooz**): Small mountain fastness in north-western Faltha, remnant of a far larger civilisation [WZ *the people*]
Windrise: Town in inland Firanes, situated where the Westway leaves the Mjolk valley
Wira Storrsen (Wee-rah **Store**-sin): Younger son of Storr of Vinkullen, a solid, blond-haired man. Slain by the Lords of Fear on the slopes of Steffl mountain [FI *wiry*]
Wisent (Wih-**sent**): Name of the Fenni clan chief's own aurochs [FN *bison*]
Withwestwa Wood (With-**west**-wuh): Extensive boreal forest of northern Plonya; part of the forest that extends across

northern Faltha. The name was originally given to the whole continent [FM *westwood*, backform of Falthwaite and Faltha]

Wiusago, Prince (Wee-you-**sar**-go) aka Long-hair: Prince of Deruys, younger but only remaining son of the Raving King of Deruys, companion to the Arkhimm [OD *wiseacre*]

Wodhaitic Sea (Woe-day-**it**-ick): Western sea bordering Faltha, specifically that ocean partly enclosed by north-western and south-western Faltha [FM *hot water*]

Wodranian Mountains (Woe-**drain**-ee-an): Large mountainous area in east central Faltha, home of the Wodrani [FM *water men*]

Wordweave aka Voiceskill: One of the word-based powers wielded by an adept in the *Fuirfad*. The Wordweave allows the user to weave another meaning into her or his words

Worship, House of: Tall tower of Instruere, a monument based on the Tower of Worship in Dona Mihst

Ylisane (Ell-iss-ayne): Queen of Sna Vaztha, most powerful monarch of Faltha, not corrupted by Bhrudwo [SVZ *frozen glass*]